Midnight at the Well of Souls

Entered by a thousand unsuspected gateways – built by a race lost in the clouds of time – the Well of Souls transforms creatures of any sort into different forms. So, spacefarer Nathan Brazil is not surprised to find himself accompanied by a batman, an amorous female centaur and a mermaid as he sets out on his strange mission across the Well World. Yet Nathan Brazil's own metamorphosis is more terrifying than any of the others – and with the gradual return of his memory comes the secret of the Well World.

Spirits of Flux and Anchor

Cassie did not feel the soul rider enter her body but suddenly she knew that Anchor was corrupt, and that, far from being a formless void from which could issue only mutant changelings and evil wizards, Flux was the source of Anchor's very existence. The price of her new knowledge is exile, yet Cassie and the Rider of her soul are the only hope for the redemption of both Flux and Anchor.

The Identity Matrix

While backpacking in Alaska, Victor Gonser, a 35 year old PhD in political science, finds himself trapped in the body of a 13 year old Tlingit Indian girl. A little later he is forced from there into the spectacularly beautiful body of an 18 year old blonde. He finds that the switches are part of a skirmish for Earth by two alien races ... and that is just the beginning!

Also by Jack L. Chalker

The Well of Souls
Midnight at the Well of Souls (1977)
Exiles at the Well of Souls (1978)
Quest for the Well of Souls (1978)
The Return of Nathan
    Brazil (1980)
Twilight at the Well of Souls:
    The Legacy of Nathan Brazil (1980)
The Sea is Full of Stars (1999)
Ghost of the Well of Souls (2000)

The Watchers at the Well
Echoes of the Well of Souls (1993)
Shadow of the Well of Souls (1994)
Gods of the Well of Souls (1994)

The Dancing Gods
The River of Dancing Gods (1984)
Demons of the Dancing
    Gods (1984)
Vengeance of the Dancing
    Gods (1985)
Songs of the Dancing Gods (1990)
Horrors of the Dancing Gods (1995)

Soul Rider
Spirits of Flux and Anchor (1984)
Empires of Flux and Anchor (1984)
Masters of Flux and Anchor (1984)
The Birth of Flux and Anchor (1985)
Children of Flux and Anchor (1985)

The Rings of the Master
Lords of the Middle Dark (1986)
Pirates of the Thunder (1987)
Warriors of the Storm (1987)
Masks of the Martyrs (1988)

G.O.D. Inc
The Labyrinth of Dreams (1987)
The Shadow Dancers (1987)
The Maze in the Mirror (1988)

Changewinds
When the Changewinds Blow (1987)
Riders of the Winds (1988)
War of the Maelstrom (1988)

The Quintara Marathon
The Demons at Rainbow
    Bridge (1989)
The Run to Chaos Keep (1991)
The Ninety Trillion Fausts (1991)

The Wonderland Gambit
The Cybernetic Walrus (1995)
The March Hare Network (1996)
The Hot-Wired Dodo (1997)

Three Kings
Balshazzar's Serpent (1999)
Melchior's Fire (2001)
Kaspar's Box (2003)

Other Novels
A Jungle of Stars (1976)
The Web of the Chozen (1978)
Dancers in the Afterglow (1978)
A War of Shadows (1979)
And the Devil Will Drag You
    Under (1979)
The Identity Matrix (1982)
Downtiming the Night Side (1985)
Priam's Lense (1998)
The Moreau Factor (2000)

Jack L. Chalker

SF GATEWAY OMNIBUS

MIDNIGHT AT THE WELL OF SOULS
SPIRITS OF FLUX AND ANCHOR
THE IDENTITY MATRIX

GOLLANCZ
LONDON

First published in Great Britain in 2014 by
Gollancz
An imprint of the Orion Publishing Group
Orion House, 5 Upper St Martin's Lane,
London WC2H 9EA

An Hachette UK Company

A CIP catalogue record for this book is
available from the British Library

ISBN 978 0 575 09771 1

1 3 5 7 9 10 8 6 4 2

Typeset by Jouve (UK), Milton Keynes

Printed and bound by CPI Group (UK) Ltd, Croydon CR0 4YY

The Orion Publishing Group's policy is to use papers
that are natural, renewable and recyclable products and
made from wood grown in sustainable forests. The logging
and manufacturing processes are expected to conform to
the environmental regulations of the country of origin.

www.orionbooks.co.uk
www.gollancz.co.uk

CONTENTS

ENTER THE SF GATEWAY ...

Towards the end of 2011, in conjunction with the celebration of fifty years of coherent, continuous science fiction and fantasy publishing, Gollancz launched the SF Gateway.

Over a decade after launching the landmark SF Masterworks series, we realised that the realities of commercial publishing are such that even the Masterworks could only ever scratch the surface of an author's career. Vast troves of classic SF and fantasy were almost certainly destined never again to see print. Until very recently, this meant that anyone interested in reading any of those books would have been confined to scouring second-hand bookshops. The advent of digital publishing changed that paradigm for ever.

Embracing the future even as we honour the past, Gollancz launched the SF Gateway with a view to utilising the technology that now exists to make available, for the first time, the entire backlists of an incredibly wide range of classic and modern SF and fantasy authors. Our plan, at its simplest, was – and still is! – to use this technology to build on the success of the SF and Fantasy Masterworks series and to go even further.

The SF Gateway was designed to be the new home of classic science fiction and fantasy – the most comprehensive electronic library of classic SFF titles ever assembled. The programme has been extremely well received and we've been very happy with the results. So happy, in fact, that we've decided to complete the circle and return a selection of our titles to print, in these omnibus editions.

We hope you enjoy this selection. And we hope that you'll want to explore more of the classic SF and fantasy we have available. These are wonderful books you're holding in your hand, but you'll find much, much more ... through the SF Gateway.

www.sfgateway.com

INTRODUCTION

from The Encyclopedia of Science Fiction

Jack Laurence Chalker (1944–2005) was a US writer and editor, though now very much better known for his fiction. He was active as a fan from an early age, and producer of a successful Fanzine, *Mirage*. As editor, he founded and edited the Mirage Press, which specialized in sf scholarship. His own work in that area began with *The New H. P. Lovecraft Bibliography* (1962) with Mark Owings, and *In Memoriam: Clark Ashton Smith* (1963), continuing with some studies and guides with Owings, who is sometimes listed as a pseudonym of Chalker, a confusion arising from his sole crediting for *The Necronomicon: A Study* (1967), which was in fact collaborative. They also worked together on *Mirage on Lovecraft* (1965) and *The Index to the Science-Fantasy Publishers: (a Bibliography of the Science Fiction and Fantasy Specialty Houses)* (1966). After the solo *An Informal Biography of $crooge McDuck* (1974), Chalker moved his attention to fiction, only returning to his earlier interest twenty years later with a new edition of his 1979 *Index*, which though technically a revision of the earlier work was in fact ten times its length, and can pragmatically be treated as a new title: *The Science-Fantasy Publishers: A Critical and Bibliographic History* (1991), still with Owings; *The Science-Fantasy Publishers: Supplement One, July 1991-June 1992* (1992) with Owings and its sequels continue the coverage. In its mature form, *Science-Fantasy Publishers* is a central reference resource.

His first novel, an ambitious singleton Space Opera, *A Jungle of Stars* (1976), proved typical in that its opposing aliens (who are both ex-gods) represent through their conflict a form of populist argument about alternative utopian worldviews, and in that its plot concentrates on members of mortal races who have been recruited to do the superbeings' fighting for them in a kind of world-arena. This underlying articulacy and the plot-device of recruitment also mark his most successful single novel, *Dancers in the Afterglow* (1978), a complex and melancholy tale of oppression and enforced metamorphosis on a conquered colony planet, in which questions of power and morality are again asked with some ease, and the human need for freedom is answered (and at the same time deeply assaulted) by transformation tropes out of Science Fantasy and nightmare. *Dancers* contains in embryo almost all of the next decade or so of Chalker's prolific career, most of which was given over to the construction of large series. On the other hand, *The*

Devil's Voyage (1981), which is almost Chalker's only associational fiction, deals with the ship that carried the A-bomb used on Hiroshima to its rendez-vous, and which was subsequently sunk and its crew eaten by sharks; but also about the security scare caused by Cleve Cartmills's 'Deadline', published in March 1944 in John W. Campbell Jr's *Astounding*.

The first of the series which would dominate the rest of Chalker's career is the **Well of Souls** sequence, which begins with his second fiction title, *Midnight at the Well of Souls* (1977) (see below), and continues with *The Wars of the Well: Exiles at the Well of Souls* (1978), *The Wars of the Well: Quest for the Well of Souls* (1978), *The Return of Nathan Brazil* (1980), *Twilight at the Well of Souls: The Legacy of Nathan Brazil* (1980), the three-part **Watchers of the Well** subseries comprising *Echoes of the Well of Souls* (1993), *Shadow of the Well of Souls* (1994) and *Gods of the Well of Souls* (1994), then finally *The Sea is Full of Stars* (1999) and *Ghost of the Well of Souls* (2000). In this series the dominant pattern of the Chalker multi-volume tale can be seen. Into a Science and Sorcery world which reveals itself in the shape of a game-board disguised as a Dystopia, recruited and metamorphosed mortals are introduced to find their way, usually stark-naked, to the heart of the Labyrinth, where godlings await them, and, perhaps, as a reward for the Godgame they have successfully played, grant them the true form they have always secretly wished to assume. It is a pattern open to abuse; not all of Chalker's fantasy series, for instance, exhibit the exuberance so freely expressed the **Well of Souls** books, or in his other major sf series, **The Four Lords of the Diamond**, which includes *Lilith: A Snake in the Grass* (1981), *Cerberus: A Wolf in the Fold* (1982), *Charon: A Dragon at the Gate* (1982) and *Medusa: A Tiger by the Tail* (1983). The clearest exception to this is the **Soul Rider** sequence, beginning with *Spirits of Flux and Anchor* (1984) (see below). Other sf series include **The Quintara Marathon** – comprising *Demons at Rainbow Bridge* (1989), *The Run to Chaos Keep* (1991) and *The Ninety Trillion Fausts* (1991); and **The Three Kings** sequence – comprising *Balshazzar's Serpent* (1999), *Melchior's Fire* (2001) and *Kaspar's Box* (2003) – where Chalker shifts ground from his usual arena into the Far Future, refreshingly.

Of Chalker's infrequent later singletons, *The Identity Matrix* (1982) (see below) and *Downtiming the Night Side* (1985) stand out; his short fiction, also infrequent, is represented by *Dance Band on the Titanic* (1988). Chalker was a novelist of considerable flair, with an ear acutely attuned to the secret dreams of freedom mortals tend to dream, but the power of his vision was less perceivable by readers during the middle years of his career, when he published many books, not all of them as fresh to the eye as his earlier works. But a selective reading – at least twenty of his novels remain vital entertainments – can bring his big career back into focus. His first thoughts about the splendours and terrors of being human in a metamorphic universe will remain. Though most of his best work was written before the millennium, he is a pioneer of the new century.

Chalker's first great series begins with *Midnight at the Well of Souls* (1977), the first tale reprinted here. It establishes the matrix for the remaining volumes of the **Well of Souls** sequence, and for much of Chalker's future sf. A rambunctious space-freighter captain named Nathan Brazil finds himself on a planet divided, like Oz on speed, into 1460 distinct districts or biomes, each capable of absorbing and metamorphosizing any conscious being who lands in one of them. As he ricochets through this world, Brazil changes sex, occupation, species and powers, without losing track of himself. He encounters dystopias and paradises, philosophies and technologies, all the ways of being human.

Even more compact than this tale, *The Identity Matrix* (1982), the nonstop singleton that closes the omnibus, lives entirely up to its title. But again, out of the churn of identity transfers and transformations, out of the challenges to our species assumptions about the nature of the universe, human souls survive, and flourish, and experience joy.

Bookended by the above, perhaps the best of Chalker's fantasy series, the **Soul Rider** sequence begins with *Spirits of Flux and Anchor* (1984), translating the constant metamorphoses of his earlier sf into a kind of surfing. The roiling universe that embraces the various protagonists of this tale is just like an endless ocean, and the best way to survive life in that ocean is to ride it. After all the turmoil and the tragedy, some joyful essence within the battered human frame opens its eyes, and sees a new horizon. Stripped of all the tomfoolery and all the hurt, that may be the essence of Chalker's message, his gift to us.

For a more detailed version of the above, see Jack L. Chalker's author entry in *The Encyclopedia of Science Fiction*: http://sf-encyclopedia.com/entry/chalker_jack_l

Some terms above are capitalised when they would not normally be so rendered; this indicates that the terms represent discrete entries in *The Encyclopedia of Science Fiction*.

MIDNIGHT AT THE WELL OF SOULS

This book is for Roger Zelazny,
Mark Owings, Applesusan, Avedon,
and Suzy Tiffany for entirely
different reasons.

DALGONIA

Mass murders are usually all the more shocking because of the unexpected settings and the past character of the murderer. The Dalgonian Massacre is a case in point.

Dalgonia is a barren, rocky planet near a dying sun, bathed only in a ghostly, reddish light, whose beautiful rays create sinister shadows across the rocky crags. Little is left of the Dalgonian atmosphere to suggest that life could ever have happened here; the water is gone or, like the oxygen, now locked deep in rock. The feeble sun, unable to give more than the deep reddish tint to the landscape, is of no help in illuminating the skyline, which was, despite a bluish haze from the inert elements still present in it, as dark as the shadows. This was a world of ghosts.

And it was haunted.

Nine figures trooped silently into the ruins of a city that might easily have been mistaken for the rocky crags on the nearby hills. Twisted spires and crumbling castles of greenish-brown stood before them, dwarfing them to insignificance. Their white protective suits were all that made them conspicuous in this darkly beautiful world of silence.

The city itself resembled nothing so much as one that might have been built of iron aeons before and subjected to extensive rust and salt abrasion in some dead sea. Like its world, it was silent and dead.

A close look at the figures heading into the city would reveal that they were all what was known as 'human' – denizens of the youngest part of the spiral arm of their galaxy. Five were female, four male, the leader a thin, frail man of middle years. Stenciled on his back and faceplate was the name *Skander*.

They stood at the half-crumbled gate to the city as they had so many times before, gazing at the incredible but magnificent ruin.

> *My name is Ozymandias.*
> *Look on my works ye mighty,*
> *and despair!*
> *Nothing beside remains …*

If those words from a poet out of their near-forgotten past did not actually echo through each of them, the concept and feeling of those lines did. And through each mind, as they had through the minds of thousands of others

3

who had peered and pecked through similar ruins on over two dozen other dead planets, those endless and apparently unanswerable questions kept running.

Who were they who could build with such magnificence?

Why did they die?

'Since this is your first trip as graduate students to a Markovian ruin,' Skander's reedy voice said through their radios, startling them out of their awe, 'I will give a brief introduction to you. I apologize if I am redundant, but this will be a good refresher nonetheless.

'Jared Markov discovered the first of these ruins centuries ago, on a planet over a hundred light-years distant from this spot. It was our race's first experience with signs of intelligence in this galaxy of ours, and the discovery caused a tremendous amount of excitement. Those ruins were dated at over a quarter of a million standard years old – and they were the youngest discovered to date. It became obvious that, while our race still grubbed on its home world fiddling with the new discovery of fire, someone else – these people – had a vast interstellar empire of still unknown dimensions. All we know is that as we have pressed inward in the galaxy these remains get more and more numerous. And, as yet, we haven't a clue as to who they were.'

'Are there no artifacts of any sort?' came a disbelieving female voice.

'None, as you should know, Citizen Jainet,' came the formal reply in a mildly reproving tone. 'That is what is so infuriating about it all. The cities, yes, about which some things can be inferred about their builders, but no furniture, no pictures, nothing of an even remotely utilitarian nature. The rooms, as you will see, are quite barren. Also, no cemeteries; indeed, nothing mechanical at all, either.'

'That's because of the computer, isn't it?' came another, deeper female voice, that of the stocky girl from the heavy-gravity world whose family name was Marino.

'Yes,' Skander agreed. 'But, come, let's move into the city. We can talk as we go.'

They started forward, soon coming into a broad boulevard, perhaps fifty meters across. Along each side ran what appeared to be broad walkways, each six to eight meters across, like the moving walkways of spaceports that took you to and from loading gates. But no conveyor belt or such was evident; the walkways were made of the same greenish-brown stone, or metal, or whatever it was that composed the rest of the city.

'The crust of this planet,' Skander continued, 'is about average – forty to forty-five kilometers thick. Measurements on this and other worlds of the Markovians showed a consistent discontinuity, about one kilometer thick, between the crust and the natural mantle-rock beneath. This, we have discovered, was an artificial layer of material that is essentially plastic but seems to have had a sort of life in it – this much, at least, we infer. Consider how much information your own cells contain. You are the products of the best genetic manipulation techniques, perfect physical and mental specimens of the best of your races adapted to your native planets. And yet, for all that, you are far more than the sum of your parts. Your cells, particularly your brain cells, store input at an astonishing and continuing rate. We believe that this computer beneath your feet was composed of infinitely complex artificial brain cells. Imagine that! It runs the entirety of the planet, a kilometer thick – all brain. And all, we believe, attuned to the individual brain waves of the inhabitants of this city!

'Imagine it, if you can. Just wish for something, and there it is. Food, furniture – if they used any – even art, created by the mind of the wisher and made real by the computer. We have, of course, small and primitive versions now – but this is generations, possibly millennia, beyond us. If you could think of it, it would be provided!'

'This Utopian Theory accounts for most of what we see, but not why all this is now ruins,' piped in an adolescent male voice, Varnett, the youngest – and probably brightest – but unquestionably the most imaginative of the group.

'Quite true, Citizen Varnett,' Skander acknowledged, 'and there are three schools of thought on it. One is that the computer broke down, and another is that the computer ran amok – and the people couldn't cope either way. You know the third theory, anyone?'

'Stagnation,' Jainet replied. 'They died because they had nothing left to live for, strive for, or work for.'

'Exactly,' Skander replied. 'And yet, there are problems with all three suppositions. An interstellar culture of this magnitude would have allowed for breakdowns; they'd have some sort of backup system. As for the amok theory – well, it's fine except that every sign shows that the same thing happened at once, all across their entire empire. One, even several, okay, but not all at the same time. I am not quite willing to accept the last theory, even though it is the one that fits the best. Something nags at me and says that they would have allowed even for that.'

'Maybe they programmed their own degeneration,' Varnett suggested, 'and it went too far.'

'Eh?' There was a note of surprise but keen interest in Skander's voice. 'Programmed – planned degeneration! It's an interesting theory, Citizen Varnett. Perhaps we'll find out in time.'

He motioned and they entered a building with a strange, hexagonal doorway. All the doors were hexagons, it appeared. The interior of the room was very large, but there was no sign as to its purpose or function. It looked like an apartment or a store after the tenants had moved out, taking everything with them.

'The room,' Skander pointed out to them, 'is hexagonal – as the city is hexagonal, as is almost everything in it if you see it from the correct angle. The number six seems to have been essential to them. Or sacred. It is from this, and from the size and shape of the doorways, windows, and the like – not to mention the width of the walkways – that we have some idea of what the natives must have been like. We hypothesize that they were rather like a top, or turnip shape, with six limbs which may have been tentacles usable for walking or as hands. We suspect that things naturally came in sixes to them – their mathematics, their architecture, maybe they even had six eyes all around. Judging from the doors and allowing for clearance, they were about two meters tall on the average and possibly wider than that at the waist – which is where we believe the six arms, tentacles, or whatever were centered, and that must be why the doorways widen at that point.'

They stood there awhile, trying to imagine such creatures living in the rooms, moving up and down the boulevards.

'We'd best be getting back to camp,' Skander said at last. 'You will have ample time to study here and to poke into every nook and cranny of the place.' They would, in fact, be there a year, working under the professor at the University station.

They walked quickly in the lighter gravity and reached the base camp about five kilometers from the city gates in under an hour.

The camp itself looked like some collection of great tents of a strange circus, nine in all, bright white like the pressure suits. Long tubes connecting the tents occasionally flexed as the monitoring computers continually adjusted the temperature and barometric pressure that kept each inflated. On such a dead world little else was needed, and the insides were lined to make punctures almost impossible. If any such did happen, though, only those in the punctured area would be killed; the computer could seal off any portion of the complex.

Skander entered last, climbing into the air lock after making certain that none of his charges or major equipment was left outside. By the time the lock equalized and allowed him into the entry tent, the others were already all or partially out of their pressure suits.

He stopped for a minute, looking at them. Eight representatives from four planets of the Confederation – and, except for the one from the heavy-gravity world, all looked alike.

All were exceptionally trim and muscular; they could be a gymnastic team without any imagination. Although they ranged in age from fourteen to twenty-two, they all looked prepubescent, which, in fact, they were. Their sexual development had been genetically arrested, and would probably continue that way. He looked at the boy, Varnett, and the girl, Jainet – both from the same planet, the name of which eluded him. The oldest and the youngest of the expedition, yet they were exactly the same height and weight, and, with heads shaved, were virtually identical twins. They had been grown in a lab, a Birth Factory, and brought up by the State to think as identically as they looked. He had once asked why they continued to make both male and female models, only half in jest. It was, of course, a redundancy system in case anything happened to the Birth Factories, he had been told.

Humanity was on at least three hundred planets, and of those all but a handful were on the same line as the world that had spawned these two. Absolute equality, he thought sourly. Look alike, behave alike, think alike, all needs provided for, all wants fulfilled in equal measure to all, assigned the work they were raised for and taught that it was the only proper place for them and their duty. He wondered how the technocrats in charge decided who was to be what.

He thought back to the last batch. Three in that number came from a world that had even dispensed with names and personal pronouns.

He wondered idly how different the human race was at this point from the creatures of the city out there.

Even on worlds like his own home world it was like this, really. True, they grew beards and group sex was the norm, something that would have totally shocked these people. His world had been founded by a group of nonconformists fleeing the technocratic communism of the outer spiral. But, in its own way, it was as conformist as Varnett's home, he thought. Drop Varnett into a Caligristian town and he would be made fun of, called names, even, perhaps lynched. He wouldn't have the beard, or the clothes, or the sex to fit into Caligristo's life-style.

You can't be a nonconformist if you don't wear the proper uniform.

He had often wondered if there was something deep in the human psyche that insisted on tribalism. People used to fight wars not so much to protect their own life-style but to impose it on others.

That's why so many worlds were like these people's – there had been wars to spread the faith, convert the downtrodden. Now the Confederacy forbade that – but the existing conformity, world to world, was the status quo it protected. The leaders of each planet sat on a Council, with an enforcement arm capable of destroying any planet that strayed into 'unsafe' paths and manned by specially trained barbarian psychopaths. But these weapons of terror could not be used without the actions of a majority of the Council.

It had worked. There were no more wars.

They had conformed the entire mass of humanity.

And so had the Markovians, he thought. Oh, the size and sometimes the color and workmanship of the cities had varied, but only slightly.

What had that youth, Varnett, said? Perhaps they had *deliberately* broken down the system?

Skander's face had a frown as he removed the last of his pressure suit. Ideas like that marked brilliance and creativity – but they were unsafe thoughts for a civilization like the one the boy had come from. It revived those old religious ideas that after perfection came true death.

Where could he have gotten an idea like that? And why had he not been caught and stopped?

Skander looked after their naked young bodies as they filed through the tunnel toward the showers and dorm.

Only barbarians thought that way.

Had the Confederacy guessed what he was up to here? Was Varnett not the innocent student he was supposed to be, but the agent of his nightmares?

Did they suspect?

Suddenly he felt very chilly, although the temperature was constant.

Suppose they *all* were …

Three months passed. Skander looked at the picture on his television screen, an electron micrograph of the cellular tissue brought up a month before by the core drill.

It was the same pattern as the older discoveries – that same fine cellular structure, but infinitely more complex inside than any human or animal cell – and so tremendously alien.

And a six-sided cell, at that. He had often wondered about the why of that – had even *their* cells been hexagonal? Somehow he doubted it, but the way that number kept popping up he wouldn't disbelieve it, either.

He stared and stared at the sample. Finally, he reached over and turned up the magnification to full and put on the special filters he had developed and refined in over nine years on this barren planet.

The screen suddenly came alive. Little sparks darted from one point in the cell to another. There was a minor electrical storm in the cell. He sat, fascinated as always, at the view only he had ever seen.

The cell *was* alive.

But the energy was not electrical – that was why it had never been picked up. He had no idea what it was, but it behaved like standard electrical energy. It just didn't measure or appear as electricity should.

The discovery had been an accident, he reflected, three years before. Some careless student had been playing with the screen to get good-looking effects and had left it that way. He had switched it on the next day without noticing anything unusual, then set up the usual energy-detection program for another dull run-through.

It was only a glimpse, a flicker, but he had seen it – and worked on his own for months more to get a filter system that would show that energy photographically.

He had tested the classical samples from other digs, even had one sent to him by a supply ship. They had all been dead.

But not this one.

Somewhere, forty or so kilometers beneath them, the Markovian brain was still alive.

'What *is* that, Professor?' Skander heard a voice behind him. He quickly flipped the screen off and whirled around in one anxious moment.

It was Varnett, that perennial look of innocence on his permanently child-like face.

'Nothing, nothing,' he covered excitedly, the anxiety in his voice betraying the lie. 'Just putting on some playful programs to see what the electrical charges in the cell might have looked like.'

Varnett seemed skeptical. 'Looked pretty real to me,' he said stubbornly. 'If you've made a major breakthrough you ought to tell us about it. I mean—'

'No, no, it's nothing,' Skander protested angrily. Then, regaining his composure, he said, 'That will be all, *Citizen* Varnett! Leave me now!'

Varnett shrugged and left.

Skander sat in his chair for several minutes. His hands – in fact, his whole body – began shaking violently, and it was a while before the attack subsided. Slowly, a panicked look on his face, he went over to the microscope and carefully removed the special filter. His hand was still so unsteady he could hardly hold on to it. He slipped the filter into its tiny case with difficulty and placed it in the wide belt for tools and personal items that was the only clothing any of them wore inside.

He went back to his private room in the dorm section and lay down on his bed, staring up at the ceiling for what seemed like hours.

Varnett, he thought. Always Varnett. In the three months since they had first arrived, the boy had been into everything. Many of the others played their off-duty games and engaged in the silliness students do, but not he. Serious, studious to a fault, and always reading the project reports, the old records.

Skander suddenly felt that everything was closing in on him. He was still so far from his goal!

And now Varnett knew. Knew, at least, that the brain was alive. The boy would surely take it the step further – guess that Skander had almost broken the code, was ready, perhaps in another year or so, to send that brain a message, reactivate it.

To become a god.

He would be the one who would save the human race with the very tools that must have destroyed its maker.

Suddenly Skander jumped up and made his way back to the lab. Something nagged at him, some suspicion that things were even more wrong than he knew.

Quietly, he stepped into the lab.

Varnett was sitting at the television console. And, on the screen, the same cell Skander had been examining was depicted *with its energy connectors clearly visible!*

Skander was stunned. Quickly his hands reached for the little pocket in which he kept his filter. Yes, it was still there.

How was this possible?

Varnett was doing computations, checking against a display on a second screen that hooked him to the math sections of the lab computer. Skander stood there totally still and silent. He heard Varnett mumble an assent to himself, as if some problem he had been running through the computer had checked out correct.

Skander stole a glance at his chronometer. Nine hours! It had been nine hours! He had slept through part of his dark thoughts and given the boy the chance to confirm his worst nightmare.

Something suddenly told Varnett he wasn't alone. He sat still for a second, then glanced fearfully around.

'Professor!' he exclaimed. 'I'm glad it's you! This is stupendous! Why aren't you telling everyone?'

'How –' Skander stumbled, gesturing at the screen. 'How did you get that picture?'

Varnett smiled. 'Oh, that's simple. You forgot to dump the computer memory when you closed up. This is what you were looking at, which the computer held in new storage.'

Skander cursed himself for a fool. Of course, everything on every instrument was recorded by the computer as standard procedure. He had been so shook up by Varnett's discovery of his work that he had forgotten to dump the record!

'It's only a preliminary finding,' the professor managed at last. 'I was waiting until I had something really startling to report.'

'But this *is* startling!' the boy exclaimed excitedly. 'But you have been too close to the problem and to your own disciplines to crack it. Look, your fields are archaeology and biology, aren't they?'

'They are,' Skander acknowledged, wondering where this conversation was leading. 'I was an exobiologist for years and became an archaeologist when I started doing all my work on the Markovian brains.'

'Yes, yes, but you're still a generalist. My world, as you know, raises specialists in every field from the point at which the brain is formed. You know my field.'

'Mathematics,' Skander replied. 'If I recall, all mathematicians on your world are named Varnett after an ancient mathematical genius.'

'Right,' the boy replied, still in an excited tone. 'As I was developing in the

Birth Factory, they imprinted all the world's mathematical knowledge directly. It was there continuously as I grew. By the time my brain was totally developed at age seven, I knew all the mathematics, applied and theoretical, that we know. Everything is ultimately mathematical, and so I see everything in a mathematical way. I was sent here by my world because I had become fascinated by the alien mathematical symmetry in the slides and specimens of the Markovian brain. But all was for nothing, because I had no knowledge of the energy matrix linking the cellular components.'

'And now?' Skander prodded, fascinated and excited in spite of himself.

'Why, it's gibberish. It defies all mathematical logic. It says that there are *no* absolutes in mathematics! None! Every time I tried to force the pattern into known mathematical concepts, it kept saying that two plus two equals four isn't a constant but a *relative* proposition!'

Skander realized that the boy was trying to make things baby-simple to him, but he still couldn't grasp what he was saying. 'What does all that mean?' he asked in a puzzled and confused tone.

Varnett was becoming carried away with himself. 'It means that all matter and energy are in some kind of mathematical proportion. That nothing is actually real, nothing actually anything at all. If you discard the equal sign and substitute "is proportional to" and, if it is true, you can alter or change *anything*. None of us, this room, this planet, the whole galaxy, the whole universe – none of it is a constant! If you could alter the equation for anything only slightly, change the proportions, anything could be made anything else, anything could be changed to anything else!' He stopped, seeing from the expression on Skander's face that the older man was still lost.

'I'll give a really simple, basic example,' Varnett said, calmed considerably from his earlier outburst. 'First, realize this if you can: there is a finite amount of energy in the universe, and that is the only constant. The amount is infinite by our standards, but that is true if this is true. Do you follow me?'

Skander nodded. 'So you're saying that there is nothing but pure energy?'

'More or less,' Varnett agreed. 'All matter, and *constrained* energy, like stars, is created out of this energy flux. It is held there in that state – you, me, the room, the planet we're on – by a mathematical balance. Something – some quantity – is placed in proportion to some other quantity, and that forms us. And keeps us stable. If I knew the formula for Elkinos Skander, or Varnett Mathematics Two Sixty-one, I could alter, or even abolish, our existence. Even things like time and distance, the best constants, could be altered or abolished. If I knew your formula I could, given one condition, not only change you into, say, a chair, but alter all events so that you would have always *been* a chair!'

'What's the condition?' Skander asked nervously, hesitantly, afraid of the answer.

'Why, you'd need a device to translate that formula into reality. And a way to have it do what you wished.'

'The Markovian brain,' Skander whispered.

'Yes. That's what they discovered. But this brain – this device – seems to be for local use only. That is, it would affect this planet, perhaps the solar system in which it lies, but no more. But, somewhere, there must be a master unit – a unit that could affect at least half, perhaps the whole, galaxy. It *must* exist, if all the rest of my hypothesis is correct!'

'Why must it?' Skander asked, a sinking sensation growing in his stomach.

'Because *we* are stable,' the boy replied, an awestruck tone in his voice.

Only the mechanical sounds of the lab intruded for a minute after that, as the implications sank home to both of them.

'And you have the code?' Skander asked at last.

'I think so, although it goes against my whole being that such equations can be correct. And yet – do you know why that energy does not show by conventional means?' Skander slowly shook his head negatively, and the mathematician continued. 'It is the primal energy itself. Look, do you have that filter with you?'

Skander nodded numbly and produced the little case. The boy took it eagerly, but instead of placing it in the microscope he went over to the outer wall. Slowly he donned protective coveralls and goggles, used in radiation protection, and told Skander to do likewise. Then he sealed the lab against entry and peeled back the tent lining in the one place where it covered a port – not used here, but these tents were all-purpose and contained many useless features.

The baleful reddish landscape showed before them at midday. Slowly, carefully, the boy held the tiny filter up to one eye and closed the other. He gasped. 'I was right!' he exclaimed.

After a painful half-minute that felt like an eternity, he handed the little filter to Skander, who did the same.

Through the filter, the entire landscape was bathed in a ferocious electrical storm. Skander couldn't stop looking at it.

'The Markovian brain is all around us,' Varnett whispered. 'It draws what it needs and expels what it does not. If we could contact it—'

'We'd be like gods,' Skander finished.

Skander reluctantly put down the filter and handed it back to Varnett, who resumed his own gazing.

'And what sort of universe would you create, Varnett?' Skander almost whispered, reaching under the protective clothing as he spoke and pulling out a knife. 'A mathematically perfect place where everyone was absolutely identical, the *same* equation?'

'Put your weapon away, Skander,' Varnett told him, not taking his gaze from the filtered landscape. 'You can't do it without me, and if you think about it you'll realize that. In only a few months they'll find our bodies and you here – or dying in the city – and what will that get you?'

The knife hesitated a long moment, then slowly slid back into the belt under the protective garment.

'What the hell are you, Varnett?' asked Skander suspiciously.

'An aberration,' the other replied. 'We happen, sometimes. Usually they catch us and that's that. But not me, not yet. They will, though, unless I can do something about it.'

'What do you mean, an aberration?' Skander asked unsurely.

'I'm human, Skander. A real human. And greedy. I, too, would like to be a god.'

It had taken Varnett only seven hours to crack the mathematics, but it would take a lot longer to make the Markovian brain notice them. Their project was so intense that the others began to take notice and inquire, particularly the research assistants. Finally, they decided to take them all in on it – Varnett because he was certain that, once in contact with the Markovian brain, he could adjust the others to his version of events, and Skander because he had no choice. While they worked the lab, the others combed the city and, using small flyers, the other cities and regions of the planet.

'You are to look for some sort of vent, entrance, gate, or at least a temple or similar structure that might mean some kind of direct contact with the Markovian brain,' Skander told them.

And time went on, with the others, good Universalists all, looking forward to carrying the news back to the Confederacy that the perfect society was within man's grasp.

Finally, one day, only two months before the next ship was due in, they found it.

Jainet and Dunna, one of the research assistants, noticed through the large filters they had constructed for the search that one tiny area near the north pole of the planet was conspicuous by the absence of the all-pervasive lightning.

Flying over to it they saw below them a deep hexagonal hole of total darkness. They were reluctant to explore further without consultation, and so radioed for the rest to come up.

'I don't see anything,' Skander complained, disappointed. 'There's no hex hole here.'

'But there was!' Jainet protested, and Dunna nodded in agreement. 'It was right there, almost directly over the pole. Here! I'll prove it!' She went over and rewound the flyer's nose camera recording disk a little more than halfway. They watched the playback in skeptical silence, as the ground rolled beneath them on the screen. Then, suddenly, there it was.

'See!' Jainet exclaimed. 'What did I tell you!'

And it was there, clearly, unquestionably. Varnett looked at the screen, then to the scene below them, then back again. It all checked. There had been a hexagonal hole, almost two kilometers across at its widest point. The landmarks matched – it was at this spot.

But there wasn't a hole there now.

They waited then, almost an entire day. Suddenly the flat plain seemed to vanish and there was the hole again.

They photographed it and ran every analysis test on it they could.

'Let's drop something in,' Varnett suggested at last. They found a spare pressure suit and, hovering directly over the hole, the light on the suit turned on, they dropped it in.

The suit struck the hole. 'Struck' is the only word they had for it. The suit hit the top of the hole and seemed to stick there, not dropping at all. Then, after hovering a moment, it seemed to fade before their eyes. Not drop, but fade – for even the films showed that it didn't fall. It simply faded out to nothingness.

A few minutes later the hole itself disappeared.

'Forty-six standard minutes,' Varnett said. 'Exactly. And I'll bet at the same time gap tomorrow it opens again.'

'But where did the suit go? Why didn't it drop?' Jainet asked.

'Remember the power of this thing,' Skander told her. 'If you were to get to it, you wouldn't descend forty-plus kilometers. You'd simply be transported to the place.'

'Exactly,' Varnett agreed. 'It would simply alter the equation and you would be *there* instead of *here*.'

'But where is *there?*' Jainet asked.

'We believe at the control center of the Markovian brain,' Skander told her. 'There would be one – the same way there are two bridges on a spaceship. The other is for emergencies.' Or male and female members on your planet, Skander had almost said.

'We'd best go back and run this all through our own data banks,' Varnett suggested. 'After all, it's been a long day for us anyway. The hole opens and closes regularly. So we can do the same things tomorrow as we can do today.'

They all muttered assent at this proposal, and several suddenly realized how tired they were.

'Someone should stay here,' Skander suggested, 'if only to time the thing and keep the camera running.'

'I'll do it,' Varnett volunteered. 'I can sleep here on this flyer and you all can go back in the other two. If anything comes up I'll let you know. Then someone can spell me tomorrow.'

They all agreed to this, so after a short while everyone but Varnett headed back to base camp.

Almost all went to sleep immediately, only Skander and Dunna taking the extra time to feed their records into the data bank. Then both went off to their own quarters.

Skander sat on the edge of his bunk, too excited to feel tired. Curiously, he felt exhilarated instead, adrenalin pumping through him.

I must take the gamble, he told himself. I must assume that this is indeed the gateway to the brain. In less than fifty days this crew will be replaced, and they'll go home to blab the secret. Then everyone will be in, and the Statists of the Confederacy will gain the power.

Was that what had happened to the Markovians? Had they become so much a communal paradise that they stagnated and died out?

No! he told himself. *Not for* them! *I shall die, or I shall save mankind.*

He went first to the lab and wiped all information from the data banks. There was nothing left when he finished; then he wrecked the machinery so none could retrieve the faintest clue. Next he went to the master control center. There the atmospheric conditions were set. Slowly, methodically, he turned off all the systems except oxygen. He waited there almost an hour until the gauges read that the atmosphere was now almost entirely oxygen everywhere in the tents.

That done, he made his way carefully to the air lock, anxious not to scrape against anything or to cause any sort of spark. Although nervous at the prospect that one of the sleepers would wake up and make that spark, he took the time to don his pressure suit and then take all the other such suits outside.

Next he took from the emergency kit of one of the flyers a small box and opened it.

Premanufactured items for all occasions. It was a flare gun.

The puncture it would make would be sealed in seconds by the automated equipment, but not before it ignited the oxygen inside.

It was over in one sudden flare, like flash paper.

After, he could see the vacuum-exposed remains of the sleepers whose charred bodies were still in their beds.

Seven down, one to go, he thought without remorse.

He boarded a flyer and headed toward the north pole. He glanced at his chronometer. It took nine hours to fly back, he had been three doing his work, and now there was another nine to return to the pole.

About an hour to spare until that hole opened up again.

Enough time for Varnett.

It seemed like days until he got there, but the chronometer said just a little over nine hours.

As he came over the horizon he searched for Varnett's flyer. It wasn't to be seen.

Suddenly Skander spotted it – down, down on that flat plain at the pole.

He braked and hovered over it. Slowly, in the gloom, he made out a tiny white dot near the center of the plain.

Varnett! He was going to be the first in!

Varnett detected movement and looked up at the flyer. Suddenly he started running for his own.

Skander came down on him, skirting the ground so low that he was afraid he would crash himself. Varnett ducked and rolled, but was unhurt.

Skander cursed himself, then decided to set it down. He still had the knife, and that might just be enough. He took the flare pistol which, while it wouldn't necessarily penetrate the suit, might cause a blinding distraction. He was not a large man, but he was a head taller than the boy and the odds were otherwise even in his mind.

Landing near Varnett's flyer, he got out quickly, flare gun in his right hand, knife in his left. Cursing the almost total absence of light and the fact that he had had to take his eyes off Varnett to land, Skander looked cautiously around.

Varnett had vanished.

Before this could sink in, a white figure jumped from atop the other flyer and hit him in the back. He went down, dropping the flare gun.

The two figures, rolling across the rocky landscape, grappled for the knife. Skander was larger, but older and in worse physical condition than Varnett. Finally, with a shove, Skander pushed Varnett away from him and came upon the boy with the knife. Varnett let him get very close; then, as the knife made a quick stab, the boy's arm reached out and caught the older man's wrist. The two struggled and groaned in their suits as Skander tried to press the knife home.

They were in that frozen tableau when, suddenly, the hole opened.

They were both already in it.

Both vanished.

ANOTHER PART OF THE FIELD

Nathan Brazil stretched back in his huge, pillowy lounge chair aboard the bridge of the freighter *Stehekin*, nine days out of Paradise with a load of grain bound for drought-stricken Coriolanus and with three passengers. Passengers were common on such runs – there were actually a dozen staterooms aboard – as freighter travel was much cheaper than passenger ships and a lot easier if you wanted to get where you were going in a hurry. There were a thousand freight runs for every passenger run to almost anyplace.

The crew consisted only of Brazil. The ships were now automated, so he was there just in case something went wrong. Food had been prepared for all before takeoff and had been loaded into the automated kitchen. A tiny ward-room was used on those occasions when someone wanted to eat outside of his stateroom or with the captain.

Actually, the passengers had more contempt for him than he for them. In an age of extreme conformity, men like Nathan Brazil were the mavericks, the loners, the ones who didn't fit. Recruited mostly off the barbarian worlds of the frontier, they could take the loneliness of the job, the endless weeks often without human company. Most psychologists called them sociopaths, people alienated from society.

Brazil liked people all right, but not the factory-made ones. He would rather sit here in his domain, the stars showing on the great three-dimensional screens in front of him, and reflect on why society had become alienated from him.

He was a small man, around 170 centimeters tall, slight and thin. His skin was dark-complexioned. Two bright, brown eyes flanked a conspicuous Roman nose which sat atop a mouth very wide, rubbery, and full of teeth. His black hair hung long to his shoulders, but was stringy and looked over-greased and underwashed. He had a thin mustache and thinner full beard that looked as if someone had attempted to grow a full brush and hadn't made it. He was dressed in a loose-fitting but loudly colorful tunic and matching pants, and wore sandals of a sickly green.

The passengers, he knew, were scared stiff of him, and he liked it that way. Unfortunately, they were still almost thirty days out and their boredom and claustrophobia would sooner or later drive them meddling into his lap.

Oh, hell, he thought. Might as well get everybody together. They have huddled back in that small lounge in the stern long enough.

He reached up and flicked a switch.

'The captain,' he intoned in a tenor voice that nonetheless had a gravelly undertone to it, making it sound a little harsh and unintentionally sarcastic, 'requests the pleasure of your company at dinner today. If you like, you may join me in the wardroom forward in thirty minutes. Don't feel put out if you don't want to come. I won't,' he concluded, and switched off the speaker, chuckling softly.

Why do I do that? he asked himself for the hundredth – thousandth? – time. For nine days I chase them around, bully them, and see as little of them as possible. Now, when I start to be sociable, I blow it.

He sighed, then reached over and dialed the meals. Now they would *have* to come up, or starve. He idly scratched himself and wondered whether or not he should take a shower before dinner. No, he decided, I had one only five days ago; I'll just use deodorant.

He picked up the book he had been reading off and on, a blood-and-guts romance on some faraway planet published centuries ago and produced in facsimile for him by a surprised and gratified librarian.

He called librarians his secret agents because he was one of the very few who read books at all. Libraries were usually single institutions on planets and were patronized by only a very few. Nobody wrote books anymore, he thought, not even this garbage. They dredged up whatever information they needed for reference from the computer terminal in every household; even then the vast majority were the vocal types that answered questions. Only the technocrats needed to read.

Only barbarians and wanderers read anymore.

And librarians.

Everybody else could just flip a switch and get a full, three-dimensional, sight-sound-and-smell creation of their own fantasies or those of a crew of dedicated fantasists picked by the government.

Pretty dull shit, he thought. Even the people were bred without imaginations. The imaginative ones were fixed – or gotten rid of. Too dangerous to have a thinker unless he thought the government's way.

Brazil wondered idly whether any of his passengers could read. The Pig probably – his name for Datham Hain, who looked very much like one – but he probably only read up on the stuff he sold or some mundane crap like that. Maybe a manual on how to strangle people twenty ways, he thought. Hain looked as if he'd enjoy that.

The girl with him was harder to figure. Like Hain, she obviously wasn't from the communal factory worlds – she was mature, maybe twenty or so, and, if she didn't look so wasted away, she might be pretty. Not built, or beautiful, but nice. But she had that empty look in her eyes, and was so damned servile to the fat man. Wu Julee, the manifest said her name was. *Julie Wu?* mused a corner of his brain. There it was again! Damn! He tried to grab onto the source of the thought, but it vanished.

But she does look Chinese, said that little corner, and then the thought retreated once again.

Chinese. That word meant something once. He knew it did. Where did those terms come from? And why couldn't he remember where they came from? Hell, almost everybody had those characteristics these days, he thought.

Then, suddenly, the thought was out of his mind, as such thoughts always were, and he was back on his main track.

The third one – almost the usual, he reflected, except that he never drew the usual, permanently twelve-year-old automaton on his trips. They were all raised and conditioned to look alike, think alike, and believe that theirs was the best of all possible worlds. No reason to travel. But Vardia Diplo 1261 was the same underneath, anyway: looked twelve, was flat-chested, probably neutered, since there was some pelvic width. She was a courier between her world and the next bunch of robots down the line. Spent all her time doing exercises.

A tiny bell sounded telling him that dinner was served, and he got up and ambled back to the wardroom.

The wardroom – nobody knew why it was called that – merely consisted of a large table that was permanently attached to the floor and a series of chairs that were part of the floor until you pulled up on a little ring, where-upon they arose and became comfortable seats. The place was otherwise a milky white plastic – walls, floor, ceiling, even tabletop. The monotony was broken only by small plaques giving the ship's name, construction data, own-ership, and by his and the ship's commissions from the Confederacy as well as by his master's license.

He entered, half expecting no one to be there, and was surprised to see the two women already seated. The fat man was up, intently reading his master's license.

Hain was dressed in a light blue toga that made him look like Nero; Wu Julee was dressed in similar fashion, but it looked better on her. The Com-worlder, Vardia, wore a simple, one-piece black robe. He noted idly that Wu Julee seemed to be in a trance, staring straight ahead.

Hain completed reading the wall plaques, then returned to his seat next to Wu Julee, a frown forming on his corpulent face.

'What's so odd about my license?' Brazil asked curiously.

'That form,' Hain replied in a silky-smooth, disquieting voice. 'It is so old! No such form has been used in my memory.'

The captain nodded and smiled, pushing a button under his chair. The food compartments opened up on top and plates of steaming food were revealed in front of each person. A large bottle and four glasses rose from a circular opening in the middle of the table.

'I got it a long time ago,' he told them conversationally, as he chose a glass and poured some nonalcoholic wine into it.

'You have been in rejuve then, Captain?' Hain responded politely.

Brazil nodded. 'Many times. Freighter captains are known for it.'

'But it costs – unless one is influential with the Council,' Hain noted.

'True,' Brazil acknowledged, talking as he chewed his synthetic meat. 'But we're well paid, in port only a few days every few weeks, and most of us just put our salaries into escrow to pay for what we need. Nothing much else to blow it on these days.'

'But the date!' Vardia broke in. 'It's so very, very old! Citizen Hain said it was three hundred and sixty-two standard years!'

Brazil shrugged. 'Not very unusual. Another captain on this same line is over five hundred.'

'Yes, that's true,' Hain said. 'But the license is stamped *Third Renewal – P.C.* How old *are* you, anyway?'

Brazil shrugged again. 'I truthfully don't know. As old as the records, anyway. The brain has a finite capacity, so every rejuve erases a little more of the past. I get snatches of things – old memories, old terms – from time to time, but nothing I can hang on to. I could be six hundred – or six thousand, though I doubt it.'

'You've never inquired?' Hain asked curiously.

'No,' Brazil managed, his mouth full of mush. He swallowed, then took another long drink of wine. 'Lousy stuff,' he snorted, holding the glass up and looking at it as if it were full of disease cultures. Suddenly he remembered he was in the middle of a conversation.

'Actually,' he told them, 'I've been curious as to all that, but the records just sort of fade out. I've outlived too many bureaucracies. Well, I've always lived for now and the future, anyway.'

Hain had already finished his meal, and patted his ample stomach. 'I'm due for my first rejuve in another year or two. I'm almost ninety, and I'm afraid I've abused myself terribly these past few years.'

As the small talk continued, Brazil's gaze kept falling to the girl who sat so strangely by Hain. She seemed to be paying not the least attention to the conversation and had hardly touched her food.

'Well,' Brazil said, suppressing his curiosity about the strange girl, '*my* career is on that wall and Citizen Vardia's is obvious, but what takes you flitting around the solar systems, Hain?'

'I am – well, a salesman, Captain,' the fat man replied. 'All of the planets are somewhat unique in the excesses they produce. What is surplus on one is usually needed on another – like the grain you have as cargo on this fine ship. I'm a man who arranges such trades.'

Brazil made his move. 'What about you, Citizen Wu Julee? Are you his secretary?'

The girl looked suddenly confused. *That's real fear in her eyes*, Brazil noted to himself, surprised. She turned immediately to Hain, a look of pleading in her face.

'My – ah, niece, Captain, is very shy and quiet,' Hain said smoothly. 'She prefers to remain in the background. You *do* prefer to remain in the background, don't you, my dear?'

She answered in a voice that almost cracked from disuse, in a thin voice that held no more tonal inflection than Vardia's.

'I do prefer to remain in the background,' she said dully, like a machine. A recording machine at that – for there seemed no comprehension in that face.

'Sorry!' Brazil told her apologetically, turning palms up in a gesture of resignation.

Funny, he thought to himself. The one who looks like a robot is conversational and mildly inquisitive; the one who looks like a real girl is a robot. He thought of two girls he had known long ago – he could even remember their names. One was a really sexy knockout – you panted just being in the same room with her. The other was ugly, flat, and extremely mannish in manner, voice, and dress – the sort of nondescript nobody looked at twice. But the sexy one liked other girls best, and the mannish one was heaven in bed.

You can't tell by looks, he reflected sourly.

Vardia broke the silence. She was, after all, bred to the diplomatic service.

'I think it is fascinating you are so old, Captain,' she said pleasantly. 'Perhaps you are the oldest man alive. My race, of course, has no rejuve – it is not needed.'

No, of course not, Brazil thought sadly. They lived their eighty years as juvenile specialist components in the anthill of their society, then calmly showed up at the local Death Factory to be made into fertilizer.

Anthill? he thought curiously. Now what in hell were *ants*?

Aloud, he replied, 'Well, old or not I can't say, but it doesn't do anybody much good unless you've got a job like mine. I don't know why I keep on living – just something bred into me, I guess.'

Vardia brightened. *That* was something she could understand. 'I wonder what sort of world would require such a survival imperative?' she mused, proving to everyone else that she didn't understand at all.

Brazil let it pass.

'A long-dead-and-gone one, I think,' he said dryly.

'I think we shall go back to our rooms, Captain,' Hain put in, getting up and stretching. 'To tell the truth, the only thing more exhausting than doing something is doing nothing at all.' Julee rose almost at the same instant as the fat man, and they left together.

Vardia said, 'I suppose I shall go back as well, Captain, but I would like the chance to talk to you again and, perhaps, to see the bridge.'

'Feel free,' he responded warmly. 'I eat here every mealtime and company is always welcome. Perhaps tomorrow we'll eat and talk and then I'll show you how the ship runs.'

'I shall look forward to it,' she replied, and there even seemed a bit of warmth in her flat voice – or, at least, sincerity. He wondered how genuine it was, and how much was the inbred diplomatic traits. It was the sort of comment that was guaranteed to please him. He wondered if he would ever know what went on in those insect minds.

Well, he told himself, in actual fact it didn't make a damned bit of difference – he would show her around the ship and she would seem to enjoy it anyway.

When he was alone in the wardroom, he looked over at the empty dishes.

Hain had polished off everything, as expected, and so had Vardia and he – the meals were individually prepared for preference and body build.

Julee's meal was almost untouched. She had merely played with the food.

No wonder she's wasting away, he thought. Physically, anyway. But why mentally? She certainly *wasn't* Hain's niece, no matter what he said, and he doubted if she was an employee, either.

Then, *what?*

He pushed the disposal button and lowered the chairs back to their floor position, then returned to the bridge.

Freighter captains were the law in space, of course. They had to be. As such, ships of all lines had certain safeguards unique to each captain, and some gimmicks common to all but known only to those captains.

Brazil sat back down in his command chair and looked at the projection screen still showing the virtually unchanging starscape. It looked very realistic, and very impressive, but it was a phony – the scene was a computer simulation; the Balla-Drubbik drive which allowed faster-than-light travel was extradimensional in nature. There was simply nothing outside the ship's energy well that would relate to any human terms.

He reached over and typed on the computer keyboard: 'I SUSPECT ILLEGAL ACTIVITIES. SHOW CABINS 6 ON LEFT AND 7 ON RIGHT SCREEN.' The computer lit a small yellow light to show that the instructions had been received and the proper code for the captain registered; then the simulated starfield was replaced with overhead, side-by-side views of the two cabins.

The fact that cameras were hidden in all cabins and could be monitored by captains was a closely guarded secret, though several people had already had knowledge of the accidentally discovered bugs erased from their minds by the Confederacy. Yet, many a madman and hijacker had been trapped by these methods, and Brazil also knew that the Confederation Port Authority would look at the recordings of what he was seeing live and question him as to motive. This wasn't something done lightly.

Cabin 6 – Hain's cabin – was empty, but the missing passenger was in Wu Julee's Cabin 7. A less-experienced, less-jaded man would have been repulsed at the scene.

Hain was standing near the closed and bolted door, stark naked. Wu Julee, a look of terror on her face, was also naked.

Brazil turned up the volume.

'Come on, Julee,' Hain commanded, a tone of delightful expectancy in his harsh voice. There was no question as to what he had in mind.

The girl cowed back in horror. 'Please! Please, Master!' she pleaded with all the hysterical emotion she had hidden in public.

'When you do it, Julee,' Hain said in a hushed but still excited tone. 'Only then.'

She did what he asked.

Less-experienced and less-jaded men would have been repulsed at the sight, it was true.

Brazil was becoming aroused.

After she finished, Wu Julee continued to plead with the fat man to give it to her. Brazil waited expectantly, half-knowing what *it* was already. He just had to see where it was hidden and how it was protected.

Hain promised her he would go get it and then donned the toga once more. He unbolted the door and appeared to look up and down the hallway. Satisfied, he walked out to his own cabin and unlocked the door. The unseen watcher turned his gaze to Cabin 6.

Hain entered and took a small, thin attaché case from beneath the wash-basin. It had the high-security locks, Brazil noted – five small squares programmed to receive five of Hain's ten fingerprints in a certain order. Hain's body blocked reading the combination, but it wouldn't have mattered anyway – without Hain's touch the whole inside would dissolve in a quick acid bath.

Hain opened the case to reveal a tray of jewelry and body paint. Normal enough, and the tray seemed deep enough to fill the whole case. No customs problems.

Working a second set of fingerprint-coded combinations through the thin plastic which hid the additional guards, the tray came loose and appeared to be floating on something else. The fat man lifted the tray out.

For the first time Brazil noticed that Hain had on some thin gloves. He hadn't seen them being put on – maybe they were already on during the scene he had just witnessed – but there they were.

The fat man reached in and picked out a tiny object that almost dripped with liquid. The rest of the case bottom, Brazil could see, was filled with the stuff. His suspicions were confirmed.

Datham Hain was a sponge merchant.

The contraband was called sponge because that was what the stuff was – an alien sponge spawned on a distant sea world now interdicted by the Confederacy.

The story came back to Brazil. A nice planet, mostly ocean but dotted with millions of islands connected in a network of shallows. A tropical climate except at the poles. It looked like a paradise, and tests had shown nothing that could hurt the human race. A test colony – two, three hundred people – was landed on the two largest islands for the five-year trial, as per standard procedure. Volunteers, of course, the last remnant of frontiersmen in the human race.

If they survived and prospered, they owned the world – to develop it or do with it what they would. But because man's test instruments could analyze only the known and the theoretical, there was no way to detect a threat so alien it hadn't even been imagined. That was the reason for the trial in the first place.

So those people had settled in and lived and loved and played and built on their islands.

For almost a month.

That was when they started to go mad, the people of that colony. They regressed – slowly, at first, then increasingly faster and faster. They turned into primitive beasts as the thing that had caught them ate away at their brains. They became like wild apes, only without even the most rudimentary reasoning ability. Finally they died, from their inability to cope with even the basics of eating and shelter. Most drowned; some killed one another.

And out of their bodies, eventually, grew the pretty flowers of the island, in new profusion.

Scientists speculated that some sort of elemental organism – based not on carbon or silicon, but on the iron oxides in the rocks of their pretty island – interacted through the air not with them but with the synthetic food rations they brought to help them until they could develop their own native agriculture.

And they had eaten it, and it had eaten them.

But there had been one survivor – one woman who had hidden in the huge beds of alien sponge along a particularly rocky shoreline. Oh, she had died, too – but almost three weeks later than the others. When she no longer returned each evening to sleep in the sponge bed.

The natural secretions of the sponge acted as a retardant – not as an antidote. But as long as a victim had a daily intake of the secretion, the mutant strain seemed inactive. Remove the substance – and the degenerative process began once again. But scientists had taken some samples of the mutant strain and of living sponge with them to study in their labs on far-off worlds. All of it was thought to have been destroyed afterward – but evidently some had not been. Some had been taken by the worst of elements and was developed in their own labs in unknown space.

The perfect commodity.

By secretly introducing the stuff into people's food, you gave them the disease. Then, when the first symptoms came and baffled all around you, the merchant would come. He would ease the pain and cause normality by giving you a little bit of sponge – as Hain was administering a dose to Wu Julee at that very moment.

The Confederacy wouldn't help you. It maintained a sponge colony on that interdicted world for the afflicted, where one could live a normal, if very primitive, existence and soak each night in a sponge bath. If, that is, the victim could be gotten there before the disease became too progressive to bother.

The sponge merchants chose only the most wealthy and powerful – or their children, if their world had families of any sort. There was no charge for the daily sponge supply, oh, no. You just did as they asked when they asked.

There was even the suspicion that so many rulers of the Confederacy were hostage to the stuff now that that was the reason no real search for an antidote or cure had ever been started.

For power was the ultimate aim of the sponge merchants.

Nathan Brazil wondered who Wu Julee was. The daughter of some big-shot ruler or banker or industrialist? Maybe the child of the Confederacy enforcement chief? More likely she was a sample, he thought. No use risking exposure.

She was his absolute slave, no question. The disease had been allowed to incubate in her just short of that critical point when the stuff multiplied exponentially. Human, yes, but probably already with her IQ halved, constantly in mild pain that started to grow as the effects of the sponge antitoxin wore off. An effective demonstration, which would keep the merchant from having to infect some innocent and let things run their full course. That was done, of course, when necessary – but it wasn't good to have a long period of time when it would be obvious to the agents of the Confederacy that a sponge merchant was at large.

He wondered idly why the girl didn't commit suicide. He thought *he* would. A victim is probably too far gone to consider it by the time he realizes it is the only option, he decided.

Brazil looked back up at the screens. Hain had repacked the case and stored it and was preparing to go to sleep. Clever, that case, the captain thought. Sponge is extremely compressible and needs only enough seawater to keep it moist. It even grew in there, he thought. As samples were dispensed, new ones would replace it. That was the reason only the minimum was ever given to a victim – get hold of enough of it, unused, and you could grow your own.

Wu Julee was lying on her own bed, one leg draped down on the side. She was breathing hard but she had a sort of idiot's smile on her face.

Relief for another day, the little sponge cube swallowed, the body breaking down the evidence.

Nathan Brazil's stomach finally turned.

What were you, Wu Julee, before Datham Hain served dinner? he mused. A student or scholar, or a professional, like Vardia? A spoiled brat? A young maiden, perhaps one day expecting to bear children?

Gone now, he thought sadly. The recordings would nail Datham Hain clean – and the syndicate of sponge merchants would let him hang, too. Most he had ever heard of were compulsive suiciders when subjected to any psych probes or the like. They would get nothing from him but his life.

But Wu Julee – without sponge, she needed eighteen days from where they would be at absolute flank speed to make that damned planet colony, and she was already near or at the exponential reproductive stage.

She would arrive a mindless vegetable, unable to do anything not in the autonomic nervous system, having spent most of the voyage as an animal. A day or two after that, it would eat her nervous system away and she would die.

So they wouldn't bother. They'd just send her to the nearest Death Factory to get something useful out of her.

They said Nathan Brazil was a hard man: experienced, efficient, and cold as ice, never a feeling for anything but himself.

But Nathan Brazil cried at tragedy, alone, in the dark, on the bridge of his powerful ship.

Neither Hain nor Wu Júlee came to dinner again, although he saw the fat man often and kept up the pretense of innocent friendship. The sponge merchant could actually be quite entertaining, sitting back in the lounge over a couple of warm drinks and telling stories of his youth. He even played a fair game of cards.

Vardia, of course, never joined in the games and stories – they were things beyond her conception. She kept asking *why* they played card games since the only practical purpose of games was to develop a physical or mental skill. The concept of gambling, of playing for money, meant even less to her – her people didn't use the stuff, and only printed it for interplanetary trade. The government provided everyone with everything they needed equally, so why try to get more?

Brazil found her logic, as usual, baffling. All his life he had been compulsively competitive. He was firmly convinced of his uniqueness in the universe and his general superiority to it, although he was occasionally bothered by the universe's lack of appreciation. But she remained inquisitive and continued asking all those questions two cultures could never answer for each other.

'You promised days ago to show me the bridge,' she reminded him one day.

'So I did,' he acknowledged. 'Well, now's as good a time as any. Why don't we go all the way forward?'

They made their way from the aft lounge, along the great catwalk above the cargo.

'I don't mean to pry,' he said to her as they walked along, 'but, out of curiosity, is your mission of vital importance?'

'You mean war or peace, something like that?' Vardia responded. 'No, very few are like that. The truth is, as you may know, I have no knowledge of the messages I carry. They are blocked and only the key from our embassy on

Coriolanus can unlock whatever I'm supposed to say. Then the information will be erased, and I will be sent home, with or without a message in return. But, from the tone or facial expressions of those who give me the messages, I can usually tell if it's serious, and this one certainly is not.'

'Possibly something to do with the cargo,' Brazil speculated as they entered the wardroom and walked through it this time and out onto another, shorter catwalk. The great engines which maintained the real-universe field of force around them throbbed below. 'Do you know how bad things are on Coriolanus?'

She shrugged. 'Not too bad, I understand. No widespread famine yet. That will happen months from now, when the harvest doesn't come in because the rains didn't come *last* season and the ground is too hard. Then this cargo will be needed. Why do you ask?'

'Oh, just curious, I guess,' he responded, an odd and slightly strained tone in his voice.

They entered the bridge.

Vardia was immediately all over it, like an anxious schoolchild. 'What's this?' and 'How's that work?' and all the other questions poured from her. He answered as best he could.

She marveled over the computer. 'I have never seen one that you must write to and read,' she told him with the awe reserved for genuine historical antiques. He decided not to respond that people these days were too mechanical for him so he couldn't bear to have a real mechanical person around, but instead he replied, 'Well, it's what you get used to. This one's just as modern and efficient as any other; I tried it on and can handle it easier. Although I have little to do, in an emergency I have to make thousands of split-second decisions. It's better to use what you can use instinctively in such a situation.'

She accepted his explanation, which was partially the truth, and noticed his small library of paperback books with their lurid covers. He asked her if she knew how to read and she said no, whatever for? Certain professions on her world required the ability to read, of course, but very few – and if that wasn't required, as it certainly wasn't for her job as a reel of blank recording tape, she could see no reason to learn.

He wondered if somewhere they simply had a single Vardia Diplo program, and they read it out, erased the whole thing, then rerecorded it for each trip. Probably, he decided – otherwise, she would have seen bridges before and encountered enough alien culture not to ask those naive questions. Most likely she was just new. It was tough to tell if her kind was fourteen or forty-four.

At any rate, he was glad she couldn't read. He had suffered a very unsettling moment when she had gone over to that computer and he had noticed that he had forgotten to turn off the screen.

The computer had been spewing its usual every-half-hour warning to him.

UNAUTHORIZED COURSE CORRECTION, it said. THIS IS NOT A JUSTIFIED ACTION. COURSE IS BEING PLOTTED AND WILL BE BROADCAST TO CONFEDERACY AS SOON AS DESTINATION IS REACHED.

And she wondered why he didn't have the talking kind of computer.

And so they continued on the new course, all but Brazil and the computer oblivious to their real destination.

A stroke of genius, he congratulated himself after Vardia had left. The courier's answers had eased his conscience on Coriolanus. They would get their grain – just late. In the meantime, Hain would continue to give Wu Julee the sponge, until that day came when they arrived over the sponge world itself. There he would lose two passengers – Wu Julee would have life, and Hain would be introduced to the colony as a pusher.

Brazil didn't think any Admiralty Board in the galaxy would convict him; besides, he already had the largest number of verbal and written reprimands in the service. Vardia, though, would never understand his reasoning.

A loud, hollow-sounding gong brought him out of his satisfied reverie. It reverberated throughout the ship. Brazil jumped up and looked at the computer screen.

DISTRESS SIGNAL FIELD INTERCEPTED, it read. AWAIT INSTRUCTIONS.

Seeing what the message was, he first flipped off the gong then flipped on the intercom. His three passengers were all concerned, naturally.

'Don't be alarmed,' he told them. 'It's just a distress field. A ship or some small colony is having problems and needs help. I will have to answer the call, so we'll be delayed a bit. Just sit tight and I'll keep you informed.'

With that he turned to the computer, giving it the go-ahead to plot the coordinates of the signal. He didn't like the idea at all – the signal had to be coming from a place far off his approved course. That invited premature discovery. Nonetheless, he could never ignore such a signal. Similar ones had saved him too many times, and the odds of anybody else intercepting it were more astronomical than his own odds at happening on it.

The ship's engines moaned, then the throbbing that was a part of his existence subsided to a dull sound as the energy field around the ship merged into normal space.

The two screens suddenly came on with the real, not the fake, galaxy – and a planet. A big one, he noted. Rocky and reddish in the feeble light of a dwarf star.

He asked the computer for coordinates. Its screens were blank for a long time, then it replied, DALGONIA, STAR ARACHNIS, DEAD WORLD,

MARKOVIAN ORIGIN, NO OTHER INFORMATION, UNINHAB-
ITED, it added needlessly. It was plain that nothing *he* knew could live here.

PLOT DISTRESS COORDINATES AND MAGNIFY WHEN DONE,
he ordered, and the computer searched the bleak panorama, quadrant by quadrant. Finally it stopped on one area and put it under intense magnification.

The picture was grainy, snowy as hell, but the scene clearly showed a small
camp. Something just didn't look right.

Brazil parked the ship in a synchronous orbit and prepared to go down
and see what was wrong. But first, he flipped on the intercom again.

'I'm afraid I'll have to seal you aft,' he told his passengers. 'I have to check
out something down on the planet. If I don't return within eight standard
hours, the ship will automatically pull out and take you to Coriolanus at top
speed, so you needn't be worried.'

'Can I come with you?' Vardia's voice came back at him.

He chuckled. 'No, sorry, regulations and all that. You'll be in contact with
me through this intercom all the time, so you'll know what's going on.'

He suited up, reflecting that he hadn't been in one of the things in years.
Then he entered the small bay below the engine well through a hatch from the
bridge and entered the little landing craft. Within five minutes, he was away.

The ship's computer took him to the spot by radio link, and he was at the
scene in under an hour. He raised the canopy – the little craft had no air or
pressurization of its own – and climbed down the side, striking the ground.
The lighter gravity made him feel ten feet tall. The ship, of course, was kept at
one gee for everybody's convenience.

He needed only a couple of minutes to survey the scene and to report his
findings back to the ship's recorders as the passengers anxiously followed his
every word. 'It's a base camp,' he told them, 'like the kind used for scientific
expeditions. Tent-type units, modular, pretty modern – seem to have
exploded somehow. All of them.' He knew that was impossible – and he knew
they knew – but those were the facts all the same.

He was just wondering aloud as to what could have caused such a thing
when he noticed the piled-up pressure suits near what would have been the
exit lock. He went over to them and picked one up, curiously.

'The suits are outside the area – empty. As if somebody threw them there.
The explosion or whatever couldn't have done it – not without some damage.
Wait a minute, let me get over to the area of the dorms.'

Vardia listened with growing fascination, and frustration that she could
see none of it, nor ask questions.

'*Yuk,*' came Brazil's voice over the intercom. 'Pretty messy death. They died
when the vacuum hit, if the explosion didn't get them. Hmmm … Seven. I
can't figure it out. The place is a mess but the explosion didn't really do more
than rip the tents to shreds. But that was enough.'

He moved over to another area that caught his eye.

'Funny,' he said, 'looks like somebody's done a job on the power plant. Well, here's what did it, anyway. Somebody jacked up the oxygen to pure and shut off the rest of the air. Just takes a spark after that. Worries me, though. There are two dozen safeguards against that sort of thing. Somebody had to do it deliberately.'

The words sent a chill through all three passengers listening breathlessly to his account. Even Wu Julee seemed caught up in the drama.

'Well, I just counted the beds,' Brazil told them, his voice keeping calm but tinged with the concern he felt. 'A dorm room for five, another one with three, and a single – probably the project chief's. Bodies in all but the chief's and one of the fivesome. Hmmm … There were seven pressure suits. Should have been nine.'

They heard him breathing and moving around, but he was infuriatingly silent for the longest period.

Finally he said, 'Two flyers are gone, so the missing ones must be somewhere else on the planet. It's a sure bet that one of them, at least, killed the others.'

Again the long silence, punctuated only with breathing sounds. All aboard the freighter were holding their breaths. It took no imagination at all to figure out that one, maybe two, madmen were loose on that planet – and Brazil was alone.

'Now here's the strangest part,' the captain reported at last. They strained for every word, cursing him for his maddening conversational tone. 'I've gotten to the rescue signal. It's about a kilometer from the camp, on a low ridge. But it isn't turned on.'

It was almost two hours more before Nathan Brazil was back aboard the ship. He didn't get out of his suit, although he left the helmet on his chair while he checked the computer. It assured him once again that it was indeed receiving a distress signal from the beacon below.

Only Brazil knew that it wasn't.

It just wasn't possible.

He unlocked the aft compartment and made his way back to the passengers, all of whom were seated in the lounge.

'So what do you make of it, Captain?' Hain asked seriously.

'Well,' replied the other hesitantly, 'I'm about to start believing in ghosts. *That signal isn't on.* To make sure, I disabled it completely before coming back. But it's still coming in loud and strong up here.'

'There must be another signal,' Vardia suggested logically.

'No, there isn't. Not only is one the standard issue – and everything else there is standard issue – but a computer that can plot a course in deep space through the underdimensions and get you to a particular port on a particular planet in the middle of nowhere doesn't screw up in plotting the coordinates of a distress signal.'

'Let's proceed on what we *do* know, then,' Hain suggested. 'We know that there *is* a signal – no, no, let me finish!' he protested as Brazil was about to cut in. 'As I said, there *is* a signal. It was set or sent by someone who, presumably, is one or both of the people who survived the – ah, disaster. Someone – or something – wants us to come down, wanted us to find the wrecked station, wants *something.*'

'A malevolent alien civilization, Hain?' Brazil retorted skeptically. 'Come on. We've got – what? – a thousand, give or take, solar systems explored to date, with more every year. We've found remains of the Markovians – one of their cities is near the camp, probably what the group was investigating – and lots and lots of animal and plant life. But no living, present-day alien civilizations.'

'But we've done only a trifle!' Hain protested. 'There are a billion billion stars around. You know the odds.'

'But not here, inside our perimeter,' the captain pointed out.

'But, he *is* right, you know,' Vardia interjected. 'Perhaps someone – or something – discovered *us.'*

'No,' Brazil told them, 'it's not that. There is some simple explanation. What happened down there was cold-blooded human murder by one of the team. For what madness, I can't guess. They can't get off the planet with what they've got. If they don't starve to death first, their pickup ship will get them.'

'You mean you aren't going to try to find them?' Vardia asked. 'But you must! Otherwise some other ship might answer them and the killers might be able to overpower them before they are forewarned!'

'Oh, the odds against anyone else hearing that signal are astronomical,' Brazil replied patiently.

'I assure you,' Hain said flatly, 'that the last thing I wish to do is stalk a murderer on an unknown world. Nevertheless, Citizen Vardia is correct. If we found them, someone else might.'

Brazil's eyebrows shot up in surprise. 'Can *you* handle a pistol?' he asked the fat man. 'Can you?' he asked Vardia.

'I can,' Hain replied evenly, 'and have.'

'That is left to the military caste,' Vardia replied, 'but I am an expert with the sword, and I have a ceremonial one with me. It will puncture a pressure suit.'

Brazil almost laughed. 'A sword? You?'

She ran to her room and came back with a gleaming, handsome blade that glittered as if it were made of the finest silver. 'It builds quick reflexes and good muscles,' she explained. 'Also, for some reason the sword is traditional in our service.'

Brazil's face grew serious again. 'And what about Wu Julee?' he asked, not of her but of Hain.

'She goes where I go,' Hain replied cautiously. 'And she will, in a pinch, help protect us with her life.'

I'll bet, Brazil thought sourly. You, anyway.

There was never any problem of pressure suits; they expanded or contracted to fit almost any known human wearer, although Hain's did give him a little problem. Each of them had worn one before, at least in the practice drill before the ship left port. They were extremely light, and, once the helmet had been set into place and the seal activated, a person hardly knew he had it on. Air was recirculated and refined through two small, light filters on the side of the helmet. The supply would last for almost a day. In an emergency situation, the lifeboat could recharge the air supply for fifteen people for a month, so there was plenty of air to spare.

Brazil led them first to the distress beacon, if only to prove to himself that he was correct. They examined it carefully, and agreed that there was no way it could be sending.

But the little lifeboat monitor connection to the mother ship still said it was.

So they climbed back in and sped northward, the mystery so pressing on them that they barely noted the Markovian ruins near the camp and along the route. The ship's computer had located the two missing shuttlecraft on a plain near the north pole, and that seemed the next likely place to investigate. If anyone was left alive, he would be there.

'Why do you think they are up there?' Vardia asked Brazil.

'My theory is that the murderer couldn't trap one of them in the base camp and that that one took a shuttle and flew off. There must have been a chase, and that plain is where they met up,' the captain replied. 'We'll know in a little while, because we're almost there.'

Being in a lifeboat with a major spatial propulsion unit, Brazil was able to make the long trip by going back up into orbit and braking back down again. Thus, the nine-hour journey was reduced to just a little over ninety minutes. He braked to the slowest speed he could maintain as they cleared a last mountain range and came upon a broad, flat plain.

'There they are!' Vardia almost shouted, and they all looked ahead at the two craft, small silver disks in the twilight, shown prominently at the edge of a slight discoloration in the plain.

Brazil circled around the spot several times.

'I can see no one,' Hain reported. 'Not a sign of life, not a pressure suit, nothing. They may still be in the craft,' he suggested.

'Okay,' Brazil replied, 'I'll set down a few hundred meters from them. Hain, you stay back just outside this boat and cover me. The other two of you stay inside. If anything happens to us, the mother ship will reclaim the boat.'

There was a soft bump, and they were down on the surface of Dalgonia. Brazil reached into the broad, black belt he wore on the outside of his pressure suit and removed one of two pistols and handed it to Hain.

The pistols didn't look like much, but they could fire short pulses of energy at rates from one per second to five hundred per second, the latter not doing much for aim but able to spread things enough to knock off a small regiment. There was a *stun* setting that would paralyze a man for a half hour or more, but both men placed their weapons on *full*.

There were seven ugly bodies far to the south.

Brazil eased out of the hatch in the eerie silence of a near vacuum, and, keeping the two shuttlecraft always in view, moved to cover behind the lifeboat. That was a relatively safe haven. Since the boat had been built to take a tremendous amount of stress and even friction, it would be impervious to any weapons likely to be in the hands of their quarry.

Hain emerged shortly after, having more trouble climbing down with his bulk despite the weak gravity. He chose a position just forward of the nose where he was mostly sheltered but could still use the edge of the boat to steady his pistol.

Brazil, satisfied, moved cautiously forward.

He reached the nearest craft in less than two minutes. 'No sign of life yet,' he told them. 'I'm going to climb up on top and have a look inside.' He mounted the rail-type ladder along the side of the shuttle and walked over to the entry hatch.

'Still nothing,' Brazil reported. 'I'm going in.'

It took only another three minutes to get inside and find nobody home. He then repeated the sequence with the second craft and found it empty too, although this one showed signs that somebody had spent many hours there.

'Come on up, anybody,' he called. 'There's no one here, or for many kilometers around. See what you make of it.'

Hain told Wu Julee to join him. Vardia climbed out last, and they all went over to the captain, who was standing near the second shuttle and looking anxiously at the ground. Brazil noted with some amusement that Vardia clutched her nice, pretty sword.

'Look at the ground here,' he said, pointing to the tracks of a person in a pressure suit coming up to a point at which the dust around was greatly disturbed for a large area.

'What do you make of it, Captain?' Hain asked.

'Well, it looks as if my theory's right, anyway. See – the first one was here, then saw the second one land, and he hid out on the back of the shuttle. When the pursuer – the guy who landed second I assume was the murderer – found nobody home, he walked around to here' – Brazil gestured at the mottled dust thrown about – 'and was jumped by the first person from on top. They fought here, then one took off across the plain, the other in pursuit. See how we get only the toe tracks coming out of the fight scene?'

Vardia was already following the tracks out onto the plain. Suddenly she stopped short and stared, incredulous, at the ground. 'Captain! Everyone! Come here!' she called urgently. They rushed up to her. She was pointing at the ground immediately ahead of her.

The fine dust was thinner here, and the rock changed color from a dull orange to more of a gray, but at first they didn't see what she meant. Brazil went over and stooped down. Then it sank in on him.

At the place where one man had stepped, just where the two strains of rock met, there was half a footprint. Not the running type – it was angled, so that a little less than half of a grown man's footprint, pressure suit pattern and all, was visible in the orange. Where it met the gray, there was unbroken dust.

'How is it possible, Captain?' Vardia asked, awed for the first time in her life – and not a little scared.

'There *must* be an explanation. It's a freakish thing – but I'd believe almost anything after all we've seen. I'm sure we'll find their prints continue farther on. Let's see.'

They all walked onto the gray area for some distance. Vardia suddenly looked back to make certain that *they* were making footprints, and was relieved to see that they were. Suddenly she stopped short.

'Captain!' she exclaimed, that toneless voice suddenly tinged with panic and fear. The rest caught it, stopped, and turned. Vardia was pointing back at the ships from which they had come.

There were no shuttlecraft. There was no lifeboat. Only a bleak, unbroken orange plain stretching off to the mountains in the distance.

'Now what the hell?' Brazil managed, looking all around him to see if they had somehow turned around. They hadn't. He looked up to see if he could spot anything leaving, but there was nothing but the cold stars as darkness overtook them.

'What happened?' Hain asked plaintively. 'Did our murderer—'

'No, that's not it,' Brazil cut in quickly, a cold chill suddenly going through him. 'No one person – not even two – could have managed all three craft, and nobody but me could have lifted that lifeboat for another two hours.'

There was a sudden vibration, like a small earthquake, that knocked them all off their feet.

Brazil broke his fall and held on in a crouch on his hands and knees. He looked up suddenly.

The whole area seemed bathed in eerie flashes of blue-white lightning, thousands of them!

'Damn me for an asshead!' Brazil swore. 'We've been had!'

'But by whom?' Vardia called out.

Wu Julee screamed.

Then there was nothing but darkness and that weird, blue lightning, now laced, it appeared, with golden sparks. They all felt the sensation of falling and turning and twisting in the air, as if they were dropping down some bottomless pit. There was no up, no down, nothing but that dizzy sensation.

And Wu Julee kept screaming.

Suddenly they were lying on a flat, glassy-smooth black surface. Lights were on around them, and there seemed to be a structure – as if they were in some building, like a great warehouse.

Things didn't stop spinning around for a while. They were dizzy, and sick. All but Brazil threw up into their helmets, which neatly and efficiently cleared the mess away. A professional spaceman, Brazil was the first to recover his equilibrium. Then he steadied himself, half sitting up on the black, glassy floor.

It was a room, he saw – no, a great chamber, with six sides. The glassy area was also a hexagon, and around it stretched a railing and what appeared to be a walkway. A single great light, also six-sided, was suspended above them in the curved ceiling. The place was huge, Brazil saw, easily large enough to house a small freighter.

The others were there. Vardia, he saw, was already sitting up, but Wu Julee, it appeared, had passed out. Hain just lay on the floor, breathing hard. Brazil struggled to his feet and made his way unsteadily to Wu Julee. He checked and saw that she was in fact still breathing but unconscious.

'Everybody all right?' he called. Vardia nodded and tried to rise. He helped her to her feet, and she managed. Hain groaned, but tried, and was game about it. He finally managed it.

'Just about one gee,' Brazil noted. 'That's interesting.'

'Now what?' asked Datham Hain.

'Looks like some breaks in that railing – the closest one is over there to your right. We might as well make for it.' Taking their silence for assent, he picked up Wu Julee's limp body and they started off. She weighed hardly anything, he noted, and he wasn't a particularly strong man.

He looked down at her, sorrow in his eyes. *What will happen to you now, Wu Julee? But I tried! God! I tried!*

Her eyes opened, and she looked up into his through the tinted helmet faceplates. Perhaps it was the gentle way he carried her, perhaps it was his expression, perhaps it was just the fact that she saw him and not Hain, but she smiled.

She got much heavier about halfway there, he noted, as his body was drained of the adrenalin that had pumped into him during the – fall? Finally he was straining at the weight, although she weighed no more than half what she should. He finally admitted defeat and had to put her down. She didn't protest, but as they continued to walk she clung tightly to his arm.

No matter what, Hain no longer owned her.

Steps of what looked like polished stone led up to the break in the rail – six of them, they noted. Finally they were all up on some kind of platform from which a conveyor belt stretched out. But it was not moving in either direction.

They all looked to the captain for guidance. For the first time in his life, Nathan Brazil felt the full weight of responsibility. He had gotten them into this – never mind that they had talked him into it, it was his responsibility – and he didn't have the slightest idea what to do next.

'Well,' he began, 'if we stay here we starve to death, or run out of air – or both. We may do so anyway, but we at least ought to see what we're into. There has to be a doorway out of this place.'

'Probably six of them,' Hain said caustically.

Brazil stepped out onto one of the conveyors, and it suddenly started moving. The movement was so unexpected that he found himself carried along farther and farther away from the rest before anyone could say anything.

'Better get on,' he called back, 'or you'll lose me! I don't know how to stop this thing!'

He was receding farther and farther, when Wu Julee stepped on. The other two immediately did likewise.

The speed wasn't great, but it was faster than a man could walk briskly. A larger, broader platform loomed ahead before Brazil could see it. So he slid off onto it, stumbled, fell down, and rolled halfway across.

'Watch out! Platform coming up!' he warned. The others saw the platform and him in time to step off, although each one nearly lost his balance in the attempt.

'Apparently you're supposed to be walking on the belt,' Vardia said. 'That way you just walk onto the platform. See? There are actually several belts just before the platform, each one going at a slightly slower speed.'

The belt suddenly stopped.

'No doorway here,' Hain noted. 'Shall we press on?'

'I suppose so – whoops!' Brazil exclaimed as he was about to step out. The other belt had started in the reverse direction!

'Looks like somebody's coming to meet us,' Brazil said jokingly, a tone that didn't match his inner feelings at all. Even so, he pulled and checked his pistol, noting that Hain was doing the same. Vardia, he saw, still held onto that sword.

They could see a giant figure coming toward them, and all stepped back to the rear edge of the platform. As the figure came closer, they could see that it was like nothing in the known universe.

Start with a chocolate brown human torso, incredibly broad, and ribbed so that the chest muscles seemed to form squarish plates. A head, oval-shaped, equally brown and hairless except for a huge white walrus mustache under a broad, flat nose. Six arms – in threes, spaced in rows down the torso – extremely muscular but attached, except for the shoulder pair, on ball-type sockets like the claws of a crab. Below, the torso melded into an enormous brown-and-yellow-striped series of scales leading to a huge, serpentine lower half, coiled, but obviously five or more meters in length when outstretched.

As the creature approached the platform, it eyed them with large, human-looking orbs punctuated with jet-black pupils. As it reached the edge of the platform, the lower left arm slapped the rail. The belt stopped just short of the platform. Then, for what seemed like forever, they just stared at each other – these four humans in ghostly white pressure suits and this creature of some incredibly alien spawning.

The alien finally pointed to them, then with its top pair of arms made a motion to remove their helmets. When it saw they made no move, it pointed again to them, then did what appeared to be a deep-breathing exercise.

'I think it's trying to tell us we can breathe in here,' Brazil said cautiously.

'Sure, *he* thinks so, but what does he breathe?' Hain pointed out.

'No choice,' Brazil replied. 'We're almost out of air anyway. May as well chance it.'

'I do,' came the unexpected voice of Wu Julee, and, with that, she unfastened her helmet – not without some trouble, for her coordination was shot. Finally the helmet fell to her feet, and she breathed in.

And continued breathing.

'Good enough for me,' said Vardia, and she and Brazil did the same. For a short time Hain continued to resist. Then, finally assured that everyone was still breathing, he removed his as well.

The air seemed a bit humid and perhaps a little rich in oxygen – they experienced a slight light-headedness that soon passed – but otherwise fine.

'Now what?' Hain asked.

'Damned if I know,' Brazil replied honestly. 'How do you say hello to a giant walrus-snake?'

'Well I'll be goddamned!' exclaimed the walrus-snake in perfect Confederation plain talk, 'if it ain't Nathan Brazil!'

ZONE
(ENTER GHOSTS)

None of the group could have been more stunned than Nathan Brazil.

'Somehow I knew you'd wind up here,' the creature continued. 'Sooner or later just about every old-timer does.'

'You know me?' Brazil asked incredulously.

The creature laughed. 'Sure I do – and you know me, too, unless you've had one too many rejuves. I know, had the same problem myself when I dropped through the Well. Let's just say that people really change around here, and let it go at that. If you'll follow me, I'll make you more comfortable and give you some orientation.' With that the creature uncoiled backward, then recoiled at a length about two meters back on the belt. 'Step aboard,' it invited.

They looked at Brazil. 'I don't think we have much choice,' he told them. Then, noticing Hain's pistol still drawn and pointed, he said to the fat man: 'Put that popgun away until we find out the lay of the land. No use in getting popped yourself.'

They stepped onto the belt, which started not when they boarded but only after the rail was given another slap by their alien host. For the first time they could hear noise – giant blowers, it sounded like, echoing throughout the great hall. The belt itself gave off its own steady electric hum.

'Do you – eat what we eat?' Hain called out to the creature.

The alien chuckled. 'No, not anymore, but, don't worry, no cannibals around, either. At least, not Type Forty-ones like you. But I think we can round up some food – some *real* food, maybe the first in everybody's except Nate's whole life.'

They rode around three belts until they came to a platform much larger than the others. Here the walls curved and twisted away from the Well. Brazil could see why the configuration hadn't been visible from afar.

Then they followed the snakeman – no mean trick, they found, with its enormous serpentine body – down a long corridor. They saw other corridors branching off, but they traveled over a thousand meters before they took one.

It led into a very large room set up something like a reception area. Comfortable, human-style chairs with plush cushions abounded, and a plastic wall covering was decorated with flowers. Here, such amenities seemed as incongruous as the alien would seem to their worlds. The creature had a sort of desk, semicircular in shape and seemingly form-fitted for him to coil comfortably behind. It held only a very ordinary-looking pen, a small pad of paper, and a seal – hexagonal of course – seemingly solid gold cast in clear plastic. The seal featured a snake coiled around a great cross, and it had a superscription around the edges in a script unfamiliar to any of them.

The snakeman lifted up a small part of his desk top to reveal an instrument panel underneath of unfamiliar design and purpose. A large red button was most prominent, and he pushed it.

'Had to reset the Well,' he explained. 'Otherwise we could get some non-oxygen breathers in and they'd be hung up in storage until somebody remembered to press the button. Let me also punch in a food order for you – you always were a steak-and-baked-potato man, Nate. So that's what it'll be.' He punched some buttons in sequence on the console, then closed it. 'Ten or fifteen minutes and the food will be here – and it'll be cooked right, too. Medium, wasn't it, Nate?'

'You seem to know me better than I do,' Brazil replied. 'It's been so long since I had a steak – maybe almost a century. I'd just about forgotten what one was. Where did you know me, anyway?'

A broad yet wistful smile crept across the creature's face. 'Can you remember an old bum named Serge Ortega, Nate? Long ago?'

Brazil thought, then suddenly it came to him. 'Yeah, sure, I remember him – but that was maybe a hundred years ago or so. A free-lancer – polite name for a pirate,' he explained to the others. 'A real rascal. Anything for a buck, was wanted almost everywhere – but a hell of a character. But you can't be him – he was a little guy, from Hispaniola, before they went Com and changed the place to Peace and Freedom.'

'I'm sorry to hear that,' the creature responded sadly. 'That means my people are dead. Who was the mold? Brassario?'

'Brassario,' Brazil confirmed. 'But all this explains nothing!'

'Oh, but it does,' the snakeman replied. 'Because I *am* Serge Ortega, Nate. This world changed me into what you see.'

'I don't see what's wrong with factory worlds,' Vardia interjected. They ignored her.

Brazil looked hard at the creature. The voice, the eyes – they *were* dimly familiair, somehow. It *did* remind him of Ortega, sort of. The same crazy glint to the eyes, the same quick, sharp way of talking, the underlying attitude of amused arrogance that had gotten Ortega into more bar fights than any other man alive.

But it had been so long ago.

'Look here!' Hain put in. 'Enough of old home week, Ortega or not Ortega. Sir, or whatever, I should very much like to know where we are, and why we are here, and when we shall be able to return to our own ship.'

Ortega gave that evil smile. 'Well, as to where you are – you're on the Well World. There's no other name for it, since that's exactly what it is. As to where it is – well, damned if I know. Nobody here has ever been able to leave it. I only know that the night sky is like nothing you ever saw before. I spaced almost two hundred years, and none of the extremely prominent features look familiar. At the very least we're on the other side of the galaxy, or maybe even in another galaxy. As to why you're here, well, you somehow bumbled into a Markovian Gate like me and maybe thousands of others did. And here you are, stuck just like the rest of us. You're here for good, mister. Better get used to it.'

'See here!' Hain huffed. 'I have power, influence—'

'Means nothing here,' Ortega responded coldly.

'My mission!' Vardia protested. 'I must perform my duties!'

'No duties, nothin' anymore but you and here,' the snakeman said. 'Understand this: you are on a world built by the Markovians – yes, I said *built*. The whole thing: lock, stock, and core. As far as we know, the whole damned thing is a Markovian brain in perfect working order, and preprogrammed.'

'I figured we were inside Dalgonia,' Brazil said. 'It felt as if we fell down into something.'

'No,' replied Ortega, 'that was no fall. The Markovians really had godlike powers. Matter transmission was a simple thing for them. Don't ask me how it works, but it does, because we got a local version here. I wouldn't understand it if somebody *did* explain it, anyway.'

'But such a thing is impossible!' Hain objected. 'It is against the laws of physics!'

Ortega's six limbs shrugged. 'Who knows? At one time flying was impossible. Then it was impossible to leave a planet, then impossible to leave a solar system, then impossible for anything to go faster than light. The only thing that makes something impossible is ignorance. Here on the Well World the impossible's a fact of life.'

At that moment the food arrived, brought in on a small cart that was obviously some sort of robot. It went up to each in turn, and offered a tray of hot food, which, when removed, revealed an identical tray beneath. Brazil removed the cover and just stared for a minute. Finally, he said, in a tone of absolute awe and reverence: 'A *real* steak!' He hesitated a moment and looked over at Ortega. 'It *is* real, isn't it?'

'Oh, yes,' the snakeman assured him. 'It's real enough. The potato and beans, too. Oh, not *quite* a cow, not *quite* a potato, and so forth, but so close you'll never be able to tell the difference. Go ahead, try it!'

Hain was already greedily tearing into his, while Vardia looked at the food, bewildered.

'What's the trouble?' Brazil managed between swallows. 'Problems?'

'It's quite safe to eat,' Ortega assured her. 'There are no microorganisms that will give you any real problems here – not until you go out, anyway. The stuff's biologically compatible.'

'No, no – it's –' she stammered. 'Well, I have never seen food like it before. How do you …?'

'Just watch me and follow my example,' Brazil laughingly replied. 'See? You cut it with a knife and fork like this, then—'

They dug into the meal, Vardia getting the hang of it, although she protested several times that she thought the food tasted terrible. But they were all too hungry to protest.

Ortega's eyes fell on Wu Julee, who just sat there staring at the food, not eating at all. 'The girl – she is ill?' he asked them.

Brazil suddenly stopped eating and looked at Hain, who had already finished and was just letting out an extremely noisy belch. The captain's face had a grave expression on it, and the fine food suddenly felt like lead in his stomach.

'She's a spongie,' Brazil said softly. Hain's eyebrows rose, but he said nothing.

Ortega's face, too, turned serious. 'How far gone?' he asked.

'Fairly bad, I'd say,' Brazil replied. 'Deep mental maybe five years old, voluntary action basically emotive only.' Suddenly he whirled in his chair and faced Hain, cold fury in his eyes. *'How about it, Hain?'* he snarled. *'Would you agree?'*

Ham's piggish face remained impassive, his tone of voice seemed almost one of relief. 'So you found out. I *thought* perhaps I was overdoing the routine at that dinner.'

'If we hadn't been trapped on Dalgonia, I'd have had you *and* her down on Arkadrian before you realized what was what,' Brazil told him.

Hain's face showed both shock and surprise. Brazil's remarks had gotten to him. Then, suddenly, a thought occurred to him and the old, smug self-confidence returned.

'It would seem, then, that I have fallen not into a terrible situation, but into a most fortunate one by this – er, circumstance,' he said calmly. 'A pity for the lady, though,' he added in mock sympathy.

'Why you son of a bitch!' Brazil snarled and leaped at the fat man's throat, spilling food everywhere. The big man was a head taller and twice the weight of the attacker, but Brazil's quickness and the sheer hatred in his soul flowed into his arms and hands as they tightened around the other's neck.

Hain thrashed and tried to push the smaller attacker away, but all he managed was to cause both of them to roll onto the floor, the small man still squeezing. Hain's mouth was open, face red, as he gasped for breath. The expression on Brazil's face was almost demonic; nothing would keep him from his goal.

Vardia watched open-mouthed, understanding the situation only in the vaguest way and finding Brazil's actions, both recounted and current, incomprehensible. In her private universe, there were no people, only cells composing a whole body. A diseased cell was simply eliminated. So there was no place in her mind for one who caused such a disease.

Wu Julee watched the two grapple impassively, her meal still on her lap.

Suddenly Ortega bounded over his desk and grabbed Brazil with massive arms. The giant creature moved almost too fast for the eye to follow; Vardia was stunned at the speed and surety with which the creature acted.

Brazil fought to get free of the grip, and Ortega's middle arm suddenly came from nowhere and punched the small man hard in the jaw. He went slack, still held aloft in the creature's strong grip.

Freed of his attacker, Hain gasped and choked for air, finally rolling flat on his back and lying there, his huge stomach rising and falling. He felt his neck, where the imprint of Brazil's murderous hands could still be seen.

Ortega began examining the unconscious man. Satisfied that no bones were broken, nor permanent damage done, he grunted and put the man down on the floor. Brazil collapsed in a heap, and the snakeman turned his attention to Hain.

'I thank you, sir,' Hain gasped, his hand going involuntarily to his throat. 'You have surely saved my life.'

'I didn't want to do it, nor would I have done so in normal times,' Ortega snapped back acidly. 'And if Nate ever catches up to you on the outside, I won't be there to save you – and, if I am, I'll cheerfully join him in tearing you limb from limb. *But I will not allow such a thing here!*' He turned his attention back to Brazil, who was just coming around.

Hain seemed taken aback by the creature's comments, then saw that his pulse pistol had fallen when they had tumbled and now was a foot or so from him on the floor. Slowly, his hand crept toward it.

'*No!*' Wu Julee suddenly screamed, but Hain already had the weapon, and was pointing it at both the snakeman and Brazil, who was sitting up, shaking his head and rubbing his jaw. Ortega's back was to Hain, but Brazil suddenly looked up and spotted the gun. Ortega saw him stare and turned to face the fat man.

'Now both of you behave and I won't do anything rash,' Hain told them in that same cool, confident tone he always used. 'But I am leaving this charming place right now.'

'How?' asked Serge Ortega.

The question seemed to bother Hain, who was used to simple answers to simple questions. 'The – the way we came in,' he said at last.

'The doorway leads to a corridor. The corridor leads to the Well in one direction – and that is strictly one way,' Ortega told him. 'In the other direction are more rooms like this – seven hundred and eighty of them, in a honeycombed labyrinth. Beyond them are housing and recreation facilities for the types of creatures that use those offices – seven hundred and eighty different types of creatures, Hain. Some of them don't breathe what you do. Some of them won't like you a bit and may just kill you.'

'There is a way out,' Hain snarled, but there was desperation in his voice. 'There *must* be. I'll find it.'

'And then what?' Ortega asked calmly. 'You're out in a world that is moderately large. The surface area is best expressed as five point one times ten to the eighth power kilometers *squared*. And you don't even know what the planet looks like, the languages, *anything*. You're a smart man, Hain. *What are the odds?*'

Hain seemed confused, hesitant. Suddenly he looked at the pistol in his hand and brightened. '*This* gives me the odds,' he said firmly.

'Never play the odds until you know the rules of the game,' Ortega warned softly, and advanced slowly toward him.

'I'll shoot!' Hain threatened, his voice an octave higher than usual.

'Go ahead,' Ortega invited, his great serpentine body sliding slowly toward the panicked man.

'All right, dammit!' Hain cried, and pulled the trigger.

Nothing happened.

Hain pulled the trigger again and again. It clicked, making contact with the solenoid firing pin, but did nothing else.

Ortega suddenly moved with that blinding speed, and the gun seemed to vanish from the fat man's hand.

'No weapon works in this room,' Ortega said crisply. Hain sat, a stupefied expression on his face, mouth half open. Possibly for the first time in his life that arrogant self-confidence was gone out of him.

'You all right, Nate?' Ortega shot to the small man, who still sat half-rising, holding his sore jaw.

'Yeah, you son of a bitch,' Brazil replied mushily, shaking his head to clear it. 'Man! You sure as hell pack a wallop!'

Ortega chuckled. 'I was the only man smaller than you once in a bar on Siprianos. I was full of booze and dope, and ready to take on the house, all of whom would have cheerfully slit my throat for the floor show. I just started to pick a fight with the bouncer when you grabbed me and knocked me cold. Took me ten weeks before I realized that you'd saved my neck.'

Brazil's jaw dropped in wonder, and the pain hit him as he did so and he groaned. Still, he managed: 'You *are* Serge Ortega!' in a tone of bewildered acceptance. 'I had totally forgotten that ...'

Ortega smiled. 'I said I was, Nate.'

'But, oh, man, how you've changed,' Brazil noted, amazed.

'I told you this world changes people, Nate,' Ortega replied. 'It'll change you, too. All of you.'

'You wouldn't have stopped me from finishing the pig in the old days, Serge.'

'I guess I wouldn't have,' Ortega chuckled. 'And I really wouldn't have now – except that this is Zone. And, if you'll sit over there, across the room from Hain,' he said, pointing to a backless couch, and, turning to Hain, continued, 'and if *you* will stop all your little, petty games and promise to sit quietly, I'll explain just what the situation is here – the rules and lack of them, and a few other things about your future.'

Hain mumbled something unintelligible and went back over to his seat. Brazil, still nursing his sore jaw, silently got up and moved over to the couch. He sank down in the cushions, his head against the back wall, and groaned.

'Still dizzy,' he complained. 'And I'm getting a hell of a headache.'

Ortega smiled and moved back behind his desk.

'You've had worse and you know it,' the snake-man reminded the captain. 'But, first things first. Want some more food? You spoiled yours.'

'You know damned well I won't eat for days,' Brazil groaned. 'Damn! Why didn't you let me get him?'

'Two reasons, really. First, this is – well, a diplomatic legation, you might say. A murder by one Entry of another would be impossible to explain to my government no matter what. But, more than that, she's not lost, Nate, and that makes your motive even flimsier.'

Brazil forgot his aches and pains. 'What did you say?'

'I said she's not lost, Nate, and that's right. Just as this detour deprived Hain of justice, it also saved her. Arkadrian was no solution, really. Obviously you felt she was worth saving when you decided to detour – but, just here, she's little more than a vegetable. Obviously Hain was decreasing the dosage as she became more and more accustomed to the pain. He was letting her rot out – but slowly enough to make the trip without problems. May I ask why, Hain?'

'She was from one of the Comworlds. Lived in the usual beehive and helped work on a big People's Farm. I mean the dirt jobs – shoveling shit and the like, as well as painting the buildings, mending fences, and suchlike. IQ genetically manipulated to be low – she's a basic worker, a manual laborer, basically mentally retarded and capable of carrying out simple commands – one at a time – but not of much in the way of original thought and action. She wasn't even good at that work, and they used her as a Party whore. Failed at that, too.'

'That is a slander of the Com people!' Vardia protested vehemently. 'Each citizen is here to do a particular task that needs doing, and is created for that task. Without people such as she as well as ones like me the whole society would fall apart.'

'Would you change jobs with her?' Brazil asked sarcastically.

'Oh, of course not,' Vardia responded, oblivious to the tone. 'I'm glad I'm not anything but what I am. I would be happy at nothing else. Even so, such citizens are essential to the social fabric.'

'And you say my people have gone that route,' Ortega said sadly, almost to himself. 'But – I would think the really basic menial stuff would be automated. A lot of it was in my time.'

'Oh, no,' Vardia protested. 'Man's future is with the soil and with nature. Automation produces social decay and only that necessary to the maintenance of equality can be permitted.'

'I see,' Ortega responded dryly. He was silent for a while, then he turned back to Hain. 'But how did you wind up with the girl? And why hook her on sponge?'

'Occasionally we need a – a sample, as it were. An example, really. We almost always use such people – Comworld folk who will not be missed, who are never much more than vegetables anyway. We control most of them, of course. But it's rather tough to get the stuff into their food, or even to get an audience with members of a Presidium, but, once you've done it, you control the entire world – a world of people programmed to be happy at whatever they're doing and conditioned from birth to blind obedience to the Party. Control the queen and you control all the bees in the hive. I had an audience with a Presidium Member on Coriolanus – took three years of hard work to wangle it, I'll assure you. There are hundreds of ways to infect someone once you're face-to-face. By that point, poor Wu Julee would have been in the animalistic state from progressively smaller doses. She would be the threat to show the distinguished Member what my – er, client, would become if not treated.'

'Such a thing would not work on *my* world,' Vardia stated proudly. 'A Presidium Member so infected would simply have you, her, and the Member all at a Death Factory.'

Hain laughed. 'You people never cease to amaze me,' he chuckled. 'You *really* think your Presidium members are like you? They're descendants of the early Party that spread out in past, mostly lost, history. They proclaimed equality and said they dreamed of a future Utopia when there would be no government, nothing. What they really wouldn't even admit to themselves was that they loved power – *they* never worked in the fields, *they* never worked at all, except giving orders and trying out plans and novel experiences. And they loved it! And their children's children's children still love it. A planetload of happy, contented, docile slaves that: will do anything commanded of them. And when that pain starts, less than an hour after infection, they will do anything to keep alive. *Anything.*'

'Still mighty risky for you, isn't it?' Ortega pointed out. 'What if you're knocked off by an egomaniac despite all?'

Hain shrugged. 'There are risks in anything. We lose most of our people as they work themselves up. But all of us are misfits, losers, or people who started at the bottom of society on the worst of worlds. We weren't born to power – we work for it, take risks for it, earn it. And – the survivors get the spoils.'

Ortega nodded grimly. 'How many – easy, Nate, or I'll clout you again! – how many worlds do you control now?'

Hain shrugged again. 'Who knows? I'm not on the Council. Over ten percent – thirty, thirty-five, maybe – and growing. And two new colonies are made for every one we win, so it's an ever-expanding empire. It'll be that someday – an empire.' His eyes took on a faraway look, a maniacal glow. 'A great empire. Perhaps, eventually, the entire galaxy.'

'Ruled by scum,' Brazil said sourly.

'By the strongest!' Hain responded. 'The cleverest, the survivors! The people who deserve it!'

'I hesitate to let such evil into *this* world,' Ortega said, 'but we have had as bad and worse here. This world will test you fully, Hain. I think it will ultimately kill you, but that is up to you. Here is where you start. But there's no sponge here, or other addictives. Even if there were, you'd have fifteen hundred and sixty different species to try it on, and some of them are so alien you won't even understand *what* they are, why they do what they do, or whether they do anything. Some will be almost like those back home. But this place is a madhouse, Hain. It's a world created by madness, I think, and it will kill you. We'll see.'

They were silent for a while, Ortega's speech having as unsettling an effect on Brazil and Vardia as on Hain. Suddenly, Brazil broke the silence.

'You said she wasn't lost, Serge. Why not?'

'It has to do with this world and what it does to people,' the snakeman replied. 'I will brief you later. But – not only do you change here, but you also get back what you've lost. You'll return to perfect health, Nate, even get back that memory of yours. You'll even remember things you don't want to remember. And, you'll be prepared – programmed if you like – for whatever and wherever you are. Not in the Comworld sense – what *you* need. This gives you a new start, Nate – but there's no rejuve here. This is a one-shot deal, people – a fresh start.

'But you will die here, sooner or later, the span depending on what you are.'

They slept on cots provided by Ortega. All were dead tired, and Brazil was also still smarting from the knockout punch given him by the great creature that seemed to be the reincarnation of his past friend. Hain slept separately from the rest, under lock and key, in an office the location of which was not told to the fiery little captain.

Ortega woke them all up the next morning. They assumed it was morning, although they hadn't actually been outside and, in fact, had no idea what the outside looked like on this strange yet somehow familiar world. An old-style breakfast of what appeared to be normal hen's eggs, scrambled, sausage, toast, and coffee awaited them, served by the same little cart that had brought the previous night's supper. Brazil noted that the mess from flying food had been carefully cleaned away.

Vardia, of course, had trouble with the breakfast.

Wu Julee seemed no worse than the night before, and in no more pain, if, indeed, she was in pain at all. With a lot of coaxing from Brazil she managed to eat some of the breakfast.

After they had finished and had returned the trays to the little cart, which hummed away on small tires with no apparent guidance, Serge Ortega pressed another button on his little hidden console, causing a screen to drop down at his right.

'Time, unfortunately, is limited here – both for you and, because I have a great many other duties, for me as well. When I got dropped into Zone long ago, I had only a brief orientation before I was thrown out on my ass. I wanted to give you a little bit more, to make it a little easier on you than it was for me.'

'Just how long ago *did* you drop here, Citizen Ortega?' Vardia asked.

'Well, hard to say. Well over seventy standard years – they still use the same years, don't they, Nate?' Brazil nodded affirmatively, and Ortega continued.

'It was during a low-colonist period, and I was gunrunning to a placer strike on some asteroids out beyond Sirius. I dumped them fine, avoided all the cops, but ran into some damned conduit out in the middle of deep space, before I could go FTL or anything. I'm told that most – maybe a majority – of the gates are on planets, and maybe this was one, too, at one time. Maybe all those asteroids were once a Markovian planet that broke up for some reason.'

'How long has this place – this planet – been here, Serge?' Brazil asked.

'Nobody knows. Longer than people were people, Nate. A coupl'a million years, it appears. Since the oldest folk in the planet's oldest race are only four hundred – and they're at death's door – the ancient history of the place is as shrouded in mystery and mythology as our own. You see, all this involves the Markovians – any of you know about them?'

'Nobody knows much,' Brazil replied. 'Some sort of super race that ran its planets from brains beneath the surface and died out suddenly.'

'That's about it,' Ortega acknowledged. 'They flourished, scientists here think, between two and five million years ago. And they were galaxy-wide, Nate! Maybe even more. Hard to say, but we have a lot of folk dropping through whose knowledge of the universe doesn't match anything we humans know. And that's the weirdest thing – a hell of a lot of them are close to human.'

'In what way do you mean that, Serge?' Brazil asked. 'Us-human or you-human?'

Ortega laughed. 'Both. Humanoid would perhaps be a better term. Well, first let me show you what you're in for, and I'll add the rest as I go along.'

The snakeman dimmed the lights, and a map showing two hemispheres flicked on the screen. It looked like a standard planetary map, but the two circles were filled with hexagons from pole to pole.

'The Markovians,' Ortega began, 'who were nutty over the number six, built this world. We don't know why or how, but we do know *what*. Each of their worlds had at least one gate of the kind that transported you here. You are now at the South Polar Zone, which doesn't show accurately here for obvious reasons. All carbon-based life comes here, and all of the hexes north of us to that thick equatorial line are carbon-based or could live in a carbon-based environment. The Mechs of Hex Three Sixty-seven, for example, aren't carbon-based, but you could live in their hex.'

'So the North Polar Zone takes care of the biologically exotic, then?' Hain asked.

Ortega nodded. 'Yes, there are the true aliens, beings with which we have literally nothing in common. Their hexes run down to the equator on the north hemisphere.'

'Is that black band at the equator just a map dividing line or is it something else?' Vardia asked curiously.

'No, that's not just on the map,' Ortega told her, 'and you were sharp to notice it. It is – well, the best I can describe it is that it's a sheer wall, opaque and several kilometers high. You can't really see it until you're at it, outside the border of the last hex by a hair. You can't get past it, and you can't fly over it or anything. It's just, well, *there*. We have some theories about it, of course, the best one being that it's the exposed part of the Markovian brain that is, it seems, of the entire core of this planet. The old name for it seems to be the Well of Souls – so it probably is just that. There's an old adage around here: "Until midnight at the Well of Souls," which you'll probably hear. It's just an old ritual saying now, although it may have had some real meaning in the distant past of prehistory. Hell, if that's the Well of Souls, then it's *always* midnight somewhere!'

'What do the hexagons represent?' Hain asked.

'Well, there are fifteen hundred and sixty of them on the planet,' Ortega replied. 'Nobody knows the reason for that, either, but at least the figure only has one six in it. Each hex is identical in size – each one of the six sides is just a shade under three hundred fifty-five kilometers, and they're a shade under six hundred fifteen kilometers across. Needless to say they didn't use our form of measurements when they built the place, and we don't know what system they had, but that'll give you an idea in our terms.'

'But what's *in* the hexes?' Brazil prodded.

'Well, you *could* call them nations with borders,' Ortega replied, 'but that would be understating things. Each is a self-contained biosphere for a particular life form – and for associated lower life forms. They are all maintained by the Markovian brain, and each is also maintained at a given technological level. The social level is left to whatever the inhabitants can develop or want to have, so you have everything from monarchies to dictatorships to anarchies out there.'

'What do you mean technological level?' Brazil asked him. 'Do you mean that there are places where there are machines and places where there are not?'

'Well, yes, that, of course,' Ortega affirmed. 'But, well, you can only get to the level of technology your resources allow within the hex. Anything beyond it just won't work, like Hain's pistol yesterday.'

'It seems to me that you would have been populated to death here,' Brazil commented. 'After all, I assume all creatures reproduce here – and then the Markovian brains keep shuttling people here as well.'

'That just doesn't happen,' Ortega replied. 'For one thing, as I said, people can die here – and do. Some hexes have very cheap life, some species live a comparatively short time. Reproductive rates are in accordance with this death rate. If populations seem to be rising too high, and natural factors – like catastrophes, which *can* happen here, or wars, which also can happen, although they are not terribly common and usually localized – don't reduce the numbers, well, most of the next batch is simply born sexually normal in every way yet sterile, with just a very small number able to keep the breed going. When attrition takes its toll, the species goes back to being born fertile. Actually the population's pretty stable in each hex – from a low of about twenty thousand to a high of over a million.

'As for Entries like you – well, the Markovians were extensive, as I said, but many of their old brains are dead and some of the gateways are closed forever for one reason or another. Others are so well disguised that a one-in-a-trillion blunder like mine is needed to find the entrance. We get no more than a hundred or so newcomers a year, all told. We have a trip alarm when the Well is activated and some of us take turns on a daily basis answering the alarms. Sheer luck I ran into you, but I take a lot of turns. Some of the folks here don't really like newcomers and don't treat them right, so I take their duty and they owe me.'

'There are representatives of all the Southern Hemisphere races here, then?' Vardia asked.

The snakeman nodded. 'Most of them. Zone's really a sort of embassy station. Distances are huge, travel is long here, and so here at Zone representatives of all of us can meet and talk over mutual problems. The Gate – which we'll get to presently – will zip me back home in an instant, although, curse it, it won't zip anybody back and forth except from here to his own hex. Oh, yes, there's a special chamber for Northerners here and one for us up at the North Zone just in case we have to talk – which is seldom. They occasionally have something we are short of, or our scientists and theirs want to compare notes, or some-such. But they are *so* different from us that that's rare.'

Brazil wore a strangely fixed expression as he said, 'Serge, you've spelled out the world as much as you can, but you've omitted one fact I think I can guess – how did a little Latin shrimp like you become a six-armed walrus-snake.'

Ortega's expression was one of resignation. 'I thought it would be obvious. When you go out the Gate the first time, the brain will decide which hex could stand a person or four and that's what you will become. You will, of course, also wind up in the proper hex.'

'And then what?' Hain asked nervously.

'Well, there's a period of adjustment, of course. I went through the Gate the way Nate remembers me, and came out in the land of the Uliks looking like this. It took me a little while to get used to things, and longer for everything to sort itself out in my head, but, well, the change also produces an *adjustment.* I found I knew the language, at least all the analogues to my old one, and began to feel more and more comfortable in my new physical role. I *became* a Ulik, Nate, while still being me. Now I can hardly remember what it was like to be anything else, really. Oh, academically, sure – my mind was never clearer. But *you* are the aliens now.'

There was a long silence as they digested the information. Finally, Brazil broke it and asked, 'But, Serge, if there are seven hundred and eighty life forms with compatible biospheres, why hasn't there been a cosmopolitanism here in the South? I mean, why is everybody stuck in his own little area?'

'Oh, there is some mingling,' Ortega replied. 'Some hexes have been combined, some not. Mostly, though, people stick to their own areas because each one is different. Besides, people have never liked other people who were different. Humanity – ours and everybody else's, apparently – has always found even slight pretexts to hate other groups. Color, language, funnyshaped noses, religion, or anything else. Many wars were fought here at various times, and wholesale slaughter took place. Such things are rare now – everybody loses. So, mostly, everybody sticks to his own hex and minds his own business. Besides, there's the factor of commonality, too. Could you *really* be good buddies with a three-meter-tall hairy spider that ate live flesh, even if it also played chess and loved orchestral music? And – could a society based on high technology succeed in capturing and subjugating a hex where none of its technology worked? A balance is kind of maintained that way – technological hexes trade for needed things like food with nontechnological farm hexes where society is anarchistic and only swords will work.'

Vardia looked up, eyes bright, at the mention of swords. She still had hers.

'And, of course, in some hexes there are some pretty good sorcerers – and their spells work!' Ortega warned.

'Oh, come on,' Hain said disgustedly. 'I am willing to believe in a lot – but magic? Nonsense!'

'All magic means is a line between knowledge and ignorance,' Ortega responded. 'A magician is someone who can do something you don't know how to do. All technology, for example, is magic to a primitive. Just remember, this is an old world, and its people are different from anything in your experience. If you make the mistake – any of you! – of applying your own standards, your own rules, your own prejudices to any of it, it will get you.'

'Can you brief me on the general political situation, Serge?' Brazil requested. 'I'd like to know a lot more before going out there.'

'Nate, I couldn't do it in a million years. Like any planet with a huge number of countries and social systems, everything's in a constant state of flux. Conditions change, and so do rulers. You'll have to learn things as you go along. I can only caution that there is a lot of petty warfare and a lot of big stuff that would break out if one side could figure out a way to do it. One general a thousand years or so ago took over sixty hexes. But he was undone in the end by the necessity for long supply lines and by his inability to conquer several incompatible hexes in his backfield that eventually were able to slice him up. The lesson's been well learned. Things are done more by crook than hook here now.'

Hain's eyes brightened. 'My game!' he whispered.

'And now,' Ortega concluded, 'you must go. I cannot keep you here more than a day and justify the delay to my government. You cannot put off leaving indefinitely in any case.'

'But there are many more questions that must be answered!' Vardia protested. 'Climate, seasons, thousands of needed details!'

'As for the climate, it varies from hex to hex but has no relationship to geographical position,' Ortega told her. 'The climate is maintained in each case by the brain. Daylight is exactly fifty percent of each full day anywhere on the globe. Days are within a few hours of standard, so that's fourteen and an eighth standard hours of day and the same of night. The axis is straight up – no tilt at all. But it will vary artificially. But – see! I could go on forever and you'd never know enough. It is time!'

'And suppose I refuse?' Vardia challenged, raising her sword.

With that same lightning-quick movement that had marked the previous day's fight, Ortega's snake body uncoiled like a tightly wound spring, snatched the sword, and was back behind the desk in less than half a second. He looked at her sadly. 'You have no choice at all,' he said quietly. 'Will you all now come with me?'

They followed the Ulik ambassador reluctantly but resigned. He led them again down that great, winding corridor through which they had entered the day before, and it seemed to them all that their walk would never end.

Finally, after what was about half an hour, they found that the corridor opened into a large room. Three sides were bare, plastic-like walls similar to those in Ortega's office but without any pattern. The fourth looked like a wall of absolute black.

'That's the Gate,' Ortega told them, gesturing to the black wall. 'We use it to go back and forth between our own hexes and Zone, and you will use it to be assigned. Please don't be afraid. The Gate will not alter your personality; and, after the adjustment period, you will find that you are even better, mentally, than you were. For the little girl, here, passage through will mean the restoration of normality, cure of the addiction, and a correction of whatever imbalances they used to limit her IQ and abilities. Of course, she may still be a rather dull farm worker, but in no event will she be worse off than she was before she was addicted.'

None of them rushed into the Gate.

Finally, Ortega prodded them. 'The doorway behind you is closed. No one, not even I, may reenter Zone until he first goes to a hex. That's the way the system works.'

'I'll go first,' Brazil said suddenly, and he took a step toward the Gate. He felt a great hand on his shoulder that stopped him.

'No, Nate, not now,' Ortega almost whispered to him. 'Last.' Brazil was puzzled, but realized the intent. The ambassador had something else to say to him without the others hearing. Brazil nodded and turned to Hain.

'How about you, Hain? Or should I go at you again? We're not in the embassy now.'

'You caught me by surprise that time, Captain,' Hain replied with the old sneer. 'But if you stop and think, you'll know I could break you in pieces. Ambassador Ortega saved *your* life back there, not mine. Yet, I will go. My future is out there.' And, with that, Hain strode confidently to the blackness and, without hesitation, stepped into it.

The darkness seemed to swallow him up the moment he entered. There was no other visible effect.

Vardia and Wu Julee each stood solidly, not moving from their places near the entrance.

Ortega turned and took Wu Julee's left arm with one of his, urging her on across the room to the dark wall. She didn't seem to protest until she was very near the darkness. Then, suddenly, she stopped and screamed, 'No! No!' Her face turned and looked pleadingly at Brazil.

'Go ahead,' he urged her gently, but she broke free of Ortega's gentle grip and ran to the captain.

Brazil looked into her eyes with a gentle pity that was almost tearing him apart inside.

'You must go,' he told her. 'You must go. I will find you.'

Still she didn't budge, but tightened her grip on him. Suddenly she was yanked from him with such force and speed that the movement knocked Brazil to the ground. Ortega pulled her away and tossed her into the blackness in one quick motion.

She screamed, but the scream stopped as the blackness absorbed her, so abrupt that it was like a recording suddenly stopped in midsound.

'This business is a bitch sometimes,' Ortega remarked glumly. He turned and looked at Brazil, who was picking himself up off the floor. 'You all right?'

'Yeah,' Brazil replied, then looked into the creature's sad eyes. 'I understand, Serge,' he said softly. Then, as if to break the mood, his tone took on that of mock anger: 'But if you're going to keep beating the hell out of me I'm leaving here no matter what!'

His tone almost broke through the snakeman's melancholy, and Ortega managed a chuckle. He put his right upper arm out and clasped Brazil to him, and there were tears in his eyes. '*God!*' the snakeman exclaimed. 'How can the greatness in people be so unloved?'

Suddenly he relaxed and turned his gaze to Vardia, who had remained motionless throughout the whole episode.

Brazil guessed what must be going through her mind now. Raised by an all-embracing state, trained and bred to a particular function, she was simply not programmed for such a disruption of her orderly, planned life. Every day for her had always been a certainty, and she was secure in the knowledge of that sameness and content with the belief that she was performing a useful task.

Now she was, for the first time, on her own.

Brazil thought for a moment, then hit upon what he hoped was a solution.

'Vardia,' he said in his best command voice, 'we set out to do a job when we landed on Dalgonia. That trail has led us here to this spot. Now it leads through there. There are seven bodies back on Dalgonia, Vardia. Seven, including at least one of your own people. There is still a duty for you to perform.'

She was breathing hard, the only sign of inner mental torment. Finally, she turned and faced the other two, then ran at the blackness of the Gate.

And was gone.

Brazil and Ortega were alone in the room.

'What was that about seven bodies, Nate?' the snakeman asked.

Brazil recounted the story of the mysterious distress signal, the mass murder on Dalgonia, and the signs of the two who had vanished as they had.

Ortega's expression was extremely grave. 'I wish I had known of this ten weeks ago when those two came through here. It would have changed things a great deal in Council.'

Brazil's eyebrows rose. 'You know them, then?'

Ortega nodded. 'Yes, I know them. I didn't do the processing, but I watched the recordings of their arrival over and over. There was a great deal of debate about them before they went through the Gate.'

'Who were they? What was their story?'

'Well, they came through together, and one of them was still trying to kill the other on the Well itself when Gre'aton – he's a Type Six Twenty-two, looks kind of like a giant locust – put a stop to it. A few of the more human-looking boys took over, splitting them up so they didn't see each other again.

'Each of them told a fantastic story, about how he and he alone had discovered some sort of mathematical relationship used by the Markovian brains. Each claimed that everything in the universe was a series of preset mathematical relationships determined by a master Markovian brain. When they were given the standard briefing, both became terribly excited, each convinced that the Well World was the master brain and that they could somehow communicate with it, maybe even run it. Each claimed the other had stolen his discovery, tried to kill the other, and was here to establish himself as god. Of course, each claimed that he was trying to stop the other from doing so.'

'Did you believe them?'

'They were mighty convincing. We used some of the standard lie-detection stuff and tried some telepathy using one of the North boys, and the results were always the same.'

'And?' Brazil prompted.

'As far as we were able to determine – and we don't have the methods for a really scientific study – *they were both telling the truth.*'

'*Whew.* You mean they're psychos through and through?'

Ortega was solemn. 'No, each truly believes he discovered what the code was, and each truly believes the other stole it, and each truly believes that he'd be good for godhead and the other would be horrible.'

'Do you really believe that godhead stuff?' Brazil asked.

Ortega turned all six arms into a giant shrug. 'Who knows? A number of folk here have similar ideas, but no one's ever been able to do anything about them. We called a Council – a *full* Council, with over twelve hundred ambassadors participating. All were given the facts. Everything was debated.

'The idea explains a lot, of course. All magic, for example. But it is so esoteric. And, as it was pointed out by some of our mathematically minded folk, even if true it probably didn't mean anything, since no one could change the brain anyway. In the end, even though a large number of members voted to kill them, the majority voted to let them through.'

'How did *you* vote, Serge?' Brazil asked.

'I voted to kill them, Nate. They are both maniacs, and both are possessed of genius. Each believed he could do what he set out to do, and both seemed to believe that it was destiny that, so soon after the discovery, they were brought here.'

'More to the point, do *you* believe it, Serge?'

'I do,' the giant replied gravely. 'Right now I think those two are the most dangerous beings in the entire universe. And – more to the point – I think that one of them, I can't tell which, has a chance of succeeding.'

'What are their names, Serge, and their backgrounds?'

Ortega's eyes brightened. 'So God in His infinite wisdom allows mercy after all! You *do* want to get them, and God has sent you to us for that purpose!'

Brazil thought for a moment. 'Serge, ever hear of a Markovian brain actually, literally, trapping people by sending out false signals or the like?'

Ortega thought for a moment. 'No,' he replied, 'as far as I know it's always accident or blunder. That's why so few come. Now do you see what I mean about God sending you to me?'

'Somebody sure did, anyway,' Brazil acknowledged dryly. 'I wish I could see those films and learn a lot about them before I tried to find two invisible needles in a planet-sized haystack.'

'You can,' Ortega assured him. 'I have all the material back in my office.'

Brazil's mouth was agape. 'But you told us there was no way back!'

Ortega shrugged monstrously again. 'I lied,' he said.

Several hours later Brazil learned as much as he was going to from the recordings, testimony, and arguments of the Council committees.

'So can you give me any leads on this Skander and Varnett? Where are they now? And what?'

'Newcomers are pretty conspicuous around here, since there are so few of them and they are so obvious,' Ortega replied. 'And, yet, I can give you nothing on either. The planet seems to have swallowed them up.'

'Isn't that unusual?' Brazil asked. 'Or, worse, suspicious?'

'I see what you mean. The whole planet saw what you saw and heard what you heard. They could have some natural allies.'

'Yeah, that's what I'm most concerned about,' Brazil said bluntly. 'The odds are that there's a monstrous race going on here, and that this place is the soul of reason compared to what everything we know would become if the wrong side was to win.'

'They could both be dead,' Ortega suggested hopefully.

Brazil shook his head in a violent negative. 'Uh-uh. Not these boys. They're clever and they're nasty. Skander's almost the archetypal mad scientist, and Varnett's even worse – a *renegade*, high-class Com. At least one of them will make it, and he'll have some way to dump his allies afterward.'

'You'll have the help of all the hexes who voted to kill them,' Ortega pointed out.

'Sure, Serge, and I'll use that when I have to. But this is really a lone-wolf operation and you know it. That Council was politically very slick. They

55

could count. Even a hex voting to kill them knew they wouldn't be killed – so what was the use of their vote? Getting there might take help – but once there, every friend I have on this world will seek godhead, and never mind that I don't know how to talk to the brain. No, Serge, I have to kill *both* of them, absolutely, irrevocably, and as quickly as possible.'

'Getting *where* might take help?' Ortega asked, puzzled.

'To the Well of Souls, of course,' Brazil replied evenly. 'And before midnight.'

Now it was Ortega's turn to look stunned. 'But that's just an old saying, like I said before—'

'It's the answer, Serge,' Brazil asserted strongly. 'It's just that nobody has been able to decipher the code and make use of it.'

'There is no answer to that. It makes no real sense!'

'Sure it does!' Brazil told him. 'It's the answer to a monstrous question, and the key to the most monstrous of threats. I saw Skander's and Varnett's eyes light up when they first heard the phrase, Serge. They seized on it!'

'But what's the question?' Ortega asked bewilderedly.

'That's what I don't know yet,' Brazil replied, pointing his finger at the Ulik animatedly. 'But *they* thought it was the answer, and *they* both think *they* can figure it out. If they can, I can.

'Look, Serge, *why* was this world built? No, not the brain; we'll accept that as bringing some sort of stability to the universe. In fact, if they're right, we're all just figments of some dead Markovian's imagination. No, *why all this?* The Well, the hexes, the civilizations? If I can answer *that*, I can answer the bigger question! And I'll find out!' Brazil exclaimed excitedly, half-rising from his chair.

'How can you be so sure?' Ortega responded dubiously.

'Because someone – or something – wants me to!' Brazil continued in the same excited tone. 'That's why I was lured here! That's why I'm here at all, Serge! That's what makes even the timing! Even now they've got a ten-week start! You, yourself, said as much back at the Gate!'

Ortega shook his head glumly. 'That was just my old Latin soul coming forth, Nate. I've been consorting with Jesuits again – yes, we have several here, from the old missionary days, came in a single ship and are out trying to convert the heathen. But, be reasonable, man! You never would have found Dalgonia were it not for the detour. You wouldn't have detoured except for Wu Julee's presence on your ship, and that could hardly have been planned, let alone your act of mercy.'

'I think it *was* planned, Serge,' Brazil said evenly. 'I think I've been conned all along. I don't know how, or by whom, or for what purpose, but *I've been had!*'

'I don't see how,' Ortega responded, 'but, even if so, how will you ever know?'

'I'll know,' Brazil said in a tone that was both firm and somewhat frightening. 'I'll know at midnight at the Well of Souls.'

They stood once again at the Gate, this time for the last time.

'It's agreed, then,' Ortega said to him. 'As soon as you pass through and get oriented, you announce yourself to the local ruler. All of them will have been notified of your coming through, with instructions to render any assistance. But at least one of them is sure to be in league with your enemies, Nate! Are you sure? What if you are swallowed up?'

'I won't be, Serge,' Brazil replied calmly. 'Chessplayers don't sacrifice their queens early in the game.'

Ortega gave one last massive shrug. 'Believe what you wish – but, be careful, my old friend. If they get you, I shall avenge your death.'

Brazil smiled, then looked at the Gate. 'Is it best to run at it, walk into it, or what?' he asked.

'Doesn't matter,' Ortega told him. 'You'll wake up as if coming out of a long sleep, anyway. May you wake up a Ulik!'

Brazil smiled, but kept his thoughts on being a seven-meter, six-armed walrus-snake to himself. He walked over to the gate, then turned for one last look at his transformed old friend.

'I hope I wake up at all, Serge,' he said quietly.

'Go with God, you ancient heathen,' Ortega said.

'I'll be damned,' Brazil muttered, half to himself. 'After all these years I might wake up a Gentile.' And, with that, he stepped through the Gate.

And in the darkness he dreamed.

He was on a giant chessboard, that stretched off in all directions. Seven pawns were down on his side – the white side. They looked like scorched and frozen bodies, lying on blackened cots.

Through the mostly faceless field of black pieces, he could see Skander and Varnett, queen and king.

Skander was a queen in royal robes, with a scepter in hand. The queen looked around, but could not spot the king. There was Wu Julee, a pawn, out front, and Vardia, a knight with bright sword flashing.

Ortega, a bishop, glided by quickly, and was struck by a black rook with the face of Datham Hain.

The queen glided quickly, trying not to trip over her long skirts, toward Hain, the scepter ready to strike that ugly, pig face, when suddenly Ortega reappeared and pushed him away.

'The black royal family has escaped, Your Highness!' Ortega's voice shouted. 'They are heading for the Well of Souls!'

The queen looked around, but there was no trace of the enemy's major pieces. Anywhere.

'But where is the Well of Souls?' screamed the queen. 'I cannot get to the king without knowing!'

A sudden burst of overwhelming, cosmic laughter came from beyond the board. It was giant, hollow, and all embracing. A giant hand gripped the queen and moved it far away to the other side of the board. 'Here they are!' the great voice said mockingly.

The queen looked around and screamed in terror. The king with Skander's face was but one square right, and the queen with Varnett's face was one square up.

'Our move!' they both said, and laughed maniacally.

Brazil awoke.

He got quickly to his feet. *Odd*, he thought curiously. *I'm more wide awake, feeling better, head clearer than I can ever remember.*

Quickly he examined his body to see what he was. With a shock he looked up around him, to the shores of a nearby lake. There were animals there, and others of his kind.

'Well I'll be damned!' he said aloud. 'Of course! That had to be the answer to the first question! I should have figured it out in Serge's office!'

Sometimes the obvious needed to be belabored.

Considering how primitive the place was, Brazil worriedly set out to see if he could find the Zone Gate.

CZILL – SPRING
(ENTER VARDIA DIPLO 1261, ASLEEP)

She was never certain why she had finally stepped through the Gate. Perhaps doing so was an acceptance of inevitability, perhaps an obedience to authority that was a part of her conditioning.

There were patterns of color, running in and out, pulsating in a rhythmic, cosmic heartbeat: yellows, greens, reds, blues – all forming kaleidoscopic patterns, a mechanical ringing sound accompanying the pulses in an odd symphonic monotone.

Then, quite suddenly, she awoke.

She was on a lush savanna, tall grasses of green and gold stretching out to low foothills in the distance. Some trees, reminiscent of gum trees, dotted the plain, with odd growths that looked like barren stubs of what once had been taller trees showing in some numbers in the distance.

With a start, she realized that the stubby trees were moving. They moved in a syncopated rhythm that was most strange. The trunks were actually legs, she realized, and it seemed as if they were all moving in great strides, yet were somehow arrested. It was like watching a track meet in slow motion. That was deceptive, though; the slower motion was apparently only an illusion, and as she watched, some of them covered pretty good distances in no time.

They all seem to have something to do or someplace to go, she thought to herself. Purpose means some sort of civilization, and I need to find out where I am and what place this is before I can get my own purpose clear.

She started toward the distant forms.

And suddenly stopped as she caught a glimpse of her own body.

She looked down at herself in wonder.

She was a sort of light green, her skin a smooth, vinelike texture. Her legs were thick and yet long and rubbery, without an apparent joint. The trunk of her body showed no signs of breasts or of a vaginal cavity; and though her feet were flat bases, her arms seemed to be of the same nature as her legs, only thinner, ending as tentacles rather than as hands. Another, shorter tentacle grew out of the main arm about ten centimeters from its tip. A thumb, perhaps?

She found that the rubbery arms worked well either way, being pliant and without apparent joint or bone, and she felt her smooth backside. No rectum, either, she found.

She ran her arm over her face. A wide slit was no doubt the mouth, yet it opened only a tiny fraction. The nose appeared to be a single, fixed, hard hole above the mouth. Growing out of the top of her head was something thin, tough, and about the size of a mortarboard, although of irregular shape.

What have I become? she asked herself, feeling fear bordering on panic.

Slowly she tried to regain control of herself. Taking deep breaths had always helped, but she found she couldn't even do that. She was breathing, all right, she could sense that – but that nostril took in only a very tiny part of the air.

She realized it was primarily a sensitive olfactory organ; she was breathing by involuntary muscle actions through the pores in her smooth, green skin.

After a while her panic seemed to subside, and she considered what to do. The distant shapes were still going about their business, she saw. She seemed to be on a road of some sort.

No matter what, she had to contact those creatures and find out just what was happening. She again started for the figures and found, with some surprise, that she covered the distance – almost a kilometer through the tall grass – in a much shorter time than she would have expected.

It *was* a road, she saw – a dirt track, really, but wide and made up of reddish-brown soil.

The creatures using it paid her no attention whatsoever, but she studied them intently. They were like herself, she knew. Those things she couldn't discover from self-examination were now apparent: two large, round, yellow eyes with black pupils, apparently lid-less. She suddenly realized that she hadn't been blinking her own eyes, and could not.

The thing growing out of her head proved to be a single large leaf of irregular shape – no two were alike. The stalk was thick and very short. Its color was a much deeper green than the body and it had an almost waxy texture.

Not knowing how to talk to them, and almost afraid to try, she decided to follow the road. It *must* go someplace, she told herself. It really didn't matter which direction – one was as good as the other.

She walked onto the road and set off toward the low hills to her left. The road really wasn't as crowded as she had thought, but at least a dozen – people? – were on the road ahead of her. She gained on a pair, and as she did she became aware that they were talking. The sounds were musical, yet she discovered that she could almost make out what was being said. As she closed to within three or four meters of the pair, she slowed, aware now that she *could* understand the strange, whispering singsong.

'... got into the Bla'ahaliagan spirit-strata stuff, and can't even be talked to these days. If the Blessed Elder doesn't get off that crap pretty soon I'm going to transfer over to cataloging.'

'Hmmmm ... Dull stuff but I can see your point,' the other sympathized. 'Crindel got stuck under Elder Mudiul on some esoteric primitive game an Entry dropped on us about three hundred years ago. Seems it has almost infinite patterns after the first few moves, and there was this project to teach it to a computer. Couldn't be done. Weird stuff. Almost went off to the Meditations and rotted, Crindel did.'

'How'd the Worthy get out of it?' the first one asked.

'Mudiul got a virus and it got the Elder quarantined for nine years,' chortled the other. 'By the time the Worthy got out the Board had closed down the project and redistributed the staff. The Old One's got off on whether rocks have souls, and that ought to keep the Worthy out of harm's way until rot wipes the Worthy.'

They went on like that for some time, and the conversation did little to clear up anything in Vardia's mind. About the only useful fact that came out of the discussion was the obvious limits of third-person-singular pronouns in the language.

She noticed that both wore gold chains around their necks as their only adornment of any kind, but, trying not to be conspicuous, she couldn't see what was fastened to them.

They had been walking for some time now, and several other things came into her mind. First, the locals seemed to live in communities. She passed groups of them here and there, their numbers ranging from three or four to several dozen. Yet there were no signs of buildings. The groupings seemed to be like camp circles, but without the fire. Occasionally she could glimpse mysterious artifacts here and there in the midst of the groups, but nothing large enough to stand out. Some groups seemed to be singing, some dancing, some both, while others were engaged in animated conversations so complex and esoteric that they melded into a tuneful chatter like a blending of insects.

Also, she was aware very suddenly, she felt neither tired nor hungry. That was a good thing, she reflected, since she had no idea what these people ate. She continued to think in her own, old language, but had no trouble understanding others with their singsong chirping so alien to her.

The two she had been following took a side path down toward a large grouping that was gathered in a particularly attractive spot. It was a pastoral setting of multicolored flowers and bushes alongside a fast-flowing stream.

She stopped at the junction of the main road and the access trail to the lake, partially blocking the side trail. Someone came up behind her and brushed past her, making her conscious of her blocking.

'I'm sorry,' she said automatically and stepped to one side.

'That's all right,' the other replied and continued on.

It was almost a full minute before she realized that she had spoken and been understood!

She hurried after the being who had spoken, now far ahead.

'Wait! Please!' she called after the creature. 'I need your help!'

The other stopped and turned, a puzzled expression on it.

'What seems to be the trouble?' the creature asked as she came up to him.

'I – I am lost and confused,' she blurted out to the other. 'I have just – just become one of you, and I don't know where I am or what I'm supposed to do.'

Realization hit the other. 'A new Entry! Well, well! We haven't had an Entry in Czill in my lifetime! Well, of course you're confused. Come! You shall sleep with us tonight and you will tell us of your origin and we'll tell you of Czill,' it said eagerly, like a child with a new toy. 'Come!'

She followed the creature down to the grove. It moved very quickly, and eagerly gathered its companions as fast as possible, excitedly telling them that they had an Entry in Riverbend, as the camp was apparently called.

Vardia took all the attention nervously, still bashful and unsure of herself.

They gathered around asking questions by the hundreds, all at once, each one canceling out the others in the general din. Finally, one with a particularly strong voice appealed for quiet over the noise, and after some work, got it.

'Take it easy!' it shouted, making calming gestures. 'Can't you see the poor one's scared to death? Wouldn't you be if, say, you went to sleep this night and woke up a Pia?' Satisfied, it turned to Vardia and said gently, 'How long have you been in Czill?'

'I – I have just arrived,' she told them. 'You are the first persons I've talked to. I wasn't even – well, I wasn't sure *how*.'

'Well, you've fallen into the worst pack of jabbering conversationalists,' the one with the loud voice said, amusement in its tone. 'I am Brouder, and I will not try to introduce everyone else here. We'll likely draw a bigger and bigger crowd as word of you gets around.'

It was interesting, she thought, that such weird whistlings and clickings should be instantly translated in her mind to their Confederacy equivalents. The creature's name was *not* Brouder, of course – it was a short whistle, five clicks, a long whistle, and a descending series of clicks. Yet that was what the name said in her mind, and it seemed to work in reverse as well.

'I am Vardia Diplo Twelve Sixty-one,' she told them, 'from Nueva Albion.'

'A Comworlder!' someone's voice exclaimed. 'No wonder it wound up here!'

'Pay the critics no mind, Vardia,' Brouder told her. 'They're just showing off their education.' That last was said with a great deal of mysterious sarcasm.

'What did you do before you came here?' someone asked.

'My job?' Vardia responded. 'Why, I was a diplomatic courier between Nueva Albion and Coriolanus.'

'See?' Brouder snorted. 'An educated one!'

'I'll still bet the Apprentice can't read!' called out that one in the back.

'Forget the comments,' Brouder urged her with a wave of its tentacle. 'We're really a friendly group. I was – is something the matter?' it asked suddenly.

'Feeling dizzy,' she replied, the ground and crowd suddenly reeling a bit. She reached out to steady herself on Brouder. 'Funny,' she muttered. 'So sudden.'

'It comes on like that,' Brouder replied. 'I should have thought of it. Come on, I'll help you down to the stream.'

It took her down to the rushing water, which had a strangely soothing effect on her. It walked her into the water.

'Just stand here a few minutes,' the Czillian told her. 'Come back up when you feel better.'

Automatically, she found, something like tendrils were coming out of small cavities in her feet and were digging into the shallow riverbed. She drank in the cool water through them, and the dizziness and faintness seemed to evaporate.

She looked at the riverbank and saw that they were all watching her, a line of fifteen or twenty light-green, sexless creatures with staring eyes and floppy leaves on their heads. Feeling suddenly excellent once more, she retracted her tendrils and walked stiffly back to the bank.

'Feel all right now?' Brouder asked. 'It was stupid of us – you naturally wouldn't have had much water in you. You're the first Entry in some time, and the first one ever for us. Please, if you feel in the least bit strange or ill, let us know. We take so much for granted.'

The concern in its voice was genuine, she knew, and she took comfort from it. *All* of them had looked concerned when she had been out in the river.

She really felt she was among friends now.

'Will you answer some of my questions, then?' she asked them.

'Go ahead,' Brouder told her.

'Well – these will sound stupid to you all, of course, but this whole business is entirely new to me,' she began. 'First off, what am I? That is, what are we?'

'I'm Gringer,' another approached. 'Perhaps I can answer that one. You are a Czillian. The land is called Czill, and while that explains nothing, it at least gives you a label.'

'What does the name mean?' she asked.

Gringer gave the Czillian equivalent of a shrug. 'Nothing, really. Most names don't mean anything these days. They probably all did once, but nobody knows anymore.

'Anyway, we are unusual in these parts because we are plants rather than animals of some sort. There are other sentient plant-beings on the Well World, eleven in the South here and nine in the North, although I'm not sure those are really plants as we understand them. We're a distinct minority here, anyway. But there are great advantages to being in the vegetable kingdom.'

'Like what?' she asked, fascinated in spite of herself.

'Well, we are not dependent on any sort of food. Our bodies make it by converting light from the sun, as most plants do. Just get a few hours of real or artificial sun a day and you will never starve. You do need some minerals from the soil, but these are common to much of the Well World, so there are few places you can't get along. Water is your only need, and you need it only once every few days. Your body will tell you when – as it did just now. If you get into a regular routine of drinking, you will never feel dizzy or faint nor will you risk your health from its lack. There is also no sex here, none of those primal drives that get the animals in such a neurotic jumble.'

'Such things have been minimized on my home planet,' she responded. 'It would appear from what you say that I will not find this place that far from my own social concepts. But, if you have no sexes, do you reproduce by some artificial means?'

The crowd chuckled at this.

'No,' Gringer responded, 'all races on the Well World are self-contained biological units that could survive, given certain ecological conditions, without any aids. We reproduce slowly, for we are among the oldest-lived folk on the planet. When something happens to require additional population, then we plant ourselves for an extended period and produce another of ourselves by fission. This is far more practical than the other way, for everything that we are is duplicated, cell for cell, so that the new growth is an exact copy that contains even the same memories and personalities. Thus, even though you will wear out in a few centuries, you will also live forever – for the growths are so identical that not even we are certain which one is which.'

Vardia looked around, studying the crowd. 'Are there any such twins here?' she asked.

'No,' Gringer replied. 'We tend to split up, stay far apart, until the years make us into different folk by the variety of experiences. We live in small camps, like this one, drawn from different occupations and interests, so that the camps provide a wide range of folk and keep things from getting too dull.'

'What do you do for work?' Vardia asked. 'I mean, most – ah, animal civilizations are devoted to food production, building and maintaining shelters, educating the young, and manufacturing. You don't seem to need any of those things.'

'This is true,' Brouder acknowledged. 'Freed from the animal demands of food, clothing, shelter, and sex, we are able to turn ourselves to those pursuits to which other races must, because of the primacy of those needs, devote only a small part of their endeavors.'

Vardia was more puzzled than ever. 'What sort of activities do you mean?' she asked.

'We think,' Brouder replied.

'What Brouder means,' Gringer cut in, seeing her uncomprehending look, 'is that we are researchers into almost every area. You may think of us as a giant university. We collect knowledge, sort it, play with problems both practical and theoretical, and add to the greater body of knowledge. Had you followed the main road in the other direction, you would have come upon the Center, which is where those of us who need lab facilities and technical tools work and where people following similar lines meet to discuss their findings and their problems.'

Vardia's mind tried to grasp it, and could not. 'Why?' she asked.

Brouder and Gringer both showed expressions of surprise. 'Why what?' Gringer asked.

'Why do you do such work? To what goal?'

This disturbed them, and there were animated conversations through the gathered crowd. Vardia was equally disturbed by the reaction to her question, which she had considered very straightforward. She thought perhaps she had been misunderstood.

'I mean,' she said, 'to what end is all of this research? You do not seem to use it yourself, so who is it for?'

Gringer seemed about to have a fit of some kind. 'But the quest for knowledge is the only thing that separates sentient beings from the most common grasses or lowest animals!' the Czillian said a bit shrilly.

Brouder's tone was almost patronizing, as if addressing a small child. 'Look,' the researcher said to her, 'what do *you* think is the end result for civilization? What is the goal of your people?'

'Why, to exist in happiness and harmony with all others for all times,' she replied as if reciting a liturgy – which is what it was, taught from the day she was produced at the Birth Factory.

Gringer's long tentacles showed agitation. Its right one reached down and pulled up a single blade of the yellowish grass that grew for kilometers in all directions. It pushed the long stalk in front of her, waving it like a pointer. 'This blade of grass is happy,' Gringer stated flatly. 'It gets what it needs to survive. It doesn't think or need to think. It remains happy even though I've pulled it up and it will die. It doesn't know that, and won't even know it when it's dead. Its relatives out there on the plains are the same. They fit your definition of the ultimate goal of civilized society. It knows nothing, and in perfect ignorance is its total perfection and its harmony with its surroundings. Shall we, then, create a way to turn all sentient beings into blades of field grass? Shall we, then, have achieved the ultimate in evolution?'

Vardia's mind spun. This sort of logic and these kinds of questions were outside her experience and her orderly, programmed universe. She had no answers for these – heresies, were they? Cornered, but as yet unwilling to give up the true faith, she regressed.

'I want to go back to my own world,' she wailed plaintively.

Brouder's expression was sad, and pity swept the crowd, pity not only at her philosophical dilemma but also for her people, the billions blindly devoted to such a hollow goal. Its rubbery tentacle wrapped itself around hers, and pulled her back into the reddish-brown, upturned soil of the camp.

'Any other questions or problems can wait,' it said gently. 'You will have time to learn and to fit here. It is getting dark now, and you need rest.'

The shadows were getting long, and the distant sun had become an orange ball on the horizon. For the first time since waking up, she *did* feel tired, and a slight chill went through her.

'Except under the artificial light of the Center we are inactive in darkness,' Brouder explained. 'Although we could go indefinitely there, we need the rooting to remain healthy and active. We gain minerals and strength from it, and it is also necessary for mental health.'

'How do I – ah, root?' she asked.

'Just pick a spot not too near anyone else, and wait for darkness. You will see,' Brouder told her. The Czillian pointed out a good spot, then moved about five long paces from her.

Vardia just stood there for a while, looking at the small community in the gloomy dusk. She discovered that, although her eyes remained open, she was having trouble seeing. Everything looked very dark, as if she were peering through a piece of film that was badly underexposed. Then she felt the myriads of tiny tendrils in her feet creep out in response to some automatic signal and extend deep into the loose soil. The chill and tiredness seemed to lift, and she felt a warmth rising within her. Every cell of her new body seemed to tingle, and she was consumed in an orgasmic feeling of extreme pleasure that canceled out thought.

All over the hex of Czill, all who were not working in the Center were similarly rooting. To an alien observer, the land would be punctuated with over a million tall, thick vines as motionless as the trees.

And yet the landscape was not motionless. Millions of nocturnal insects set up a chorus, and several small mammals scurried around looking for food and, in the process, moving, aerating, and fertilizing the soil. They provided the carbon-dioxide-from-oxygen conversion needed for atmospheric balance in this hex. The teeming legions of life coexisted with the daylight Czillians in perfect balance. They existed under the thousands of stars in the night sky the sleeping plant-people could not see.

Because her eyes were lidless she saw the awakening even as she underwent it. It was strange to come out of that infinitely pleasurable sleep and see the morning simply fade in. Several of the others were in her field of vision, and she saw that the sleeping position was very stiff. Tentacles ran down and almost blended with the trunk, the legs almost forming a solid front.

She noted absently that picking one's spot for the night was more important than had been first indicated. The unrooting was apparently triggered by the sun's rays falling on the single leaf atop the head, so the more objects scattered about blocked the sun's first rays, the slower one was to be freed. She felt her own tendrils retract and suddenly she could move freely, as if a paralysis had worn off.

Brouder came up to her. 'Well? Do you feel better?' it asked cheerfully.

'Yes, much,' she replied, and meant it. She *did* feel better, her fears and insecurities fading into a tiny corner of her mind. For the first time she noticed that Brouder wore a neck chain similar to the ones on the two she had followed. Now she looked at the tiny object suspended from it.

It was a digital watch.

Brouder looked at it and nodded. 'We're early,' it said, then looked somewhat sheepish. 'I always say that, even though we always wake up at the same time.'

'Then why wear a watch?' she asked. 'It *is* a watch, isn't it?'

'Oh, yes,' the Czillian affirmed. 'I need it to tell me the time and day so I can make my meetings at the Center. It's been hectic lately, and I am always afraid that I'm going to get trapped and not be able to come home nights.'

'What are you working on?' she asked.

'A very strange project, even for this place,' came the reply. 'We are attempting to solve a probably unsolvable riddle that is endemic to this world – a great deal of the Center is devoted to it right now. And the worst part is that most of us feel it is unsolvable.'

'Then why bother with it?' she asked. The Czillian looked at her, a grave expression coloring its body movements.

'Because, while we are the best equipped to work on the problem, others are also at work on it. If there is any chance it *is* solvable, the ultimate knowledge will be ours. In others' hands, that knowledge might threaten the very survival of us all.'

Here was something Vardia could understand, and she pressed her new friend for more information. But the Czillian dismissed further inquiry for the time being. She had the strong impression that the work was of too high a grade for her to be trusted, even though she was now one of them.

'I am going to the Center now,' Brouder told her. 'You should come with me. Not only will that give you a chance to see a little of our country – it's your country now, you know – but only at the Center can you be tested and assigned.'

She agreed readily and they started off, back down the road she had followed the day before. As they walked, Brouder pointed out the land and vegetation and sketched out the country for her. 'Czill is six hundred fourteen point eight-six kilometers across, as is every other hex on the Well World except the equatorial hexes.'

She marveled at the knowledge that the measurement it used bore no relationship to the metrics of her own world, yet was translated to the decimal points instantly inside her head.

'We have, of course, six neighbors, two of which are ocean species. Our seven great rivers are fed by hundreds of streams like the one at our camp. The rivers in turn empty into a great ocean – one of three in the South – covering almost thirty hexes. This one of ours is the Overdark Ocean. One of the sea folk is a marine mammal, half-humanoid and half-fish. They are air-breathers, but live most of their lives underwater. They are the Umiau, and you might run into a few at the Center. We are always cooperating on a number of projects, particularly oceanographic studies, since we can't visit their world except in pressure suits. The other ocean species is a nasty group called the Pia – evil characters with great brains and humanoid eyes. But they have ten tentacles with slimy, adhesive suckers and a gaping mouth with about twenty rows of teeth. You can't really talk to them, although they are quite intelligent. They tend to eat anybody not of their race.'

Vardia shuddered, imagining such horrors. 'Then why don't they eat the Umiau?' she asked.

Brouder chuckled. 'They would if they could, but, as with all hexes near antagonistic species on the Well World, natural limitations are designed into the system. The Umiau's land is near the mouth of three rivers and the low salt content isn't to a Pia's liking. Also, the Umiau do have certain natural defenses and can swim faster and quicker. They're in some kind of uneasy truce now, anyway, since the Umiau, although they aren't fanatical about it, can and will eat Pia, too.'

They remained silent for a while, until they came to a major fork in the road.

'We go to the left,' Brouder said. 'Don't ever go down that right fork – it leads to the camps of the diseased and isolated.'

'What sort of diseases?' she asked uneasily.

'About the same number as anywhere else,' Brouder replied. 'But every time we discover an immunizing agent, something new mutates in the viruses. I wouldn't worry about it, however. The average Czillian life span is over two hundred and fifty years, and if nothing serious happens to change that, you'll twin several times anyway. The population's a stable million and a half – crowded, but not so much that we cannot have empty spaces and camp room. Our births and deaths are almost exactly even – the planet's master brain sees to that. Besides, since we don't really age in the sense most other things do, and since we can regenerate most of our parts that go bad or get injured, there's naturally a constant death factor to keep the population in bounds. The master brain only interferes in critical situations.'

'Regenerate?' Vardia asked, surprised. 'Do you mean that if I lose an arm or leg it will grow back?'

'Just so,' Brouder affirmed. 'Your entire pattern is held within every cell of your body. Since respiration is direct, through the pores, as long as your brain's intact, you'll come back. It's painful – and we don't experience much pain – but possible.'

'So the only area I have to protect is my head,' she remarked.

Brouder laughed a high, shrill laugh. 'No, not your head, certainly not! Either foot,' it said, pointing to her strange feet that looked like inverted bowls with spongy lids for soles.

'Do you mean I'm walking on my brains?' she gasped incredulously.

'Just so, just so,' affirmed Brouder. 'Each controls half of your body, but each has the total content of the body's input, including thought and memory. If we were to chop you off at the bottom of the stalk, your two feet would dig into the ground and each would sprout a new you. Your head contains sensory input neural circuits only – in fact, it's mostly hollow. Chop it off and you'd just go to sleep and dig in until you grew a new one.'

Vardia marveled at this news as much as she had at Ortega back at Zone. But this isn't some alien creature I just met, she told herself. It is *me* it is talking about.

'There's the Center,' Brouder said as they came over a rise.

It was a great building that seemed to spread out for kilometers across the horizon. There was a great bubble in the center that reflected light like a mirror, then several arms – six of them, she noted with dry amusement – made of what appeared to be transparent glass – spread out symmetrically. She saw skyscrapers of the same transparent material, a few twenty or more stories, rising around the bubble and opposite the tips of the arms.

'It's incredible!' she managed.

'More than you know,' Brouder replied with a touch of pride. 'There our best minds work out problems and store the knowledge we obtain. The silvery rails that thread through the walls and ceilings are artificial solar light sufficient to keep us awake and fed through the night, and if you look to the horizon you'll see the River Averil coming in. The Center's built over it, giving us a constant water source. With light and water provided – and some vitamin baths – you can work around the clock for seven to ten days. But sooner or later it catches up with you and the longer you stay awake the longer you will have to plant in the end.'

Something made her think of Nathan Brazil and that book he had been reading, the one with the lurid cover.

'You have a library here?' she asked.

'The best,' the other boasted. 'It has everything we've ever been able to collect, both from our studies on this planet and from Entries like yourself who provide history, sociology, and even technical information.'

'Any stories?' she asked.

'Oh, yes,' came the reply. 'And legends, tales, whatever. The Umiau are particularly fertile in that department. The river's how they get up to the Center.'

'What keeps the Pia away, then?' she asked apprehensively.

'They can't take fresh water, and they'd have to breathe it, remember? The Umiau are mammals so they don't care what sort of water they're in.'

Brouder went on to explain the social structure of the Center. It was headed by a small group of specialists called Elders, not because they were old but because they were the best in their fields. Below them were their assistants, the Scholars, who did the research and basic project work. Brouder was a Scholar, as was Gringer. Under them were the Apprentices who learned their fields and waited for their chance to prove themselves and advance. The bottom level was the Keepers – the cleaners, gardeners, and technicians who maintained everything so that everyone could get on with his work. The Keepers chose their own lives and professions and many were retired upper-level folk who had decided they had gone as far as they could, or who had reached dead ends. But some just liked to do what they did.

Brouder took her inside and introduced her to a Scholar whose name was Mudriel. Basically, the Scholar was an industrial psychologist, and over the next several days – weeks, in fact – Vardia was kept busy with interviews, tests, and other experiments to see her total profile. In addition, they began to teach her to read the Czillian language. Mudriel, in particular, was pleased with the speed and ease with which she was mastering it.

Every evening they sent her out to a special camp near the Psych Department but out of the shade of the building. The nights saw a strange forest grow up on all sides of the Center as thousands of workers of all ranks came out and rooted. Some stayed rooted for days, even several days, sleeping off long, around-the-clock stints at work.

Vardia seemed to be Mudriel's only customer, and she remarked on it.

'You are the first Entry to be a Czillian in our lifetimes,' Mudriel explained. 'Normally, I study various departments and workers to see if they are ruining their health or efficiency, or are misplaced. It happens all the time. Sometimes, whenever possible, we bring Entries from other hexes here for debriefing. When that is not possible, I go to them. I am one of perhaps a thousand, no more, who has been in the Northern Hemisphere.'

'What's it like?' she asked. 'I understand it's different.'

'That's the word for it,' Mudriel agreed, and gave a brief shudder. 'But we have some just as bad on our side, in one way or another. Ever think of interviewing a Pia in its own domain when it's trying to be helpful and eat you at the same time? I have.'

'And yet you've survived,' she said in admiration.

Mudriel made a negative gesture. 'Not always. I've been down to my feet once, practically wrecked for weeks three or four times, and killed twice.'

'Killed!' Vardia exclaimed. 'But—'

Mudriel shrugged. 'I've twinned four times naturally,' it replied matter-of-factly, 'and once when I was left with only my brains. There are still four of me. We stay in the same job and take turns on the travel to even out the risk.'

Vardia shook her head in wonder, a gesture more human than Czillian.

While most twins were turned to other fields by the Psych Department, ones with critical jobs or super-specialized knowledge and skills often worked together side by side. Vardia met several people at the Center several times to mutual confusion.

One day Mudriel called her into its office, where it was thumbing through an enormously thick file.

'It's time to assign you and go on to other things,' the psychologist told her. 'You've been here long enough for us to know you better than we know almost any other Czillian. I must say, you've been a wonderful subject, but a puzzling one.'

'In what way?' Vardia asked. As time went by she had become more and more accustomed to her new form and surroundings, and less and less had felt the social alienation of that first night.

'You have normalized,' Mudriel pointed out. 'By this time you are feeling as if you were born one of us, and your past life and that which went with it is a purely intellectual memory experience.'

'That's true,' Vardia acknowledged. 'It almost seems as if all my past happened to someone else, that I just watched it unfold.'

'That's true of all Entries,' replied Mudriel. 'Part of the change process, when the biological changes adjust and remake the psyche. Much of our personality and behavior is based on such biological things. In the animals, it's glands, enzymes, and the like, but with us it's various different secretions. Hormonal imbalances in your former race cause differences; by artificially injecting certain substances into a male of your species who was sexually developed, he could be given female characteristics, and vice versa. Now, time has rebalanced your mind with your new body, and it is for the best.'

'What puzzles you about me, then?' Vardia prodded.

'Your lack of skills,' replied the psychologist. '*Everybody* does something. But you were apparently raised to be highly intelligent yet totally ignorant. You could carry messages and conversations with ease, yet do nothing else. Your ignorance of much of your own sector amazes us.

'You were, in effect, a human recording machine. Did you, for example, realize that in the eighty-three days you've been with us you've had a longer existence than ever in your short life?'

'I – I don't know what you mean,' Vardia stammered.

Mudriel's expression and tone were of mixed pity and disgust. 'They bred you with an extremely high intelligence, but while you grew up, they administered extremely deep programming to make certain you never used it. Over all this was lightly placed the persona known as Vardia Diplo Twelve Sixty-one, a number whose implications are distasteful to me. This made you curious, inquisitive, but only on the surface. You could never act on any information gained, nor did you have any desire to. The persona was mainly to help others feel comfortable. When you reached your destination, an embassy employee would put you under hypnosis, read off the message – and, in the process, wipe your memory. Then the same persona would be reimposed with a reply message, if any. Had you reached Coriolanus, this would have been the case. You now have vivid memories of your Captain Brazil and the other passengers, and of Dalgonia. All of these would have been gone. Any whom you knew who had previously encountered you would be strangers to you. They would just assume, as you would, that it was another Vardia Diplo they knew. Think back – what do you remember of your life before boarding Brazil's ship?'

Vardia thought back with the clarity and detachment she now possessed. She remembered saying good-bye to the Political Office staff, walking out, riding to the spaceport, boarding the shuttle.

Nothing before.

'I never realized –' she began, but Mudriel cut her off.

'I know,' the psychologist said. 'Part of the deep program. It would never even occur to you. And you didn't even know the message you carried, the one that they would go to these lengths to keep private. By programmed exercises you kept yourself in perfect physical condition, and if challenged or cornered you would fight suicidally to free yourself. If trapped, you would have triggered a series of impulses that would have brought about your suicide.' Mudriel saw the mixed apprehension and disbelief in Vardia's eyes.

'Don't worry,' the psychologist assured her. 'We have removed the deep programming. You will remain you. Would you like to hear the message you carried?'

Vardia nodded dully, her mind in a fog.

The psychologist took out a tiny translucent cube and popped it into a well in a small recorder on a table nearby.

Vardia suddenly heard her voice – her old voice, incredibly, although she no longer possessed the vocal cords to speak that way, saying in a tinny way: 'The Commissariat introduces you to Datham Hain, who, with a companion, came on the same ship as the courier. Citizen Hain is on a mission of vital importance to the Commissariat and requires dinner appointments with several Members of the Presidium of Coriolanus, as many as can be accommodated. You are to follow whatever might be his instructions to the letter, without question or hesitation. Keep the courier until at least one such meeting has been arranged, then reprogram it to report on that meeting, said reprogramming to be in Hain's presence and with his approval. All glory to the People's Revolution, all glory to its prophets.'

The psychologist studied Vardia closely as the recording closed. The ex-courier was obviously stunned and shaken, but that shock treatment had to be administered. All over the Entry's body, the Czillian read the mental struggle that had to be taking place within.

It was a terrible thing to destroy someone's complacent world-picture.

Finally, the psychologist asked gently, 'Would you like to go root and meditate? Take as long as you want.'

Vardia shook her head negatively. 'No,' she said at last, in a half-whisper, 'no, I'm all right.'

'I know,' the psychologist soothed. 'It is a terrible thing to find the lie in life. That is one reason we are dedicated here to the uncovering of truth. There are societies and people just as bad on this world, maybe even worse. Hain himself is here somewhere, and probably has already fallen in with a bad bunch. Such societies are the enemies of all civilization, and it is with them that we war. Will you join us in the fight?'

Vardia stood silent a few moments more. Then, suddenly, something seemed to snap within her, and with a fierceness and intensity that surprised even her she said, 'Yes!'

The psychologist gave the Czillian equivalent of a smile and turned back to the file it had before it.

Picking up a stamp, it brought it down on an empty block on the front of the file. In Czillian it read: *Ready for Assignment.*

The last processing was over, and Vardia Diplo 1261 was extinguished.

Vardia the Czillian left the office.

THE AKKAFIAN EMPIRE
(ENTER DATHAM HAIN, ASLEEP)

Datham Hain had entered the Gate with a false sense of bravado, but he was scared to death. He had nightmares of awful proportions, bringing forth every fear in his long life. These surfaced as the Markovian brain picked, analyzed, and classified each subject according to some long-lost, preset reasoning.

He awoke suddenly, with a start, and looked around. It was the strangest look in his experience.

He realized immediately that he was now color-blind, although instead of merely the blacks, whites, and shades of gray, there was a mild sepia-tone effect that made certain things look fuzzy and others stand out. His depth perception was remarkable, he realized. At a glance he could tell exactly how far everything in view was from everything else, and his vision seemed to be enlarged to a 180-degree field. That was amazing, as amazing as the view itself.

He seemed to be on a ledge overlooking an incredible landscape far below. The land was bleak and sandy, broken only by hundreds of cones that looked almost like perfectly formed volcanoes. He strained to get a better look, and found, suddenly, the scene magnifying itself, each time by a factor of two. As it did, a hardly noticed hairline-split midway in his vision also magnified, so that it became a huge bar separating the scene into right and left views. It was as if he were peering through two windows while standing in front of the post that separated them.

There were things down there, and they were moving. Hain stared in fascination at them, a corner of his mind wondering why he was fascinated instead of horrified or repelled. They were great insects, ranging in size from one to almost four meters long, the median height being almost a meter. They had two large, apparently multifaceted eyes fixed, like a fly's, forward in the head. Below the eyes were huge mandibles flanking a mouth resembling a parrot's beak. With surprise he saw one creature stop while a long, snaky black tongue emerged to clean the face.

The body was oblong and seemed to have hair on it – the resolution of Hain's vision was so fine that he could almost count the hairs. And yet – yes, flush against the body in the hair were wings, several pairs of them. The rear of the body exposed a barren, bony tip that undoubtedly was a stinger.

Hain tried to imagine the fate of anyone stung with something that size.

The head seemed to be on a hinge or circular joint, as some of the creatures moved it slightly in one or another direction.

For the first time he saw the feelers, giant things that seemed to have a life of their own, moving every way but forward – including straight up. They ended in hair-covered nodules.

The eight legs were thick and were also covered with hair, longer and down-angled. They were multi-jointed, and he saw a pair of the creatures using their forward legs like hands to move a rock away from a pathway it was blocking. He could see that the tips were not hair but spikelike and were covered with a secretion that looked sticky.

The insects moved with amazing speed sometimes, and, every once in a while, one would take to the air briefly. Apparently they couldn't fly very far with all that weight, but could manage a short hop when they felt like it. As Hain watched, he saw that some of them were operating machines! One looked like a snowplow, and it was clearing dust and debris from the road-ways as it was pushed forward; others seemed to have no obvious purpose.

With the realization that these were not animals but one form of sentient life on the Well World, something else hit, as well. He tried to turn his head to see himself, but could not. He opened his strangely rigid mouth and stuck out his tongue. It was more than three meters long, as controllable as an arm, and covered with an incredibly sticky substance.

I'm one of them, he told himself, more in wonder than in fear.

He raised his head up and brought his two forward legs into view. He had been right, he saw. Three joints, all bendable in any direction. The tips *were* spikes, like hard rubber, and he experimented by reaching out and picking up a small rock. As his legs touched the rock, a sticky secretion gave him a grip. When he let go, the secretion turned to a solid film and fell away like used skin.

He noticed immediately that, when the dropped rock hit, he did not hear it. Rather, he *felt* it, as a sharp, single pulsation. The antennae, he told himself. They sense air movement, but not as sound.

Suddenly he was aware that he was getting thousands of tiny pulses through them, and, incredibly, he almost sensed the source and distance of each.

This has possibilities, thought Datham Hain.

Using his tongue he surveyed his own body, being careful not to come near the stinger at the rear which he now realized he could feel when he wanted to. No use in possibly poisoning myself this early in the game, he thought cautiously.

He was about three meters long and almost a meter high, he discovered. About medium-sized for those creatures down there.

He flexed his wings – six pairs, he found – long but looking extremely thin and frail to support his weight. He decided he wouldn't try them out until he knew more about his anatomy. Even birds have to be taught to fly, he thought, and sentient creatures probably had less instinct – if any at all – than the lower species.

Now how do I get down off this ledge? he wondered. Finally, he decided to experiment, moving his body close to the edge. As his front legs touched the side they secreted that substance and stuck, he saw with satisfaction.

Emboldened, he pushed off and started walking down the side.

Doing so was incredibly easy, he found, confidence growing with each step. He realized he could probably walk on a ceiling, if the sticky stuff would support his weight. The main problem would be getting used to the fact that there was so much of him in back of his head. The legs worked in perfect coordination, as if he had been born with them; but the body was hard and rigid, and took some practice to maneuver without spilling end over end.

It took several minutes to descend the low cliff, although he realized that, with practice, he could probably come back and do it in seconds. Once down, he faced a problem that his reason wouldn't solve for him. He wanted to get introduced quickly, to get settled in here, and to check out the sociopolitical system, the geography, and the like. Also, he was feeling hungry, and he hadn't the slightest idea what these creatures ate.

But how did they communicate? Not only language, but even the *means* weren't all that apparent.

Well, that Ortega had said that the brain would provide for such things, he told himself; but he was exceedingly nervous as he approached one of the creatures coming down the road.

The other saw him and stopped.

'What are you doing just standing there, Markling?' the newcomer challenged sternly. 'Don't you have any work to do?'

Hain was stunned. The language was a series of incredibly rapid pulsations transmitted in some way from the creature's antennae to his own, yet he had understood everything! All but the last word, anyway. He decided to try to talk back.

'Please. I am newly born to this world, and I need help and guidance,' he began, then felt his own antennae quiver incredibly quickly as he talked. It worked!

'What the hell?' responded the gruff stranger, although not really in those terms. Hain's brain automatically seemed to translate into familiar symbols. 'You sick or something?'

'No, no,' Hain protested. 'I have just come from Zone, where I have just awakened as one of you.'

The other thought about that for a minute. 'I'll be damned! An Entry! Haven't had one in over ten years!' Suddenly the old skepticism returned. 'You're not just saying that to shirk, are you?'

'I assure you that I am what I say, and that up until a very short time ago I was of a totally different race and form.'

'You adjust pretty well,' the other noted. 'Most of 'em have the creeping fits for days. Well, I'll take you over to the nearest government house and it'll be their problem. I have work to do. Follow me.' With that, it started on down the road, and Hain followed.

His guide was almost a third larger than he was, Hain saw. Most of the creatures he passed seemed to be about the same size or smaller than he. A few big ones were around, and they seemed to be the bosses.

They walked past several of the huge cones, then up the side of one that looked no different from the rest and into the hole on top. Hain noted that the opening was so even because it was rimmed with metal, like an open hatch. He almost lost his nerve on entering. The aboveground part of the cone, about ten meters worth, was hollow to the outside structure. They were not only walking down, but at an angle.

When they passed ground level, they walked onto a floor which was also some kind of metal. Tunnels lined with tile, with neon or some similar lighting stretching down in long tubes, led away like spokes on a wheel. They were wide enough to hold two of the creatures abreast, and they passed several as his guide led him down a near one.

Doorless openings into large chambers filled with all sorts of strange stuff, often with dozens of the creatures working, were passed before they reached one with a hexagon in lights over the doorway. Inside the hex was a wide gray ring, then a smaller black one, then a white dot. It reminded Hain with some amusement of the view of his guide's posterior, with its menacing stinger.

Several small and medium-sized creatures were working, apparently at some sort of paperwork, Hain noted with curiosity. Huge printing machines, like typewriters, were all over, with television screens displaying what the creatures, using their forward legs, were typing on a strange keyboard. The keyboard was a series of apparently identical cubes, forty or fifty of them, which lit momentarily as they were touched. A crazy dot pattern emerged on the screens in no apparent logical order or pattern. When the screen was filled, a hind leg would kick a large stud and the screen would go blank – and they would be back to typing again.

So I can't read the language, Hain noted to himself. Well, can't have everything.

The guide waited patiently until somebody noticed him and looked up from its keyboard.

'Yes?' asked the worker and the communicated tone was one of irritated nastiness.

'Found this Markling on the road, claims to be an Entry,' said the big guide in that same annoyed tone he had used with Hain.

There was that word again. What in seven hells was a Markling, anyway?

'Just a moment,' the clerk or whatever it was said, 'I'll see if His Highness will see you.'

The office worker went into a side door and stayed several minutes. Hain's hunger was increasing, and so was his apprehension. A hereditary empire, he thought. Well, it could be worse.

Finally the clerk reappeared. 'His Highness will see the Entry,' she said – for some reason Hain automatically thought of his guide as masculine and the receptionist and most of the other workers as feminine. The guide moved forward.

'Just the Entry,' said the clerk sharply. 'You will return to your duties.'

'As you say,' the other replied, and turned and left.

Hain gathered up his courage and entered the doorway.

Inside was the biggest creature he had ever seen. But there was something else unusual about him.

The hairs on his body were white.

Hain suddenly realized just how hereditary this monarchy was.

There were some boxes and bags around of more or less conventional design, and one of those typewriters with a much larger screen. Nothing else. The big one reared back on the last four of his eight legs. Hain was impressed and cowed; he hadn't seen anyone else doing that.

'What's your name, Entry?' the big white one demanded imperiously. The tone, Hain realized by now, was conveyed by the intensity of the signal.

'Datham Hain, Your Highness,' he replied in the most respectful way he could.

The official ran his tongue over his beak in thought. Finally, he went over to the typewriter and started punching up something – something short, Hain saw, because the screen was still almost empty when the large creature punched the send bar or whatever it was. A moment's wait. Then the screen started to fill with those funny dots.

The official read the message carefully, studying it for several minutes. Finally it turned back to him as he stood there impatiently, needing almost four meters to negotiate the move.

'Ordinarily, Hain, we'd just train and condition you to a position and you'd fit in or die.' Hain's heart – if he still had one – sank. 'But,' the royal official continued, 'in this case we have special use for you. Too bad you turned up a Markling, but that's to be expected. You'll be quartered near here – I'll have one of my assistants show you where. There's a commissary three doors down. Most of you Entries come through starving, so go in there and eat your fill. Don't worry about what it is – we can eat just about anything. Wait in your quarters until I get instructions from Imperial Headquarters.'

Hain still stood there, digesting all this. Finally, he said, 'Your Highness, might I be permitted one question?'

'Yes, yes,' the other said impatiently. 'What is it?'

'What's a Markling?'

'Hain,' replied the official patiently, 'life is hard and cheap in the Akkafian Empire. Infant mortality is extremely high, not only from normal factors imposed by nature but for other reasons you'll find out sooner or later for yourself. As a result, to ensure racial continuation, about fifty females are born for every male.

'A Markling is a female Akkafian, Hain. You've had a sex change.'

Datham Hain was led by one of the office staff to the commissary, which proved to be a large room filled with strange animals, plants, and worms, some still alive. Feeding as an Akkafian was not pleasant, at least to Hain's unnormalized psyche, but it was necessary. The creatures frankly didn't taste all that bad – in fact, they didn't taste very much at all, but they filled the void in what seemed to be multiple stomachs. If he didn't think about what he was eating, the changeling discovered, it went down all right.

That tongue, like a sticky whip, was infinitely controllable. Live prey were simply picked up, thrown to the rear sting area to be paralyzed, then held and fed by the mandibles a little at a time through the beak.

Discovering that he was now a she wasn't much of a shock to Hain; the odds were that sexuality was so different among these people that it probably didn't make much difference anyway. What *was* disquieting was that the males seemed to be in firm charge. The Nirlings, as the males were called, were larger and controlled the government and supervisory positions and the technology that kept them in power. The females, mostly neutered, did the work, apparently compulsively. Hain had seen no evidence of force or coercion; the workers carried out their tasks dedicatedly, unquestioningly, and uncomplainingly. Hain understood the system to a degree. It was not unlike that of the Comworlds, where people were bred to work.

The only trouble, he – no, she – thought, is that I am on the low end of the scale. To be an alien creature, to be totally different – these things she could accept. To be female she could accept. To be a slave to such a system was intolerable.

After feeding they took her to a rest area. This race worked at whatever it did around the clock, and individuals were spelled by others so they would get rest at scheduled intervals.

The staging area rose for several storeys – a large, underground wall of cubicles each of which was just large enough to hold a single creature. About half were filled as they entered, and Hain was assigned a number and told to go into it and wait for instructions.

Hain climbed up the side easily and entered the assigned cubicle. It was warm, and extremely humid, which felt oddly more comfortable than the drier air of the offices. There was a carpet of some sort of animal hair, and a small control panel with two buttons, one of which was depressed. Curious, she pressed the other one. She had apparently found a radio which was broadcasting a series of sound patterns whose pulses were oddly pleasing and calming. A wave of relief swept over her insect body and she found herself drifting off into a dreamless sleep.

The office clerk noted with some satisfaction that Hain was asleep, then went over to the superintendent's control console at the base of the rest area. The superintendent was emptying the catch trays of waste and other products, and she showed surprise when she recognized a clerk of the baron's household.

'By order of His Highness,' the clerk commanded, 'the Markling in One Ninety-eight is to be kept asleep until called for. Make certain the pacifier remains on at shift change.'

The superintendent acknowledged the order and went into her office. A panel of plastic buttons laid out and numbered corresponding to the cubicles was before her, with many of the buttons lit, including Hain's. The superintendent held down number 198 with one foreleg while punching a small red control off to one side with the other.

Hain was locked into blissful sleep until the button was depressed again.

The clerk expressed satisfaction, and returned to the baron's office to report. The great white Nirling nodded approval and dismissed her back to her desk.

After a while, he went over to his communications console and punched the number for the Imperial Palace. He didn't like to call the palace, since the king and the ambitious nobles surrounding him were unstable and untrustworthy. Barons were low on the pecking order, but they had a much longer survival rate because they *were* away from the palace. Make your quota and the living was pretty good.

Communication was by audio only, so things had to be spelled out. Although the Akkafians had no ears, they 'heard' in much the same way as creatures who did. Sound, after all, is a disruption of the surrounding atmospheric pressure by varying that pressure. Although he had never heard a sound as such, the baron's hearing was better than most creatures on the Well World.

After a long period, somebody at the palace woke up and answered. The Imperial Household was getting sloppy and degenerate, the baron reflected. Perhaps one day soon it would be time for a baronial revolt.

Of course, the titles and such were not the same as human equivalents, but if Hain could have overheard the conversation, it would have been translated much like this:

'This is Baron Kluxm of Subhex Nineteen. I have an emergency topic for immediate transmittal to His Majesty's Privy Council.'

'The Privy Council is not assembled,' came a bored reply. 'Can't this wait, Baron?'

Kluxm cursed silently at the insolence and stupidity of even the household help. The operator was probably one of the king's Marklings.

'I said *emergency*, operator!' he emphasized, trying to keep his temper from showing. 'I take full responsibility.'

The operator seemed unsure of herself, and finally decided in good bureaucratic fashion to pass the buck.

'I will transfer you to General Ytil of the Imperial Staff,' she said. 'He will decide.'

Before Kluxm could even reply he heard the relay switch, and a new, male voice answered. 'Ytil,' it said curtly.

The baron had even less use for imperial military men; they generally went to war with other hexes when shortages developed every few years, and invariably lost them. However, he decided that Ytil would do for the same purpose as the operator had; after he explained the situation, it was somebody else's problem.

'I had an Entry today, one of the ones we'd been told to watch for.'

'An Entry!' Ytil's voice was suddenly very excited. The waves were so bad that the general's voice started to give Kluxm a headache. 'Which one?'

'The one called Datham Hain. As a common Markling breeder,' he added.

Ytil's voice still quivered with excitement, although the last plainly disappointed him. 'A Markling breeder! Pity! But to think we got one! Hmmmm. Actually, this might work out to our advantage. I've got to go over my files and recordings of Hain at Zone, but, if I remember, he's the greedy and ambitious type.'

'Yes, that's what my file said,' Kluxm acknowledged. 'But she was abnormally respectful and quiet while here. Seems to have adjusted to our form extremely well.'

'Yes, yes, that's to be expected,' Ytil replied. 'After all, no use antagonizing everyone. Hain's smart enough to see the social structure and her limits in it right off. Where is she now?'

'In a rest area near my office,' Kluxm replied. 'She's on lull music and has a full stomach, so she's out for two or three days until hunger sets in again.'

'Excellent, excellent,' approved Ytil. 'I'll call the Privy Council together and we'll send someone for her when we're ready. You are to be commended, Baron! A fine job!'

Sure, Kluxm thought glumly to himself. For which you'll take all the credit.

But credit was not what was on Ytil's mind as the general scurried down the palace corridor after terminating the conversation. He stopped in a security room and picked up a tiny, black, jewel-like object on a large chain. Carefully he placed it over his right antenna and then went down to the lowest level of the palace.

The guards weren't very curious about him; it was normal to have high-ranking military and diplomatic people using the Zone Gate.

The Akkafian general walked quickly into the darkness at the end of the basement corridor.

And emerged in Zone.

ZONE - THE AKKAFIAN EMBASSY

The Markling receptionist looked startled as General Ytil emerged through the Zone Gate.

Each hex had a gate somewhere, which would transport anyone to Zone instantaneously, and from Zone to his home hex. There were 780 such gates to the offices of each of the Southern Hemisphere races, as well as the one master Gate for Classification through which all entries passed and the huge input-only Gate in the center. It made things very easy for interspecies contact.

General Ytil dismissed the startled exclamation and apologies of the receptionist and made his way immediately to the Imperial Ambassador's office.

The Baron Azkfru had barely been tipped off by the clerk when the general rushed in the door. The ambassador could see the obvious excitement and agitation in Ytil's every movement.

'My Lord Baron!' the general exclaimed. 'It has happened! We have one of the new Entries as it was foretold!'

'Calm down, Ytil,' Azkfru growled. 'You're losing your medals for dignity and self-control. Now, tell me rationally what this is about.'

'The one called Hain,' Ytil responded, still excited. 'It turned up earlier today over in Kluxm's barony as a Markling breeder.'

'Hmmmm ...' Azkfru mused. 'Too bad she's a breeder, but it can't be helped. Where is this Entry now?'

'In lull sleep, safe for two or three more days,' the general told him. 'Kluxm thinks I've notified the Imperial Household and the Privy Council. He's expecting someone to pick her up.'

'Very good,' Azkfru replied approvingly. 'It looks like things are breaking our way. I never put much stock in fortune-tellers and such crap, but if this has happened then Providence has placed a great opportunity in our hands. Who else knows of this besides Kluxm and yourself?'

'Why, no one, Highness,' Ytil replied. 'I have been most careful.'

Baron Azkfru's mind moved quickly, sorting out the facts and deciding on a course of action with a speed that had guaranteed his rise to the top.

'All right, return to your post for now, and nothing of this to anyone! I'll make all the necessary arrangements.'

'You're making the deal with the Northerners?' Ytil asked.

Azkfru gave the Akkafian equivalent of a sigh. 'Ytil, how many times do you need to be reminded that *I* am the baron? You *take* orders, and leave the questions and answers to your betters.'

'But I only –' Ytil began plaintively, but Azkfru cut him off.

'Go, now,' the ambassador said impatiently, and Ytil turned to leave.

Azkfru reached into a drawer and pulled out a pulse rifle. *This* one worked in Zone, at least in his offices.

'Ytil!' he called after the other, who was halfway out the door.

Ytil stopped but couldn't turn. 'My Lord?' he called back curiously.

'Good-bye, fool,' Azkfru replied, and shot the general repeatedly until the white-haired body was a charred ruin.

Azkfru buzzed for his guard, and thought, *Too bad I couldn't trust the idiot, but his incompetence would give the show away.*

The guard appeared, and looked down at the general's remains nervously but without curiosity.

'The general tried to kill me,' he explained without any effort to be convincing. 'I had to defend myself. It appears that he and the Baron Kluxm are at the heart of a baronial revolt. After you dispose of this carrion, go to Kluxm's, and eliminate his whole staff and, of course, the baron. Then go to the rest area and bring a Markling named Hain to my estate. Do it quietly. I'll report the revolt.'

They nodded, and it took them only a few minutes to eat the body.

After they had left, he buzzed for a clerk.

'You will go to the Classification Gate and enter. It will take you to the North Zone. When you get there don't leave the Gate room, but simply tell the first inquirer that you want to talk to Ambassador Thirteen Forty, and wait for that person. When it comes, tell it who you are, who sent you, and that we are ready to agree. Got that?'

The clerk waved her antennae affirmatively and repeated the message.

Dismissing her, he attended to the last detail. He flipped the intercom to the receptionist's desk.

'The General Ytil wasn't here,' he told her. 'Understand? You never even heard of him.'

The clerk understood all too well, and rubbed out Ytil's appearance in her logbook.

It was a big gamble he was taking, he knew, and it would probably cost him his life. But the stakes! The stakes were too great to ignore!

THE BARONY OF AZKFRU, AKKAFIAN EMPIRE

Datham Hain's massive body, now in a drugged sleep, rested in the center of the lowest floor of the Baron Azkfru's nest. The room was filled with computer banks flashing light-signals and making clicking and whirring sounds. Four large cables were attached to Hain's head at key points, and two smaller ones were fixed to the base of her two antennae. Two neutered Markling technicians with the symbol of the baron painted between their two huge eyes checked readings on various dials and gauges, and checked and rechecked all the connections.

Baron Azkfru's antennae showed complete satisfaction. He had often wondered what the Imperial Household would say if they knew he had one of these devices.

There would be civil war at the very least, he thought.

The conditioner had been developed by a particularly brilliant Akkafian scientist in the imperial household almost eighty years before, when the ambassador himself was just a youngling. It ended the periodic baronial revolts, and assured the stability of the new – now old – order by making revolution next to impossible. Oh, you couldn't condition everyone with certainty, so it was done subtly. Probably every baron dreamed of overthrowing the empire – it let the pressure and frustration out.

But none of them could do it. Because, although they could dream about it, they couldn't disobey a direct imperial command.

But Azkfru could.

His father had duplicated the device here in the earliest days of its development. Here, slowly, methodically, key ones were deconditioned and reconditioned. Even so, he reflected, you couldn't change the basic personality of the conditioned. That was why Ytil had to go – too dumb to keep quiet.

As for Kluxm – well, it was known for some particularly strong-willed Nirlings to break free, although never with any prayer of support from the rest of the conditioned leadership.

'We are ready when you are, Highness,' called one of the Markling technicians. Azkfru signaled satisfaction and went down to the floor.

Quickly and efficiently two additional cables similar to the ones on Hain were placed on his own antennae. When he now said something, it would be placed in the machine, amplified, processed, and fed directly into the brain of Datham Hain in such a way that it would be taken as acceptable input and engraved in the other's mind.

The baron signaled a go-ahead, and the technicians touched the last controls.

'Datham Hain!' the ambassador's brain called out.

Hain, although unconscious, answered, 'Yes?'

'Your past to this point you retain, but it is an academic past, there to call upon if needed but irrelevant to your present and future,' the baron told her. 'What is important to you, what is the *only* thing of importance to you, is that you are a breeder Markling of the Barony of Azkfru. Your destiny is whatever the Baron of Azkfru wishes, and that is acceptable and normal to you. My will is your will, your *only* will. You exist to serve me alone. You would never betray me, nor allow harm to come to me. You are my own, my property, and that is all that is good and happy in your mind or life. When you serve me you are happy, and when you do not you are unhappy. That is the measure of your joy in life. I am your leader, your lord, and your only god. Your worship is normal. Do you understand this?'

'I understand, my lord,' replied Hain mechanically.

The baron signaled to the technicians to break contact, which they quickly did, then unfastened the two cables from his antennae.

'How did it take?' Azkfru asked one of the technicians.

'The subject is receptive,' replied one of the technicians, part of whose *own* conditioning was never to consider the idea that she might have been conditioned. 'However, her psychological profile is one of extreme selfishness. That might eventually cancel the conditioning, producing mental breakdown.'

'What do you advise, then?'

'Go along with the idea,' the technician suggested. 'Go back into her mind and tell her that her only avenue to wealth and power is through you and no one else. That's something her mind can completely accept, and it will be acted upon in concert with the standard conditioning you've already administered. Then, after she's awake and you are interviewing her, hold out the highest possible position a breeder Markling could attain.'

'I *see*,' the baron replied, and he did see. That made everything perfect. 'Let us complete the conditioning,' he commanded.

*

Datham Hain awoke with a very strange set of feelings and yet not aware that over ten days had passed since she was first introduced to the land of the Akkafian.

A Markling with the insignia of the Baron Azkfru entered and saw that she was awake. 'You must be starved,' the newcomer said pleasantly. 'Follow me and we will take care of that.'

Starvation was close to what Datham Hain actually felt at that point, and she needed no further urging to follow the servant. The feeding room was filled with pens of large, white-ribbed worms that were indigenous to the soil of the land. Hain had no qualms this time about eating such prey, and found them most satisfying.

'The baron raises his own *fikhfs*,' the guide explained as she gorged herself. 'Only the best for this household, till midnight at the Well of Souls.'

Hain suddenly stopped eating.

'What was that you just said?' she asked.

'Oh, it's just a saying,' the other replied.

Hain forgot it for the moment and continued eating. When it was clear that her hunger had been satisfied, the guide said, 'Now, follow me into reception, and you'll meet the baron.'

Hain obediently followed down several long and particularly plush corridors to a wide anteroom covered in that downy fur with a low-volume 'music' background, pleasant but not lulling as the other had been.

'Just relax for now,' the baron's servant told her. 'His Highness will call you in when he is ready.'

Relaxing was just the thing Hain felt least like doing; extremely awake and alert, she wished idly for something active to do, something to look at. A rack in one corner held a series of scrolls in that funny writing, but it was just random dots.

Not even any pictures, she thought glumly.

She paced nervously, awaiting the baron's pleasure.

The baron was already entertaining a guest – or guests, he wasn't sure which. Although he had communicated with a representative of whatever government this creature or creatures had, he had never met any of them and knew nothing about them. He still didn't, he realized sourly, and he didn't like the situation, either. The Northern Hemisphere was a place so alien to him that he felt more kinship with the most different of the Southern races compared to the closest of the North.

The object of his speculation and apprehension was floating about three meters in front of him. Yes, floating, he decided – no visible means of support or locomotion. It looked like a slightly upcurved strip of crystal from which a set of dozens of small crystal chimes hung down, the whole thing about a meter long and ending just short of the floor. On top of the crystal strip floated a creature that seemed to consist of hundreds of rapidly flashing lights. Their pattern and their regularity suggested that they existed in a transparent ball fitting in the crystal holder – but, try as he would, he couldn't make out the ball he somehow felt was there.

The Diviner and The Rel might be looking at him in an equally odd and uneasy way, he realized, but he would never know. He would not like to be, would not ever be, in its world. But it was in his, and that gave him a small measure of comfort.

'Will this Hain stay loyal to you?' The Rel asked, apparently using its chimes to form the words, which gave it a total lack of tone or coloration.

'My technicians assure me so,' replied Azkfru confidently. 'Although I fail to see why she is necessary to us in any event. I feel uneasy trusting everything to someone so new and unknown.'

'Nevertheless,' replied The Rel, 'it is necessary. Remember that The Diviner predicted that you would receive one of the outworlders, and that the solution to our problems was not possible without an outworlder present.'

'I know, I know,' Azkfru acknowledged, 'and I am grateful that it was me who was contacted by your people. We have as much stake in this as you, you know.' He fidgeted nervously. 'But why are you sure that this one is the outworlder needed?'

'We're not,' The Rel admitted. 'The Diviner only knows that one of the four who came in that party is needed to open the Well. One was destined for Czill, one for Adrigal, one for Dillia, and one for here. Of the four, yours was known to be psychologically the most receptive to our offer.'

'I see,' Azkfru said, uncertainty mixed with resignation in his tone. 'So twenty-five percent was better than zero percent. Well, why not just grab the others so we're sure?'

'You know the answer to that one,' The Rel responded patiently. 'If we missed just one of these Entries, it would hide and we couldn't monitor it. This way, we will know where they are and what they are doing.'

'Urn, yes, and there's the second prediction, too.'

'Quite so,' The Rel affirmed. 'When the Well is opened all shall pass through. Thus, if we keep one of them with us, we will stand the best chance of going through with them.'

'I still wish I were going with you,' the baron said. 'I feel uneasy that the only representative of my people will be a conditioned alien of known untrustworthiness.'

'One of you is going to be conspicuous enough,' The Rel pointed out. 'Two of you is an advertisement for hundreds of other uneasy governments. Right now, neither of us knows if our agreement is duplicated by others with any or all of the other three.'

That idea made Azkfru more uncomfortable than ever.

'Well, damn it, you – or half of you, or whatever – is The Diviner. Don't you *know?*'

'Of course not,' replied The Rel. 'The present is as closed to The Diviner as it is to you. Only random snatches of information are received, and that in rather uncontrolled fashion. Getting this much is more than we usually get on anything. Hopefully more pieces will fit together as we progress.'

Rather than disturbing him further, this news reassured him instead. So the damn thing wasn't omnipotent, anyway. Still, he wished he knew more about the creature that stood before him. What *were* its powers? What tricks did it have up its sleeve?

The fear that most consumed him was of a double cross.

The Diviner – or The Rel – seemed to sense this, and it said, 'Our hexes are as alien as can be. We have no commonality of interest or activity. You are an incomprehensible people to us, and your actions are equally so. Never would we be here, in peril of our sanity, were it not for the urgent single commonality our races share: survival. We are satiated in the summing process, and active in the coefficient of structure. Our sole object is to keep everything just the way it is.'

The baron didn't understand any of it, but he *did* understand that mutual survival was a common bond, and the assurance that they wanted to preserve the status quo. The trouble was, he could say exactly the same thing and not mean a word of it.

And now all of his future rested on Datham Hain.

The baron gave the Akkafian equivalent of a sigh of resignation. He had no choice in the matter. That conditioning *must* hold!

'How soon do you wish to begin?' he asked the Northerner.

'A lot depends on your end,' The Rel pointed out. 'Without Skander the whole scheme falls apart, the sum clouds and changes to an infinite number.'

'And you can point him out, only you,' the baron replied. 'I'm ready when you are.'

'No more than a week, then,' The Rel urged. 'We have reason to suspect that Skander will move out of reach shortly after that.'

'Very well,' the baron sighed, 'I'll condition two of my best Markling warriors. You don't need Hain for this part, do you?'

'No,' responded The Rel. 'That will do nicely. We'll have to work at night and hide out during the day, so it will take a good day to set us up once there. Another two days to get there, inconspicuously, if possible. Can you be ready within a day period from this moment?'

'I think so,' the baron replied confidently. 'Anything else?'

'Yes. While you prepare the two assistants I should like to talk to one who understands structures and electrical systems. Is that possible?'

'Well, yes,' the baron affirmed with some surprise. 'But why?'

'It will be necessary to perform some minor sabotage to ease our task,' The Rel explained enigmatically. 'Although we have studied it, we want to confirm our necessary actions to be doubly certain, hopefully with one who comprehends such things.'

'Done,' Azkfru told the creatures. 'Now I must attend to other matters. Go out the side there and an assistant will take you to a room that will be private. I will send the technicians to you.'

'We go to prepare,' intoned The Rel, and floated out the designated exit.

Azkfru waited several minutes until he was certain the Northerner was well away, then went over to the doorway to his main waiting room and pressed the opening stud with his right foreleg.

'Enter, Mar Datham,' he said imperiously, and quickly got back to the dais that served as his work area. He struck his most awesome pose.

Datham Hain entered on the words, a shiver going through her at their majesty. Almost hypnotically, she entered the office.

She stopped as she saw him, and bent down automatically in a gesture of extreme subservience. Orgiastic spasms shook her, and she cowed in awe and fear.

He is God, she thought with absolute conviction. He is the epitome of greatness.

'My Lord and Master, I am your slave, Datham Hain. Command me!' she intoned and meant every word of it.

The sincerity carried over to Azkfru, who received it with satisfaction. The conditioning had stuck.

'Do you give yourself to me, Mar Datham, body and soul, to do with as I would, forever?' he intoned.

'I do, Master, my Lord God, I do! Command me to die and I shall do so gladly.'

Great now. Forever, if she was around all the time. But she would have only a few interviews until he had to trust her with all he had. Well, here goes the kicker, Azkfru thought.

'You are the lowest of the low, Mar Datham, lower than the *fikhfs* that breed to be eaten, lower than the defecations of the least of those *fikhfs*,' he intoned.

And it was so, she realized. She felt as low and as small as she could ever get. She felt so tiny and unimportant that she found it hard to think at all. Her mind was a complete blank, yet basking on pure emotion in the presence of Him who was All Glory.

'You will remain lowly scum,' the Master pronounced, 'until I have other use for you. But as you are the lowest of the low, so can you be raised to the heights by my command.' Now came the clincher. 'A great task will be placed in your hands, and your love and devotion to me above all else will determine all that is in your future, whether it be the mindless cleaners of the defecation pits or,' he paused for added emphasis, 'perhaps even the chief concubine of a king.'

Hain groveled all the more at this thought suddenly placed in her witless head.

'And your name shall now be *Kokur*, nor will you answer to any other but it, and so you will stay and so you will be until you have successfully carried out my tasks. Then only will you be restored to a name, and then that name will be great. Go, now. My servant shall show you your duties until I shall call you for the task.'

She turned and left the office quickly, on quivering legs.

When the door closed behind her, the baron relaxed.

Well, he thought, it is done. For the next few days, if The Diviner and The Rel were successful, Datham Hain would truly be as low as one could get. Although consciously obedient and happy, that nasty subconscious would be helplessly humiliated by the job and the status, and that was perfect. After a few days, Hain would be willing to do anything to get out of there, and she would be offered a permanent return to that miserable state as opposed to elevation as high as she could possibly reach.

Hain would serve him, he felt confidently.

Kokur wasn't a name, it was a job description.

Until The Diviner and The Rel returned, Datham Hain would work in the defecation pits, piling up the huge amounts of crap his barony produced – including her own – and then treating it with a series of chemicals and agents that would change its composition into a horrible but physically harmless mess. Hain would not only work there, she would sleep in it, walk in it, and, as her sole diet, eat it. And the only name she could respond to or think of herself as was *Kokur*, which meant dung-eater.

When off with The Diviner and The Rel, it would be a constant and humiliating reminder of her lowly status and her lifelong fate for failure, a reminder that would even reach others through the translating devices used around the Well World.

Datham Hain would be a most obedient slave.

Actually kind of attractive, he thought. Too bad she's a breeder.

DILLIA – MORNING
(ENTER WU JULEE, ASLEEP)

Wu Julee awoke from a dreamless sleep and looked around. She felt strange and slightly dizzy.

The overriding fact that hit her was that the pain was gone.

She closed her eyes and shook her head briskly. The dizziness worsened for a moment, then things seemed to steady.

She looked around.

She was in a beautiful forest, the likes of which she had never seen before. Trees grew straight as poles fifty or more meters in the air, almost disappearing into a slight morning mist. The undergrowth was equally lush and a vivid green. Beautiful flowers grew wildly all around her. There was a trail nearby, a nicely maintained one made of deep sawdust lined with small, irregular stones. There was a slight but steady roaring sound in the distance, but it didn't seem threatening, only curious.

The path seemed to lead toward the roar in one direction, and she decided to follow it. Walking felt strange to her, but she thought little of it. She felt strange all over. She walked slowly down the trail about a kilometer, and it led her to the source of the increasing roar.

She came upon a waterfall, dropping majestically in three stages down the side of a mountain whose gray rocks were well worn by uncounted years of erosion. The falls fed a stream, or river, which flowed swiftly but rather shallowly over a rocky bottom seen clearly through the greenish tinge to the water's surface. Here and there, she saw logs and remnants of logs that had fallen due to weathering or age. Many were covered with mossy yellow-green growths and several were nurse trees, their dead and decaying limbs providing a haven from which newer trees of a different type were growing. Small insects hummed and buzzed all around, and she watched them curiously.

A sudden crackle of underbrush made her turn with a start. She saw a small, brown-furred mammal with a rodent's face and a broad flat tail jump into the stream carrying a twig in its mouth. Her eyes followed it until it made the opposite shore and ran into the underbrush formed by swampy weeds and long grains of grassy plants diagonally opposite her.

Still acting without conscious thought, like a newborn child seeing the world for the first time, she went up to the stream just far enough down that she wasn't caught in the spray from the great falls.

She looked down at her reflection. She saw the face of a young woman barely in her teens, a face that looked back at her. Not beautiful, but pleasant, with long brown hair falling down over small but well-formed breasts.

She reached up with one hand and brushed back the hair on one side. Her skin was a light brown, her palms a slightly lighter color but seemingly made of a tougher skin. I've got pointy ears, she thought, seeing them revealed by the brushed-back hair. And they *were* pointed, the insides a soft pink. Although not really large, she realized that they would probably protrude slightly if she stood perfectly erect. On some sort of impulse, she tried to wiggle her ears – and they moved noticeably!

Then she looked down at her body. At the waist the very light down that began just below her breast thickened into hair of the same color as her skin. Her eyes moved down to two stocky legs that ended in large, flat hooves.

That's strange, she thought. Hooves and pointed ears that wiggle.

For no reason in particular she turned her body at the waist almost half-way around, and looked in back of her. A long, sturdy-looking equine body supported by two hind legs was clearly visible – and a tail! A big, brushy tail she found she could wiggle.

What am I? she thought in sudden fear. Where is this?

She tried to remember, but could not. It's as if I was just born, she thought. I can't remember anything. Not my name, not anything.

The reflection and the body looked totally strange to her.

I remember the words, she thought. I know that this is a stream and that is a waterfall and that that person in the water is a reflection of me, and I'm a young girl.

She hadn't even realized she was a girl until then. There was a term for this, she thought, and she tried to remember it. Amnesia, that was it. People who couldn't remember their past. Somehow she felt that she had never been to this place before, and that something was different about her, but she couldn't think of what. She just stood there by the edge of the stream for several minutes in stunned silence, not knowing what else to do. Several insects buzzed around her rear, and with an automatic motion she brushed them away with her tail.

Suddenly her ears picked up the sound of laughing – a girl and a boy, she thought. They were coming down the trail! Quickly, almost in panic, she looked around for a place to hide, but found none before the pair came trotting down the path. They look like the top half of people stuck onto the bodies of working ponies, her mind thought. Her face turned quizzically at the thought. What were people anyway, if not these? And what were ponies?

The two beings were not really large, but the boy was almost a head taller and proportionately larger than the girl. The male was a golden color, with silver-white hair down to his shoulders and a full beard, neatly trimmed, of the same color. The girl, curiously, was a mottled gray mixed with large black spots, and this coloration extended to her upper torso. Her hair was a mixed gray and black, her gray breasts much fuller than the amnesiac onlooker's.

No navels, she thought inanely. We don't have navels.

The pair saw her and stopped almost in midlaugh. They surveyed her curiously, but without any trace of hostility or alarm. 'Hello!' called the boy – he looked no more than fourteen or fifteen, the girl about the same. The voice was a pleasant tenor, with a slight, indefinable accent. 'I don't think we've seen you here before.'

She hesitated a moment, then replied hesitantly, 'I – I don't think I've ever been here before. I – I just don't know.' Tears welled in her eyes.

The two centaurs saw that she was in some distress and rushed up to her.

'What's the matter?' the girl asked in a high-pitched adolescent voice.

She started to cry. 'I don't know, I can't remember anything,' she sobbed.

'There, there,' the boy crooned, and began to stroke her back. 'Get it all out, then tell us what's going on.'

The stroking had a calming effect, and she straightened up and wiped her eyes with her hand.

'I don't know,' she managed, coughing a little. 'I – I just woke up down the trail and I can't remember anything – who I am, where I am, even what I am.'

The boy, who was even larger in comparison to her than he was to his companion, examined her face and head, and felt the skull.

'Does it hurt anywhere when I do this?' he asked.

'No,' she told him. 'Tickles a little all over, that's all.'

He lifted up her face and stared hard into her eyes.

'No glaze,' he commented, mostly to himself. 'No sign of injury. Fascinating.'

'Aw, come on, Jol, what'd you expect to find?' his companion asked.

'Some sign of injury or shock,' he responded, almost in a clinical tone. 'Here, girl, stick out your tongue. No, I mean it. Stick it out.'

She did, feeling somewhat foolish, and he examined it. It was a big tongue, flat and broad, and a gray-pink in color.

'All right, you can stick it back in now,' he told her. 'No coating, either. If you'd have had some kind of shock or disease, it'd show.'

'Maybe she's been witched, Jol,' the spotted gray centaur suggested, and drew back a little.

'Maybe,' he conceded, 'but, if so, it's nothin' to concern us.'

'What d'you think we oughta do?' his girlfriend asked.

Jol turned and for the first time Julee saw he had some kind of saddlebag strapped around his waist.

'First we take our shower,' he answered, removing an irregular bar of what must have been soap, some cloths, and towels from the bag, then unstrapping it and letting it fall to the ground. 'Then we'll take our mystery girl here to the village and let somebody smarter than we are take over.'

And they proceeded to do just that. After some more hesitation, she joined them, following their actions and sharing a towel.

'You don't have to get too dry,' the girl, whose name was Dal, told her. 'You'll air-dry pretty good.'

Together the three of them set off back down the trail.

As they left the forest the village and lands beyond came into view.

It was a beautiful land, she thought. The stream flowed out of majestic, snow-capped mountains which spread out on both sides to reveal a rich valley and gently rolling hills.

The village – a collection of rough but sturdy log buildings by the side of a blue-green lake – bustled with activity. The fields were properly plowed and planted, and she saw a few centaurs checking and tending between stalks of unknown grain.

The whole place didn't seem as if it could support, or had, more than a few hundred people, she thought and commented on that to her companions.

Jol laughed. 'That proves you must be from downlake,' he said. 'Some pretty big communities down there. Actually, there's close to a thousand in the valley, here, but we're spread out all over the landscape. Only fifty or sixty live in town all the time.'

The main street was broad and maintained much like the trails, of which she had seen quite a few, a thick covering of sawdust making the paving.

Most of the buildings had an open side facing the street. The largest building was the first one they reached. It contained a huge forge on which several male and female centaurs worked hot metal. She saw with curiosity one woman lift a hind leg while a brawny male, wearing a protective bib, hammered something on her foot, apparently painlessly.

Other buildings proved to be stores selling farm implements, seed, and the like. There was even a barbershop and a bar, closed at the moment but unmistakable in its huge kegs and large steins.

'Is it always this warm and humid here?' she asked Jol.

He chuckled again in that friendly way he had about him. 'No, this is a four-season hex,' he explained enigmatically. 'Then we all get out our *gammot* fur coats and hats and gloves and romp in the cold snow.'

A *gammot*, she discovered, was one of the large rodents she had spied down by the stream.

'It must be a huge coat,' she remarked, and Dal and Jol both laughed.

'You *really* do have amnesia!' Dal responded. 'The hair on our bodies and a nice, thick layer of fat put on in summer and fall are pretty good insulators. Only our hairless parts need protection.'

'You can see the fireplaces and chimneys,' Jol pointed out. 'In the fall the fronts are put back on and they become warm as today inside.'

Julee started to ask what happened when it rained, but she saw that the roofs and ledges were angled and the buildings so placed that it would take a really terrible storm to get much rain inside.

'It looks as if anyone dishonest could steal anything he wanted here,' Julee commented.

They both stopped and looked at her strangely. 'That just isn't done here – not by any Dillian,' he huffed.

His reaction startled her, and she apologized. 'I – I'm sorry. I don't know why I think like that.'

'We do get some alien traders from other hexes in once in a while and they've tried taking stuff,' Dal put in to defuse the issue. 'Won't do 'em no good here, though. Only way in is by the lake – forty kilometers, almost as deep as it is long. Nobody can beat us in the woods, and anybody who wants to climb six kilometers of mountain at steep grade and below zero temperatures would lose more than he could take.'

They reached a small building about two-thirds of the way down the thirty or so buildings of the town's lone street. A wooden sign hung on a post, a hexagonal symbol of two small trees flanking a huge one, burned in with some sort of tool. Inside stood an elderly centaur with long, white hair and unkempt beard reaching down below his nipples. He had once been coal black, she realized, but now the body hair was flecked with silvery white.

He would look very officious standing there at his cluttered desk, she thought, amused, if he wasn't sound asleep and snoring loudly.

'That's Yomax,' Jol told her. 'The closest thing we've got to a government in the village. He's sort of the mayor, postmaster, chief forester, and game warden here. He always opens up at seven o'clock like the duty book says, but since the boat doesn't get in until eleven-thirty, he usually goes back to sleep until just before then.' He yelled, 'Hey! Yomax! Wake up! Official business!'

The old man stirred, then wiped his eyes and stretched, not only his arms but also his entire long body.

'Hmph! Whazzit?' he snorted. 'Some damned brat's always foolin' with me,' he muttered, then turned to see who stood there.

His eyes fixed on Wu Julee, and he suddenly came fully awake.

'Well! Hello!' he greeted in a friendly but puzzled tone. 'I don't remember seein' you around before.'

'She's lost her memory, Yomax,' Jol explained. 'We found her down by Three Falls.'

'She don't know nothin' about nothin',' Dal put in. 'Didn't even know 'bout winter and coats and all.'

The old man frowned, and came up to her. Ignoring Jol's protests that he had done it already, Yomax proceeded to go through the same examination Julee had had earlier – with similar negative results.

Yomax scratched his beard and thought. 'And you don't remember *nothin'?*' he asked for the fifth or sixth time, and for at least that many times she answered, 'No.'

'Mighty strange,' he said. Then, suddenly, he brightened. 'Lift your right foreleg,' he instructed. She did, and he grasped the hoof firmly and turned it up.

'I think she's been witched,' Dal maintained.

'Com'mere and lookit this,' Yomax said softly. The other two crowded in to see.

'She ain't got no shoes!' Dal exclaimed.

'Not only that,' the old one pointed out, 'there's no sign that she ever had any.'

'Don't prove nothin',' Dal persisted. 'I know lots'a folks what don't wear shoes, particularly up-valley.'

'That's true,' admitted Yomax, dropping the leg and straightening up, for which Julee was thankful. She felt circulation start to return. 'But,' the old centaur continued, 'that's a virgin hoof. No deep stains, no imbedded stones, nothing. Hers are like a newborn's.'

'Aw, that ain't possible,' Jol said scornfully.

'I told ya she was witched,' Dal insisted.

'You two get along and do your chores or whatever,' Yomax told them, waving them away with his hands. 'I think I know at least part of what this is about.'

They left reluctantly and then started to return. Yomax had to bellow at them several times.

'Now, then, young lady,' he began, satisfied of some privacy at last, 'let me throw some names at you. Let's see if any of 'em strike a bell.'

'Go ahead,' she urged him, intrigued.

'Nathun Brazzle,' he began, trying to make do with the strange names on a paper he had fished from a crowded drawer in his desk. 'Vardya Dipla Twelve Sixty-one. Dayton Hain. Wo Jolie. Anythin'?'

She shook her head slowly from side to side. 'I've never heard any of those names before,' she told him. 'At least – I don't think so.'

'Hmmm ...' the old man mused. 'I'm sure I'm right. Only possible explanation. Well, tell you what. Got one test when the boat comes in. Old Entry from the same neck of the woods as these folks – ten, fifteen years ago. He pilots the ferry now, since old Gletin refused to see how old he was and went overboard in a storm 'couple years back,' Yomax told her. 'He'll still remember the old language. I'll git him to spout some of that alien gibberish at ya, and we'll see if ya understand it.'

They passed the time talking until the ferry arrived, the old man telling about his land and people with pride and affection. During the course of his rambling but entertaining memoir/travelogue, which she was sure was almost half-true, a great many facts emerged. She learned about the Well World, and what the hexes were. She learned about Zone and gates, and the strange creatures that wandered around. She found that, although the Dillians lived to be well over a hundred Well World years on the average, the population was relatively small. Females went into heat only every other year, then only for a short period, and invariably bore but a single young – which had about an even chance of surviving its first year.

If you made it through puberty, about a twenty percent chance, then you would live a long life – because you would already be immune to most of what would kill you.

The various colors – Yomax said there were hundreds of combinations – of the people didn't seem to meld with interbreeding, she was told, since all color genes were recessives.

'Rank comes with age,' Yomax told her. 'When you get too old to plow, or build, or chop and haul wood, they put you in charge of things. Since nobody likes to admit they're old when the job's so little – you saw how much respect I got from the young ones – I wound up bein' about everything the village needs.'

The mother was the ultimate authority in child-rearing, he explained, but the family group shared moral responsibility. Since customs like marriage and inheritances were unknown – everything was simplistically communal – people formed family groups with other people they liked, without much regard to sex. The groups were mostly traditional now, but occasionally new ones of three to six would be formed by the young after puberty.

The entire hex was a collection of small towns and villages, she learned, because of the low birthrate and also because of innate limits on technology here. Anything more ambitious than the most basic steam engine just wouldn't work in Dillia.

That kept things extremely simple and pastoral, but also stable, peaceful, and uncluttered.

'In some hexes you can't even tell what sort of place it once was,' Yomax told her. 'All them machines and smelly stuff, everybody livin' in air-conditioned bubbles. Then they want to come *here* to get back to nature! They do some tourist business in other parts of the country, but this place is so isolated nobody's discovered it yet. And, when they do, they'll find us damned hostile, I can tell you!'

With that impassioned statement, there came the long, deep sound of a steam whistle, its call echoing across the mountains.

Yomax grabbed a simple cloth sack tied with twine and invited her down to the lakefront about 150 meters from town. She saw a simple wooden wharf with several huge posts, nothing more. A few townspeople waited just off the dock, apparently having business downlake or awaiting passengers.

Coming up on the wharf was the strangest craft she had ever seen. A giant oval raft, it looked like, with another raft built on top of it and supported by solid log cross-bracing. In the middle was a single, huge, black boiler, with a stack going up through the second tier and several meters beyond, belching white smoke.

A single centaur, black and white striped all over, a crazy-looking broad-brimmed hat on his head, stood at a large wheel, which was flanked by two levers. The levers went down through to the boiler level and seemed to do nothing but signal a brown centaur-engineer to turn some control or other on the boiler. The boiler was attached by what looked more like thick rope than chain to a small, wooden paddle wheel in the back.

About twenty varicolored Dillians stood on the first deck, some between oaken trunks full of unguessable cargo. Under the cross-bracing there seemed to be a counter and some kegs and steins. A large bale of grain flanked it.

Wu Julee could guess that this was the snack bar. She had already had a brunch with Yomax and discovered that the centaurs were herbivores who occasionally cooked various dishes but mostly ate raw grains and grasses grown in their fields. Tasted good, too, she had found.

Ropes from wooden posts on the side of the primitive steamer were tossed to a couple of villagers on the dock who tied the boat off. Satisfied, the captain went to the back and came down an almost disguised grooved ramp to the first deck.

Yomax tossed the mail to a crewman who idly threw it toward the center of the boat. The captain picked up a similar sack and jumped off to the dock, clasping hands with Yomax and then handing the old official the sack.

Yomax introduced the steamer captain to Wu Julee.

'This here's Klamath,' the old man told her. 'Not a proper name for a good Dillian, but he was born with it.'

'Please to meet you, Lady um ...?' The captain's expression prompted a lead.

'She don't know her name, Klammy,' Yomax explained. 'Just kinda showed up all blanked out early this morning I think she's an Entry, and thought maybe you could help.' Quickly he explained his language idea to the captain.

'Harder than you think,' the captain replied thoughtfully. 'It's true that I think in the old tongue, but everything's instantly and automatically translated in and out. It'd be easier if I could write something for her.'

Julee shook her head sadly. 'I am certain that I never learned to read. I just know it.'

'Hmmm ... Well, Yomax, you're the control,' Klamath said. 'It's going to take a lot of concentration to get out some old word stuff through the translation process, and I'm not really going to know if I'm successful or not. It all sounds the same to me. If she understands it and you don't, then we'll have it made.'

Klamath took chin in hand in a thoughtful pose, trying to think of something he could do to break through the barrier. Suddenly he brightened. 'Worth a try,' he said at last, 'but even if she doesn't understand it, it won't prove much. Well, here goes.

'Using the Three KY spectroanalysis program, stellar motion can be computed by phase-shifting observations using the infraspectrometer circuits in the navigational matrix for visual course plots,' Klamath intoned. Suddenly he stopped and turned to Yomax. 'How was that?' he asked.

'I got maybe one word in four,' the old man replied. 'How about the lady here?'

Julee shook her head in bewilderment. 'A lot of big words but I didn't understand what they meant.'

'Can you remember a big word?' Klamath prompted.

She thought for a minute. 'Ma – matrix, I think,' she said hesitantly, and, she looked totally perplexed, 'phase shifting?'

Klamath smiled. 'Good old basic navigation manual!' he exclaimed. 'You're from my part of the universe, all right. There's just no equivalent for that stuff in this language.'

Yomax nodded, an expression of satisfaction on his face. 'So she's one of the last four.'

'Almost certainly,' Klamath nodded. 'I've been keeping track of them since I know one, at least slightly. He's almost a living legend among spacers, and we know where he is and where the one called Vardia is. You must be that girl that was sick; that would explain the memory problems.'

'Who am I, then?' she asked excitedly. 'I want to know.'

'Probably a girl named Wu Julee,' Klamath told her.

'Wu Julee,' she repeated. The name sounded strange and totally unfamiliar to her. She wasn't sure she liked it.

'I'll be heading back downlake in an hour or so, and when I get to Donmin I'll see the local councilman and pass the word along,' Klamath said. 'In the meantime, you might as well stay here. It's about the best place to relax and enjoy things, and that might be just what you need.'

Their course of action agreed to, they all went to the local bar. She felt somewhat left out of the conversation after that, and the thick, dark ale made her slightly giddy. She excused herself and wandered out onto the main street.

Jol and Dal were there, and, seeing her, rushed up for the news.

'They say I'm an Entry,' she told them. 'Someone named Wu Julee. They said I was sick.'

'Well, you're healthy now,' Jol replied. 'And whatever you had got cured on the way in. Maybe your memory will come back, too, after a while.' He stopped and fidgeted nervously for a time, glancing once in a while to Dal. Finally the spotted female threw up her hands.

'All right, all right. May as well,' she said enigmatically.

'Sure it's all right with you?' Jol responded.

'Why not?' his girlfriend replied, resigned.

Jol turned back to Wu Julee. 'Look,' he said eagerly, 'we – Dal and me – we been thinkin' of putting together our own family, particularly with Dal pregnant and all. There's so few folks our age up here, and we aren't gettin' along with our own families too good now. Why don't you come in with us?'

Julee hesitated a moment, then replied, 'I'd like that – if it's all right with Yomax.'

'Oh, he won't mind,' Dal replied. 'He's been itchin' to see us take jobs anyhow, and if we form the group we'll have to to get our share of the harvest.'

And *it was* that easy.

They picked a spot fairly deep in the woods upvalley and started by building a primitive but efficient trail to the site. It required little clearing, but it did wind in and out between the giant trees. Borrowing a large handsaw and with some help from a forester they chopped down two trees near a tiny creek and burned out the stumps. Villagers helped them clear the area and cut up the trees into useful sizes, as well as providing smaller, more useful logs and hauling reddish clay used for insulation.

Wu Julee – the others nicknamed her Wuju, which she liked better – threw herself into the work, putting any thoughts of Klamath and governmental problems out of her mind. She hadn't seen the captain after the first day, since the boat came only once a day and stayed barely over an hour. Weeks passed.

They put in the sawdust floor, and built a stone cairn to use as a stove and winter heater, fueled with wood left over from the project. The cabin had a large central area with crude tables and a work area, and five stalls – bedrooms, really, with leaning supports, since the Dillians slept standing up. The extra stalls were for Dal's increasingly obvious new arrival and a spare in case someone else would join them. Jol and Dal took her trapping in the woods, and showed her how to skin and weave the animal furs and the skin from various plants into clothing. Once settled in, she and Jol were assigned to survey and check some back-country trails, particularly noting log bridges that might not stand the weight of winter snows. It was easy and pleasant work, and she enjoyed the peace and natural wonder of the mountains. When winter came they would help dig out snowed-in cabins and ensure safe paths around the small lakeside community.

In late summer Dal dropped her foal, large and fully formed but barely covered in a soft, neutral, downy fur, with reddish, wrinkly skin that made the boy-child look like a wizened old man.

Although born looking physically eight or nine in size and proportion – and able to stand, walk, even run within a few hours of birth – the child would be toothless for over a year and could only feed by nursing. It needed almost constant supervision, even though hair developed in the first few weeks affording a measure of protection. Born only with the instincts of a wild animal, the boy would have to learn how to reason, to speak, to act responsibly. It was difficult for Julee to get used to at first, since after the first month the child looked like a boy of about ten.

But he would look that way for years, they told her, perhaps eight or ten, until puberty. Until then they would be his world; after that, he would have to pull his own load.

But this peaceful, almost idyllic existence was interrupted by the start of her nightmares. They often involved racing pain, torture, and an evil, leering monstrous face that demanded horrible things of her. Many nights she woke up screaming, and it took hours to calm her down.

She began seeing the town Healer – the Dillian wasn't a doctor, because they had never been able to talk one into moving up into the isolated wilderness, but she could treat minor injuries and illnesses and set broken bones and the like. Anything really serious required using the old treadmill-powered raft to get the patient downlake. That was not really as difficult as it sounded because there was a fairly strong current that led to the falls at the downlake town.

Talking to the Healer helped, but the sleeping powders didn't. As fall started turning the leaves a riot of colors, and the snow began to creep down from the mountaintops, with occasional cold winds breaking through the still comfortable warm air, she was drawn and looked not at all well. Drinking the warm, potent ale seemed to help for a while, but she was more and more in a state of intoxication which made her less useful and harder to live with.

The villagers and her two companions were concerned but felt helpless as she seemed to deteriorate daily. The nightmares became worse and more frequent, the drinking increasing to compensate. She had been there almost twelve weeks, and she was miserable.

One particularly chilly day she came from the little bar in a high state of inebriation that even the cold wouldn't moderate, wandering down to the dock as the steamboat came in. She stared at a figure dressed in rugged furs sitting on the top deck, outside the little pilothouse that had been erected when the season changed.

It was alien. It looked human, but had only two legs and no hindquarters. Its features were hidden under a big fur hat, but it seemed to be smoking a pipe – a habit only a few of the oldest around did because of the difficulty of getting the weeds to stuff into it. She wasn't sure if this was a creature of her drunk or of her nightmares, and she just stared at it.

The boat tied up and the creature, or vision, joined the captain in walking down to the first level and onto the dock. Klamath spotted her, and pointed. The funny two-legged creature, so small next to the Dillians, nodded and walked over to her.

She drew back apprehensively, stifling a sudden and overwhelming urge to run.

The creature approached her cautiously and called out, in Dillian, 'Wu Julee? Is that you, Wu Julee?' The voice seemed familiar, somehow. He stopped about two meters from her, took the huge, curved pipe from his mouth, and pulled off the furry headpiece.

Wu Julee screamed and screamed, then suddenly seemed, to collapse, hitting the ground hard in a dead faint.

Klamath and many of the villagers rushed up to her in concern.

'Damn!' said the creature. 'Why do I always have that effect on women?'

For the shock of seeing his face had brought it all back to her suddenly and in full force. The only change the Well World had made in Nathan Brazil was his clothes.

THE BARONY OF AZKFRU, AKKAFIAN EMPIRE

The Baron Azkfru was furious.

'What do you mean he wasn't there?' he stormed.

The Diviner and The Rel remained impassive and apparently unperturbed as usual.

'We had no problems concealing ourselves through the first day,' The Rel reported, 'and acted about an hour after nightfall. When we approached the structure where Skander almost had to be, The Diviner sensed a change in the balancing equation. A new factor had been introduced. Skander had been there, but had left.'

'What do you mean a new factor?' snarled the Baron.

'In the most basic terms,' The Rel explained patiently, 'someone knew we were coming and what we were after. So either by direct warning or the indirect action of others, Skander was not there when we were. It was much too dangerous to remain there any length of time awaiting a possible return, so we broke off and returned here.'

Azkfru was stunned. 'A leak? Here? But, that's impossible! It couldn't have been any of my people – they're too thoroughly under my control. And, if anyone from the Imperial Palace had a reconditioned plant here, I wouldn't still be alive now. If there's a leak, it must be on your side.'

'It is possible our intentions were divined in the same way we divine the actions of others,' The Rel admitted, 'but it is impossible for any in my own leadership to have betrayed us, and you, yourself, saw to the security when we came cross Zone. A release of information on your side remains the most likely explanation.'

'Well, we'll dismiss the blame for now,' Azkfru said more calmly, 'and proceed from here. What do we do now?'

'Skander is still the only link we have to concrete knowledge of the puzzle,' The Rel pointed out. 'And, its location is known, if presently unattainable. The Diviner states that Skander's research was incomplete, and it must return to the learning place sooner or later. We are now attuned to that, and will know when. It is suggested that we bide our time until this Skander is again within our grasp. We did not compromise the plan, we just about proved it. It is still workable.'

'Very well,' growled Azkfru. 'Will you stay here?'

'We miss our homeland and constructive endeavor,' The Rel replied, 'but the mission is too vital. We will remain. Our needs are few, our requirements simple. A dark, bare cell will be sufficient, and an avenue to the surface every once in a while to stand beneath the stars. Nothing more. In the meantime, I would check your own security. It will profit us little if such a thing happens again!'

Soon after The Diviner and The Rel were seen to, the baron flew to the Imperial Palace and, securing a Zone pass, returned to his office in Zone. He was confident that he wouldn't be alive if it were any of his own people, so that left alien intervention – which meant Zone.

The offices, even the walls, were practically torn apart. It took almost two days and the destruction of more than half the embassy to find it. A tiny little transmitter inserted in his communications unit in his own office! His technicians examined it, but could be of little help.

'The range is such that it would carry to over four hundred other embassies,' one explained to him. 'Of the four hundred, almost three hundred are functional and used, and, of those, more than half are technologically capable of creating such a device, while the rest could probably purchase it untraceably, and almost all could place the device during a slow period when you were away.'

He had most of his office staff ritually executed anyway, not that it made him feel any better – just less foolish.

Someone had heard him kill General Ytil.

Someone had spied when The Diviner and The Rel had come through, and listened to their initial conversations in his office.

No more, he knew. But that was bad enough.

Someone else now knew at least *what* Skander was.

He had no choice, though, he realized. He had to wait.

Almost fifteen weeks.

THE CENTER IN CZILL

Vardia was assigned a basic Apprentice's job, doing computer research. She learned fast – almost anything they taught her – even though she couldn't make a great deal of sense out of her part of the project she was on. It was like seeing only one random page from a huge book. In itself, nothing made any sense. Only when put together with thousands of other pages did a picture finally emerge, and even then the top researchers had the unenviable job of fitting all the pages together in the proper order.

She enjoyed the life immensely. Even though she didn't understand her work, it was a constructive function with purpose, serving the social need. It was a comfortable niche. Here, indeed, is social perfection, she thought. Cooperation without conflict, with no basic needs beyond sleep and water, doing things that meant something.

After a couple of weeks on the job she began feeling somewhat dizzy at times. The spells would come on her, apparently without cause, and would disappear just as mysteriously. After a few such episodes she went to the central clinic. The doctors made a few very routine tests, then explained the problem to her.

'You're twinning,' the physician said. 'Nothing to be concerned about. In fact, it's wonderful – the only surprise is that it has happened so fast after joining us.'

Vardia was stunned. She had met some twins off and on at the Center, but the idea that it would happen to her just never occurred to her.

'What will this do to my work?' she asked apprehensively.

'Nothing, really,' the doctor told her. 'You'll simply grow as each cell begins its duplication process. A new you will take shape growing out from your back. This process will make you a bit dizzy and weak, and, near its completion, will cause some severe disorientation.'

'How long does the process take?' she asked.

'Four weeks if you continue a normal schedule,' was the reply. 'If you're willing to plant day and night, about ten days.'

She decided to get it over with if she could. Although everyone else seemed excited for her, she, herself, was scared and upset. Her supervisor was only too glad to give her time off, as she had not worked on the project long enough to be irreplaceable. So she picked a quiet spot away from the Center and near the river and planted.

There was no problem during the nights, of course, but during the day, when she had to root by exercising the rooting tendrils voluntarily, she quickly became bored. Except for early morning and just before dusk, she was alone in the camp or else surrounded by unconscious Czillians sleeping off long round-the-clock work periods.

On the third day, she knew she had to have water and uprooted to go down to the stream. Doing so was more difficult than she would have thought possible. She felt as if she weighed a ton, and balance was a real problem. She could reach back and feel the growth out of her back, but it didn't make much sense.

At the river's edge she saw a Umiau.

She had seen them at the Center, of course, but only going from one place to another. This was the first one she had seen close up, and it just seemed to be lying there, stretched out on the sand, asleep.

The Umiau had the lower body of a fish, silvery-blue scales going down to a flat, divided tail fin. Above the waist it remained the light blue color, but the shiny scales were gone, leaving a smooth but deceptively tough skin. Just below the transition line was a very large vaginal cavity.

The Umiau had two large and very firm breasts, and the face of a woman who, were she in Brazil's world, would have been considered beautiful despite hair that seemed to flow like silvery tinsel and bright blue lips. The ears, normally covered by the hair, were shaped like tiny shells and set almost flush against the sides of the head, and, Vardia saw, the nose had some sort of skin flaps that moved in and out as the creature breathed, probably to keep water out when swimming, she guessed. The long, muscular arms ended in hands with long, thin fingers and a thumb, all connected by a webbing.

Vardia stepped in to drink, and, as she did so, she saw other Umiau on and off along the banks, some swimming gracefully and effortlessly on or just beneath the surface. The river was shallow here, near the banks, but almost two meters deep in the center. On land they were awkward, crawling along on their hands or, at the Center, using electric wheelchairs.

But, as she saw from the swimmers in the river's clear water, in their own element they were beautiful.

Most, like the sleeper nearby, wore bracelets of some colorful coral, necklaces, tiny shell earrings, or other adornments. She had never understood jewelry as a human, and she didn't understand it now.

They all looked alike to her except for size. She wondered idly if they were all women.

Finishing her drink, she made her way, slowly, to the shore. She made large splashes and was terrified she would fall.

The noise awakened the sleeper.

'Well, hello!' she said in a pleasant, musical voice. The Umiau could make the sounds of the Czillian language, and most of them at the Center knew it. Czillians could not mock any other, so all conversations were in the Czillian tongue.

'I – I'm sorry if I awakened you,' Vardia apologized.

'That's all right,' the Uniau replied, and yawned. 'I shouldn't be wasting my time sleeping, anyway. The sun dries me out and I have a fever for hours after.' She noticed Vardia's problem. 'Twinning, huh?'

'Y-yes,' Vardia replied, a little embarrassed. 'My first time. It's awful.'

'I sympathize,' the mermaid said. 'I passed the egg this cycle, but I'll receive it next.'

Vardia decided to root near the stream for a while, and did. 'I don't understand you,' she told the creature hesitantly. 'Are you, then, a female?'

The Umiau laughed. 'As much as you,' she replied. 'We're hermaphrodites. One year we make an egg, then pass it to another who didn't, where it's shot with sperm and develops. The next year, you get the egg passed to you. The third year you're a neuter; then the cycle starts all over again.'

'You cannot abstain, then?' Vardia asked innocently.

The Umiau laughed again. 'Sure, but few do, unless they get themselves sterilized. When the urge hits, honey, you do it!'

'It is pleasant, then?' Vardia persisted innocently.

'Unbelievably,' the Umiau replied knowingly.

'I wish this was,' Vardia pouted. 'It is making me miserable.'

'*I* wouldn't worry about it,' the Umiau told her. 'You only do it two or three times in your very long lives.' The mermaid suddenly glanced at the sun. 'Well, it's getting late. It's been pleasant talking with you, but I have to go. Don't worry – you'll make out. The twin's coming along fine.'

And, without another word, it crawled into the water more rapidly than Vardia would have suspected possible and swam away.

The next few days were mostly boring repetitions of the earlier ones, although she did occasionally talk to other Umiau for brief periods.

On the ninth day when she needed water again, she discovered she had little control over herself. Every forward movement seemed to be countered by the twin now almost fully developed on her back. Even her thoughts ran confused, every thought seeming to double, echoing in her mind. It took immense concentration to get to the water, and, in getting out, she fell.

She lay there for some time, feeling embarrassed and helpless, when she suddenly realized a curious fact, a thought that echoed through her mind.

I'm I'm seeing seeing in in both both directions directions, her mind thought.

Getting up was beyond her, she knew, and she waited most of the afternoon for help. The confusing double sight didn't help her, since both scenes seemed to be double exposures.

She tried to move her head, but found she couldn't without burying it in the sandy bank. Finally, an hour or two before sunset, others came for rooting and pulled her out and helped her back to a rooting spot.

The tenth day was the worst. She couldn't think straight at all, couldn't move at all, couldn't judge scenes, distances, or anything. Even sounds were duplicated.

The sensation was miserable and it seemed to go on forever.

On the eleventh day nothing was possible, and she was in a delirium. About midday, though, there was a sudden release, and she felt as if half of her had suddenly, ghostlike, walked out of her. Everything returned to normal very suddenly, but she felt so terribly weak that she passed out in broad daylight.

The twelfth day dawned normally, and she felt much better, almost, she thought, euphoric. She uprooted and took a hesitant step forward. 'This is more like it!' she said aloud, feeling light and in total control again.

And, at exactly the same moment, another voice said exactly the same thing! They both turned around with the same motion.

Two identical Vardias stood looking, amazed, at each other.

'So you're the twin,' they both said simultaneously.

'I'm not, you are!' they both insisted.

Or am I? each thought. Would the twin know?

Everything was duplicated. Everything. Even the memories and personality. That's why they kept saying and doing the same things, they both realized. Will we ever know which is which? they both thought. Or did it matter? They both came out of the same body.

Together they set out for the Center.

They walked wordlessly, in perfect unison, even the random gestures absolutely duplicated. Communication was unnecessary, since each knew exactly what the other was thinking and thought the same thing. The procedure was well established. Once at the reception desk, they were taken to different rooms where doctors checked them. Pronounced fit and healthy to go back to work, each was assigned to a part of the project different from that she had previously been working on, although with similar duties.

'Will I ever see my twin again?' asked the Vardia who was in Wing 4.

'Probably,' the supervisor replied. 'But we're going to get you into divergent fields and activities as quickly as possible so each of you can develop a separate path. Once you've had a variety of experiences to make you sufficiently different, there's no reason not to see each other if you like.'

In the meantime the other Vardia, having asked the question sooner and having received the same answer, was settling in to a very different sort of position, even though the basic computer problem was the same.

She began working with a Umiau, for all the world identical to the one she had talked with along the riverbank. Her name – Vardia's mind insisted on the feminine for them even though they were neither – and both – was Endil Cannot.

After a few days of feeling each other out, they started talking as they worked. Cannot, she thought, reminded her of some of the instructors at the Center.

Every question seemed to get a lecture.

One day she asked Cannot just what they were looking for. The work so far consisted of feeding legends and old wives' tales from many races into the computer to find common factors in them.

'You have seen the single common factor already, have you not?' Cannot replied tutorially. 'What, then, is it?'

'The phrase – I keep hearing it off and on around here, too.'

'Exactly!' the mermaid exclaimed. 'Until midnight at the Well of Souls. A more poetic way of saying forever, perhaps, or expressing an indefinite, like: We'll keep at this project until midnight at the Well of Souls – which seems likely at this rate.'

'But why is it important?' she quizzed. 'I mean, it's just a saying, isn't it?'

'No!' the Umiau replied strongly. 'If it were a saying of one race, perhaps even of bordering races, that would be understandable. But it's used even by *Northern* races! A few of the really primitive hexes seem to use it as a religious chant! Why? And so the saying goes back as far as antiquity itself. Written records go back almost ten thousand years here, oral tradition many times that. That phrase occurs over and over again! Why? What is it trying to tell us? That is what I must know! It might provide us with the key to this crazy planet, with its fifteen hundred and sixty races and differing biomes.'

'Maybe it's literal,' Vardia suggested. 'Maybe people sometime in the past gathered at midnight at some place they called the Well of Souls.'

The mermaid's expression would have led anyone more knowledgeable in all-too-human emotions to the conclusion that the dumb student had finally grasped the obvious.

'We've been proceeding along that tack here,' Cannot told her. 'This is, after all, called the Well World, but the only wells we know of are the input wells at each pole. That's the problem, you know. They are *both* input, not opposites.'

'Must there be an output?' Vardia asked. 'I mean, can't this be a one-way street?'

Cannot shook her statuesque head from side to side. 'No, it would make no sense at all, and would invalidate the only good theory I have so far as to why this world was built and why it was built the way it was.'

'What's the theory?'

Cannot's eyes became glazed, but Vardia could not tell if it was an expression or just the effect the Umiau had when closing the inner transparent lid while keeping the outer skin lid open.

'You're a bright person, Vardia,' the mermaid said. 'Perhaps, someday, I'll tell you.'

And that was all there was to that.

A day or two later Vardia wandered into Cannot's office and saw her sitting there viewing slides of a great desert, painted in reds, yellows, and oranges under a cloudless blue sky. In the background things got hazy and indistinct. It looked, Vardia thought, something like a semitransparent wall. She said as much aloud.

'It is, Vardia,' Cannot replied. 'It is indeed. It's the Equatorial Barrier – a place I am going to have to visit somehow, although none of the hexes around it are very plentiful on water, and the trip will be hard. Here, look at this,' she urged, backing the slides up several paces. She saw a view taken through the wall with the best filters available. Objects were still indistinct, but she could see just enough to identify one thing clearly.

'There's a walkway in there!' she exclaimed. 'Like the one around the Zone Well!'

'Exactly!' the mermaid confirmed. 'And that's what I want to know more about. Do you feel up to working through the night tonight?'

'Why, yes, I guess so,' she replied. 'I've never done it before but I feel fine.'

'Good! Good!' Cannot approved, rubbing her hands together. 'Maybe I can solve this mystery tonight!'

Stars swirled in tremendous profusion across the night sky, great, brilliantly colored clouds of nebulae spreading out in odd shapes while the starfield itself seemed to consist of a great mass of millions of stars in swirls the way a galaxy looked under high magnification. It was a magnificent sight, but one not appreciated by Vardia, who could not see it with her coneless eyes as she worked in the bright, artificial day of the lab, or by unseen onlookers out in the fields to the south.

At first they looked like particularly thick grains of the wild grasses in the area. Then, slowly, two large shapes rose up underneath the stalks, shapes with huge insect bodies and great eyes.

And – something else.

It sparkled like a hundred trapped fireflies, and seemed to rest atop a shadowy form.

'The Diviner says that the equation has changed unnaturally,' said The Rel.

'Then we don't go in tonight?' one of the Akkafian warriors asked.

'We must,' replied The Rel. 'We feel that only tonight will everything be this auspicious. We have the opportunity of an extra prize that increases the odds.'

'Then the balance – this new factor – is in our favor?' asked the Markling, relieved.

'It is,' The Rel replied. 'There will be two to carry back, not one. Can you manage it?'

'Of course, if the newcomer isn't any larger than the other,' the Markling told The Rel.

'Good. They should be together, so take them both. And – remember! Though the Czillians will all sleep as soon as the power-plant detonator is triggered, the Umiau will not. They'll be shocked, and won't see too well or get around too much, but there may be trouble. Don't get so wrapped up in any struggle that you sting either of our quarry to death. I want only paralysis sufficient to get us back to the halfway island.'

'Don't worry,' the warriors assured almost in unison. 'We would not fail the baron like that.'

'All right, then,' The Rel said in a voice so soft it was almost lost in the gentle night breeze. 'You have the detonator. When we rush at the point I have shown you, I shall give a signal. *Then* and only then are you to blow it. Not sooner, not later. Otherwise the emergency generators will be on before we are away.'

'It is understood,' the Markling assured the Northerner.

'The Diviner indicates that they are both there and otherwise alone in their working place,' The Rel said. 'In a way, I am suspicious. This is too good fortune, and I do not believe in luck. Nonetheless, we do what we must.

'All right – *now!'*

DILLIA-UPLAKE

Wu Julee groaned and opened her eyes. Her head was splitting and the room was spinning around.

'She's comin' around!' someone's voice called out, and she was suddenly conscious of a number of people clustering around her.

She tried to focus, but everything was blurry for a few moments. Finally, vision cleared enough for her to see who each was, particularly the one non-Dillian in the crowd.

'Brazil!' she managed, then choked. Someone forced a little water down her throat. It tasted sour. She coughed.

'She knows you!' Yomax yelled, excited. 'She remembers things agin!'

She shut her eyes tightly. She *did* remember – everything. A spasm shook her, and she vomited the water.

'Yomax! Jol!' she heard the Healer's voice call. 'You louts take her behind! Captain Brazil, you pull; I'll push! Let's try and get her on her feet as soon as possible!'

They fell to their tasks and managed to pull it off with several tries. No thanks to me, Brazil thought. Man! These people have muscles!

She was up, but unsteady. They put side panels padded with cloth under her arms and braced them so she could support herself. The room was still spinning, but it seemed to be slowing down. She still felt sick, and started trembling. Someone – probably Jol – started stroking her back and that seemed to calm her a little.

'Oh, my God!' she groaned.

'It's all right, Wu Julee,' Brazil said softly. 'The nightmares are past, now. They can't hurt you anymore.'

'But how –' she started, then threw up again and kept gagging.

'All right, all of you outside now!' the Healer demanded. 'Yes, you, too, Yomax! I'll call you when I'm ready.'

They stepped out into the chill wind. Yomax shrugged, a helpless look on his face.

'Do you drink ale, stranger?' the aged centaur asked Brazil.

'I've been known to,' Brazil replied. 'What do you make it out of?'

'Grains, water, and yeast!' said Yomax, surprised at the question. 'What else *would* you make ale out of?'

'I dunno,' Brazil admitted, 'but I'm awfully glad you don't either. Where to?'

The three of them went down the main street, Brazil feeling like a pygmy among giants, and up to the bar, front on now.

The place was full of customers – about a dozen – and they had trouble squeezing in. Brazil suddenly became afraid that he would be crushed to death between equine rumps.

The conversation stopped when he entered, and everyone looked at him suspiciously.

'I just love being made to feel welcome,' Brazil said sarcastically. Then, to the other two, 'Isn't there a more, ah, private place to talk?'

Yomax nodded. 'Gimme three, Zoder!' he called, and the bartender poured three enormous steins of ale and put them on the bar. He handed one to Jol and the other to Brazil, who almost dropped it when he found out how heavy the filled stein really was. Using two hands, he held on and followed Yomax down the street a few doors to the oldster's office.

After Jol stoked the fire and threw some more wood in, the place seemed to warm and brighten spiritually as well as literally. Brazil let out a long sigh and sank to the floor, resting the stein on the floor beside him. As the place warmed up, he took off his fur cap and coat. Underneath he didn't seem to be wearing anything.

The two centaurs also took off their coats, and both of them stared at him.

Brazil stared back. 'Now, don't you go starting that, or I'll go back to the bar!' he warned. The Dillians laughed, and everybody relaxed. Brazil sipped the brew, and found it not bad at all, although close to two liters was a bit much at one time for him.

'Now, what's ail this about, mister?' Jol asked suspiciously.

'Suppose we swap information,' he offered, taking out his pipe and lighting it.

Yomax licked his lips. 'Is that – is that *tobacco?*' he asked hesitatingly.

'It is,' Brazil replied. 'Not very good, but good enough. Want some?'

Yomax's expression, Brazil thought, was as eager and unbelieving as mine was when I saw that steak at Serge's.

Was that only a few months ago? he asked himself. *Or was it a lifetime?.*

Yomax dragged out an old and battered pipe that resembled a giant corncob and proceeded to fill it. Lighting it with a common safety match, he puffed away ecstatically.

'We don't get much tobacco hereabouts,' the old man explained.

'I never would have guessed,' Brazil responded dryly. 'I picked it up a fair distance from here, really – I've traveled nine hexes getting here, not counting a side trip to Zone from my home hex.'

'Them rodent fellas are the only ones in five thousand kilometers with tobacco these days,' Yomax said ruefully. 'That where?'

Brazil nodded. 'Next door to my home hex.'

'Don't think I remember it,' the old official prodded curiously. 'Except that you look like us, sort of, from the waist up, I don't think I ever seen your like before.'

'Not surprising,' Brazil replied sadly. 'My people came to a no-good end, I'm afraid.'

'Hey! Yomax!' Jol yelled suddenly. 'Lookit his mouth! It don't go with his talkin'!'

'He's using a translator, idiot!' snapped Yomax.

'Right,' the small man confirmed. 'I got it from the Ambreza – those "rodent fellas" you mentioned. Nice people, once I could convince them that I was intelligent.'

'If you and they was neighbors, why was *that* a problem?' Jol asked.

The sadness crept back. 'Well – a very long time ago, there was a war. My people were from a high-tech hex, and they built an extremely comfortable civilization, judging from the artifacts I saw. But the lifestyle was extremely wasteful – it required enormous natural resources to sustain – and they were running out, while the by-products curtailed good soil to the point where they were importing eight percent of their food. Unwilling to compromise their life-style, they looked to their neighbors to sustain their culture. Two hexes were ocean, one's temperature was so cold it would kill us, two more weren't worth taking for what they had or could be turned into. Only the Ambreza Hex was compatible, even though it was totally nontechnological. No steam engines, no machines of any kind not powered by muscle. The Ambreza were quiet, primitive farmers and fishermen, and they looked like easy prey.'

'Attacked 'em, eh?' Yomax put in.

'Well, they were about to,' Brazil replied. 'They geared up with swords and spears, bows and catapults – whatever would work in Ambreza Hex – with computers from home telling them the best effective use. But my people made one mistake, so very old in the history of many races, and they paid the price for it.'

'What mistake was that?' asked Jol, fascinated.

'They confused ignorance with stupidity,' the man explained. 'The Ambreza were what they appeared to be, but they were not dumb. They saw what was coming and saw they had to lose. Their diplomats tried to negotiate a settlement, but at the same time they scoured other hexes for effective countermeasures – and they found one!'

'Yes? Yes? And that was …?' Yomax prompted.

'A gas,' Brazil said softly. 'A Northern Hemisphere hex used it for refrigeration, but on my people it had a far different effect. They kidnapped a few people, and the gas worked on them just as the Northerners said it would. Meanwhile the only effect on the Ambreza was to make them itch and sneeze for a while.'

'It killed all your people?' asked Yomax, appalled.

'Not killed, no – not exactly,' the small man replied. 'It made, well chemical changes in the brain. You see, just about every race is loosely based on, or related to, some animal past or present.'

'Yup,' Yomax agreed. 'I once tried to talk to a horse in Hex Eighty-three.'

'Exactly!' Brazil exclaimed. 'Well, we came from – were a refinement of, really – the great apes. You know about them?'

'Saw a few pictures once in a magazine,' Jol said. 'Two or three hexes got kinds of 'em.'

'That's right. Even the Ambreza are related to several animals in other hexes – including this one, if I recall,' Brazil continued. 'Well, the gas simply mentally reverted everyone back to his ancestral animalism. They all lost their power to reason and became great apes.'

'Wow!' Jol exclaimed. 'Didn't they all die?'

'No,' Brazil replied. 'The climate's moderate, and while many of them – probably most of them – did perish, a few seemed to adapt. The Ambreza moved in and cleared out the area afterward. They let them run free in small packs. They even keep a few as pets.'

'I ain't much on science,' the old man put in, 'but I *do* remember that stuff like chemical changes can't be passed on. Surely their children didn't breed true as animals.'

'The Ambreza say that there has been slow improvement,' answered the small man. 'But while the gas has to be extremely potent to affect anybody else, it appears that the stuff got absorbed by just about everything – rocks, dirt, and everything that grows in it or lived in it. For my people, the big dose caused initial reversion, but about one part per *trillion* keeps it alive. The effect is slowly wearing out. The Ambreza figure that they'll be up to the level of basic primitive people in another six or seven generations, maybe even start a language within five hundred years. Their – the Ambreza's, that is – master plan is to move the packs over into their old land when they start to improve. That way they'll develop in a non-technological hex and will probably remain rather primitive.'

'I'm not sure I like that gas,' Yomax commented. 'What worked on them might work on us.' He shivered.

'I don't think so,' Brazil replied. 'After the attack, the Well refused to transport the stuff anymore. I think our planetary brain's had enough of such things.'

'I still don't like the idea,' Yomax maintained. 'If not that, then somethin' else could get us.'

'Life's a risk anyway, without worrying about everything that *might* happen,' Brazil pointed out. 'After all, you could slip on the dock and fall in the lake and freeze to death before you got to shore. A tree could fall over on you. Lightning could strike. But if you let such things dominate your life, you'll be as good as dead anyway. That's what's wrong with Wu Julee.'

'What do you mean?' Jol asked sharply.

'She's had a horrible life,' Nathan Brazil replied evenly. 'Born on a Comworld, bred to do farm labor, looking and thinking just like everybody else, no sex, no fun, no nothing. Then, suddenly, she was plucked up by the hierarchy, given shots to develop sexually, and used as a prostitute for minor visitors, one of whom was a foreign pig named Datham Hain.'

He was interrupted at this point and had to try to explain what a prostitute was to two members of a culture that didn't have marriage, paternity suits, or money. It took some doing.

'Anyway,' he continued, 'this Hain was a representative of a group of nasties who get important people on various worlds hooked on a particularly nasty kind of drug, the better to rule them. To demonstrate what it did if you didn't get the treatment, he infected Wu Julee first and then let the stuff start to destroy her. There's no cure, and on most worlds they just put such people to death. Most of those infected, finding their blood samples matching Wu Julee's blood, played Hain's game, taking orders from him and his masters.'

'The stuff kind of does to you, but very painfully, what that gas did to my Hex Forty-one, only it also depresses the appetite to nonexistence. You eventually mindlessly starve to death.'

'And poor Wuju was already pretty far gone,' Jol interpolated. 'In pain, practically an animal, with all that behind her. No wonder she blotted all memories out! And no wonder she had nightmares!'

'*Life's* been a nightmare to her,' Brazil said quietly. 'Her physical nightmare is over, but until she faces that fact, it still lives in her mind.'

They just stood there for several minutes, there seeming to be nothing left to say. Finally, Yomax said, 'Captain, one thing bothers me about your gas story.'

'Fire away,' the man invited, sipping more of the ale.

'If that gas stuff was still active, why didn't it affect you, at least slightly?'

'I honestly don't know,' Brazil responded. 'Everything says I should have been reduced to the level of the hex, including Ambreza chemistry. But I wasn't. I wasn't even physically changed to conform to the larger, darker version of humanity there. I couldn't explain that – and neither can the Ambreza.'

The Healer stuck her head in the door, and they turned expectantly.

'She's sleeping now,' she reported. '*Really* sleeping, for the first time in more than a month. I'll stay with her and see her through.'

They nodded and settled back for a long wait.

Wu Julee slept for almost two days.

Brazil used the time to tour the village and look at some of the trails. He liked these people, he decided, and he liked this isolated place, cut off from everything civilized except for the one daily boat run. Standing on a ledge partway up a well-maintained cross-country trail, he was oblivious to the cold and the wind as he looked out at the mass of snow-covered mountains. He realized suddenly that almost the whole mountain range was in the next hex, and he speculated idly on what sort of denizens lived in that kind of terrain.

After spending most of a day out there, he made his way back to the village to check on Wu Julee's progress.

'She came around,' the Healer informed him. 'I got her to eat a little something and it stayed down. You can see her, if you want.'

Brazil *did* want, and went in.

She looked a little weak but managed a smile when she saw him.

She hasn't really changed radically, he thought, at least not from the waist up. He would have known her anywhere – despite the different coloration and the lower body, the pointy ears, and all. She actually looked healthier than she had under the influence of that vicious drug, the product of eating better and of exercising.

'How are you feeling?' he asked, idly wondering why that stupid question was always the first asked of obviously sick people.

'Weak,' she replied, 'but I'll manage.' She let out a small giggle. 'The last time we saw each other I had to look up to you.'

Brazil took on a pained expression. 'It never fails!' he wailed. 'Everybody always picks on a little man!'

She laughed and so did he. 'It's good to see you laugh,' he said.

'There's never been much to laugh about, before,' she replied.

'I told you I'd find you.'

'I remember – that was the worst part of the sponge. You *know*, you are aware of all that's happening to you.'

He nodded gravely. 'Throughout the history of man there's always been some kind of drug, and people stuck on it. The people who push the stuff are on a different kind of drug, one so powerful that they are not aware of its own, ravaging, animalistic effect on them.'

'What's that?'

'Power and greed,' he told her. 'The ugliest – no, the second ugliest ravager of people ever known.'

'What's the ugliest, then?' she asked him.

'Fear,' he replied seriously. 'It destroys, rots, and touches everyone around.'

She was silent for a moment. 'I've been afraid most of my life,' she said so softly he almost couldn't make out the words.

'I know,' he replied gently. 'But there's nothing to fear now, you know. These are good people here, and this is a spot I could cheerfully spend the rest of my life in.'

She looked straight at him, and her youthful looks were betrayed by the eyes of someone incredibly old.

'They *are* wonderful,' she admitted, 'but it's *their* paradise. They were born here, and they know nothing of the horrors around them. It must be wonderful to be that way, but I'm not one of them. My scars seem huge and painful just because of their goodness and simplicity. Can you understand that?'

He nodded slowly. 'I have scars, too, you know. And some of them are more than I can take at times. My memory's coming back – slowly, but in extreme detail. And, like Serge said, they're mostly things I don't want to remember. Some good times, some wonderful things, certainly – but some horrors and a lot of pain, too. Like you, I blotted them out, more successfully it seems, but they're coming back now – more and more each day.'

'Those rejuve treatments must have done a lot to your memory,' she suggested.

'No, nothing,' he said slowly. 'I've never had a rejuve treatment, Wu Julee. Never. I knew that when I blamed them for such things.'

'Never – but that's impossible! I remember Hain reading your license. It said you were over five hundred years old!'

'I am,' he replied slowly. 'And a lot more. I've had a hundred names, a thousand lives, all the same. I've been around since Old Earth, and before.'

'But that was bombed out centuries ago! Why, that was back almost before history!'

His tone was casual, but there was no doubting his sincerity. 'It's been dropping like a series of veils, little by little. Just today, up in the mountains, I suddenly remembered a funny, little, Old Earth dictator who liked me because I wasn't any taller than he was.

'Napoleon Bonaparte was his name ...'

He slept on furs in Yomax's office for several days, seeing Wu Julee gain some strength and confidence with every visit.

But those eyes – the scars in her eyes were still there.

One day the steamboat came in, and Klamath almost fell in the lake rushing out to meet him.

'Nate! Nate!' the ferry captain called. 'Incredible news!' From his expression it was nothing good.

'Calm down, Klammy, and tell me about it.' He spied a block-printed newspaper in the waterman's hand, but couldn't read a word of the language.

'Somebody just busted into that university in Czill and kidnapped a couple of people!'

Brazil frowned, a funny feeling in his stomach. That was where Vardia was, where he was going next.

'Who'd they snatch?' he asked.

'One of yours, Vardia or something like that. And a Umiau – they're sorta mermaids, Nate – named Cannot.'

The little man shifted uneasily, chewing on his lower lip.

'Anybody know who?'

'Got a good idea, though they deny it. Bunch o' giant cockroaches with some unpronounceable name. Some of the Umiau spotted them in the dark when they shorted out the power at the Center.'

Slowly the story came out. Two large creatures resembling giant flying bugs blew the main power plant, causing the artificial sunlight to fail in one wing of the Center. Then they crashed through the windows of the lab, grabbed Vardia and Cannot, and took them away. The leaders of the culprit's race were confronted at Zone, but pointed out that there were almost a hundred insectival races on the planet and denied they were the ones. Their tight monarchy, resembling a Comworld with fancy titles, was leakproof – so nobody was sure.

'But that's not the most sensational part!' Klamath continued, his voice rising again. 'These Umiau got super-upset at all this, and one of them let slip the truth about Cannot.

'Seems they and the top dogs of the Center had a real secret to keep. Cannot was Elkinos Skander, Nate!'

Brazil just stood there, digesting the information. It made sense, of course. Skander would use the great computers of the Center to answer his big questions, getting everything he needed so that, when he was ready, he could mount an expedition under his direction to the interior of the Well World. Power and greed, Brazil thought sourly. Corrupting two of the more peaceful and productive races on the planet.

Well, they wanted it all, and now all they've got left is their fear, he reflected.

'I'll have to go to Czill now,' he told the ferry captain. 'It looks as if my job is starting.'

Klamath didn't understand, but agreed to hold the boat until Nathan could say good-bye to Wu Julee.

She was standing unsupported and looking through a book of landscape paintings by local artists when he entered. His expression telegraphed his disquiet.

'What's the matter?' she asked.

'They've broken into a place a couple of hexes over and kidnapped Vardia and Skander, the man who might be the killer of those seven people back on Dalgonia,' he told her gravely. 'I have to go, I'm afraid.'

'Take me with you,' she said evenly.

The thought had never occurred to him. 'But you're still weak!' he protested. 'And here is where you belong. These are your people, now. Out there is nothing but worse and worse. It's no place for you!'

She walked over to him and looked down with those old, old eyes.

'I have to,' she told him. 'I have to heal the scars.'

'But there're only more scars out there,' he countered. 'There's fear out there, Wu Julee.'

'No, Nathan,' she replied sternly, using his first name for the first time. She tapped her forehead. 'The fear is in here. Until I face it, I'll die by inches here.'

He was silent for a while, and she thought he still wouldn't take her.

'I'm easier to care for than you are,' she pointed out. 'I'm tougher of skin, more tolerant of weather, and I need only some kind of grass and water.'

'All right,' he said slowly. 'Come if you must. You can get back to Dillia through a gate from anywhere, anyway.'

'That's what I've got to know, Nathan,' she explained. 'I'm cured of sponge, but I'm still hooked on that ugliest drug, fear.'

'You sure you're well enough?'

'I'm sure,' she replied firmly. 'This will give me what I need.'

She put on a coat and they went outside. When they told Yomax and the others that she was going along, the same round of protests started all over again, but her mind was made up.

'I'll tell Dal and Jol,' Yomax said, tears welling in his eyes. 'But they won't understand, neither.'

'I'll be back, old man,' she replied, her voice breaking. She kissed him lightly on the cheek.

Klamath sounded the steam whistle.

They stepped on the board first floor of the steamship and entered the partially closed cargo door that enclosed the lower deck from the colder weather.

Five hours later they landed in the much larger village of Donmin downlake. Compared to the uplake community, it was a bustling metropolis of fifteen or twenty thousand, stretching out across broad, cleared plains. The streets were lit with oil lamps, although Brazil had no idea what sort of unrefined, natural oil they used. It smelled like fish, anyway.

He reclaimed a well-made but crude backpack from the shipping office and said good-bye to Klamath, who wished them luck.

The packs, Wu Julee found, were largely filled with tobacco, a good trade commodity. One pouch had some clothing and toiletries.

Using the tobacco, Brazil managed to trade for some small items he thought they would need, then got a room for them at a waterfront inn, where they spent the night.

The next day they set out early across the trails of Dillia toward the northeast. She had trouble staying back with him, having to walk in almost uncomfortable slow motion. After several kilometers of particularly slow going, she suggested, 'Why don't you ride me?'

'But you're already carrying the pack,' he protested.

'I'm stronger than you think,' she retorted. 'I've hauled logs heavier than you and the pack put together. Come on, climb on and see if you can keep from falling off.'

'I haven't been on a horse since I went to the first Wilson inauguration,' he muttered incomprehensibly. 'Well, I'll try.'

It took him three tries, even with her help, to mount her broad, stocky body that reminded him so much of a Shetland pony. And he fell off twice, to her derisive laughter, when she started to trot. She finally had to put her arms behind her to give him something to hold on to. When her circulation started going, he had to hold on to the much-less-reassuring pack. His own circulation was in no great shape. His legs discovered a hundred new muscles he had never known before, and the agony almost obliterated the soreness of his rump from bouncing.

But they made good time, the kilometers flying by. Near dusk they reached the Dillian border, through the last village and seeing here and there only an isolated farmhouse. It started to snow, but it was only a flurry at first and didn't really bother either of them.

'We're going to have to quit soon,' he called to her.

'Why?' she mocked. 'Scared of the dark?'

'My body just won't take much more of this,' he groaned. 'And we'll pass into the Slongorn Hex in a little while. I don't know enough about it to want to chance it in the dark.'

She slowed, then stopped, and he got off. Pain shot through him but it was the aching sort, not the driving sharpness of riding. She was amused at his discomfort.

'So who couldn't make the trip because they were too weak?' she teased. 'Look at the brave superman now! And we've already stopped five times!'

'Yeah,' he grunted, stretching and finding that that only made it hurt in different places. 'But that was only so you could eat. Lord! Do you people stuff yourselves!'

And they did, he thought, consume an enormous quantity to support their large bodies.

'Will we have to camp here?' she asked, looking at the darkening woods with no sign of lights nearby. 'If we do, we'd better get some good shelter. It looks like the snow may pick up.'

'If that road we passed about a kil and a half ago was the turnoff to Side-crater Village, there should be a roadhouse not too much farther on.' He checked a frayed and faded map he had in the pack.

'Why not go back to the village?' she suggested.

'Almost eight kils down a dead end?' he replied skeptically. 'No, we'll go on and hope the roadhouse is still in business. But I'll walk for a while, no matter what!'

As darkness fell the snow did pick up, and started to stick. The wind whistled through the trees, keeping time with the subtle, quiet sound of the snow hitting against trees, bushes, and them.

Visibility dropped to almost zero.

'Are we still on the road?' she yelled to him.

'I don't know,' he admitted. 'We should have come to that roadhouse by now. But we don't have any choice. We'd never build a fire in this stuff now. Keep going!'

'I'm getting real cold, Nathan!' she complained. 'Remember, more than half of me is exposed!'

He stopped, and brushed the snow off her backside. Insulating layer of fat or not, he realized she couldn't continue too much longer.

'I'm going to climb on!' he yelled above the wind. 'Then go on as fast as you can! We've *got* to come to something sooner or later!'

They pushed forward, he clinging to her back, but it was slow going against the wind. They continued on for what seemed like hours in the blowing cold and darkness.

'I don't know how much longer I can go on!' she called to him at last. 'My ass is frozen solid now.'

'Come on, girl!' he shouted. 'Here's that adventure you wanted! Don't give up now!'

That spurred her on, but it seemed hopeless as the snow continued to pile up.

'I think I see something ahead!' she shouted. 'I can't be sure – I think my eyes are covered with icicles!'

'Maybe it's the roadhouse!' he shouted. 'Head for it!'

She pushed on.

Suddenly, as if they passed through an invisible curtain, the snow was gone – and so was the cold. She stopped suddenly.

He got off and brushed the snow from him. After a few moments to catch his breath, he walked back several steps.

And back into the blowing snow and cold.

He went back to her.

'What is it, Nathan?' she asked. 'What happened?'

'We must have missed the roadhouse,' he told her. 'We've crossed the border into Slongorn!'

Her body began to thaw rapidly, and painfully. Her eyes misted, then started to clear.

Looking back, she could see nothing but billowing, snowy fog.

In any other direction, the spectacular night sky of the Well World shone cloudlessly around them.

'We might as well camp right here,' he suggested. 'Not only am I too tired to go any farther, but there's no use chancing unfamiliar territory. Anything that might cause us problems is unlikely to be this close to the border, and we always have a convenient if chilly exit if we find any real problems.'

'It's hard to believe,' she said as he unstrapped the pack and removed a couple of towels, wiping his face and hair, then starting to give her the much more difficult rubdown. 'I mean – coming out of that awful storm and into this – winter to summer, just like that.'

'That's the way it can be,' he replied. 'Sometimes there's no clear dividing line, sometimes it's dramatic. But, remember, despite the fact that things interlock on this world – tides, rivers, oceans, and the like – each hex is a self-contained biological community.'

'All of a sudden I'm starting to sweat,' she noted. 'I think I'll take these heavy fur clothes off.'

'I'm ahead of you,' he responded, drying her rear and tail. She twisted around and saw that he had removed almost all of his clothing. He looks even punier naked, she thought. You can just about see every rib on his body, even through that carpet of black chest-hair.

He finished and came around to her front. Together they stood and looked at the landscape eerily illuminated in the bright starlight.

'Mountains, trees, maybe a small lake over there,' he pointed out. 'Looks like a few lights off in the distance.'

'I don't think we're on the road,' she commented. They seemed to be on a field of short grasses. She reached down almost automatically and picked a clump.

'I'm not sure you ought to eat that right now,' he warned. 'We don't know all the ground rules here.'

She sniffed the grass suspiciously. Although Dillians were moderately nearsighted, their senses of smell and hearing were acute. 'Smells like plain old grass,' she said. 'Kind of short, though. See? It's been cut!'

He looked at the stuff and saw that she was right. 'Well, this is logically either a high-technology hex or a nontechnological one, judging from the pattern I've seen,' he noted. 'From the looks of things, it's high.'

'The grass has been cut in the last day or two,' she observed. 'You can still smell it.'

He sniffed, but didn't notice much, and shrugged. He never had much of a smeller despite the Roman nose, he thought.

'I'm going to chance it,' she decided at last. 'It's here, and I need it, and we have two or three days before we'll get through here.' She took about three steps, then stopped.

'Nathan?'

'Yes?'

'What kind of people live here? I mean, what—'

'I know what you mean. I couldn't get a really good description out of anyone. It's not the most traveled route, mostly a through route. The best I could get was that they were two-legged vegetarians.'

'That's good enough for me,' she replied, and started picking clumps of grass and chewing them.

'Don't get too far away!' he called. 'It's too damned hot to build a fire, and I don't want to attract the wrong people. We might be – probably are – trespassing.'

Satisfied as long as he could still see her, he stretched out the furs to dry and stripped completely. After discovering that some of the grass was stiff and sharp, he spread the three wet towels out to form a mat, then got out a couple of large bricks of cooked confection he had bought back in Donmin. He sat on the towels and ate about half of one bar, which was hard and crunchy but filling, and then came down with a terrible candy-thirst.

He reached for the flagon containing water, but decided to leave its half-empty contents if he could. No telling what the water was like here.

He got up and went over to the border, only a few meters away. He could hear the howling winds and see the blowing snow. Some of the cold radiated out a few centimeters from the border. He got down on his knees, reached into the cold, and came up with a handful of snow.

That did the job.

He went back and stretched out on the towels. He still ached from the day's ride, but not nearly as bad. He knew the pain would come back when he mounted the next day, though. Maybe in three or four days he would get used to riding. By his own estimates, they were still almost nine hundred kilometers from the Center.

She came back after a while and surveyed him lying there on the towels.

'I thought you'd be asleep,' she said.

'Too tired to sleep,' he responded lazily. 'I'll get off in a little while. Why don't you get some? You're doing all the work, and there's a lot yet to do. In the next few days we'll sure find out if they have pneumonia on this world.'

She laughed and the laugh developed into a major yawn.

'You're right,' she admitted. 'I'll probably fall over in the night, though. Nothing to lean on here.'

'Ummm-humm,' he half-moaned. 'Can you sleep lying down?'

'I have, once or twice, mostly on the end of drunks,' she replied. 'It's not normal, but if I don't crush my arm, I can. Once we go to sleep we're just about unconscious and unmoving for the night.'

She came up close to him and knelt down, then slowly rolled over on one side, very close to him and facing him.

'Ahhh ...' she sighed. 'I think this is going to work, tonight, at least.'

He looked at her, still half-awake, and thought, Isn't it funny how human she looks like that? Some of her hair had fallen over in front of her face, and, on impulse, he reached over and put it in back of her gently. She smiled and opened her eyes.

'I'm sorry, I didn't mean to wake you,' he whispered.

'That's all right,' she replied softly. 'I wasn't really asleep. Still ache?'

'A little,' he admitted.

'Lie with your back to me,' she told him. 'I'll rub it out.'

He did as instructed and she twisted a little to free her left arm then started a massage that felt so good it hurt.

After a few minutes he asked her if there was something he could do in return, and she had him stroking and rubbing the humanoid part of her back and shoulders. Doing so was awkward, but she seemed satisfied. Finally, he finished and resumed his position on the towels.

'We really ought to get some sleep,' he said quietly. Then, almost as an afterthought, he leaned over and kissed her.

She reached out and pulled him to her, prolonging the embrace. He felt terribly uncomfortable, and, when she finally let him go, he rolled back onto the towels.

'Why did you *really* come with me?' he asked her seriously.

'What I said,' she replied in a half-whisper. 'But, also, I told you I remember. I remember *all* of it. How you gambled to save my life. How you held me up in the Well. And – how you came out of your way to find me. I saw the map.'

'Oh, *hell*,' he said disgustedly. 'This will never work. We're two different kinds of creature, alien to each other.'

'You've been wanting me, though. I could feel it.'

'And you know damned well our bodies don't match. Anything like sex just won't work for us now. So get those ideas out of your head! If that's why you're here, you should go back in the morning!'

'You were the only clean thing I ever ran into in that dirty old world of ours,' she said seriously. 'You're the first person I ever met who *cared*, even though you didn't know me.'

'But it's like a fish falling in love with a cow,' he retorted in a strained, higher-than-normal tone. 'The spirits are there but they happen to come from two different worlds.'

'Love isn't sex,' she replied quietly. 'I, of all people, know that better than anyone. Sex is just a physical act. Loving is caring as much or more about someone else than you do about yourself. Deep down inside you have the kind of feeling for others that I've never really seen before. I think some of it rubbed off. Maybe, through you, I'll face down that fear inside of me and be able to give myself.'

'Oh, *hell!*' Brazil said sourly, turning his back to her.

In the quiet that followed, they both went to sleep.

The centaur was huge, like a statue of the god Zeus come to life, and it mated with the finest stallion. He came out of his cave at the sound of footsteps, then saw who it was and relaxed.

'You're getting careless, Agorix,' the man said to him.

'Just tired,' the centaur replied. 'Tired of running, tired of jumping at every little noise. I think soon I will go into the hills and end it. I'm the last, you know.'

The man nodded gravely. 'I have destroyed the two stuffed ones in Sparta by setting the temple on fire.'

The centaur smiled approvingly. 'When I go, there will be naught but legends to say that we were here. That is for the best.' Suddenly tears flowed from his great, wise eyes. 'We tried to teach them so much! We had so much to offer!' he moaned.

'You were too good for this dirty little world,' the man replied with gentleness and sympathy.

'We came of our own choice,' the centaur replied. 'We failed, but we tried. But it must be even harder on you!'

'I have to stay,' the man said evenly. 'You know that.'

'Don't pity me, then,' the centaur responded sharply. 'Let me, instead, mourn for you.'

Nathan Brazil awoke.

The hot sun was beating down on him, and had he not already been tanned from earlier travels, he would have had a terrible sunburn.

What a crazy dream, he thought. Was it touched off by last night's conversation? Or was it, like so much lately, a true memory? The latter scared him a little, not because the dream was obscure, but because it would explain a lot – and in a most unpleasant direction.

He put it out of his mind, or tried to.

Suddenly he realized that Wu Julee was gone.

He sat up with a start and looked around. There was a large indentation in the grass where she had been, and some divots kicked up where she had gotten up, but no sign of her.

He looked around, noting several things about the landscape.

For one thing, they had been fairly lucky. Although the area around *was* a grassy hill, it sloped down into dank, swampy wetlands not far away. There were odd buildings, like mushrooms, scattered about near the swamp and through it, but no sign of any real activity. He looked back at the border. It was a snowy forest scene that greeted him, but the storm had passed and the sky was quickly becoming as blue there as it was overhead. He walked over to the border, got some snow, and rubbed his face with the cold stuff.

Blinking the sleep from his eyes, he turned back to look for Wu Julee. He spotted her at last, coming back toward him at full gallop.

He turned and packed the towels away in the pack, removing from the clothing pouch a bundle of black cloth. He unfolded it and looked at it. He had had it made in another hex, awfully nonhuman, but it had seemed right when he had tried it on.

The pants fitted, and his feet slipped into shoe-shaped bottoms with fairly tough, leathery soles on the outside. The material was of the stretchy type, and it seemed to adhere to him like a second skin, as did the pullover shirt. He had two of the latter, and chose the one with no sleeves over the other, which had form-fitting gloves.

It works, he thought to himself, and fairly comfortable, too. But it's so form-fitting and so thin I still feel naked. Oh, well, at least it'll keep the sun out.

He wished for sunglasses, not for the first time. But the first group he had hit who made them were the Dillians, and the smallest was a bit too large for him.

Wu Julee came up to him at that point, looking excited.

'Nathan!' she called, 'I've been out exploring and you'll never guess what's over the next hill!'

'The Emerald City,' he retorted, even though he knew that expression would draw a blank look. In fact, it went right past her.

'No! It's a road! A *paved* road! And it has cars on it!'

He looked puzzled. 'Cars? This close to the border? What kind of cars?'

'Electric ones, I think,' she replied. 'They don't go all that fast, and there aren't many of them, but there they are. There's a little parking lot up by the border. The Dillian roadhouse is a hundred meters or so farther on!'

'So we did miss it in the storm and got off the track!' he said. 'They must supply the roadhouse with various things, and use the roadhouse as a business base. Funny you never heard of them.'

'I've been uplake all my time here,' she reminded him. 'The only others I ever heard about were the mountain people, and I never saw any of them.'

'Well, what do these people look like?' he asked curiously. 'We'll have to travel through most of their hex.'

'They're the strangest – well, you'll have to see. Let's get going!'

He strapped the pack on her and climbed aboard. She seemed particularly happy and eager and, well, *alive* this morning, he thought.

They moved along at a fast clip, and the old pains came back almost immediately, although he was getting to the point where he was going up when she was and down when she did. It helped a little, but not much.

They cleared the top of the hill in about five minutes, and he saw immediately what she meant. A half-dozen vehicles were parked in a little paved area near the border. They were mostly open, except for one with a roof of canvas or something like it. None of them had seats, and, from the looks of the one with the top, their drivers were very tall and drove by a two-lever combination. The road was wide enough for one car to pass another, and it had a white line painted down the center of the black surface.

She stopped near the lot. 'Look!' she said. 'Now you'll see what I mean by weird people!'

And she was most definitely right, Brazil decided. The last time he had seen anything remotely resembling it was on a long-ago, month-long bender.

Imagine an elephant's head, floppy ears and all, but no tusks, with not one but *two* trunks growing from its face, each about a meter long and ending in four stubby, jointless fingers grouped around the nostril opening. Mount the head on a body that looked too thin to support such a head, armless and terminating in two short, squat, legs and flat feet that made the walker look as if he were slightly turning from side to side as he walked. Now paint the whole creature a fiery red, and imagine it wearing green canvas dungarees.

Nathan Brazil and Wu Julee didn't have to imagine it. That was exactly what was walking at a slow pace toward them.

'Oh, wow!' was all he could manage. 'I see just what you mean.'

The creature spotted them and raised its trunks, which seemed to grow out of the same point between and just below the eyes, in a greeting. 'Well, hello!' it boomed in Dillian in a voice that sounded like an injured foghorn. 'Better weather on this side of the line, hey?'

'You can say that again,' Brazil responded. 'We almost got caught in the storm and missed the roadhouse. Spent the night over in the field, there.'

'Heading out, then?' the Slongornian asked pleasantly. 'Going to tour our lovely country? Good time of year for it. Always summer here.'

'Just passing through,' replied Brazil casually. 'We're on our way to Czill.'

The friendly creature frowned, which gave it an even more comical aspect that was hard to ignore. 'Bad business, that. Read about it last night.'

'I know,' Nathan replied seriously. 'One of the victims – the Czillian – was a friend of mine. Ours,' he quickly corrected, and Wu Julee smiled.

'Why don't you go into the roadhouse, have breakfast, and try to bum a ride through?' the creature suggested helpfully. 'All of these trucks'll be going back empty, and you can probably hitchhike most of the way. Save time and sore feet.'

'Thanks, we'll try it,' Brazil called after the Slongornian as that worthy climbed into the covered truck and started backing it out, controlling the steering with a trunk on each lever. The truck made a whirring noise but little else, and sped off down the road at a pretty good clip.

'You know, I bet he's doing fifty flat out,' he said to Wu Julee as the truck disappeared from view. 'Maybe we can move faster and easier than we figured.'

They walked over the border to the incongruously snow-clad roadhouse. The cold hit them at once, Wu Julee being unclad except for the pack, and his clothing not much more than protection from the sun. They ran to the roadhouse, and she was inside almost a minute ahead of him.

Five Slongornians stood at a counter shoving what appeared to be hay down their throats with their trunks. One drained a mug of warm liquid somewhat like tea and then squirted it into its mouth. The innkeeper was a middle-aged female Dillian who looked older than her years. Two young male centaurs were sorting boxes in the back, apparently arranging the deliveries the Slongornians had made.

And there was one other.

It's a giant man-sized bat! Brazil thought, and that is what it did look like. It was taller than he was by a little bit, and had a ratty head and body with blood-red eyes; its sharp teeth were chewing on a huge loaf of sweetbread. Its arms were slightly outstretched and they melded into the leathery wings, the bones extended to form the structural support for the wings. It had long, humanoid legs, though, with a standard knee covered in wiry black hair like gorillas' legs, and ending in two feet that looked more like large human hands, the backs covered with fur. The thing was obviously double-or triple-jointed in the legs, since it was balanced on one with no apparent effort while holding the loaf in the other, the leg brought up level with the mouth.

The creature seemed to ignore them, and no one else in the place seemed to pay any attention. They turned and ordered breakfast, a thick porridge in a huge bowl served steaming hot with wooden spoons stuck in the stuff. Wu Julee just ordered water with it, while Nathan tried the pitch-black tea. It tasted incredibly strong and bitter, and had an odd aftertaste, but he had found from the days he had spent in Dillia that the tea woke him up and got his motor started.

It didn't take long for one of the Slongornian truck drivers to strike up a conversation. They seemed to be an extraordinarily friendly and outgoing people, and when curious about this strange-looking one in their midst felt no hesitancy in starting things off. Between comments about the weather, the porridge, and the hard and thankless life of truck drivers, Brazil managed to explain where he was going and as much of his reason as he had told the one in the parking lot.

They sympathized and one offered to take them the nineteen kilometers to his base in the nearest Slongornian city, assuring them that they could prob-ably hitch rides from terminal to terminal across the country.

'Well, Wu Julee, no exercise and no aches today,' Nathan beamed.

'That's nice,' she approved. 'But, Nathan – don't call me by that name any-more. It's somebody else's name – somebody I'd rather not remember. Just call me Wuju. That's Jol's nickname, and it's more my own.'

'All right,' he laughed. 'Wuju it is.'

'I like the way you say it,' she said softly. He reflected to himself that he didn't feel comfortable with the way *she* had said *that*.

'Excuse me,' said a sharp, nasal, but crystal-clear voice behind them, 'but I couldn't help overhearing you on your travel plans, and I wondered if I could tag along? I'm going in the same direction for a while.'

They both turned, and, as Brazil expected, it was the bat.

'Well, I don't know …' he replied, glancing at the willing truck driver who cocked his head in an unmistakable why-the-hell-not attitude.

'Looks like it's all right with the driver, so it's all right with us, ah – what's your name? You've already heard ours.'

The bat laughed. 'My name is impossible. The translator won't handle it, since it's not only a sound only we can make but entirely in the frequencies beyond most hearing.' The creature wiggled his enormous bat ears. 'My hearing has to be acute, since, though I have incredible night vision, I'm almost blind in any strong light. I depend on my hearing to get around in the day. As for a name, why not call me Cousin Bat? Everyone else does.'

Brazil smiled. 'Well, Cousin Bat, it looks as if you're along for the ride. But why not just fly it? Injured?'

'No,' Cousin Bat replied, 'but this cold's done me no good, and I've traveled quite a distance. Frankly, I'm extremely tired and sore and would just as soon let machines do the work instead of muscle.'

The bat went over to settle his bill, paying in some kind of currency that Brazil guessed was valid in Slongorn, which would be used to pay for the supplies.

He felt a sudden, hard pressure on his arm, and turned. It was Wu Julee – Wuju, he corrected himself.

'I don't like that character at all,' she whispered in his ear. 'I don't think he can be trusted.'

'Don't be prejudiced,' he chided her. 'Maybe he feels uncomfortable around horses and elephants. Did you have bats on your home world?'

'Yes,' she admitted. 'They were brought in years ago to help control some native bugs. They did, but they were worse than the bugs.'

Brazil shook his head knowingly. 'I thought so. Well, we'll meet some even more unpleasant characters along the way, and he seems straight enough. We'll find out. If he's honest, he'll be a great night guard and navigator.'

She resigned herself, and the matter was settled for the moment.

Actually, Brazil had an ulterior motive. With Cousin Bat around, there was less likelihood of the emotions of the night before getting aired or strengthened, he thought.

The ride was uneventful. Cousin Bat took the floor next to the Slongornian driver and promptly went to sleep, while Wuju and Brazil sat in the rear bed, the only place she could fit.

The Slongornian city was modern enough to have traffic jams as well as signals and police. Had it not been for the mushroom-shaped buildings and the total incongruity of the inhabitants, it would have been very comfortable. They waited there for two hours before another truck going in their direction was sufficiently empty to fit Wuju in the back, and even then she was uncomfortably cramped. Still, it was faster than her own speed.

Shortly after nightfall, they were more than halfway across the hex. Cousin Bat was wide awake by this time. Since there were no inns that could accommodate someone of Wuju's size and build, they made camp in the field of a friendly farmer.

The bat had looked like a cartoon version of a villain by day, but in the dark he took on a threatening aspect, his red eyes glowing menacingly, reflecting any light.

'You going to fly on now, Cousin Bat?' Brazil asked after they were settled.

'I will fly for a while,' the creature replied, 'partly for the exercise, and partly because there are some small rodents and insects roaming about here. I am sick and tired of wheat cakes and the like. My constitution is not constructed for such fare. However, Murithel, which is the next hex, is a bit nasty I'm told. I'll stick with you to Czill, if you'll have me.'

Brazil assured him he would, and the bat leaped up into the evening sky with a flurry of leathery wings and vanished.

'I still don't like him,' Wuju insisted. 'He gives me the creeps.'

'You'll have to get used to him,' he told her. 'At least, until I find out what his game is.'

'What?' she yelped.

'Oh, he's a phony, all right,' Brazil said. 'Remember, in the old life I was nothing much but a truck driver like these folks here. I was even delivering grain. Truck drivers see a little of everybody and everything, know isolated facts about all sorts of things from the people they run into. They knew where our flying companion's home hex was. It's nine hexes north-northwest of here – almost exactly the opposite direction to the way we're going, at least the wrong point on a V.'

'Now who's getting nervous?' she retorted. 'He could be going someplace on business. He certainly hasn't told us much about what he does.'

'I know what he does,' Brazil replied evenly. 'One of the other drivers saw him flying south, toward Dillia, two days ago.'

'So?'

'He was coming to meet us, Wuju. He stayed at that roadhouse knowing we'd have to come that way to get to Czill. He almost missed us in the storm, but we managed to blunder into him anyway.'

'Then let's get away, Nathan. Now. He might – kill us, or kidnap us, or something.'

'No,' he said thoughtfully.. 'Nobody goes that far out of his way to kill somebody. You just hire it done and that's that. If it's kidnap, it's the same gang that got Vardia and Skander, and if we joined it would solve one of my problems. But I smell something different here – I don't think he's one of their side, whoever they are.'

'Then he's on our side?' she asked, trusting his judgment.

Nathan Brazil turned over on his towels and yawned. 'Baby, you better remember now that the only side anybody's ever on is his own.'

He slept far better than she that night.

Cousin Bat, looking tired, woke them up in the morning, but it was hours before they got a ride, and they made poor time. Brazil was plainly worried.

'I'd hoped to get to the border before nightfall,' he told them, 'so we could see what was what tomorrow. Now, we won't get there until midday, and not really in until nightfall.'

'That suits me,' the bat replied. 'And both of you can make do in the dark. I suggest we make the border, look over the terrain, but not enter until darkness falls. Better to keep to the dark for movements.'

Brazil nodded approval. 'Yeah. At least that'll put the Murnies on the same footing, and with your eyes we ought to be able to even out the odds.'

Wuju looked alarmed. 'What are the Murnies?' she asked.

'I see we've got the same information,' Cousin Bat said. 'The Murnies are the folk of Murithel, of which we have over three hundred kilometers to traverse. They are a nasty bunch of carnivorous savages that seem to be half-plant and half-animal. They'll try to eat anything that doesn't eat them.'

'Can't we go around them, then?' she asked, appalled at the idea of crossing such a land.

'No,' Cousin Bat replied. 'Not from here. An arm of the ocean comes in to the east, and from what I've heard of the Pia we'll take the Murnies on dry land. To go up the other way we'd go through Dunh'gran, a land of nicely civilized flightless birds, but then we'd have to cut through Tsfrin, where the giant, crablike inhabitants are quite antisocial – not to mention armor-plated – and down in through Alisst, about which I know nothing. Not to mention about fourteen hundred kilometers.'

'He's right, Wuju,' Brazil said. 'We'll have to try to sneak through the Murnies.'

'Any weapons?' Cousin Bat asked.

'I've got a light-pistol,' Brazil told him. 'In the pack, there.'

'No good,' the bat replied. 'Nontechnological hex. Those great weapons are never any use where you need them.'

Brazil rooted around in the pack and pulled out a gleaming short sword. Looking at Wu Julee, he asked, 'Remember this?'

'It's that Com girl's!' she exclaimed. 'So that's what that damned thing was that kept hitting me on the side! How in the world did you wind up with it?'

'It was left in Serge's office at Zone,' he reminded her. 'I went back there a few days after arriving in my home hex. I found the Zone Gate, dodged Ambreza guards, and jumped in, managing to get word to Ortega before those giant beavers made me into a domesticated pet. Old Serge gave it to me. Said it might come in handy. Ever used one?'

She looked at it strangely. 'I – I don't think I've ever even killed a bug. I don't know if I could.'

'Well, you'll have to find out now,' he told her. 'Your arm muscles and speed make it a better weapon for you than for me.'

'What will you use, then?' she asked.

'Five thousand safety matches and a can of flammable grease,' he replied cryptically. 'You'll see. What about you, Cousin Bat?'

'Carrying a weapon would keep me off-balance, but I can always pick and drop rocks,' the creature replied. 'Besides, my teeth and my airborne punch are extremely effective.'

'Okay, then,' Brazil nodded, reasonably satisfied. 'We're as good as we're gonna get. Remember, our *best* hope is no fight at all – to sneak through and that's that.'

Wuju took the sword and tried a few awkward thrusts. She didn't look sure or confident. 'What – what do I aim at if I have to use it?' she asked uncertainly.

'The head's always the best,' Cousin Bat told her. 'Even if it isn't the brain, at least it's the eyes, nose – things that matter. A second choice is the genitals, if any.'

No roads led to the Murithel border, and they had to walk the last several kilometers in the dark.

'We'll stay on this side through tomorrow,' Brazil said tensely. 'Then, near sundown, we'll go.'

They spent the night talking, except for an hour or so when Cousin Bat left for his nightly feeding. Brazil tried to keep Wuju awake most of the night, so they would sleep the following day, but well before the night was half over she had succumbed.

He decided to let her sleep, and spent the earlier hours talking to the bat. The creature was easy to talk to, but gave little useful information and rather glib lies.

Brazil resisted the temptation several times to come right out and ask Cousin Bat who he really was and what he wanted, but never quite got to the point of doing so.

Both finally were asleep by morning.

Wuju was up first, of course, but she didn't stray far from them. Brazil slept until almost midday, and Bat finally had to be awakened later on when he showed every sign of sleeping until dark.

Murithel was clearly visible from their camp. It didn't look very menacing; in fact, it looked beautiful.

Brazil had one of those uneasy memories again. He remembered a place long vanished and forgotten. He'd been standing on a barren hill overlooking some rough but scenic landscape. A couple of thousand meters from that hill ran a line of trees lending color to the landscape. What he could see of Murithel reminded him of that long ago day, and gave him the same feelings, for the river that had fed those trees was something called the Little Bighorn, and a few years before he had seen it, others had as well. He bet that that landscape had looked as quiet and peaceful as this one did to that general who came into primitive territory.

How many Indians are behind those rocks and trees? he asked himself.

The landscape was formed of low, rocky mountains and rolling hills, some made up of bright orange rock eroded into strange and eerie patterns. Others were more a dull pink, with clumps of trees here and there and grass on the tougher portions. A line of trees betrayed a small river or stream off to their left. The sky was cloudy and the sun reflected strange shadows off the landscape.

'I think it's beautiful,' Wuju said. 'But it looks so *strange*. Even the sky seems to be a lighter blue, with yellows and greens in it. But it's so rough and rugged – how will we know that we're going the right way?'

'No problem on a clear night,' Brazil replied. 'Just head toward the big, bluish-orange nebula. Looks as if it's clouding up in there, though.'

'I agree,' the bat put in, concern in his voice. 'We might have some rain. Bad for navigation, bad for flying if need be. It'll slow us down.'

'But it'll also keep the Murnies down,' Brazil pointed out. 'If we get rain, we keep going as long as it's possible. The Slongornians say that that low pinkish range of hills with the little bit of green goes pretty much northeast for almost half the distance. I'd say we get to it and follow it. Looks as if there may be caves and shelters there, too.'

The bat nodded approval. 'I agree. If I were to live in such a place, I'd make my camps and villages along river and stream courses, on the flats but in defensible positions. If we stay away from such places unless absolutely necessary, we might just make it.'

'As close to sunset as possible, I want you to reconnoiter the area from the air,' Brazil told Cousin Bat. 'I want to know as much about what's in there, reasonable paths and the like, before we go.' He went over and pulled the sword out of the pack, and changed his shirt to the long-sleeved one with gloves. With Bat's help, they tore the shirt he had been wearing, twisted and tied it to make a makeshift scabbard fixed around Wuju's neck and draped to one side so all but the hilt was in the shirt.

'That ought to hold,' he said with satisfaction, 'if the sword doesn't tear through the material and if you remember to hold the cloth when taking out the sword.' Next he removed a small, battered tin and took out something that looked like oily grease.

'What's that?' she asked, curious.

'Slongornian cooking fat,' he replied, applying the stuff to his face and neck. 'Something in it is like a dye. Bat's black and you're brown, but my light skin will be a giveaway in close quarters. I want to be able to blend in.'

Satisfied, they settled back to wait for sundown.

THE BARONY OF AZKFRU, AKKAFIAN EMPIRE

Vardia regained consciousness slowly. Even with the aid of what looked like a sunlamp, it was almost half an hour before she could make any movement at all.

The Umiau she knew as Cannot groaned softly. With great effort she turned her head a little and saw that the mermaid was having a similar struggle to regain muscle movement.

'Son of a bitch!' the Umiau swore in Confederacy plain talk.

She would have gasped had she the physical equipment for it. She recognized the dialect at once, though she hadn't heard it since she was in Ortega's office in Zone.

'You – are – from – the – Confederacy,' she managed, the voice sounding strangely distant and fuzzy.

'Of course,' the mermaid growled. 'That's what all this is about. I am Elkinos Skander.'

Vardia stretched and flexed, feeling far surer of herself with every passing moment.

The Umiau stared at her for a moment, a puzzled frown on her face. 'You mean you really haven't any idea about what's going on?'

Vardia shook her head. 'No, nothing.'

Skander was thunderstruck. It simply hadn't occurred to her that anyone hadn't known at least part of the story. 'Look,' she began, 'you're Vardia, right? You came in with that party from Dalgonia?' She nodded, and the mermaid continued. 'Well, I came in a few weeks ahead of you.'

Now it was Vardia's turn to be astonished. 'Then you – it was *your* tracks we followed!'

'Indeed they were!' Skander replied and proceeded to tell her the entire story – the discovery, the opening of the gate, even the murders. Only the point of view had changed on the latter.

'I returned to the camp instead of staying on station,' Skander lied. 'By the time I arrived, this rascal Varnett had already killed them. There was no way out, no chance of holding him off, so I made for the Gate. I hadn't any real idea where it would take me, or if it would kill me; but I was being chased by a madman. I had no choice. When I arrived, the Gate had not yet opened, and Varnett caught me. We struggled – he was much younger, but I was in far better condition – and the Gate opened beneath us.'

He went on and told how they were separated, interrogated for several days, and finally allowed to pass through the same Gate she had gone into. 'I don't know what happened to Varnett,' Skander finished. 'I woke up a Umiau and damned near drowned those first few hours. The Umiau spotted me and I was taken immediately to government Center by two police. They kept me locked up until I normalized, and while there I was apprised of the unique situation here and of my own new situation. When I heard about the Center and the contacts with your people, we decided to strike a bargain – me with my new people, and my people with yours – to solve the problem of this planet once and for all and,' the mermaid concluded, with a strangely fiery look in her eyes like those of a religious fanatic, 'whoever does solve it will control this world at the very least, and perhaps all of them.'

'But none of our people has ever sought power,' she objected.

'*All* people seek power,' Skander replied firmly. 'Few, however, are ever given the opportunity to grab it.'

'I still can't see my people wanting to rule the world or whatever,' she said stubbornly. 'Perhaps yours, but not mine.'

Skander shrugged. 'Your people are a mystery to me, just as mine would be to yours. Maybe they only wanted to add the ultimate knowledge. Maybe they still wouldn't have done it, but for one factor.'

'Which is?' she asked, still unwilling to accept what she was hearing.

'Varnett, of course. He's out there; he has the same formulae I do for contacting the brain, and he's at least as smart, perhaps smarter than myself. We couldn't take the chance. If anyone was to break the final puzzle and control the brain of this world, it would better be the Umiau – and the Czillians, of course,' the scientist added hastily.

'So how did we come to this?' Vardia asked, waving her tentacles around at the barren dirt chamber with its incongruous electrical outlet.

'Because I was stupid,' Skander replied harshly. 'Someone found out who I was – how I don't know. But our ambassador at Zone got a warning that someone was out to kidnap me, and so I cleared out and lay low for several weeks. I relied on the fact that most species can't tell individuals of another species apart. I came back, eventually, using a colleague's name and office, and tried to complete the last few days' work. That's why we were pushing it around the clock. I'd already solved half the puzzle and hoped I could crack the rest. I even had you transferred up – not for what you *were* doing, but because I could talk conversationally to you about the Dalgonian Gate and your own experiences.'

Now she was really puzzled. 'Why would my experiences be any different than yours?'

'Because the Gate should have closed behind us!' Skander exclaimed excitedly. 'We – Varnett and I – opened it when we cracked the code. Our minds opened it. But there's no reason why the thing remained active – if it has. The resupply ship should have been in shortly after you and gone through the same motions – then most of them should have arrived here.'

Vardia thought back, and told about the strange emergency signal.

'Another funny thing. I hadn't really thought about it, but—'

'Go on!' Skander prompted. 'What was it?'

'I – I'd swear that your two ships *vanished* – just weren't there – before the Gate opened.'

The Umiau was suddenly very excited. 'Vanished! Yes, that would explain it! But, tell me, who else was in your party? I glanced at the information but didn't pay much attention at the time.'

'There was a big, ugly fat man, I don't remember his name,' she recalled, straining. It all seemed so long ago. 'He turned out to be a sponge merchant – and he had this girl, Wu something, who was all fouled up on the stuff.'

'No one else? Wasn't there a pilot?'

'Oh, yes, Nathan Brazil. A funny little man no bigger than I was. But old – his pilot's license was pre-Confederacy!'

Suddenly Skander laughed and rocked back against the wall on her long fish's tail, clapping her hands once in amusement.

Vardia didn't understand at all and said so.

'They've kidnapped the wrong person!' the Umiau replied, still chuckling.

'That's very interesting, Dr Skander, but where does that leave us?' came a weird, unearthly yet quiet, voice that seemed to be made up of pulses and chimes, although both kidnap victims understood every word. They both turned, as The Diviner and The Rel glided out of a nook hidden in shadows.

'What the hell are you?' Skander said, more in wonder than in fear.

'We are, I'm afraid, behind your rough treatment and discomfort,' The Rel replied.

'You're not from around Czill,' Vardia observed almost accusingly. 'Nothing like you is related to the kind of life we have here.'

'We are from the Northern Hemisphere,' The Rel explained. 'However, we were obliged, upon learning of Dr Skander's mission through means not worth explaining to you, to forge an alliance. You are in the Akkafian Empire, on the other side of the ocean from Czill.'

'Those big bugs,' Vardia put in. 'The ones that came through the glass – they're not …'

'They are,' The Rel replied. 'I fail to see why that should disturb you. So far we haven't found much difference in any of you Southern races.'

'No difference!' Vardia exclaimed, upset by the comment. 'Why, just look at the two of us! And – how can you compare us to those bugs?'

'Form doesn't matter,' observed The Rel. 'Only content. I find most of your actions and reactions incomprehensible, but consistent. As for those bugs, we'll have one with us for quite some time, I fear. I have arranged it so that we draw only the weakest link in this society, but it takes no deduction to assume that the creature will be incredibly brave and loyal in our defense until that final moment when we are at the controls of the planetary brain. Then, of course, it will kill us all.'

Skander opened her mouth but said nothing. The score was perfectly clear, except The Diviner and The Rel's role and side.

'That's all very well,' Vardia said at last, 'but won't these people think of that?'

'Oh, they will perform what is known as the double cross,' The Rel replied casually in that same, even tone. 'But The Diviner's talents are real. We will make it – all but one of us. We shall do this.'

'Which one?' Skander asked quietly.

'I have no idea, and neither does The Diviner,' replied The Rel. 'Perhaps it's one of you, or the Akkafian. Perhaps it is we, for no Diviner can foretell its own demise.'

They digested that awhile. Finally, Skander broke the new silence.

'You say you're not like us. But here you are, kidnapping me, trying for the same goal as all the other races would if they had the chance. Power is still the name of the game.'

'You misunderstand us,' The Rel said. 'We have power. We have powers we choose not to reveal at this time. We have no wish to interfere in your petty goals, wars, sex, politics, or anything else. Our goal is simply to make certain that no one ever gets into that control center again.'

'Well, so you say,' Skander replied skeptically. 'But the fact remains that, for now, you're our only hope of getting out of here and getting away from the bugs.'

'Remember that!' The Rel said. 'I am your only protection. And – oh, yes, for some additional measure of protection, I would suggest that Czillian Vardia change its name for the entire expedition, and that you both remember to use that different name. I will make certain that our companion does not know your identity, either.'

'But why?' Vardia asked, particularly puzzled now. 'Who is this companion.'

'A greatly changed and mentally preconditioned Datham Hain, the fat man of your party,' The Rel told her. 'It would be better if it did not know that one of our party knows everything about its past activities. Although a conditioned slave, deep down Hain is still Hain. I suggest you remember what it did to others before, what kind of person it is.'

'Oh,' was all she could manage. She thought for a moment. 'Then I'll call myself Chon, which is a common name in Czill, and easy to remember and respond to.'

'Very good,' The Rel replied. 'Remember it. We will leave as soon as possible. In the meantime, may I remind you of several facts. First, let me point out, Dr Skander, that there is little water in this land. These people can move on the ground at close to ten kilometers per hour, up to twice that in the air; and they have nasty stingers. As for you, Czillian, move out of the sunlight and you'll root. You know that. That lamp is all that keeps you awake. The light here is not intense enough on its own to keep you awake.' And with that it glided out the door.

Skander beat her fist on the hard ground, and Vardia stayed still, but the message had been received and understood.

There was no escape.

MURITHEL – ONE HOUR FROM DAWN

Wuju had some trouble with the uneven, rocky ground, but they had managed to advance more than forty kilometers into the hex without meeting any of its dominant life form.

There was a flutter of wings and Cousin Bat landed just ahead of them. 'There's a fairly good cave with rock cover a little farther up,' the dark one whispered. 'It's a good place to make camp. There's a small tribe of Murnies over on the other side of those trees, there, but they look like a hunting party, likely to stay on the plains and river basin.'

Brazil and Wuju looked where the bat pointed, but could see nothing but pitch darkness.

Cousin Bat led the way up to the cave. It was already getting light when they approached it, and they lost no time at all in getting in. It was a good location, high up on the cliff atop some ancient rock slide. They could see for kilometers but, thanks to the shape of the rocks and boulders around the cave, could not be seen from the plain below. It was damp and had a small family of tiny, toadlike reptiles living there, but these were quickly chased. It wasn't all that deep a cave, but it would hide the three of them.

'I'll take the first watch,' Brazil said. 'Wuju's dead tired now, and you, Bat, have been flying around half the night. All I've been doing is riding.'

They agreed, and he assured them he would call Wuju when he was too tired to carry on.

Brazil took a comfortable perch near the cave mouth and watched the sun rise.

Still light-headed over this air, he thought. It was obviously quite different in composition from what he was used to, although he had been through worse getting to Dillia from his own ill-fated Hex 41. Much richer in oxygen, lower in nitrogen, he decided. Well, the other two had gotten used to it and he would, too, in time.

The air was cool and crisp but not uncomfortable. Probably eighteen degrees Celsius, he thought, with high humidity. The threatened rainstorm still looked threatening, but hadn't materialized yet.

The sun was well over the distant mountains when he saw his first Murnies. There they were – a small bunch, less than a dozen, running with spears after a deer-like creature. They were over two meters high, he guessed, although it was hard to figure at a distance. They were almost rectangular, a uniform light green in color, very thin – incredibly so, for he almost lost ones that turned sideways. They were kind of lumpy, looking at the distance something like light-green painted bushes. Two arms, two legs – but they melted into a solid when one stood straight and still.

He was amazed that he could see some features from this far away. Their big yellow eyes must be larger than dinner plates, he thought, and those mouths – huge, they seemed to go completely across the body, exposing a reddish color when they were opened wide. And they had teeth – even from here he could see they were pointed daggers of white of a size to fit those mouths.

They were sloppy hunters, but eventually they cornered the brownish deer-thing, surrounded it, and speared it to death.

Don't they ever throw the spears? he wondered. Maybe those thin, wide arms couldn't get enough strength or balance.

As soon as the creature fell, they pounced upon it, ripping pieces of it and shoving it into their mouths, fighting each other to get extra bites. Those hands must have pretty good claws to tear like that, he thought.

In just a few minutes, they had finished off the entire deer-thing, which must have weighed at least 150 kilos, he guessed. They even ate the bones. When they finally picked up their spears and went off down the plains, there was no sign of the prey they had eaten except a torn-up patch of dirt and grass.

Seven days, he thought. At the rate we're going, seven days in *their* country. And that's if everything goes *right*. And there's bound to be lots more of them, a lot thicker group.

No problem alone, of course. Even easier with Cousin Bat, whoever he worked for.

Why the hell did I allow her to come along?

Why had he?

That act of courage in taking off her pressure helmet in Zone? Was that what he liked in her, deep down?

Pity, maybe. Certainly that had motivated him at the start.

Thinking back, he kept remembering how she had clung to him in Zone, looked to him for support, defying Hain even that close to the end.

What was love, anyway? he mused. She said it was *caring*, caring more about someone else than about yourself.

He leaned forward and thought a minute. Did he *really*, deep down, care if the Murnies got the bat? He realized he wouldn't shed a tear for the creature. Just one more in a long list of dead associations. Was he going to Czill because Vardia was kidnapped? No, he decided, luck of the draw, really. He was going to Czill because it was the only lead he had to Skander, and that project was – well, wasn't that caring?

What's it to me if Skander takes over and remolds the universe in his own crazy image? He had met a lot of nice people, happy people, old friends and new acquaintances, in his long life and here on the Well World. He cared about them, somehow, even though he knew deep down that, in a pinch, they probably wouldn't do the same for him. Maybe it's for that unknown one who would, he thought. Nathan Brazil, ever the optimist.

Had anybody ever cared?

He thought back, idly watching a much larger group of Murnies chasing a fair-sized herd of the deer-things. How many times had he been married, legally or socially? Twenty times? Thirty? Fifty? More?

More, he thought wonderingly. About every century. Some had been nice lookers, some real dogs. Two of them had even been men. Had any of them really *cared* about him?

Not one, he thought bitterly. Not one, deep down in their selfish little hearts. Lovers, hell. The only friends who hadn't betrayed him in some manner or the other were those who hadn't had the chance.

Would he really care if the Murnies ate *him?*

Just tired, the centaur had said. *Tired of running, tired of jumping at every little noise.*

I'm tired, too, he thought. Tired of running nowhere, tired of that tiny belief, often foresworn, that somewhere, somewhere, was someone who would *care*.

If all that were true, why *did* he care about the Murnies? Why did he feel fear?

The wild ports, the happy drugs, the whores and dives, the endless hours alone on the bridge.

Why have I lived so long? he asked himself. Not aging wasn't enough. Most people didn't die of old age, anyway. Something else got them first.

Not him.

He had always survived. Banged up, bleeding, nearly dead thousands of times, and yet something in him would not let him die.

He remembered the Flying Dutchman suddenly, sailing the world's oceans with a ghost crew, alone but for one short leave every fifty years, doomed until a beautiful woman would love him so much that she would give up her life for him.

Who commands the Dutchman? he asked the winds.

Who curses him to his fate?

It's psychology, he thought. The Dutchman, Diogenes – I'm all these people. It's why I'm different.

All those millions over the centuries who killed themselves when nobody cared. Not me, I'm cursed. I can't accept the universality of shallow self-interest.

That fellow from – what was the name of that country? England. Yes, England. Orwell. Wrote a book that said that a totalitarian society sustains itself by the basic selfishness of everybody. When the chips were down, his hero and heroine betrayed each other.

Everybody thought he was talking of the fears of a future totalitarian state, Brazil thought bitterly. He wasn't. He was talking about the people around him, in his own enlightened society.

You were too good for this dirty little world, he had said, but he had stayed. Why? In failure?

Whose failure? he wondered, suddenly puzzled. He almost had the answer, but it slipped away.

There was movement in back of him and he jumped and jerked around.

Wuju came up to him slowly. He looked at her curiously, as if he had never seen her before. A chocolate brown girl with pointy ears welded to the working half of a brown Shetland pony. And yet it worked, he thought. Centaurs always looked somehow noble and beautiful.

'You should have called one of us,' she said softly. 'The sun's almost straight up. I thought you were asleep.'

'No,' he replied lazily. 'Just thinking.' He turned back to gaze over the valley, now seemingly swarming with Murnies and deer-things.

'About what?' she asked casually, starting to massage his neck and shoulders.

'Things I don't like to think about,' he replied cryptically. 'Things I hid away in little corners of my mind so they wouldn't bother me, although, like all ghosts, they haunt me even when I don't know it.'

She leaned over and kissed him on the cheek. 'I do love you, Nathan,' she whispered.

He got up and walked toward the back of the cave, patting her gently on her equine rump as he did so. There was a puzzled half-smile on his face, and he said, as he stretched out near Cousin Bat, in a voice so low it was really to himself, 'Do you, Wuju? Do you, really?'

THE BARONY OF AZKFRU, AKKAFIAN EMPIRE

The baron was, if anything, more majestic than before, and Datham Hain was at her lowest ebb, at the brink of suicide from weeks now in the dung pits.

'You have your name back, now, Mar Hain,' the baron pronounced in that godlike tone he had.

That was a small gesture, yet to Hain it was as momentous as being crowned supreme ruler of the galaxy, for it restored a measure of her self-respect. It also bound the Entry all the more to the baron, from whom all blessings flowed.

'I have now a task for you, of the utmost difficulty,' the baron told her. 'It will require loyalty and devotion, as well as all of your intelligence and cunning. If you fail me, you are lost forever; if you succeed, you shall sit beside me in an honored place as chief concubine of, not your baron, but at the very least the emperor, perhaps not only of this empire.'

'You have but to instruct this humble slave and I will obey though there be no reward and the cost be my life,' Hain groveled.

I'll bet, the baron thought sarcastically. Once more he regretted having to trust such a one as this on so important a mission. Blast that Northerner! Yet, The Diviner had so far been a hundred percent correct on everything, and he dared not go against the creature, at least not until the final moments.

'Listen well, Mar Hain,' the baron said carefully. 'Soon you will meet three aliens. You will have a translation device implanted so that you can follow all conversations. Also, two of them are Entries, and may be able to communicate in the nontranslatable tongue of your old life – so it is better if you feign both ignorance and stupidity whenever possible.

'You will be going on a great journey together. Now, here is what you are to do ...'

'Those filthy bugs!' Vardia, now calling herself Chon, exclaimed as they set her down on a road with the others and flew off, making irritating buzzing noises as they did so.

'Let's have no racial slurs,' Hain said sternly. 'They think even less of you, and they are my people.'

'Come on, you two, cut it out!' Skander snapped. Unable to walk, they had built a saddle which left the mermaid perched only mildly comfortable atop Hain's back. 'We have a long and probably difficult journey ahead of us. Our lives may depend on each other, and I don't want all this carping!'

'Quite so,' The Rel agreed. 'Please remember, you two, that although you were kidnapped, we all have a common goal. Save all disputes for the time we reach our goal, not during the journey.'

They were at the imperial border, manned by bored sentries. The change in the landscape was tremendous. The arid, hilly, pinkish-gray land of the Akkafians ended abruptly as if there were some physical barrier, perfectly straight, stretching from horizon to horizon.

'All of you put on your respirators,' The Rel instructed, needing none for itself. They still didn't know if it breathed. Hain's was bulky, the great insect looking as if she were wearing some sort of giant, distorted earmuffs behind her eyes. Vardia's hung on a strap around her neck and was attached to her lower legs by two cables ending in needles which were inserted in her skin. Skander's was a simple mask over mouth and nose, with tubes leading to a tank also on Hain's back. Vardia's alone contained not an oxygen mixture but pure carbon dioxide. There was a mechanism by which the waste contents in her canister could be exchanged with those of Skander and Hain.

The hex they faced was bleak enough; the sky showed not the various shades of blue common to much of the world, but an almost irritatingly bright yellow.

'Sound will travel, but slowly and with great distortion,' The Rel told them.. 'The atmosphere has enough trace elements to allow us to get by with such simple devices, but that is mostly due to seepage – the other hexes surrounding it naturally leak a little. We will be able to refresh our tanks from supplies along the way, but under no circumstances remove your masks! There are elements all about which will not harm your exteriors but will, nonetheless, cause physical problems or even death if taken in great quantities in the lungs for any period of time.'

Vardia looked out over as much of the landscape as the glare permitted her to see. A very jagged, burnt-orange landscape, filled with canyons and strange, eroded arches and pillars. What erodes them? she wondered idly. And what sort of creatures could live in such a hostile place? Carbon-based life? All the South was supposed to be, yet there could be nothing carbon-based about anything able to stand such a place..

'Hain,' The Rel instructed, 'remember to keep your beak tightly shut at all times. You don't want to swallow the stuff. And, Skander, keep that blanket tightly on your lower parts and you'll get and retain enough moisture to keep you from drying up. The respirator's been designed that way. All set? Then, any last-second questions?'

'Yes, I have a couple,' Vardia said nervously. 'What sort of creatures will we meet, and how will we possibly cross this place and survive?'

'The creatures are basically autonomatons, thinking machines,' The Rel replied. 'This is a high-technological hex; more so, in fact, than the one we've been in. The only reason they coexist is that the Akkafians couldn't exist here for very long, nor is there anything of use to them in The Nation, while the people of this hex would break down in an atmosphere more conducive to your form of life. Come! We've wasted enough time! You'll see how we survive as we go along.'

With that The Diviner and The Rel floated quickly across the border. Vardia, a helpless feeling inside her, followed; and Hain and Skander brought up the rear.

Skander and Vardia both had the same impression: as if they were suddenly in an environment of kerosene. The odor permeated their bodies and penetrated their breathing. The atmosphere also felt heavy, almost liquid; and, while invisible, it rippled against their bodies like a liquid, even though it was plainly a gas. Moreover, it burned slightly, like a strong alcohol. It took them awhile to get used to it.

The Rel paced them at close to Vardia's maximum stride; Hain followed at the same pace, between eight and ten kilometers per hour. In less than an hour they came upon a paved road, although the paving stone looked like a single long ribbon of smoothly polished jade. And, as with most roads and trails in the various hexes, this one contained traffic.

The first thought they all had was that no two denizens of The Nation were alike. There were tall ones, thick ones, thin ones, short ones, even long ones. They moved on wheels, treads, two, four, six, and eight legs, and they had every imaginable type of appendage and some not very imaginable as to purpose. Although all obviously machines of dull-silver metal, all looked as if they had been fashioned in a single stroke. No bolts, joints, or any other such were visible; they bent and flexed the metal like skin, and in any way they wanted.

Vardia understood and marveled at this.

Each one was made for a single purpose, to fulfill a single need of the society. It was built to order to do a job, and this it did where and when needed. It was, she thought, the most practical of all the societies she had seen, the perfection of social order and utilitarianism – a blend of the best of the Comworlds' concepts with the lack of physical dependencies of the Czillians.

She only wished she understood what the people of The Nation were doing.

There were structures, certainly, more and more of them as they went on. Some were recognizable as buildings, although as varied and oddly shaped as the inhabitants of this strange land. Other structures seemed to be skeletal, or spires, twisted shapes of metal, and even apparently girders of some sort arranged in certain deliberate but baffling ways. Functionally built workmen rushed to and fro. Some were building, of course, but many seemed to be digging holes and filling them up again, while others carried piles of sand from one point and dumped them to form new piles of sand elsewhere. None of it made sense.

They continued to follow The Diviner and The Rel. They went on through this landscape for hours without stopping and without any of the creatures taking the slightest notice of them. More than once, in fact, both Hain and Vardia had had to move out of the way quickly to avoid being run over by some creature or by the creature's load.

They came upon a building that seemed to be made of the same stuff as the creatures themselves, but was shaped something like a large barn. The Diviner and The Rel surprised them by turning in at the building's walkway. It waited until they were all at the rather large sliding doorway, then glided up to a very large button, then back, up again, and back again.

'Do you wish me to push it?' Vardia asked. The response sounded like garbled nonsense to her own ears. The Rel jumped up and down, and The Diviner's lights blinked more agitatedly, and so Vardia pushed the button. The door slid aside with entirely the wrong sounds, and the strange creature that led them glided inside. They followed and found themselves in a very large but barren chamber. Suddenly the door slid shut behind them, and they were in total darkness, illuminated only by the oddly non-illuminating blinks of The Diviner.

They had gotten so used to the strange sensations produced by the atmosphere of the place that the gradual absence of them was almost as harsh as their original exposure to them.

There were whirring, clicking, and whooshing noises all around them, going on for what seemed to be several minutes. Then, finally, an inner door slid open to reveal another large barren chamber, this one lit by some kind of indirect lamps in the ceiling. They went in.

'You may remove your breathing apparatuses now,' The Rel told them clearly. 'Skander, will you pull Mar Hain's up and off? Thank you. Now, Hain, can you gently – gently – remove the two tubes from Citizen Chon's legs? Yes, that's right.'

They all breathed in fresh air. It was stuffy, weak, and slightly uncomfortable to Vardia; to the others, it was exhilarating.

'You'll be all right in a little while, Citizen Chon,' The Rel assured her. 'The atmosphere is mostly pure oxygen, with just a trace of carbon dioxide. This will be added, both from our companions and artificially, in a little while.'

There was another hissing sound, and one of the metallic creatures came out of a side door that had been almost invisible in the back wall. It was humanoid, about the same height as Vardia's 150 centimetres, and was featureless except for a triangular screen on the head.

'I trust all is satisfactory?' it said, in a voice pleasantly and unexpectedly filled with human tonality. It sounded, in fact, like an eager, middle-aged hotel clerk, far more human than The Rel's monotone.

'The green one, there, the Czillian, is a plant, not an animal,' The Rel told the creature. 'It requires carbon dioxide of at least point five percent. Will you raise the level? It is in much discomfort.'

'Oh, I am so very, very sorry,' the robot replied so sincerely that they almost believed it. 'The matter is being adjusted.'

Just like that Vardia *could* sense a difference, growing with every minute. She found it much easier to breathe, and the feeling that she was going to black out evaporated. Obviously these things were all linked together. The Czillian marveled at their efficiency, quietly envying their unity.

'What environments do you require?' the creature asked.

'Types Twelve, Thirty-one, One Twenty-six, and Thirteen Forty,' The Rel told it. 'Adjoining, with private intercom, please.'

'It is being prepared,' the robot assured them, and bowed slightly.

'What sort of a place *is* this?' Skander asked sharply.

The robot reared back, and Vardia swore that its featureless face had a shocked expression to match the tone of the reply.

'Why, this is a *first-class* transient hotel, of course. What else?'

One at a time they were taken to their rooms by small wheeled robots with place for luggage and the like. They put all their gear in storage, except for the air tanks, which were ordered cleaned and refilled, with particular attention to Vardia's getting the right gas.

Strong hands lifted Skander gently out of the saddle and onto the back of one of the carts. The scientist found herself traveling at high speed down a lighted tunnel, and deposited next to a room with no apparent exterior markings. It opened automatically, and the cart glided inside and stopped.

Skander was amazed. It was a swimming pool, with a dry slope going gently down into blue water which became deeper and deeper as it went toward the back of the room – the pool was perhaps fifteen meters long by about ten wide. In the water, clearly visible, were several small fish of the kind the Umiau liked the most, and clumps of the blue-green seaweed that was the other staple of their diet.

Skander rolled off and happily plunged into the water. It was only about four meters deep at its deepest point, but it felt wonderful.

The little cart left, the door closing behind it. It returned for Hain, who was too large for it. Another cart appeared in seconds, and the two, working in concert, took Hain down the same tunnel to the next door, which was furnished in the *zagrt* fur of the best nobles and was stocked with a nice supply of the juicy white worms.

Next, Vardia was taken to a room that had a rich black soil and good artificial sunlight. The room even had a chain dangling from its center, labeled, in Czillian, *Pull for darkness. All guests awakened in eight hours after darkness pulled or twelve hours after occupancy.* There was a small pool of clear water in the corner, and even a small desk with paper and pen.

She guessed from her own surroundings what the others' must be like, and only wished she could see The Diviner and The Rel's room. That would almost certainly tell more about the mysterious creatures than anything seen so far.

There was a mild crackling sound in their rooms, and then The Rel's odd, toneless voice came to the other three.

'Please enjoy this night at the baron's expense,' it said. 'Tomorrow I shall arrange transportation for us which will take us to the border. We shall not have such pleasant and easy accommodations after this, so enjoy it. After tomorrow, things get tough.'

Vardia took a long drink and then sank her roots into the rich soil that felt incredible, indescribable. With a feeling of total well-being, she turned off the lights.

Skander was the last to sleep, since the Umiau had been cooped up in the saddle harness and was enjoying the freedom of the waters. At last she, too, crawled up the bank and pressed the light switch on the wall.

Each of them slept soundly (except possibly for The Diviner and The Rel, who didn't seem to need it – the others weren't sure), and all were awakened not only by the automatic turning on of the lights but by the voice of The Rel.

The creature conveyed emotion for the first time, not by tone but by the sharp, fast, excited way it spoke. 'Something is terribly wrong!' it told them. 'We are being detained for some technicality! We cannot leave today!'

'Do you mean,' Skander's voice came to all of them in a tone of almost total disbelief, 'that we're under arrest?'

'It would seem so,' replied The Rel. 'I cannot understand it.'

MURITHEL – SOMEWHERE IN THE INTERIOR

'We're in some kind of trouble,' Nathan Brazil said half under his breath.

For three days now they had moved along the rocky mountain ledges, mostly under cover of darkness guided by Cousin Bat's exceptional night vision and inbred sonar. They had passed hundreds, perhaps thousands of the bloodthirsty Murnies, often coming close to their villages in the dark, quietly working around their dulled campfires.

They had been exceptionally lucky, and they knew it. But now they had run out of mountains.

The mountains – hills, really – ended abruptly in a jagged cliff, stretching off at an angle away from the direction they had to go. Ahead, toward the east, flat, unbroken prairie spread out to the horizon.

The land was still dry this time of year, yet yellow grasses topped with pinkish blossoms carpeted the prairie. Also covering the plains were herds of thousands, perhaps tens of thousands, of the antelope that were the Murnies' staple diet.

Murnie camps also dotted the plains, in small groups of three or four skin tents, never more than seven groups in a bunch, arranged in a circle.

Even as Brazil looked at the scene, appreciating their position, something, some wrongness ahead of him, nagged at his mind.

'How the hell are we ever going to get through them?' Wuju asked nervously. 'We can't fight them all, even in the dark.'

'Well, let's camp here for the day,' Cousin Bat suggested, 'and tonight I'll take a trip across and see how far we really have to go to reach cover. Maybe you'll think of something by the time I get back.'

They agreed it was the only thing they could do, so they carved out a niche in the rocky ledge and tried to sleep, first Brazil on guard, then Bat, and finally Wuju. The sequence was almost a routine by now.

Nathan Brazil was dreaming more of his strange dreams when he felt hands gently shaking him. 'Nathan!' Wuju whispered urgently. 'Wake up! It's almost dark!'

He got up and tried to shake the sleep from his eyes. He was dizzy and upset from the small amount of food he had allowed himself from the dwindling supply in the packs. The deprivations were taking their toll on him. Wuju had it almost as bad, since there was precious little grass on the trail for one of her bulk. Yet she had never complained.

They all smelled like concentrated sweat and feces, and Brazil wondered idly if Murnies had good smellers. With no baths for three days and only leaves for toilet paper, he was certain that, in reverse circumstances, he could smell his party five kilometers upwind.

Cousin Bat was already waiting for the sun to sink completely behind them. Brazil went up to him quietly.

'You ready, Bat?' he asked the night creature.

'Not bad,' came the reply. 'The wind's wrong. If that plain's too broad I might have to come down at least once. I don't like that.'

Brazil nodded. 'Well, I want you to land if possible, or at least skim close enough to get me a handful of those weeds.'

'Got something in mind?' the other asked.

'Maybe,' he replied. 'If we're lucky – and if we don't have to run to the border.'

'I'll see what I can do,' the bat replied dryly. 'We've got to clear this bunch in one sweep, you know. Once committed, we'll have no place to hide.'

Brazil looked at the creature strangely. 'You know, I can't quite figure you out,' he said.

'What's to figure?' Bat replied. 'It's my neck, too, you know.'

'Why not just fly over and away? You might not make it all the way in a stretch, but you could pick your own places. Why stick with us?'

The bat gave that ratty smile, exposing those triple rows of sharply pointed little teeth.

'To tell you the truth, I thought about it a number of times, particularly in the last few days. It's extremely tempting – all the more so now – but I can't do it.'

'Why not?' pumped Brazil, puzzled.

The bat thought for a minute. 'Let's just say that, once before, I was in a position to help some people I knew were in danger. I don't want more people on my conscience.'

'We all have our crosses to bear,' Brazil said in an understanding tone. 'Myself more than most.'

'It boils down to more than just conscience, Brazil,' responded Cousin Bat earnestly. 'I've known some other men. They, like me, wanted power, wealth, fame – all the reasons for striving. They'd lie, cheat, steal, torture, even kill, for those. I want these things, too, Brazil, but what more right do I have to them than they? Perhaps, though I don't know for sure, the fact that they would abandon you and I would not makes me superior to them. I'd like to think so.'

And with that, as the last rays of the sun disappeared behind the rocks to the west, Cousin Bat took off into the dark.

A few seconds later, Wuju sidled up behind Brazil. 'What a strange man,' she said wonderingly.

He gave a mirthless chuckle. 'Bat, you mean? He let his guard down more there than I'd expected. It's the most personal thing we've gotten in all these days. But, no, strange is not the correct word for him. Unusual, perhaps, even uncommon. If he was telling the complete truth there, he's also a good friend, a particularly nasty enemy – and, quite possibly, one of the most potentially dangerous men I've yet met on this planet.'

She didn't understand what he was talking about but didn't pursue it, either. Something much more important was on her mind.

'Nathan,' she asked softly, 'are we going to die?'

'I hope not,' he replied lightly, trying to break the mood. 'With luck—'

'The truth, Nathan!' she interrupted. 'What are our chances?'

'Not good,' he responded truthfully. 'But I've been in spots as bad or worse in my long life. I survive, Wuju. I –' His voice broke off abruptly, and he averted his eyes from hers. She understood, and there were small tears in her eyes.

'But the people around you don't,' she finished. 'That's it, isn't it? That's *your* cross. How many times have you been a lone survivor?'

He looked out into the darkness for a minute. Then, without turning, he said, 'I can't count that high, Wuju.'

Cousin Bat returned in a little over an hour. Brazil and Wuju were doing something just inside the shelter, and he was curious.

They looked up from their work as he approached, and Brazil asked the simple but all-important question: 'Well?'

'Five kilometers, give or take,' the bat replied evenly. 'Before you get any farther there's a steep drop to a river valley, mud sides with slow, shallow water. It's barely flowing.'

Brazil seemed to brighten at the news, particularly of the river's speed and shallowness. 'Can we get a straight run, more or less?' he asked.

The bat nodded. 'Once we get down, I'll position you and point you in the right direction. I'll stay over you once you get started to keep you on the right track.'

'Good! Good!' Brazil enthused. 'Now, what about the antelope?'

'Tens of thousands of them,' the other replied. 'Together in big groups. Nothing too near us, though.'

'Excellent! Excellent!' Brazil seemed to get more excited with every word. 'And now the clincher – did you get some of that grass?'

Cousin Bat turned and walked back to where he had landed, picking up a clump of straw with one foot. Holding it, he hobbled back to them and dropped the grass at Brazil's feet.

The man picked it up expectantly, feeling it, even biting it. It was somewhat brittle, and gave a slight snap when it was bent too far.

'Just out of curiosity, what are you doing?' the bat asked.

Brazil reached down into a pouch and removed a small handful of the tiny sticks inside.

'Safety matches,' he explained. 'Haven't you noticed it, or thought about it, you two? Haven't you *seen* out there on the plain?'

They both looked at him with blank expressions. 'I haven't seen anything except antelope, Murnies, and grass,' said Wuju, trying to think.

'No! No!' Brazil responded, shaking his head animatedly. 'Not what you *see!* What you *don't* see! Look out there into the darkness! Tell me what you see.'

'Nothing but pitch darkness,' Wuju said.

'Nothing but sleeping antelope, Murnies, and grass,' Bat said.

'Exactly!' Brazil said excitedly. 'But what you *don't* see, anywhere out there, is something we've seen in every Murnie camp we've passed up to this point.'

They still didn't see it, and he continued after a pause. 'Look, why do the Murnies build campfires? Not to cook their food – they eat it raw, even live. It's because they think this is cold! And to protect themselves from the dog packs at night, of course. It must be very important to them or we wouldn't have seen the campfires so consistently. *But there are no fires out there on the plains!* No dots of light, no sparks of any kind! And the riverbed's wide but slow and shallow is it flowing. You see what it means?'

'I think I do,' Wuju replied hesitantly. 'It's the dry season. Out there on the grasslands, the danger of a brushfire exceeds their fears of the dogs or their desire for warmth.'

'It must be like a tinderbox out there,' Brazil pointed out. 'If they are afraid of any fire at all, it must be so dry that anything will set it off. If the wind's right, we can make things so hot for them down there that the least thing they'll be concerned about is us.'

'Wind's about as right as you can get,' the bat said quietly.

'Okay, then,' Brazil responded. He removed all his clothes, and jumped, stark naked, up on Wuju's back, his back against hers. He pulled the shirt around his chest just under his armpits. 'Take the ends on both sides, Wuju, and tie them tight around you. No! Pull it *tight*, damn it! As tight as you can! Yes, that's better.' Next the stretchy pants were pulled around his waist and tied in front of her. It was several minutes before he was satisfied that he was solidly attached to her, riding backward. Tied just in front of him were the packs, the two pouches full of safety matches within easy reach. Then he applied the rest of the Slongornian cooking fat to as much of his exposed parts as he could. It was a sloppy job, but it would do in the dark.

Cousin Bat nodded approvingly. The two men looked at each other wordlessly, and the bat turned and started down the rocky ledge. Wuju followed, Brazil cursing to himself at his inability to see anything ahead of them, thinking he forgot something, and feeling with every step that he was slipping off even though the knots remained secure.

'Stop!' he yelled suddenly, and everyone froze. 'Your hair, Wuju! Tie it down. Use the scabbard – you have to hold the sword anyway. I don't want to set it on fire or have it blowing in my face.'

She did what he asked silently, draping her hair forward and over her left breast so it wouldn't interfere with the sword in her right hand. Now Brazil was roped in three ways, and he felt as if he were cut in pieces. Which was just the way he wanted it.

They had gone over the plan many times, but he was still nervous. Wuju could sprint at more than thirty-five kilometers per hour, but that was just for short distances. She would have to go all out for over five kilometers, then down into a ditch, and keep running as long as she could.

Cousin Bat took off and circled for what was only a minute but seemed to be an hour. Finally they heard him come up behind them. 'Now!' the flying creature ordered. *'Go!'*

Wuju took off across the plains at full speed.

Brazil watched the grasses disappear behind her and held onto the pack for dear life. He was sitting on a bony place and being bounced around for all he was worth. Although it was a clear night and he had excellent night vision, Brazil already could not see the rocky hills they had left.

Come on, Wuju! he thought tensely to himself. *Keep going!*

'Turn slightly right.' Bat's voice came from somewhere above, and she did as instructed. 'Too much!' She heard the bat's voice, probably just two or three meters above her head: 'That's it! Now straight!'

Brazil panicked as he felt the upper bindings loosen, and he grabbed all the harder on the pack sides. And still she roared ahead at top speed! He could hear her take sobbing breaths and feel her horselike half inhale and exhale mightily, but still they went on.

We're going to make it! he thought excitedly. If I can only hold on to this goddamn pack for a few more minutes, we'll be through them before they realize what happened!

Suddenly the knots from the top two bands broke, sending the elastic clothing into the night and propelling him forward, headfirst, into the pack.

'Nathan!' he heard her call breathlessly at the break and jerk.

'I'm all right!' he called back. 'Keep going!'

Suddenly there were sounds around them, grunts, groans, and yells.

'Nathan!' she screamed. 'They're ahead of us!'

'Run right at them at top speed!' he yelled. 'Slash with your sword!' He grabbed at the matches, struck several against the hard leather straps. They flared, but immediately went out because of the wind caused by her rapid movement.

Suddenly she was heading into them, and they were roaring and clawing at her. She knocked the first several down and found, to her surprise, that the sword seemed to slice into them like butter. Once, twice more, she slashed at them, and they screamed in deep agony and clutched at wounds.

And then she was through them!

'Any ahead?' Brazil yelled.

'Not yet,' came Bat's voice. 'Keep going!'

'There's plenty behind us!' Nathan called. 'Slow down to a gallop so I can get at least one match lit!'

Wuju slowed and he tried again. They stayed lit in his hands, but went out before they hit the ground.

'Brazil!' Bat's voice called urgently. 'A whole bunch of them! Coming up fast to your right!'

Suddenly a group of six or seven came at them out of the grasses. Nathan felt a searing pain in his right leg. One Murnie jumped and hit Wuju's back-side, tearing a deep gash in her just in front of the pack. She screamed, stopped, and reared, slashing out at them with her sword.

Brazil hung on somehow, and tore off one of the pouches of matches with strength that surprised him. He struck one and threw it into the pouch. The matches caught with a *whoomph* and he threw the pack out onto the grass.

Nothing for a minute, and she bolted for the Murnies at an apparent open-ing. They had formed a hunting circle and their spears were ready.

They expected the charge, but their traditional ways didn't allow for their quarry to have a sword, and the formation broke!

Suddenly the whole world caught fire.

The suddenness and volatility was what stunned them all.

My god! Brazil thought suddenly. *It's as if the stuff were made of cellulose!*

He could see Cousin Bat, saw the creature come down on a Murnie and kick with those powerful, handlike feet rolled up as fists. The giant green sav-age went down and didn't move.

The whole world suddenly became bright. Ahead she saw the stream val-ley, like a crack in the land.

The Murnies started running and screaming. The antelope panicked and ran in all directions, trampling many Murnies underfoot to get away.

She jumped into the ravine, and the momentum and steep sides caused her to lose her balance. She went sprawling down the hill. Brazil felt himself suddenly free as he was flung away onto the bank. He was stunned for a min-ute, then he picked himself up and looked around. There was a glow still from the fire above, but down in the valley there was a still, near-absolute darkness.

Feeling numb and dizzy, he ran down the valley in the direction Cousin Bat had said the river flowed. He looked around for Wuju but couldn't see her anywhere.

'Wuju!' he screamed hoarsely. '*Wuju!*' But his voice was no match for the riot of noise above him, the cries of burning animals and panicked Murnies, many of whom were plunging over the bank into the valley.

He ran down the muddy shore and into the river and followed it. The rocky bottom cut his feet. But he was oblivious to pain, running like a scare-crow, mindlessly, aimlessly down the river.

Soon the glow and the sounds were far behind him, but still he pressed on.

Suddenly he tripped and fell facedown in the water. He continued, crawling forward, then somehow picked himself up and started again.

The fetid odor of swamp mud was all around him and all over him, yet he continued. Until, quite abruptly, everything caught up to him and he collapsed, unconscious before he hit the water, stones, and mud.

THE NATION – A FIRST-CLASS HOTEL

They had not, as it happened, been arrested. They had been quarantined. The way the robot manager explained it, an analysis of the particles found in their waste gases had revealed two of them to have certain microscopic life forms that could cause corrosion problems in The Nation. They were, therefore, being held until their laboratories could check out the organisms, develop some sort of serum, and introduce it to them so they could safely get across the country without causing difficulties.

For Hain this was her first real vacation since entering this crazy world, and she lazed, relaxed, and seemed in no hurry to go on.

The Diviner and The Rel accepted the situation indignantly but with resignation; it kept pretty much to itself.

Since their hosts had evacuated the wing in which the four were staying, they were allowed to visit one another. Vardia was the only mobile person who cared to do so; she started going to Skander's room regularly.

The Umiau welcomed the company, but refused to talk about her theories on the Well World or to discuss the object of their journey for fear that other ears were listening.

'Why do we have to go through with this?' Vardia asked the scholar one day.

The Umiau raised her eyebrows in surprise. 'We're still prisoners, you know,' she pointed out.

'But we could tell the management,' the Czillian suggested. 'After all, kidnapping is a crime.'

'It is, indeed,' the mermaid agreed, 'but that is also unheard of cross-hex. The fact is, these people don't *care* if we're prisoners, victims, or monsters. It just isn't their concern. I've tried.'

'Then we must escape once we're back on the road,' she persisted. 'I've already seen a map – it's in a desk in my room. The next hex borders the ocean.'

'That won't work,' Skander replied firmly. 'First of all, we have no idea as to the powers of this Northerner, and I don't want to test them. Secondly, Hain can fly and walk faster than you, and either one of us is just a few good mouthfuls for her. No, put that out of your mind. Besides, we'll not be ill-served in this. In the end, I have the ultimate control over us all, because they can't do a thing without the knowledge I possess. They are taking me where I want to go and could not get myself. No, I think we'll go along with them – until midnight at the Well of Souls,' she added with a devious chuckle.

'That's about how long we'll be kept here,' Vardia said grumpily.

The Umiau reclined lazily in the shallow end of the pool. 'Nothing we can do about this. Meantime, why not tell me something about yourself? You know all about me, really.'

'I really don't have much of a history before coming here,' she responded modestly. 'I was a courier – wiped clean after every mission.'

The mermaid clucked sympathetically. 'But surely,' she urged, 'you know about your world – the world of your birth, that is. For instance, were you born or hatched? Were you male or female? What?'

'I was produced by cloning in Birth Factory Twelve on Nueva Albion,' she said. '"All reproduction is by cloning, using the cellular tissues of the top people in history of each occupational group. Thus, all Diplos on or of Nueva Albion were cloned from the Sainted Vardia, who was the go-between in the revolution several centuries ago. She kept contact between the Liberation Front on Coriolanus and the Holy Revolutionaries in reactionary Nueva Albion. Thus, I carried her genes, her resemblance, and her job. My number, Twelve Sixty-one, said I was the sixty-first Vardia clone from Birth Factory Twelve.'

Skander felt a sourness growing in her stomach. So that's what mankind has come to, she thought. Almost two-thirds of mankind reduced to clones, numbers – less human than the mechs of this absurd Nation.

'Then you were a woman,' the Umiau said conversationally, not betraying her darker inner thoughts.

'Not really,' she replied. 'Cloning negates the need for sexes, and sexes represent sexism which promotes inequality. Depending on the clone model, development is chemically and surgically arrested. All glands, hormone production, and the like are removed, changed, or neutralized permanently, in my case on my eleventh birthday. We are also given hysterectomies, and males are castrated, so that it is impossible to tell male or female after the turning age. Every few years we were supposed to get a complete treatment that kept the aging processes arrested and freshened the body, so that one couldn't tell a fifty-year-old from a fifteen-year-old.'

Outwardly the Umiau remained impassive, but internally Skander was so depressed that she felt nauseated.

Ye gods! the archaeologist swore to herself. A small, carefully bred cadre of supermen and superwomen ruling a world of eunuch children raised to unquestioning obedience! I was right to have killed them! Monsters like that – in control of the Well! Unthinkable!

They should all be killed, she knew, hatred welling up inside of her. The masters who were the most monstrous of spawn, and the masses of poor impersonal blobs of children – billions of them, probably. Best to put them out of their misery, she thought sadly. They weren't really people anyway.

Suddenly her thoughts turned to Varnett. Same idea, Skander thought. Although the boy hadn't come from a world as far gone as Nueva Albion, it would go that way in time. Names disappear on one world, sex on another, then all get together to form a universe of tiny, mindless, sexless, nameless organic robots, programmed and totally obedient – but so, so happy.

Varnett – brilliant, a truly great mind, yet childish, immature, in thousands of ways as programmed as his cousins whom he despised. What sort of a world, what sort of a universe, would Varnett create?

The Markovians had understood, she reflected. They knew.

I won't betray them! she swore intensely. I won't let anyone wreck the great dream! I will get there first! Then they'll see! I'll destroy them all!

MURITHEL – SOMEWHERE IN THE INTERIOR

Cousin Bat circled around feeling helpless. Maybe I can pick him up, he thought, looking at Brazil's battered and bleeding body in the mud. He's not a very big fellow, and I've moved some pretty heavy rocks with these legs.

He was about to give it a try when a group of Murnies came running up the valley. They got to Brazil's unconscious body before Bat could do anything at all, and the night creature thought, It's all over. They'll chomp him into pieces for a late snack now.

But they didn't. Four of the savages stayed with the body, while two others made for the top of the valley and the plains above. Fascinated, Bat stayed with them, balancing on the air currents.

The two returned a few minutes later with a litter made with tough branches for poles and, apparently, woven grass for the stretcher. Carefully they placed Brazil on the litter. One Murnie picked up the front, the other took the rear. They climbed the bank effortlessly, and Bat followed them, still invisible in the dark.

Darkness had returned to the plain as well. Bat was amazed to see hundreds, perhaps thousands, of Murnies beating a large, smoldering area about a thousand meters from the valley where they had plunged. It was a well-coordinated, well-rehearsed fire brigade, with the bulk of the Murnies beating out the last sparks with skin blankets, while an apparently endless chain of the creatures ran a bucket brigade from the creek all the way to the fire scene.

These are savages? Bat asked himself wonderingly. The teamwork and skillful handling of the fire he could not reconcile in his mind with the toothy carnivores who chased live prey with primitive spears and attacked them fiercely with spear and claw.

Brazil's unmoving form was hauled into a small camp away from the fire scene. A particularly huge Murnie, his light green skin laced with dark brown, examined the man and started barking orders. Even though Bat's translator would – should – pick up what the big one was saying, he dared not get close enough to hear.

The big Murnie got a bucket of water and started to wash Brazil's wounds with a gentleness that surprised the bat. Others brought a large hide case and a number of leaves. The big one opened the laces on the case, and from its interior pulled out varicolored jars of what looked like mud and more leaves, some apparently kept soaked in some solution in jars.

Slowly, methodically, the big one administered the muds to Brazil's open wounds, and used the leaves to form a compress for the man's head.

He's a doctor! Cousin Bat realized suddenly. They're treating him!

Bat felt better, almost relaxed enough to leave, but he did not.

Those wounds are tremendous, he noted. The man's lost huge amounts of blood, and probably has multiple breaks, concussion, and shock. Even if the medicine man knew the art of transfusion, there is none to give the blood.

Brazil will be dead within hours, no matter what magic this creature can work, Bat realized sadly. But what can I do? And, if they somehow cure him – what then? Prisoner? Pet? Plaything? Slave?

The Murnie medicine man gestured, and a smaller tribesman came into camp leading a huge stag antelope. It was the largest such animal Bat had ever seen, light brown with a white stripe running from the back of the head to the stubby tail, a large set of eerie-looking antlers atop that head. The stag was docile, too much so to be normal, Bat knew. It was drugged or some-thing. He saw with amazement that the deerlike animal wore a collar of carefully twisted skin, from which a small stone dangled.

Someone owns that animal, Bat reflected. Do these savages of the plain breed their food?

Into camp from different directions came five more Murnies, looking like the witch doctor – really large ones, with that curious brown discoloration, more pronounced on some than others.

Six, thought the bat. Of course it would be six. Primitives went in for mys-tic numbers, and if any number had power here that one certainly did.

They put the stag so that it faced Brazil, and all six moved close. Three of them placed their right hands on the unflinching stag, and took the right hands of the other three in their left. The other three all placed their left hands on Brazil's body.

Bat stayed aloft as long as he could, but finally decided he had to land. He was just coming out of the fight, and the exhilaration and extra pep that had flowed through him had waned. Reluctantly, he made for the valley and flew along until he found a place with no Murnies in the immediate vicinity. He landed, breathing hard, thinking of what he could do.

In a few minutes he had his wind back, and decided on a plan that the odds said were ridiculous.

He had to try.

No more running, he told himself. If I can do it, I'll do it.

He took off and flew back to the camp, seeing that he was in luck. The stag was staked to a post in the ground, apparently asleep, away from Brazil, who was covered with the mud compounds and leafy stuff, still in the open.

Brazil weighed around fifty kilos, he guessed. The litter? Five more? Ten? I can't do it, he thought suddenly, fear shooting through him. That much weight, for all that distance!

Suddenly he thought of the Dillian girl. He had lost track of her while following Brazil, but he couldn't take the time now. Nothing he could do in her case regardless, he knew. But she had run all out, all that distance on the ground, never stopping, cut and speared – way beyond her limits, while hungry and weak.

You've been eating well, Bat told himself sternly. You're as big and strong and healthy as you'll ever be. If she can do it …

Without another thought he swooped down to Brazil, and took one side of the litter, folding it over so he held both branches in his feet with Brazil wrapped in the middle. He took a quick glance around. So far so good. Now – could he take off, no ledge, no running start, with this load?

He started beating his great wings furiously, aided by a timely gust of wind that rustled the grass across the plain. He rose, and beat all the more furiously. Too low! he thought nervously. Got to get height!

The furious flapping brought Murnies running from their tents, including the big one.

'No! No! Come back!' the medicine man screamed, but the wind picked up and Bat was on his way, over the stream and down along its course, the unconscious Brazil hanging from the folded litter. Cousin Bat did not believe in gods or prayers, yet he prayed as he struggled to keep up speed, height, and balance. Prayed he would make it to Czill and to modern medicine without killing Brazil, himself, or both.

With shock and dismay the medicine man watched Bat fly into the darkness.

'Ogenon!' he called in a deep, rough voice.

'Yes, Your Holiness?' a smaller, weaker voice replied.

'You saw?'

'The body of the honored warrior has been taken by the one who flies,' Ogenon responded in a tone that seemed to wonder why such a stupid question had been asked.

'The flying one is ignorant of us and our ways, or he would not have done this,' the medicine man said as much to himself as to his aide. 'He flew east, so he's taking the body to Czill. I'll need a strong runner to get to the border. Now, don't look at me like that! I know how foul the air is over there, but this has to be done. The Czillians must realize when they see the warrior's body and hear the winged one's story what has happened, but, if the body survives – not likely – they will not know of the survival of the essence. Go!'

Ogenon found a warrior willing to make the trip in short order, and the medicine man instructed him what to say and to whom, impressing on the runner the need for speed. 'Do the message in relays,' the old one said. 'Just make sure it is continuous and that it is not garbled.'

Once the instructions were given and the runner was off into the darkness, the large Murnie turned again to his aide, who was looking extremely bleary-eyed and was yawning repeatedly.

'Get awake, boy!' snapped the elder. 'Now, locate the six-limbed creature and tell me where it is.'

'That's simple, Your Holiness,' Ogenon responded sleepily. 'The six-limbed one is under treatment at the Circle of Nine. I saw it being dragged there.'

'Good,' the old one replied. 'Now, you'll have to go to the Base Camp and bring an elder to me, Elder Grondel by name.'

'But that's –' Ogenon started to protest, yawning again.

'I know how far it is!' the big one roared. 'You can make it there and back before dawn!'

'But suppose the Revered Elder won't come,' the aide wailed, trying to get out of the assignment and to get back to sleep.

'He'll come,' the medicine man replied confidently. 'Just describe to him the three alien creatures we've had here this night, and tell him particularly of the honored warrior and of what has happened. He'll beat you here, I'll wager, even though he's eighty years old! Now, off with you! *Now!*'

Ogenon went, grumbling about how everybody kicked him around and he always had to do everything.

Once out of sight, the elder couldn't hold back his own yawns anymore, yet he didn't return to his tent and mat but sat down in the, for him, very chilly night air.

All he could do now was wait.

*

Wuju relived the nightmare run for hours, then, suddenly, woke up.

I must still be dreaming, she thought. Everything was fuzzy and she was feeling quite high. She couldn't believe what she saw.

She was in a Murnie camp, in the earliest light of dawn, and there were horribly loud and grotesque snores all around her. Sitting in front of her, arms around its knees, was the biggest Murnie she had ever seen – taller than she, and she stood over two meters. It was also oddly colored, on the whole a deeper brown than she, laced only here and there with spots of the light green that was the usual color of these strange creatures.

From a distance they had looked like walking rectangular bushes. But here, up close, she saw that they had a rough skin that folded and sagged, like partially melted plastic, all over their body. They looked like a large trunk of a body with no head, she thought. The eyes, huge as dinner plates, were located where the breasts should be, and perhaps thirty centimeters below them was that enormous mouth, a huge slit that seemed almost to cleave the trunk in two. There was no sign of hair, genitals, or, for that matter, a nose and ears.

The drug or whatever it was seemed to be wearing off more and more. This isn't a dream! she thought suddenly, as fear ran through her. She tried to move, but found her legs were all roped to stakes deep in the ground, and her hands were tied behind her. She struggled in panic to pull free, and the sound woke up the big brown Murnie. Its huge eyes opened, deep yellow with perfectly round, black irises that reflected the light almost like a cat's.

'Do not struggle,' the creature said to her. The words were mushy, as if they were uttered in the midst of a roar, but they were understandable. It was speaking a language it knew but its mouth was not suited to its use.

'I said do not struggle!' the Murnie repeated, getting up and stretching in a very human fashion. 'You are quite safe. No one will harm you. Can you understand me? Nod if you can.'

Wuju nodded fearfully, panic still all over her face.

'All right, now listen well. It is difficult for me to speak this tongue, and I must concentrate carefully to get the words out. You can understand me, but I cannot understand you, I don't think. Say something.'

'What – what is all this?' she almost screamed.

The Murnie scratched his behind with his huge, wide hand. The arms were almost to the ground when drooping by his side. 'I thought so. I could not understand a word. You have no translator. You must concentrate hard, like me. Think, then answer. What language am I using?'

She thought for a second, then suddenly realized the truth. 'Confederacy!' she exclaimed, amazed. 'You are an Entry!'

'All right. I got Confederacy but nothing else. That is because all Entries continue to think in their original tongue. What they say is automatically transformed in the neural passages to the language of the native hex. You can understand me, therefore you can speak it as I do if you think hard, make your mouth form the word you think. Take it slowly, one word at a time. Tell me your name and the name of your companions. Then try a simple phrase, one word at a time.'

Wuju concentrated, the fear and panic evaporating. Once this one had been one of her own kind! A potential friend she would need most of all here. As she started to speak she saw what he meant, and adjusted.

'I-ahm-Wuju,' she managed, and it almost sounded right. Her mouth and tongue wanted to make a different set of words. 'Moy frandiz ahar Nathan Brazil ind Cooseen Baht.'

'Nathan Brazil!' the big Murnie exclaimed excitedly, suddenly very wide awake. The rest of what he said was unintelligible.

My god! she thought. Does everybody on this crazy planet know Nathan?

The Murnie suddenly frowned, and scratched the side of his head thoughtfully. 'But the other was an old-culture man by description,' he mused, suddenly looking at her again with those huge yellow eyes. 'You mean he still looked like his old self?' She nodded, and his great mouth opened in surprise. 'I wonder why he wasn't changed in the Well?'

'Whahr est Nathan?' she managed.

'Well, that's really the problem,' the Murnie answered. 'You see, he's sort of in two places at once.'

He was a former freighter pilot like Brazil, the native told her, on the line for over two hundred years, facing his fourth rejuve and with all his family and friends dead, his world so changed he couldn't go home. He had decided to commit suicide, to end the loneliness, when he got a funny distress signal in the middle of nowhere. He had veered to investigate, when suddenly his ship had seemed to cease to exist around him, and he had fallen into the Zone Well and wound up a Murnie.

'They are good people,' he told her. 'Just very different. They can use nothing not found in nature or made by hand. No machines at all. They are bisexual, like us – although an alien couldn't tell who was who. Strong families, communal, with a strong folk art and music – herdsmen who breed the antelope we eat. Very hostile to strangers, though – they would have killed you last night.'

'Den woi om I ailoif?' she managed.

'You're alive,' he replied, 'because you killed about two dozen warriors, directly that is, plus the fibre and the like.'

She didn't understand, and said so.

'The Murnie nation accepts death naturally,' he explained. 'We don't fear it, nor dwell on it. We live for each day. It's far more enjoyable that way. What are respected most and valued most are honor and courage. You all displayed that last night! It took raw courage to run the plain, and great honor to keep going until you dropped rather than give in. If you had surrendered, they would still have killed you. But they found both you and Brazil, badly wounded, unconscious in different parts of the stream bed. It would have been cowardly and dishonorable to have killed you. You had gained respect – so they dragged each of you to the camp nearest where you were found, and your injuries were tended to. Our medicine is quite advanced – this is a rough hex.'

'Nathan!' she exclaimed. 'Ist hay arriot?'

'He was banged up much worse than you,' the Mumie replied gravely. 'You're going to hurt for a while when the herbal anesthetic wears off, but you have nothing more than four or five deep scratches on your back and a lot of bruises. We have treated them, but they will ache.' He paused for a second. 'But Brazil, he was much worse. I don't know how he kept going. It's not pos-sible. He should be dead, or, at best, totally paralyzed, yet he walked almost a kilometer down that streambed before collapsing. What an incredible will he must have! The Murnies will sing stories of him and tell of his greatness for centuries! In addition to the hundreds of minor bone breaks, the enormous amount of blood he lost from gaping wounds, and a badly lacerated leg, he had a broken back and neck. He got a kilometer with a broken back and neck!'

She thought of poor Nathan, twisted and bleeding, paralyzed and comatose. The thought made her sick, and it was several minutes and several attempts before she could concentrate on speaking Confederacy again. Tears welled up in her eyes, and she couldn't stop crying for several minutes. The fierce-looking Murnie stood there feeling helpless and sympathetic.

Finally she managed, 'Ist – hay ist stull aliff?'

'He is still alive,' the Murnie replied gravely. 'Sort of.'

'Hay ist oncun – uncrunchus?'

'Unconscious, yes,' the Murnie replied. 'I said, remember, that this was a rough hex that prized honor and courage, and had a lot of knowledge and wisdom within its limits. Because Murithel is totally nontechnological, the inhabitants have turned, aside from herbal compounds and muds, to the powers of the mind. Some of these doctors – and they *are* doctors – have enormous mental powers. I don't understand the powers, and I doubt if they do. These people study and concentrate over half their lives to develop the powers. By the time they're strong enough to be useful, the wise men – Holy Ones we call them – are elderly, sometimes with only a few years to live and to teach the next generation.' He paused again, and started pacing nervously, trying to think of how to say it.

'When Brazil was brought in so battered and close to death,' he said carefully, 'he was already, because of his tremendous courage, the most legendary character ever to be here. The Holy One who examined him did what he could, but saw that death was probable no matter what. He summoned five others – six is a magic number here, for obvious reasons – and they performed a Transference of Honor. It has only been done three or four times since I've been here – it shortens the life spans of the Holy Ones by a year or more. They reserve it for the greatest of honor and courage.' He stopped again, his tone changing. 'Look, I can see you don't understand. It is difficult to explain such things when I don't understand it, either. Umm … Are you a follower of any religion?'

The idea of religion was extremely funny to her, but she answered gently, 'No.'

'Few of us are – or were, in my day, and I'm sure it's worse now. But here, against these hills and on these plains, you learn that you are ignorant of almost everything. Call it mechanical, if you will, a part of the Markovian brain's powers, like our own transformations and this world itself, but accept it: that which is us, our memories, our personality, whatever, can be not only transformed but transferred. Now I – stop looking at me like that! I am *not* insane. I've seen it!'

'Arrh sou stelling moi daht Nathan ist naow e Murnie?' she asked, unwilling to believe but unwilling to disbelieve, either. Too much had already happened to her on this crazy world.

'Not a Murnie,' he replied evenly. 'That would involve superimposing his – well, they call it his "essence" – on somebody else. No, when someone's so respected that he rates a Transference of Honor, he is transferred to the best thoroughbred breeding stag or doe. Don't look so shocked – they are of such high quality that they are instantly recognized. No one would eat them, or even bother them.

'If, then, the body can be successfully brought back to health – which is rare or the Holy Ones would never do the Transference in the first place – he is switched back. If not, he is revered, cared for, and has a happy and peaceful life on the plains.'

'Nathan est un ahntlupe?' she gasped. It was becoming easier to talk, although her pronunciation was still terrible.

'A beautiful pure stag,' the Murnie acknowledged. 'I've seen him. He's still drugged. I didn't want him coming out of that state until you and I were both there to explain it to him.'

'Ist der – ist der unny chants dot hes boody wall liff?' she asked.

'Will his body live?' the Murnie repeated. 'I'm sure I don't know. I honestly doubt it, but I would have said that the Transference of Honor was more likely than going a kilometer with a game leg, a broken back, and busted neck. The outcome will depend on how much damage he receives beyond what's already done.'

Then he told her of Cousin Bat's rescue. 'He obviously could not consider us civilized or Brazil anything more than the victim of primitive medicine. Would you? So he plucked Brazil's body up and is even now taking it to Czill where they have a modern hospital. If the body survives the trip – and from what was told me I doubt if it survived the night, let alone the trip – the Czillians will know what happened. One of our people is getting the news to them sometime today just in case. They can sustain the body's functions indefinitely if it's still alive, though an empty vessel. Their computers know of the Transference of Honor. If they can heal the body, it can be returned here for retransference, but that is not something to pin your hopes on.

'I said I experienced three Transferences in my eighty years. Of them all, none of the bodies lasted the night.'

Nathan Brazil awoke feeling strange. Everything looked strange, too.

He was on the Murnie plain, he could see that – and it was daylight.

So I've survived again, he thought.

Things looked crazy, though, as if they were seen through a fish-eye camera lens – his field of vision was a little larger than he was used to, but it was a round picture vastly distorted. Things around the periphery looked close up; but as the view went toward the center of the field of view, everything seemed to move away as if he were looking down a tunnel. The picture was incredibly clear and detailed, but the distortion as things around the field of view bent toward the fixed center made it difficult to judge distances. And the whole world was brown – an incredible number of shades of brown and white.

Brazil turned his head and looked around. The distortion and color blindness stayed constant.

And he felt funny, crazy, sort of.

He thought back. He remembered the mad dash, the fire, falling off Wuju – then everything was dark.

This is crazy, he thought.

His hearing was incredibly acute. He heard everything crystal-clear, even voices and movements far away. It took him several minutes to sort out the chatter, finally assigning about eighty percent of it to things he could see.

There were Murnies moving around, and they all seemed to be light brown to him, although he remembered them as green. Suddenly he heard footsteps near him, and he turned to see a huge Murnie that was all very deep brown coming toward him.

I must be drugged, he told himself. These are after-effects of some drug they gave me.

The big Murnie ambled up to him.

I must be standing upright on a rack or something, he thought. I'm as tall as he is, and he's at least two meters, judging by his size, large compared to the run-of-the-Murnie crowd around.

Two grossly distorted Murnie hands took his head, lowered it slightly, so the creature was looking right into Brazil's eyes.

The Murnie grunted, and said, in Confederacy, 'Ah! Awake, I see! Don't try to move yet – I want to let you down easy before that. No! Don't try to talk! You can't, so don't bother.'

The creature walked a few steps in front of him and sat down tiredly on the grass.

'I haven't slept in over a day and a half,' the Murnie said with a sigh. 'It feels good just to relax.' He shifted to a more comfortable position, and considered where to begin.

'Look, Nate,' he began, 'first things first. You know I'm an Entry, and I've been told I'm not the first one who knew you that you've run into here. It kinda figures. Well, if your mind can go back ninety years, you might remember Shel Yvomda. Do you? If so, shake your head.'

Brazil thought. It was an odd name, he should remember it – but there were so many people, so many names. He tried to shrug, found he couldn't, and so moved his head slowly from side to side.

'Oh, well, it doesn't matter. They call me the Elder Grondel now, Elder because I've lived longer than fifty years here and that makes for respect. Grondel is their name – means The Polite Eater, because I continue to be civilized. I'm one of two people in Murithel who can still speak Confederacy. We would have lost it, except we ran into each other and practice for old times' sake. Well, enough of that. I guess I'd better tell you what happened. You aren't gonna like this, Nate.'

Brazil was stunned, but he accepted the situation and understood why they had done it and why they had thought it necessary. He even felt a deep affection for Cousin Bat in spite of the fact that he had fouled up the works.

As they sat there, the last of the drug wore off, and he suddenly found himself free to move.

He looked as far down as possible first, and thought, crazily, This is what Wuju must have seen when she first appeared in Dillia. Long, short-furred legs, much more graceful than hers, with dark hooves.

He turned his head and saw his reflection against the tent nearby.

He was a magnificent animal, he thought with no trace of humor. And the antlers! So that's why his head felt so funny!

He tried to move forward, and felt a tug. The Murnie laughed, and unfastened him from the stake.

He walked around on four legs for the first time, slowly, just around in circles.

So this is what it feels like to be changed, he thought. Strange, but not uncomfortable.

'There are some hitches, Nate,' Grondel said. 'It's not like a transformation. The body you have is that of a great animal, but not a dominant species. You've got no hands, tentacles, or any other thing except your snout to pick things up with, and you've got no voice. These antelope are totally silent, no equipment to make a noise. And your only defenses are your speed – which is considerable, by the way, cruising at fifteen or more kilometers per hour, sprints up to sixty – and a tremendous kick with the rear legs. And the antlers – those are permanent; they don't shed and won't grow unless broken off.'

Brazil stopped walking and thought for a while. Arms he could do without if necessary, and the rest – but not being able to talk bothered him.

Suddenly he stopped and stared at himself. All the time he had been thinking, he had been automatically leaning over and munching grass!

He looked back at Grondel, who just was watching him curiously.

'I think I can guess what you just realized,' the Murnie said at last. 'You just started munching grass without thinking. Right?'

Brazil nodded, feeling stranger than before.

'Remember – you, *all* of that inner self that's you – was transferred, but it was superimposed on the remarkably dull antelope brain and nervous system. Superimposed, Nate – not exchanged. Unless you directly countermand it, the deer's going to continue acting like a deer, in every way. That's automatic, and instinctive. You're not man *into* deer, you're man *plus* deer.' Brazil considered it. There would be some problems, then, particularly since he was a brooder, given to introspection. What did a deer do? Ate, slept, copulated. Hmmm … The last would cause problems.

There were, as Grondel had said, many hitches.

How do I fit inside this head? he wondered. All of my memories – more, perhaps, than any other man. Weren't memories chemical? He could see how the chemical chains could at least be duplicated, the brainwave pattern adjusted – but how did this tiny brain have room for it all?

'Nate!' He heard a call, and looked up. Grondel was running toward him from whatever distance this fish-eye vision couldn't tell him. He would get used to it, he thought.

He had moved. As he brooded, he had wandered out of the camp and over almost to the herd! He turned and ran back to the camp, surprised at the ease and speed with which he ran, but he slowed when he realized that the distorted vision would take some getting used to. He almost ran the Murnie down.

He started to apologize, but nothing came out.

The Murnie sympathized. 'I don't know the answer, Nate. But get used to it before doing anything rash. Your body's either dead or it'll be even better the longer you give it in Czill. Hey! Just thought of something. Come over here to this dirt patch!'

He followed the Murnie curiously.

'Look!' Grondel said excitedly, and made a line in the dirt with his foot. 'Now you do it!'

Brazil understood. It was slow and didn't look all that good, but after a little practice he managed to trace the letters in the dirt with his hoof.

'WHERE IS WUJU?' he traced.

'She's here, Nate. Want to see her?'

Brazil thought for a second, then wrote, very large, 'NO.'

The Murnie rubbed out the old letters so it was again a virgin slate. 'Why not?' he asked.

'DOES SHE KNOW ABOUT ME?' Brazil wrote.

'Yes. I – I told her last night. Shouldn't I have?'

Brazil was seething; a thousand things raced through his mind, none of them logical.

'DON'T WANT,' he had traced when he heard Wuju's voice.

'Nathan?' she called more than asked. 'Is that really you in there?'

He looked up and turned. She was standing there, looking awed, shaking her head back and forth in disbelief.

'It's him,' Grondel assured her. 'See? We've been communicating. He can write here in the dirt.'

She looked down at the marks and shook her head sadly. 'I – I never learned how to read,' she said, ashamedly.

The Murnie grunted. 'Too bad,' he said. 'Would have simplified things.' He turned back to Brazil. 'Look, Nate, I know you well enough to know that you'll head off for Czill as soon as you're confident of making the trip. I know how you feel, but you *need* her. *We* can't go, wouldn't if we could. And somebody's got to know you're you, to keep you from straying, and to do your talking for you. You need her, Nate.'

Brazil looked at them both and thought for a minute, trying to understand his own feelings. Shame? Fear?

No, dependence, he thought.

I've never been dependent on anyone, but now I need somebody. For the first time in my long life, I need somebody.

He was dependent on Wuju, almost as much as she had been dependent on him in the early stages of their relationship.

He tried to think up logical reasons for that not being the case, to rationalize his feelings, but he could not.

He traced in the dirt, 'BUT I'M NOW BIGGER THAN YOU ARE.'

Grondel laughed and read it to her. She laughed, too.

Then he wrote: 'TELL HER ABOUT DEER PART.' Grondel understood, and explained how Brazil was really two beings – one man, one animal – and how he had already lapsed into deer while thinking.

She understood. When still, such as during the night, he would have to be staked like a common deer to keep him from wandering away. And he couldn't even drive his own stake!

Dependence. It grated on him as nothing ever had, but it had the feel of inevitability.

He hoped fervently that his body was still alive.

Grondel had finally collapsed in sleep and was snoring loudly in a nearby tent.

Brazil and Wuju were alone for the first time, he suffering the indignity of being staked so he couldn't wander off.

They had worked most of the day on his getting used to the body, adjusting to the vision and color blindness, the supersensitive senses of hearing and smell. The speed in his sprint amazed him and Wuju both. As fast as she had seemed when he was human, she now seemed terribly slow, ponderous, and exhausted while he was still feeling great. He also discovered that his hind-leg kick could shatter a small tree.

A few things were simplified, of course. No packs needed now, he could eat what she ate. No drag on speed – he could run as fast as Cousin Bat could fly, maybe faster for short periods.

If only he could talk! Make some sort of sound!

Wuju looked at him admiringly. 'You know, you're really beautiful, Nathan. I hope they have mirrors in Czill.' She still talked mildly distorted, but Grondel had been forcing her to use the old language so much during the past day and a half that it was becoming easier, like a second language.

She came and stood beside him, pressing her equine body against his sleek, supermuscled antelope body. She started to rub him, actually pet him gently.

His mind rebelled, though he didn't try to pull away or stop her.

I'm getting excited as hell! he thought, surprised. And, from the feel of it, there was a lot of him to get excited.

His first impulse was to stop her, but instead he moved his head over and started nuzzling her neck with his muzzle. She leaned forward, so his antlers wouldn't get in the way.

Is it the animal, or do I want to do this? a corner of his mind asked, but the thought slipped away as irrelevant, as was the thought that they were still two very, very different species.

He stroked her equine back with the bottom of his snout and got to the bony hind end. She sighed and slipped off the leash that was attached to his hind leg. They continued.

This was a crazy, insane way to have sex, but the deer in him showed him how.

Wuju finally had what she wanted from Nathan Brazil.

Brazil awoke feeling really fine, the best in many long years. He glanced over at Wuju, still asleep, although the sun had been up for an hour.

Isn't it funny, he thought. The transformation, the commitment, the crisis, and the way those people had served me have all come together to do what nothing else had.

He remembered.

He remembered it *all*, all the way back.

He understood, finally, what he had been doing before, what he was doing now, why he survived.

He considered the vessel he wore. Not of his own choosing, of course, but it was serviceable if he could just get a voice.

How great a change to know it all! His mind was absolutely clear, certain, now that everything was laid out before him. He was in total control now, he knew.

Funny, he thought, that this doesn't change anything. Knowledge, memory, wisdom aside, he was the culmination of all of the experiences in his incredibly long life.

Nathan Brazil. He rolled the name around in his mind. He still liked it. Out of the – what? – thousand or more names he had had, it had the most comfortable and enigmatic ring.

He let his mind go out across the land. Yes, definitely some sort of breakdown. Not major, but messy. Time dulls all mechanisms, and the infinite complexity of the master equation was bound to have flaws. One can represent infinity mathematically but not as something real, something you can see and understand.

And yet, he thought, I'm still Nathan Brazil, still the same person I was, and I'm here in Murithel in the body of a great stag and I've still got to get to the Well before Skander or Varnett or anyone else does.

Czill. If what he had heard was right, they had computers there. A high-technology hex, then. They could give him a voice – and news.

Grondel emerged from a tent and came over to him. He strained at the rope on his left hind leg, and the Murnie understood and freed him. He went immediately to the big patch of bare dirt that was his writing pad. Grondel followed, grumping that he hadn't had anything to eat yet, but Brazil was adamant and anxious.

'What's on your mind, Nate?' he asked.

'HOW FAR HERE TO CZILL CENTER,' Brazil traced.

'Already, huh?' Grondel muttered. 'Somehow I knew it. Well, about a hundred and fifty kilometers, maybe a title more, to the border, then about the same into the Czillian capital. I'm not sure, because I've never left this hex. We don't get along well with our neighbors, which is fine with us.'

'MUST GO,' he scratched, 'IN CONTROL OF SELF NOW. IMPORT-ANT.'

'Ummm … Thought you weren't going there across Murithel for a vacation. All right, then, if I can't dissuade you. What about the girl?'

'SHE COMES TOO,' he scratched, 'WILL WORK OUT EASY CODE FOR BASIC STUFF, STOP, GO, EAT, SLEEP, ETC.'

And that was the way they worked it out, Brazil thinking of as many basic concepts as he could and using a right leg, left leg, stomping code for them. Twelve concepts were the most he could work on short notice without fear that she would mix them up. He also had to assure them several times that he would not wander away or stray again. She accepted it, but seemed dubious.

They ate their fill of the grasses. Grondel would ride Wuju with them to the border. Though Nathan was safe as a branded, purebred stag, she was not. A Murnie accompanying them would ease her passage.

They followed the stream, passing first the spot where his body had lain, the mud and bottom still disturbed from the action. They made exceptionally good time, and Brazil enjoyed the experience of being able to move quickly and effortlessly, so powerful that the mud couldn't trap him, nor could the brisk pace tire him. He just wasn't built for riding, though; and Wuju had to carry Grondel, which slowed her more than usual. It didn't matter.

They made the border shortly after dark on the second day. On the morning of the third, after Grondel had refreshed Wuju on the stomp code, they bade him good-bye and crossed into Czill. The air was extremely heavy with an almost oppressive humidity, the kind that wets you with a fine, invisible mist as you move through it. The air was also oppressive with carbon dioxide, which seemed to make up one or more percent of the atmosphere, although oxygen was so far above their previous norms that it made them feel a little light-headed. Were it not for the great humidity, Brazil thought, this would be a hell of a place for fires. As it was, he would be surprised if a match would burn.

They ran into Czillians soon enough, strange-looking creatures that reminded him of smooth-skinned cactuses with two trunks and carved pumpkin heads. Neither he nor Wuju had a translator now, so communication was impossible, but at the first village center they reached, they managed a primitive sort of contact.

The place looked like a great, transparent geodesic dome, and was one of the hundred or more subsidiary research villages outside the Center. The Czillians were surprised to see a Dillian – they knew what Wuju was, but as far as any could remember none of her race had ever reached Czill before. They regarded Brazil as a curiosity, an obvious animal.

About the only thing Wuju could get across to them were their names. She finally gave up in frustration and they continued on the well-maintained road. The Czillians sent the names and the information of their passage on to the Center, where it was much better understood.

Brazil paid a lot of attention to Wuju, and their lovemaking continued nightly. She was happy now and didn't even wonder how Brazil, who led, was picking the right direction at every junction as if he had been there before. In her mind the only question that mattered was about his human body. She felt a little guilty, but she hoped the body would not be there or would be dead.

She had him now, and she didn't want to lose him.

Late in the morning of the second day, they came to what was obviously the main highway of the hex, and followed it. It was another day and a half before they got to the Center, though, since it was not in the center of the hex as Grondel had thought, but was situated along the ocean coast.

They arrived just as darkness was falling, and Brazil stomped that they would sleep first. No use going in when there was only minimum staff, he thought.

As he made love to her that night, part of her mind was haunted. *The rest of him is inside that building,* she thought, and it upset her. *This might be their last night.*

Cousin Bat woke them up in the wee predawn hours.

'Brazil! Wuju! Wake up!' he shouted excitedly, and they both stirred. Wuju saw who it was and greeted him warmly, all her past suspicions forgotten.

Bat turned to Brazil unbelievingly. 'Is that *really* you in there, Brazil?'

Brazil nodded his antlered head affirmatively.

'He can't talk, Cousin Bat,' Wuju explained. 'No vocal cords of any kind. I think that upsets him more than anything else.'

The bat grew serious. 'I'm sorry,' he said softly to Brazil. 'I didn't know.' He snorted. 'Big hero, plucking the injured man from the jaws of certain death. All I did was make a mess of it.'

'But you *are* a hero!' Wuju consoled him. 'That was an incredibly brave and wonderful thing.' Well, there was no avoiding it. The question had to be asked.

'Did he – is his body still alive?' she asked softly.

'Yes, it is, somehow,' Bat replied seriously. 'But – well, it's a miracle that it's alive at all, and there's no medical reason for it. It's pretty battered and broken, Wuju. These doctors are good here – unbelievable, in fact. But the only thing that body will ever be good for is cloning. If Brazil were returned to it, he'd be a living vegetable.'

They both looked at Brazil expectantly, but the stag gave no indication whatsoever of emotion.

Wuju tried to remain normal, but the fact that a great deal of tension had suddenly drained from her was obvious in the lighter, more casual tone she used. 'Then he's to stay a deer?'

'Looks that way,' Bat responded slowly. 'At least they told me that the injuries were already too severe for me to have caused the final damage. They can't understand how he survived the Murnie blows that broke his neck and spinal column in two places. Nobody ever survived damage like that. It's as good as blowing your brains out or getting stabbed through the heart.'

They talked on until dawn, when the still landscape suddenly came alive with awakening Czillians. Bat led them into the Center, and took them to the medical wing, on the river side.

The Czillians were fascinated by Brazil and insisted on checking him with electroencephalographs and all sorts of other equipment. He was impatient but submitted to the tests with growing confidence. If they were this far advanced, perhaps they could give him a voice.

They took Nathan down to a lower level after a while and showed him his body. Wuju came along, but one quick glance was all she needed and she rushed from the room.

They had him floating in a tank, attached to hundreds of instruments and life-sustaining devices. The monitors showed autonomic muscle action, but no cranial activity whatsoever. The body itself had been repaired as much as possible, but it looked as if it had been through a meat grinder. Right leg almost torn off, now sewn back securely but lifeless in the extreme. The giant, clawed hand that had ripped the leg had also castrated him.

Brazil had seen enough. He turned and left the room, climbing the stairs back to the clinic carefully. They were not built to take something his size and weight, and the turns were difficult. He didn't fit in the elevators, which were designed for Umiau in wheelchairs.

Having a 250-plus-kilo giant stag walk into your office can be unsettling, but the Czillian doctor tried not to let it faze it. The doctor heard from Bat, who had heard it from Wuju, that Brazil could write. Since soft dirt was one thing that was very plentiful in Czill, it had obtained what appeared to be a large sandbox filled with dry, powdery gray sand from the ocean shore.

'What do you want us to do?' the doctor asked.

'CAN YOU BUILD ME VOICE BOX,' Brazil scratched.

The doctor thought a minute. 'Perhaps we can, in a way. You might know that the translator devices, which we import, sealed, from another hex far away, work by being implanted and attached to neural passages between the brain and the vocal equipment – whatever it is – of the creature. You had one in your old body. We now have nothing to attach the translator to in your case, and putting anything in there would interfere with eating or breathing. But if we could attach a small plastic diaphragm and match the electrical impulses from your brain to wires leading to it, we might have an external voice box. Not great, of course, but you could be understood – with full translator function. I'll tell the labs. It's a simple operation, and if they can come up with anything, we might be able to do it tomorrow or the next day.'

'SOONER THE BETTER,' he scratched, and started to leave to find Bat and Wuju.

'Just a minute,' the doctor called. 'As long as you're here, alone with me, I'd like to take up something you might not know.'

Brazil stopped, turned back to it, and waited expectantly.

'Our tests show you to be – physically – about four and a half years old. The records show that the average life span of the Murthiel antelope is between eight and twelve years, so you can expect to age much more rapidly. You have four to eight more years to live, no more. But that is at least that many years longer than you would have lived without the transfer.' It stopped, looking for a reaction. The stag cocked his head in a gesture that was unmistakably the equivalent of a shrug. He walked back to the sandbox.

'THANKS ANYWAY,' he scratched, 'NOT RELEVANT,' he added cryptically, and left.

The doctor stared after him, puzzled. It knew that everyone said Brazil might be the oldest person ever to live, and certainly he had shown incredible, superhuman life and stamina. *Maybe he wants to die*, it mused. *Or maybe he doesn't think he can, even now.*

The operation was a simple one, performed with a local anesthetic. The only problem the surgeon had was in isolating the correct neural signals in an animal brain so undesigned for speech of any kind. The computers were fed all the neural information and some samples of him attempting speech. They finally isolated the needed signals in under an hour. The only remaining concern was for the drilling in the antlers, but when they found that the bony growths had no nerves to convey pain, it simplified everything. They used a small Umiau transistor radio – which meant it was rugged and totally waterproof. Connections were made inside the antler base, and the tiny radio, only about sixty square centimeters, was screwed into the antler base. A little cosmetic surgery and plastic made everything but the speaker grille blend into the antler complex.

'Now say something,' the surgeon urged. 'Do it as if you were going to speak.'

'How's this?' he asked. 'Can you hear and understand me?'

'Excellent!' the surgeon said enthusiastically, rubbing its tentacles in glee. 'A landmark! There's even a suggestion of tone and emphasis!'

Brazil was delighted, even though the voice was ever so slightly delayed from the thought, something he would have to get used to. His new voice sounded crazy to his ears, and did not have the internal resonance that came with vocal cords.

It would do.

'You'll have a pretty big headache after the anesthetic wears off,' the surgeon warned. 'Even though there are no pain centers in the antlers, we did have to get into the skull for the little wire contacts.'

'That won't bother me,' Brazil assured them. 'I can will pain away.'

He went out and found the bat and Wuju waiting anxiously in the outer office.

'How do you like my new voice?' he asked them.

'Thin, weak, and tinny, very mechanical-sounding,' Bat replied.

'It doesn't sound like you at all, Nathan,' Wuju said. 'It sounds like a tiny pocket radio, one that a computer was using. Even so, there's some of you in it – the way you pause, the way you pronounce things.'

'Now I can get to work,' Brazil's strange new voice said. 'I'll have to talk to the Czillian head of the Skander project, somebody high up in the Umiau, and I'll need an atlas. In the meantime, Wuju, you get yourself a translator. It's really a simple operation for you. I don't want to be caught in the middle of nowhere with you unable to talk to anybody again.'

'I'll go with you,' said the bat. 'I know the place fairly well now. You know, it's weird, that voice. Not just the tiny sound from such a big character. It doesn't seem to come from anywhere in particular. I'll have a time getting used to it.'

'The only part that's important is your calling me a big character,' Brazil responded dryly. 'You don't know what it's like to go through life being smaller than everybody else and suddenly wind up the largest person in a whole country.' Brazil felt good; he was in command again.

They walked out, and Wuju was left alone, internally a mass of bewildering emotion. This wasn't turning out the way she had thought at all. He seemed so cold, so distant, so *different* – it wasn't Nathan! Not the voice, she thought. It was something *in* the voice, a manner, a coldness, a crispness that she had never felt before.

'Get a translator' he had told her, then walked out to business without so much as a good-bye and good luck.

'I want to go down to the old body one last time,' Brazil said to the bat, and they made their way down the stairs to the basement room.

Bat, too, had noticed a change in his manner, and it disturbed him. He wondered whether the transformation had altered or changed Brazil's mind. Some forms of insanity and personality disorders are organic, he thought.

Suppose the deer brain isn't giving the right stuff in the right amounts? Suppose it's only partially him?

They walked into the room where his body was floating, still alive according to all the screens and dials. Brazil stood by the tank, just looking at the body, for quite some time. Bat didn't interrupt, trying to imagine what he would be thinking in the same circumstances.

Finally Brazil said, almost nostalgic in tone, 'It was a good vessel. It served me for a long, long time. Well, that's that. A new one's as easy as repair this time. Let it go.'

As he uttered the last word, all the meters fell to zero and the screens all showed a cessation of life.

As if on command, the body had died.

Brazil turned and walked out without another word, leaving Bat more confused than ever.

'There's no question that Skander solved the riddle,' the Czillian project chief, whose name was Manito, told Brazil and Cousin Bat. 'Unfortunately, he kept the really key findings to himself and was very careful to wipe the computer when he was through. The only stuff we have is what was in when he and Vardia were kidnapped.'

'What was the major thrust of his research?' Brazil asked.

'He was obsessed with our collection of folklore and legends. Worked mostly with those, and keying in the common phrase: *Until midnight at the Well of Souls.*'

Brazil nodded. 'That's safe enough,' he replied. 'But you say he dropped that line of inquiry when he returned?'

'Shortly after,' the Czillian replied. 'He said it was the wrong direction and started researching the Equatorial Barrier.'

Brazil sighed. 'That's bad. That means he's probably figured the whole thing out.'

'You talk as if you know the answer, too,' the project chief commented. 'I don't see how. I have all the raw data Skander did and I can't make sense of it.'

'That's because you have a puzzle with millions of pieces, but no concept of the size and shape of the puzzle even to start putting things together,' Brazil told her – he insisted on thinking of all life forms that could do the act of reproducing, growing a new being, as she. 'Skander, after all, had the basic equation. There's no way you can get that here.'

'I can't understand why you let him use you so,' Bat put in. 'You – both races – gave him a hundred percent protection, cooperation, and access to all the tools he needed without getting anything in return.'

The Czillian shook her head sadly. 'We thought we were in control. After all, he was a Umiau. He couldn't exist outside his own ocean because he couldn't travel beyond it. And there was, after all, the other – the one who disappeared. He was a mathematician. Whose data banks was he consulting? Was he brilliant enough not to need them? We couldn't afford *not* to back Skander!'

'Any idea where they are?' Brazil asked.

'Oh, yes, we know where they are – fat lot of good it does us. They are currently being held captive in a nation of robots called, simply enough, The Nation. We received word that they were there, and, since we have a few informational trades with The Nation, we pulled in all our IOU's to hold them there as long as possible.'

Brazil was suddenly excited. 'Are they still there? Can we get them out?'

'Yes, they're still there,' Manito replied, 'but not for long. There's been hell to pay from the Akkafians. Their ambassador, a Baron Azkfru, has threatened to bomb as much of The Nation as he can – and he can do a good deal of damage if that's all he's out for. That's the line. They'll be released today.'

'Who's in the party?' Bat asked. 'If it's weak enough we might be able to do something yet.'

'We've thought of that already,' the Czillian responded. 'Nothing that wouldn't get our person killed along with the rest. Aside from Vardia and Skander, there's an Akkafian – they are huge insects with great speed, the ability to fly, and nasty stingers, and they eat live prey – named Mar Hain, and a weird Northerner we know little about called The Diviner and The Rel. If they're one or two I can't find out.'

'Hain!' Brazil exclaimed. 'Of course, it would be. That son of a bitch would be in the middle of anything dirty.'

'You know this Hain?' Bat asked curiously.

Brazil nodded. 'The gang's all here, it looks like.' He turned to Manito suddenly. 'Did you bring the atlas I asked for?'

'I did,' the Czillian replied, and lifted a huge book onto a table. Brazil walked over to it and flipped it open with his nose, then started turning pages with his broad tongue. Finally he found the Southern Hemisphere map and studied it intently. 'Damned nuisance,' he said. 'Antelope don't need very good vision.'

'I can help,' the Czillian said, and walked toward the stag. 'It is in Czillian, anyway, which you can't read.'

Brazil shook his head idly from side to side. 'It's all right. I see where we are now, and where *they* are. We're about even – two hexes up on this side to the Ghlmon Hex at the northern tip of the ocean. They've gotten two up the eastern side of the same ocean to pretty much the same spot.'

'How can you possibly know that?' the Czillian blurted out, stunned. 'Have you been here before? I thought—'

'No,' Brazil replied. 'Not *here*.' He flipped a few more pages, studying a close-up map of a particular hex. Then he flipped again, studied another, then to yet another. All in all, he carefully examined five hexes. Suddenly he looked up at the confused Czillian.

'Can you get me in touch with some Umiau big shot?' he asked. 'They owe us something for Skander. They've got Slelcron, which is a nontech hex and so is fine from our point of view, and Ekh'l, which could be anything at all these days. We've got Ivrom, which I don't like at all, but there's no way around it, and Alisstl, which will make Murithel look like a picnic. We can contend with Ivrom, I hope, but if we went through the Umiau hex, on a boat of some kind, we could avoid the nasty one and maybe even gain some time on the others. If they stick near the coast – and I think they will, because those are the best roads by far – we might just beat them there and intercept them here,' he pointed with his nose to the map, 'at the northern tip of the bay here, in Ghlmon.'

'Just out of curiosity,' Bat said, 'you said that the Umiau were warned the first time about a kidnap try on Skander. Now, you said you heard they were in The Nation. Who told you those things?'

'Why, we don't know!' the Czillian answered. 'They came as, well, tips, passed in common printer-machine type in our respective languages, to our ambassadors at Zone.'

'Yes,' Bat persisted, 'but who sent them? Is there a third set of players in the race?'

'I was hoping *you* could tell me that,' Brazil said flatly.

Bat's eyes widened. 'Me? All right, I admit I knew who you were back in Dillia, and that I joined you on purpose. But I don't represent anyone except myself, and the interests, of my people. We got word the same way the Czillians and Umiau did, at Zone. Said where you'd be, approximately when, and that you were going after Skander and Varnett. We couldn't find who sent it, but it was decided that we had a stake in the outcome. I was elected, because I've done more traveling than most of my people. But – me? The third party? No, Brazil, I admit only to not being truthful with you. Surely by now you know that I'm on your side – all the way.'

'That's too bad,' Brazil replied. 'I would very much like to know our mysterious helper, and how he gets his information.'

'Well, he seems to be on our side,' Bat said optimistically.

'Nobody's on any side but his own,' Brazil snapped back. 'Not you, not me, not anybody. We're going to have a tough enough time just dealing with the Skander party. I don't want to reach the goal of this chase and have our helpful third party finish off the survivors.'

'Then you propose to give chase?' the Czillian asked stupidly.

'Of course! That's what all this is about. One last question – can you tell me the last major problem Skander fed to the computer?'

'Why, yes, I think so,' the Czillian replied nervously. She rummaged through some papers, coming up with two. 'He asked two, in fact. One was the number of Entries into hexes bordering the Equatorial Zone, both sides.'

'And the answer?'

'Why, none on record. Most curious. They're not true hexes anyway, you know. Since the Equatorial Barrier splits them neatly in half, they are two adjoining half-hexes, each side – therefore, twice as wide as a normal hex and half the distance north and south, with flat equatorial borders.'

'What was the second question?' Brazil asked impatiently.

'Oh, ah, whether the number six had any special relation to the Equatorial Zone hexes in geography, biology, or the like.'

'And the answer?'

'Still in the computer when the unfortunate, ah, incident occurred. We did, of course, get the answer, even though it was on a printout which the kidnappers apparently took with them. The material was still in storage, and so we got another copy.'

'What did it say?' Brazil asked in an irritated tone.

'Oh, ah, that six of the double half-hexes, so to speak, were split by a very deep inlet all the way up to the zone barrier, evenly spaced around the planet so that, if you drew a line from zone to zone through each of the inlets, you'd split the planet into absolutely equal sixths.'

'Son of a bitch!' Brazil swore. 'He's got the whole answer! Nothing will ever surprise me again!'

At that moment another Czillian entered the room and looked at the bat and the stag confusedly. Finally she picked the bat and said, shyly, 'Captain Brazil?'

'Not me,' Bat replied casually, and pointed a bony wing at the stag. 'Him.'

She turned and looked at the creature that was so obviously an animal. 'I don't believe it!' she said the way everyone did. Finally she decided she might believe it and went over to the great Murithel antelope, and repeated, 'Captain Brazil?'

'Yes?' he answered pleasantly, curious in the extreme. *Captain* Brazil?

'Oh,' she responded softly, 'I – I realize I've changed a great deal, but nothing like *you*. Wow!'

'Well, who are – um, that is, who *were* you?' he asked, intrigued.

'Why, I'm Vardia, Captain,' she replied.

'But Vardia was kidnapped by the bugs!' Bat exclaimed.

'I know,' she replied. 'That's what's really upset me.'

A ROAD IN THE NATION

'Quarantine, hell!' Skander grumbled, strapped in again atop Hain's back, irritated by the yellowish atmosphere and the discomfort of the breathing apparatus. Her voice was so muffled by the mask that none could understand a word.

'Stop grumbling, Skander,' The Rel responded. 'You waste air and can't be understood by anybody but me anyway. You are quite right, though – we've been stalled.'

Vardia, whose head and vocal mechanism were not related in any way to her respiratory system, asked, 'Who could be responsible? Who knew we were here, would be staying at that particular hotel? Perhaps our people have tracked you down.' There was hope in her voice.

'Don't get yourself that excited, Czillian,' The Rel replied. 'As you can see, the delaying action slowed us but did not stop or deter us – nor did it liberate you. No, this smells of darker stuff. Of the one who planted the hidden listening device in the baron's office at Zone and prevented our escapade weeks earlier.'

This was the first Vardia had heard of that incident, and it made her think back to the many things that had happened to her. That distress signal where one could not have been operating. The vanishing of the two shuttlecraft on Dalgonia, and the disappearance of their lifeboat. The opening of the Well Gate only after they were all securely in it. Captain Brazil's firm belief that he was being suckered by someone.

That strange snakeman, Ortega. Over seven hundred chances, and Brazil is met by the only person at Zone who knew him. Coincidence?

She suddenly felt furious, thinking of all of it in detail. Someone *was* using her – using all of them – moving them like pieces in a game.

What about the hex assignments? Skander to a place where she had all the tools at her disposal, corrupting a peaceful people in the process. She to the hex next door, assigned – actually *assigned!* – to work with Skander and kidnapped with her. By whom? Someone working for that bastard Datham Hain!

And Captain Brazil! She had gotten the word when Brazil had entered Zone, looking exactly the same as he had before. Why didn't the Gate change him? And that pathetic little addict – dumped into a hex almost perfect for getting back to being human without pressures. Brazil had been hung up on her, she recalled. Probably they were together now.

Why? she wondered. Sex? That was something the animals did, she told herself. She had never understood it, or why people liked it; and if her own twinning was any indication, it was a most unpleasant experience. Why was a distinguished, high-ranking person of such a responsible position as Captain Brazil willing to jeopardize his career and his life for the sake of some wasted girl he never knew – didn't know, in fact, even through Zone? Even if he had saved her, she wouldn't have contributed anything. She was practically an animal then. More sense to get her to a Death Factory where her remains would help fertilize a field.

Perhaps this was why the Com philosophy was developing and spreading, she thought. It was rational, planned. Like being a plant, or one of these robots. Even Hain's dirty crew couldn't stop the march of such perfection of order, she felt sure. The sane hexes here proved it.

'We will have better service, and a shorter stay, at other hotels,' The Rel informed them, breaking Vardia's reverie. 'I think we will be out of this place where we are so unpopular in two days. Slelcron will be no faster but easier. No one communicates with the Slelcron. We will be ignored but unimpeded. As for Ekh'l – well, I have no information there, but I feel confident that, no matter what happens, we will not be beaten.'

'You seem pretty sure of yourself,' Vardia commented. 'More prophecy from The Diviner?'

'Logic,' The Rel replied. 'We were impeded for someone's purpose. Why? To what end? So they can beat us to the equator? I doubt it. It would be easier to kill us than detain us so. No, they will have to come out to us at the equator. They want to be there when we arrive because they know who and where we are, but not what Dr Skander knows – how to get to the Well. They want in with us – indeed, they may be allies, since they will assuredly take steps to see that no one else beats us to the goal. And maie no mistake about it, there is another expedition. The Diviner has said that we will not enter until all the recent Entries combine. That is fine – as long as we are in charge.'

'We will be,' Hain suddenly said.

NEAR THE IVROM BORDER IN THE UMIAU NATION

They presented a sight unprecedented on the Well World: a broad raft of logs, pulled along by ten Umiau wearing harnesses. On the raft were a Dillian centaur, a giant stag, a two-meter-tall bat, and a Czillian, plus a well-depleted bale of hay and a box of dirt.

'Why can't the Umiau just take us all the way up?' Vardia asked Brazil.

The stag turned his head. 'I still can't get used to the idea that you are in two places at once, so to speak,' he said through his radio speaker. The splashing and sound of the wind on the water made it hard to hear his little box if you weren't positioned just right.

'I have a hard time thinking that the little captain I came here with is a huge deer,' she replied. 'Now answer the question.'

'Too dangerous,' he told her. 'We're going as far up as possible, but you eventually start getting some nasty currents, whirlpools, and other stuff. They don't get along too well with the inhabitants, either. The Umiau would make out, but those nasty fish with the twenty rows of teeth would chew up this raft and us before we could be properly introduced. No, we'll take our chances with a hundred and sixty kilometers of Ivrom.'

'What is Ivrom, Nathan?' Wuju asked. She had gotten the translator, and overcome most of her reservations. He treated her gently, and said only the right things, and she had eased up. There was still that something different about him, that indefinable something they all sensed but couldn't put their fingers on.

Wuju had talked it out with Cousin Bat. 'How would you feel,' Bat had asked her, 'if you'd awakened not a Dillian but a regular horse? And looked down at your own dead body? Would you still be the same?'

She had accepted that explanation, but Bat didn't believe it himself. What had changed in Brazil was the added air of total command, of absolute confidence and certainty. And he had as much as admitted he knew the answer to the total puzzle. He could get in to the control center, control the world – or more.

Bat was more encouraged now, really. So much the better. The man with the answers had no hands, couldn't even open a door by himself. Let him get in, Bat thought smugly. Let him show how to work things.

'Nathan!' Wuju said louder. 'What is Ivrom? You haven't told us!'

'Because I don't know, love,' he replied casually. 'Lots of forest, rolling hills, plenty of animals, most familiar. The atlas said there were horses and deer there. It's a non-technological hex, so it's the sword-and-spear bit again, probably. The intelligent life form is some kind of insect, I think, but nobody's sure. Those active volcanoes to our left – that's Alisstl, and it's a formidable barrier. The people there are thick-skinned reptiles who live in temperatures close to boiling and eat sulfur. Probably nice folks, but nobody drops in.'

She looked over at the range of volcanic mountains. Most were spouting steam, and one had a spectacular lava fountain along a side fissure. She shivered, although it wasn't cold.

'This is the way to travel if you can!' Brazil said with enthusiasm, taking a deep breath of the salty air. 'Fantastic! I used to sail oceans like this on big ships, back in the days of Old Earth. There was a romance to the sea, and those who sailed it. Not like the one-man space freighters with their computers and phony pictures of winking dots.'

'How soon will we land?' Wuju asked him, a bit ill at the rolling and tossing he liked so much. She was happy to see him obviously enjoying himself, talking like his old self again, but if it was at the cost of this kind of upset stomach, she would take land.

'Well, they've gone exceptionally fast,' he replied. 'Strong devils, and amazing in their element. I'll have to remember that strength. Wouldn't do to underestimate our Dr Skander.'

'Yes, but *how long?*' she insisted.

'Tomorrow morning,' he replied. 'Then it'll be no more than a day or so to Ghlmon – we won't have to cross the whole hex of Ivrom, just one facet – and another day to the top of the bay in Ghlmon.'

'Do you really think we'll meet them – the others, that is – up there?' Vardia asked. 'I'm most anxious to free my other self – my sister – from those creatures.'

'We'll meet them,' Brazil assured her, 'if we beat them – and we certainly should at this rate. I know where they have to go. When they get there, we'll be ready for them.'

'Will I be able to scout this Ivrom tonight?' Cousin Bat called out to him. 'I'm sick and tired of fish.'

'I'm counting on you, Bat,' Brazil replied laughing. 'Eat up and tell us what's what.'

'No more midnight rescues from the jaws of death, though,' Bat replied in the same light vein.

'You never know, Bat,' Brazil replied more seriously. 'Maybe this time I'll rescue *you.*'

The Umiau had been remarkably uninformed about Ivrom, which wasn't as strange on the face of it as it would seem. The Umiau were water creatures, and their need was for technological items they could not manufacture. An alliance with the Czillians was natural; their other neighbors they at least knew from watery experience, even if they didn't get along too well with all of them, and Alisstl was too hot to handle. Ivrom, named from the old maps and not by the inhabitants, was peaceful forests and meadows, no major rivers, although it had hundreds of tiny creeks and streams. It was a nontechnological hex, so it wasn't easy to get to, even harder to move around in, and probably not worth the trouble. Of course, the major problem was that no one who had ever set out for Ivrom – to study, for contact, or to go through it – had ever been seen or heard from again. For that reason the party stopped on a reef, over a submerged shoal in deep water, and anchored for the night even though there would still have been time when they arrived to have made camp on or near the beach.

It did look inviting, too. The air was sweet and fresh, about twenty degrees

Celsius, surprisingly comfortable humidity for a shore area because of the inland breeze, a few light, fluffy clouds but nothing that looked threatening, and a deep blue sky.

The shoreline revealed a virgin sandy beach, flat and yellow and stretching down the coast. The breakers and some obvious storms had forced driftwood onto the shore, where it had built up near the beginning of the forest. It was a very dense forest, rather dark from the thickness of the underbrush and giant evergreens, but nothing looked suspicious or sinister. As twilight deepened, they could make out an occasional small deer and a number of other animals much like muskrats, marmots, and other woodland creatures.

It reminded Brazil of a number of really pleasant places on Old Earth before they were paved over. Even the animals and birds, now flocking to roosts in the tall trees, seemed very Earthlike – far more than even the most familiar hexes he had been through.

He wished he could recall more about the place, but he couldn't. Nobody could keep track of everything, he thought, even though the mind behind Ivrom had obviously paid a great deal of attention to a Type 41 habitat.

Insects, his mind kept telling him. But that was the kind of fact that you heard once or twice rather than recalled from personal experience, and it registered but was not something you had paid attention to at the time. Everything has changed so much it probably wouldn't matter anyway, he thought. Evolution and natural processes like erosion and deposition, diastrophism and the other forces operated in accordance with the logic of each hex, so things were constantly changing on the Well World as they were everywhere in the universe.

Darkness totally obscured the shoreline for all but Cousin Bat, who reported that he couldn't see anything they hadn't seen by day.

'Well, maybe something,' Bat corrected. 'I can't be sure at this distance, though. Looks like tiny, little, blinking lights, on and off, on and off, all over the forest – moving around, too, but slowly.'

Lightning bugs, Brazil thought. Was he the only person from their little corner of the galaxy who could remember lightning bugs?

'Well, go on in, then,' Brazil told the bat after a while, 'but be careful. Looks peaceful, but the place has a really spooky reputation, and except for the fact that my mind keeps insisting that the life form there is insects, I can't think of anything else to tell you. Just watch out for insects, no matter how small or insignificant – they might be somebody we'd rather make friends with.'

'All right,' Bat responded calmly. 'Insects are a normal part of my diet, but I won't touch them if I can help it. Just a quick survey, then I'll be back.'

They agreed and Bat took off into the darkness.

When the sun came up the next morning, Cousin Bat still had not returned.

JUST OVER THE NATION – SLELCRON BORDER – MORNING

The Rel stopped just ahead as the air suddenly cleared and they walked into bright sunshine.

'You may all remove your breathing apparatuses and discard them,' it told them. 'The air is now quite safe for all of you.'

Skander reached up and took off her mask, but stowed it in the pack case. 'I'll keep mine, and I think you others should, too,' the Umiau cautioned. 'I have no idea what the interior is like, but it's possible we may need the couple hours of air left in these tanks. If the mechanism is self-operating, it may not exist in any atmosphere.'

'I am well aware of that, Doctor,' The Rel replied. 'I, too, can not exist in a vacuum – The Diviner requires argon and neon, and I require xenon and krypton, which, thankfully, have been present in the quantities we need in all of the hexes so far. We had weeks to prepare for this expedition, you know, and I fully expected us ultimately to have to face a vacuum – in which those little respirators will do us no good whatsoever. The packs contain compressed pressure suits designed for each of us.'

'Then why didn't we use them in that hellhole we just went through?' Hain grumbled, outraged. 'That stuff burned!'

'That was a hex of sharp edges and abrasives where the suits might have suffered premature damage,' The Rel replied. 'It was a discomfort, no more. I thought it best not to take any risks with pressurized equipment until we have to.'

Hain grumbled and cursed, and Skander wasn't much better – she was drying out rapidly and itched terribly. Only Vardia was now perfectly comfortable – the sun was very strong, the sky was blue and cloudless, and she even somehow sensed the richness of the soil.

'What is this, place, anyway?' Skander asked. 'Any chance of a shady stream where I can wet down?'

'You'll survive,' The Rel responded. 'We will alleviate your discomfort as soon as we can. Yes, there are almost certainly streams, lakes, and ponds here. When I find one shallow enough and slow enough that it will not be your avenue away from us, you will get your wish.'

The place was thinly forested, but had tremendous growth of bushes and vines, and giant flowers – millions of flowers, as far as the eye could see, rising on stalks from one to three meters high, bright orange centers surrounded by eighteen perfectly shaped white petals.

Huge buzzing insects went from flower to flower, but the actions were individualistic, not as they would move in a swarm. Each was about fifty centimeters long, give or take, and very furry; and though their basic color was black, they had stripes of orange and yellow on their hind sections.

'How beautiful,' Vardia said.

'Damned noisy, if you ask me,' Skander yelled, noting the tremendous hum the insects' wings made as they moved.

'Are the insects the life form?' Hain asked. The Rel had to move back close to the huge beetle to be heard.

'No,' the Northerner replied. 'As I understand it, it is some sort of symbiosis. The flowers are. Their seeds are buried by the insects, and if all goes well the braincase develops out of the seed. Then it sprouts the stalk and finally forms a flower.'

'Then maybe I can eat a few of the buzzing bastards,' Hain said eagerly.

'No!' The Rel replied quickly. 'Not yet! The flowers drop seeds, so they do not reproduce by pollination. The bees bury the seeds, but little else – yet they are obviously gaining their food from the center of the flowers. See how one lands there, and sticks its proboscis into the orange center? If the flowers feed them, they must do something for the flower.'

'They can't uproot,' Vardia said sympathetically. 'What's the use of having a brain if you can't see, hear, feel, or move? What kind of a dominant species is that?'

The ultimate Comworld, Skander thought sarcastically, but said aloud, 'I think that's what the insects do. If you keep watching one long enough, it goes to one other flower, then returns to the original. It might go to dozens of flowers, but it returns between trips to a particular one.'

Vardia noticed a slight lump in the grass just ahead of them. Curiously she went over to it and carefully smoothed the dirt away.

'Look!' she called excitedly, and they all camd to see. 'It's a seed! And see! An egg of some kind attached to the outside! Each insect attaches an egg to each seed before burying it! It's grown attached! See where the seed case is growing over the egg, secreting that film?'

Skander almost fell out of her saddle peering over Hain's hard shell to see, but the glance she got told the story.

'Of course!' the scientist exclaimed. 'Amazing!'

'What?' they all asked at once.

'That's how they communicate – how they get around, don't you see? The insect's like a robot with a programmable brain. They grow up together – I'll bet the insect hatches fully formed and instinctively able to fly when the flower opens. Whatever it sees, hears, touches, it communicates to the flower when it returns. I'll bet after a while they can send the creatures with messages, talk to each other. And every time the insect gets to another flower, the old hands give information for it to take back. The creatures live, but they live their lives secondhand, by recording, as it were.'

'Sounds logical,' The Rel admitted. 'Hain, I would suggest you eat anything *but* those flowers and the black, striped insects. You could get huge numbers of them, we all could, but if we upset them we could face a programmed army of millions of the things. I want to be peaceful.'

'All right,' Hain agreed grumpily. 'But if there's nothing else to eat, the hell with them.'

At that moment one of the huge insects flew right into their midst and started carefully but quickly re-burying the exposed seed and egg. Satisfied, it flew off to a nearby flower and buried its head in the flower's center. They watched it carefully, both for intent and out of curiosity. Finally it seemed satisfied and backed out, flying over to them and hovering menacingly in front of them, darting from one to the other. They stayed still, but Hain's antennae radiated, 'If that thing makes one wrong move, I'll eat it regardless.'

Finally the creature got to Vardia, flew all around her, then suddenly jumped on her head, and before she could make a move it pushed its sharp, mosquito-like proboscis into the top of her head just under the leafy growth. They were all too stunned to move for several seconds. Suddenly Hain said, 'I'll zap it.'

'*No!*' Skander shouted violently. 'You might leave that thing in her. Wait a minute and let's see what happens.'

Vardia had no pain centers but she did have sensitive nerves, and they felt the thing enter and probe until it touched a particular set of nerves, the ones that sent messages to and from her head and brains.

Quite suddenly everything went dark, and a strange voice much like her own thoughts, only stronger, asked, 'Who and what are you and what are you doing here?'

She could think of nothing but answering. The alien thought was so powerful it was hypnotizing. It was more demand than question.

'We are just passing through your hex on our way to the equator.'

She felt the proboscis withdraw, and the lights came on again. She was in control and saw the thing heading away at high speed.

'Va – Chon,' Skander corrected. 'What happened?'

'It … it spoke to me. It asked who we were, and I said we were just people going through the hex toward the equator. Man! It's strong! I have the strangest feeling that I would have to answer anything it asked – and do whatever it said.'

The Rel drifted over and lifted itself up so it could examine her head with whatever it used for sensory equipment. As it drifted just a few centimeters from her up to her head, she felt a strange tingling. Obviously it did not float – something supported it.

The Diviner and The Rel seemed satisfied and floated back down. 'No sign of a wound of any kind,' the creature said. 'Amazing. One of the flowers got curious, and since you were the only member of the vegetable kingdom around, it picked you. Stay still and let it happen again. Assure them we'll do no harm and get through as quickly as possible. Tell them we're following the coast and will take care.'

'I don't think I can tell them anything they don't ask,' Vardia responded weakly. 'Oh, oh, here it comes again!'

The creature did not have to probe the second time; it went straight to the proper nerve endings, 'READOUT!' came the command, and suddenly she felt herself being drained, as if that which was her very essence was being sucked up into a bottle through a straw. The process took several minutes.

'Look!' Skander cried. 'My god! She's rooted! Un-moving in bright daylight! What did that thing do to her?'

The insect moved back into the mass of flowers.

'We can't do anything but wait,' The Rel cautioned. 'We don't know the rules here. At least those insects seem to be dominant only on the plants. Take it easy and let things run their course.'

Hain and The Rel both moved toward her, where she stood rooted and motionless. Hain pressed against her skin, and got no response, nor any from the blank eyes.

'Are we going to have to camp here?' Hain asked at last in a disgusted tone. 'Why not just leave her?'

'Patience, Hain,' The Rel warned. 'We can't afford to proceed until this drama plays itself out, even if it takes hours. We have only a little more than two hundred kilometers in this hex but we want to survive it.'

They waited, and it took hours.

Vardia felt suspended in limbo, unable to see, hear, feel, or do anything else. Yet it wasn't like being asleep – she knew that she existed, just not where.

Suddenly she felt that sucking feeling again, and suddenly she was aware of someone else. She couldn't understand how she knew, but something else was there, all right. Suddenly that force of thought she had felt when the insect had first penetrated her head was all around her.

'I MELD WHAT IS YOURS TO ME AND WHAT IS ME TO YOU,' the voice that was pure thought said, and it was so.

There was an explosion in her mind, and she clung desperately to control, to her own personality, even as she felt it being eroded away, mixed into a much larger and more powerful, yet alien, set of thoughts, memories, pictures, ideas.

Why do you resist? asked a voice that might have been her own thoughts

186

or someone else's. Submit. This is what you have always wanted. Perfect union in uniformity. Submit.

The logic was unassailable. She submitted.

'It's coming back!' Skander yelled, and the other two followed the path of the insect to Vardia's head and watched it bury its sharp proboscis as before. This time it stayed an abnormally long time – perhaps three or four times longer than it had the last trip. Finally it finished and withdrew, buzzing off back to its home flower. They watched as her body came back to life, the eyes moving, looking about. She uprooted, and moved her tentacles around, shook her legs.

'Chon! Are you all right?' Skander called out, concerned.

'We are fine, Dr Skander,' replied Vardia in a voice that was hers yet strangely different. 'We may proceed now, without any problems.'

The Diviner's little flashing lights became extremely agitated. The Rel said, 'The Diviner says that you are not the one of our party. Who or what are you? The equation has been altered.'

'We are Chon. We are everything that ever was Chon. The one you call Chon has been melded. It is no longer one but all. Soon, as even now it happens, all will be Chon and Chon will be all.'

'You're that damned flower!' Hain said accusingly. 'You swapped minds with the Czillian somehow!'

'No swap, as you call it, was involved,' it told them. 'And we are not that damned flower as you said, but *all* the flowers. The Recorders transfer and transmit as you surmised, but the process may be and usually is total at first sprout, or how else should we get our information, our intellect? A new bloom is a blank, an empty slate. We merge.'

'And you merged with the Czillian?' The Rel said more than asked. 'You have all of its memories, plus all that was you?'

'That is correct,' the creature affirmed. 'And, since we have all of the Czillian experience within us, we are aware of your mission, its reason, and goal, and we are now a part of it. You have no choice, nor do we, since we cannot meld with you.'

Skander shivered. Well, Vardia got her wish at last, the mermaid thought. And we've got problems.

'Suppose we refuse?' Skander shot at the new creature. 'One gulp from Hain here and you're gone.'

The creature in Vardia's body stepped boldly in front of Hain and looked at the big insect's huge eyes.

'Do you want to eat me, Hain?' it asked evenly.

Hain started to flick her sticky tongue, but something stopped her. Suddenly she didn't want to eat the Czillian, not at all. She liked the Czillian. It was a good creature, a creature that had the interest of the baron at heart. It was the best friend she had, the most loyal.

'I – I don't understand,' Hain said in a perplexed tone. 'Why should I want to eat it? It's my friend, my ally. I couldn't hurt it, never, or the pretty flowers and insects, either.'

'It's got some kind of mental power!' Skander screamed, and tried to free herself from the saddle in panic. Suddenly Hain spread out, lowering her shell to the ground, legs extended outward.

Skander was free of the harness and looked around for a place to leap. Her darting eyes met the lime disks of the Czillian, and suddenly all panic fled. She couldn't remember why she was afraid in the first place, not of the Czillian, anyway.

The thing came right up to the mermaid, so close they could touch. A Czillian tentacle stroked the Umiau's hair, and the mermaid smiled and relaxed, content.

'I love you,' Skander said in a sexy voice. 'I'll do anything for you.'

'Of course you will,' the Slelcronian replied gently. 'We'll go to the Well together, won't we, my love? And you'll show me everything?'

The Umiau nodded in ecstasy.

The Slelcronian turned to The Diviner and The Rel, who stood there a few meters away, viewing the scene dispassionately.

'What are you going to do with me?' The Rel asked in the closest it could come to sarcasm. 'Look me in the eye?'

For the first time the creature was hesitant, looking uncertain, puzzled, less confident. It reached out its mind to the Northern creature, and found nothing it could contact, understand, relate to. It was as if the creature was no longer there.

'If we cannot control you, you are at least irrelevant to us,' Vardia's voice said evenly. The Diviner and The Rel didn't move.

'I said the equation had changed,' The Rel said slowly. 'I didn't say which way. The Diviner is always right, it seems. Until this moment I had no idea whatsoever how we were to control Skander once in the Well, or why the addition of the Czillian tipped things more in our favor. It's clear now.'

The Rel paused for a moment. 'We have been in charge of this project from its inception,' The Rel continued. 'We have used a judicious set of circumstances and The Diviner's amazing skills to make our own situation. We lead. Now we lead without worry.'

'What power do you possess to command us?' scoffed the new Vardia. 'We are at this moment summoning the largest of our Recorders to crush you. You are no longer necessary.'

'I have no power at all, save speech and movement,' The Rel admitted as eight huge insects hummed thunderously into view over the flowery fields.

'The Diviner has the power,' The Rel added, and as it spoke the flashing lights of The Diviner grew in intensity and frequency. Suddenly visible bolts shot out from the blinking creature and struck the eight Recorders at the speed of light.

The Recorders' outlines flashed an electrical white. There was a tiny roll of thunder as each of the creatures vanished, caused by air rushing in to take the place where it had been. It sounded like eight distant cannon shots.

'Hmmm …' The Rel said in its flat tone, 'that's a new one. The Diviner is full of surprises. Shall we go? I should not like to spend more than two nights in your charming land.'

The Slelcronian mind in Vardia's body was staggered and crushed. Something seemed to deflate inside, and the confident glow in its eyes was replaced by respect mixed with something new to its experience – fear. 'We – we didn't know you had such powers,' it almost gasped.

'A trifle, really,' The Rel replied. 'Well? Do you want to join us or not? I hope you will – it's so much simpler than what The Diviner would have to do to get Skander's cooperation, and I'm certain that, in the interest of your people, both of them, you'd rather we made it before anyone else.'

The stunned creature turned to Skander and said, shakily, 'Get back into your harness. We must go.'

'Yes, my darling,' Skander replied happily, and did so.

'Your lead, Northerner,' the Slelcronian said.

'As always,' The Rel replied confidently. 'Do you know anything about Ekh'l?'

THE BEACH AT IVROM – MORNING

'Looks peaceful enough,' Vardia commented as they unloaded the raft onto the beach. 'Very pleasant, really.'

'Reminds me of the Dillian valley area, upvalley in particular,' Wuju added, as they strapped the bulky saddlebags around her.

'Something in here doesn't like people, though,' Brazil reminded them. 'This hex has no embassy at Zone, and expeditions into it have always vanished, as Bat did last night. We have only this one facet of the hex to travel, but that's still over one hundred kilometers, so I think we'll stick to the beach as long as possible.'

'What about Bat, then?' Wuju asked in a concerned voice. 'We can't just abandon him, after all he's done for us.'

'I don't like doing so any more than you do, Wuju,' Brazil replied seriously, 'but this is a big hex. He can fly at a good speed and over obstacles, and by now he could be just about anywhere. We might as well be looking for a particular blade of grass. As much as I'd like to help him, I just can't take the risk that whatever's here will get one or all of us.'

'Well, I don't like it,' Wuju said adamantly, but there was no assailing his logic on any grounds except emotion. 'We survived the Murnies,' she reminded him. 'How much worse can it be here?'

'Much,' he replied gravely. 'I survived Murithel by luck, as did you – and we knew who the enemy was and the problems. This is even more chancy, because we *don't* know what's here. We've *got* to leave Bat to the Fates. It's Bat or all of us.' And that settled that.

With Bat gone, Brazil regretted more and more his lack of arms or other appendages that could hold and use things. Although this was a nontechnological hex, several good and somewhat nasty items would be usable, and these were given to Wuju and Vardia. The centaur was given two automatic, gunpowder-powered projectile pistols, worn strapped to gunbelts worn in an X – and carrying extra ammunition clips – across her chest. Vardia had two pistols of a different kind. They squirted gas kept under pressure in attached plastic bottles. When the trigger was pulled hard, a flint would ignite the gas, which could be liberated at a controlled rate. The flamethrower was good for about ten meters, and needn't be very directional to be effective. Wuju, of course, had never fired a pistol and had no luck with the little practice gotten in in the ocean. But these were still effective short-range weapons, psychologically if nothing else, and they made a lot of noise going off.

'We stick to the beach,' Brazil reminded them. 'If we're lucky, we'll be able to get the whole way without going into the forest.'

As satisfied as they could be, they thanked the Umiau who had pulled them this far, and the mermaids left.

Brazil said 'Let's go,' in a voice more filled with tension than excitement.

The sand and huge quantities of driftwood slowed their progress, and they found on several occasions that they had to walk into the shallows to get around some points, but the journey went well.

They made good time. By sundown, Brazil estimated that they had traveled more than halfway. Since his vision was extremely poor after nightfall, and Vardia was better off rooting, they stopped for what they all hoped would be their only night in the mysterious hex.

The sandy soil was not particularly good for the Czillian, but she managed to find a hard, steady place near the beginning of the woods and was set for the night. He and Wuju relaxed nearby as the surf crashed on hidden rocks just beyond the shoreline, then gently ran up with a sizzling sound onto the beach.

Something was bothering Wuju and she brought it up. 'Nathan,' she said, 'if this is a nontechnological hex like Murithel, how come your voice works? It's still basically a radio.'

The idea had never occurred to Brazil and he thought about it. 'I can't say,' he replied carefully, 'but on all the maps and the like this is nontech, and the general logic of the hex layout dictates the same thing. It can't work, though, unless it's a byproduct of the translator. They work everywhere.'

'The translator!' she said sharply. 'Feels like a lump in the back of my throat. Where do they come from, Nathan?'

'From the North,' he told her. 'From a totally crystalline hex that grows them as we grow flowers. It's slow work, and they don't let many of them go.'

'But how does it work?' she persisted. 'It's not a machine.'

'No, not a machine in the sense we think of machines,' he replied. 'I don't think anyone knows how it works. It was, if I remember right, created in the same way as most great inventions – sheer accident. The best guess is that its vibrations cause some kind of link with the Markovian brain of the planet.'

She shivered a little, and Brazil rubbed close to her, thinking the dropping temperature was the cause. 'Want a coat?' he asked.

She shook her head negatively. 'No, I was thinking of the brain. It makes me nervous – all that power, the power to create and maintain all those rules for all those hexes, work the translators, even change people into other things. I don't think I like the idea at all. Think of a race that could build such a thing! It scares me.'

Brazil rubbed her humanoid back with his head, slowly. 'Don't worry about such things,' he said softly. 'That race is long gone.'

She was not distracted. 'I wonder,' she said in a distant tone. 'What if they *were* still around, still fooling around. That would mean we were all toys, playthings – all of us. With the power and knowledge to create all this, they would be so far above us that we wouldn't even know.' She shook him off and turned to face him. 'Nathan, what if we were just playthings for them?'

He stared hard into her eyes. 'We're not,' he responded softly. 'The Markovians are gone – long dead and gone. Their ghosts are brains like the one that runs this planet – just gigantic computers, programmed and automatically self-maintained. The rest of their ghosts are the people, Wuju. Haven't you understood that from what you've learned by this trip?'

'I don't understand,' she said blankly. 'What do you mean the people are the Markovian ghosts?'

'"Until midnight at the Well of Souls,"' he recited. 'It's the one phrase common to all fifteen hundred and sixty hexes. Think of it! Lots of us are related, of course, and many people here are variations of animals in other hexes. I figured out the solution to that part of the puzzle when I came out of the Gate the same as I went in – and found myself in a hex of what we always thought

191

of as "human." Next door were one-and-a-half-meter-tall beavers – intelligent, civilized, highly intellectual, but they were basically the same as the little animal beavers of Dillia. Most of the wildlife we've seen in the hexes that come close to the type of worlds our old race could settle are related to the ones we had back there. There's a relationship for all of them.

'These hexes represent home worlds, Wuju,' he said seriously. 'Here is where the Markovians built the test places. Here is where their technicians set up biospheres to prove the mathematics for the worlds they would create. Here's where our own galaxy, at least, perhaps all of them, was engineered ecologically.'

She shivered again. 'You mean that all these people were created to see if the systems worked? Like an art class for gods? And if it was good enough, the Markovians created a planet somewhere that would be *all* like this?'

'Partly right,' he replied. 'But the creatures weren't created out of the energy of the universe like the physical stuff. If so, they'd be the gods you said. But that's not why the world was built. They were a tired race,' he continued. 'What do you do after you can do it all, know it all, control it all? For a while you delight in being a race of gods – but, eventually, you tire of it. Boredom sets in, and you must be stagnant when you have no place else to go, nothing else to discover, to reach.' He paused, as the breaking waves seemed to punctuate his story, then continued in the same dreamy tone.

'So their artisans were assigned to create the hexes of the Well World. The ones that proved out were accepted, and the full home world was then made and properly placed mathematically in the universe. That's the reason for so much overlap – some artisans were more gifted than others, and they stole and modified each other's ideas. When they proved out, the Markovians came to the Well through the gates, not forced but voluntarily, and they passed through the mechanism for assignment. They built up the hexes, struggled, and did what none else could do as Markovians – they died in the struggle.'

'Then they settled the home worlds?' she gasped. 'They gave up being gods to suffer pain and to struggle and die?'

'No,' he replied. 'They settled on the Well World. When a project was filled, it was broken down and a new one started. What we have here today is only the youngest worlds, the youngest races, the last. The Markovians all struggled here, and died here. Not only all matter, but time itself, is a mathematical construct they had learned and overcome. After many generations, the hexes became self-sufficient communities if they worked. The Markovians, changed, bore children that bred true. It was these descendants, the Markovian seed, who went to the Well through the local gates to what we now call Zone, that huge Well we entered by. On the sixth day of the sixth month of each six years they went, and the Well took them, in a single sweep like a clock around the Well, one sweep in the middle of the night. It took them, classified them, and transported them to the home world of their races.'

'But surely,' she objected, 'the worlds had their own creatures. There is evolution—

'They didn't go physically,' he told her evenly. 'Only their substance, what the Murnies called their "essence," went. At the proper time they entered the vessels which had evolved to the point of the Well. That's why the translator calls it the Well of Souls, Wuju.'

'Then we are the Markovian children,' she breathed. 'They were the seeds of our race.'

'That's it,' he acknowledged. 'They did it as a project, an experiment. They did it not to kill their race, but to save it and to save themselves. There's a legend that Old Earth was created in seven days. It's entirely possible – the Markovians controlled time as they controlled all things, and while they had to develop the worlds mathematically, to form them and create them according to natural law, they could do millions of years work rather quickly, to slide in their project people at the exact moment when the dominant life form – or life forms – would logically develop.'

'And these people here – are they all Entries and the descendants of Entries?' she asked.

'There weren't supposed to be any,' he told her. 'Entries, that is. But the Markovians inhabited their own old universe, you know. Their old planets were still around. Some of the brains survived – a good number if we blundered into even one of them in our little bit of space. They were quasi-organic, built to be integral with the planet they served, and they proved almost impossible to turn off. The last Markovian couldn't shut his down and still get through, so they were left open, to be closed when time did to the old worlds what it does to all things left unmaintained.'

'Then there are millions of those gates still open,' she speculated. 'People could fall in all the time.'

'No,' he replied. 'The gates only open when someone wants them to be open. It doesn't have to be a mystical key – although the boy Varnett, back on Dalgonia, caused it to open by locking into his mind the mathematical relationships he observed. It doesn't happen randomly, though. Varnett was the exception. The key *is* mathematical, but anyone near one doesn't have to know the key to operate the Gate.'

'What's the key, then?' she asked, puzzled.

'Spacers – thousands of them have been through the Well, not just from our sector but from all over. I've met a number. It's a lonely, antisocial job, Wuju, and because of the Fitzgerald Contraction and rejuve, it is a long one. All those people who came here through gates got signals on the emergency band that lured them to the gates. Whether they admit it or not, they all had one thing in common.'

'What was that?' she asked, fascinated.

'They all wanted to or had decided to die,' he replied evenly, no trace of emotion in his voice. 'Or, they'd rather die than live on. They were looking for fantasy worlds to cure their problems.

'Just like the Markovians.'

She was silent for a while. Suddenly she asked, 'How do you know all this, Nathan? The people here don't, those children of the Markovians who didn't leave.'

'You got that, did you?' he responded admiringly. 'Yes, when the last were changed, they sealed the Well. Those who didn't want to go, lost their nerve, or were happy here – they stayed, with only a memory, perhaps even regret once it was done, for they kept the phrase "until midnight at the Well of Souls" alive as the symbol of forever. How do I know all this? I'm brilliant, that's why. And so is Skander – that's why we're going where we have to go.'

She accepted his explanation, not noticing the evasion. 'But if everything is sealed, why bother?' she asked. 'Skander can't do any harm, can he?'

'Deep beneath our feet is a great machine,' he told her seriously. 'The Markovian brain is so powerful that it created and maintained the home worlds as it maintains this one; the brain keeps the equations that sustain all unnaturally created matter, that can undo the fabric of time, space, and matter as it created them. Skander wants to change those equations. Not just our lives but our very existence is at stake.'

She looked at him for a long time, then turned idly, staring into the forest, lost in her thoughts.

Suddenly she said, 'Look, Nathan! The flying lights are out! And I can hear something!'

He turned and looked into the forest. They *were* insects of some kind, he thought, glowing as they flitted through the forest. The light, he saw, was constant – the blinking that had been apparent from shore was an illusion, caused by their passage behind the dense foliage. The darkness was too complete for his deer vision to get any detail, but the floating, gliding lights were clear. There was something very familiar about them, he thought. I've never been here, yet I've seen this before.

'Listen!' Wuju whispered. 'Hear it?'

Brazil's fine-trained ears had already picked it up even over the crashing of the waves.

It was music, haunting, strange, even eerie music, music that seemed to penetrate their very bodies.

'It's so strange,' Wuju said softly. 'So beautiful.'

The Faerie! he thought suddenly. Of course there'd be Faerie! He cursed himself for not thinking of it before. This close to the equator there was bound to be magic, he realized. Some of those authoritarian sons of bitches had snuck onto Old Earth and it had been hell getting rid of them. He looked anxiously at Wuju. She had a dreamy look on her face, and her upper torso was swaying in time to the music.

'Wuju!' he said sharply. 'Come on! Snap out of it!'

She pushed him away and started forward, toward the woods. He rushed up and tried to block her way, but she wouldn't be deterred. He opened his mouth and tried to grab her arm, but it wouldn't hold.

'Wuju!' he called after her. 'Don't go in! Don't desert us!'

Suddenly a dark shape swooped down from the sky at him. He ducked by lowering his forelegs and started running. It swooped again, and he cursed the poor vision that kept him from taking full advantage of his reflexes.

He heard maniacal laughter above him, and the mad thing swooped again, brushing him this time.

They're forcing me into the forest! he realized. Every time he moved in any direction but in the creature's, laughing and gibbering, it would swoop in and block his way.

'Cousin Bat! Don't do it! It's Nathan Brazil!' he called to the dark shape, knowing the effort was futile, that the bat was under a Faerie spell.

Brazil was in the woods now, where Bat couldn't follow by flying. He saw the creature standing there, outlined in the starlight glare on the ocean, looking up and down the beach.

He looked around, and barely made out a large form heading away about eight meters farther in.

It's useless, he realized. The music's got her and Bat's got me.

I've faced them down before, he thought, and won. Maybe again, because they don't know that. No choice here, though. If I don't follow they'll send some other creatures after me.

He could barely see despite the light from the flitting bugs that grew thicker and thicker as he entered the forest, but he smelled Wuju's scent and followed it.

After what must have been twenty minutes, he emerged into a clearing in the woods.

A toadstool ring, he thought grimly.

Under a particularly huge tree was a wide ring composed of huge brown toadstools. The music came from here, made by the thousands of insects that swarmed in the center of the ring. Wuju was in the ring, too, almost covered by the creatures, so thick now that they lit up the place like a lamp. She was dancing and swaying to the eerie music of their wings, as were a number of other creatures, of varying shapes and sizes.

The music grew in intensity and volume as more and more of the creatures of light came to the ring. Sitting in the hollow of the great tree, still and observing, was a glowing insect much, much larger than the others – perhaps close to a meter. It had the oval shape of a beetle, and a light, ribbed underside that was highly flexible. Two long, jointed hind legs were held in front of it in a bent but relaxed position, and two forelegs, longer and with sharp-toothed ridges, that seemed to be leading the insect orchestra, waving in perfect time. It sat like this, underside exposed, leaning against the tree, a face on a telescoping neck down on the chest, watching things. The face was strange, not insect-like at all, nor was the position of the sitter nor the fact that it had only four limbs. It appeared to have a tiny, scruffy moustache, topped by a perfectly round and black nose, and two almost human eyes that reflected the glare of the proceedings with an evil and ancient leer.

There was a sudden darkness above, and Cousin Bat landed in the middle of the circle, bowed to the large onlooker, and joined the dance. The strange eyes of the lead bug darted around the circle, then over to Brazil, whose form was just barely visible still hidden by the forest.

Suddenly the leader's forelegs went into a V shape, and the music stopped, everyone staying perfectly still; even the bugs seemed frozen in midflight.

The lead bug, who Brazil knew was the Swarm Queen, spoke to Cousin Bat, and Brazil found it interesting that the translator carried it as the voice of an incredibly tiny and ancient old woman.

So are the legends of witches born, he thought sardonically.

'You have brought only two! I charged you to bring all three!' the Swarm Queen accused Bat.

Bat bowed, his voice flat and mechanical. 'The other is a plant, Highness. It is rooted for the night, asleep beyond any recall except the morning sun.'

'That is unacceptable,' the Swarm Queen snapped. 'We have dealt with this problem before. Wait!' She turned to Brazil, and he felt the piercing eyes fall on him.

'Deer! Come into the circle!' the Swarm Queen ordered, and Brazil felt himself moving slowly, haltingly, toward the circle despite no order on his part. He felt the energy grow to almost overpowering proportions as he crossed the toadstool ring.

'The ring binds you all! Bound be ye till my return, or till morning, till midnight at the Well of Souls,' she intoned, then flipped over on her stomach, supported by all four legs. The back had long, integral wings and seemed to glow with the same stuff as her underside, although Brazil knew that was mostly reflection.

'You will show me,' she said to the bat, and Bat immediately took off, the Swarm Queen following with a tinkling sound that was like a single note in the eerie Faerie symphony.

Brazil tried to recross the circle of toadstools, found he couldn't. He idly kicked at one, but it proved to be more rock than toadstool, and his hoof met with a clacking sound but nothing else.

He looked at the inhabitants of the circle. All, like Wuju, were frozen, like statues, although he could see that they were breathing. There was a monotonous, yet pleasant, hum from the Faerie, marking place.

Many of the other creatures were vaguely humanoid; all were small, a few monkey-like, but all were distorted, hellish versions of their former selves.

Brazil remembered the encounters on Old Earth. Since the Faerie created their own press to suit themselves, they had a pretty good reputation in folklore and superstition. He had never discovered how they had managed to get in. Oh, some representatives of many other races had – some as volunteers to teach the people, some because their home worlds had closed before they personally had reached maturity and Old Earth had the room and a compatible biosphere.

He wondered idly if those primitive peasants who told such wonderful stories of the Faerie would still like them if they knew that these folk doubled as the basis for witches and many evil spirits. Once created by some Markovian mind, they could not be wiped out; they had to run their course and survive or fail as the rules said.

They had done too well. They worked their magic and dominated their own hex, using the collective mental powers of the swarm directed and guided by the Swarm Queen who was mother to them all, and tried to spread out. They managed to interfere in thirteen other Southern hexes where the mathematics did not forbid their enormous powers, before the Markovians finally moved to limit them to their own hex.

Here they were in their own element, and supreme. How many thousands, maybe hundreds of thousands, of swarms existed in this hex? Brazil wondered. I beat them outside of their own element once, but can I do it here?

About an hour passed, with Brazil, the only moving thing in the ring, getting more and more nervous; yet he held onto a streak of optimism deep inside. If they couldn't succeed with Vardia before daybreak, these nocturnal creatures would go back to their tree burrows, Swarm Queen included. How long to dawn? he wondered.

A sudden thought came to him, and he started carefully to draw a pentagram around the circle. He tried to be casual, so it didn't look as if he were doing much of anything; but his hoof managed to make the mark in the grassy meadow. This was a long shot, he knew, but it might stall the Swarm Queen until morning.

He was about halfway around when brush crackled and he saw Vardia walk onto the knoll and into the circle, the Swarm Queen resting on her sun leaf. There was a shadow above, and Bat landed back in the circle. As soon as

Vardia was across the toadstool ring, the Swarm Queen flew back over to her seat under the tree and resumed that casual and unnatural sitting position.

Too late, he thought, and stopped the pentagram. I'll have to accept the spell and break it.

The Swarm Queen looked thoughtful for a few minutes. Then, quickly, she looked at the circle. 'Be free within the circle,' she said almost casually in that tiny, old-woman's voice.

Bat staggered a few seconds, then caught himself and looked around, surprised, He saw the others and looked amazed.

'Brazil! Vardia! Wuju! How'd you get here?' he asked in a puzzled tone.

Wuju looked around strangely at the assemblage. She saw Brazil and went over to him. 'Nathan!' she said fearfully. 'What's happening?'

Vardia looked around and barely whispered, 'What a strange dream.'

Bat whirled, spied the Swarm Queen, and started to walk toward her. He got to the circle, and suddenly couldn't make his feet move. He flapped his wings for a takeoff, but didn't go off the ground.

'What the hell is this?' Bat asked strangely. 'Last I remember I was flying near the shoreline when I heard this strange music – and now I wake up here!'

'These creatures seem to –' Wuju began, but the Swarm Queen suddenly snapped, 'Stand mute!' and the Dillian's voice died in midsentence.

The Swarm Queen glanced up at the barely visible sky.

'There's a storm coming,' she said more to herself than to anyone. 'It will not be over until after dawn. Therefore, the simplest thing should be the best.' She looked up at the buzzing swarm, then flipped over and walked into the circle. Brazil could feel 'the power building up. The Swarm Queen flipped again lightly, and sat on the side of a toadstool, inside the ring, forelegs behind her to steady her.

'What shall we do with the interlopers?' she asked the swarm.

'Make them fit,' came a collective answer from the swarm.

'Make them fit,' the Swarm Queen echoed. 'And how can we make them fit when we have so little time?'

'Transform them, transform them,' suggested the swarm.

The Swarm Queen's gaze fell on Wuju, who almost withered at the look and clung to Brazil.

'You wish him?' the Swarm Queen asked acidly. 'You shall have him!' Her eyes burned like coal, and the humming of the swarm intensified to an almost unbearable intensity.

Where Wuju had been, there was suddenly a doe, slightly smaller and sleeker than Brazil's stag. The doe looked around at the lights, confused, and then leaned down and munched a little grass, oblivious to the proceedings.

The Swarm Queen turned to Vardia. 'Plant, you want so much to act the animal, so shall you be!'

The buzzing increased again, and where Vardia had stood was another doe, identical to the one that had been Wuju.

'It's easier to use something local, that you know,' the Swarm Queen remarked to no one in particular. 'I have to hurry.' She turned her gaze on Cousin Bat.

'You like them, be like them!' she ordered, and Bat, too, turned into a doe identical in every way to the other two.

Now she turned to Brazil. 'Stags should not think,' she said. 'It is unnatural. Here is your harem, stag. Dominate them, rule them, but as what you are, not what you pretend to be!'

The swarm increased again, and Brazil's mind went blank, dull, unthinking.

'And finally,' pronounced the Swarm Queen, 'so that so complex a spell, done so hurriedly, does not break, I bequeath to the four the fear and terror of all but their own kind, and of all things which disturb the beasts. They are free of the circle.'

Brazil suddenly bolted into the dark, the other three following quickly behind.

There was the rumble of thunder, the flash of lightning.

'The circle is broken,' intoned the Swarm Queen.

'We go to shelter,' responded the swarm as it dispersed. The other creatures came alive, some gibbering insanely, others howling, as the lightning and thunder increased.

The Swarm Queen flipped and walked quickly over to her tree and into the base.

'Sloppy job,' she muttered to herself. 'I hate to rush.'

The rain started to fall.

Even though it *was* a sloppy spell, it took Brazil almost a full day and night to break it. The flaw was a simple one: at no time during the encounter had the Swarm Queen heard him talk, and it just hadn't occurred to her that he could. The input-output device on the translator continued to operate, although it did little good for the rest of the night in the storm and throughout the next day, when the nocturnal Faerie were asleep.

When the creatures emerged at nightfall, though, they talked. The conversations were myriad, complex, and involved actions and concepts alien to his experience, but they did form words and sentences which the transceiver mounted in his antlers delivered to his brain. These words, although mostly nonsense, gave a continual input that banged at his mind, stimulated it, gave it something to grab onto. Slowly self-awareness returned, concepts formed, forced their way through the spell's barrier.

That spark inside of him that had always ensured his preservation would not let him lapse or quit. Concepts battered at his brain, forcing word pictures in his mind, building constructs which burst into his consciousness.

It was like a war against an invisible barrier, something inside him attacking, always beating at the blocks that had been placed.

Suddenly, he was through. Memories crowded back, and with them came reason. He felt exhausted – he was totally worn out from the struggle, yet he knew that precious time had been wasted, and more roadblocks raised.

He looked around in the dark. It was very hard to see anything except the flitting shapes of the Faerie, but he knew that he must be deep inside the hex. He looked around. Asleep nearby were the three transformed members of the expedition, absolutely identical even to scent. The Swarm Queen *had* been in a hurry and had used but a single model.

Realizing there was little that could be done until shortly before dawn, lest he give himself away to some curious Faerie by acting undeer-like, he relaxed and waited for the sky to lighten.

With daylight came safety, and the freedom to move. He spent over an hour trying to make some kind of contact with the three does, but their stares were blank, their actions totally natural. The spell could not be broken from without as far as they were concerned.

For a while he considered abandoning them; they would follow him to the border, of course, but would be unable to cross it. The stakes certainly warranted it; logic dictated it.

But he knew he couldn't do it. Not without a good try.

He started off, wishing he could trace the wild, crazy route they had used to get where they were. He decided that the best thing to do would be to head due east; no matter what, that would bring him to the ocean sooner or later, and from there he could get his bearings.

He moved with the swiftness that only a deer could have in the forest, and the three followed him loyally, almost slavishly. Part of the spell, he guessed. The Swarm Queen had bound Wuju to him, and then duplicated her transformation precisely on the other two, which simplified things a great deal.

He made the ocean before nightfall, but had no way of telling if he were north or south of the Faerie colony he sought. He decided that he had accomplished enough for one day, and that the next day would tell the story.

He awoke later than intended, the sunlight already glaring down on the ocean, causing diamond-like facets to cover the surface.

Which way? he wondered. Am I north or south of our last position?

He finally decided to go north; at worst, this would take him to the Ghlmon border and where he had to go. If he didn't run into the place he was looking for, he would have to abandon them for a while and return later to straighten the matter out. About an hour up the beach he came upon the packs, still sitting in the sand where they had camped the first night. They were wet and sand-blown, but still intact.

As the does romped in the surf or sniffed at the strange-smelling things in the sand, he worked feverishly, cursing his lack of hands. It took ten minutes to open a pack, and several more to work one of the flame guns that Vardia had carried out of the pack. The next task was somehow to pick it up.

He finally managed a grip of sorts with his mouth. It was awkward, and he dropped it many times as he went back into the forest, but each time he patiently turned it just right and handled it again.

It seemed like hours getting the flame pistol through that forest, but at last he came upon the clearing of ominously familiar character: the toadstool ring and the great tree. It was too well etched in his memory to be simply a similar place of some other swarm, and his deer's nose confirmed the proper scents.

Carefully he searched for a large, uneven rock, and with great difficulty rolled it to within a meter of the hollow area that was the Swarm Queen's throne, at the base of the big tree. He managed to prop the flame gun sideways against the rock, so that it was mostly upright and pointed at the hollow.

Satisfied, he went and got sticks from the forest and built a crude pentagram around the pistol and rock. Next he positioned himself so his forelegs were on either side of the pistol, the left one serving as a backstop for the grip area which also contained the gas, the right one just to the right of the trigger.

He nodded to himself in satisfaction, and briefly checked the sun and the location of his three does, all of whom were idly grazing nearby. About two hours to sundown, he thought. Just about right.

He brought his right foreleg to bear on the trigger. The pistol jiggled but remained in the right general direction. There was a hiss of escaping gas, but no flame. He released it, realizing that the flint igniter mechanism would require a hard and quick jerk on the trigger.

He knew that, if he did that, he might lose control of the gun, even have it suddenly jump up and burn him. He sighed and made up his mind. Tensely, he planted his left foreleg against the gun butt and his right just touching the large, unguarded trigger made for Czillian tentacles.

Suddenly, in one sudden motion, he pulled against the trigger hard with his right leg. It jumped a little, but stayed firm.

And remained unignited.

Steeling himself, he tried again. Once more it failed to ignite, because he had flinched and not pushed the trigger straight back. He wondered idly if he could succeed, given his physical limitations. If not, he would just have to abandon his companions.

He tried one more time, using extra force. The pistol ignited, but the thing almost jerked out of his precarious hold. Carefully, without releasing the trigger, he gingerly managed to point the thing back in the general direction of the tree. Just to the left of the tree the area was smoldering, some of it still afire.

Now the jet of flame focused on the tree hollow, and he could see the bark smolder and catch, the fire almost enveloping the tree like something liquid and living. Smoke billowed up, the scent disturbing to his nostrils. Birds screeched, and forest animals ran for cover in panic.

Suddenly he heard what he had been waiting for: a tiny, weak voice coughing. The Swarm Queen had more than one exit available, and she crawled dizzily out of the top of the tree trunk, near the point where the four main branches went off. She was blind, sick, and groping feebly, starting to make her way up the side of one of the branches.

'Swarm Queen!' he called, not letting up on the flame. 'Shall I burn you or will you meet my conditions under pain of reversal?'

'Who are you that dares do this to me?' she managed, coughing and groaning in fear and misery as she maintained her dignity.

'He who was wronged by you, and he who drove your ancestors off distant planets!' he replied boldly, but idly and somewhat fearfully wondering how much more of a charge the pistol had. 'Do you yield under pain of reversal?'

The large bug hadn't made it up the branch, almost overcome by the smoke and feeling the flames. Brazil was suddenly afraid she would fall into the fire before she yielded.

'I – I yield!' she called. 'Turn off your cursed fire!'

'Say the whole thing!' he demanded.

'I yield under pain of reversal, dammitall!' she screamed nervously.

At that moment the charge ran out of the gun and it sputtered and died. Brazil let go, and looked at it strangely. *A few seconds longer,* he thought, *and I'd have lost.*

'Get me down before I burn!' screamed the Swarm Queen, who was still very much in danger. The flames continued to smolder in the tree and around the trunk, although without the added fire they were slowly turning to glowing red against the charred and blackened side.

'Jump straight ahead and fly to the ground,' he told her. 'You know the distance.'

She could have done so before, of course, but the heat and fire always induced panic in these creatures.

She landed shakily and sat, trembling, for several minutes. Finally she regained her composure and peered up at him with those old and evil semi-human eyes, squinting. She was not totally blind in the light, but her vision was quite poor.

'You're the deer!' she gasped in amazement. 'How did you break the spell? How do you talk at all?'

'Your spells cannot hold me for long,' he told her. 'That which inhabits this simple vessel is your superior. But it *does* bind my companions, and it is for their sake that I charge you.'

'You have three charges only!' she spat, looking at the still smoking, blackened tree. 'Consider them carefully, lest I kill you for what you have done to my home and my honor!'

'Honor be damned,' Brazil replied disgustedly. 'If you had any, there would have been no need to invoke a reversal. Remember *that* well. Should you default on the charges, it is I who will be Swarm Queen and you who will be a deer!'

'State the charges, alien,' she responded in a bitter tone. 'They will be honored.'

Brazil thought carefully.

'One,' he said. 'My three companions and I shall cross the border into Ghlmon, traversing the distance from here to there without spell or any form of interference that would cause danger or delay.'

The Swarm Queen's eyebrows rose, and she said, 'Done.'

'Two: the spells shall be removed from my three companions, and they shall regain all mental faculties, all memory, and shall be restored to their original forms.'

'Done,' the Swarm Queen agreed. 'And the third?'

'You shall cast a spell to be effective when we cross the Ghlmon border that will erase all memories, effects, and signs of us four having been here, including those from your own mind.'

'A pleasure,' she said. 'So shall it be when darkness falls.'

'Until midnight at the Well of Souls,' he responded.

And she was stuck. Should any of the conditions cease to function or be unfulfilled, the original spell would bounce back at her.

Nightfall came in about two hours. There were still some wisps of smoke from the tree, but little else to show the struggle. When the swarm emerged from its thousands of holes in the surrounding trees, it found the queen disturbed, but they sensed that a battle had been fought and that she had lost. Since their power could only be focused through her, they had to go along.

The three does had scattered during the fire, but all had timidly returned by dusk and were herded into the toadstool circle without much difficulty.

The Swarm Queen's eyes burned with hatred, but she followed orders. As the swarm gathered in the circle and hummed its strange music, she pronounced the first charge, for their safe conduct, then turned to the second.

'The three within the circle shall be restored in mind and body to their original selves!' she pronounced, and as she said it, it was so.

Brazil gasped, cursing himself for a fool in remembering the literalness of charges.

In the circle stood Vardia, not as a Czillian, but as she had looked those first days on his ship – human, about twelve years old, thirty or so kilos, with shaven head.

Next to her, looking even more confused, was not the Dillian Wuju but Wu Julee, obviously a healthy and unaddicted one, but about forty-five kilos, long black hair, and decent-sized but saggy breasts.

And there was a stranger there. He was a boy, about Vardia's apparent physical age, with short hair and pre-pubescent genitals, about 150 centimeters tall, muscled, and fairly well proportioned.

'Well, Master Varnett,' Brazil said, bemused. 'Out of the woodwork early, I guess.'

EKH'L

The Diviner and the Rel and the Slelcronian in Vardia's body surveyed the towering, snow-capped mountains ahead of them.

The mountains, majestic and all-encompassing, ran right to the sea. A small beach was visible, composed of blackish sand. Out into the water they could see sea stacks, the remnants of long-extinct volcanic activity. The sky was a leaden gray, and the air was terribly cold off the ocean.

'Clouds will be moving in soon,' Hain remarked behind them. 'Rain or snow likely all along the beach. We'd better get started.'

'Can we make it without going into the mountains?' the Slelcronian asked apprehensively. 'What if we run out of beach?'

'Friend Hain, here, can cling to the sheer walls if necessary,' The Rel replied confidently, 'and she can ferry us around that way. No, this looks like rough, slow going but one of the easiest steps. The border with Yrankhs is just a few meters beyond the waterline, so we're not likely to meet the denizens of Ekh'l – a kind of flying ape, I believe. The Yrankhs are not ones we'd like to meet – flesh-eaters all – but they are water-breathers and not likely to bother us unless we decide to swim.'

'The fog's coming in,' Skander noted. 'We'd better get going.'

'Agreed,' responded The Rel, and they started down to the beach.

It was easy going, relatively speaking. The beach did disappear for several miles at one point or another, but although it ate up a lot of time, there was no problem in Hain ferrying them across one by one.

After almost three days, including delays from both terrain and a cold, bitter rain that stopped them for several hours, they were about three-quarters of the way to the Ghlmon border. The only living things they had encountered were seabirds in the millions, crying out in rage at the intruders. Once or twice they thought they caught sight of something huge flying about the mountaintops on great white wings, but the creatures never came close and no one was sure.

At a particularly long break in the beach, which took Hain over an hour to negotiate each way, the only incident of the slow passage occurred.

Hain set off first with the Slelcronian and the supplies, leaving The Diviner and The Rel alone with Skander on the beach.

Skander sat munching some dried fish, apparently unconcerned about the pace or the rough portage ahead. Then, satisfied that Hain was out of sight and hearing along the rocky cliff, the Umiau looked up at The Rel. It was hard to tell the front from the back of the creature even if she knew the Northerner *had* a front or back.

Slowly, almost imperceptibly, she started edging down toward the nearby ocean breakers.

Less than five meters from the water, The Rel noticed, and started coming toward Skander at a surprisingly fast speed. 'Stop!' the creature called. 'Or we shall stop you!'

Skander hesitated a fateful moment, then made a break for the beckoning waves.

The Diviner's glowing, winking lights became extremely intense, and something shot out from the globe, striking with a loud crash just in front of the mermaid. Skander rolled but did not stop.

Another bolt shot out, striking Skander in the back, and she gave a cry then went limp, the water actually touching her outstretched arm. The body was motionless, eyes staring, but the sharp rise and fall of the chest showed that she lived.

The Rel glided up to the creature and halted next to the body.

'I wondered just how long that mind of yours would be controlled by that silly hypnotism,' it said in its even, toneless voice. 'But you forgot the Slelcronian lesson. Don't worry – you will be able to move soon. A fraction more voltage and your heart would have stopped, though. The only reason that you live is that we need you. The same for the others – Hain for transportation, the Slelcronian because its powers might be useful in a pinch. Now, you'll be coming around shortly. But remember this! If you escape you are of no use to me. If we must choose between losing you and killing you, you are most surely dead. Now, you may move – the *correct* way. And shall we say nothing of this to our companions, eh?'

Skander surrendered, as movement returned. She still felt numb, but not merely of body. The Rel continued in control, and she had no doubt that she was trapped.

Hain returned in a little over two hours, and, after a short rest, was able to handle the two of them.

'We're almost there,' the great insect told them. 'You can see the damned place from the last stretch of beach. It looks like a piece of hell itself.'

Hain was right. Ghlmon looked like a place one would run *from*, not to. The shoreline curved off to the northwest, and the land of Ghlmon started abruptly, the last of the Ekh'l mountains just slightly inching into the new hex. It was a land of blowing sand, dunes ranging in all directions right down to the sea. Outside of the ocean, there was no sign of water, vegetation, or any break in the oranges and purples of the swirling sand.

'You really would have to be crazy to go there willingly, wouldn't you?' Hain said slowly, more to herself than to the others.

'No water at all,' Skander sighed.

'No soil, nothing but sand,' the Slelcronian added unhappily.

'The first truly pleasant place we've seen in the South,' said The Rel.

Skander turned to The Rel. 'Well, O leader, how do we proceed?' she asked sarcastically.

'We keep to the coast,' the Northerner responded casually. 'Hain can continue to catch fish. The Slelcronian will have to go without vitamins for a day or two, but it will get plenty of sun. Better water in that stream back there,' The Rel told the plant creature.

While the Slelcronian did so, Skander asked, 'What about you, Rel? Or don't you eat?'

'Of course we eat,' The Rel replied. 'Silicon. What else?'

In a few minutes, they crossed the border.

The wind was close to forty kilometers per hour, the temperature around forty degrees Celsius. It was like going from midwinter into the worst day of summer, and the swirling sand bit deeply into all of them.

They were still within sight of the Ekh'l mountains when they had to stop for the day. Skander collapsed on the hot sand and shook her head exhaustedly. 'What kind of creatures could possibly live in this hell?' she mused.

Almost as if to answer the question, a tiny head popped out of the sand near them. Suddenly, it leaped out of the sand, revealing a small, two-legged dinosaur, about a meter high, with short, stubby arms terminating in tiny but very human hands. It had a very long tail which seemed to balance it.

It was a darker green than the Czillian, but this was broken by what appeared to be a tiny, rust-colored vest and jacket. The creature came up to them and stopped. Its flat head and raised eyes set on each side of a spade-shaped mouth surveyed them with quick, darting motions. Suddenly it leaned back on its tail in a relaxed posture.

'I say, old fellows,' it said suddenly in a casual tenor that seemed to come from deep inside its throat – suggesting a translator in use – 'Are you the good guys or the bad guys?'

IVROM

'This turning you all back into what we think of as human has some definite drawbacks,' Nathan Brazil, still a giant stag, complained as they walked up the beach. The packs were on him, since none of the other three could now manage the heavy load.

'You think *you* have problems,' Wu Julee responded. 'We're all stark naked and none of the clothing in the packs fits anymore.'

'Not to mention feeling hunger, and pain, and cold again,' Vardia put in. 'I had forgotten these sensations, and I don't like them. I was happier as a Czillian.'

'But how is it possible?' Wuju asked. 'I mean, how could things done by the Markovian brain be so undone?'

'Why not ask Varnett?' Brazil suggested. 'He's the brain that got this mess started, anyway.'

'You all are yelling about trivialities,' Varnett sulked. 'I could *fly*. And before I set out to catch you, Brazil, I experienced sex. For the first time, I experienced sex. Now I'm back in this retarded body again.'

'Not that retarded,' Brazil responded. 'You were arrested chemically, but that's all out of your body now. Just as the sponge is out of Wuju. You should mature normally, in a couple of years, depending on your genes and your diet. Good looking, too, if I remember rightly, since you're based on Ian Varnett. I remember him as one hell of a womanizer – particularly for a mathematician.'

'You *knew* Ian Varnett?' the boy gasped. 'But – he's been dead some six hundred years!'

'I know,' said Nathan Brazil wistfully. 'He got caught up in the great experiment on Mavrishnu. What a waste. *You* know it was a waste, Varnett – I saw your Zone interviews.'

'There has always been trouble with Varnetts on Mavrishnu,' the duplicate of the great mathematician, made from cells of the long-dead original's frozen body, said with a gleam in his eye. 'They tried three or four early on, but I'm the first one in more than a century. They needed him again, at least, his potential. I wasn't the first to interrupt Skander at his real work and inquiries – a lot of skillful agents put everything together. They were raising me for a different, more local set of problems, but I was already proving to be, I think, too much of a problem. They set me up on Dalgonia to see if I could crack Skander's work, figuring that whether I did or didn't they could get me when I returned.'

The group continued talking as they walked down the beach, unhampered – as the charge to the Faerie required – by any obstructions.

'How much *do* you know, Varnett? About all this, that is,' Brazil asked.

'When I saw the cellular sample of the Dalgonian brain in the computer storage, I recognized the mathematical relationship of the sequence and order of the energy pulses,' the boy remembered. 'It took about three hours to get the sequence, and one or two more to nail it down with the camp's computers. I only had to look at the thing to see that the energy waveforms represented there bore no resemblance to anything we knew, and the matter-to-energy-to-matter process within the cells was easily observed. I combined what I saw with what we theorized *must* be the reason the Markovians had no artifacts. The planetary brain created anything you wanted, stored anything you wanted, on demand, perhaps even by thought. That gave me *what* was going on in that relationship, although I still haven't any idea *how* it's done.'

Vardia was impressed. 'You mean it was like the spells on us here – they just *wished* for something and it was there?'

'That's how the magic works here,' Varnett affirmed. 'The only way such a concept is possible is if, in fact, *nothing* is real. All of us, these woods, the ocean, the planet – even that sun – are merely constructs. There is nothing in the universe but a single energy field; everything else is taking that energy, transmuting it into matter or different forms of energy, and holding it stable. That's reality – the stabilized, transmuted primal energy. But the mathematical constructs that are so stabilized are in constant tension, like a coiled spring. The energy would revert to its natural state if not kept in check. These creatures – the Faerie – have some control over that checking process. Not enough to make any huge changes, but enough to change the equation slightly, to vary reality. That's magic.'

'I don't understand what you're saying too well,' Wuju put in, 'but I think I get the basic idea. You're saying that the Markovians were gods and could do or have anything they wished for, just like that.'

'That's about it,' Varnett admitted. 'The gods were real, and they created all of us – or, at least, the conditions under which we could develop.'

'But that would be the ultimate achievement of intelligence!' Vardia protested. 'If that were true, why did they die out?'

Wuju smiled knowingly and looked to Nathan Brazil, once the only human, now the only nonhuman in the party, who was being uncharacteristically silent.

'I heard someone say why they died,' Wuju replied. 'That someone said that when they reached the ultimate, it became dull and boring. Then they created new worlds, new life forms here and there – and all went off as those new forms to start from the beginning again.'

'What a horrible idea,' Vardia said disgustedly. 'If that were true, it means that even perfection is imperfect, and that when our own people finally reach this godhood, they'll find it wanting and die out by suicide, maybe leaving a new set of primitives to do the same thing all over again. It reduces all the revolutions, the struggles, the pain, the great dreams – everything – to nonsense! It means that life is pointless!'

'Not pointless,' Brazil put in suddenly. 'It just means that grand schemes are pointless. It means that you don't make your own life pointless or useless – most people do, you know. It wouldn't make any difference if ninety-nine percent of the people of the human race – or any other – lived or not. Except in sheer numbers their lives are dull, vegetative, and nonproductive. They never dream, never read and share the thoughts of others, never truly experience the fulfilling equation of love – which is not merely to love others, but to be loved as well. That is the ultimate point of life, Vardia. The Markovians never found it. Look at this world, our own worlds – all reflecting the Markovian reality, which was based on the ultimate *materialist* Utopia. They were like the man with incredible riches, perhaps a planet of his own designed to his own tastes, and every material thing you can imagine producible at the snap of his fingers, who, nonetheless, is found dead one morning, having cut his own throat. All his dreams have been fulfilled, but now he is there, on top, alone. And to get where he was, he had to purge himself of what was truly of value. He killed his humanity, his spirituality. Oh, he could love – and buy what he loved. But he couldn't buy that love he craved, only service.

'Like the Markovians, when he got where he'd wanted to be all his life, he found he didn't really have anything at all.'

'I reject that theory,' Vardia said strongly. 'The rich man would commit suicide because of the guilt that he had all that he had while others starved, not out of some craving for love. That word is meaningless.'

'When love is meaningless, or abstract, or misunderstood, then is that person or race also meaningless,' Brazil responded. 'Back in the days of Old Earth one group had a saying, "What shall it profit a man, if he shall gain the whole world, and lose his own soul?" Nobody listened then, either. Funny – haven't thought of that group in years. They said God was love, and postulated a heaven of communal love, and a hell for those who could not love. Later on that got crudded up with other stuff until the ideas were gone and only the artifacts were left. Like the Markovians, they paid more attention to *things* than to *ideas* – and, like the Markovians, they died for it.'

'But surely the Markovian civilization was heaven,' Vardia said.

'It was hell,' Brazil responded flatly. 'You see, the Markovians got everything their ancestors had ever dreamed of, and they *knew* it wasn't enough. They *knew* that something attainable was missing. They searched, poked, queried, did everything to try and find why the people were miserable, but since everything they had or knew was a construct of themselves, they couldn't find it. They decided, finally, to go back and repeat the experiment, little realizing that it, too, was doomed to failure – for the experiment, our own universe, was made in a variety of shapes and forms, but it was still in their own image. They didn't even bother to make a clean start – they used themselves as the prototypes for all the races they'd create, and they used the same universe – the one they'd lived in, rose in, and failed in. That's why their artifacts are still around – the two artifacts they had – their cities and their control brains.'

Varnett let out a gasp. 'Suddenly I think I see what you mean. This Well World we're on, if you're right, not only provided the trial-lab runs for the new races and their environments, and the way of changing everything to match – it was also the control!'

'Right,' Brazil affirmed grimly. 'Here everything was laboratory-standard, lab-created, monitored, and maintained by automatic equipment to keep it that way. Not all of them – just a representative sample, the last races to be created, since they were the easiest to maintain.'

'But our race here destroyed itself,' Varnett protested. 'I heard about it. Does that mean we're out of it? That the best we can do is destroy ourselves, destroy others, or, perhaps, reach the Markovian level and wind up committing suicide anyway? Is there no hope?'

'There's hope,' Brazil replied evenly. 'And despair, too. That religion of Old Earth I told you about? Well, those who believed in it had the idea that their God sent his son, a perfect human being filled with nothing but goodness and love, to us humans. Son-of-God question aside, there really *was* such a person born – I watched him try to teach a bunch of people to reject material things and concentrate on love.'

'What happened to him?' Wuju asked, fascinated.

'His followers rejected him because he wouldn't rule the world, or lead a political revolution. Others capitalized on his rhetoric for political ends. Finally he upset the established political system too much, and they killed him. The religion, like those founded by other men of our race in other times, was politicized within fifty years. Oh, there were *some* devoted followers – and of others like this man, too. But they were never in *control* of their religion, and became lost or isolated in the increased institutionalizing of the faiths. Same thing happened to an older man, born centuries earlier and thousands of miles away. He didn't die violently, but his followers substituted *things* for *ideas* and used the quest for love and perfection as a social and political brake to justify the miseries of mankind. No, the religious prophets who made it were the ones who thought in Markovian terms, in political terms – the founder of the Com, for example, saw conditions of material deprivation that made him sick. He dreamed of a civilization like that of the Markovians, and set the Com on its way. He succeeded the best, because he appealed to that which everyone can understand – the quest for material Utopia. Well, he can have it.'

'Now, hold on, Brazil!' Varnett protested. 'You say you were there when all these people were around. That must have been thousands of years ago. Just how old are you, anyway?'

'I'll answer that when we get to the Well,' Brazil responded. 'I'll answer all questions then, not before. If we don't get to the Well before Skander and whoever's with him, it won't make any difference, anyway.'

'Then they could supplant the Markovians, change the equations?' Varnett asked, aghast. 'I at one time thought I could, too, but logic showed me how wrong I was. My people – my *former* people, those of the night – agreed with me. It was only when word came that Skander might make a run for it that they decided to send me to head him off. That's why I joined up with you, Brazil – you said you were going to do the same thing back in Zone. Our mysterious informant told us to link up with you if we could, and I did.'

'Now how could –' Brazil started, then suddenly was silent for a moment, thinking. Suddenly the voice box between his antlers gave off a wry chuckle. 'Of course! What an idiot I've been! I'll bet that son of a bitch has bugged every embassy in Zone! I'd forgotten just what kind of a devious mind he had!'

'What are you talking about?' Wuju asked, annoyed.

'The third player – and a formidable one. The one who warned Skander against kidnap, got Varnett to link up with me. He knew all along where Varnett, here, and Skander were. He just wanted to be there for the payoff, as usual. I was his insurance policy, in case anything went wrong – and it did. Skander was kidnapped, and out of control or immediate surveillance. At least he has managed to delay one or another party on the way to the Well so that we're supposed to get there at about the same time – where he'll have a reception party waiting for us. He warned Skander so I'd have time to get to Grill, about even with them on the other side of the ocean. When we were trapped with the Murnies, he pulled strings to get the Czillians to put pressure on The Nation to bottle them up until we were even again! I don't wonder that he might have some influence with the Faerie – maybe the Skander party somehow got bogged down, too!'

'Who the hell are you talking about, Nathan?' Wuju persisted.

'Look!' Brazil said. 'There's Ghlmon, the last hex before the equator! See the burned-out reddish sand? It goes across two hexes in width, a half-hex tall.'

'*Who?*' Wuju persisted.

'Well,' Brazil replied hesitantly, 'unless I am wildly mistaken, somewhere out in that sunburned desert we'll meet up with him.'

'Are we going to cross the border today?' Varnett asked, looking at the sun, barely above the horizon.

'Might as well,' Brazil responded. 'It's going to be pretty tough on all of us there, so we'd better get used to it. The heat's going to be terrible, I think, and my fur coat's going to be murder, while your naked skins will be roasted. So we'd better push on into the night as much as we can, following the shoreline as we have. Days may be unworkable there.'

Wuju had an infuriated look on her face, but Brazil speeded up, forcing them into a jog to keep up, and within a few minutes they crossed the border.

The heat hit them like a giant blanket, and it was humid, too, this close to the ocean. Within minutes of crossing the border, they had slowed to almost a crawl, the three humans perspiring profusely, Brazil panting wildly, tongue hanging out of his mouth. Finally, they had to stop and rest. Dusk brought only slight relief.

Wuju looked again at Brazil with that I'd-like-to-kill-you expression. Hot, winded, the sand burning her feet and, when she sat down, her rear, she remained undeterred.

'Who, Nathan?' she persisted, gasping for breath.

Brazil's stag body looked as uncomfortable as anyone's, but that mechanical voice of his said evenly, 'The one person who could know for certain that I would go after Skander, and that I would get to you in Dillia before going anywhere, was the only person who could tell Varnett where to find me and why. He was a pirate in the old days. You couldn't trust him with anything if he could make a shekel going against you, yet you could trust him with your life if there were no profit in it. That's what I forgot – the stakes are high here; there's a bigger profit potential than anyone could think of. He told me I could get help from everyone of all races, but trust none – including him, as it turned out. Although he figured I wouldn't think of him as an opponent since we'd been good friends and I owed him. He was almost right.'

Understanding hit her at last, and she brightened. '*Ortega!*' she exclaimed. 'Your friend we met when we first entered Zone!'

'The six-armed walrus-snake?' Vardia put in. '*He's* behind all this?'

'Not *all* this,' came a voice behind them – a clipped, casual male voice that carried both dignity and authority. 'But he still is happy everything has turned out right.'

They all whirled. In the near-darkness, it was hard for any of them to see properly, but the creature looked for all the world like a meter-tall dinosaur, dark green skin and flat head, standing upright on large hind legs, while holding a curved pipe in a stubby hand. He also appeared to be wearing an old-fashioned formal jacket.

The creature puffed on the pipe, the coals glowing in the dark.

'I say,' it said pleasantly, 'do you mind if I finish my pipe before we travel? Terrible waste otherwise, y'know.'

WEST GHLMON

The four of them looked curiously at the strange creature. Brazil could only think that he should have been in *Alice in Wonderland.* The others took the appearance of the new arrival more calmly, having grown used to strange creatures and strange ways by this time.

'You were sent by Serge Ortega?' Brazil asked evenly.

The creature took its pipe out of its mouth and assumed an insulted expression. 'Sir, I am the Duke of Orgondo. This is Ghlmon. The Ulik have no authority here. They are merely our neighbors. We were approached only a few days ago by Mr Ortega about this matter, and we are, of course, much concerned. The Ulik interest is – well, frankly, closer to ours. We know them and understand them. We've gotten along for thousands of years with them. With their help we managed to survive when the environment here changed and the soil turned to sand. But all of you – Mr Ortega included – are here at our sufferance, and we will brook no intrusions into sovereignty.'

'What's he saying?' Vardia asked, and the others added their confusion. For the first time, Brazil realized that now they could understand only people with translators and those speaking Confederacy. Their own translators had gone along with their former bodies.

'Pardon me, Your Grace,' Brazil said politely. 'I will have to translate, for, I fear, my companions have no translators.'

The lizard looked at the three humans. 'Hmmm … Most curious. I had been told to expect a Dillian, Czillian, and a Creit. We heard that you would be an antelope, and that so far is the only correct information. You are Mr Brazil, are you not?'

'I am,' Brazil replied. 'The male is Mr Varnett, the female with breasts is

Wuju, and the undeveloped female is Vardia. We did, after all, have to come through Ivrom. That, in itself, is an accomplishment, I should think – to have come through unaltered would have been a miracle.'

'Quite,' nodded the Ghlmonese. 'But we had no doubt you would come through, although there's been hell to pay for the three days you disappeared. We figured you'd been bewitched, and started moving some diplomatic mountains to find who had you.'

'Then that bewitching stuff wasn't part of Ortega's tricks?' Brazil responded. 'He seemed awfully confident we'd get through.'

'Oh, no, he figured that you would get stuck,' the duke replied casually. 'But we of Ghlmon are more adept at the arts than those filthy savages in Ivrom. It was only a matter of finding you. We already had the other party, so nothing was disturbed no matter how long it took,'

'So what's the next move now?' Brazil asked calmly.

'Oh, you'll be my guests for the night, of course,' the duke said warmly. 'Tomorrow, we'll get you on a sandshark express and take you to the capital at Oodlikm, where you will link up with Ortega and the other party. From that point it will be Ortega's show, although we'll be watching.'

Brazil nodded. 'This game is getting so crowded you need a scorecard.' He provided a running translation of the conversation so that the others could follow what was going on. Finally the creature's pipe went out, and it tapped the bowl and shook out the last remains of whatever it had been smoking. It smelled like gunpowder.

'Places have been prepared for you,' the duke told them. 'Ready to go? It's not far.'

'Do we have a choice?' Brazil retorted.

The little dinosaur got that hurt look again. 'Of course! You may go back across the border, or jump in the ocean. But, if you plan to stay in Ghlmon, you will do what *we* wish.'

'Fair enough,' the stag replied. 'Lead on.'

They followed the little dinosaur along the beach in silence for a little over a kilometer. There, by the side of the sea, a huge tent of canvas or something very similar had been erected. A flag was flying from the tent's center mast. Several Ghlmonese stood around nearby, and tried not to look bored to death.

Two by the tent flap snapped to attention as the duke approached, and he nodded approvingly. 'Everything ready?' he asked.

'The table is set, Your Grace,' one replied. 'Everything should be suitable.'

The duke nodded and the sentry held back the flap so he could enter and kept it open for the others to pass through.

Inside, the place looked like something out of a medieval textbook. The floor was covered with thick carpeting like a handwoven mosaic. Actually made up of hundreds of small rugs, it looked like a colorful series of lumps.

In the center was a long, low wooden table with strange-smelling dishes on it. There were no chairs, but the human members of the party were quickly provided with rolls of blankets or rugs that propped them up enough to make things comfortable.

'Simple, but it will have to do,' the duke said, almost apologetically. 'You will find the food compatible – Ambassador Ortega was most helpful here. We didn't expect you in these forms, of course, but there should be no problem. Pity you couldn't be entertained in the castle, but that is impossible, I fear.'

'Where *is* your castle?' Brazil asked. 'I haven't seen any structures but this one.'

'Down below, of course,' the duke replied. 'Ghlmon wasn't always like this. It changed, very slowly, over thousands of years. As the climate became progressively drier, we realized that we couldn't fight the sand, so we learned to live beneath it. Air pumps, constantly manned by skilled workmen, keep the air coming in from vents to the surface – which crews keep clear. Sort of like living under the ocean in domes, as I have heard is done elsewhere. The desert's our ocean – more than you think. We can swim in it, albeit slowly, and follow guide wires from one spot to another, coming up here only to travel long distances.'

Brazil translated, and Vardia asked, 'But where does the food come from? Surely nothing grows here.'

'We are basically carnivores,' the duke explained after the translation of the question. 'Lots of creatures exist in the sand, and many are domesticated. Water is easy – the original streams still exist, only they now run underground, along the bedrock. The vegetable dishes here are for your benefit. We always keep some growing in greenhouses down under for guests.'

They ate, continuing the conversation. Brazil, not knowing how much the Ghlmonese were actually in on the expedition, carefully avoided any information in that direction, and it was neither asked for nor brought up by his host.

After eating, the duke bade them farewell. 'There's a good deal of straw over there for padding if you can't sleep on the rug,' he told them. 'I know you're tired and won't disturb you. You have a long journey starting tomorrow.'

Vardia and Varnett found soft places near the side of the tent and were asleep in minutes. Wuju tried to join them, but lay there awake for what seemed like hours. Her insomnia upset her – she was tired, aching, and uncomfortable, yet she couldn't sleep.

The torches had been extinguished, but she could make out Brazil's large form in the gloom near the entrance. Painfully, she got up and walked over to him.

He wasn't asleep either, she saw. His head turned as she approached. 'What's the matter?' he asked.

'I – I dunno,' she replied hesitantly. 'Can't sleep. You?'

'Just thinking,' he said, an odd, almost sad tone in his electronic voice.

'About what?'

'This world. This expedition. Us – not just the two of us, all of us. It's ending, Wuju. No beginnings anymore, just endings.'

She looked at him strangely in the darkness, not comprehending his meaning. Unable to pursue it, she changed the subject.

'What's going to happen to us, Nathan?' she asked.

'Nothing. Everything. Depends on who you are,' he replied cryptically. 'You'll see what I mean. You've had a particularly rough time, Wuju. But you're a survivor. Tough. You deserve to enjoy life a little.' He shifted uncomfortably, then continued.

'Just out of curiosity, if you had a choice, if you could return to our sector of the universe as anything or anybody you wanted to be, what would you choose?'

She thought for a minute. 'I've never considered going back,' she replied in a soft, puzzled tone.

'But if you could, and you could be who and where you wanted – like the genie with the three wishes – what would you choose?'

She chuckled mirthlessly. 'You know, when I was a farmer, I had no dreams. We were taught to be satisfied with everything. But when they made me a whore in the Party House, we'd sometimes sit and talk about that. They kept the males and females separate – we never saw any males except Party locals and favored workers. We were programmed to be supersexy and give them a hell of a time. I'm sure the male jocks were equally fantastic for the female bigwigs. They shot us full of hormones, thought we couldn't think of anything but sex – and, it's true, we craved it, constantly, so much so that during slack times we were in bed with each other.

'But the Party people,' she continued, 'they knew things, went places. Some of them liked to talk about it, and we got to know a lot about the outside world. We'd dream about getting out into it, out perhaps to other worlds, new experiences.' She paused for a moment, then continued in that dreamy, yet thoughtful, somewhat wistful tone.

'Three wishes, you said. All right, if we're playing the game, I'd like to be rich, live as long as I wanted, and be young all that time, and fantastically good-looking, too. Not on a Comworld, of course – but that's four, isn't it?'

'Go on,' he urged. 'Never mind the three. Anything else?'

'I'd like to have you under those same conditions,' she replied.

He laughed, genuinely pleased and flattered. 'But,' he said, serious again, 'suppose I wasn't there? Suppose you were out on your own?'

'I don't even want to think about that.'

'Come on,' he prodded. 'It's only a game.'

Her head went up, and she thought some more. 'If you weren't there, I think I'd like to be a man.'

If Brazil had had a human face, it would have risen in surprise. 'A man? Why?'

She shrugged, looking slightly embarrassed. 'I don't know, really. Remember I said young and good-looking. Men are bigger, stronger, they don't get raped, don't get pregnant. I'd like to have children, maybe, but – well, I don't think any man could turn me on except you, Nathan. Back in the Party House – those men who came. I was like a machine to them, a sex machine. The other girls – they were real people, my family. They *cared*. That's why the Party gave me to Hain, Nathan – I'd gotten to the point where I couldn't turn on to men at all, only women. They felt, they cared, they weren't – well, weren't *threatening*. All of the men I met were – except you. Can you understand that?'

'I think I can,' he responded slowly. 'It's natural, considering your background. On the other hand, there are many worlds where homosexuality is accepted, and you can get children by anything from cloning to artificial insemination. And, of course, men have just as many problems and hang-ups as women. The grass isn't greener, just different.'

'That might be the fun of it,' she replied. 'After all, it's something I've never been – like I'd never been a centaur before, and you'd never been a stag. I *know* what it's like to be a woman – and I don't particularly care for it. Besides, we're only playing.'

'I guess we are,' he responded. 'Since we are, would you rather go back to being a Dillian than what you are now? You can, you know – just go back to Zone through the local Gate and back through again. You'll be readjusted to the original equation. That's the most common way of breaking spells around here, you know. That's the way I'd have handled things if I'd had the time back in Ivrom rather than risking that facedown with the Swarm Queen.'

'I – I'm not sure I *could* go back to Dillia,' she said softly. 'Oh, I loved being that big and strong, loved the country and those wonderful people – but I didn't fit. That's what was driving me crazy in the end. Jol was a wonderful person, but it was *Dal* I was attracted to. And that doesn't go over in Dillia socially – and, if it did, it's impractical.'

He nodded. 'That's really what you meant when you told me long ago about how people should love people no matter what their form or looks. But what about me? Suppose I turned into something *really* monstrous, so alien that it bore almost no resemblance to what you knew?'

She laughed. 'You mean like the bat or a Czillian or maybe a mermaid?'

'No, those are familiar. I mean a real monstrosity.'

'As long as you were still you *inside*, I don't think anything would change,' she replied seriously. 'Why do you talk like that, anyway? Do you expect to turn into a monster?'

'Anything's possible on this world,' he reminded her. 'We've seen only a fraction of what can happen – you've seen only six hexes, six out of *fifteen hundred and sixty*. You've met representatives of three or four more. There's a lot that is stranger.' His voice turned grim. 'We have to meet the new Datham Hain shortly, you know. He's a giant female bug – a monster if ever there was one.'

'Now his outside matches his foul inside,' she snapped bitterly. 'Monsters aren't racial, they're in the mind. He's been a monster all his life.'

He nodded. 'Look, trust me on this. Hain will get what he deserves – so will everybody. Once inside the Well, we'll all be what we once were, and then will come the reckoning.'

'Even you?' she asked. 'Or will you stay a deer?'

'No, not a deer,' he replied mysteriously, then changed the subject. 'Well, maybe it's better over. Two more days and that'll be it.'

She opened her mouth to prod, then closed it again. Finally, she asked, 'Nathan, is that why you've lived so long? Are you a Markovian? Varnett thinks you are.'

He sighed. 'No, not a Markovian – exactly. But they might as well continue to think I am. I may have to use that belief to keep everything from blowing apart too soon.'

She looked stunned. 'You mean all this time you've been dropping hints that you were one of the original builders, and it was all a *bluff*?'

He shook his head slowly. 'Not a bluff, no. But I'm very old, Wuju – older than anyone could imagine. So old that I couldn't live with my own memories. I blocked them out, and, until arriving here on the Well World, I was mercifully, blissfully ignorant. No mind in history can function long with this much storage input. The shock of the fight and transformation in Murithel brought the past back, but there's so *much!* It's next to impossible to sort it all out, get a handle on it all. But these memories still give me the edge – I know things the rest of you don't. I'm not necessarily smarter or wiser than you, but I do have all that experience, all that accumulated knowledge of thousands of lifetimes. That gives me the advantage.'

'But they all think you're going to work the Well for them,' she pointed out. 'Everything you've said indicates that you know how.'

'That's why Serge kept us alive,' he explained. 'That's why we've been coddled and prodded. I have no doubt that the little voice box on top my antlers has an extra circuit monitored by Serge. He's probably listening right now. I don't care anymore. That's why he could help us, know where we were and what happened to us. That's why we're going to meet him; that's how all this was prepared in advance. Just in case he can't use me, he'll use Skander, or Varnett – he thinks.'

'I can see why he'd be concerned with you three,' she replied, 'but why the rest of us? Why me, for example?'

If Brazil could have smiled, he would have. 'You don't know Serge – the old Serge. I'd been so lulled by that talk about a wife and kids I'd forgotten how little this world changes the real you, deep down. Hain – well, Hain is useful to keep Skander in check as well as for transportation. I don't know who else is along, but be sure they're there only because Serge has some use for them or he hasn't been able to figure out how to dispose of them properly.'

'But why me?' she repeated.

'They must have some tame nasties on the Comworlds,' he replied sardonically. 'You're a hostage, Wuju. You're his handle on me.'

She looked uncertain. 'Nathan? What if it really came down to that? Would you do what he asked for me?'

'It won't come to that,' he assured her. 'Believe me, it won't. Varnett has already figured out why, although he's forgotten in his youthful excitement.'

'Then what *will* you do?'

'I will lead them all to the Well – Skander can do that anyway, so could Varnett. I intend to show them everything they want. But they will learn that this treasure hunt is full of thorns when they discover what the price really is. I'll bet you that, once in the control room of their dreams, they will think the price is too high.'

She shook her head in wonder. 'I don't understand any of this.'

'You will,' he replied cryptically, 'at midnight at the Well of Souls.'

The trip was uncomfortable and bumpy. They traveled on a huge wooden sled with runners. Pulling them swiftly were eight huge beasts they could not fully see – sandsharks, the Ghlmonese called them. Only huge gray backs and huge, razor-sharp fins were visible as they pulled their heavy load and were kept in check by a Ghlmonese driver with reins for each of the huge creatures.

The sandsharks were giant mammals who lived in the sand as fish lived in water. They breathed air – a single huge nostril opened whenever their great backs broke the surface – and moved at eight to ten kilometers per hour.

By the end of the day the travelers were all sore and bruised, but more than halfway there. They spread rugs out on the sand, and ate food heated by the fiery breath of their driver. There was no problem sleeping that evening, despite the hot air, blowing wind, and strange surroundings.

The next day was a repeat of the first. They passed several other sleds carrying Ghlmonese, and occasionally saw individuals riding in huge saddles on the backs of sandsharks. Once in a while they would see a cluster of what appeared to be huge chimneys with crews keeping the openings from being blocked by sand. Far below, they knew, there were towns, perhaps large cities.

Finally, near dusk of the second day, structures appeared ahead of them, growing rapidly larger as they approached. These proved to be a network of towers and spires made of small rocks, reaching fifty or more meters in the air, like the tops of some medieval fortress.

They slowed, and came to a halt near two towers with a wide gate between. A number of Ghlmonese stood around; others were busy going to or from unknown places.

An officious-looking dinosaur, in ornate red livery, came up to them. 'You are the alien party from Orgondo?' he asked gruffly.

'They are,' their driver replied. 'All yours and welcome. I have to see to my sharks. They've had a tough journey.'

'Which of you is Mr Brazil?' the official inquired.

'I am,' Brazil replied.

The official looked surprised, since Brazil was, after all, still a giant stag, but he recovered quickly. 'Come with me, then. The rest of you will be taken to temporary quarters.' He motioned to some other Ghlmonese, also in the red livery, and they came up to escort the party. Although the smallest of the humans was a head taller than any of the guards, no one felt like arguing.

'Go with them,' Brazil instructed his group. 'There'll be no problems. I'll join you as soon as I can.'

They had no choice, and walked to the tower nearest them. Brazil turned to the official. 'What now?' he asked.

'Ambassador Ortega and the other alien party are camped out near the base of The Avenue,' the official replied. 'I am to take you to them.'

'Lead on,' Brazil urged, unconcern in his voice.

The Avenue proved to be a broad trench, thirty or more meters across, that was just beyond the towers and spires. It was also more than fifteen meters below ground level, but, despite only the most rudimentary stone buffers, the sand didn't seem to blow into the obviously artificial culvert, but over and past it.

Broad stone stairs led down to the flat, almost shiny surface below. Brazil had some trouble negotiating the stairs, but finally made it. The buildings of Oodlikm seemed to line The Avenue on both sides, like medieval castles used to be built into the sides of steep river valleys back on Old Earth. There were many stairways and hundreds of doors, windows, and even ports for defense along both sides of The Avenue wall. As for the valley itself, its level, jewellike surface seemed to stretch to the ocean on Brazil's right, and off to the horizon on his left.

Brazil's hooves clacked on the shiny surface. He towered over countless stalls selling all sorts of things and over the crowds which gaped at him and made way as he passed. He and his escort walked toward the ocean, past the last shops, and finally to what was obviously a more official, less commercial section, across which had been hastily erected a barricade with a heavy wooden gate and armed guards.

The official approached the gate, showed a pass he produced from his coat pocket, After the guards inspected his pass carefully, the gates opened and they passed through. Inside were more guards – huge numbers, in fact. In the center of The Avenue were an Akkafian, a Czillian, a Umiau in what looked like a square bathtub, and – something else.

Brazil studied The Diviner and The Rel, and the last pieces fit into place. The role of the Northerner had been unclear to him from the start, and he knew nothing of the creature's hex, physically or culturally. He was certain that the thing was at the heart of much of the mischief that had been worked, though.

Darkness had fallen, and the stars started showing through. Small gaslights had been lit, giving the entire scene an eerie glow.

'Remain with the others,' the official instructed him. 'I will get Ambassador Ortega.'

Brazil went over to the alien creatures, ignoring all except the Umiau.

'So you're Elkinos Skander,' he said flatly.

The mermaid gave a puzzled look. 'So? And who or what are you?'

'Nathan Brazil,' he replied crisply. 'That name means little to you? Perhaps it will be better to say that I am here to avenge seven murders.'

The Umiau opened her mouth in surprise. 'Seven – what the hell do you mean?'

Brazil's independent eyes showed Skander on the right, and the interest of the other three on the left. The others were all watching the two tensely.

'I was the captain of the freighter who found the bodies on Dalgonia. Seven bodies, charred, left on a barren world. None of them ever did you harm, nor was there any reason for their deaths.'

'I didn't kill them,' Skander responded in a surly tone. 'Varnett killed them. But, what of it? Would you have preferred to open this world to the Coms?'

'So that was it,' Brazil said sadly. 'The seven died because you feared that their governments would get control. Skander, *you* know who killed them, and *I* know who killed them, but even beyond that is the fact that they needn't have died even for so dubious a reason. The Gate would not have opened for them.'

'Of course it would!' Skander snapped. 'It opened when Varnett and I found the mathematical key to the computer. And it was still open for you and your party to fall through!'

Brazil shook his head slowly. 'No, Skander. It opened only because the two of you *wanted* it to open. That's the key, you know. Even though you didn't know that the Gate didn't lead to the Dalgonian brain, but to here, you knew that some sort of Gate must exist and you wanted desperately to find it. You had already decided to kill Varnett and the others before you found it. Varnett knew it. He had a desire to find the Gate, and the fear of death to fix it.

That's what opened it up, not your mathematical discoveries. It hadn't opened since the Markovians, and it wouldn't have opened again unless the conditions were right.'

'Then how did *you* fall through?' Skander retorted. 'Why did it open for you?'

'It didn't,' Brazil replied evenly. 'Although I should have known it was there.'

'But it *did* open for us, Brazil,' Hain put in.

'Not for you, Hain, or for me, or for Vardia, either,' Brazil told them. 'But, within our party, there was one person who had lost all hope, who wanted to die, to escape fate's lot. The brain, sensitized to such things, picked this up and lured us to Dalgonia with the false emergency signal. We went up to where the shuttles left by Skander and Varnett were still parked, walked out onto the Gate floor, and, when Wu Julee was well within the field, the Gate triggered – sending all of us here.'

'I remember you, now!' Skander exclaimed. 'Vardia told me about you while we were imprisoned in The Nation! She told me how the ships seemed to vanish. When I heard all that, I assumed you had engineered the whole thing, that you were a Markovian. The evidence fitted. Besides, it stands to reason that you don't leave a control group like those on the Well World without someone to monitor the control.'

'The fact that it was the girl and not Brazil who triggered the Gate doesn't necessarily invalidate your conclusions, Doctor,' came a smooth, husky voice behind them. They turned to see the huge form of Serge Ortega, all five meters of snake and two meters of his thick, six-armed body.

'Serge, I should have known better,' Brazil said good-humoredly.

All six arms of the Ulik shrugged. 'I have a pretty good racket here, Nate. I told you I was happy, and I am. I have most of the embassies at both zones bugged, and the conversations recorded. I find out what's happening, who's doing what to whom, and if there's anything of interest to me and to my people I act on it.'

Brazil nodded, and would have smiled if the stag body allowed it. 'It was no accident that you were the one who met us, was it? You already knew I was there.'

'Of course,' Ortega replied. 'Small cameras installed in two or three points around the Well go on whenever someone comes through. If they're old-human I get there first. Nobody cares much, since the Zone Gate randomly assigns them to other hexes.'

'You didn't meet me when I came through,' Skander pointed out.

Ortega shrugged again. 'Can't *live* in the damned office. Bad luck, though, since I then lost sight of you for a long time. These others were already in and assigned before I managed to track Varnett down, although the Umiau are so lousy at secrecy your cover was blown about a month after you came.'

'You've been following me since Czill, haven't you, Serge?' Brazil asked. 'How did you manage it?'

'Child's play,' the Ulik replied. 'Czill has a high technological level but no natural resources, and some problems in handling hot metal anyway. We supply parts for their machines – we and many others – only ours have slight modifications. A resonator for the translator, for example, takes only one almost invisible extra circuit to broadcast – if you know the right frequency. The range isn't fantastic, but I knew where you were, and in most instances mutual back-scratching, past IOU's, and the like were all that was needed. I think I know what you are, Nate, and I think you know you should play the game my way.'

'Or you'll kill the others?'

The snakeman looked hurt, but it was exaggerated. 'Why, Nate! Did I say any such thing? But, regardless, I have Skander, here, and, if all else fails, Varnett. I'd prefer you, Nate. I don't think you're any different from the Nathan Brazil I've known all these decades. I'm willing to bet that that personality of yours isn't a phony front or a construct, but the real you, no matter what your parents were. You know me better than anybody, so you know my actions and what I'll do in any case. Will you lead the party in?'

Brazil looked at his old acquaintance for a moment. 'Why everybody, Serge? Why not just you and me?' he asked.

'Ah, come on, Nate! What do you take me for? You know how to get in; I don't. You know what's in there – I don't. With the others I get an expert check on your actions and descriptions, and a little insurance from their own self-interest. The Northerner, here – it's working for a group so different from any of us I can't figure out anything about them. Nonetheless, like Hain, here, and the plant, they're all looking out for their own interests. So are your people, really. Nobody's going to let anybody else get the upper hand. You'll all even be armed – armed with pistols that can kill any of you, but can't kill me. I've taken immunity shots from Hain's stinger, so that's no threat, and I am so much physically stronger than any of you that I'll be happy to take you on. Nate knows how quick I can move.'

Brazil sighed. 'Always figuring the angles, aren't you, Serge? So tell me, if this was your game all along, why did we have to fight and walk so far? Why not just get us all together and bring us to this point?'

'I hadn't the slightest idea where you were going,' replied Ortega honestly. 'After all, Skander was still looking, Varnett had given up, and nobody else knew. So I just let the expeditions lead me here. When it became clear where *both* expeditions were headed, I arranged to slow things down until I could get here ahead of you. Easier than you think – Zone Gate to Ulik, then over. Hell, man, I've been to that Equatorial Zone hundreds of times. There's no way in that anybody's ever found, and a lot have tried over the years.'

'But we now know that the entrance is at the end of The Avenue,' The Rel said suddenly. 'And, from Skander, I perceive that the time of entry is midnight.'

'Right on both counts,' Brazil admitted. 'However, that knowledge alone won't get you in. You need the desire to get to the Well center, specifically, and a basic equation to tell the Well you know what you're doing.'

'The Varnett relationship,' Skander said. 'The open-ended equation of the Markovian brain slides. That's it, isn't it?'

'Sure,' Brazil acknowledged. 'After all, it wasn't supposed to keep any Markovians out. The conditions of this world are such that the relationship is simply indecipherable. It's only one in a million that the two of you discovered it, and almost one in infinity that you'd get to where you could use it. You could never have used it on Dalgonia since it requires an answer for completion, an addition. It's sort of "What is your wish?" and you have to give that wish in mathematically correct form. In this case, though, the simple completion is done by the brain if you ask the question – the reverse.'

'But if he is a Markovian, why could he not just contact the brain and save himself all the problems he's had here?' the Slelcronian asked.

Brazil turned to the plant person, a puzzled tone in his voice. 'I thought you were Vardia – but that tone just doesn't sound like her.'

'Vardia merged with a Slelcronian,' The Rel explained, telling of the flower creatures and their strange ways. 'It is possessed of a good deal of wisdom and some fairly efficient mental powers, but your friend is such a tiny part of the whole that the Czillian is essentially dead,' The Rel concluded.

'I see,' Brazil said slowly. 'Well, there were too many Vardias here anyway. Ours is the original – back to human, again.' He turned to Serge again. 'So are Wuju and Varnett.'

'Varnett?' Skander sat up suddenly, spilling water. 'Varnett is with you?'

'Yes, and no tricks, Skander,' Ortega warned. 'If you try anything on Varnett I'll personally attend to you.' He turned back to Brazil. 'That goes for you, too, Nate.'

'There will be no problems, Serge,' Brazil assured him tiredly. 'I'll take you all inside the Well, and I will show you what you want – what you all want. I'll even answer any questions you want, clear up any uncertainties.'

'That suits us,' Ortega responded, but there was a note of caution in his voice.

THE AVENUE – AT THE EQUATOR

The journey up The Avenue had been without event, and none had tested Ortega's defenses. They were all going where they wanted to go, and, as the Ulik had said, each one had his own selfish interests at heart. All during the journey Brazil had been talkative and friendly, yet there was a sadness deep within him they could all feel, although he tried to laugh it off. The four members of Brazil's party kept to themselves. Hain kept looking at Wuju strangely, but bided her time, and Skander seemed resigned to Varnett's existence in the party.

And now, in the afternoon's waning sun, they stood at the Equatorial Barrier itself, imposing and seemingly impenetrable.

It was like a wall, partially translucent, that rose up until it merged with the deep blue, cloudless sky. The barrier itself didn't look thick, and felt smooth and glassy to the touch, yet it had withstood attempts by many races on both sides to make as much as a mark on it. It went off to each side of them from horizon to horizon, like a giant, nonreflecting glass wall.

The Avenue seemed to merge into it, and there was no sign of any small crack, fissure, or even juncture of the odd paving of The Avenue with the surface of the barrier. They seemed to become one.

Brazil went up to the wall, then turned to face them. They waited expectantly.

'We can't enter until midnight, so we might as well be comfortable,' he told them.

'Do you mean twenty-four hundred?' the real Vardia asked.

'No, of course not,' Brazil replied. 'For one thing, the Well World's days are about twenty-eight and a quarter standard hours, as you know, so the time twenty-four hundred has no meaning here. Midnight means exactly that – the middle of the night. Since a total day is exactly twenty-eight point three three four standard hours, and since the axis is exactly vertical, that means the light period is fourteen point one six seven hours, and so is the darkness. Midnight, then, comes seven point zero eight three five hours after sunset. The figures were determined by physical necessity when building the place. They just came out that way. Believe me, Markovian clocks were quite different from ours, and the time could be precisely determined.'

'Yes, but how will *we* determine it?' The Rel asked. 'There are a couple of timepieces here, but they are by no means that exact.'

'No need,' Brazil assured the Northerner. 'Hain, fly up to the surface there and watch the sun. When it vanishes to the west, then tell us immediately. Be

225

conservative – err on the side of sunlight. We'll check watches for seven hours from that point. After that, we can simply wait to open the wall. We'll have only about two minutes, so it's important that everyone goes as soon as the wall opens. The ones who don't will be left out here.'

'What about the atmosphere inside?' Skander asked. 'We have only a few pressure suits here.'

'No problem there, either,' Brazil responded. 'All of us are compatible with the oxygen-nitrogen-carbon mix that's common, in one sense or another, with the sectors on both sides of The Avenue. There will be a compromise adjustment, but while the mixture might make a few of us temporarily light-headed, it shoudn't pose any problem. This system will automatically follow us, section by section, as we go down. The only problem we might have, and it's minor, is some strongly differing gravitational pulls due to the lines of force flowing from here. None will be a *real* problem, just uncomfortable occasionally.'

His explanation seemed to satisfy them, and they sat down or otherwise relaxed, waiting for the proper time.

'Are you really – really me?' Vardia hesitantly asked the Slelcronian, who was awake only because of a small, lamplike gadget fastened over the headleaf.

The Slelcronian paused and thought carefully. 'We are you, and we are more than you,' it replied. 'All your memories and experiences are here, along with the millions of the Slelcronians. You are a part of us, and we are a part of you. Through the Recorder, you are a part of the total synthesis, not just the isolated portion in this body.'

'What's it like?' she asked.

'It is the ultimate stage to which any can aspire,' the creature told her. 'No individuality, no personality to corrupt. No jealousy, greed, anger, envy, or those other things that cause misery. All alike, all identical, all in communion. As plants we require nothing save water and sunlight, and carbon dioxide to breathe. When another is needed, we make a seed and mate it to the Recorders; it grows, and immediately after bloom becomes as we. The Recorders do not think, and get their food from our bodies.'

'But – what do you *do?*' she asked curiously. 'What is the purpose to your life?'

'Universal happiness in a stable order,' the Slelcronian replied unhesitatingly. 'Long have we yearned to spread the synthesis. Now, through this body and your experience, we can return to Czill and multiply. We shall work with the devices of Czill to create a synthesis of animal with plant. We shall expand, eventually, to the Well World, and, with the aid of the Well, to the corners of the universe. All shall become one with the synthesis, all shall enjoy perfect equality and happiness.'

She thought a minute. 'And what if you can't do it with the animals?'

'We will,' the Slelcronian replied confidently. 'But, should it not be so, then the superior shall eliminate the inferior, as it is in the laws of nature since the beginning of time.'

This isn't me, she thought. This can't be me. Or – or is it? Is this not what my society strives for? Is this not why we clone, why genetic engineering is eventually planned to make everyone identical, sexless, equally provided for in every way?

A sudden question struck her, and she asked, 'And what will you do once you have accomplished this all-encompassing synthesis? What then?'

'Then there will be perfection and harmony and happiness,' replied the Slelcronian as if reciting a litany. 'Heaven will be ours and it will be forever. Why do you ask such a question? Are we not you? Did you not in fact accept the offered synthesis?'

The question disturbed her, for she had no answer. What had changed? How had the paths of Vardia I and II differed so radically in the last few weeks that such question would even occur to her?

She turned away, and her eyes fell on Wu Julee and Nathan Brazil. They had some sort of symbiotic relationship, she thought. It was observable, no matter what form they had been in. When he could have clearly escaped the Ivrom spell, he had risked himself to free her.

She sat down, the chill of the night making the hardness of The Avenue feel like an ice cube on her bare behind.

What had she seen that her sister had not? Emotion? Love? Some different sort of relationship? Kindness? What?

What had her sister seen? A nation of great bugs all out to do each other in and lord it over the others. Hain. Skander. That weird Northern creature. A world of machines. They represented something far different from Nathan Brazil, Wuju – and Varnett, with guilt over seven dead people he probably couldn't have saved anyway. Guilt over doing the right and proper thing? Impossible! Yet – she remembered him coming in in the early morning, carrying Brazil's battered and broken body. Exhausted, weak, half-crazed from the burden, yet unwilling to sleep or eat until Brazil had been tended to. Standing over that body, only technically alive, and weeping.

Why?

She thought again of the Slelcronian and its dreams. The perfect society. Heaven. Forever.

The Markovians had it, had the ultimate in material existence.

And they had deliberately wrecked it for death, misery, pain, and struggle on countless worlds in countless forms.

What *was* perfection, anyway? What did the Markovians lack that gave the lie to the grand dream?

They forgot how to love, Brazil had said. But what was love?

Have we already forgotten it?

The thought upset her, and she couldn't explain why. For the first time in her life, she felt alienated, alone, outside, left out.

Cheated.

And she had no idea what was missing.

For the first time, and perhaps the first of any being on the Well World, she knew what it must have been like to be a Markovian.

Was this, then, what Nathan Brazil felt? Was this why he felt he was cursed? Did he live all those millennia searching for the missing factor in the Markovian dream, hoping that someone would discover it?

But, no, she concluded. He knew what it was. He had tried to explain it.

Suddenly she shivered, but not from the chill. She had never thought, never brooded like this before, never faced the chill of reality before.

Oh, nonexistent, uncaring gods! she thought bitterly. What a curse more horrible than anything imaginable.

Suppose Nathan Brazil had what was missing, deep inside – and no one else did?

'Hello, Vardia,' said a voice behind her. She turned with a start, and saw Wuju standing there. 'You've been sitting there looking strange for the longest time.'

She smiled weakly, but said nothing.

Wuju smiled and sat down beside her. 'Yikes! This pavement's cold!'

'If you just sit you don't notice it,' Vardia told her.

'Everyone's so somber and serious now,' Wuju noted. 'Even me.'

Vardia looked at her strangely. 'It's the mission – the end of the mission. In there is anything you want. Just wish for it. And all of us are going in. I don't know about anyone else, but I just discovered I don't know what to wish for.'

'I wish we weren't going,' Wuju said grimly. 'If I had one wish, it'd be that this never had to end. Here – this journey, Nathan, all of you. It's been the happiest time of my life. I'm afraid that nothing will be the same after we're in there. Nothing.'

Vardia took her hand and patted it. Now why did I do that? she wondered, but she continued doing it.

'I don't know what's going to happen,' Vardia said calmly. 'I only know that I must change. I *have* changed. Now I must understand how and why.'

'I don't like this at all,' Wuju responded in that same tone of foreboding. 'I don't like the idea of things being changed by a whim. No one should have that kind of power – least of all these sorts. I don't like being a figment, an afterthought. I'm scared to death. I told Nathan, but he just shook his head and went away. I don't understand that, either. I can face death, now – and evil, too. But I can't face the fear of what's in there. Not alone.'

'You're not alone,' Vardia said with a gentleness that surprised her.

Wuju looked over at Brazil, standing facing the wall, unmoving, stoic, alone. She started to tremble.

'I can't face it alone!' she wailed weakly.

'You're not alone,' Vardia repeated, squeezing her hand tighter.

Elkinos Skander watched the two women with interest. So the robots have retained a little humanity after all, he thought with satisfaction. But it's buried so deep within them that it took the Well World to bring any of it out.

And for what?

Things weren't working out quite the way he had planned at all, but except for the Slelcronian and, perhaps, that Northerner, it was all right, particularly if the robots like Vardia could feel.

Surely they wouldn't object to his requests of the Well.

He looked over at Hain, motionless in the darkness.

'Hain? You awake?' Skander asked softly.

'Yes. Who could sleep now?' came the bug's response.

'Hain, tell me. What do you expect to get in there? What do you want of the Well?'

Hain was silent for a moment. 'Power,' she replied at last. 'I would make the Baron Azkfru emperor of the Well World, this galaxy, perhaps the universe. But, with this mob, I'll settle for his being emperor for the longest of time in Akkafan, with such other power left to future effort. My Lord, the baron, can do anything except fight this machine.'

Skander raised his mermaid's eyebrows in surprise. 'But what do *you* get out of it?'

'I shall be the baron's queen,' Hain replied excitedly. 'I shall be at his throne, second only to him in power. I shall bear the broods that will rule for eternity, the product of Azkfru and myself! The workers, even the nobles, shall defer to me and my wishes, and envy me, and my subjects will sing my praises!' Hain paused, carried away by her own vision.

'I was born in a run-down shack in a hole called Gorind on Aphrodite,' she continued. 'I was unwanted, sickly. My mother beat me, finally cast me out into the mud and dust when she saw I'd never be a miner. I was nine. I went into the city, living off the garbage, stealing to make do, sleeping in cold back doorways. I grew up grubbing, but in the shadow of the rich, the mineowners, the shippers from whom I stole. One day, when I was fifteen or so, I raped and killed a girl. She struggled, called me names – tried to scratch me, like my mother. They caught me, and I was about to be psyched into a good programmed worker when this man came to see me in my cell. He said he had need of people like me. If I agreed to serve him and his bosses, he would get me out.'

'And you accepted, of course,' Skander put in.

'Oh, yes. I went into a new world. I found that the rich whom I'd envied dreamed of greater riches, and that power came not from obeying the law but from not getting caught. I rose in the organization. I ate well, grew fat, ordered people around. I have – had – my own estate on a private world of the bosses. Staffed all by women, young women, held to me by sponge. Many were slaves; others I had reduced to animals. They roam naked in the forest on the estate, living in trees, eating the swill I put out for them like barnyard animals.'

Skander had an eerie feeling in his stomach, yet he followed Hain's statements with morbid fascination. 'But that's gone now,' Skander said as calmly as he could manage.

'Not gone,' Hain replied, agitated. 'I will be mother now.'

There was nothing Skander could say. Pity was for what Hain was or could have been, not what the creature was now.

'What do you want out of all this, Skander?' Hain asked suddenly. 'Why all this trouble, all this effort? What do you want to do?'

'I want to restore humanity to itself,' Skander replied fiercely. 'I want to get rid of the genetic engineers, the philosophers of political sameness on the Comworlds. I want to turn us around, Hain! I want to make people human again, even if I have to destroy civilization to save mankind. We're becoming a race of robots, Hain. We wipe out the robots or we abdicate the universe to other races. The Markovians died of stagnation, Hain, and so will we unless it's stopped!'

Hain had never liked fanatics, saviors, and visionaries, but there was nothing else to do but talk. 'Tell me, Skander. Would you go back? If you could, I mean. Suppose you get your wish. Would you go back or stay here?'

'I think I could end my days here if I got what I want,' Skander replied honestly. 'I like this place – the diversity, the challenges. I haven't had time to enjoy being Umiau. But, then, I'd like to see what our little race would be if my plan were fulfilled. I don't know, Hain. Would *you* go back?'

'Only as the Queen Mother of the Akkafians,' Hain responded without hesitation. 'At the side of my beloved Lord Azkfru. Only to rule would I return, Skander. For nothing less.'

Ortega slithered over to them. He had small pistols in his hands, and he put one next to Skander and the other in front of Hain.

'Pistols for all,' he said lightly. 'Nice little energy jobs. They will work in there, like in any high-tech hex. They'll work on everybody except me. A dandy little circuit prevents that.'

Skander reached over, picked up the pistol, felt it. Suddenly the Umiau scientist looked into Ortega's wide brown eyes.

'You expect us to kill each other, don't you?' he said softly. 'You expect all hell to break out after we get to the Well and learn how it operates. And then you'll finish off the winner.'

Ortega shrugged, and smiled. 'Up to you,' he replied calmly. 'You can compromise with me, or with each other, or do as you say and shoot. But I will be in at the payoff no matter what.' He slithered away to distribute guns to the others, chuckling softly.

'That bastard,' Hain commented. 'He hasn't seen what The Diviner and The Rel can do, has he? Wonder what sort of defense he has for that?'

'I think he knows,' Skander responded. 'That's one slick pirate there. He's counting on us to take care of the Northerner. And, damn his eyes, we have to! We have to, or that blinking little son of a bitch will zap all of us!'

'Just be thankful that snake *did* get transported to the Well World,' Hain said flatly. 'Otherwise, he'd be running the whole damned galaxy by now.'

Varnett came over to Brazil, who was still standing facing the Equatorial Barrier. 'Brazil?' he said softly. 'You awake?'

Nathan Brazil turned slowly, looking at Varnett.

'Oh, yes, I'm awake,' Brazil told him. 'I was just thinking. I've enjoyed this escapade, you know. Enjoyed it a great deal. Now it's over, ended. And it ends like all the other episodes in my life. So I have to pick up and keep on once again.'

Varnett was puzzled. 'I don't understand you at all, Brazil. You're in the pilot's seat. You alone know what's in there – you *do* know, don't you? You have a girl who loves you, and a future. What's eating you?'

Brazil shook his head slowly.

'I have no future, Varnett,' he replied. 'This part of the great play is over. I already know the ending, and I don't like it. I'm trapped, Varnett. Cursed. This diversion helped, but not much, because it brought back too much pain and longing as well. And as for Wuju – she doesn't love *me*, Varnett. She has a deep need to be loved. She loves a symbol, something that Nathan Brazil did to and for her, something in the way he reacted to her. But she wants of me what I can't give her. She wants her dream of normality.' He shifted, stretching his legs out in front of him. He continued to face not the others, but the barrier.

'I'm not normal, Varnett,' he said sadly. 'I can give her what she wants, needs, deserves. I can do it for all of you. But I can't participate, you see. That's the curse.'

'Sounds like grandiose self-pity to me,' Varnett said derisively. 'Why not take what you want if you can do all that?'

Brazil sighed. 'You'll know soon enough. I want you just to remember this, Varnett. I want you to keep it in your head throughout all that happens. Inside, I'm no different from the rest of you.'

'What would you want, if you could have anything at all?' Varnett asked him, still bewildered.

Brazil looked at the other seriously, sadly. There was agony and torment within him.

'I want to die, boy. I want to die – and I can't. Not ever. Not at all. And I want death so very much.'

Varnett shook his head uncomprehendingly. 'I can't figure you, Brazil. I just can't figure you.'

'What do *you* want, Varnett?' Brazil asked sharply, changing tone. 'What would you wish for yourself?'

'I've thought a lot about that,' the other replied. 'I'm only fifteen years old, Brazil. Just fifteen. My world has always been dehumanized people and cold mathematics. I'm the oldest fifteen of my race, now, though. I think, perhaps, I'd like to enjoy life, enjoy a *human* life – and somehow make my contribution to progress. To stop this headlong rush of the human race into a Markovian hell and try to build the society they hoped would evolve from their tens of thousands of cultures and races. There's a greatness here in the Markovian Well, a potential unrealized, perhaps, but great nonetheless. I'd like to see it reached, to complete the equation the Markovians couldn't.'

'So would I, boy,' Brazil replied earnestly. 'For only then could I die.'

'Seven hours!' Ortega's voice broke through the stillness. 'It's almost time!' His voice cracked with excitement.

Brazil turned slowly to face them. They were all scrambling to be near the barrier.

'Don't worry,' he assured them. 'It'll open for me. A light will go on. When that light comes on, walk into the barrier. When you do, it'll be as nothing. Only *I* will change, but be ready for it. And understand something else – *I* will lead. I have no weapons, but the Well will give me a form unfamiliar to you. Don't be upset by it, and don't get trigger-happy with each other. Once we're all inside, I'll take you down to the Well of Souls, and I'll explain everything along the way. Don't do anything hasty, because I'm the only one who can get you down with certainty, and I'll not forgive any breaches. Clear?'

'Big talk, Nate,' Ortega said confidently, but there was an unease in his manner. 'But we'll go along if you do.'

'I gave you my word, Serge,' Brazil said. 'I'll keep it.'

'Look!' the Slelcronian cried. 'The light's gone on!'

In back of Brazil a section of the floor corresponding to The Avenue was lit into the Equatorial Barrier.

'Let's go,' Brazil said calmly, and turned and stepped into the barrier. The others, tension on their faces, followed him.

Suddenly Skander cried out, 'I was right! I was right all along!' and pointed ahead. The others looked in the indicated direction.

There were several gasps.

Wuju stifled a small scream.

The Well had changed Nathan Brazil, just as he had warned.

MIDNIGHT AT THE WELL OF SOULS

The creature stood at the end of The Avenue, where it passed through a meter-high barrier and stopped.

It looked like a great human heart, two and a half meters tall, pink and purple, with countless blood vessels running through it, both reddish and bluish in color. At the irregular top was a ring of cilia, colored an off-white, waving about – thousands of them, like tiny snakes, each about fifty centimeters long. From the midsection of the pulpy, undulating mass came six evenly spaced tentacles, each broad and powerful-looking, covered with thousands of tiny suckers. The tentacles were a sickly blue, the suckers a grainy yellow. An ichor of some sort seemed to ooze from the central mass, although it was thick and seemed to be reabsorbed by the skin as fast as produced, creating an irregular, filmy coating.

And it stank – the odor of foul carrion after days in the sun. It stung their nostrils, making them slightly sick.

Skander began babbling excitedly, then turned to them. 'See, Varnett?' he said. 'See what I told you? Six evenly spaced tentacles, about three meters tall! That's a Markovian!' All traces of animosity were gone; this was the professor lecturing his student, in pride at the vindication of his theories.

'So you really was a Markovian, Nate,' Ortega said wonderingly. 'Well, I'll be damned.'

'Nathan!' Wuju called out. 'Is that – that thing really you?'

'It is,' Brazil's voice came, but not as speech. It formed in each of their brains, in their own languages. Even The Diviner received it directly, rather than through The Rel.

Skander was like a child with a new toy. 'Of course! Of course!' he chortled. 'Telepathy, naturally. Probably the rest, too.'

'This is a Markovian body,' Brazil's voice came to them, 'but I am not a Markovian. The Well knows me, though, and, since all lived as new races outside, it was only natural that we be converted to the Markovian form when entering the Well. It saved design problems.'

Wuju stepped out ahead of them, drawing close to the creature.

'Wu Julee!' Hain shouted insanely. 'You are mine!' The long, sticky tongue darted out to her, wrapped itself around her. She screamed. Ortega spun quickly toward the bug, pistols in two hands.

'Now, now, none of that, Hain!' he cautioned carefully. 'Let the girl go.' He pointed the pistols at the Akkafian's eyes.

Hain hesitated a second, deciding what to do. Finally the tongue uncoiled from Wu Julee, and she dropped about thirty centimeters to the floor, landing hard. Raw, nasty-looking welts, like those made by rope burn, showed on her skin.

The creature that was Nathan Brazil walked over on its six tentacles, until it loomed over her. One tentacle reached out, gently touched her wound. The smell was overwhelming. She shrank from the probe, fear on her face.

The heartlike mass tilted a little on its axis.

'Form doesn't matter,' it mocked her voice. 'It's what's inside that counts.' Then it said in Brazil's old voice: 'What if I were a monster, Wuju? What then?'

Wuju broke into sobs. 'Please, Nathan! Please don't hurt me!' she pleaded. 'No more, please! I – I just can't!'

'Does it hurt?' he asked gently, and she managed to nod affirmatively, wiping the tears from her eyes.

'Then trust me some more, Wuju,' Brazil's voice came again, still gentle. 'No matter what. Shut your eyes. I'll make the hurt go away.'

She buried her head in her hands, still crying.

The Markovian reached out with a tentacle, and rubbed lightly against the angry-looking welt on her back and sides. She cringed, but otherwise stayed still. The thing felt clammy and horrid, yet they all watched as the tentacle, lightly drawn across the wound, caused the wound to vanish.

As the pain vanished, she relaxed.

'Lie flat on your back, Wuju,' Brazil instructed, and she did, eyes still shut. The same treatment was given to her chest and sides, and there was suddenly no sign of any welt or wound.

Brazil withdrew a couple of meters from her. There was no evident front or back to him, nor any apparent eyes, nose, or mouth. Although the pulpy mass in the center was pulsating and slightly irregular, it had no clear-cut directionality.

'Hey, that's fantastic, Nate!' Ortega exclaimed.

'Shall we go to the Well?' Brazil asked them. 'It is time to finish this drama.'

'I'm not sure I like this at all,' Hain commented hesitantly.

'Too late to back out now, you asshole,' Skander snapped. 'You didn't get where you were without guts. Play it out.'

'If you'll follow me,' Brazil said, 'and get on the walkway here; we can talk as we ride, and probably panic the border hexes at the same time.'

They all stepped onto the walkway on the other side of the meter-tall barrier. The Avenue's strange light went out, and another light went on on both sides of the walkway, illuminating about half a kilometer to their left.

'The lights will come on where we are, and go out where we aren't,' Brazil explained. 'It's automatic. Slelcronian, you'll find the light adequate for you despite its apparent lack of intensity. You can get rid of that heat lamp. Just throw it over the barrier there. It will be disposed of by the automatic machinery in about fourteen hours.' The Markovian's tentacle near the forward part of the walkway struck the side sharply, and the walkway started to move.

'You are now on the walkway to the Well Access Gate,' he explained. 'When the Markovians built this world, it was necessary, of course, for the technicians to get in and out. They were full shifts – one full rotation on, one off. Every day from dozens to thousands of Markovian technicians would ride this walkway to the control center and to other critical areas inside the planet. In those days, of course, The Avenue would stay open as long as necessary. It was shortened to the small interval in the last days before the last Markovian went native for good, to allow the border hexes some development and to keep out those who had second thoughts. At the end, only the three dozen project coordinators came, and then irregularly, just to check on things. As any technician was finally cleared out of the Well, the key to The Avenue doors was removed from his mind, so he could not get back in if he wanted to.'

They moved on in eerie silence, lighted sections suddenly popping on in front of them, out in back of them, as they traveled. The walkway itself seemed to glow radiantly; no light source was visible.

'Some of you know the story of this place already,' Brazil continued. 'The race you call the Markovians rose as did all other species, developed, and finally discovered the primal energy nature of the universe – that there was nothing but this primal energy, extending outward in all directions, and that all constructs within it, we included, are established by rules and laws of nature that are not fixed just because they are there, but are instead *imposed*. Nothing equals anything, really; the equal sign is strictly for the imposed structure of the universe. Rather, everything is relative to everything else.'

'But once the Markovians discovered the mathematical constructs governing stability, why didn't they change them?' Skander asked. 'Why keep the rules?'

'They didn't dare try to tackle the master equations, those governing physical properties and natural laws,' Brazil replied. 'They could alter things a little, but common sense should tell you that in order to change the master equation you first have to eliminate the old one. If you do that, what happens to you and the rest of the universe? They didn't dare – so they imposed new, smaller equations on localized areas of the preexisting universe.'

'Not gods, then,' Vardia said quietly. 'Demigods.'

'*People*,' Brazil responded. 'Not gods at all. People. Oh, I know that this form I've got is quite different than you'd think, but it's no more monstrous or unusual than some of the creatures of this world, and less than some. The many billions of beings who wore bodies like this were a proud race of ordinary people with one finger on the controls. They argued, they debated, strove, built, discovered – just like all of us. Were their physical forms closer to the ones we're familiar with, you would possibly even like them. Remember, they achieved godhood not by natural processes, but by technological advancement. It was as if one of our races, in present form, suddenly discovered the key to wish fulfillment. Would we be ready for it? I wonder.'

'Why did they die, Brazil?' Skander asked. 'Why did they commit suicide?'

'Because they were not ready,' Brazil replied sadly. 'They had conquered all material want, all disease, even death itself. But they had not conquered their selves. They reveled in hedonism, each an island unto itself. Anything they wanted, they just had to wish for.

'And they found that wasn't enough. Something was missing. Utopia wasn't fulfillment, it was stagnation. And that was the curse – *knowing* that the ultimate was attainable, but not knowing what it was or how to attain it. They studied the problem and came up with no solutions. Finally, the best amplified Markovian minds concluded that, somewhere in their development, they'd lost something – the true fulfillment of the dream. The social equation did not balance, because it lacked some basic component. One plus two plus three equals six, but if you don't have the plus two in there, it can't possibly reach more than four.

'Finally, they came to the conclusion that they were at a dead end, and would stagnate in an eternal orgy of hedonism unless something was done. The solution seemed simple: start over, try to regain the missing factor, or rediscover it, by starting from the beginning again. They used a variety of races and conditions to restart, none Markovian, on the idea that any repetition of the Markovian cycle would only end up the same.'

'And so they built this world,' Varnett put in.

'Yes, they built this world. A giant Markovian brain, placed around a young but planetless sun. The brain *is* the planet, of course, everything but the crust. Gravity was no problem, nor was atmosphere. They created an outer shell, about a hundred kilometers above the surface. The hexagons are all compartments, their elements held in all directions by fields of force.'

'So it was built to convert the Markovians to new forms?' Skander asked.

'Double duty, really,' Brazil told them. 'The finest artisans of the Markovian race were called in. They made proposals for biospheres, trying to outdo one another in creativity. The ones that looked workable were built, and volunteers went through the Zone Gate and became the newly designed creatures in the newly designed environments. Several generations were needed for even a moderate test – the Markovians didn't mind. A thousand years was nothing to them. You see, they could build, pioneer-style, but they were still Markovians. A lot of generations born in the biome and of the new race were needed to establish a culture and show how things would go. Their numbers were kept relatively stable, and the fields of force were much more rigid then than now. They had to live in their hex, without any real contact with other hexes. They had to build their own worlds.'

They were riding *down* now, at a deceptively steep angle. Down into the bowels of the planet itself.

'But why didn't the first generation establish a high civilization?' Varnett asked. 'After all, they were just like us, changed outside only.'

'You overestimate people from a highly technological culture. We take things for granted. We know how to turn on a light, but not why the light comes on. None of us could *build* most of our artifacts, and most civilized races become dependent on them. Suddenly dumped in a virgin wilderness, as they all were, they had no stores, no factories, no access to anything they didn't make themselves out of what was available. A great many died from hardship alone. The tough ones, the survivors, they built their own societies, and their children's societies. They worked with purpose – if the test failed, then they died out. If they succeeded – well, there was the promise that the successful ones would someday go to the Well of Souls at midnight, and there be taken to a new world, to found a new civilization, to grow, develop, perhaps become the progenitors of a future race of gods who would be fulfilled. Each hoped to be the ones whose descendants would make it.'

'And you were here when that happened,' Wuju said nervously.

'I was,' he acknowledged. 'I assisted the creator of Hex Forty-one – One Eighty-seven, the hundred and eighty-seventh and last race developed in that hex. I didn't create it, simply monitored and helped out. We stole ideas from each other all the time, of course. Dominant species in one hex might be a modified pattern of animals in another. Our own race was a direct steal from some large apes in another hex. The designer liked them so much that not only did the dominant race turn out to be apes, but they were almost endlessly varied as animals.'

'Hold on, Brazil,' Skander said. 'These others might not know much about things, but I'm an archaeologist. Old Earth developed over a few billion years, slowly evolving.'

'Not exactly,' Brazil replied. 'First of all, time was altered in each case. The time frame for the development of our sector was speeded up. The original design produced the life we expected, but it developed differently – as giant reptiles, eventually. When it was clear that it wouldn't do to have our people coexist with them, a slight change in the axial tilt caused the dinosaurs to die out, but it placed different stresses on other organisms. Minor mammals developed, and to these, over a period of time, we added ours to replace the ones logically developing in the evolutionary scale. When conditions seemed suitable for us, when apelike creatures survived, we began the exodus. Soon the temperate zones had their first intelligent life. Again, with all the resources but nothing else. They did well, astonishingly so, but the long-term effects of the axial tilt produced diastrophism and a great ice age within a few centuries. Our present, slow climb has been the product of the extremely primitive survivors of those disasters. So, in fact, has it been with all your home worlds.'

'Is there a world, then, or a network of worlds of the Akkafians?' Hain asked.

'There was,' Brazil replied. 'Perhaps there is. Perhaps it's larger and greater and more advanced than ours. The same with the Umiau, the Czill, the Slel-cronians, the Dillians, and others. When we get to the Well itself, I'll be able to tell you at least which ones are still functioning, although not how, or if they've changed, or what. I would think that some of the older ones would be well advanced by now. My memory says there were probably close to a million races created and scattered about; I'll be curious to see how many are still around.'

They had been going down for some time. Now they were deep below the surface, how deep they couldn't say. Suddenly a great hexagon outlined in light appeared just under them.

'The Well Access Gate,' Brazil told them. 'One of six. It can take you to lots of places within the Well, but it'll take you to the central control area and monitoring stations if you have no other instructions. When we get to it, just step on it. I won't trigger it until everyone is aboard. In case somebody else does, by accident, just wait for the light to come back on and step on again. It'll work.'

They did as instructed, and when all were on the Gate, all light suddenly winked out. There followed a twisting, unsettling feeling like falling. Then, suddenly, there was light all over.

They stood in a huge chamber, perhaps a kilometer in diameter. It was semicircular, the ceiling curving up over them almost the same distance as it was across. Corridors, hundreds of them, led off in all directions. The Gate was in the center of the dome, and Brazil quickly stepped off, followed by the others, who looked around in awe and anticipation.

The texture of the place was strange. It seemed to be made up of tiny hex-agonal shapes of polished white mica, reflecting the light and glittering like millions of jewels.

After they stepped off the Gate, Brazil stopped and pointed a tentacle back over it.

Suspended by force fields, about midway between the Gate and the apex of the dome, was a huge model of the Well World, turning slowly. It had a ter-minator, and darkness on half of its face, and seemed to be made of the same mica-like compound as the great hall. But the hexagons on the model were much larger, and there were solid areas at the poles, and a black band around its middle. The sphere seemed to be covered by a thin transparent shell com-posed of segments which exactly conformed to the hexagons below.

'That's what the Well World looks like from space,' Brazil told them. 'It's an exact model, fifteen hundred sixty hexagons, the Zones – everything. Note the slight differences in reflected light from each hex. That's Markovian writing – and they are numbers. This is more than a model, really. It's a separate Markovian brain, containing the master equation for stabilizing all of the new worlds. It energizes the Well, and permits the big brain around us to do its job.'

'Where are the controls, Nate?' Ortega prodded.

'Each biome – that is, planetary biome – has its own set of controls,' Brazil told him. 'This place is honeycombed with them. Each hex on the Well World is controlled as a complement to the actual world. Most controls, of course, do not have corresponding hexes. What we're left with today are the last few hexes created and some of the failures – not necessarily the ones that died out, but the ones that didn't work out. The Faerie, for example. Some of them snuck into the last batch of transits, and several of the others who were lefto-vers from closed and filled projects, some Dillians, some Umiau, and the like, who wanted to get out of the Well World and thought they could help, came, too. Not many, and they were disrupted by civilization's rises and falls, and became the objects of superstition, fear, hatred. None survived the distance on Old Earth, but we didn't get many to begin with, and reproduction was slow. But, come, let's go to a control center.'

He walked toward one of the corridors on his six tentacles, and they fol-lowed hesitantly. All of them held their pistols tightly, at the ready.

They walked for what seemed an endless time down one of the corridors, passing closed hexagonal doors along the way. Finally Brazil stopped in front of one, and it opened, much as the lens of a camera opens. He walked in, and they followed quickly, anxious not to lose sight of him even for a moment.

The room lit up as they approached. It was made of the same stuff as the great hall and the corridors. There were, however, walls of obvious controls, switches, levers, buttons, and the like, and what looked like a large black screen directly ahead of them. None of the instruments held any sort of clue as to what they were, or had anything familiar about them.

'Well, here it is, and it's still active,' Brazil announced. 'Let me see,' he mur-mured, and went over to a panel. Their faces showed sudden tension and fear, and all of the pistols were raised, trained on him. The Diviner's blinking lights started going very, very fast.

'Don't touch nothin', Nate!' Ortega warned.

'Just checking something here,' Brazil responded, unconcerned. 'Yes, I see. In this room is the preset for a civilization that has now expanded. It's inter-stellar, but not pangalactic. Population a little over one and a quarter trillion.'

'If it's a high-tech civilization, then it is not ours,' the Slelcronian said with some relief.

'Not necessarily,' Brazil replied. 'The tech levels here on the Well World were not imposed on the outside at all. They were dictated by the problems you might find in your own world. A high-tech world had abundant and easily accessible resources, a low-tech much less so. Since the home world had to develop logically and mathematically according to the master rules of nature, some worlds were better endowed than others. By making the trial hex here a low-tech, no-tech, or the like, we simply were compensating for the degree of difficulty in establishing technological civilization on the home world, not preventing it. We made them develop alternatives, to live without technology so they'd be better prepared on their home worlds. Some did extremely well. Most of the magic you find here is not Well magic, but actual mental powers developed by the hexes to compensate for low-tech status. What they could use here, they could use there.'

'The Diviner says you are truthful,' The Rel commented, one of the first things the Northerner had said since they set out. 'The Diviner states that you were responsible for its prophecy that we would be here.'

'In a way, yes,' Brazil replied. 'When I went through the Zone Gate, the Markovian brain recognized me as a native of Hex Forty-one and sent me there. However, in its analysis, it also found what I, myself, didn't know – that I had an original Markovian brainwave pattern. It then assumed that I was here to give it further instructions or to do work. When it concluded this, The Diviner, extremely sensitive to such things, picked up the message, however garbled.' He paused, and that central mass tilted toward them a little.

'And now,' he said, sadness in his voice, 'here we are, in the control center, and you've all got fear on your faces and your guns trained on me.' *Even you, Wu Julee*, he thought, immeasurable sadness coursing through him. *Even you.*

'I tried to give mankind rules for living which would avert a second disaster like the first, would keep it from self-destruction. Nobody listened. Nobody changed. Type Forty-one was badly flawed – and it beat the odds anyway, this time. It made its way to the stars, and that was an outlet for its aggression, although, even there, even now, its component parts are looking at ways to dominate one another, kill one another, rule one another. And the drive for domination is there even in the nonhumans, you, Northerner, and you, Slelcronian. Look at you all now. Look at yourselves! Look at each other! Do you see it? Can you feel it? Fear, greed, horror, ambition burning within you, consuming you! The only reason you haven't killed one another by now is your common fear of me. How dare you condemn a Hain, a Skander – a society? How dare you?

'How many of you are thinking of the people these controls represent? Do you fear for them? Do you care about them? You don't want to save them, better their lives. That fear is inside you, fear for your own selves! The basic flaw in the set-up equation, that burning, basic selfishness. None of you cares for any but yourself! Look at you! Look at what monsters you've all become!'

Their hearts pounded, nerve ends frayed. The Diviner and The Rel were the first to respond.

'What about yourself, Nathan Brazil?' The Rel chimed. 'Isn't the flaw in us simply a reflection of the flaws in yourself, in your own people, the Markovians, who could not give us what we lack because they did not themselves possess it?'

Brazil's reply was calm, in contrast to his previous outburst.

'The Markovians wanted to live in this universe, not run it. They had already done that. Destiny was a random factor they believed necessary to the survival of us all. That's why they closed down the Well. None of us would be here except for a freak set of circumstances.'

'Where are the controls, Nate?' Ortega asked.

'We'll find them ourselves,' Hain snapped. 'Varnett cracked the big code, he should be able to crack this one, too.'

Brazil's voice held deep sorrow. 'Pride is a weakness of all things Markovian, and you're a reflection of it. Now, if you'll ease up and allow me one touch on the panel in back, I'll show you the controls. I'll tell you how to operate them. Let's see what happens then.'

Ortega nodded, pistols at the ready. Brazil reached out with a tentacle and touched a small panel behind him.

The large black screen went on – but it wasn't exactly a screen. It was a great tunnel, an oval stretching back as far as the eye could see. And it was covered with countless tiny black spots, trillions of them at the best guess. And between all the various black spots shot frantic electrical bolts in a frenzy of activity, trillions of blinking hairline arcs jumping from one little black area to another.

'There's your controls,' Brazil said disgustedly. 'To change the ratios, all you have to do is alter the current flow between any two or more control spots.'

He looked at them, and there was the deepest fear and horror on their faces. They're afraid of me, he thought. All of them are in mortal fear of me! Oh, my God! Wuju who loved me, Varnett who risked his life for me, Vardia who trusted me – all afraid. I haven't harmed them. I haven't even threatened them. I couldn't if I wanted to. How can they ever understand our common source, our common bond? he thought in anguish. We love, we hate, we laugh, we cry, live – that I am no different from themselves, only older.

But they did not understand, he realized. I am God to the primitives, the civilized man of great power at a point where knowledge is power, surrounded by the savages.

That's why I'm alone, he understood. That's why I'm always alone. They fear what they can't understand or control.

'One control panel,' he said softly. 'One only. What are a few trillion lives? There is their past, their present, their potential future. All yours. Maybe their equation is the basis for one or more of you in this room. Maybe not. It's somebody's. Maybe it's yours. Okay, anybody, who wants to touch the first and second control spots, change the flow? Step right up! Now's your chance to play God!'

Varnett walked carefully over to the opening, breathing hard, sweat pouring from his body.

'Go on,' Brazil urged. 'Do your stuff! You might cancel out somebody, maybe a few trillion somebodies. You'll certainly alter someone's equation in some way, make two and two equal three in somebody's corner. Maybe none of us will be here. Maybe none of us will ever have been here. Go on! Who cares about all those people, anyway?'

Varnett stood there, mouth open, looking like a very frightened fifteen-year-old boy, nothing more. 'I – I can't,' he almost sobbed.

'How about you, Skander? This is where you wanted to be. And you, Hain?' His voice rose to a high, excited pitch. 'Diviner? Can you divine this one? Vardia? Serge? Wuju? Slelcronian? *Any of you?*'

'*In the name of God, Brazil!*' Skander screamed. '*Stop it!* You know we don't dare do anything as long as we don't understand the panel's operation!'

'He's bluffing!' Hain snarled. 'I'll take the chance.'

'*No!*' Wuju screamed, and swung her gun around on the great bug. 'You can't!'

'I'll even show you how,' Brazil said calmly, and took a step.

'Nate! Stay away from there!' Ortega warned. 'You can be killed, you know!'

Brazil stopped, and the pulsating mass bent toward Ortega slightly. 'No, Serge, I can't. That's the problem, you see. I told you I wasn't a Markovian, but none of you listened. I came here because you might damage the panel, do harm to some race of people I might not even know. I knew you couldn't *use* this place, but all of you are quite mad now, and one or more of you might destroy, might take the chance, as Hain just showed. But none of you, in your madness, has thought to ask the real question, the one unanswered question in the puzzle. Who stabilized the Markovian equation, the basic one for the universe?'

There was a pumping sound, like that of a great heart, its *thump, thump, thump* permeating them. Their own hearts seemed to have stopped, all frozen in an eerie tableau. Only the thumping seemed real.

'I was formed out of the random primal energy of the cosmos,' Brazil's voice came to them. 'After countless billions of years I achieved self-awareness. I was the universe, and everything in it. In the aeons I started experimenting, playing with the random forces around me. I formed matter and other types of energy. I created time, and space. But soon I tired of even those toys. I formed the galaxies, the stars, and planets. An idea, and they were, as congealed primal energy exploded and flung transmuted material outward from its center.

'I watched things grow, and form, according to the rules I set up. And yet, I tired of these, also. So I created the Markovians and watched them develop according to my plan. Yet, even then, the solution was not satisfactory, for they knew and feared me, and their equation was too perfect. I knew their total developmental line. So I changed it. I placed a random factor in the Markovian equation and then withdrew from direct contact.

'They grew, they developed, they evolved, they changed. They forgot me and spread outward on their own. But since they were spiritually reflections of myself, they contained my loneliness. I couldn't join with them as I was, for they would hold me in awe and fear. They, on the other hand, had forgotten me, and as they rose materially they died spiritually. They failed to grow to my equal, to end my loneliness. Their pride would not admit such a being as myself to fellowship, nor could their own fear and selfishness allow fellowship even with each other.

'So I decided to become one of them. I fashioned a Markovian shell, and entered it. I knew the flesh, its joys and its pains. I tried to teach them what was wrong, to tell them to face their inner fears, to rid themselves of the disease, to look not to a material heaven but within themselves for the answers. They ignored me.

'And yet the potential was there. It is still there. Wuju's response to kindness and caring. Varnett's self-sacrifice. Vardia's need for others. Other examples abound, not just about us, but about all our people. The one who sacrifices his life to save others. The compassion there, sometimes almost buried by the overlying depravity. It peers through – isolated, perhaps, but it is there. And as long as it is there, I shall continue. I shall work and hope for the day when some race seizes that spark and builds on it, for only then will I no longer be alone.'

They said nothing for several seconds. Then, quietly, Ortega responded, 'I'm not sure I believe all this. I've been a Catholic all my life, but somehow God to me has never been a little spunky Jew named Nathan Brazil. But, assuming what you say is true – which I don't necessarily accept – why haven't you scrapped everything and started again? And why continue to live our grubby little lives?'

'As long as that spark is present, I'll let things run, Serge,' Brazil replied. 'That random factor I talked about. Only when it's gone will I go, give up, maybe try again – maybe, finally die. I'd like to die, Serge – but if I do I take everything with me. Not just you, everybody and everything, for I stabilize the universal equation. And you are all my children, and I *care*. I can't do it as long as that spark remains, for as long as it remains you are not only the worst, but the best of me.'

The *thump, thump, thump* continued, the only sound in the room.

'I don't think you're God, Nate,' Ortega replied evenly. 'I think you're crazy. Anybody would be, living this long. I think you're a Markovian throwback, crazy after a billion years of being cut off from your own kind. If you was God, why don't you just wave your tentacles or something and get what you want? Why all this journey, and pain, and torment?'

'Varnett?' Brazil called. 'You want to explain it mathematically?'

'I'm not sure I don't agree with Ortega,' Varnett replied carefully. 'Not that it makes much difference from a practical point of view. However, I see what you're driving at. It's the same dilemma we face at that control board, there.

'Let's say we let Skander do what he wants, abolish the Comworlds,' the boy continued. 'Let's say Brazil, here, shows him exactly how to do it, just what to press and in what sequence and in what order. But the Com concept and the Comworlds developed according to the normal human flow of social evolution, right or wrong. They are caused by countless past historical events, conditions, ideas. You can't just banish them; you've got to change the equation so that they never developed. You have to change the whole human equation, all the past events that led to their formation. The new line you created would be a completely different construct, things as they would be without any of the crucial points that created the Coms. Maybe it was an outlet. Maybe, bad as it was, it was the only outlet. Maybe man would have destroyed himself if just one of those factors wasn't there. Maybe what we'd have is something worse.'

'Exactly,' Brazil agreed. 'For anything major you have to change the past, the whole structure. Nothing just vanishes. Nothing just appears. We are the sum of our past, good as well as bad.'

'So what do we do?' wailed Skander. 'What can we do?'

'A few things can be done,' Brazil replied calmly. 'You – most of you – sought: power. Well, *this* is power!' With that the Markovian moved toward the control panel.

'My God! He's going in there!' Skander screamed. 'Shoot, you fools!' The Umiau fired its pistol at the Markovian. In a second, the others followed, pouring a concentrated energy pulse into the mass sufficient to disintegrate a building.

The Markovian creature stopped, but seemed to absorb the energy. They poured it into him, all of them, even Wuju, with great accuracy.

He was still there.

The Diviner's lights blinked rapidly, and searing bolts shot out, striking the Markovian body. There was a glow, surrounding the creature in stark outline, and then it faded.

Brazil was still there.

They stopped firing.

'I told you you couldn't hurt me,' Brazil said. 'None of you can hurt me.'

'Bullshit!' Ortega spat. 'Your body was torn to ribbons in Murithel! Why wasn't this one?'

'Of course! Of course!' Skander exclaimed excitedly. 'This body is a direct construct of the Markovian brain, you fools! The brain won't allow it to be harmed, since it's really part of the brain itself!'

'Quite so,' Brazil responded. 'Nor, in fact, do I have to go in there at all. I can instruct the brain from right here. I've been able to do that since we first entered the Well itself. I merely wanted to give you a demonstration.'

'It would seem that we are at your mercy, Markovian,' The Rel said. 'What is your intention?'

'I can affect things for anyplace from here,' Brazil told them. 'I merely feed the data into the brain through this control room, and that's that. It's true there's a control room for each type, but they are all-purpose, in case of problems, overcrowding when we built the place, and so on. Any control room can be switched to any pattern.'

'But you said –' Ortega started to protest.

'In the words of Serge Ortega,' Brazil replied, a hint of amusement in his voice, 'I lied.'

Wuju broke from them and ran up to him, and prostrated herself in front of him, trembling. 'Please! Please don't hurt us,' she pleaded.

There was infinite compassion in his voice. 'I'm not going to hurt you, Wuju. I'm the same Nathan Brazil you knew from the start of this mess. I haven't changed, except physically. I've done nothing to you, nothing to deserve this. You know I wouldn't hurt you. I couldn't.' The tone changed to one not of bitterness, but of deep hurt and agony, mixed with the loneliness of unimaginable lifetimes. 'I didn't shoot at *you*, Wuju,' it said.

She started crying; deep, uncontrollable sobs wracked her. 'Oh, my god, Nathan! I'm so sorry! I failed you! Instead of trust, I gave you fear! Oh, god! I'm so ashamed! I just want to die!' she wailed.

Vardia came over to her, tried to comfort her. She pushed the girl away.

'I hope you're satisfied!' Vardia spat at him. 'I hope you're pleased with yourself! Do anything you want to me for saying this, but don't torture her anymore!'

Brazil sighed. 'No one can torture someone like that,' he replied gently. 'Like me, you can only torture yourself. Welcome to the broader human race, Vardia. You showed compassion, disregard for yourself, concern for another. That would have been unthinkable in the old Vardia. If none of you can still understand, I intend to do something *for* you, not *to* you. For the most part, anyway.' He angled to address all of them.

245

'You're not perfect, none of you. Perfection is the *object* of the experiment, not the component. Don't torture yourself, run away from your fears. Face them! Stand up to them! Fight them with goodness, mercy, charity, compassion! Lick them!'

'We are the sum of our ancestral and actual past,' The Rel reminded him. 'What you ask may indeed be possible, but the well of fate has accented our flaws. Is it reasonable to expect us to live by such rules, when we find it difficult even to comprehend them?'

'You can only try,' Brazil told it. 'There is a greatness in that, too.'

The *thump, thump, thump* continued.

'What is that noise?' Ortega asked, ever the practical man.

'The Well circuits are open to the brain,' Brazil replied. 'It's awaiting instructions.'

'And what will those instructions be?' Varnett asked nervously.

'I must make some repairs and adjustments to the brain,' Brazil explained. 'A few slight things, so that no one can accidentally discover the keying equation again. I'm not sure I'd like to go through this exercise again – and, if I did, there's no guarantee that some new person might not take that chance, damage the structure, do irreparable harm to trillions who never had a chance. But, just in case, the Well Access Gate will be reset to respond only to me. Also more of an insurance factor has to be added, to summon me if things go wrong.'

Skander gave an amazed chuckle. 'That's *all?*' he said, relieved.

'It is most satisfactory to me,' The Rel pronounced. 'We were concerned only that nothing be disturbed. For a short while there, we lost sight of that – but we are back in control of ourselves again.'

'Very minor adjustments are possible without disturbing anything,' Brazil told them. 'I can't do anything grandiose without upsetting a few things. I will, however, do some minor adjustments. For one thing, I am going to make sure that nothing like the Ambreza gas that reduced Type Forty-one humans on this world to apes will pass again, and I'm going to slap some local controls on technological growth and development, so that such an adjustment won't be necessary again, not here.

'And, because I can't bear to see them like that, I'm going to introduce a compound to the Type Forty-one atmosphere that will break the gas molecules down into harmless substances, while at the same time I'm going to make it a nontechnological hex absolutely, I don't know what they'll come up with, but I'll bet it's better than their current lot.'

'What about us?' Hain asked.

'I will not change what you are inside,' Brazil told them. 'If I do that, you will not have lived at all. To do anything otherwise would be to invite paradox, and that might mess up everything. Thus, I have to deal with you as you are.'

Brazil seemed to think for a moment, then said, in a voice that sounded as if it came from thunder, 'Elkinos Skander! You wanted to save the human race, but, in the process, you became inhuman yourself. When the end justifies *any* means, you are no better, perhaps worse, than those you despise. There are seven bodies back on Dalgonia. Seven human beings who died trusting you, helping you, who were victims of your own lust for power. I can't forget them. And, if I alter the time line, bring them back, then all this didn't happen. I pity you, Skander, for what you are, for what you could have become. My instructions to the brain are justice as a product of the past.'

Skander yelled, 'It wasn't me! It was Varnett! I wanted to save the worlds! I wanted—'

And suddenly Skander wasn't there anymore.

'Where did it go?' The Rel asked.

'To a world suited for him as he is, in a form suited to justice,' Brazil responded. 'He *might* be happy there, he might find justice. Let him go to his fate.'

Brazil paused a moment, then that huge voice came back. 'Datham Hain!' it called. 'You are the product of a horrible life. Born in contagion, you spread it.'

'I never had a chance except the way I took!' Hain shouted defiantly. 'You know that!'

'Most products of a bad environment turn out worse,' Brazil admitted. 'And yet, some of the greatest human beings came out of such miserable lots and conquered them. You didn't, yet you had the intelligence and potential to do so. Today, you stand as a contagion. I pity you, Hain, and because I pity you I will give you a localized wish.'

Hain grew slightly larger, her black color turning to white. She saw it in the fur on her forelegs.

'You turned me noble!' she exclaimed, pleased and relieved.

'You're the most beautiful breeder in the kingdom of the Akkafians,' Brazil said. 'When I return you to the palace, you won't be recognized. You'll be at the start of a breeding cycle. The Baron Azkfru will see you and go mad with desire. You will be his brood queen, and bear his royal young. That is your new destiny, Hain. Satisfied?'

'It is all that I could hope for,' Hain replied, and vanished.

Wuju looked at Brazil, a furious expression on her face. 'You gave that son of a bitch *that?* How could you reward that – that monster?'

'Hain gets the wish, but it's not a reward, Wuju,' Brazil replied. 'You see, they withheld from their newcomer one fact of Akkafian life. Most Marklings are sterile, and they do the work. A few are raised as breeders. A breeder hatches a hundred or more young – but they hatch *inside* the mother's body and eat their way out, using the breeder's body for their food.'

Wuju started to say something, then formed a simple, *'Ooooh'* as the horror of Hain's destiny hit her.

'Slelcronian!' Brazil pronounced. 'You present me with a problem. I don't like your little civilization personally, and I don't like you much, either. I've adjusted things slightly, so the Recorders now only work with Slelcronians, not with any sentient plant. But you, personally – you're a problem. You're too dangerous to be let loose in the technology of Czill; you know too much. At the same time, you know too much of what is here to go back to Slelcron. It occurs to me, however, that you've really not altered the expedition in any significant way. If you had *not* taken over Vardia, nothing would have changed. Therefore, you didn't – and, in fact, couldn't.'

Nothing seemed to change, but there was a difference in the Czillian body.

'So what are you going to do with me and my sister?' Vardia the Czillian asked. As far as everyone in the room was concerned, except for Brazil, the Slelcronian takeover had never happened. Slelcron was merely the funny place of the flowers and the giant bees, and their passage had been uneventful. Even so, the human Vardia had found her sister the Czillian as cold as the Slelcronian had been. She had gone through the same mental anguish as she had before and felt alienated from her sister.

Everything was as it had been before.

'Vardia, you are your old self, and no longer your sister,' Brazil pointed out. 'I think you'd be happiest returning to Czill, to the Center. You've much to contribute, to tell this story the way it happened. They won't be able to make use of what you say to get in, but it may cause the thinkers there to consider what projects are really worthwhile. *Go!*'

She vanished.

Now only Brazil, The Diviner and The Rel, Varnett, Wu Julee, Ortega, and the original Vardia were left.

'Diviner and Rel,' Brazil said, 'your race intrigues me. Bisexual, two totally different forms which mate into one organism, one of which has the power and the other the sensory input and output. You're a good people, with a lot of potential. Perhaps you can carry the message and reach that plateau.'

'You're sending us back, then?' The Rel asked.

'No,' Brazil replied. 'Not to the hex. Your race is on the verge of expanding outward in its sector. It is near the turning point where questions of goals are asked. I'm sending you to your own people on their world with the message I gave you here. The Diviner's gift will distinguish you. Perhaps you can turn your people, perhaps not. It's up to you. Go!'

The Diviner and The Rel vanished.

'Varnett,' Brazil said, and the boy jerked as if he was shot.

'What's in that little bag of tricks for me, Brazil?' he asked with false bravado.

'There are degrees of Comworlds, some better than others,' Brazil noted. 'Yours isn't too far gone yet. Even Vardia's can change. The worst of the lot is Dedalus. It went the genetic engineering route, you know. Everyone looks alike, talks alike, thinks alike. They kept males and females, sort of, but the engineers thought of even that. The people are hermaphroditic – small male genitals atop a vagina below. They breed once, in an exchange, then lose all sexual desires and prowess. Each has one child, which is, of course, identical to the parents, turned over to and raised by the state. It's a grotesque anthill, but it may represent the future.

'They don't even have names there. Obedience and contentment are engineered into them. Yet, the Central Committee retains power. This small group retains its sexual abilities, and the members are slightly different. The population is programmed to obey any one of those leaders unquestionably. The Committee was a perfect target, and they're controlled by the sponge syndicate. That sort of genetic engineering is, I fear, what the spongers have in mind for everyone eventually – with themselves on top.

'I give you the chance to change things. As the Murnies did with me, I do to you. You will be the Chairman of the Central Committee of Paradise, formerly called Dedalus. You'll be the new Chairman. The old one just kicked the bucket, and you're now unfrozen to take command. If you meant what you told me, you can kick the spongers out of their most secure planethold and restore that planet to individual initiative. The revolution will be easy – the people will obey unquestionably. Your example and efforts could dissuade others from taking the Dedalus course. It's up to you. You're in charge.'

'What happens to the new Chairman's mind?' Varnett asked. 'And my body?'

'Even swap,' Brazil told him. 'The new boy will wake up a bat over in your old hex. He'll make out. He's born to command.'

'Not *that* madhouse,' Varnett chuckled. 'Okay, I accept.'

'Very good,' Brazil told him. 'But, I leave you this out. Should you ever want, any Markovian Gate will open for you – to bring you back here, for good. You'll be in a new body, so nobody knows what you would wind up as. You'd be here until you died, but you have that option.'

Varnett nodded soberly. 'Okay. I think I understand,' he said, and vanished.

'Serge Ortega,' Brazil sighed. 'What in hell am I going to do with an old rascal like you?'

'Oh, hell, Nate, what's the difference?' Ortega responded, and he meant it. 'This time you won.'

'Are you really happy here, Serge? Or was that just part of the act?'

'I'm happy,' the snakeman replied. 'Hell, Nate, I was so damned bored back in the old place I was ready to kill myself. It's gotten too damned civilized, and I was too old to go frontier. I got here, and I've had a ball for eighty years. Even though I lost this round, it's been great fun. I wouldn't have missed it for the world.'

Brazil chuckled. 'Okay, Serge.'

Ortega vanished.

'Where did you send him?' Vardia asked hesitantly.

'Eighty's about the average life span for a Ulik,' Brazil replied. 'Serge didn't start as an egg, so he's a very old man. He has a year, five, maybe ten. I wouldn't put it past him to beat the system, but why the hell not? Let him go back to living and having fun.'

'And so that leaves us,' Wuju said quietly.

There was a sudden flicker in the image of the Markovian, then a sparkling graininess. The shape twirled, changed, and suddenly standing there in front of them was the old, human Nathan Brazil, in the colorful clothes he had first worn on the ship a lifetime ago.

'Oh, my god!' Wuju breathed, looking as if she were seeing a ghost.

'The God act's over,' he said, sounding relieved. 'You should see who you're really dealing with.'

'Nathan?' Wuju said hesitantly, starting forward. He put up his hand and stopped her, sighing.

'No, Wuju. It couldn't work. Not now. Not after all this. It wouldn't work anyway. Both of you deserve much better than life's given you. There are others like you, you know – people who never had the chance to grow, as you did. They can use a little kindness, and a lot of caring. You know the horrors of the sponge, Wuju, and the abuse to which some human beings subject others. And you, Vardia, know the lies that underlie the Com philosophy. I've talked to both of you, observed you both carefully. I've fed all this information plus as much data as could be obtained from a readout by the brain while you were in this room. The brain responded with recommendations on what would be best for you. If we're wrong – the brain and I – after a trial of what I'm going to do, then you both have the same option that is open to Varnett. Just get near a Markovian Gate – you don't have to jump into it. Just get passage on a ship going near a Markovian world. If you want, the Gate will pluck you out without disturbing the ship, passengers, or crew. You'll somehow mysteriously vanish. And you'll wind up in Zone again. Like Varnett, you will have to take potluck with the Zone Gate again. Once here, again, there will be no returning.

'But try it my way for a while. And remember what I said about your own contributions. Two people *can* change a world, if they wish.'

'But what –' Wuju started to ask, but was cut off in midsentence.

The two bodies didn't vanish, they just collapsed, like a suit of clothes with the owner gone. They lay there in a heap on the floor.

Brazil went over and carefully rearranged them so they looked as if they were sleeping.

'Well, now what, Brazil?' he asked himself, his voice echoing in the empty hall.

You go back, and you wait, his mind told him.

What about the bodies? he wondered. Somehow he couldn't just vaporize them. Though their owners were gone, they lived on as empty vegetables.

But there was nothing else to do, of course. They were just memories for him now, one a strange mixture of love and anguish. He was prolonging the inevitable.

There was a crackle, and the bodies were gone, back to primal energy.

'Oh, the hell with it,' said Nathan Brazil, and he, too, vanished.

The control room was empty. The Markovian brain noted the fact and then dutifully turned off the lights.

ON 'EARTH,' A PLANET CIRCLING A STAR NEAR THE OUTERMOST EDGE OF THE GALAXY ANDROMEDA

One moment Elkinos Skander had been perched atop Hain's back, looking at the control room and those in it. Then, suddenly, he wasn't.

He looked around. Things looked funny and distorted. He was color-blind except for a sepia tone that lent itself to everything.

He looked around, confused. I've gone through another change, he realized. My last one.

A rather pleasant-looking place, he thought, once he got used to the distorted vision. Forests over there, some high mountains, odd-looking grass, and strange sort of trees, but that was to be expected.

There were a lot of animals around, mostly grazing. They look a lot like deer, he noted, surprised. A few differences, but they would not look out of place on a pastoral human world.

He looked down at himself, and saw the shadow of his head on the grass.

I'm one of them, he suddenly realized with a shock. *I'm a deer. No antlers like those big males over there, so I must be a doe.*

A deer? he thought quizzically.

Why a deer?

He was still meditating on this, when suddenly the grass seemed to explode

251

with yells and strange shapes; great, rectangular bodies with their facial features in their chest, and big, big teeth.

He watched as the Murnies singled out a large doe not far from him and surrounded it. Suddenly they speared it several times, and it went down in wordless agony and lay twitching on the ground, blood running, but still alive.

The Murnies pounced on it, tearing at it, eating it alive.

To be eaten alive! he thought, stunned, and suddenly blind panic overtook him. He started running, running away from the scene.

Up ahead another band of Murnies leaped out of nowhere and cornered another deer, started to devour it.

They're all over! he realized. *This is their world! I'm just food to them!*

He ran narrowly avoiding entrapment several times. There were thousands of them here, and they all were hungry.

And even as he ran in exhausted, dizzy circles, he knew that even if he avoided them today he would have to avoid them tomorrow, and the day after, and the day after, and wherever he ran on this planet there would be more of them.

Sooner or later they'll get me! he thought in panic. *By god! I'll not be eaten alive! I'll cheat Brazil of his revenge!*

He reached the highlands by carefully pulling himself together.

Now that he had decided on a course of action, he felt calm.

There! Up ahead! his mind said joyfully. He stopped and looked over the edge of the cliff.

Over a kilometer straight down to the rocks, he saw with satisfaction. He ran back a long ways, then turned toward the cliff. With strong resolve, he ran with all his might toward the cliff and hurled himself over it.

He saw the rocks coming up to meet him, but felt only the slight shock of pain.

Skander awoke. The very fact that he awoke was a shock, and he looked around.

He was back on that plain at the edge of the forest. His shadow told him.

He was a deer again.

No! his mind screamed in horror. *I'll cheat the bastard yet! Somehow I'll cheat him!*

But there were a lot of deer and a lot of Murnies on that world, and Skander still had six more times to die.

PARADISE, ONCE CALLED DEDALUS, A PLANET NEAR SIRIUS

Varnett groaned, then opened his eyes. He felt cold. He looked around him and saw a number of people peering at him anxiously.

They all looked exactly alike. They didn't even look particularly male or female. Slight breasts and nipples, but nothing really female. Their bodies were lithe and muscular, sort of a blend of masculine and feminine.

All of them had small male genitals where they should be, but, from his vantage point, he could see a small cavity beneath them.

None of them had any body hair.

If you did it upside down and the other was right side up, he thought, you could give and receive at the same time.

'Are you all right?' one asked in a voice that sounded like a man's voice but with a feminine lilt.

'Do you feel all right?' another asked in the identical voice.

'I – I think so,' he replied hesitantly, and sat up. 'A little dizzy, that's all.'

'That will pass,' the other said. 'How's your memory?'

'Shaky,' he replied carefully. 'I'm going to need a refresher.'

'Easily done,' the other replied.

He started to ask them their names, then suddenly remembered. They didn't use names on *his* planet.

His planet! *His!*

'I'd like to get right to work,' he told them.

'Of course,' another replied, and they led him from the sterile-looking infirmary down an equally sterile corridor. He followed them, got into an elevator, and they rode up to the top floor.

The top floor, it seemed, was an office complex. Workers were everywhere, filing things, typing things, using computer terminals.

Everybody else was slightly smaller than he was, he realized. Not much, but in a world where everyone was absolutely identical such a slight difference was as noticeable as if Cousin Bat had entered the room.

His office was huge and well-appointed. White wall-to-wall carpeting, so thick and soft his bare feet practically bounced off it. There was a huge desk, and great high-backed chair. No other furnishings, he noted, although their lack made the place look barren.

'Bring me a summary of the status of the major areas of the planet,' he ordered. 'And then leave me for a while to study them.'

They bowed slightly, and left. He looked out the glass window that was the wall in back of his desk.

A complex of identical buildings stretched out before him. Broad, tree-lined streets, some small parkland, and lots of identical-looking shapes walking about on various business.

The sky was an off-blue, not the deepness of his native world, but it was attractive. There were some fleecy clouds in the sky, and, off in the distance, he saw signs of cultivated land. It looked like a rich, peaceful, and productive place, he thought. Of course, weather and topography would cause changes in the life-styles planet-wide, but he wagered those differences were minimal.

The aides returned with sheaves of folders bulging with papers. He acknowledged them curtly, and ordered them out.

There were no mirrors, but the lighting reflected him in the glass windows.

He looked just like them, only about fifty millimeters taller and proportionately slightly larger.

He felt his male genitals. They had the same feel as the ones he had had as Cousin Bat, he thought.

He reached a little lower, and found the small vaginal cavity.

He spread some papers around to make it look as if he had been studying them. He would, in time, of course, but not now.

He saw a small intercom on the desk and buzzed it, taking a seat in the big chair. At the far end of the room a clerk almost beat the track records entering, coming up to the desk and standing at full attention.

'I have found indications,' he told the clerk seriously, 'that several members of the Presidium may be ill. I want a team of rural doctors – based, as far as possible, away from here – to be brought to my office as soon as possible. I want that done *exactly* and at once. How long before they can get here?'

'If you want them from as far away from government centers as possible, ten hours,' the clerk replied crisply.

'All right, then,' he nodded. 'As soon as they arrive they are to see me – and no one else. *No one* is even to know that they have been sent for. I mean absolutely no one, not even the rest of the office.'

'I shall attend to it personally, Chairman,' responded the clerk, and turned to leave. So much for the spongies, he thought.

'Clerk!' he called suddenly, and the other halted and turned.

'Chairman?'

'How do I arrange to have sex?'

The clerk looked surprised and bemused. 'Whenever the Chairman wishes, of course. It is a great honor for any citizen.'

'I want the best specimen here in five minutes!' he ordered.

'Yes, Chairman,' responded the clerk knowingly, and left.

His eyes sparkled, and he rubbed his hands to-gather gleefully, thinking about what was to come.

Suddenly Nathan Brazil's visage arose from the corners of his mind.

He said he'd give me my chance, he thought seriously. And I'll make good on it. This world will be changed!

The door opened, and another inhabitant of Paradise entered.

'Yes?' he snapped.

'I was told to report to you by the clerk,' the newcomer said.

He smiled. The world would be changed, yes – but not right away, he thought. Not until I've had much more fun.

'Come on over here,' he said lightly. 'You're about to be honored.'

ON THE FRONTIER – HARVICH'S WORLD

He groaned, and opened his eyes. An older man in overalls and checkered shirt, smelly and with a three-days' growth of beard, was bending over him, looking anxious.

'Kally? You hear me, boy? Say somethin'!' the old man urged, shouting at him.

He groaned. 'God! I feel lousy!' he managed.

The old man smiled. 'Good! Good!' he enthused. 'I was afeared we'd lost you, there. That was quite a crack on the nog you took!'

Kally felt the left side of his head. There was a knot under the hair, and some dried blood. It hurt – throbbed, really.

'Try to stand up,' the old man urged, and gave him a hand. He took it, and managed to stand shakily.

'How do ya feel, boy?' the old man asked.

'My head hurts,' he complained. 'Otherwise – well, weak but okay.'

'Told ya ya shoulda got a good gal ta help with the farm,' the old man scolded. 'Ifn I hadn'ta happened along you'd be dead now.'

The man looked around, puzzled. It *was* a farm, he saw. Some chickens about, a ramshackle barn with a couple of cows, and an old log shack. It looked like corn growing in the fields.

'Somethin' wrong, Kally?' the old man asked.

'I – uh, who are you?' he asked hesitantly. 'And where am I?'

The old man looked concerned. 'That bump on the noggin's scrambled your brains, boy. Better get into town and see a doctor on it.'

'Maybe you're right,' the other agreed. 'But I still don't know who you are, where I am – or who I am.

'Must be magnesia or somethin',' the old man said, concerned. 'I'll be damned. Heard about it, but never seed it afore. Hell, boy, you're Kally Tonge, and since your pa died last winter you've run this farm here alone. You was borned here on Harvich,' he explained, pronouncing it *Harrige*, 'and you damned near died here.' He pointed to the ground.

He looked and saw an irrigation pump with compressor. Obviously he had been tightening the top holding nut with the big wrench and had kicked the thing into start. The wrench had whirled around and caught him on the head.

He looked at it strangely, knowing what it must mean.

'Will you be all right?' the old man asked concernedly. 'I got to run down the road or the old lady'll throw a fit, but if ya want I can send somebody back to take ya inta the doc's.'

'I'll see him,' Kally replied. 'But let me get cleaned up first. How – how far is it into town?'

'Christ, Kally! Ya even talk a little funny!' the old man exclaimed. 'But Depot's a kilometer and a half down the road there.' He pointed in the right direction.

Kally Tonge nodded. 'I'll go in. If you get a head injury, it's best to walk. Just check back in a little while, just in case. I'll be all right'

'Well, okay,' the old man responded dubiously. 'But if I don't hear ya got in town, I'm comin' lookin',' he warned, then walked back to the road.

He's riding a horse! Kally thought wonderingly. And the road's dirt!

He turned and went into the shack.

It was more modern than he would have guessed, although small. A big bed with natural fur blankets in one corner, a sink, a gas stove – bottled gas underneath, he noted – and the water was probably from a water tank near the barn. A big fireplace, and a crude indoor shower.

There was a small refrigerator, too, running off what would have been a tractor battery if he had had a tractor.

He noted the toilet in one corner, and went over to it. Above it hung a cracked mirror, some scissors, and toiletries.

He looked at himself in the mirror.

His was a strong, muscular, handsome face in a rugged sort of way. The hair was long and tied off in a ponytail almost a meter long, and he had a full but neatly trimmed beard and mustache. The hair was brown, but the beard was reddish.

He turned his head, saw that the knot was almost invisible in the hair. Brushing it back revealed an ugly wound.

He died in that accident, he thought. Kally Tonge died of that wound. And I filled the empty vessel.

He stripped and took the mirror off its nail hanger, looking at himself. He saw a rugged, muscular body, well toned and used to work. There were calluses on the hands, worn in from hard farm labor.

The wound *did* hurt, and while he was certain it wouldn't be serious now, it would be better to go into town. It would also help to explain his mental lapses.

He put on a thick wool shirt and work pants, and some well-worn leather boots, and went back outside.

The place was interesting, really. It looked like something out of ancient history, yet had indoor plumbing, electricity, albeit crude, and several other signs of civilization. In the midst of this primitiveness, he noticed with amusement that he wore a fancy wristwatch.

It was not cold, but there was a chill in the wind that made him glad he had picked the thicker shirt. They were short on rain here, he noted; the dirt road was rutted and dug up, yet dry and caked.

He walked briskly down the road toward the town, looking at the scenery. Small farms were the rule, and many looked far more modern than his. There wasn't much traffic, but occasional people passed on horseback or in buckboards, giving him the impression that modern vehicles were either in short supply or banned.

And yet, despite the lack of recent rain, the land was good. The tilled soil was black and mineral-rich, and where small compressors pumped water from wells or nearby creeks into irrigation ditches, the land bloomed.

He came upon the town much faster than he had anticipated. He didn't feel the least bit tired or uncomfortable, and he had walked with a speed that astonished him. The town itself was a study in contrasts. Log buildings, some as tall as five stories, mixed with modern, prefabricated structures. The street wasn't paved, but it went for several blocks, with a block or two on either side of the business district composed of houses, mostly large and comfortable. There was street lighting, and some of the businesses had electric signs, so there was a power plant somewhere, and, from the look of things, running water and indoor plumbing.

He studied some of the women, most of whom were dressed in garb much like his own, sometimes with small cowboy hats or straw broad-brimmed hats on their heads. There weren't nearly as many women as men, he noted, and those that were here looked tough, muscular, and mannish.

The town was small enough so that he spotted the doctor's office with no difficulty and headed for it. The doctor was concerned. He had quite a modern facility, with a minor surgery and some of the latest machines and probes. Clearly medical care was well into the modern era here. The X-rays showed a severe concussion and fracture. The doctor marveled that he was alive at all, as he placed medication and a small bandage on the wound after sewing seven stitches.

'Get somebody to stay with you the next few days, or look in on you regularly,' the doctor advised. 'Your loss of memory's probably only temporary, and not that uncommon in these cases. But a lot of damage was done. The brain was bruised, and I want someone to see that you don't have a clot in there.'

He thanked the doctor, assuring him that he would take care of himself and be watched and checked.

'Settle the bill at the end of the month,' the doctor told him.

This puzzled him for a minute. The bill? Money? He had never used it himself, and, back on the street, he pulled out a thin leather wallet, which looked like the survivor of a war, and opened it.

Funny-looking pieces of paper, about a dozen of them. They had very realistic pictures, almost three-dimensional, on them, the fronts showing the same man three times, the others two other men and a woman. The backs showed a remarkably realistic set of farm scenes. He wished he could read the bills. He would have to find out what each one was and remember the pictures.

A three-story log building's lights went on in the coming twilight, and he saw from the symbol on the sign that it was a bar and something else. He didn't recognize the other symbol, and couldn't read the words. Curious, he walked over to it.

There was a rumbling of thunder in the distance.

She awoke, feeling nauseated, and threw up.

The bile spilled on the cheap rug, and in it, as she gagged uncontrollably, she could see bits and pieces and even whole pills of some kind.

The spasms lasted several minutes, until it seemed there was nothing else to give. Feeling weak and exhausted, she lay back on the bed until the room steadied. The stench of the bile permeated her.

Slowly, she looked around. A tiny room, with nothing but a bed much too large for it and a wicker chair. There was barely fifty centimeters' clearance on either side of it.

The walls and ceiling seemed to be made of logs, but the construction was so solid it might as well have been rock. It was dark in the room, and she looked for a light. Spying a string hanging above her, she pulled it, and a weak, naked light bulb suspended from the ceiling flicked on. The glare hurt her eyes.

She raised her head slightly and looked down at her body. Something was definitely different.

Two extremely large but perfectly formed breasts met her eye, and her skin seemed creamy smooth, dark-complexioned but unpigmented.

Her gaze slid down a little more, and she saw that the rest of her body matched the breasts – curving in all the right places, definitely.

She felt – strange. Tingly all over, but particularly in the areas of her breasts and crotch.

She was nude from the waist up, but hanging on sultry hips was a pantslike garment of fine-woven black lace, to which hundreds of tiny sequins of various colors were attached.

She felt her face, and found that she had some sort of hairdo. There were also long, plastic earrings hanging from pierced ears.

She looked around in the gloom, found a small cosmetics case with a mirror in it, and looked at her face.

It is a beautiful face, she thought, and she was not being vain. Maybe the most beautiful face I've ever seen. Cosmetics had been carefully applied to bring out just the right highlights, but the face was so perfect that they seemed almost intrusive on its beauty.

But whose face was it? she wondered.

She noticed a box next to the cosmetics case on the floor, and picked it up idly. It was a pillbox – open, and empty. There was a universal caution symbol on it, but she couldn't read the writing. She didn't need to.

This girl, whoever and whatever she was, had killed herself. She had taken all those pills and overdosed. She had died here, in this room, moments before – alone. And the moment that girl had died, she had been somehow inserted into the body, and the physical processes righted.

She stared again at that beautiful face in the mirror.

What would make someone who looked like this and experienced such feelings as she now did commit suicide? So very young, she thought – perhaps no more than sixteen or seventeen. And so very beautiful.

She tried to get up, but felt suddenly light-headed and strange. She flopped back down on the bed and stared up at the light bulb, which, for some reason, had become fascinating.

She found herself gently caressing her own body, and it felt fantastic, like tingling jolts of pleasure at each nerve juncture.

It's the pills, a corner of her mind told her. You didn't get all of them out of your system.

The door opened suddenly, and a man looked in. He was dressed in white work clothes, like kitchen help. He was balding and fiftyish, but he had a tough, hard look to him. 'Okay, Nova, time to –' he began, then stopped and looked at her, the empty box, and the bile and vomited-up pills on the floor and the side of her bed.

'Oh, shit!' he snarled angrily, and exploded. 'You went for the happy pills again, didn't you? I warned you, dammit! I wondered why a sexy high-top like you would work this jerkwater! They tossed you out of the others!' He stopped, his tone going from fury to disgust.

'You're no good to anybody, not even yourself,' he snapped. 'I told you if you did this again, I'd toss you in the street. Come on! You hear me?' he started yelling. 'You're going out and now! Come on, get up!'

She heard him, but the words didn't register. He looked and sounded somehow funny, and she laughed and pointed to him, giggling stupidly.

He grabbed her by the arm and pulled her up. 'Jesus!' he exclaimed. 'You're a hell of a piece. Too bad your insides don't match your outsides. Come on!'

He pulled her out into the hall and dragged her down a flight of wooden stairs. She felt as if she were floating, and made flying motions with her free arm and motor sounds with her voice.

A few other young women peered out from second-floor rooms. None of 'em pretty as me, she thought smugly.

'Stop that giggling!' the man commanded, but it sounded so funny she giggled more.

The downstairs was a bar, some sawdust on the floor, a few round tables, and a small service bar to one side. It was dimly lit, and empty.

'Oh, hell,' he said, almost sadly, reaching into a cash drawer behind the bar. 'You ain't even earned your keep here, and you burned your clothes on the last flyer. Here – fifty *reals*,' he continued, stuffing a few bills in the lace panty. 'When you come to out in the street or the woods or the sheriff's office, buy some clothes and a ticket out. I've had it!'

He picked her up as if she weighed nothing, and, opening the door with one hand, tossed her rudely into the darkening street. The chilly air and the hard landing brought her down a bit, and she looked around, feeling lost and alone.

She suddenly didn't want to be seen. Although there were few people about, there were some nearby who would see her in a few moments. She saw a dark alleyway between the bar and a store and crawled into it. It was very dark and cold, and smelled a little of old garbage. But at least she was concealed.

Suddenly the streetlights popped on, and deepened the shadows in which she sat confused. The shock of where she was and her situation broke through into her conscious mind. She was still high, and her body still tingled, particularly when rubbed. She still wanted to rub it, but she was aware of her circumstances.

I'm alone in a crazy place I don't know, practically nude and with the temperature dropping fast, she thought miserably. How much worse can things get?

As if in answer, there was a rumbling and a series of static discharges, and the temperature dropped even more.

Tears welled up in her eyes, and she started crying at the helplessness of her position. She had never been more miserable in her life.

A man was crossing the street, walking toward the bar. He stopped suddenly. Lightning flashed, illuminating her for a brief moment. He looked puzzled, and came toward the alley. She was folded up, arms around her knees, head down against them. She rocked as she cried.

He saw her and stared in disbelief. Now what the hell? he thought.

He reached out and touched her bare shoulder, and she started, looked up at him, saw the concern on his face.

'What's the matter, little lady?' he asked gently.

She looked up with anguished face and started to speak, but couldn't.

She was, even in this state, the most beautiful thing he had ever seen.

'Nothing's that bad,' he tried to soothe her. 'Where do you live? I'll take you home. You're not hurt, are you?'

She shook her head negatively, and coughed a little. 'No, no,' she managed. 'Don't have a home. Thrown out.'

He squatted next to her. The lightning and thunder continued, but the rain held off still.

'Come on with me, then,' he said in that same soft tone. 'I've got a place just down the road. Nobody there but me. You can stay until you decide what to do.'

Her head shook in confusion. She didn't know what to do. Could she trust him? Dare she take this opportunity?

A strange, distant voice whispered in her brain. It said, *'Can you feel it? Fear, greed, horror, ambition, burning within you, consuming you! … Perfection is the object of the experiment, not the component. … Don't torture yourself, run away from your fears. Face them! Stand up to them! Fight them with goodness, mercy, charity, compassion. …'*

And trust? she wondered suddenly. Oh, hell! What have I got to lose if I go? What do I have if I don't?

'I'll go,' she said softly. He helped her up, gently, carefully, and brushed the dirt off her. He's very big, she realized. I only come up to his neck.

'Come on,' he urged, and took her hand.

She hesitated. 'I don't want – want to go out there looking like this,' she said nervously.

'There's nothing wrong with the way you look,' he replied in a tone that had nothing if not sincerity. 'Nothing at all. Besides, the storm's about to break, I think. Most folks will stay inside.'

Again she looked uncertain. 'What about us?' she asked. 'Won't we get wet?'

'There's shelter along the way,' he said casually. 'Besides, a little water won't hurt.'

She let him lead her down the deserted street of the town and out into the countryside. The storm continued to be visual and audible, but not as yet wet. The landscape seemed eerie, illuminated in the flashes.

The temperature had dropped from about fifteen degrees Celsius to around eight degrees due to the storm. She shivered.

He looked at her, concerned, feeling the tremors in her hand.

'Want my shirt?' he asked.

'But then you'll be cold,' she protested.

'I like cold weather,' he responded, taking off his shirt. His broad, muscled, hairy chest reactivated those funny feelings in her again. Carefully he draped the shirt around her. It fit her like a circus tent, but it felt warm and good.

She didn't know what to say, and something, some impulse, caused her to lean into him and put her arm around his bare chest. He responded by putting his arm around her, and they resumed walking.

Somehow it felt good, calming, and her anxieties seemed to flee. She looked up at him. 'What's your name?' she asked in a tone of voice she didn't quite comprehend, but was connected, somehow, in its throaty softness to those strange feelings.

'W –' he started to say, then said, instead, 'Kally Tonge. I have a farm not much farther down the road.'

She noticed the bandage on the side of his head. 'You're injured.'

'It's nothing – now,' he replied, and chuckled. 'As a matter of fact, you're just what the doctor ordered – literally. He said somebody should be with me through the night.'

'Does it hurt much?' she asked.

'Not now,' he replied. 'Medicine's pretty advanced here, although as you know the place is rather primitive overall.'

'I really don't know much about this world,' she replied truthfully. 'I'm not from here.'

'I could have guessed that,' he said lightly. 'Where *do* you come from?'

'I don't think you've ever heard of it,' she replied. 'From nowhere now, really.'

'What's *your* name?' he asked.

She started to say 'Nova,' the name the man had called her, but instead she said, 'Vardia.'

He stopped and looked at her strangely. 'That's a Com name, isn't it?' he asked. 'You're not from any Comworld!'

'Sort of,' she replied enigmatically, 'but I've changed a lot.'

'On the Well World?' he asked sharply.

She gasped, a small sound of surprise escaping her lips. 'You – you're one of the people from the Well!' she exclaimed. 'You woke up in that body, as I did! That head wound killed Kally Tonge and you took over, as I did!'

'Twice when I needed someone you comforted me, even defended me,' he said.

'*Wuju!*' she exclaimed, and an amazed smile spread over her face. She looked him over critically. 'My, how you've changed!'

'No more than you,' he replied, shaking his head wonderingly. '*Wow!*'

'But – but, why a man?' she asked.

His face grew serious. 'I'll tell you sometime. But, good old Nathan! He sure came through!'

The storm broke, then, and the rain started coming down heavily.

They were both soaked through in seconds, and her fancy hairdo collapsed. He laughed, and she laughed, and he picked her up and started running in the mud. Just ahead he saw his shack, outlined in the lightning flashes, but he misjudged the turn to his walk with his burden. They both tumbled into the road, splashing around and covered with thick black mud.

'You all right?' he shouted over the torrent.

'I'm drowning in mud!' she called back, and they both got up, laughing at each other.

'The barn's closer!' he shouted. 'See it over there? Run for it!'

He started off, and she followed, the rain getting heavier and heavier. He reached the door way ahead of her, and slid it aside on its rollers. She reached it, and they both fell in. The place had an eerie, hollow sound, the rain beating on the sheet-metal roof and wood sides of the barn. It was dark, and smelled like the barn it was. A few cows mooed nervously in their stalls.

'Wooj?' she called.

'Here,' he said, near her, and she turned.

'Might as well sit it out here,' he told her. 'There's a pile of hay over there, and it's a thousand meters to the shack. Might as well not go through the deluge twice.'

'Okay,' she replied, exhausted, and plopped into the hay. The rain continued to beat a percussion symphony on the barn.

He plopped beside her. She was fussing with her lace pants.

'The mud's all caked in them, and the sequins are scratching me,' she said. 'Might as well get them off, for all the good they'll do as clothing anyway, even if they are all I've got in the world.'

She did, and they lay for a while side by side. He put his arm around her and fondled her breast.

'That feels good,' she whispered. 'Is – is that what I've been feeling? I thought it was still the pills. Is this what you felt with Brazil?'

'I'll be damned!' he said to himself. 'I always wondered what an erection felt like to a man!' He turned and looked at her. 'I'll show you what it's really like, if you want,' he said softly.

'I – I think that's what he wanted,' she replied.

'Is it what *you* want?' he asked seriously.

'I think I do,' she whispered, and realized that it *was* what she wanted. 'But I don't even know how.'

'Leave that to an expert,' he replied. 'Although I'm not used to this end of things.' He put both arms around her, kissed her and fondled her.

And he kicked off his pants, and showed her the other side of being a woman, while discovering himself what it was to be a man.

The rain was over. It had been over for a couple of hours, but they just lay there, content in the nearness of each other.

The door was still half-open, and Vardia, still dazed and dreamy from her first sexual experience, saw the clouds roll back and the stars appear. 'We'll get you some clothes in the morning,' he said at last. 'Then we'll tour the farm. This rain should do everything good. I was born on a farm, you know, but not my own farm.'

'People – non-Com people – they do that *every* day?' she asked.

He chuckled. 'Twice if they're horny enough. Except for a couple of days each month.'

'You – you've done it both ways,' she said. 'Is it different?'

'The feeling's definitely different, but it's the same charge,' he replied. 'An important part, male or female, is that you do it when you want with someone you want.'

'Is that love?' she asked. 'Is that what Brazil was talking about?'

'Not the sex,' he replied. 'That's just a – a component, as he would say. Without the object – without love, without feeling for the other person, without *caring*, it's not pleasant at all.'

'That's why you're a man now,' she said. 'All the other times – they were the wrong kind, weren't they?'

'Yes,' he replied distantly, and looked out at the stars. She clenched his hand tightly in hers.

'Do you think he was really God?' Vardia asked quietly.

'I don't know,' he replied with a sigh. 'What if he wasn't? When he was in the Well he had the power. He gave me my farm, a good, healthy young body, a new chance. And,' he added softly, 'he sent you.'

She nodded. 'I've never lived like this,' she said. 'Is it all as wonderful as tonight?'

'No,' he replied seriously. 'There's a lot of hard work, and pain, and heartache – but, if it all comes together, it *can* be beautiful.'

'We'll try it here,' she said resolutely. 'And when the fun is gone, if ever, or when we're old and gray, we'll take off for a Markovian world, and go back and do it again. That's a good future.'

'I think it is,' he responded. 'It's more than most people ever get.'

'This world,' she said. 'It must never become like the others, like the Com. We must make sure of that.'

At that moment there was a glow far beyond the horizon, and suddenly a bright arrow streaked upward in the dark sky and vanished. A few seconds later, a distant, roaring sound came to them.

'Poor Nathan,' he said sadly. 'He can do it for everyone but himself.'

'I wonder where he is now?' she mused.

'I don't know what form he's in,' he replied, 'but I think I know where he is and what he's doing, and thinking, and feeling.'

They continued to gaze at the stars.

ABOARD THE FREIGHTER *STEHEKIN*

Nathan Brazil lay in the command chair on the bridge and gazed distantly at the fake starfield projected in the two window screens. He glanced over to the table atop the ancient computer.

That same pornographic novel was there, spread open to where he had last been reading it. He couldn't remember it at all, but, he reflected, it didn't matter. They were all alike anyway, and there was plenty of time to read it again.

He sighed and picked up the cargo manifest, idly flipping it open.

Cargo of grain, bound for Coriolanus, it read. *No passengers.*

No passengers.

They were elsewhere now – the rotten ones in their own private hells, the good ones – and the potentially good – with their chances. He wondered whether their dreams were as sweet as they had imagined. Would they forget the lessons of the Well, or try for change?

In the end, of course, it didn't really matter.

Except to them.

He closed the manifest and threw it across the control room. It banged against the wall and landed askew on the floor. He sighed a long, sad sigh, a sigh for ages past and the ages yet to be.

The memories would fade, but the ache would remain.

For, whatever becomes of the others or of this little corner of the universe, he thought, I'm still Nathan Brazil, fifteen days out, bound for Coriolanus with a load of grain.

Still waiting.

Still caring.

Still alone.

SPIRITS OF FLUX AND ANCHOR

For Mike Resnick
– from one madman to another.

1

Anchor

There was no need to tell anyone in Anchor Logh that the man in black was dangerous. Any stringer who rode the Flux was more than dangerous – he was someone to be feared for more reasons than one.

Cassie watched the man ride in on his huge white horse and felt a sudden chill at the very sight of him. She had a particular reason for that chill, being of The Age and with the Census Celebration barely three days away, although she didn't really believe she was in any danger. The quota this year was the lowest in her lifetime, thanks to an unusually abundant harvest and a high number of deaths among the Honored Elders, and her odds, like all those with her birth year, were barely one in a hundred. In fact, only four stringers had been invited to the Celebration this year and, it was said, only two had accepted, the rest preferring fatter pickings in other Anchors with more potential victims – and profits. That fact alone made the appearance of this one even more of a standout than it normally would have been.

He was a tall, lean, muscular man with coal-black hair and a handlebar moustache, and in normal circumstances and with a normal background he would have been considered a handsome man, even a desirable man, by those Cassie's age and older. But he was not a normal man with a normal background, and it was clear to any who looked upon him that this was so. There was just *something* about him, something you couldn't put your finger on, that radiated a fearsome chill to all he passed. His face was worn and aged well beyond his years, his skin seemed tough as leather, and his eyes, a weirdly washed-out blue, radiated contempt for World and its offerings. He was dressed in black denim, including black boots, gloves, and a wide-brimmed black hat that had one side of its wide brim tied up in stringer fashion, and a black leather jacket lined with weathered sheepskin that must have once been white.

Weathered … That was a good word for him. His boots, his clothes, even his sawed-off shotgun with the fancy carved handle that hung from his silver-decorated belt in a special holster – they all were weathered almost beyond belief.

He rode slowly, imperiously, right past Cassie, but those cold, distant eyes took no notice whatsoever of the thin, slightly built girl nor of much of anyone or anything else, either. She shivered a bit, then turned and began walking back towards the communal farm where she had been born and raised.

The farm lay at the end of a winding, rutted dirt road, about a kilometer back from the main highway, and on either side of the girl stretched broad fields of grass dotted with grazing cows. She knew every rut in that road by heart, and every cow as well, but somehow, today, they seemed more distant and remote than anything ever had.

It was a bright, cloudless day, and the Holy Mother was in all Her divine glory in the sky, filling Anchor Logh with her brightness and slightly coloring the landscape with subtle and different shadings. It was a glorious sight, yet She was always there when the clouds parted, and Her visage was so omnipresent, so taken for granted, not just by Cassie but by all those on World, that the Holy Mother was rarely paid attention to except when one was praying – or sinning.

Today, though, the Holy Mother seemed particularly close and needed, and Cassie stopped and looked up at Her reverently, seeking some comfort and inspiration. The sparkling bands of gold, orange, deep red and emerald green that gave the slight color shifts to the land showed the beauty and glory of Heaven and reminded all humankind of the Paradise it had lost and could regain, in the same way as night showed the emptiness of Hell, the distant, tiny stars representing the lost souls that might be consumed by darkness if not redeemed.

After a time she moved on, a lonely little figure walking back to the only home she'd ever known. Although the day was pretty, there was a chill in the air, and she wore a heavy checked flannel shirt and wool workpants.

Cassie had the kind of face that could be either male or female, and this, along with her tendency to keep her black, slightly curly hair clipped extremely short – as well as her slight build – often got her mistaken for a boy, an error her low, husky soprano did nothing to correct. She'd been the last of four children, all girls, and her parents had really wanted a boy. Particularly her father, a smith who wanted very much to pass on the family trade as his father had to him, and his father's father before that. She had not been spared that knowledge, and was often reminded of that fact.

Perhaps because of this, or at least in trying to please them, she'd always been a tomboy, getting into fights and walking, talking, and now working with the boys, herding, milking, and even breaking horses. Tel Anser, the hard old supervisor in the corral, often held her up as an example to the boys he worked with, teasing them that she was far more of a man than any of them. That didn't win her any popularity contests, of course, but she didn't really mind. She was proud of the comment.

Still, she was a lonely girl. Partly because of the way she was, she never got asked to dances, never, in fact, had even been asked for, let alone been out on, a single date. Those few boys who *did* accept her did so as an equal and a friend – and that meant as just one of the boys. It was hard, sometimes, sitting around and listening to them compare notes on girls they were attracted to, driving home by their very indifference to her sex the fact that she would never be the object of such conversations, either by them or by others.

Still, the flip side of that never appealed to her much, either. Perhaps if she'd been pretty, or sexy, or at least cute, or had big breasts and a big ass she might have thought differently, but she didn't have those attributes and never would.

That meant, at least, never having to dress in those silly, fancy outfits and do all that highpitched giggling and gushing about that absolutely *dreamy* boy in the third row in school, or flirting, putting on phony perfumes and painting eyes, cheeks, lips – well, it just seemed so damned silly and *stupid* to her, if not downright dishonest. She never saw why girls had to go through all that stuff anyway, when boys scored extra points just by taking a bath.

She'd never gotten along with, nor much liked, her sisters, either. Of course, part of that was in being the youngest, and, therefore, the target for older siblings, but, later on, it was because she neither liked nor identified with them or their concerns and they knew it. Well, now she was riding and herding and milking while her oldest sister was pregnant with her second kid, the next was trying hard to have her first while working in the commune laundry, and the third was an apprentice bull cook who seemed content. Some wonderful ambition *that* was.

Ambition was very much on Cassie's mind right now, for she was The Age, graduated from general school, and on her way to either higher education or an assigned trade depending on how she did on the massive battery of tests she'd take after Census.

She'd always had an affinity with animals, particularly horses, who were prettier, stronger, and far more loyal and dependable than most people she'd met, and this had not gone unnoticed by those who were always referred to as 'the powers that be.' She was aiming for one of the two slots open for veterinarian's training. *Then* she'd show them! Then she'd show them *all!* Status, a true profession, rank that commanded respect, top pay, and a skill that was vitally needed.

Her father was working iron when she entered the smithy, and she stood and watched until the red-hot metal had been skillfully shaped and formed and dunked into the water. He spotted her then, standing there, and frowned. 'Well, Cass? Parcel man have anything for us today?'

She looked suddenly disgusted with herself and shook her head. 'I'm sorry, Pa. I – I guess I forgot to check.'

'*What!* Didn't you go out to the highway like I told you to?'

'Yeah, I went, only …'

'Only *what?*'

'Well, soon as I got there a stringer rode by and I just sort of forgot anything else. I'm sorry, Pa.'

Her father sighed. He was a huge, superbly muscled man with thick black hair and a full beard, looking every bit the smith he was, and he had a hell of a mean streak in him and the short temper to bring it out. He didn't usually let it get the better of him, though, unless he'd been drinking, and while she braced for at least a hard and foul tongue-lashing, it never came. Like everyone else in Anchor Logh, her father had once been The Age himself, facing his own Census. As rough as he was now, and he'd been even rougher back then, he knew what the sight of a stringer this close to Census would have done to *him* back then, and he was never the sort of man to hold anyone to a higher standard than that to which he held himself.

Instead he said, 'Well, don't fret about it. The Holy Mother knows you got enough on your mind right now.'

Feeling very relieved, she decided she should make amends anyway and so she responded, 'Want me to go back out there now? I don't mind. I got nothing much to do.'

'Naw, that's all right. I hav'ta go out there myself in an hour or two anyway, and if there's anything I guess it'll wait 'til then. You just get along now and enjoy yourself.'

She thought for a moment, the crisis already far in the past in her mind, and decided to take advantage of her father's unusual good nature. 'Maybe I could take Leanspot into the city, then? I got to return some books to the Temple library and pick up some others.'

He thought it over. Under ordinary circumstances he'd have given a flat no, but she *was* The Age, and if she couldn't take care of herself and gain self-confidence now, she sure as hell better know it.

'Yeah, sure,' he said at last. 'Take all the time you want. But if you stay past nightfall, you'd best stay at the Temple overnight. With this crowd coming in and Census coming up you don't want to take no chances, you hear?'

She nodded soberly. 'I promise.'

In point of fact, people were very safe in the city unless they aided and abetted their own downfalls. Citizens had full rights and protections and those were jealously guarded and enforced by the government and police. Minors – those under The Age – were even more zealously protected. Naturally, if someone went over to one of the Main Street dives and flashed a lot of money around, or solicited immoral favors and lived to regret it, there wasn't much to be done, but, on the whole, anyone could walk in any part of the city in safety even late at night.

Citizenship, however, came with being counted in the Census, which was always on a predetermined date. That left those like Cassie, who'd reached The Age well before Census, in the position of being neither minors nor citizens, and during that period they were vulnerable to those who saw profit in this loophole. There were tales of young men and women being abducted and held through Census and the registry. If not caught in the Paring Rite, which was a fate worse than death, and if they then did not register as citizens, the law regarded them not as people at all, and, therefore, recognized no rights in their case. They became, in fact, property, animals like horses or cows or pigs in so far as the government was concerned – the property of the abductor or whomever the abductor transferred them to. They were even registered, as animals, with the Veterinary Office. The law, even the church, would actually support the owner over the victim, and this condition would last for life.

It was explained by the church that such things were the Holy Mother's will, since She dictated the laws governing World, and meant that this life was forfeit to some terrible deed or lifestyle in the life immediately past that required a lifetime's punishment to expunge. There was no way to get out of it, then, since anyone who tried to escape or thwart this working out of punishment would be doomed to the same fate in every subsequent life until the evil done was cleansed. Cass had never, to her knowledge, seen such people, but she knew they existed, usually traded from Anchor to Anchor through the stringers so that there would be no family revenge.

She kissed her father and went back to the block where she lived. It was one of several dozen buildings, all four stories high, composed literally of large prefabricated cubes that locked together. Because of the design, though, the buildings were asymmetrical, each row of cubes set slightly in or out of the row and with four large ones at its base, five slightly smaller on top, the end two protruding, six still smaller atop that, then five of the same size on top. The size cubicle you got depended on your family size and ranking within the commune. Once they'd lived in the relatively palatial ground level, but now she climbed the stairs to the second story. A family of six needed more space than a family of four, and with two daughters married off it was only the high regard for her father that had moved the farm council to allow them to live even where they were now.

At this time of day there was no one home. Mom was on the other side of the farm, in the Administration Building, working her usual job in accounting, and Tam was in the bakery today, so it seemed unnaturally quiet and still. It was just a basic three-room apartment, the living room and two decent-sized bedrooms, but it was home. She found a long match and lit one living room lamp, then went back to the bedroom she and Tam shared and lit the lamp there. Throwing some of Tam's clothes out of the way, she rooted in the closet and came up with a basic change of clothing and a small toiletries bag which she packed quickly. While picking and choosing the toiletries she looked up at herself in the small mirror and stared into her own face for a moment.

Dark brown eyes stared back at her out of a young boy's face. For not the first time she reflected that she'd make a better boy than girl all around. Except, of course, she didn't care for girls much and she *did* like boys. She chuckled a bit to herself, remembering the several times at fairs elsewhere in the Riding she'd drawn the adolescent attentions of more than one girl who'd made that mistake. They'd often said she'd outgrow it, but that was obviously not going to happen now. She was stuck with the physique of permanent boyish adolescence, although she'd never grow more than her current 163 centimeter height nor reach 50 kilos no matter how much she exercised and how much she ate. Or worry about packing a bra, either.

She sighed and turned away and zipped up the travel bag, picked it up, and left the cube, putting out the lights on the way.

Only then did she remember the books she was supposed to be taking back to the library, and she returned for them. It was, she decided, just going to be one of those days.

2

Rider

We are the spirits of Flux and Anchor and some call us demons. It is possible that we are such, for certainly we know not our natures or origins. Everything is born, yet we were not born. At least, I can remember no such experience, nor can any of my kind. It may be true, as some of us argue, that since no human clearly remembers his or her birth it might just be the same with us, yet that makes no sense to me. Humans are born, and humans die, yet we who are the Soul Riders do not die, and our number is constant and fixed to the number of Anchors on World.

Certainly it seems as if I have been thus forever, yet there must have been an origin at some time in the far past, or at least a coming to World, since it is clear that World has a no more infinite past than infinite future. It, too, was born, whether by creation of the Holy Mother as the church says or by more natural and predictable processes, and the time of its borning is written in the rocks of Anchor and the decay rate of Flux. It has been here, although not in this form always, no more than four or five billion years at best, and humans have been here a far shorter time than that – a few thousand years at best. And yet I can remember no time without humans.

If humans and World were both born, and will both surely die, as will all things known to us in the universe, then why and how do we exist as we do?

The Holy Church says that we are demons left from the Great Rebellion, when angels in their pride rose up and slew angels and threatened to usurp the Holy Mother's domination of the universe in foolish and futile insurrection. It was then, or so it is written, that the Holy Mother acted, changing the angelic seditionists to foul and horrible monstrosities whose outer forms and very existence mirrored their most terrible inner selves and exiled them to Hell, sealing the seven gates to Hell against their coming again into this universe save by proxy.

The misguided, misused, and misshapen ones who followed the Seditionists in their terrible mutiny, and those who took no side in the fray, were changed to human form by the Holy Mother after Her inevitable victory, in that way to suffer pain and torture and purify themselves in life after life until they again be cleansed and worthy to reenter the kingdom of Heaven shown so tantalizingly close in the day sky. It is also written in the holy books that the gates of Hell will be reopened one day by the evil ones known as the Seven Who Wait, who roam World supervising the misery of human existence and take joy in inflicting it. When and if those gates are again reopened, Hell will pour once more into World, and humanity will be caught once again in the midst of battle between Heaven and Hell and will again be forced to make a terrible choice. Then will humanity have a second chance at Paradise, and depending on their souls' progress through the lives they lived, they will choose rightly or wrongly. Those who choose correctly this time around will be allowed back into Heaven, while the rest shall be permanently recast into foul Hell.

But if that's true, where does it leave us? Just as we are neither born nor die, what is our purpose and role in this scheme if it be true? We have been around a long time and have long memories, and know that holy books are often adjusted, and religions go through social evolution the same as governments. And yet there is some consistency and truth in all of it which gives us pause.

The Seven Who Wait exist. The gates of Hell exist, and there is certainly something foul and evil beyond them. That something is so seductive to some humans, but not to any of us. It is that sense of overwhelming evil emanating from those terrible sealed gateways that drives us ever onward on our missions. We fight the Seven and their agents wherever and whenever we can, and we seek them out for this battle. We alone are feared by them, for we are the immortal last line of defense.

And, still, while we do the work of the church it continues to brand us demons, agents of the Seven, Hell-spawns and half-creatures. They will not listen to more rational pleas, nor change their view, for they do not understand us and so fear us as much as the Seven do. Nor is this fear without some justification, for this is a place of certainty in its beliefs, a place where everything has an explanation and where Heaven and Hell can be glimpsed. We are the wild cards, the unexplainable in the midst of the totally explained, and if we do not understand our own selves then how can they be expected to do so?

It is certain that somebody, somewhere knows the answer. Someone who *knows why World has the holy name that must not be spoken aloud, the cryptic and unintelligible Forfirbasforten. The church says it is an angelic name bestowed on World by the Holy Mother and is not for humans to know or understand, but someone does. Someone, or something, directs our actions in unknown and unseen ways, so that we go to a new host at just the right moment, and live their lives with them unknown and unseen to them until they have need of us against the Seven. Perhaps it is the Nine Who Guard, but I have encountered some of them many times and they seem as mystified by our presence and natures as are we ourselves, although, at least, they understand that we are not enemies but allies in their unending battle and do not fear us.*

Some say that humanity did not originate on World at all, but came here from some other, better place. That is, of course, consistent with both the evidence and scripture, but did we come with them? Or were we, perhaps, here before, the original inhabitants of this place caught in the middle of a great war we were powerless to do anything about? Some believe this, and see us as the ghosts and racial memories of such a race, yet this is not at all consistent with cosmology, for it would put us outside the Holy Mother's creation until wrenched into it, and that opens up a series of philosophical knots that can never be untied.

I think, perhaps, that we were once humans ourselves, and walked the face of World directly. It is possible that, for some reason, our souls were not placed into new bodies but remained suspended in the spirit world, bound to World but not of it. Why this should be so I do not know, but it was clearly not a random choice, as our numbers, as I said, are quite fixed.

I prefer to think of us as once-great warriors, the best of our human race, who were so valued that we were appointed the last line of defense against the forces of evil, supporting first the church and then the Nine Who Guard.

If what they say of birth and death are true, intellect survives memory, but memory dies as it gets in the way of true intellectual, or spiritual, growth. Thus we have no memories of our human lives, no sense of all those trillions of stimuli that flood in and confuse the mind even as it grows. Perhaps, I certainly hope, we were the ones who reached purification far ahead of the masses and were thus given our guardian duties with no need to be born and reborn again and again.

And yet I feel that I was once a soldier. Certainly I feel most comfortable when mated with one, and it certainly fits my own theory of origin, as well as our long and complex work.

I digress as I float, my random thoughts going out to any of my kind who may be in the area and less inclined to introspection. Very well, I will stop, for matters press, and I feel myself drawn from the Flux, where I have been these past seven lifetimes, back again at last to Anchor. Whoever or whatever guides our destinies has a new job for me, and I am anxious to begin.

I emerge from the energy flow and there bursts upon me the clean, crisp certainty of Anchor. Which Anchor it is I do not know, but it seems somehow familiar, and welcomes me as some long-lost relation. This is an odd sensation, worthy of further study on its own.

I drift above the hills and treetops, and below me burn the souls of Anchorfolk, the sheer density and clarity of their life matrices telling me that this is a large Anchor indeed. The specific features are beyond my present perceptive abilities, yet all around me screams not merely life but, most importantly, unambiguous life, its mathematical symmetry and distinct solidity oddly reassuring. I have been too long in the Flux.

I sense the capital ahead of me now, with a density of souls that I can scarcely handle, and in its center, a shining beacon, its Focal Point. It is truly odd, this particular Focal Point, for it seems to broadcast directly to me. It seems right somehow, in a way I cannot explain. It is almost as if it sends to me a half-completed equation, for which I am myself the other half, and which, if joined, will give the answer to it all. The answers are here. The threat is large and the time is short. That much I am certain of.

Ah, but no, I am to be stopped short of the Focal Point, the answer so close and yet so disturbingly out of reach. I am directed not at the Focal Point, but at a human soul who lives below, and even now I descend for the mating. Down, down, to ground level, and forward to the soul whose matrix will mate with my own. The one is moving, yet I come upon it, envelop it, mate with it and draw within those recesses of its mind it does not even know exist. I bind myself, and see, hear, and feel once more as humans do. I ride a new soul.

Cassie walked from the cubicle towards the stables, her bag hanging from her shoulder, deep in thought. Suddenly she stopped as a cold chill came over her, and for a brief moment she felt both dizziness and nausea. It passed quickly, though, leaving her standing there a moment, puzzled, and wondering if she should go at all now. She must be coming down with something – she was still a good ten days from her period. But, no, she felt fine now.

Just nerves, she told herself, and continued walking towards the stables.

3

Stringer

Matson wasn't his real name. No stringer ever allowed his or her real name to be known – that way led to potential blackmail, for anyone could then determine the stringer's relationship to others and have a hold on them. Stringers feared only that someone would have something on them, something that would eat into their absolute independence and freedom. They did not fear challenge, and particularly did not fear death, since it was better to die free than live with any strings at all, including compromises of their lifestyle. To have it any other way would be to be harnessed just as surely as they harnessed their characteristic mule trains, the long strings, or ropes, giving them their name and title.

Matson was a stringer in his mid-thirties, which meant he was a very good stringer indeed in an occupation that often saw you dead in the Flux while still in your teens or twenties. He'd been around a lot in his time, and he still enjoyed the constant challenges of the job.

He'd left his duggers and mules at the clear spot at the western gate. At the moment he was deadheading, and he hated like hell to do that – all expenses and no profits. This particular Anchor's census, though, should make up for it. He'd heard that only one other stringer was close enough to take advantage of the bargain, and that meant a good deal of business. Usually there were so many stringers you had trouble even filling your local Fluxland orders and paying back your I.O.U.s for the quarter, but here, even with a small census, he'd wind up with half the crop.

It did not trouble him to deal in human beings, just as he also dealt in gold, silver, various manufactured goods, and anything else that was in demand in one place and surplus in another. While he lived by a strict personal moral code, this was the way of World, a system he'd been brought up to accept and believe in and, since 'right' and 'wrong' are always defined by the culture of a place, this sort of traffic – for which there was good socioeconomic justification – was simply taken for granted.

It was a good two days' ride from the Anchor wall to the capital, and a pretty boring one at that. Farming Anchors were perhaps the least interesting of all, all the more so because these people considered themselves free and autonomous. Theirs was a happy little worldlet, and most would never leave nor want to.

They were as domesticated and spiritually dead as their cows, he thought sourly.

He amused himself by playing mental word games and by double and triple checking his mnemonic tricks that allowed him to keep all his orders, requests, I.O.U.s, and accounts in his head. Permanent records were dangerous to a stringer's freedom, too, even if you could keep decent account books in the Flux.

Still, it would be good spending a couple of days in a real city, one that was what it looked like and wouldn't change or dissolve on you because of a paranoid wizard's bad dreams, and to sleep in a nice, comfortable bed, drink some decent booze, and maybe fool around a little.

He reached the city before nightfall, and went immediately to Government House to register himself and then paid the usual brief courtesy call on the local temple, writing out his specific requirements for their perusal, while also dropping off a box of the local Sister General's cigars. It always paid to do a little homework before coming in to a new town.

Next he went over to Main Street – dull name for the entertainment district, the kind of name you'd expect a bunch of cow herders to come up with – and checked into a decent hotel. Capital districts were always nice if only because they alone had electricity, which included hot and cold running water and in-room baths. Since the hotel was taking care of his horse, he quickly stripped and ran the bath water, then slipped into the hot tub. It felt *really* good. He never realized just how many minor muscle aches and pains he lived with until they were taken away. About the only trouble was, they always made the damned bath tubs about a finger's length too short.

Still, he leaned back, lit a cigar, then reached over and picked up the small pile of papers he'd been given at his two prior stops. One set was a bunch of orders for various goods the Anchor needed, and these he would either try and fill or, if a better trip came along, he'd pass along to some other stringer going this way for the usual finder's fee. Also included was a smaller list of what was usually called 'desired personnel,' and those were more high-ticket items. He might find and arrange transport for the two needed gunnery instructors, although why they needed them for this place was beyond him, but he suspected that they were going to have to pay and pay big and actually hire by enticement the electrician with experience and the civil engineer, and they'd be damned lucky if they got either one at any price. Anchorfolk didn't like to travel in the Flux at all, and for good reason. Making it worth the while of this level of skill to travel would cost them before, during, and after. Still, he'd see what he could do.

He had only raw numbers on his own outgoing goods. They would have to check their census and see how many of the unlucky losers fit what he needed to fill other orders. He liked the numbers, though. A hundred and six to go out, fifty-six females and fifty males, split between two stringers. True, he'd have to make a good stab at filling the Anchor's orders, but he liked this kind of arrangement. No up-front outlay and the goods came on consignment.

After bathing, he unpacked a bit and rummaged through his pack to find civilized clothing. Although he'd be here three to five days, he did not even glance at the drawers and closets in the room. He never unpacked any more than he had to, the quicker to make a getaway if it were ever needed.

Dressed in the same manner as when he arrived, but with all clean clothes save hat and boots, he rearranged his belt, removed the shotgun holster and its deadly occupant and clipped on a knife in its scabbard and the bullwhip. He liked the bullwhip – it had such an intimidating effect on the locals, particularly the self-styled toughs.

Finally, he shaved, all except the moustache. It was still just coming in, but he'd been suffering lately from a series of runny noses and decided that a moustache was the best local cure for a constantly chapped upper lip. Finally satisfied, he left his room and went down to the street, looking first for a restaurant and a good meal. Before he was ten meters down the street, though, he stopped, seeing a black-clad figure riding in on a spotted horse. The second stringer had arrived.

'Arden!' he called out. 'Good to see you!'

The horse stopped and the rider stared for a moment. 'Matson? That you? Well, I'll be damned!'

She was several years younger than he, but still tough and long on experience. She was tall, lean, and lanky, but well proportioned, and if the strain of the job showed as much in her face as it did in his it made that face no less pretty, and while she hadn't bothered to put on a wig as yet to hide her shaven head, her oval face seemed complimented by its very baldness. She jumped down off the horse and walked over to him. 'It's been a long time,' she said softly.

He nodded. 'Tuligmon, two years ago.'

She grinned. 'How sweet! You remembered!'

'How could I forget? You beat me out of some of the best damned merchandise I've seen since I started stringing.'

She laughed. 'Well, no contest this time, unless a couple of wild card stringers show up. Good stuff here and it's all ours, my dear.'

'Well, since we're not competitors this time, what do you say to a night on the town? Um, such as it is, anyway.'

'You're on! But let me check in and get cleaned up a little first.'

'I'm not starving. I'll wait for you in the hotel bar.'

He'd first met Arden years ago, when she was just out of her teens and he was a big, experienced stringer in his mid-twenties and anxious to show off to the younger generation. That was over in Anchor Mahri, a depressing factory land half a world from here. She'd been such a sexy, wide-eyed innocent, hanging on his every word and vamping him constantly, and he'd started regarding her less as a stringer than as just another barroom girl with not much future. She'd hung around with him while he'd made some of his calls and discussed orders and deals, and he hadn't thought much of it. She'd even moved into his hotel room.

Of course, one morning he awakened to find her gone, and thought little of it, until he made his rounds to firm up his deals and found that she had been there first. Not just to one, but to every damned account on his list – and with a better offer and a take it now or forget it style. She'd taken note of every single item of business he did and every offer under discussion and beaten him by just the exact deal that would make them switch. She'd given him one hell of a sour stomach and a worse wallop in the pocketbook, but he also admired her gutsy style. He was pretty sure afterward that, given a day alone with a recalcitrant prospect, she would wind up owning his business.

She also had a quick mind, a superbly trained body and the reflexes to make it work for her, and more talent with the Flux than anybody he'd ever met. She could hold her own in any fight, and he'd heard the stories of some of those as well.

She joined him in about half an hour, having washed up and changed into her city clothes. They were still stringer black, of course, but made out of some tight, clingy material that seemed to form-fit itself to her body and make her seem, while fully clothed, almost naked. At least it left very little to the imagination. She also wore her dress boots, with the heels so high it gave her the sexiest walk in the world.

'Well? Shall we go?' she prompted.

He nodded and signed the tab. 'I guess steak would be the best in a place like this. At least farmers make good home-grown beer and booze.'

They barely noticed the stares and nervous looks they got from those they passed. Stringers were used to such things, and both Matson and Arden were experienced enough that they no longer even got the slight charge from knowing they were feared by all the 'decent' folk of Anchor and Flux. Like monarchs, they tended only to notice when such reactions were absent.

The food *was* good, and perfectly prepared, although the wine was lousy. While the beer and booze were good, this was clearly not grape country. They relaxed with shop talk, mostly telling tales of good and bad experiences and filling one another in on people and places the other hadn't been to, at least in a long time. Neither, of course, discussed future plans or routings – she would never give away anything by reflex, and she'd sure taught him long ago not to, either. So it surprised him, after dinner and after checking out a couple of inferior bar shows, when she said, 'You know, I've been thinking of quitting for a while. Going to a Freehold and contribute while there's still time.'

That stopped him. 'Huh? *You?*'

'So what's wrong with me?'

He chuckled. 'That would take too long to list, but it's all mental. No, I just can't see you taking off all that time and becoming a mama to a screaming kid, that's all. I think you'd go nuts.'

'Most mothers do, I'm told. But, you know, I've been a lot of places and seen and done a lot of things. I'm very well off, so that's not a problem, and it's one thing I've never done.'

'You've never cut off your left arm, either. But if that's the way you feel, why not just do it? You could have any man you want.'

'Uh huh. And there's one I have in mind who, I think, will make half of the best new stringer in a century. I decided that fate would make the decision if I met him again in time, and it looks like I have.'

He stared at her. 'You're serious?'

'I'm serious. I made the decision the moment I saw you, riding in here.' She flashed him her patented evil grin. 'I already arranged with the hotel to share your room.'

He thought of the sheets of business documents there and felt a mild chill. She caught it and laughed. 'Yes, I saw them. Want to see mine? The same stuff. We're not competing here, remember?'

He smiled and shrugged. 'Okay, then. The shows here are pretty lousy anyway.'

She smiled and patted his bottom. 'Let's go put on our own, then. The next few days are exactly the right time for it.'

Bending to fate, he followed her back to the hotel.

4

Temple

'Where ya goin', Cass?'

She stopped and turned to see Dar and Lani. Dar was a big, strapping farmboy with a tan complexion set off by flaming red hair, while Lani was a pretty, tiny – shorter and lighter than Cassie by far – and extremely overendowed young woman. Cassie's father had once cruelly joked that Lani got not only her own attributes but the ones that were supposed to go Cass as well. Both had been in her class through school; Lani was a little more than a month older than Cass, Dar just a week younger than she.

Cassie would have liked Lani to have been as short in brains as she was endowed in beauty, just to provide some symmetry to life, but the truth was it was Dar who was rather slow – one teacher had used the term 'vacuous' – while Lani was quite bright and in line for a scholarship to teacher's training or perhaps into agricultural research. It said something about the beauty that, while she could have had any boy not only in the commune but probably in the entire Census, she had chosen Dar, whose mind was nil but who was certainly pleasant and cheerful and, like so many large men, uncommonly gentle, but who was also, from all reports, rather well endowed himself.

Both were simply too nice to stay mad at, and Dar had been one of those boys who'd always been a friend.

'I'm going into the city,' she told them. 'I have some books to return and some more I need to take out. The exams are only a couple of weeks away.'

They both nodded. Lani said, 'I think it's a little too late for the books now. These tests aren't like the ones in school, remember. Relax, Cass. You're a natural for the vet's spot.'

She smiled at the compliment. 'I guess you're right, but I can't help worrying and studying anyway. It can't hurt, and maybe it'll help if I *do* get the slot. Anyway, it beats sitting around being bored.'

'Yeah, you're right about that bored stuff,' Dar agreed. 'In fact, we were thinking of going into the city ourselves. Census Carnival opens tonight, remember.'

Cass was surprised at herself for not remembering that. The fact was, she never thought of things that cost money, because communards didn't have it or need it. All was provided by the council, with bonuses for the best work being used for catalog purchases. That's why they went to the capital so seldom despite its closeness.

'You have money for that this early?'

'Sure,' Dar responded, 'and so do you. A hundred cubits of silver on account, for coming of The Age.'

She had, quite frankly, forgotten all about that, although she had the slip for it in her overnight bag where she'd stuffed it after they gave it to her. It was redeemable almost everywhere if cash was available, and cash was readily available during Census Celebration. 'I'd been thinking of putting that away for later,' she told them.

'Aw, c'mon! That's not what that's for,' he retorted. 'Hell, you get staked after classification, plus expense money. *This* money's strictly for having a good time. What say we all go into town and go to the Carnival? Just relax and let loose for a while, have some fun.' He looked suddenly uncertain and turned and looked at Lani, but she gave him a nod and a smile.

Cassie thought it over for a moment. 'Well, okay. Maybe you're right. I knew I was going to have to stay over tonight anyway, since it's already so late. Go and get your things. I'll wait for you here.'

The Census Celebration was part of the system dictated by the holy scriptures, and it was a curious blend of circus, government report, and public execution. Its root was in the absolute prohibition of any sort of birth control on the part of the individual – although the priestesses who were midwives had the authority and duty to terminate the life of any baby determined by a host of very strict standards to be defective – and the concurrent duty of all married couples to have as many children as they could. Large families had greater status in the community, preferential treatment, and huge allowances.

Unfortunately, an Anchor could support only a finite number of people. Each year a massive census was taken across the entire 680 square kilometers of Anchor Logh, a census of people, animals – everyone and everything that consumed things. This was then compared with the harvests, known reserves, and anticipated demands for the following year, and a total number of supportable people was determined, which was then compared against the total numbers of young men and women reaching age 18 – The Age – between census periods. The difference, less the average birth-death differential for the past five censuses, was the number of surplus people, and that surplus had to be disposed of.

The church and holy books gave ample theological backing to this cruel rite, since the selection was done in the most random and fairest of ways by a great lottery on the last day of Census Celebration. The Holy Mother, of course, operated in such a circumstance, and those selected were actually selected by Her for reasons of atonement or whatever other reasons She might have that were inscrutable to humans. The Paring Rite, as it was called, was a most sacred and holy rite, performed by the Sister General herself on the front steps of the holy Temple. Those 'pared' in the rite were forbidden citizenship and became Property of the People. As such, they were sold or bartered to the stringers as any other goods and removed from Anchor Logh. What the stringers did with them was the subject of wild speculation and terrible stories, most contradictory, but nobody really knew for sure since no one returned to tell the tale.

And so it was with some horror that, as the three rode towards the city, Cassie remarked, 'I saw a stringer riding in today.'

The light mood of the other two seemed to vanish at once. Dar shivered. 'Them vultures! Demon bastards from the Flux!' Neither of the women was going to argue that the stringers were actually essential to the economy of World; that they alone kept commerce of all kinds going. And even if they had, for they actually knew this, it would not have changed their opinion in the slightest. Anyone who rode the Flux for a living simply couldn't be human and remain mentally and spiritually whole.

Cassie had seen the Flux once. They all had, on an overnight field trip in school. It was a terrible and frightening sight, a wall of nothingness surrounding World. Although they all knew World was round, since it had been made by the Holy Mother in the image of Heaven, it still looked like the edge of the earth.

There were a fair number of people in Anchor Logh who had gone through the Flux in a stringer's train, of course. Many professional schools were located in other Anchors, and occasionally needed professionals were imported. The Sister General herself had come from an Anchor far away. But stringers controlled your mind in the Flux, and the images of the journey were either too muddied or too bizarre and fantastic to believe when others were told of those trips. Usually, after a time in Anchor, those who recalled and told of those trips found the experience hard to believe or accept as well.

Only the stringers knew for certain what, if anything, was out there in the Flux, and even if you had nerve enough to ask one – well, who could believe a stringer?

Spirits lightened again when they reached the city. Already there were huge crowds of people in from the outlying ridings and the streets of the city were festooned with multicolored lights and decorations and there was a festive air. They headed straight for the carnival grounds, oblivious of the time, and it was a fantastic sight indeed. This year the government had outdone itself in rides and sideshows and attractions, all powered by the electrical energy supplied by the sacred modules located well beneath the Temple. Although the crowd was large, it felt *good* to be with so many merry people in such close quarters.

Anticipating that all young people of The Age would be physically present as required by law, and knowing that each had their hundred cubit marker, the Central Bank had a booth set up to cash in the markers, and after standing in line for quite a while all three were, for the first time in their lives, cash solvent. They wasted no time in enjoying the money.

For the first time in a very long time Cassie felt good. For a few hours all the worries and tensions of the day and the time slipped away, as did much of the loneliness. It was easy, for a time, to even pretend that it was she and Dar there at the Carnival, with Lani the guest instead of herself.

It was quite late before they pooled their money and saw just how quickly it could vanish and knew that it was time to leave. Cassie came to the conclusion with extreme reluctance, as it also brought her back to reality. Dar and Lani planned to stay at the Youth Hostel, where lodging and basic meals were free to commune members. She recalled her books, and said, 'I have to stay over at the Temple. I think it's too late to return these tonight. Want to stay over there, Lani?'

The pretty girl looked slightly embarrassed, and Dar sort of shuffled his feet. Finally Lani responded, 'Uh, Dar can't stay there, Cass. You know that.'

She started to reply, but then thought better of it as the social wall went up once again. Having been so mentally up that evening, her euphoria came crashing down with more than usual force. They were not a threesome. They had never been a threesome. They were two plus one, and guess who was the odd girl out?

'Oh, that's right. I don't know why I said that – forget it,' she recovered as best she could. 'You go on and have a good time. I'll see you tomorrow.'

They seemed relieved now to break it off, and she wanted away from them at this moment, too, so it was after quick and perfunctory goodbyes that they went their separate ways.

Church and state were inexorably linked in Anchor Logh, as in most Anchors, yet they were quite separate institutions. As the Holy Mother was female, only women could enter the priesthood or hold any office in the church. To balance this, only men could hold office in the Anchor government or in riding or commune governments as well. However, since the government acted in ways holy scripture dictated, and because legal disputes with the government were settled by special priestesses who decided things according to their interpretation of scripture, the fact was that women ran the Anchor. This, too, balanced out quite a lot, since priestesses took vows of not only poverty and obedience but absolute chastity as well, vows that, once taken, could not be withdrawn. Only virgins could enter the order, those with an intact hymen. When they did, they were no longer subject to the Paring Rite, but they became, forever, not citizens but the Property of the Church, and second thoughts and reconsiderations were strictly for the next life.

These thoughts went through her own mind as she walked to the Temple.

She had left Leanspot at the Youth Hostel stables and brought her luggage with her. Now she redeemed it from the check stand near the carnival entrance and started off towards the Temple. Off to one side of the route was the brightly lit gaiety of Main Street, but she had no intention of going there, or, in fact, anywhere near there. Particularly with stringers in town. She approached Temple Square and stopped a moment to look at the massive structure, an impressive block of some unknown reddish material from which rose nine great pyramidal spires, the central one reaching some one hundred meters into the air. The whole building was indirectly floodlit with multicolored lights, and the sight was nothing if not awe-inspiring.

The huge stage and platform had already been erected against the front steps of the magnificent building, in preparation for the Paring Rite that would come now in only three days. The sight only added to her sense of gloom and despair, and she went around to the side and mounted the long stone stairs to the Temple's great bronze doors as quickly as she could.

She saw an unusual number of priestesses about, not only in the scarlet robes and hood of the temple but in whites, blues, greens, and just about every other color as well, indicating local church and provincial staff had already arrived in great numbers for the holiest days of the year.

She had occasionally toyed with the idea of joining the priesthood herself, for it was a tempting opening to potential power, position, and prestige. She certainly would have no trouble with the celibacy part, but she'd always hesitated because it meant living in a woman's world, cut off from the outside for more than three years of intense religious education leading to ordination, then more years in advanced education in a secular school where her devotion would be tested. The novitiate period, it was said, was the toughest time, since you were already a priestess bound for life and yet you would be tempted by all the things you gave up.

Except, of course, what had she to give up? The shaving off of all her hair, head and body, as required of novices, would hardly detract anything from her already nonexistent sex appeal. She had never liked the loss of self-control brought on by hard drinking or light drugs, and she'd never much liked being around those who took them, so she could forgo the usual social life of a campus, and as for owning nothing and subsisting only on charity – well, she'd basically had that for her entire life anyway ...

Slowly she walked around the huge platform and up the one hundred steps to the Temple entrance. When she reached those great bronze doors, though, she did not enter immediately but instead turned back and stared again at the broad platform below, looking out at the massive, empty but well-lit square beyond. Empty now, but not three days from now.

It looked more sinister and frightening in the darkness. She felt an odd chill run through her, and an unreasoning churning in the pit of her stomach, and her already deep depression grew even more intense. She reached into her bag and took out one of the books she was returning and stared at the cover. *Introduction to Biochemistry*, it said.

Who am I trying to kid? her black mood asked. *I couldn't even understand the first two exercises in this thing.* She turned and pulled open the door and stepped into the Temple antechamber, but she did not turn and go downstairs to the small section with complimentary rooms for people with Temple business who were obliged to stay the night. Instead, she walked straight ahead to a second set of doors and entered the Inner Temple itself, not quite understanding why.

Although deserted at this hour, the altar flames burned brightly in the colors of the Holy Mother, casting a different colored glow on each of the huge statues of the Loyal Angels. To her eyes those Angels seemed to come alive, and they all looked down directly at her and smiled invitingly. She prostrated herself before the main altar, her innermost fears surfacing and driving her, although she neither understood nor realized this. Her black depression, fed by her frustration at what the books had told her she did not know or understand, and by the sight of that platform in Temple Square, had transformed and magnified her insecurities to the point where she could no longer bear them.

And so she had fled, quite naturally, to the Holy Mother, where all this was instantly transformed in her mind. Nobody else wanted her, but the Holy Mother did. She felt this with such a sense of conviction at revealed truth that she never doubted for a moment that the Holy Mother and Her blessed

Angels were speaking straight to her. *Come to the mother church*, they seemed to whisper to her. *Come to the church and banish all insecurity, all fear, all uncertainty. Give us your soul, and we will guide your destiny perfectly.*

It was suddenly all so simple, so clear in her mind. A sisterhood of equals, bound together in piety and love. Reason fled and was replaced by emotional ecstasy. As if in a dream she got up, bowed again to the altar, then went to the sacristy door and then through it into the Temple complex itself. She had never been back there before, and she was thinking not at all, so she just walked in search of a priestess, any priestess, to tell her she was ready to commit her life, body and soul, to the church.

There was, however, no one in the back administrative area, for it was meditation time and very late now, and she continued to walk in her daze down darkened halls and up and down flights of stairs. In all that time she met no one, but time had lost its meaning to her and she did not seem to notice the futility of her search.

Finally there was a room down at the end of a hall that was brightly lit and she heard muffled voices coming from it. She walked towards it, but paused nervously in the darkness before going on, some measure of sanity and self-control returning as interaction with other human beings faced her. She had not wavered in her decision, but now she seemed to realize that she was where she had no business being, and she became afraid that the discovery of her presence here, in forbidden quarters, might be some sort of violation that would impede or exclude her from the sisterhood.

Cautiously and nervously she peered inside the doorway to see who was in there. The sight almost sent her into shock again, but a far different kind than the one that had churned her emotions only moments earlier.

The room was a large one, and three women sat within. The one in a plush, comfortable chair to the left of a projection console would have been instantly recognizable anywhere in Anchor Logh – but not quite like this.

Her angelic Highness, Sister General Diastephanos, sat in that chair in a state more of undress than anything else, puffing away on a big, fat cigar. Sharing the chair, and equally in a state of undress, was undoubtedly a Temple priestess, and she was essentially sitting on the Sister General's lap. There was no mistaking the placement of this unknown woman's arms and the reciprocated gentle gestures from the Sister General.

The third woman in the room was still in her priestly robes, the rich mottled silver of administrative services. She sat at the projector controls, occasionally looking over at several small blinking screens, and appeared totally oblivious to the grotesque scene going on just to her left.

Diastephanos sighed. 'Enough, Daji. We have to get through this *sometime* tonight, you know, or we'll be working all the way up the Paring Rite.' The other woman untangled herself and got to her feet, pouting a bit like a hurt little child, but she went obediently over to another chair, pulled it up, curled up in it and relaxed to watch. 'Next,' Her angelic Highness ordered curtly.

The projectionist touched a switch, and a photograph of a boy appeared on the screen, under which was an enormous amount of typed data that seemed to be an abbreviated life history. Cassie could hardly suppress a gasp. She *knew* that boy! She'd gone to school with him!

'Good looking bull,' Daji remarked absently in a high-pitched voice that sounded vacuous but was also oddly accented. Her comment was ignored by the others.

'Okay socially, but the brains of a head of cabbage,' the projectionist noted matter-of-factly, looking down at the screen. 'Barely literate, fourteen separate disciplinary incidents starting at age eight. A real brawler. He'd be a good soldier as long as he only had to take orders, not give them.'

'Wall guard type, then?' the Sister General suggested.

'Hardly. Oh, sure, if he could be bent into shape, but it's doubtful that he'd be receptive to military discipline.'

'Sounds tailor-made, then,' the high priestess noted. 'Didn't that stringer Matson put in an order for replacement field soldiers?'

The projectionist checked her data. 'Um, yes. Up to ten for Persellus, if we had them. No sex preference as usual.'

'What's it matter out in the Flux? What's the old bitch offering for them?'

'The usual. The goddess, you might remember, has a real gift for duplicating printed circuit boards even though she hasn't the slightest idea what they are or what they're used for. Fratina has been complaining about how she's had to cannibalize a backup unit to keep the water treatment system running, and I could use a couple of extra memory modules. Three like this one and we'll be set on that score.'

Her angelic Highness thought for a moment. 'Persellus would be close by. How many have we given Matson already?'

'Eleven so far, but they're mostly girls. You know the taste of some of our local customers.'

The high priestess chuckled. 'Do I ever! Well, we'll give him muscle-brain here and two others for the parts list you supply – draw it up and supply the patterns for her. We've got a lot of leeway in assignments with only two stringers but we're in a weaker position. Arden wants a lot of beef, too, if I remember.'

'Well, there's the two males and two females, perfect physical specimens, for Taladon. For experimental purposes, it says here.'

'Gad! And we're almost completely through the list *now*. Looks like we're going to have to have a second run-through and give up some people we don't want to.'

The projectionist touched the switch again and a new boy's face and record appeared. 'Nope, forget him,' she muttered.

'What? He some kind of genius?'

'No, he's a snot-nosed absolute bastard with an asshole where his brain should be, but he's also Minister Alhred's son.'

The Sister General sighed. '*Another* political goodie! Holy Mother of Heaven! No *wonder* this takes so long!'

Cassie knew she should turn right now and chalk up her earlier feelings to the shortest religious conversion on record, but her shock and horror at all this was mixed with a horrid fascination as well. The sexual habits of the Sister General were but a momentary shock. As disillusioning as it was to one who had so recently decided to join the church, it was no more than was commonly rumored and whispered about all priestesses by half the population. No, what was the true and total shock was what those women were doing in that room. It was something quite obvious, yet it undercut the very foundation of Cassie's entire system of beliefs, and those of her whole society and culture. *They were fixing the Paring Rite!* They were exempting the privileged, and evaluating and choosing who would go and who would stay according to their own personal criteria.

She watched as two more boys were evaluated and quickly passed over because they had aptitudes for jobs that were needed in Anchor Logh. It was obvious by the comments, though, that all of these were the finalists in a long selection process that probably began as soon as the numbers had been turned in months ago. These, then, were the worst of the worst, those of The Age who, for political or personal reasons, were of least use to the Anchor. The fact that a Minister's son, the child of a high-ranking government official, had made it down this far indicated that such a relationship was handy but not a guarantee of safety. It was, rather, a political club to be held over a recalcitrant politician.

Sin, too, was a criteria, but not necessarily for the boy or girl under review. From the off-handed comments about the 'orders' they had taken from Fluxlands, whatever they were, for various types, it was clear that being too smart, or asking too many questions about the system and the church, could be just as dangerous as having as much brains as a head of cabbage. Troublemaking parents could be punished by having their child chosen, too, the selection being a confirmation by the Holy Mother of their parental sins, while some were chosen simply because they fit a specific requirement of some other place in need. This was well across the fine line separating natural balance of population in the Anchors and divine punishment from real crime.

This was out-and-out slavery, the selling of human beings as property.

Reluctantly, Cassie decided she'd better get out of there, even though she'd love to just stay and see who was still to come up on that screen. Maybe – her? She shuddered at the thought and turned to go, then realized that she was totally and completely lost. How many corridors and stairways *were* there in this place, anyway? She moved as quietly as possible away from the door and towards the nearest stairwell anyway, remembering that she'd seen no one on the way and that, at least, she might have all night to figure it out. She reached the opening to the stairs, turned in – and ran smack into two of the largest, meanest-looking Temple Wardens she'd ever seen. Both women, even in the dim light, looked like they could pick her up with one finger each and chew her to bits for lunch – and enjoy every minute of it. Her heart sank, but she couldn't help wondering just how long they'd been there.

There was no use in even trying to make a break for it. Even if she managed the unlikely feat of getting away from these two, they knew this place inside out and she had no idea where she was. One of the wardens gave a smirk and gestured with her finger for Cassie to turn around and retrace her steps. She had no choice, really, and walked as directed back to the lighted room. She hesitated at the doorway and got a rude shove into the room that almost sent her sprawling on her face.

The three women inside all turned and stared at her. Finally the Sister General said, 'Well, well, well … The sewer rats are growing very large this year, I see.'

'She was pretty blatant about it,' one of the wardens noted. 'Tripped every alarm on the main board. The only reason she got this far was she got lost real fast. Her trail's so tangled you can't even figure it out on a security chart and floor plan without getting lost yourself.'

'How long was she outside the room here?'

'Ten, fifteen minutes. After the first minute, when she decided to stay and watch, we didn't feel there was any reason for interrupting Your Highness before we had to. Actually, we were just going to pick her up on her way out, if she could manage it – we were betting on that, see – but she stayed around here so long we figured you'd want to deal with her personally.'

'Oh, yes, I do indeed,' the Sister General purred. 'Come here, child.'

She was none too gently prodded towards the leader of the Temple. When she was standing right in front of the woman, the high priestess reached out and grabbed her arm, pushing back the sleeve and seeing there the slim bracelet that all wore until they were registered.

'It figures,' the priestess muttered to herself. 'We get two or three a year around this time. Huah, check her out on the board.' She looked again at the bracelet and studied its tiny charm. 'CXT-4799-622-584M,' she read.

The projectionist nodded and punched the numbers into a keypad. The screen stayed blank. 'Nope. Not on our Bad Girl list,' Huah said, and keyed in some more commands. This time the screen flickered and Cassie's picture and data came up on it. They definitely updated their files constantly – it was her very recent graduation picture.

The women studied it for a moment. 'Very high I.Q., but only average in school. A dreamer, butch beyond the usual age for such things,' the projectionist noted. 'Rather *be* one of the boys than be with one, but still classified heterosexual. Prefers horses to people.'

'Kinky,' Daji put in. It was ignored, as usual.

Cassie was forced to stand there silently as the details of her life and interests were read out, including many incidents and anecdotes she had long forgotten. It was obvious that these files were extremely elaborate and would have been impossible to keep and keep straight without the strange powered devices that worked only here in the city and with the constant cooperation of local priestesses, government officials, and spies that had to permeate the whole of Anchor Logh. It was here that their destinies were plotted, not in Heaven, that was clear – but they were plotted on the basis of very complete information.

'We had her down for psychological counseling,' the projectionist concluded, 'but she's really good with animals. Wanted a vet's slot but doesn't have the mental self-discipline for the boring and routine work required to get the degree. Currently we had her down as a good church prospect – she'd be an excellent midwife, for example – with the usual twist of giving her a choice between that and a menial job like stable hand.'

'That's all I came in for – to apply for the novitiate,' Cassie blurted out. 'I didn't mean to do anything wrong!'

'Too bad,' the Sister General commented without a trace of sorrow or pity in her voice. 'Well, girl, you surely understand that that way is out now. Even if we could overlook your sacrilege to the Temple and what you saw in this room – nobody would ever believe you anyway, no matter how you blabbed – we can't overlook the fact that *you* would know. You'd be a latent rebel, never fully able to take church doctrine or discipline, uncontrollable by us or the government without extreme measures, and you're smart enough to figure ways around those. You could be the source for some major inconveniences at some point down the road, and we can't have that. When we identify a potential agent of such instability, we really have no choice.'

'What could *I* do?' Cassie asked, half-pleading.

'Who knows? Perhaps nothing. Very likely nothing. But a society like ours works and survives because it is in a very delicate balance. It works primarily because its people *believe* it works, and believe that they live in a free democracy where jobs and promotions are based solely on merit and loyalty to the system, and that it's possible for the lowest – or a child of the lowest – to become the highest. It doesn't take much to upset that balance. That is really why we do all of this, and why we do it this way. Left to itself, this land would get periodically out of balance, opening the way for radical ideas and resultant radical changes. The whole thing would collapse into anarchy, and the living would envy the dead. It's happened before, child, more than once, long ago and far away. No matter what you think of us, we take our responsibility very, very seriously and are totally bound to scripture. The church's sole mission is to preserve stability, to shore up the system and eliminate its weakest and most threatening spots, so that the Holy Mother's plan can continue. By your own actions you have made yourself a potential source of such instability, and you have learned the truth decades before you were ready to understand and handle it.'

She was about to continue when a buzzer sounded on the projectionist's console. The controller reached over and picked up a small oblong-shaped object that was apparently some sort of communications device and talked in a low tone for more than two minutes. The rest of them waited, wondering what it was about.

Finally the projectionist was finished and she turned to the Sister General. 'More headaches. That was Ranatan over at the Lazy Bull on Main Street. Seems that last year he got a new girl for the upstairs room from another dive in Anchor Thomb. Now the stringer Arden told him his chit's been called, and he's pulled an abduction to pay up.'

The Sister General frowned. 'Damn. Anybody we know?'

'Not on our list, if that's what you mean. I remembered her when we were checking slots. A real looker, Ranatan says, although she's got some brains. Wait a moment.' She punched in a code and checked a screen.

'Anybody we can live without?' the Sister General asked hopefully.

'Yeah. Good I.Q. and solid aptitudes, but not in anything we aren't already overstocked in. I guess we can spare her, but Ranatan owes us one now, coming up with this so late. Says he forgot about it until his marker was called.'

'I'll bet,' the high priestess sneered.

'One problem, though. She has a steady boyfriend, and he woke up from the sapping Ranatan's boys gave him in a rotten and angry mood. He's raising holy hell with the local cops right now. Farmhand type. Not on our list but he could easily be our third soldier.'

The Sister General nodded. 'Arrange it. Since there'll be something of a cover-up necessary to pacify the police and families, better use the tunnel and bring 'em here. Keep 'em on ice until after Paring Rite, then just add her in with the crowd and make sure they leave at night. You know the routine.'

The administrator nodded. 'What about her and the boy?' By 'her' it was clear that this meant Cassie.

'We'll keep 'em on ice until Paring Day. Use two of the cells below, ninth level. Somebody can work out cover stories for them staying in town. As for Ranatan's girl, put her in with this one until then. We'll have to check with the stringers and see who's heading in the right direction to make delivery.'

'Check,' responded the administrator crisply, and that was that.

5

Rite

The cell was not, strictly speaking, a jail, but it was clear from some of the graffiti on the walls that it had served as one many times. In point of fact, it was the kind of barren cubicle that novices used when living and studying at the Temple. Under other circumstances, Cassie thought ruefully, she might have been in a similar or identical cell in this very place as a priestess-in-training.

The box-like cell was roughly three meters wide and three deep, with old and rotting straw on the floor. The rear of the place contained two fixed wooden 'beds' of sorts, one on each side; really nothing more than two rectangular boxes filled with more straw. In front of these were two small shelves mounted on each wall, empty now and probably for some time, although, hanging from a nail in one was a tiny oil lantern that provided some, but not much, illumination. Sitting on the floor near the door was a very old chamber pot that was cold, shallow, and rust-encrusted. The door itself was of solid wood with the hinges on the outside and a tiny window in the middle. The window was not barred, but it was barely large enough to get a hand through. The door, however, *was* barred, and with a very solid plank.

The wardens had stripped her completely before shoving her in, and had warned her that should she cause any problems while there, they would be perfectly willing to bring down some manacles and a gag, too, if need be. She didn't intend to make any trouble, though – at least not right now. Even if she managed a miracle, where could she go and what could she do with both church and state against her? Anchor Logh was a big place, but the Sister General had been right about one thing – the people believed totally in the system because the alternatives were so horrible. She might make it back home for a couple of days, but once her number was picked in the Paring Rite even her own parents, sad and grieving as they might be, would turn her in.

She felt curiously ambivalent about her future. The fact was, the high priestess had been correct about her. She had seen too much, and she had lost her faith. The system was based on the scriptures, and now she had caught the church red-handed circumventing its own system. If the church could do *that*, it must follow the scriptures only when it was convenient for it to do so, and if the *church* didn't really buy those holy writings, how in hell could she?

She wondered again about the stringers who'd invoked such horror in her. It was obvious that *they* knew it was all a sham, for they participated and even profited by it. Perhaps that explained their callous attitude towards everything and everyone. They *knew* it was all phony, strictly business and cynically amoral. If you knew that right from the start, as they most certainly did, and you also knew that there wasn't a damned thing you could do about it, what sort of person might you become? The answer to that one made stringers at least understandable as people, although she still couldn't agree with or like anyone who assisted so eagerly in perpetuating the fraud for personal gain.

The church equated disorder with evil. The Seven Who Wait really personified that disorder, and, thus, were depicted as the ultimate evil. Did the Seven, in fact, exist, or were they a convenient invention of the church to scare people with, she wondered? Perhaps it was a grisly sort of joke on all of them, even the church. Perhaps this was not some testing ground but Hell itself, and they were in fact the fallen angels, suffering pain and anguish and being reborn again and again, forever, into eternal punishment, with Heaven so tantalizingly in sight and always totally out of reach, everyone living rigid and mostly unhappy lives because they were working towards ultimate salvation – an ultimate salvation that would be forever denied them. Now *that* made sense – and would be the ultimate joke. Perhaps this is the secret the stringers knew, that it was all for nothing and that nothing really counted.

She shivered, only partly from the damp chill of the cell. Well, if that *were* the way of World, then something, however minor, could and must be done about it. If the angels rebelled against the Holy Mother and created disorder, and if those angels now ran World, then it was time they got a little disorder of their own. It was not in stability that hope lay, but in rebellion. Somehow, some time, she swore to herself, I will help be the instrument of that.

Strong words from someone who knew that she was to be cast into the Flux, a prisoner and slave, in a matter of days, and who was now pacing a tiny cell, stark naked and alone.

How long she was there, alone with uncounted tiny vermin and her own sour thoughts, it was impossible to say, but occasionally the heavy bar that kept her door securely closed would move back and a warden, backed up by another, would enter, leave a bowl of foul-smelling gruel, a cup of water, and check the chamberpot. She'd also slept, off and on and fitfully, although she was never quite sure for how long. The small oil lamp continued to burn, and she was afraid to turn it off for fear it would remain that way.

Still, three 'meals' into her imprisonment, the door opened again, but it was not for food. She just stood there, amazed, as two wardens tossed another naked figure into the cell. 'Let your roommate there tell you the rules,' one warden sneered, and the door was slammed shut and barred once more.

Cassie stared at the figure now picking herself up off the floor. 'Lani? Oh, Holy Mother of World! Not *you*, too!'

The other got up, frowned, and stared at her. Finally something seemed to penetrate the shock. 'Cass?'

Quickly Cassie helped her friend over to one of the beds. 'Sit here, or lie back,' she soothed. 'There's mites and everything else in here but they'll get you no matter where you are so you might as well be as comfortable as you can.'

It took some time for the small, attractive girl to get a grip on herself, but Cassie was patient, knowing that time was the one thing they had plenty of. Eventually Lani was able to talk about it, sort of, in small bits and pieces, and the story came out.

The truth was, there wasn't much to tell. After leaving Cassie at the fairgrounds, she and Dar had headed for the youth hostel. On their way they'd come close to the bright lights and raucous sounds of Main Street, and both had, more or less on impulse, gone over there. It was just curiosity, really – the area was always denied them in the past, and now that they were The Age it was open to them both. Open, yes, but dangerous. They had finally gone into a bar, just to see what one was like, and had been befriended by this nice young fellow working there. He'd been very easy to talk to, and *extremely* nice and friendly without being anything more than that, and eventually he offered to buy them one drink each just to celebrate their coming of age. It seemed so nice, so reasonable ...

Nor, in fact, was there much more to the story. She had more or less awakened in a room much like a hotel room, but she felt too dizzy and sleepy to see much or tell much about it. She was conscious only of being bound, somehow, and of several people coming in and out at various times, some giving her sweet-tasting things to drink that put her out once more, others just standing there and having some sort of conversation or other that she couldn't follow, although she seemed to think it was about her. Finally somebody came in with a novice's white robes and bundled her, still drugged, out a back door and down a series of back streets to some sort of tunnel, and through there to here. She was just coming down from the drugs, and just realizing her status.

'I've been abducted!' she suddenly said, sitting up straight. 'Oh, Holy Mother protect me from my sins! Abducted!' She started to shake a little, and began sobbing quietly. Cassie felt sorry for her and let her cry it out, giving what comfort she could. Finally Lani seemed to realize Cassie's own situation. 'You – you've been abducted, too!'

Cassie sighed. 'Not quite, but I might as well have been.' Quickly she outlined her own story, and why she was now there. 'So, you see, I'm above board from their point of view. I'll be picked in the Paring Rite. You won't. You'll just – disappear.'

Lani shook her head in shock and wonder. 'What's to become of us after that, Cass? What can we *do*?' Another thought suddenly struck her. 'Poor Dar! He must be worried sick!'

'Yeah, just like us,' Cass told her. 'He made such a fuss they copped him, too. He's probably somewhere in a hole like this one until Paring Rite, then they'll let him out just long enough to get picked. It's less messy that way.'

Lani still could not quite accept it. 'The church in league with stringers and kidnappers ... I'm sorry, Cass, it's just so – *hard* to accept, even now. And – why *me*?'

Cassie sighed. 'You were handy. You were, sorry to say it, foolish enough to walk into a joint with your bracelet showing, and the bar owner owed a favor to some bar owner in an Anchor far away. I saw them operate, Lani. They put in orders for people – size, shape, physical stats, you name it – like they were ordering a horse or new plow.'

'But what would anyone want with *me*? I mean, was it just because we were the first ones dumb enough or naive enough to walk in there, or what?'

Cass shook her head. She'd been pretty naïve herself, and maybe she still was, but she didn't recall *ever* being *that* naïve. 'Uh, Lani, a bar doesn't exactly want you for your brains.'

For a moment the other girl looked puzzled; then, slowly, the light dawned, and she seemed to wilt a bit. 'Oh,' she managed, sounding shocked. 'Oh, oh, oh ...' She sighed. 'What can we *do*?' she wailed.

Cassie shrugged. 'What *can* we do? Oh, sure, if you could escape you might kick up a fuss, but nobody would believe the church was involved, so nobody would find me or Dar, and all it means is that they'd get some other girl in your place and your number would be picked like mine and Dar's will be. They don't like problems, Lani.'

'I'd make a stink they *couldn't* sweep away,' Lani retorted bitterly.

'If you managed anything, they'd just kill you. That's the kind of people they are, Lani. I've watched them in action. Look on the bright side. At least you're going to an Anchor, and you know why and for what. If you're very lucky, and if they don't mess with your mind or something – you're smart. You'll figure something out. You always have a chance at getting them back. Me – I don't know. I'm being sent into the Flux, whatever that means. If I get back I'll be the first I ever heard of to do it.'

Lani just shook her head sadly and was silent for a moment. Finally she said, 'You just don't *know*, Cass. My field is – was – biology. I read up on it a lot. Some of the drugs they have ... I can even tell you right now the formula for the drug they probably used on me. And the ones they *will* use on me when I get – where I'm going. Somehow, when you read about them in cold, scientific language you never think of them being used on people, particularly anybody you know. Particularly not me ...' She seemed to lapse into a sort of impersonal world of horror.

'First they'll give me a series of doses of aphalamatin. It's used on the criminally insane, mostly. It burns out certain localized areas of the cerebral cortex, leaving you very nice and happy all the time and very, very compliant – you'll do just about *anything* to please, like a little kid, and you're dumb enough you can't even add without using your fingers. Then, after a tubal of course, they'll give me massive hormonal injections to get me super-endowed and horny all the time, and ...'

'For Heaven's sake, stop it!' Cassie screamed, reaching down and shaking her. 'You've got to *fight* them! Fight as long as you can, with whatever you have! Sure, maybe it's impossible, but, damn it, you fight anyway! Maybe, just maybe, we can do something, *anything* to get these bastards!'

Lani just sat there and didn't seem to hear. Cassie finally gave up in disgust and tried pacing around a bit. Maybe it was possible to be *too* smart, she thought. Anybody who ever figured the odds on anything radical and believed them probably would never try it. As for her, she couldn't name a dozen drugs and wasn't sure what half of *them* did, except stop a bleeding cut or cure a headache, but she wasn't about to give up, or count the odds. Her bitterness and hatred was far too strong and too deep for this, and while Lani's surrender to the inevitable frustrated and disgusted her, it only reinforced her own anger.

The fact was, she couldn't really blame the girl. Like herself, Lani had been brought up very secure in the system and was a solid true believer. Unlike her, Lani had not witnessed the total betrayal of that system firsthand. Lani was here because she was pretty; Cassie was here because she knew too much. It was a major difference. Secure in her knowledge that the system was rigged, a total sham, she had no qualms whatsoever about betraying it. Lani, on the other hand, faced her unpleasant future still shackled with the beliefs of her upbringing, beliefs shaken only by Cassie's admittedly biased account and by no real supporting evidence. Lani had only Cassie's word they were in the Temple.

Lani, then, had surrendered to the total fatalism that the church and scripture brought, and as the hours wore on she seemed to wrap herself more and more in the comfort of those beliefs.

'It is the will of the Holy Mother,' Lani pronounced at last, and relaxed a bit. 'It was my own past sins that led me to go to Main Street, and this is my payment. Well, I will do it. I will be the best damned stripper, dancer, whore, or whatever they will me to be. The Holy Mother's will be done!'

Cassie could do nothing but sigh and get more disgusted. This, of course, was the trouble, and why things worked so well for the people who ran it. They probably wouldn't have to use a single drug on Lani, or much of anything else.

That, in fact, discouraged Cass the most. A rebellion was impossible if only one rebel existed. Lani in fact showed just how formidable a task rebellion was, and why it was unheard of in Anchor Logh. What could a liberator do when the slaves of the system would fight like hell against the rebels for their right to remain slaves?

Still, perhaps unwittingly, the Sister General had offered some slight hope. There *had* been rebellion elsewhere, in other Anchors. The old bitch as much as admitted it. And, by their conversation, it was certain that there was more than nothingness in the Flux. There were, in fact, real places with real rulers and real names, although just what sort of place would be ruled by somebody who thought herself a goddess was hard to imagine.

Well, let the sheep be led to the slaughter if they wanted. She, Cassie, would have none of it. She would probably die or suffer terribly; even she was logical enough to realize this. But she'd die or suffer *fighting*, and if there was any chance, any chance at all, for something more she would have what revenge she could.

They came for her after what seemed like an eternity. At first she had welcomed Lani's company, but by now the poor girl was far gone into her own fantasy rationalization, practicing being sexy and alluring and seemingly looking forward to her fate with a near messianic fanaticism that Cass found bizarre in the extreme. Separation was now a relief.

Of course, Cassie and Dar had to be produced for the Paring Rite, for the same reason Lani had to stay hidden. They took Cass out of the cell and upstairs to a comfortable dressing area, where she found all her clothes neatly cleaned and pressed. She put them on and gave the wardens no trouble. If nothing else had, Lani had convinced her that whatever future she had was not in Anchor Logh, but out there, somewhere, in the terrible Flux. The system was simply too good for easy solutions. Revenge, and revolution, must come from without, for it would certainly never come from within. That she knew now with a certainty equalling the certainty that her name would be picked today in the Paring Rite. In a way, she was like Lani – she'd stopped bemoaning her fate and actually welcomed getting it over with.

Anything rather than go back to that damned, cursed cell with its other occupant.

They kept her in the ante-room while things started up outside. She could see their plan, and it was really pretty clever. No matter who was outside, or what family had attended, she was to be released just before the 'lottery', out a side entrance. She'd be out there, free, but pinned in one location by the crowd and with no time at all to do much of anything before being called. It would look very convincing – and there was absolutely nothing she could do about it, damn them.

Outside, the great square was filled with people, overflowing down the side streets as far as the eye could see. Speakers had been set up all over town so that the sacred rite and its result would be known to all, and at exactly mid-day it all began with the grand processional.

It was still an impressive sight, even to one who knew that it was all just a different version of carnival showmanship. At the mid-hour the great gong sounded from the high steeple, not its usual six times but, for the only time in the year, thirteen times. As the gong started, the great bronze doors opened as if on their own, and the processional began from within.

First came the novices, all in bright white cloaks with hoods up, then the associates and professional orders, headed by their superiors – the Midwife General, the Judiciary General, the Educator General, and all the others, followed by their members. They fanned out, providing a riot of colors in their formal robes and vestments, on both sides of the platform. Now came the ranking priestesses of each parish, large or small, from the entire Anchor, followed by their associates and assistants, and, finally, the ranking members of the priestly guilds of the Temple itself. Below, in the square, directly in front of the platform, were roped-off rows of chairs, and now the processional filed down the steps on both sides of the platform and filed into those seats, novices in the back, Temple personnel in front, everybody else in between.

Finally the Sister General herself appeared, dressed in a robe of sparkling gold inlaid with gems that contained all the colors of all the orders below, carrying her gold sceptre of office and wearing a crown made up entirely of colorful flowers. She looked in every respect the absolute monarch she actually was, subject only to the orders of Her Perfect Highness, the Queen of Heaven, who was safely in her palace in Holy Anchor half a world away.

She walked to a small, flower-covered lectern that had been set up for her in the front and center position on the platform, and stood there while aides lit incense in small stands flanking the high priestess. The day was cloudy and damp, but nobody seemed to mind.

She raised her right arm and the entire crowd went down on one knee, or as far down as the packing would permit.

'Peace be unto you, and the blessings of the Holy Mother be with you always,' she intoned, the small hidden mike carrying her blessing clearly throughout the city.

'And to you and the Holy Mother Church,' came the mass response. Even Cassie found herself mouthing the required responses, although she viewed the whole procedure cynically. Even so, she couldn't help but wonder what the effect on this crowd would be if they'd seen the same majestic-looking Sister General the way *she* had.

There followed the long and complex sacramental service, through which the local priestesses of the various churches represented their parishioners, interspersing prayers and responses. As it was winding down, though, the chief of administration for the Temple and two wardens brought down the large wire mesh drum and placed it behind the Sister General, anchoring it firmly in pre-drilled slots in the platform base. At that time a warden inside came up to Cassie and said, 'All right, you – down and out that door there.' And, with that, she found herself pushed out the side and onto the street right in the midst of the throng. She looked around on the off-chance that somebody familiar would be there, someone who, at least, could carry news of what was going on for Dar and Lani as well, but she saw no one.

The Paring Rite itself began.

'Sisters and brothers, we are gathered here today for a most sacred and holy duty,' the Sister General began. 'The Holy Mother and Her Angels have directed the welfare of this Anchor for the past year and have determined it is in all ways in accord with the holy scriptures and divine will. People were born, people died, in accordance with the divine cycle of death and rebirth, so that we who once failed our great test could, by Her infinite mercies, regain the richness of Heaven.

'Those souls which are darker than others, and which must learn much more to reach this holy perfection, are revealed to us in the Paring. This is surely the most clear illustration of divine will and direct intervention in our affairs, for it is the Holy Mother who determines the size of the harvest, the death and birth rate, and so, by comparing the two, creates the miracle by which souls who need purification in the Flux that surrounds us are revealed to us. This year the number is fifty males and fifty-six females, out of a blessedly large generation, showing us indeed that Anchor Logh is among the most blessed of the communities of World.

'Now,' she continued, 'through Her divine intervention, the names of those souls will be made known to us. Do not judge anyone of a family of the chosen to be in any way blamed for that selection. To blame another is to substitute the will of humankind for the wisdom of the Holy Mother, and She will not hold blameless those who cast aspersions on any family member. Likewise, do not grieve for those who are chosen, for they are not lost, but rather found, and through their Paring and subsequent purification they, too, gain in the eternal quest for perfection. Do not judge them – let the Holy Mother alone do that, or you, yourself, may be judged wanting by Her in your next life, and may have been so judged in the past.'

Nice of her, Cassie thought sourly. *Next thing you know she'll be saying that we're the lucky ones.* She wondered idly where Dar was. Probably stuck in a crowd just like her, and even less understanding of just what was happening to him and why.

'When each child becomes an adult, she or he was given a bracelet and charm by the local parish to which that person belonged,' the Sister General went on. The explanation was hardly necessary, but it was required of the Rite. 'Those people are here now. For most, this will be the day of their true

301

coming of age. Those whom the Holy Mother does not choose will report, as soon as they can after returning to their homes, to their local parish church and receive a registry number, and then they shall go to the government house in their communities and register and receive the rights, privileges, responsibilities, and duties of full citizens.'

She turned and looked back at the huge drum behind her. 'Here are copies of the charms each wears. Seven times does the drum spin, and then the Holy Mother will tell us the names one by one.'

The administrative chief and one of the wardens started the thing spinning the requisite number of times, then, finally, brought it to a stop. The hundreds of gold and silver colored amulets made quite a racket.

'We will now begin to read the divine will,' the Sister General told them. With that she moved back, opened the small door in the drum, and without looking at anything save the crowd, now hushed and tense, she drew the first small tag. Cassie couldn't see much of the spectacle, but she *had* been wondering how they fixed it.

The first tag was handed to the administrative chief, who took it and then consulted a large bound volume – the birth register. 'JRL-4662-622-125K,' she announced. 'Dileter of Kar Riding, come forward to the platform.'

As easy as that, Cassie reflected. Who was *ever* going to check all those numbers against the charms drawn and find out that what the clerk was reading had actually been worked out in advance and had no relation to the charm whatsoever?

As each number was read out, there was a collective sigh, or moan, from the crowd, plus occasional shrieks, wails, and protests from those called or from their friends and family. Dar was the ninth called. Cassie was the fourteenth. They were taking no chances on giving them any freedom at all.

Resigned, she made her way, with difficulty, through the crowd, which only gave way when she told each obstruction in turn she'd been called. Then they were very solicitous and their pity just dripped from them, yet it was mixed with a strong sense of relief as well. *It's not me. It's not someone I know.* And, in the midst of it all, the acute observer could pick out a small fortune in betting slips changing hands with each and every pick of the Sister General. Cass hated them for their pity and for their hypocrisy as well. *I'm coming back, you bastards!* she swore silently. *I'm coming back to tear down this damned city and wipe those looks off your holier-than-thou faces.*

She reached the platform and was actually assisted up by two wardens as if she were some sort of honored guest. Talk about hypocrites! She was led over to where those called were assembling in neat rows. Most of them looked scared to death or still in shock, and one or two were trembling uncontrollably or sobbing softly to themselves. Occasionally someone would pass out in shock when a name was called, and there were several unconscious bodies around by the end of it.

Finally, it was over. The last number had been called, and the crowd knew it, and gave the hundred and six lost souls on the stage the final indignity.

They cheered. They clapped. They built their joy into a thunderous crescendo that echoed off all points of the square and throughout the city, sweeping over the sobbing and shaking friends and family of those on stage who would now be declared property, then dead, never to be seen or heard from again.

Out of a class of 3,941, 3,835 rejoiced, as did their friends and families. Although a hundred and six were now condemned, it was a small fraction of the total, and would soon be forgotten except for the parents, siblings, friends, and relatives of those now gone. Even that, in time, would fade, as it always did, the same as if those hundred and six had been felled by accident or injury.

It was not so surprising that three of the unlucky picks did not show up for the public honor; rather, it surprised Cassie that so few had run for it. They didn't have a prayer, though, as the Sister General pointed out as soon as the crowd let her get a word in.

'Know you all that the Holy Mother has chosen three and looked for them and they are not here,' she announced. 'Know that all those declared property of the state must surrender within one day of the first bell of Paring Rite. Know, too, that if those we will now designate are not turned over to the Temple here within that period they will be declared agents of evil and discord. *Any* who help them shall suffer the same fate as they. *Any* who do so much as give them a cup of water, or simply not report them at once and aid in their apprehension, shall be guilty of a mortal sin beyond any redemption in this life and punished by terrible torments in their next, and shall forfeit all rights, citizenship, and property and themselves become property of the state. Even one who hides this from us cannot hide from the Holy Mother, who shall wreak a terrible vengeance on those who help thwart Her divine will.'

She read the names and numbers once again, and gave the benediction. The lottery drum was already removed to one side, and she turned and walked regally back up the steps to the Temple, and inside. Wardens flanked the miserable chosen, many of whom had to help their comrades merely stand, and they were then directed back into the Temple as well. Even Cassie found herself trembling slightly now that it was done, and more than a little scared. Knowing that it was fixed and that it was all a lie did nothing to change the fact that she had been declared property and banished, and was now going to the same unknown fate as those around her.

6

Mules

They were ushered into a lower level room that was large but spartan. In fact, it was often used as a small gym by the Temple priestesses, and the remains of some gym apparatus were still there, pushed against a far wall. The entire group was lined up in seven rows of fifteen each, without regard to much of anything. Wardens with nasty looking batons were posted all over the place, but the bulk of the personnel were priestesses in medical yellow. While the wardens kept them in line and menaced someone here and there who made a sound or flagged in position, the nurses measured out a clear-looking liquid into small cups and put them out on tables.

'All right – first row, walk to that table there and each take a cup,' the chief warden instructed. 'Then get back into line.'

They did as they were instructed, some sniffing or looking dubiously at the unfamiliar substance. It smelled a lot like lemonade.

Cass stood in the third row and waited her turn with the rest. She looked, of course, for others she might know in the group, as some of the others did as well, and saw several familiar faces. Her riding seemed particularly wicked this time out.

Finally she got her drink and was back in line, and after a while everyone had one. 'Now, first row, drink all of the liquid and, when finished, turn the cup upside down,' the warden instructed, 'then sit on the floor where you are.'

They did as instructed, although a couple of attempts to hold the stuff in their mouths brought sharp and painful blows from the batons and yelps of pain, and one was singled out, pinned down, and had a cup force-fed down his throat. The object lesson was well-taken; nobody in any of the subsequent rows failed to drink their cups dry.

Cassie had had more than a few qualms about downing the stuff after Lani's grisly catalog of horrible drugs, but the drink turned out to be some sort of tranquilizer. It produced an odd effect. She felt her body getting very sleepy, very distant, to the point where she was barely conscious that it was there at all, and her emotions seemed to be equally suppressed, yet her mind remained seemingly clear and sharp, and she was both conscious of and interested in the proceedings around her. In fact, it was an effective hypnotic, putting them all under yet retaining their undivided attention.

The head nurse went to each of them and checked to make certain that the drug had taken effect, then came back and stood in front of them. 'You will give me your total attention and cooperation,' she began, and instantly she had it. 'The first row will get to its feet now.' All of the first row moved as one.

'Take two steps forward, first row,' she instructed, 'then remove every piece of clothing you have on you and place it in a bundle in front of you.' Again, they did as instructed, without regard to modesty or sex. The curious thing was, they felt wide awake and totally alert – they just did what they were told as if they had no control whatsoever over their body movements.

'Now you will all pick up your clothing and hold it in front of you. That's right. Now, you will all turn to your right, so that you form a line, and walk slowly to the large box over there, drop your clothes in it, then go to the first table next to the box.'

The procedure was repeated for each one. At the first table non-Temple doctors of both sexes gave each a fairly routine physical, then they were directed to the second, where their heads were shaved clean, first with some sort of powered razors, then with a creamy compound that removed any last vestiges of hair, right down into the pores and to the base of the roots. This was the first mark of those chosen in the Paring Rite. If, somehow, one or more got away, they would be forever marked by total and complete baldness.

The second mark was the most degrading, and was administered by a very strange chair-like machine. Each in turn was told to sit in the large contraption, their rears against a metal plate of some sort. An attendant punched a button, and, when they got up, there was an indelible long number tattooed in purple on their behinds. Similarly, they were told to put their right thumbs in a hole in a small device, and that gave a purplish stain that made the fingerprint really stand out. Boys, Cassie noted, also had the shave and cream treatment for facial hair of any sort.

Finally, they were given a series of injections, purposes unknown, then broken up into small groups and taken to smaller rooms where they were given a basic meal to eat – some sort of stew, not very good, but far better than the crap they'd given her in the cell – and then were taken to basic showers and rinsed from head to toe. This done, they were taken back to the gym, where all of the equipment had been cleared and the floor covered with huge, gray cushioned mats of the usual sort found in school gymnasiums, and the chief warden told them, 'All right. You will remain here until it is time to leave. All exits will be guarded by wardens who would just love to make an example of somebody trying to leave. There is a basic bathroom through those small doors over there if you need to take a crap. Anybody still thinking of leaving before we let you should remember your stigmata and know that these will make you known to one and all. There is no place to run in Anchor Logh.' And, with that, she departed.

The drug was wearing off rapidly now, and Cassie could feel the sting on her ass where the number had been tattooed, but a side effect of the stuff was that it made you terribly tired and sleepy. Most of them, herself included, just sank down on the mats and passed out.

It was an unpleasant sleep and an unpleasant awakening, although in a sense it was better because, once it was determined that what had happened was no nightmare, there was a sense on the part of most of the group to adapt to the situation as something new to be faced, with unpleasant future realities shunted to a back part of the mind.

Cassie awoke with a mild headache and a little dizziness that soon passed, and she looked around. Some of the others had apparently been awake for some time, while others were still in various stages of half-sleep, but there was some moving around, whispered talking, and once in a while somebody would stagger to the bathroom.

They were a strange sight, all these people with no clothes or hair and numbers on their asses, but since *everybody* was that way it soon seemed somewhat normal, sort of like a uniform binding them together. Cassie got up and, after a false start or two, started to walk around and see if she could find anybody she knew. A large boy sitting up against a wall called to her. 'Hey! Cass! Is that you?'

She smiled, turned, and went over to him. Hairless, Dar looked more the country bumpkin than ever.

'I saw you come up when you were called,' he told her. 'I really wasn't expecting to see you here, though.' His face darkened. 'I kind of figured it'd be Lani.'

She sat down beside him, paused, trying to collect her thoughts, then said, 'Lani's not with our group, Dar, but she'll probably go out with us. I've seen her.' Carefully, hesitantly, she told the story from the point at which they'd split up at the Carnival until she'd been shoved outside for the Paring Rite. She spared nothing, but was as gentle as she could be.

He took it well, although for a moment he just sat there, thinking hard. Finally he said, 'Damn. And I always figured she was so much smarter'n me. That's just dumb foolishness.' He paused a moment more, then added, 'But, like you said, this is *all* just dumb foolishness, isn't it?'

She smiled wanly. 'That's about it. I'm a little surprised at how you're taking it all, though. Don't you go along with her that it's the divine will?'

He snorted. 'Divine will – hell! I already figured that any goddess that would do this mean thing to nice people like you and Lani wasn't much worth a damn. It ain't fair, that's all, and who wants a bunch of gods who ain't fair?'

She almost kissed and hugged him for that, but kept still. Eventually he told her of his own experiences, of getting the knockout drinks at the bar and waking up in the youth hostel, trying to see Lani, and being told she wasn't there. He'd become something of a wild man at that, realizing that she'd been abducted and blaming himself for it. He'd stormed back to the bar looking for the guy who'd done it and, when he couldn't find him, he'd started tearing the bar apart. In the end, the cops came and arrested *him* and had refused to listen to his protests about Lani. A cop *did* take his statement, when he'd calmed down enough to give one, and promised to check for the missing girl, but they'd left him locked up.

Finally a magistrate, who was, of course, a Temple priestess, had heard his case, but refused to even allow any testimony on Lani's disappearance. She told him there was no excuse for such misbehavior, that there were proper channels if he had a problem, and she sentenced him to remain in jail until Paring Rite, which he had.

'I kind of figured my number was up then, and Lani's too,' he told her. 'I mean, when that bitch of a judge wouldn't even *listen* about a kidnapping – hell, I smelled rotten meat. Then, when I was called so quickly, that just cinched it.'

She nodded, feeling better than she had in a long time. It was good to be believed, and to find a kindred spirit in all this mess. They talked for a while, mostly on inconsequential things, and Dar remarked, 'Hey – you know, it's funny.'

'Huh? What's funny?'

'Well, here we are, all naked and all, with a bunch of guys and girls, and nobody's the least bit turned on, if you know what I mean. I mean, if you can't be bad *now*, when can you?'

She hadn't really noticed it before, but he was right. Dar was, in fact, as amply endowed in his area as Lani was in hers, yet she felt not the slightest urge or inclination there. At first she just put it down to the situation, or the public nature of the room, but now she realized that this wasn't explainable by that at all. In fact, even if some of the boys were restrained, others like Dar would not be, and their sexual arousal would be impossible to hide.

'It must be those shots they gave us,' she decided. 'I guess one of them just, well, turned us all off.'

Dar sighed. 'Yeah. It ain't enough to make us bald and dye us purple. They got to make us mules, too.' He looked at her. 'Too bad, too. I got to admit, Cass, I never much thought of you except as one of the boys, but, like this, well, you're kind'a cute. Ain't no mistaking you for a boy, anyway.'

She grinned broadly, leaned over, and kissed him gently on the cheek. 'That's the nicest thing any boy's ever said to me. I appreciate it, Dar. I really do.'

'Yeah, too bad. The mind's willin' but the motor just won't start.' They sat there a while longer, and eventually several others recognized them and came over and joined them. They were a mixed lot from the riding, and also somewhat mixed in their reactions to all this. Cass was surprised to find how few were deep-down religious about it all. It's easy to see someone else get picked for sin, but pretty tough to get picked for it yourself when others whom you *know* are far worse than you were freed to live normal lives. Not that there weren't a few wail-and-doom fanatics, but not many.

Some friends, old and new, banded together with them for at least a brief association. There were Suzl and Nadya, two girls who crushed Cassie's old belief – or hope – that the pretty and sexy ones would be nothing without hairdos, makeup, and careful dressing, and Canty and Ivon, one a short, squat boy with a mischievous streak, the other built like a bull. Ivon, the big, muscular one, was pretty bright, but he had both a temper and an attitude that showed a bull like lack of fear – and lack of self-control.

'Turned us into damned mules, that's what they did,' Ivon grumped. 'Shaved, sexless, and branded. I suppose a halter's next.'

The shots seemed to have affected them all more than they'd expected. 'I was in the middle of my period yesterday,' Suzl noted. 'Now – nothing. I wonder what else those shots did? I wonder if it's permanent?' That last was the unspoken primary fear of all of them.

Cassie reassured them at least that there was evidence of civilization in the Flux, between the Anchors and having trade with them. What sort of civilization could exist there none of them could imagine, and Cassie decided it was better not to mention the place that wanted perfect specimens for experimental purposes. What they had now was bad enough.

They were fed at intervals, again in small groups, and there was some variety despite the basic lack of quality in the food. Two of the three missing ones also arrived during that period, both girls who said that they had been hustled away by parents or other relatives and had just bought a little more time. They had paid for that time, though, and dearly. Every hair on their bodies had been removed, and not by machine, either – even their eyebrows – and they had been tattooed by hand, without anesthetic, not merely with the number on their rump in the standard purple but all over in various colors. They had been tied down and anybody who was around was given a needle and told to write or draw something. From the looks of them there had been an awful lot of people around, and most had cruel or obscene minds.

The third missing one, they were told, would not be coming at all. She had gone someplace and found a large knife, then entered the Temple and began hacking and stabbing everyone she met, screaming that she was one of the Seven Who Wait, wreaking vengeance on the Holy Mother and Her church. It'd taken seven wardens to subdue her, and in the process they'd beaten her to death. Talk was she'd taken several in church robes with her to the next incarnation. They didn't know her name, but she became something of an instant hero to the group in the gym.

They were just beginning to get used to the routine and their new situation when the moment they dreaded arrived. The doors opened and in walked not Temple wardens but uniformed soldiers of the border guard, looking tough and nasty. The group was formed up into its now standard rows, and an officer of the guard stepped forward with a list.

'When I call your name, you will step forward and form a new set of ranks to my left,' he instructed them. 'Failure to move immediately or not carry out *any and all* orders any member of the Guard may give you without question will result in you experiencing more pain than you have ever felt in your lives. There will be no talking or whispering or gesturing of any sort. I don't care if you have to shit – do it in line. Now, listen and move when I call your name.'

Fifty-two names were called out, slightly more boys than girls, which left Cassie's group with a decided female numerical superiority. Whether by chance or what, Dar, Ivon, Suzl, and Nadya all remained with Cassie's group, although Canty and several other friends were split.

Now the roll was called for the remaining people, just to make sure that everybody was in fact in the correct group, and both were formed up into regular rows, four across for the smaller group, with one straggler in the odd-numbered other group. They were then told to extend their arms and stand that far away from the person next to them, which they did. There was the sound of clanking metal from the doorway, and everyone in both groups stiffened.

The guards were quite efficient. First worn-looking collars of some cheap metal were placed around their necks, then tough rope of some unnatural-looking but extremely tough white material was passed through rings on either side of the collar until they were all linked together. More of the rope was then passed through other collar loops right to left, so that they were linked and secured in a cross-hatched pattern. Some adjustments were made for height, but not a lot of attention was paid to niceties that might make things more reasonable or comfortable. Now waistbands of similar metal were brought out and more of the strange rope was used to have them affix the waistbands as the neckbands were.

There were some attempts to miss loops, of course, but the guards were sharp-eyed and dealt with anyone causing trouble by pointing and shooting small hand-held pistols of some sort at the offenders, who received bloody welts where they were hit and screamed in agony. Few examples needed to be made.

Finally, it was done, and the final indignity was performed by a guard who used his pistol to melt and seal all the endings, effectively welding them into this incredible position. The officer of the guard stepped forward once more.

'Stretch yourself out so that both of your ropes are tight,' he instructed. '*Keep 'em tight*! No slack. Some people have short legs, some long. Be responsible for your own ropes – the one across and the one directly in front of you. So long as you keep those ropes as tight as you can, you won't get into any trouble. If anybody isn't doing their part, one of us will deal with that person. If anybody falls, you are not, repeat, not to stop, but to yell out for help. Those of you in the lead, you will match the pace of the sergeant of the guard. You will move when we tell you, stop *instantly* if commanded to do so. Now, let's practice.'

Cassie was unprepared for the wrenching motion that twisted her around as they began, and there were many people stumbling and falling. The officer and sergeant yelled and screamed and cursed and made all sorts of comments, yet seemed to have almost infinite patience and self-assurance that, sooner or later, they would get it down pat. They did not. Finally, the officer sighed, and brought out a chest of leg manacles. These, however, were not strung together with rope but with rigid telescoping rods that could be adjusted, then locked into position.

Again they practiced, and this time the rods, running only front to back on both legs, acted like pistons. When those in front moved their left legs forward, those farther back had no choice but to do the same. For most it was a terribly unnatural gait, but after what seemed like hours of marching they managed some semblance of order. At least nobody was likely to fall down.

The rods could be twisted to telescope, revealing a ball joint that allowed them to sit, so long as they just about hugged their knees, and it was only after a number of perfect marches that they were allowed the luxury. By the end of the day they ached all over, yet they were never released and, in fact, were fed in line – some sort of tasteless meat cake, a small stale loaf of bread, and some fruit juice. That last was the most welcome, and they downed it eagerly.

It contained, of course, more of the previous day's hypnotic drug, as many, including Cassie, had suspected, but none of them cared. The thirst could not be denied, and at least the stuff made all the aches and pains seem to disappear.

After the drug had taken effect, the guard moved rapidly, ordering them to their feet and affixing the rods in place once again. Again they marched, but this time corrective measures were easily implemented. To Cassie, as to them all, the most important thing in the world, the *only* thing that mattered, was keeping a perfect pace with the ropes taut.

And, with that, the large doors to the gym were opened, and both groups were marched out, down a corridor, and out through a delivery entrance into the back of Temple Square.

The chill was still in the air, and there was a light, misty rain. It had obviously rained far harder in the hour or two preceding their exit, for it was quite wet. Night had fallen, but police were posted at all intersections to block off the curious as the sad marchers passed. Once out of the city the roads were unpaved, and the rain had turned them into a sea of thick, gooey mud, although the type of dirt used and the stone mixture in it did not make it particularly slippery, only messy.

The sergeant of the guard knew his stuff, and kept the pace exactly right, also sensing what they could not – when they had to break – and halting them at regular intervals. Each time they were given cups of juice that contained drug boosters. Finally, near dawn, they were marched into a field guarded from view on all sides by thick trees and halted, fed, and given a different drink. Within minutes of finishing, all had lapsed into the deepest sleep they had ever known.

They slept through the day, but when they awakened near dark they were all so wracked with tremendous pains through their bodies that they almost fought to drink the hypnotic that would take that pain away, and the pattern repeated.

They continued to move only after dark, thus avoiding meeting very many curious onlookers or creating the kind of crowd that always seemed to materialize around accidents, and thanks to the drugs and the preset pace one time seemed to merge into another, until they had completely lost track of how long they had been marching. It was certain, though, that the distance was over a hundred kilometers from the capital to the west gate, and their pace was quite deliberate but slow. In a sense the entire period seemed like some sort of hazy nightmare in which there was only the clanking, the occasional chanting and commands of the guards, and the single set of purposes. *Keep the ropes taut. Keep the pace exactly ...*

The most curious thing, for those able to think about it at all, was that, after a while, they awoke with less and less pain and linked up and marched with perfect adjustment without being told.

And then, late one night, they reached the west gate, the high fortified wall stretching out into the darkness on both sides of them, its inner guard walkway illuminated by torches every few meters. The whole structure, including the gate structure itself, was made of solid stone. The wall was four meters thick, with a stone guard station every fifty meters around the entirety of the Anchor. The gate added another three meters on each side, and had a headquarters building on top. The inner gates were of solid steel, a third of a meter thick themselves, and it took an entire team of mules just to turn the mechanism to open or close them. Inside was a passage called, with good reason, the Deathway: a stone opening through the wall that had its own small openings from which guards could not only monitor anyone and anything inside but fire upon it as well.

Above, just inside the gates on both sides, hung a heavy steel portcullis held up on a winch. A single kick of a lever by any guard could cause both to drop, imprisoning anyone inside who managed to jam the gates. The gates themselves were on a clever mechanism that had the outer gates always open if the inner ones were closed and vice-versa. It was said that vats of boiling hot oil could be unleashed in the Deathway with the same ease as dropping the portcullis.

The officer and sergeant of the guard halted them, then rode forward to the gate itself. There they were met by other uniformed border guards and there was a long conversation. Then there were some shouts, men ran one way or another, then a single shouted signal, and, slowly, the massive closed gates began to open.

It was a dramatic event in and of itself, but as they opened more and more a figure was revealed framed between them. It was the stringer Matson, on his white horse, idly smoking a cigar.

As soon as there was clearance he eased his mount slowly forward, then approached the sad-looking column, stopping here and there but taking a ride completely around the group. He mumbled something to himself and then rode back over to the guards watching him.

'A pretty miserable-looking lot,' he commented sourly. 'You could have at least sized them to make it easier.'

The officer shrugged. 'Not my problem. After ten days with 'em on the trail seasoning them up for you on the juice, I ain't too particular about anything except gettin' rid of 'em. You don't like their condition, *you* take the next batch out from the city.'

Matson snorted. 'That *ain't* my responsibility,' he responded sarcastically. 'How well seasoned are they?'

'Meekest group in years,' the officer told him. 'Hardly any trouble at all. Today they were barely on the juice at all and they made the best time of the trip. You could take them ropes and rods off now and I bet they'd keep perfect distance and interval and even sit just right., Ain't but a handful complained about any aches or pains when they woke up today, either. Some of 'em got real good leg muscles, even the women, and they're all in better shape than they ever been in their lives. 'Cept in the head,' he added.

Matson nodded, a sour expression on his face. 'Okay, then, get those damned rods off and remove the strings. I can't take 'em through all at once, you know.'

'You got to sign for them first,' the officer reminded him. An orderly who had been standing nearby brought up a clipboard with pen attached. Matson took it and looked over the forms carefully. They matched the ones he was carrying in his head.

'All present, if you want to count 'em,' the officer assured him.

'I already *have* counted them, and checked their general condition,' the stringer replied curtly. He scribbled a signature on the sheet. 'All right – let's get 'em over to my side.'

It was a strange experience to have the leggings and ropes removed. It had been such a seemingly endless time with them that their removal seemed almost an unnatural, out-of-balance thing to the exiles. The drug used, which was occasionally used for religious indoctrinations and retreats by the church and by guards in basic training, was quite a powerful conditioner. Highly repetitive actions performed over a sustained period were reinforced a hundredfold or more each time, and they had been almost continuously under for more than ten days. The officer was not exaggerating – freed of all linkages, they all still stood as if bound, and guards had to actually restrain the rear part of the party to keep it from following the first group through the gates and in the Deathway.

Matson went with the first group so he could effectively reassemble them on the other side. The inner gate slowly closed, and, as it did, the outer gate opened to reveal a large, brightly lit tent city crowded with strange and misshapen creatures. This area, technically referred to as the Anchor apron, was as close as most from the Flux were ever allowed into Anchor. Beyond the apron, barely visible in the darkness and reflecting none of the light from wall or apron, was the Flux itself.

7

Flux

It really wasn't until they had been fed, bedded down, and slept for some time that their senses started to return to them. Cassie awoke with a strangely disoriented feeling, not quite understanding where she was or what had happened. Opening her eyes and looking around only helped slightly, for the sights of the tent city and its milling throngs of very strange human beings and very scruffy animals did little to orient her or the others. It was only when she looked up and saw the Flux before her, then turned and saw the great wall and gate behind, that she understood exactly what was going on.

It took a moment more to realize that the leggings, rods, and even the ropes were now gone, although the collar and waistband remained, the latter hanging rather loosely on her hips. Her muscles ached, but not with the terrible pain of the first – what, days? – out. They had just been used to their maximum, pressed to their limits, and were letting her know it.

All of these discomforts were minor compared to seeing the Flux – and from outside the gates. It was a terrifying sight, even more than it had been when she'd stood on top of that wall back there as a young schoolchild and stared at it.

There was no difference, really, between the apron and the Anchor itself. The wall had been built well in from the Flux boundary for a number of reasons, some practical and some superstition. There was grass here, and well-worn paths, and it felt quite normal. Still, the Flux lay just beyond.

It rose upwards as far as the eye could see, blocking off the sky and everything else from view. It looked like a great, infinite wall of opaque glass, a light reddish tan in color, and it *shimmered* something like an early morning fog in the fields. Inside there seemed to be tiny little flashes of energy, so small they would not even be noticed in isolation but so numerous that they could not be ignored. The overall effect was of a smooth wall or container holding a mass of fog-shrouded, moving sequined material.

There were a number of grumbles and groans as the group slowly awoke to the new day and the same realizations that Cassie had felt. They had very little time to socialize, though, for Matson, looking sharp in his black outfit, hat, boots, and with his shotgun, knife, and whip on his belt, strode over to them from a nearby tent.

'All right – everybody up on their feet!' he ordered. 'We're going to have a little orientation talk and then you'll get food and drink but with no drugs to help you along. That part's over. And don't give me any trouble or any shit or I'll skip food and water in your case for starters, and once we're in the Flux you'll wish you'd never been born.'

There was no problem now. They were too scared to do much more than obey. Scared – and curious.

'All right. Now, my name's Matson and I own you. Yeah, I know that sounds funny, but it's literally and legally true. You stopped being people when your numbers got drawn. Now, that means that there's no place to run, no appeals, no protection. I'm the law, the absolute authority and if I don't like you I can do anything I want with you and I don't even have to have much of a reason. If I wake up in a bad mood and decide that the first two of you I see will have their arms chopped off because I feel like it, that's the way it'll be. You remember that. And you remember, too, that anybody who gives me lip can have his or her tongue cut out with a gesture from me and I won't even lose any sleep over it. Do you understand?'

There were a few mumbled assents. The rest had progressed in one short moment from being scared to being terrified.

Matson looked slightly peeved. 'When I talk to you as a group I expect to be answered by the group. Now, let's try that again. Do you understand me?'

'Yes,' came an almost uniform response.

'When you talk to me you call me "sir" always. Now, what was that again?'

'Yes, SIR!' they responded.

'Louder! Sometimes it's hard to hear in the Flux, so shout everything, you understand?'

'YES, SIR!' they screamed at him.

He nodded. 'That's better. All right. Let's start with the apron here. Those people that you see are Flux people. They usually live in the Flux, except when they have business here, although some of them are permanent residents of the aprons, dealing in goods and services for stringers like me. Just in case you never heard the term before, they are called duggers. Duggers are one kind of group that lives in the Flux. Forget that bullshit they sold you in school and church – the Flux is full of life, and death, and is anything but empty. In fact, a lot of stuff that keeps the Anchors going comes from Fluxlands. Anchors trade for the stuff, and what they trade is often information or services, but is also people. You, to be exact, in this case.'

He paused to let that sink in.

'Now, you may wonder why the hell the Flux needs people. Part of the reason is that it's a pretty hard, violent place compared to Anchors. They have a very high death rate. The odds are that your own lives will be short, but don't let that upset you too much. There are still a lot of folks out there who live to ripe old ages, and some who live so long they seem almost immortal. Children are born in the Flux, too, but the infant mortality rate is very high, and the odds are against somebody growing to adulthood there. Again, that doesn't mean everybody. I was born in the Flux, and I've lived more than twice as long as any of you.'

Again he paused, looking at their faces to see how they were taking it.

'Okay, then. Right now you're imagining some wild, savage kind of Anchor or something. Well, forget it. In fact, if you want to stay alive, forget every single bit of science or logic that you were ever taught. All that applies only to Anchors. In fact, that is the real difference between Anchor and Flux.

'In Anchors, everything's following a clearly defined set of natural laws. You drop a stone, it falls at a specific rate to the ground thanks to gravity. That's a good example. In the Flux, there are no natural laws. None. There *are* standard conditions – what we call "default conditions," but those exist only where not modified. You will not go floating into the air. You will be able to breathe it, and the temperature is rather warm although usually extremely dry. But these are all defaults, not fixed conditions. They are subject to change. You can take *nothing* for granted in the Flux. Nothing.

'Now – what changes these conditions? Well, the fact is, the Flux is as you see it over there. That's the default, too. A big nothing. What looks like fog, though, isn't fog at all – it's energy. The Flux *does* obey one natural law – energy can neither be created nor destroyed, but it *can* be changed. When you put a match to oil in a lamp you let out the energy in the oil. When you were in the city, though, you saw electric lights and powered gadgets. That power came from turning some matter, some solid stuff, into energy. You can do that in the Flux, too – but there you can also do it backwards!'

That caught some of them off balance. Those who had been able to follow things so far tried to figure out his last comment and fit it in, the others just stood there trying to look like they understood it all.

'What that means,' he went on, 'is that energy, what you see back there, can be changed into matter. Solid things. If you're good enough, or smart enough, you can do almost anything there. Those who can totally control it are like gods. In fact, some of 'em think they *are* gods and act like it, too. We call 'em wizards – master magicians. They really *do* have the power of gods in the Flux, and they run things. They're the ones who created the Fluxlands, the independent places in the Flux, and they run them like gods as well. Watch out for them.

'As for the rest, there are those who have varying degrees of skill in manipulating the Flux. Some of 'em are what we call false wizards. They, say, turn you into a bird. *You* think you're a bird, and everybody else thinks you're a bird, and when you jump into the air off the cliff you and everybody else thinks you're flying. But you're still you, and you can't fly, so you crash and die. Watch out for the false wizards. In their own way they're more dangerous than the real ones.'

He looked them over, then allowed a half-smile to come over his face. He knew they didn't understand much of it, and probably the ones that did didn't believe a word of it, but that was okay. This lecture would come in handy when they saw the reality of Fluxlands.

'Now, within the next day we'll be going into the Flux itself,' he told them. 'You'll be on my strings, but relatively free and loose. It might be possible for somebody to escape.' He turned back towards his tent. 'Jomo! Kolada! Front and center!'

From the direction of the tents came two creatures that probably were human once. One of them, Jomo, must have weighed a hundred and fifty kilos or more, but that was not what struck anyone who looked at him. His face was a mottled, misshapen mass with the standard features barely recognizable in it. His hands were massive, clawlike things that seemed useless for grasping much, and his shoeless feet were enormous caricatures of what feet should be. He looked, in fact, very much like Cassie's vision of a troll from the old children's stories. He wore only a skirt-like rag fastened by a crude belt.

Kolada was even worse. It was hard to tell if the creature was male or female. It was tall and humanoid, but its entire body was covered by tremendously thick brown hair including the face, from which gaped an animal-like mouth with two fangs rising up from the lower jaw and a pair of blood-red eyes that seemed to shine with an inhuman fury. Its arms were so long that they just about reached the ground, terminating in two huge paw-like hands.

'These two duggers are my chief driver and my point guard,' Matson told them. 'To answer your question even though you haven't asked, both are, or were, human just like you. Both, at different times, escaped from stringer trains into the Flux. Anybody who does that and either has no natural power over it or doesn't run into somebody who lives there will be dead quickly, for there's no food and water you don't make yourself in the void, nor any way at all to get your bearings to know where you are, where you've been, and where you're going. Only stringers and wizards know their position in the Flux, and we make certain that nobody else ever finds out how we do it. No dugger can do it, and they try all the time.

'Now, if you're wondering what happened, both of them *did* run into others, but they ran into different sorts. Jomo has a little of the real Flux power, you see, but no control. We've all got our little fears and insanities in the back of our minds. Well, see what Jomo's do to him. He doesn't always look like this. Sometimes he looks worse, occasionally better. Kolada, on the other hand, ran into somebody with real power in the Flux, somebody who was very, very dangerous. In a story far too long to go into here, that person changed a nice, normal Anchor woman into the creature you see here. And, because it was a wizard, she's absolutely stuck like this unless somebody even more powerful changes her, for she has no Flux powers at all.

'Most of the people on the apron, the duggers, have similar stories. They're all quite mad and they've all been changed in one way or another by wizards or their own minds. But they're the rare lucky ones. They survived in the Flux, and, after a while, they signed on with stringers like me and have about as much security and stability as it's possible to have in there – and some independence. In the Flux, most people more or less belong to other people, because whoever has the most power over the Flux can control everybody below them. Duggers belong to no one except themselves. These people work for me and they get paid for it. Now, if anybody wants to take a risk on surviving long enough to become a dugger, now you've seen what duggers are like, you just escape. That's it. Get some food over there at the big tent and come back here to eat.'

They went in orderly silence. The earlier lecture hadn't had much effect, but the duggers had, and as they entered the apron camp and saw that Matson's 'employees' were among the least exotic variations around, the effect was greatly enhanced. The whole place was a terrible, crawling creep show. Most had little appetite when they returned to their grassy spot.

The small group reformed for the first time since back in the gym, but they were a sober lot.

'Did you see that one that looked like a squirmy, squishy thing?' Nadya asked, shivering a bit.

'And how about the one with the wavy things coming out of its head?' Ivon added.

'I think I've seen more than I want to right now,' Cassie put in. 'I don't need to catalog it. It's tough enough to eat now, and I was *starving* ten minutes ago.'

They nodded agreement, but most managed to get something down nonetheless. At least the food was palatable – some sort of warm meat and vegetable pies and a very sweet cake, with some sort of wine that was not at all sweet but a good thirst-quencher. Ultimately, though, the conversation returned to their own fates, past and future. They talked about their long drugged march, and compared aches, pains, and bruises, as well as leg muscles which were pretty outstanding, even on the girls. Finally, it was Nadya who noticed. 'Hey – what happened to the other group?'

They all looked around. Sure enough, there was no sign of the first group, the one that was to go with the other stringer. Jomo, who was looking to the mules grazing nearby, heard, turned, and in a gruff, barely human voice, said, 'They go before you wake up with Missy Arden. They well into Flux now.'

Rather than be startled by the dugger's attention, they all turned and looked towards the imposing Flux itself. The void, Matson had called it. The void between the Fluxlands. After a while they snapped out of it and attention turned to the future, although it was mixed with a little caution. Jomo had accomplished his main purpose of letting them know that they were being overheard.

'What do you think is going to happen to us?' Dar asked at last. 'I mean, once we go – in there?'

Cassie sighed. 'I don't know, but it doesn't sound very promising, does it?'

'Do you buy this magic business?' Ivon put in. 'Sounds like those crazy old stories to me.'

'I think he's telling the truth. Some of it, anyway,' Suzl opined. 'If what he was saying was true about the Flux energies, then it's very possible to have magic and a whole little set of mini-godhoods. The only thing I can't figure out is why some people have the power and others, probably most, do not. It seems to be something you're born with, anyway, if the story of Jomo is right, not something you learn or get from your parents, although practice probably makes you better and better.'

Nadya looked worried. 'They have made a lot of changes in us, you know, so I can see how that might be taken further. I wonder, though, if they can change your mind like they can change your looks?'

'They can do it with drugs and conditioning in Anchor,' Cassie pointed out, 'so why not in Flux as well? What's really odd, though, is that the changes seem to be so real, so permanent. I mean, if it was just in Flux, then these people would change back to their old selves here in Anchor, right? They didn't. That means to me that we've got some real trouble in there. Anything they did to us in Anchor can be changed around in Flux, but anything done to you in Flux is *permanent.*'

Nadya looked at the Flux. 'A world of magicians, madmen – and slaves. It's horrible.'

Cassie thought of the Sister General, the machines, the Paring Rite, and Lani's catalog of terrible drugs, and could only wonder just how different it was from Anchor Logh after all. In a way, it just might be a more direct, more honest and open version of the world from which they had come.

It took quite some time to form the stringer train, and it was an impressive affair. There were twenty mules, all loaded down with things in large packs, as well as two horse-drawn wagons driven by duggers. Between the mules and the wagons Matson placed his human cargo, four abreast in familiar pattern, and linked together with common thin rope of the sort used on farms for clotheslines. He had expertly reformed and sized them so that the shortest were in front and would thus set the pace. The lines were then tied off to the last pair of mules ahead of them. None of the lines were intended to keep anyone captive, it was pointed out to them, but merely to give some logical distribution to the train and set a logical pace. It was also their lifeline, Matson added, for it was very, very easy to get lost in the Flux, and with a train this size, even with a dozen or more duggers managing it, it would not be possible to keep an eye on all parts of it at once.

All the duggers were mounted on horses except the impressive Jomo, who preferred being on foot, the better to get wherever he needed in the mule train. They noticed that Matson and all the duggers had small bugles or some similar instrument on their saddles or in their belts. These, it turned out, were the means of communication along the train, and each stringer had his own private codes so that none could easily trick him with false signals.

After the train had been completely assembled, Matson rode slowly all the way down it from front to back on one side, then back up to the front on the other, stopping occasionally, shouting orders to adjust or fix this or that, positioning and repositioning people and things. This went on for some time until he was completely satisfied and then rode quickly up to the front and stopped. He unclipped his bugle from his saddle, raised it to his lips, and, turning back, blew a series of sharp notes of differing length and pitch, repeating the same pattern three times. The duggers on the wagons to the rear returned a slightly different signal twice, and they saw the hairy creature called Kolada suddenly ride forward and vanish into the Flux at full gallop. They waited then another minute or two, then Matson gave one last, long blast on his horn which was returned by all of the other duggers. The train began to move forward, towards the Flux.

Dar and Ivon were both big men, so they were well back in the group, but Nadya, Cassie, and Suzl had maneuvered themselves to be near one another, being only slightly different in height, and Matson had allowed it. They began to walk towards that huge, shimmering wall.

'Here we go,' Cassie muttered under her breath. First Matson vanished into the stuff, followed by Jomo and his mules. As the great Flux region came ever closer, they all felt themselves stiffen, felt an urge to break and run, but duggers on both sides kept shouting and growling curses at them and they slowed and staggered a bit but went on. The first rows went in and essentially vanished from view, then it was Cassie's row and they were through before they even realized it.

They entered an eerie world such as none of them had ever known before.

There are a few times in everyone's life when they feel totally and completely helpless, at the mercy of fate. The bull that suddenly appears out of nowhere and charges when it's fifty meters to the nearest fence. The time when you're patching the roof and grab frantically for something to break the fall, only nothing's there. Cassie and the others felt that way now, which is why even the roughest and most boisterous of them were meek and quiet through this experience. They were caught in the web of deceit in Anchor Logh and now they were tethered and bound together by the stringer's spidery lines.

The effect of suddenly entering the Flux was too much for some who had endured so much. Somebody screamed, somebody else started sobbing hysterically, as they were pulled, helplessly, by the mules away from the Anchor that was all the reality they'd ever known, away from all that was safe and sane and real, into the terrible, shimmering void.

There was a sensation of dry heat, like being in an oven that had not yet quite warmed up to intolerable temperatures. The raw Flux was around them all now, producing an odd, slightly tingling sensation that was more eerie-feeling than uncomfortable.

There was also a terrible absence of sensation. It was dead quiet in a way that simply could not exist in Anchor, the only sounds those of the train itself, and even those beyond the immediate people in front and back seemed curiously damped or muffled. The air, too, was perfectly still and had none of the odors that were always present in normal air. No scent of grass, or the very subtle fragrances of things you never even knew were there until they were gone. The effect was to heighten the sense of smell of everyone in the group, but the only source for that was the now very pungent body odor that was already hard to take even back on the apron.

Nor had Matson been exaggerating when he warned them that they would have no sense of direction in the Flux. Every direction looked exactly like every other direction, and there were no landmarks, no markers of any sort. Even the ground was more sensed than seen; it felt slightly soft and spongy, and visually, they and the train walked as spirits through empty air on a surface that was totally invisible and indistinguishable from the air around them. It was extremely disorienting, and only the solidity of something underfoot, seen or not, allowed them to keep their balance. It was still better, they found, if you didn't look down.

The duggers on either side of the train dropped back in alternation, checking on the marching lines. They seemed somehow different now, far less deformed if no less mad, and they seemed to radiate an air of comfortable confidence. This was their element, and they were comfortable with it.

Some of them still slobbered and drooled and made bizarre, often animal-like sounds, but they never seemed to look the same way twice. For a while Cassie thought they might be different people. She soon made a sort of game of it, something to occupy her mind in the midst of the terrible nothingness, watching the one nearest her on her side as best she could. The dugger seemed almost hunchbacked one time, then ramrod straight the next. The creature went from fat to thin, almost but not quite while you were looking at it. One time she was sure she saw a beard on the dugger, yet the next time it went by it seemed clean-shaven and even had rather formidable breasts. The clothes, too, so tattered and filthy on the apron, seemed to undergo changes in color, design, and newness. It was both frightening and confusing. The horse, though, seemed solidly real.

Matson was unchanged through it all, but in constant motion, riding up and down, back and forth, making certain that all was going well. He was all business and he had no patience with anyone or anything that was out of step. Once in a while, of course, somebody in the group would become disoriented and slip, and there would be a yell from those around, a blast from the nearest dugger's bugle, and this would bring everything to a stop as the blast was echoed by all – and bring Matson at full and angry gallop. Maybe nobody else knew where they were, but he did, and he had a schedule he wanted to keep.

It was strange, though, that gallop, and those of the dugger horses. The horse was making no sound as its hooves struck invisible ground, although you could hear the great beast breathing hard and the sounds of saddle and rider.

Suddenly, in the row in front of her, one girl stepped in some mule droppings, slipped, and fell. There was the yell, the bugles, the very efficient stop, and here came Matson. He stopped and looked down at the fallen girl in disgust.

'We can't keep having this,' he said, mostly to himself. 'You! Get up – *now!*'

The girl gaped at him, then broke down and started sobbing, but she simply couldn't bring herself to her feet. Matson spat, gave a disgusted sigh, and made a casual gesture in her direction with his hand.

Energy flew from that hand in a pencil-thin line, striking the girl in the head, and she screamed in terrible agony. Just as quickly as it had appeared, the beam was gone, and the victim almost collapsed in relief. Matson waited a moment, then asked, casually, 'Want me to do it again?'

'No! Please! I—'

Another, very brief jolt was sent. 'Please *what*?'

'P – Please, sir!'

He nodded. 'Now get up and resume your place in line. You just had your warning. Next time it gets tough.'

'That son of a bitch,' some boy in the back muttered loudly. 'One day I'll kill the bastard for that.'

The stringer's head shot up, and his eyes seemed to glisten. 'Well, well, well … The gallant tough guy standing up for the little lady. How chivalrous. Trouble with chivalry, boy, is that then you got to make good on it.' He rode back several rows and looked directly at the offending boy, although it was impossible to see how he could have identified the speaker. 'I don't want to break you, son, because my customers are buying that spirit of yours, but I think I'll put a mark on you so I can remember you.'

Cassie found it hard to turn around and see properly without twisting the line, but she managed, as did most of them forward of the incident. She remembered the face of the boy Matson was confronting – he'd been the strong one with the 'brain of a cabbage' they were talking about as some sort of soldier.

Matson seemed to concentrate a moment, then he fixed his eyes intently on the outspoken boy. Energy flashed and coalesced around him, but only for a few seconds, and then vanished. The watching duggers chuckled, and those among the exiles who didn't scream either gasped or gaped.

The boy was in every way the same as he'd been from the shoulders down, but above that point he now had the perfectly proportioned head of a mule. The mule-mouth opened to say something, but only a mule's bray came out. His hands went up and felt along his neck and head, and you could feel the horror in his body movements.

'What I can do I can also undo, punk,' Matson told him. 'You give me no more trouble and I *might* be able to remember what your head used to look like and give it back to you. Any time you make threats in the Flux to *anybody* you be sure you can back 'em up all the way. There's worse things than being dead.' He moved forward on his horse and looked again at the girl whose fall had precipitated it all. 'Now, little lady, if you can't hack the pace, I can always use another pack mule. That's how I got most of the ones I'm using now anyway. Time is money, and I don't have much use for somebody who can't make the grade.' With that he raised his bugle, gave his command notes, and the train started forward once more through the void.

'It's *impossible*!' somebody muttered, and it was what the others were thinking. 'It can't be real! It just *can't* be!'

'It's magic, that's what it is,' a girl said worriedly. 'He's an evil wizard back in his own foul home.'

Matson was all the way forward again before he allowed himself a self-satisfied grin. The challenge had come very early this time, and he was glad of it. The earlier you acted, and the earlier you used your little bag of parlor tricks, the less trouble you had later on. That mule-head alone would hold them for a while. Like most stringers he was a false wizard, a weaver of totally convincing illusions, but they were good enough for kids like this. He liked to imagine what it would be like to be a *real* wizard, but he always had doubts. He liked to think that he'd still be a stringer, but you never could tell what that kind of power would do to any human.

8

Cult

After a while, the monotony of the void replaced any sense of fear or awe in their minds over the Flux. Their fear was still real, of course, and focused partly on their unknown fates and partly on their fear of Matson's frightening powers.

Every few hours they would break from their slow but steady pace and get something to eat. One of the wagons in the rear had a sort of mini-kitchen in it, and while the meals were not very tasty nor varied they were nutritious and filling, and everyone, Matson included, ate the same thing. The other wagon contained an enormous quantity of hay in small bales which were apportioned out to the mules by the ever-doting Jomo. It was clear that part of Matson's mania for a schedule once they started out was due to a tight supply allowance.

There was little trouble with the group after the initial episodes with Matson. If anybody had any rebellious thoughts they had only to look at the poor fellow trying to get the stew down his mule's throat to think the better of it.

Once she'd gotten over the initial shock of the magical transformation, however, Cassie could see some hope in it as well. 'Look,' she pointed out to Nadya and Suzl, 'if he can just wave his hands and make somebody half-mule, then nothing is permanent here. Nothing. That means we might have hair again, for example, and those poor girls with the body tattoos might one day look as good as they ever did. Maybe better.'

'Or worse,' the gloomier Nadya responded. 'All we've seen coming out of this Flux are monsters of one kind or another. These duggers, the mule head, that sort of thing. Maybe our new masters, whoever and whatever they are, just want us as raw material for animals or something. Matson, remember, said some of his mules were once human.'

'Maybe,' Cassie admitted, 'but I think it can work both ways. All we can do is hope right now.'

'I just wish we'd get somewhere,' Suzl put in. 'I'm sick and tired of this march, march, march. Good or bad, I want to just get it over with. A day or two more of this and I might turn into one of those drooling slobberers myself.'

They all pretty much felt that way, but the train's progress was slow and steady, the sleep periods seemingly dictated by Matson's feeling of how tired the marchers were and Jomo's feel of when the horses and mules needed rest. Time seemed to have lost its meaning for them all, although Matson, who carried an elaborate pocket watch, seemed to know exactly *when* as well as where they were. For the rest of them, the 'days' were measured only by sleep breaks and were broken down by feeding periods. It never seemed to get completely dark or completely light in the Flux, so there was no way at all to guess what it might be in 'real' time.

They were five 'days' into the Flux when the first break in the monotony came. They were proceeding normally after a meal break when suddenly a horse and rider appeared ahead of them and closed on Matson. He ordered the train to a halt and waited as the rider neared and stopped. It was the animal-like Kolada.

Kolada rode the 'point,' which meant she was often well ahead of the train, perhaps half a day ahead, following some sort of route mark that stringers had laid down but which few were given the power to see or read. Whatever the news it wasn't good, for there were sudden bugle signals of a type they had not heard before and the duggers whipped into action with a frenzy. All strings on mules and people were suddenly dropped, and the mules themselves were led into a circular pattern with the wagons at opposite ends closing each circle. Cinches were loosened, so that the packs formed a crude outer barrier around the mules. The duggers took out their weapons and checked them, then set up patrols both inside and outside the circle. The human cargo was loosed inside the circle and told just to sit.

Jomo took charge of the entire party, moving very fast for a huge man and giving orders in a combination of words and gestures to the other duggers. Matson took one of the duggers with him, leaving ten mounted and one afoot to guard the train, and the three of them went off at full gallop in the direction from which Kolada had just come.

None of the duggers would pay any attention to the fifty-four confused and frightened young people unless they got out of line, in which case the offender was rudely struck with fist or rifle butt. In more than one way this frightened them still more, if only because, no matter what Matson's disposition or powers were, he was human and a known quantity. Now they were completely at the mercy of these animalistic creatures.

They spent a nervous hour or more sitting there, talking low and speculating a lot, until there was a sudden shout from one of the duggers ahead and they heard bolts slide into place and the whole crew tense up.

It was Matson, though, and they relaxed. He rode up to Jomo and talked for some time, and they could see from the look on his face that there was something up ahead that had considerably shaken the iron man. His face looked almost dead white, and, if anything, he looked twenty years older.

He talked in low, clipped sentences to Jomo, who nodded and then gave a series of signals. Rapidly, the train was reassembled in a loose manner, with the duggers spacing themselves out and keeping guns at the ready. Although they ran the strings back along the mules, they only ran one string on each side back from the mules to the wagons, leaving the young people free inside this makeshift boundary. With a few quick bugle blasts, the train began to move.

It was a good hour or more before they reached the spot, but this was a different sort of march, tinged with danger and excitement. Many of the young people actually welcomed the diversion, but Cassie, along with many others, did not. It was like approaching an accident on the main highway from a distance. You wanted to see what was going on but you knew that when you got there you would find nothing good.

The scene was one of almost inconceivable carnage, the most horrible sight any of them had ever seen. Clearly the mess, spread out almost as far as the eye could see, had once been a stringer train not unlike their own, but one that had been hit with a deadly ferocity by some overwhelming force. There was blood all over, human blood mixing with that of animals, and dead bodies strewn all over the landscape. If you looked hard enough, it was possible to see that this had once been a formation similar to the one they'd assumed back a ways, but it had proved totally inadequate for whatever had hit them.

Matson had recovered some of his composure and came back to the group. He took a deep breath, then said, 'All right. Now you see it. I told you this was a rough place, and now you see how rough it can get. I'm telling you this because I'm going to need your cooperation to go through that mess and see what, if anything, can be salvaged and what we can learn about the bastards who did this. You're going to need a strong stomach for two reasons, so anybody who just can't handle it can remain here or come back here when it gets too much for you. One reason is that it's even uglier than you can tell from here. Some of the animals and people have been partly – eaten.'

The group stiffened almost collectively at this.

'The second reason is that this was – oh, hell, it was the other train from

Anchor Logh that should have been a day or more ahead of us. You will know or recognize some of those bodies.'

Some gasps, chokes, and sobs began from various parts of the group at this news. Matson didn't wait for it to subside.

'Now, not everybody is here, that's clear. That's one reason I need your help. If there's anybody you know who was in that train whose remains aren't there now, I want to know about it. We're only another hard day's ride from help, and if we know who to look for we might be able to save them. Also, whoever did this is still around. This happened only a matter of hours ago at best, from the state of the remains. We have to act fairly quickly, because the Flux tends to break down dead organic matter pretty quickly. I need to keep the duggers armed and on guard, so it's up to you. Volunteers?'

A dozen or so hands went up, including Cassie's, and he nodded and told them to come forward. They did, and walked straight into Hell itself.

Assuming the same size train, more than half the mules had been killed, the rest run off with the attackers. All of the remaining packs had been thoroughly ransacked, with the unwanted part of their contents just strewn about haphazardly. Both wagons had caught fire and been rendered useless, but it was clear that some of the contents there had been salvaged and prob-ably loaded on the remaining mules – and, perhaps, on the backs of the survivors.

All of the human bodies were stripped naked if they hadn't been to begin with, but it was easy to tell the duggers from the other group of exiles by their shape if nothing else. It was a stomach-churning chore to gather up all those bodies and lay them out so they could be potentially identified and counted. Several times members of the party suddenly felt sick; a few threw up, a few more finally ran back to the rest, but were quickly replaced by others whose curiosity or consciences now prodded them.

Most of the victims had been shot, some several times, but others were run through with arrows or spears. Some who had obviously been only wounded when the train was overrun had been put to death, most often by beheading but occasionally by slow dismemberment, the horror still on their faces. Many of the bodies had been chewed, with huge chunks of flesh just ripped from them, but it was unclear just what had done the chewing. What *was* clear was that whoever had overrun the train had been human, and probably in numbers far larger than the train's defenders.

Still, laid out, the bodies included some that could not be accounted for by duggers or exiles. These, too, had been treated just as harshly as the others, but they were clearly from some different place entirely.

For one thing, they resembled duggers but had some regularity to their dehumanizing aspects. They were mostly very tall, chunky females reminis-cent of the kind that became Temple wardens, but all had undergone animalistic metamorphosis that might show madness on the part of the perpetrator but at least showed some conscious planning.

The most obvious thing was that they all had thick heads of hair that apparently hadn't been cut in years. The shortest hair length was below the waist. Their fingers seemed unnaturally long, too, and terminated in very long, thick, sharp claws. Some of the bodies seemed covered from the waist down in very short fur with animalistic patterns and colorations, almost horse-like in texture and appearance, and all of these had tails resembling various animals – rabbit, horse, cat, they were all represented. Perhaps the most striking thing was their faces, though, with bushy, oddly upturned brows, and pink animal-like noses over mouths that seemed abnormally wide and which contained oversized, slightly protruding canines.

Although in a state of shock over the carnage, Cassie couldn't resist questions. 'What – what *are* they?' she asked Matson.

'People,' he responded dryly. 'Members of a cult. Looks like they got a fair number, too.' This last was said without any sense of exhilaration or pleasure. Matson had been curiously more cold and withdrawn since they began, but there was no trace of meanness, authoritarianism, or any other emotional mannerism. He was either holding something in very deeply or forced upon himself a remarkable detachment for the scene.

'Cult?' she prompted, treating him less like the slave master than as just someone else to talk to.

He nodded. 'Say you get a dugger type with some talent for the Flux who not only gets out here but can survive. He or she goes nuts, of course, but it's a crafty sort of nuts. Eventually these kind of people pick up other lost balls out here, maybe one day stumbling across a stringer train and catching a few escapees, something like that, or getting people trying to flee a Fluxland. This person gets 'em and imposes his particular kind of madness on them. They become his followers, his worshippers, his slaves – his playthings. If there's enough power available in the leader or in the collection they form a pocket in the Flux. A place where they can live and feed themselves. A real tiny little worldlet. They're around, usually near stringer trails, so they can sneak up and collect our garbage. This one is a lot more than that, though. There are few of 'em that can have the power to take on and lick a stringer train, and those few get known, we switch routes, and they wind up isolated. That's what's so weird about this one.'

'Huh?'

'Arden was the best stringer I ever knew, bar none. It would take an army to do this much damage to one of her trains, and she had the biggest, meanest duggers you ever saw. That's them over there. Any cult big enough and smart enough to take her is big or smart enough to take a Fluxland. It just couldn't remain hidden this long, then show up here, on a trail with no previous trouble. Something smells here. Smells bad. *I want these bastards!*'

That last was said with such sudden force and emotion that she stepped back from him. Inside him, not too far from that totally businesslike surface, was an explosion she would not like to see directed at her, even unthinkingly.

She went over to where the bodies were being laid out. It was almost complete now, but she had to force herself to look at them. It was a sight that no church vision of Hell could equal. Those dead warriors from this strange cult – how animalistic were they inside? More than they were outside? If so, could *they* or their kind have ripped out those pieces of flesh with their jaws? It was horrible to contemplate, but there seemed no other conclusion. What kind of sickness could breed ones like those?

Jomo, ugly and primitive as he was, was the only dugger she didn't fear. He came over to her and frowned, the effect producing hundreds of ripples in his broad hairless forehead. 'Saw you talkin' to Master Matson. Best you not if you know what good for you.'

'Why? He didn't seem to mind.'

Jomo looked over at the mass of corpses. 'You see any you know in this bunch?'

She nodded. 'Several.'

Jomo pointed a stubby finger at one off by itself, the figure of a woman, head shaved – or what was left of it. Most of the body was a bloody mess. 'That one not like you. That one Missy Arden. Great woman.'

'Oh, I see ...'

'No, you not see at all! *Missy Arden carry Matson child!*'

Suddenly she understood, and felt foolish. Of course, it made sense, only she had not, frankly, thought of stringers as having sex, let alone children. They were like doctors, teachers, priestesses – when you met them in a store in town or maybe saw them in a public bathroom it was, somehow, shocking and unusual, as if they didn't do the sort of things real people did.

If Jomo was right, and he had no reason to lie, then Matson right now was at his most dangerous, and that could be as fearsome as these cult members.

'Coduro!' Matson bellowed, and a dugger on horseback reigned up, turned, and came over to him.

'Yeah, boss?'

'I give you my string,' he said flatly. 'Can you see it?'

The dugger looked startled. 'Yeah! I – *can!*' It seemed to awe him, although the others had no idea what was going on.

'You take the string to Persellus. We'll have some time because this cult or whatever it has to stash its booty. Maybe enough time for us, maybe not, but if you start now you should be able to avoid them. They might have a sentry or two just up the string, though, so be careful.'

The dugger grinned, a sight that was in itself pretty gruesome to behold, and lifted his rifle. 'I think maybe I like that.'

'Well, don't let 'em bog you down, either. I want you in Persellus even if you have to kill your horse to do it, and you give the first important official you can meet the whole story. Tell 'em we're coming in, but also tell 'em the size and description of these bastards. We need protection to get in, even if I speed it up, and we better get this pest hole and eliminate it before *they* get strong enough and bold enough to make a try on Persellus. You tell 'em it's somebody with real wizard power. Tell 'em anything you want, but *get them here with a big force as soon as you can!*'

'Got'cha, boss. Rolling!' the dugger responded, then reared back on his horse and took off into the void which rapidly swallowed him up.

Matson walked back over to the mass of now neatly laid out bodies, and counted. Eleven of the beast-women, twelve duggers, Arden, of course, and twenty-nine refugees from Anchor Logh who would grow no older. He looked that last group over, then frowned and walked up and down between the bodies, nodding and mumbling to himself, then looked up and saw Cassie. 'You!'

She was startled. 'Yes, sir?'

'Notice anything funny about this group? Anything particular strike you?'

She frowned, coming over although she really didn't want to come near that terror again. Absently she looked down at one of the bodies and suddenly could not suppress a sob. *'Oh, Holy Angels! It's poor Canty!'* she managed.

Matson grunted, then took out and lit a cigar. 'Cut the hysterics. We don't have time for it. I lost somebody close to me here, too. She's dead, and so's he. If you don't want us to be you'll put them behind you until you get a chance to do something about it and concentrate on us. Now, how many boys were in that Paring Rite shit?'

She fought back the tears as best she could. 'Fifty,' she told him.

He nodded. 'And we have twenty-two in our group, so there were twenty-six in Arden's. We've got twenty-nine bodies from the other group here, and only three are female.'

She snapped out of it and gasped. 'And some of them were executed after they lost!'

He nodded. 'Whoever our bastard is, he only likes the girls. All those fighters were women, and he took all the women while killing all the men. That sounds like Rory Montagne, but that son of a bitch doesn't have enough power for all this.'

Despite Jomo's warning, and despite her own situation, she could not break away. It was obvious that, no matter what happened to her later, right now Matson needed a relatively sane human to talk to and she had more or less elected herself. 'Who is this Rory Montagne?'

'A cult leader from way back, but thousands of kilometers from here. He's a woman-hater, and, therefore, a church-hater as well.'

'Seems to me he *likes* women, maybe too much,' she pointed out.

'Oh, no. His hatred of the church is so absolute that his mission in life is the capture, submission, and humiliation of women. Every woman represents the church to him, and every time one becomes his slave or plaything he's scored in his own warped mind. But – he never had this kind of strength or power before. They've been hunting him as long as I can remember, but he's always been a nuisance rather than a real threat. I can see why his attack was particularly savage, though. When he saw a woman stringer he just couldn't help himself.' He paused for a moment, then seemed suddenly galvanized into action. 'Can you ride a mule bareback?'

'I can ride anything with four legs,' she assured him. 'So can half of us.'

Matson turned and called in the duggers. 'We're going to fast march,' he told them. 'All speed. Cut loose all but totally essential cargo, and get the rest into the wagons. Toss what you have to. Spare rations only.' They nodded and set to work. He turned back to Cassie. 'Pick your best riders. I want two on each mule. Jomo is already cutting them loose and rigging basic bridles. The rest will cram into the two wagons and I don't care about comfort. I don't care how it's done, but everybody rides, understand?'

She nodded, then hesitated. 'Uh – what about the bodies? Shouldn't we bury or cremate them or something?'

'No time. Doesn't matter, anyway. In a week the Flux will have absorbed them, and in a month the rest will be gone, too. Anything that doesn't move for any length of time goes back to energy. Don't stand and worry about those things. They're dead. Move it!'

She did. Four of the twenty mules still had to carry supplies, so that left sixteen available. She went back, not really explaining anything, and started making choices. She wanted the largest people on the mules, to make more room in the wagons, so most of the boys were paired up, and that took eleven of the mules. Reserving one for herself and, she decided, Nadya, she assigned the rest to the larger girls with some riding experience. That still left twenty-two people to fit someplace, and some food and hay had to remain in the wagons. She managed to get twelve in the cook's wagon, although very cramped and uncomfortably, but because of the bulk she only could get eight in the hay wagon. When she could get no volunteers among the girls to sit next to the driving duggers, who were the worst sort of the lot, she pulled Ivon and the poor fellow with the mule's head off their mounts, replaced them with girls, and stuck them on the wagon seats.

Ivon didn't seem too thrilled, but he had too much self-image to refuse to do it. The driver, a hulking, hunched creature with bulging, mismatched eyes and a tongue hanging out of its mouth, giggled and snorted at him and seemed to be having a good time sensing his discomfort.

Matson placed one wagon, the hay wagon, at the head of this new train, and the other in the rear. It looked very strange, but it was a much shorter train now and easier to guard. Jomo had improvised a four-across bridle and rein combination for the four remaining pack mules, and managed them while somehow perched in front of the pack on one of them. Cassie, in the first row of mules with riders, admired the troll-like man's tremendous skill.

They were underway before Nadya, hanging on to her for dear life, asked, 'What suddenly made you an honorary dugger?'

Cassie smiled. 'I don't know. I guess I've been a professional shoulder to cry on all my life. I never could figure it out but I'm not asking questions.'

They did make better speed, but the combination of mules and mostly inexperienced mule riders did not make for a really good pace, and mules tended to set their new pace and come to a halt when they wanted a drink from the canisters under the hay wagon or when they were just too tired. Matson's powers could give them more energy and will, but even he could only do so much with a mule, and it was almost fifty kilometers to this land of Persellus.

They made very good time, but there came a time when the mules and even the horses really couldn't be pushed much further. They needed a rest, and the riders, although still haunted by visions of the slaughter they'd just left behind, particularly the visions of the dead faces of people they'd known and shared a lot with over the past weeks, could take only so much on mule back, bare as their own bottoms were.

Finally Matson called a halt, and they got down, many feeling terrible pain from muscles they had seldom used. They were not allowed to rest just yet, though. The mules had to be tended first, and this time individually, and the stringer and his duggers arranged a security line, or as much of one as they could with most of the packs and hay left behind. The mules would be their primary fortress, although the remaining hay bales were hauled out and spaced around the encampment as firing positions. Only then were they allowed to eat the hard bread and cold beans that was all that was saved, and get drinks of water themselves.

When they were finished, Matson walked over to the group. 'Any of you know how to shoot a rifle or shotgun?' he asked them.

There was no response. All save the border guards and the police were forbidden any access to firearms in Anchor Logh.

'I was afraid of that,' Matson sighed. 'All right, we're still going to sleep in shifts. I want at least two of you up with each dugger at each gun position, and I want a few more on watch in the gaps. It may bore the hell out of you but you just remember your friends back there and what happened to them. If you'd rather live, then you try and not be bored. If you see *anything*, and I mean *anything* out there, or even if you just imagine you do, you sing out. The first one that goes to sleep on duty gets to be another of my mules. The first one who misses something and doesn't give a warning will wish he or she *was* a mule!' He looked over at Cassie. 'You! What's your name?'

'They call me Cassie, sir.'

He snorted. 'Too long. You're Cass. Anybody ever call you that?'

'A lot of people.'

'Better to have a strong, one-syllable name that can be yelled in a pinch anyway. You're strong and you have a knack with people. I'm putting you in charge and that means the rest of you take orders from her like you would from me or my people. Cass, you pick your guards for each period, then get some sleep.'

She was amazed. 'Yes, *sir*!' she responded, shaking her head a bit. She was no more amazed and awe-struck by the sudden promotion than the rest of them, some of whom looked a little resentful. Well, so what? she told herself. Maybe she'd become a dugger herself or something. It sure beat some of the alternatives.

The attack began slowly, with a cautious sounding out. Two duggers, looking battered and bleeding, reeled into view and began half walking, half crawling towards the circle. The alarm was sounded almost immediately, and in an instant everyone was awake and tensely at what positions they could take.

'Don't shoot! Don't shoot! We're from the Arden train!' one of them called out weakly.

'You stop now or this scattergun's gonna end things for you in the next three seconds,' Matson shouted back. 'How the hell do I know who or what you are?'

'We're from the train, the Arden train,' gasped the talkative one, but both stopped where they were. 'Happened hours ago. They were all around us ...'

'What was her whip's name?' he shouted back, unmoved. 'You have three more seconds!'

'Whip – what?' the wounded dugger gasped, looking confused.

'If you don't even know the name of Cuso, then there's no reason to let you live,' the stringer said icily, raising his shotgun.

'Oh, *Cuso!* Sure, sure. I thought you meant—'

'*Her name was Herot, you scum!*' Matson snarled at them and opened fire.

The air was suddenly alive with shapes; terrible, nameless, gibbering monsters who were all hating eyes and gaping, tooth-filled mouths, the dark monsters of nightmare and madness, dripping blood and screaming foully at them.

Matson and his duggers opened up on them, ignoring the flying things and at all times shooting low. From the mass of the monstrous attackers came occasional screams of agony as bullets and shot found their mark in the sea of terrible illusion.

But there was one hell of a lot of them. Matson took a moment to concentrate, and his head snapped back, then forward again with his eyes suddenly burning with power and concentration. 'Armies of the void, attend me!' he commanded loudly over the din of battle, and suddenly, around the outer perimeter of the train appeared hundreds of huge, dark apelike shapes with eyes of red fire. The monsters, so huge and thick that they completely shielded the train, started roaring back at the attacking shapes and then slowly advanced outward.

It was a clever maneuver, Matson's best trick. The attacking cult had only limited power on its own, and that concentrated in its leader, but it used illusion with great skill and cunning, creating for their prey what they themselves feared most and sending it forth in the hopes that those nightmares might equally terrify others.

But there were wizards in the Flux as well as illusionists; wizards who had the power to create out of the void a true and living demon army. Matson and his duggers knew that everything sent against them now was illusion, but the attackers could have no such assurance that the reverse was also true.

And so the stringer, himself a master of illusion, cast upon them a hundred demonic beasts at least as horrible as those being hurled at him, but Matson's beasts all had the same name and it was Doubt, and it had an immediate effect.

The mad shapes attacking the train shimmered, winked in and out, and seemed to lose much of their steam as their creator hesitated in the face of the counterattack. And because of their creator's diverted attention, when the monsters winked out it revealed the ones behind them.

Automatic rifles on wide spray had a devastating effect, even in the void; in the midst of a fading scenario of Hell, bullets found mark after mark, causing odd shapes to cry out and fall back, some dropping in their tracks and laying there in pools of their own blood.

Matson halted his own shooting routine and concentrated once more. 'Armies of the void, back to guard this train!' he shouted.

The huge demonic shapes paused, then did a backwards step in perfect unison, then another and another. Matson only hoped he'd been in time. No matter how crazy or frenzied some of these culties were, they'd notice, if given a chance, that for the past few, seconds the train had been shooting *through* their allegedly real phantom army. Although the Anchor people could just crouch down and wonder, the duggers understood immediately what the problem was and ceased firing, taking the time to shift positions and thus not be where they would be expected.

Matson stuck the stump of an unlit cigar in his mouth and peered out at the void, which was suddenly deathly quiet and still once more. Jomo, Cass, and several others helped reload new clips into rifles as the break lengthened. 'How many did you make, Jomo?' the stringer asked.

'We shoot twelve, maybe more,' the big mule driver responded. 'They was at least as many left.'

Matson nodded agreement. 'Yeah, I figure we still got another dozen, maybe fifteen out there. Bastards. I wonder if any of 'em noticed our more than natural shooting?'

At that moment explosions went off all around them, the concussions knocking several of them back, and from all sides huge, lizard-shaped creatures reared up and hissed defiance.

'I think maybe somebody notice!' Jomo called back, and began shooting again into the now crowded void.

'Well, we'll just see how *they* like their eardrums broken!' Matson called back. He made a series of sweeping gestures with his hand and went around in a nearly three hundred and sixty degree circle as the duggers continued their shooting.

Cass continued to supervise the reloading, so that all of the ones who could shoot had an almost continuous supply of firepower. She saw Dar come up to her operation, near Matson, and look at the rifles and then Matson. She frowned. 'What are you thinking?'

'Lani – she has to be with *them*. It don't look so hard. One shot …'

'One shot and you'll kill yourself and maybe all of us!' she screamed back at him. 'He's the only chance we got. Dar! They killed all the boys last time!'

He looked at her strangely. 'You've gone completely over to him, ain't you? You forgot what he is, and you don't give a damn any more about the rest of us.'

Before she could reply he launched himself at her. At that moment all of Matson's mentally placed charges went off in a great circle of fireworks so effective that it pushed over not only the attackers but half the train as well.

Dar recovered first, and, in his crazed mental state, struck Cass hard on the jaw with his fist, knocking her cold. In the recovery and follow-up shooting to the concussions, nobody really noticed him pick up her limp body and sprint for a weak spot in the line to the rear of Matson. The giant lizard-things, frozen for a moment in the shock of the explosions, did not deter him one bit, for he did not believe in them. A dugger saw him running with her, but as his rifle was on spray he didn't dare shoot for fear of hitting the unconscious captive on his shoulder. By the time an alarm was shouted and his rifle readjusted, Dar, carrying the unconscious Cass like a sack of potatoes, was behind the monsters and out of sight of the train.

9

Pocket

Cass awoke to a scene out of nightmare. All around her was the void, yet she was not in it any more. She tried to turn and see just how far it was, but couldn't manage, and it was only then that she realized that she was bound to a flat slab of some kind, arms and legs out in spreadeagle fashion, while something also held her through the neck and waist rings, making much movement impossible.

After the first few fuzzy moments she remembered what had happened, remembered Dar's crazy lunge – and then what?

The slab was angled slightly upward, so she had a view of what was in front of her. It was in fact an eerie and impossible scene, an outcrop of reddish rock rising up perhaps fifty meters over which spilled a small waterfall whose effluent landed in a pool below but did not seem to either drain to a creek or flood. There was a cave in back of the waterfall, but it was impossible to tell who or what might be inside. Around the pool were a number of palm trees and small bushes, and there seemed to be a few trees and bushes growing here and there all around the place. The void was just in back of the large rock, and she couldn't imagine where the water was coming from.

She was not alone. It seemed that there were an endless number of slabs set back from the pool area in an eerie sort of amphitheater, and while it was difficult to see much at that level she was certain that each slab held someone, similarly bound as she was.

Around the pool and waterfall there were – shapes. She was far enough away and at a bad angle so that at first she could not identify them, but suddenly she knew what they were. They were women, very much like those bodies at the massacre site. Primitive, part animal, some scampering about with animal-like motions, others crouched down and eating or gnawing on something. They looked like the visions of Hell painted by the church in sermon after sermon. In fact, except for the eerie warm light the whole scene resembled a painting of Hell that hung in the temple at Anchor Logh.

For a moment her upbringing broke through her skepticism. *Have I died?* she wondered. *Did Dar's blow or the attackers of the train kill me?* But no, she decided at last. She might have believed it if she hadn't seen those bodies, but she knew better. Those were real savages who attacked, and so were these. She wondered, though, if Dar had gone on to kill Matson and thus allow the second train to be overrun as well. She could hear, but not see, the noises of mules off to her right.

Suddenly the savage women near the pool stopped what they were doing and scattered, making agitated noises. From the cave behind the small waterfall emerged a group of four of the women carrying on their shoulders a body seemingly strapped to a cross-like structure made of wood. They walked through the waterfall and down a small path to the right side of it, then around the pool, finally approaching Cass and the others on the slabs. There was a neatly drilled hole in the rock at the base of the grisly amphitheater, and the structure and its occupant were hoisted into place so that the base of the cross was securely in the hole. It swayed a moment, but then settled and held firm. Cass gasped as she finally recognized the figure on the cross.

It was Dar.

He looked dazed and only semi-conscious, but in some pain. He seemed to be bound with tight metal clamps around his wrists and by strong rope through the neck and waist rings. It held him secure and helpless, but hardly comfortably.

A large figure now emerged from the cave and walked slowly down the path, around the pool, and up to the hapless man on the cross. This newcomer was dressed entirely in black robes without adornment of any kind, although he wore a large golden medal on a chain around his neck. It was impossible to tell what was stamped on the round medallion from Cass's vantage point.

The primitive women seemed to treat this dark one with reverence and awe, and gathered silently to watch. It was hard to do much counting, but there seemed to be no more than seven or eight of them.

The dark one threw back his hood to reveal a round, distinguished looking face with a carefully cropped goatee and short hair, black once but now tinged with gray. He looked over at the savage women and made a gesture, and they prostrated themselves and virtually grovelled at him. He smiled and turned to the ones on the slabs.

'Why, hello!' he said cheerfully, in a cultured if highly accented voice, almost as if he hadn't really noticed them before. 'You are all doubtlessly wondering why I've brought you here today, not to mention where this is, who I am, and what will happen now. I shall be most happy to explain it all to you.'

He gave a benign smile and then continued. 'I am Roaring Mountain, high priest of the powers of darkness, anointed so by the Seven Who Come Before, which you might know as the Seven Who Wait.'

There were a few sounds at this, but no great outcry. Most of them had expected as much, if nothing else, from the familiar scenario.

'This is my holy place,' he went on, 'my *temple*, if you will, a place of life in the midst of the void established for my own and Hell's convenience. No, you are not dead, nor are you dreaming. You have instead received a signal honor. You have gone to Hell while still alive.'

He sighed, but it was clear that he was quite a ham actor and enjoying every moment of this.

'Now, then, that takes care of two of the questions. As to what I, and my followers, and this place are doing here – we are, quite simply, guarding one of the seven gates to Hell. It is not far from here, and while it is guarded by a different sort we can take it, given sufficient personnel, at the time and convenience of our own choosing. And *that*, of course, is what *you* are doing here.'

Cass could already see, with some horror, where he was going with this, but like the rest she could do nothing but watch.

'When we struck our first blow not long ago, we had thirty-five soldiers in the cause, but many of them were outcasts in the void and thus did not have the reason or discipline to be more than, shall we say, rifle fodder. Only ten now remain, alas, but there is cheer, for now we have an additional twenty-six of *you*.'

Cass began doing some mental arithmetic. Arden's train had twenty-four survivors, plus her, plus Dar, there. She felt at least a tingle of excitement and relief that Matson had obviously beaten off the attack. Roaring Mountain had obviously lost too many in the first attack, which must have been nearly suicidal, to have a chance of taking theirs. So she'd been abducted by Dar, who'd escaped the train and been taken prisoner by these people. She had to wonder if Dar had enough sense left in his head to have some second thoughts about that. There was no doubt that this strange man was the same one Matson had guessed was behind it all. Roaring Mountain. Rory Montagne.

'Now, what we will require to eventually *liberate* this gate I estimate at about one hundred smart, dedicated troops. The attack on the first train brought us a tremendous quantity of arms and ammunition which we are still cataloging, not to mention explosives and other useful devices. It also brought us twenty-five fresh, sharp young people to be the vanguard of that new army.'

Cass frowned. Twenty-five? That couldn't be right.

'Oh, I know what you're thinking,' the dark man went on. 'Me? Work for Hell? Never! But consider – it was your own church that cast you out. It was your own kind who branded you, tortured you, then sold you as slaves. It is they who deserve the punishment, not you! See! With your own group rode one of the harlots of the church!' He snapped his fingers, and two of his savages went out of view and came back with a small figure dressed in a white robe, hands bound. But it couldn't be a novice – this woman had a fair amount of hair.

Cass gaped, recognizing Lani instantly. So that was how they'd gotten her out of the Anchor. She looked uncertain and frightened, but she looked up at the man on the cross and gave a short cry as she recognized Dar. The demonic priest's eyebrows went up. 'Ah, then you know this fellow. Very good. Darkness provides symmetry, always. *Now look only at me!'* He reached out and pulled her face around until he was staring down into her eyes. She stiffened, then seemed to relax so well that the two savages had to help support her.

'Just like all the others,' the dark man sneered, an expression of madness creeping over his face. 'Just like all those harlots in robes who are the chief whores, selling out their people and themselves. It is an abomination for women to so rule and control men!' He reached down and ripped off the white robe, revealing her voluptuous naked body. She had, Cass had to admit to herself, one hell of a body.

This, too, did not escape the attention of Roaring Mountain. His madness faded into a broad grin, and he made a few signs with his hand in front of her face. She stiffened, almost like a statue, and the dark man motioned the support away. At that moment Dar seemed to come to. He groaned and looked down at the little scene in front of him in confusion. 'Lani?' he managed.

Roaring Mountain turned and looked at the man on the cross. 'Well, this is unexpected timing. You, sir, present me with a problem. A moral dilemma, if you will. On the one hand, you defected, bringing with you a much-appreciated offering. On the other hand, Hell's minions in this holy cause must be female, for it is fitting that the just cause of Hell be carried out by those very types who oppose us so desperately. Nor, of course, could I allow the distraction of you to be around while we get about our work. Tell me – this girl here. Sister, perhaps? Or lover?'

Dar still seemed completely confused by the situation. 'Lover,' he responded.

'Ah! So they start their whoring younger than even I believed.' He thought for a moment, then nodded to himself. From his robe he produced a large, sharp knife similar to the one Matson had. 'To kill you would be an injustice. Therefore, we must be delivered from temptation and all will work out.' He turned to Lani. 'Girl? Open your eyes and look upon the man up there.'

She did, although still in a trance-like state.

'Do you know him?'

'It is Dar,' she responded woodenly.

He nodded. 'And you want Dar, don't you?'

'Yes.'

'You know what you want from him. You can see it hanging there, can't you?'

Lani seemed to tremble slightly. 'Yes. Oh, yes.'

'But who do you belong to now? Who must have your total devotion?'

'You, Master.'

'Then you must prove your devotion. You must give me what you want most.' He handed her the knife, and she took it. 'Now go to that which you want most and bring it to me.'

They all held their collective breaths, but the savages seemed amused as well as fascinated by the grisly sadism of their master.

Lani walked over to Dar, the knife outstretched. At last he understood at least this much and screamed, 'Lani! In the name of all that's holy, no! *Please!*' he sobbed.

The knife moved. Dar screamed, and suddenly there was blood all over. The girl knelt down and picked up the severed genitals and brought them back to Roaring Mountain, laying both the grisly object and the knife at his feet, kneeling in front of them.

Sparks flashed from the dark man's hand, and Dar stopped screaming and was still. The blood and wound on him vanished, and in the pubic region there was a very natural-looking female vaginal cavity, complete with pubic hair.

'He is otherwise unchanged,' Roaring Mountain told his captive audience. 'I took the model from his own lady love, so in this sense they are one.' He chuckled over his gruesome humor. 'Dar! Awaken free of pain!'

Dar's body moved, then his eyes opened and again he looked confused. Two of the savages released his bonds and he fell limply to the rocky floor but soon shook his head and got up. All of the onlookers who could still either bear to watch or hadn't passed out just from the shock and horror of the scene waited to see what would happen now.

'Arise, Lani,' the priest of Hell commanded, and she did. 'Girl, you have been punished for your sins and purged of them. Boy, you have also received justice. Do you both understand that?'

Both just nodded.

'Very well. Then the two of you are the vanguard of our new army. You, Dar, will be my general, and you, Lani, will be his aide. Both of you will lead, together, the mighty crusade. Do you agree?'

Lani, still mostly under his spell, breathed, 'Yes, Master.' Dar, who still hadn't sorted it all out, asked, 'Then we'll be together?'

'Yes, of course. You have paid a high price for it, why not?'

Dar nodded and squeezed Lani's hand. The sight was bizarre. 'Then we'll fight for you.'

Roaring Mountain sighed. 'Ah, true love conquers all. Both of you can go back in the cave and get to know each other better if you wish. We have more business here.'

Cass had watched the whole thing and felt sick at it, but she found her emotions mixed. Those two certainly deserved each other, that was for sure, and she felt little pity about their enduring fate, either, for Roaring Mountain had obviously greatly enhanced their lust for one another while rendering that lust impossible to consummate the way they wanted it. The true sickness in the scene was the dark one below, and his powers, which were obviously real – or were they? Matson's had certainly looked real, and they were but illusions.

Roaring Mountain approached the slabs and looked down at his first helpless captive. For a while he caressed, cajoled, and stroked her helpless figure in a scene of particular horror considering that the onlookers could only witness their own fate. It looked like rape was inevitable, but suddenly the dark one stopped, that look of mad fury coming back into his face. 'All the same! All the same!' he snapped, sounding both insane and violent. Suddenly Cass realized the source of that madness and that insane hatred. It was the only thing that made sense.

Roaring Mountain was himself full of lust, but he was also impotent. The man with the power to make women worship him and to change the sex of another couldn't get it up himself. How he must be filled with hate! No wonder he could abide no normal male around. Dar, in fact, would have to be his favorite, for the mad wizard had bestowed on the boy the ultimate impotence.

'Nonetheless, you are mine!' he roared, and made a pass over the girl with his right hand. Two of the savages then ran up and undid the bonds, and the dark one held out his hand and pulled the hapless girl to her feet.

She was transformed. She was in fact extremely well built herself, although it was impossible to know how much had been exaggerated by Roaring Mountain's frustrations. From her extremely narrow waist down her body was now covered in a fine brown hair terminating in two very large cloven hooves which the legs had been reconfigured to support, and from the end of her spinal column now grew a short, stubby, goat-like tail. She had a rich head of hair once more, too, of the same brownish color, but her face below her eyes had elongated a good five centimeters, giving her what could only be described as a pug-like snout. Finally, through her hair, rose two short, blunt goat-like horns.

'Behold the first of a new race,' Roaring Mountain thundered. 'This shall be the model for the future of all harlots of World!' He sounded coldly furious now, and stretched out both hands at the captive multitude. At the end he issued some commands, and the first row was released. All were helped to their feet, and all looked exactly like the first creature he had made.

Cass, in the third row, could only wait for it with mounting horror. Far worse than the transformation, for there was nothing permanent in the Flux and anything done could be undone, was the totally silent submissiveness of the newly made creatures who but moments before had been captive girls just like she. The dark priest did the second row, and they became as the first. It was only when the first group came up to unbind the second that they were close enough for Cass to see the depth of the transformation. In one way, Roaring Mountain was right – this was a whole new race, and she was next to join it!

Well, at least I'll finally have some tits, she thought inanely, her grip on sanity very, very thin.

'Hold!' commanded a deep, booming, authoritarian voice behind them, and Roaring Mountain stopped, then turned and himself dropped to his knees, as did all the savages and transformees, following his lead.

The speaker and object of this worship walked into view. He was *enormous*, standing fully three meters high and fully proportioned with muscles to match. He also had a goat-like head with huge ram's horns, deep purple skin covering his human-looking body, and he wore a loose-fitting robe of crimson satin open at the chest but tied off with a belt at the waist.

'Oh, great Prince of Hell, we welcome thee,' Roaring Mountain intoned.

'Oh, get up from there,' the giant goat-man muttered disgustedly. 'We have business to discuss.'

'I was just in the holy process of –' the dark priest began, getting up hastily.

'Of turning excellent raw material into mindless savages. Yes, I know. I'm beginning to wonder about you, I really am. I fear the hangups that attracted us to one another may be too much for you to do a decent job. Well, we'll see.' The creature looked up at the dozen or so girls still tied down. 'You couldn't be satisfied with the one train. No, you had to go after another one without replacing your losses from the first attack.' He sighed. 'Sometimes, oh Roaring Mountain, I think I should transform you into a giant asshole.'

The priest looked stricken. 'Please, Master! I can explain!'

'Bullshit! I went and carved this homey pocket in a very convenient location and handed you the nucleus of an army. If you had any sense you'd have struck at the first train, forgotten the second, and now be well on your way to training that expanded force. Instead, here you are creating a new wild animal species with barely more than you had before! Worse, yet, you didn't take that second train. They'll be back in force, hunting for this pocket now.'

The priest looked suddenly concerned. 'Then hadn't we better do something?'

The goat-man cleared his throat impatiently. 'Yes, I think we better. Any captives from that second train? I mean, any you haven't already transformed into mindless idiots?'

'One, Master – no, two!' He looked up at Cass and pointed. 'That one there, for example.'

The mysterious giant nodded his goat's head and walked up the rocky surface between the slabs and looked down at her. After what she had just witnessed and now expected to go through, she was anything but taken aback by this great apparition.

'What's your name, girl?' the goat-man demanded to know.

'Cass,' she told him. There was no use in being coy, particularly when she knew she was facing the power behind this little throne.

'Now, then, Cass – you were with the second train?'

'Yes, sir.'

'Whose train was it? What was the name of the stringer?'

'Matson, sir.'

'Um. Damn. And I suppose he sent a dugger ahead to Persellus when he saw the remains of the first train?'

'Yes, sir. Straightaway.'

He turned to Roaring Mountain. 'Another stupid mistake. I don't suppose you left anybody to take care of that little detail?'

The priest shrugged. 'How was I to know there'd be a second train by so soon? Besides, I lost a lot of troops there.'

'Idiot.' He turned back to Cass. 'You don't seem particularly frightened by me.'

'In the past few days I've been sold to a stringer, forced marched in the void, cleaned up after a massacre, been in a fight, and just now I witnessed a castration and the turning of a lot of good people into animals, and I was about to join them myself when you showed up. I'm sorry, sir master wizard or whatever you are. I just don't think I have any more fright left.'

The giant was impressed. 'Now *this* is something special, priest. A hundred like this and we could rule World. And you were about to turn her into a slavish goat-woman!' He paused a moment, controlling his temper. 'Do you know who and what I am?'

'A wizard. Isn't that what they call people like you?'

The goat man crouched down, and she could see that the goat head was not some sort of mask. Either it was all illusion or else the man had literally changed himself into this whatever it was. She decided on the latter, noticing that he wore a ring with a serpent design on his right ring finger. She also noticed that he was most certainly left-handed.

'I'm one of the Seven Who Wait,' the creature told her. 'Does that bother you?'

'Not particularly,' she answered honestly. 'The church hadn't exactly impressed me for honesty and sincerity. I see no reason why your side should be much different.'

He looked at her for a moment. 'There is great power in you,' he told her. 'I can feel it. Tremendous latent power that even now makes tentative probes at my defenses. Your very calmness, your intelligence, and your almost magnetic ability to get into the worst of situations makes me suspicious. I have seen this combination before, in many bodies, with many faces.' He sighed and got up and turned to Roaring Mountain. 'Come. Your fun here can wait. We must talk and soon, for I must be quickly gone from here. I warn you though not to try your tricks with that one. What she has within her is stronger than you. For your own sake, kill her.'

Cass suddenly felt some fear return, particularly when the priest grinned and said, 'I'll do it right now.'

'No! Not until I am gone.' Was that a worried tone in the master wizard's voice? What sort of power, she wondered, did *she* have that even one of the Seven, if that was who he was, would not like to take on?'

The two men of evil walked away, and Roaring Mountain went to the cave. Dar met him at the entrance just inside the waterfall and they exchanged a few words. Then Dar nodded, and the evil priest rejoined his master and they went off out of view. Dar hesitated a moment, then walked out and over to the slabs, then up to Cass herself. None of the savages or goat-women made any attempt to stop him.

Roaring Mountain had given Dar practically everything, she saw. His build, already considerable, was now totally filled and so muscular that you could see every flex or movement in them, and his already strong, lean, handsome face was somehow altered into near total perfection, set off by a crop of thick, black hair. If there *were* male gods, then he was the absolute perfection of them – with one detail importantly missing. He was Roaring Mountain's pet joke.

'Come to gloat?' she asked him sourly. 'Or cry on my shoulder, which isn't very good for that sort of thing right now.'

'He ordered me to kill you,' he told her. 'As soon as goat-face was gone.'

She sighed. 'Well, go ahead. Get it over with.'

'I'm not going to do it, Cass.' He reached down and freed the restraints binding her to the slab. She sat up uneasily, a little suspicious but feeling that she had nothing to lose.

'Now what am I supposed to do? Run and be eaten alive by those *things* over there?'

He shook his head slowly. 'No. They won't hurt you. Look, I did a dumb thing. I did a *lot* of dumb things. I just kept thinking of Lani, and that she was out here, and then I saw you start acting like that stringer's partner and it all just sort of snapped. I kind of deserve this, I guess, but you don't.'

She suddenly felt a little uneasy. 'Where's Lani now, Dar?'

'Dead,' he said softly. 'I killed her. I –' his voice choked a bit – 'I put her out of her misery, really. That bastard made me a woman who looks like a man, thinks like a man, wants like a man. He made her all sex, frenzied like, and only for me – and I couldn't do a damned thing. She was in torture from his games, Cass – I gave her peace.'

She was silent a moment, not wanting to desert him but fearful that Roaring Mountain, who couldn't be far off, might return at any second. 'What do you want me to do?'

'Look, they have to have a war party heading this way. I say we take our chances, get into the void, and wait. The odds ain't great, but even if we did it's better than staying here.'

She was surprised. 'We? You're coming, too?'

He nodded. 'Oh, I thought about killing myself, but I got this real urge inside me to pay 'em back. Pay 'em *all* back, like you said back in the gym at the start. I want to get these bastards, and particularly I want to get the ones that caused this back in Anchor Logh. Will you come?'

She thought a moment. 'What about the others here?'

'No time, and too big a risk. Either they'll be rescued or they won't, but if we take the whole mob they'll catch us sure.'

'All right, then. Let's move.'

They walked in back of the slabs and she found it a level area above the encampment, mostly more of the sheet rock with little growing. She could see the whole thing from up there and was shocked to see how tiny the place really was. They had less than twenty meters to reach the void, and they made it before any alarms were sounded, holding hands so they would not get separated.

As soon as they were in the void itself she stopped him. 'What's the matter?' he asked nervously.

'We don't want to get too far from the pocket or we'll just wind up lost and alone,' she told him. 'I say let's walk just a hundred paces in a straight line, counting from now. If we can't see the pocket from there, then we stop and wait there.'

'Fair enough for a start,' he agreed, and began the counting process. At a hundred paces they stopped and looked back. There was a very slight, almost imperceptible lightening of the void in the direction from which they'd come, but otherwise there was no way to know that anything was there. It provided the only orientation they had, so they decided to settle for it. There was nothing to do now but sit down on the soft, spongy, invisible ground and wait until they had to return or strike out blindly in search of food and water.

'I wanted to bring a canteen, at least,' Dar told her, 'but all that stuff was over by the mules and so were they.' They sat in silence for a while, and Cass lay back and tried to relax as much as she could. Although they were most probably dead people at this point, the immediate terrors were out of the way and she found herself suddenly unable to stop shaking and crying a bit. She just didn't fight it any more, and let it come, and it was a long time flowing from her. Dar held her and tried to comfort her, and it was some time before she realized that he was crying, too.

Coduro had brought half the armed might of Persellus, from the looks of it, including two officers of high rank that were real wizards, albeit of lesser powers.

'One of mine went nuts and defected, carrying off a girl,' he told them. 'We beat them off and cost them some lives, but with all the captives he's got this bastard has another army at his command. How many troops you got with you?'

The colonel, a bearded man in his fifties but in prime condition and looking ready for a fight, responded, 'Fifty experienced soldiers, a chief noncom, and the captain and myself. But how are you going to find a tiny pocket in all this space? They could be *anywhere* by now. We came as an escort, not a raiding party.'

'Well, I'll lead you to his pocket,' the stringer told him. 'I don't know why except I kind of took a liking to her, but I put my string on the girl he carried off. It'll lead us right to them.'

'Well! That's different! Tremendous stroke of luck, though.'

Matson suddenly hesitated. It *was* an odd thing, him putting that string on the only one that was captured. He'd never done anything like that before in his life, and he didn't know why he'd done it this time. He shrugged, went about his business, and didn't think much more on it as he recreated the strong defensive position. He didn't think the cult could possibly have turned all those captives into troops that could be used effectively in so short a time, but he didn't want to return here and find out he was wrong, either. Finally he remounted his horse and went over to the soldiers. 'Let's go get 'em,' he said enthusiastically.

Rory Montagne, he thought as he rode. A minor real wizard, able to make changes in individual human and animal bodies but that was all. He certainly wouldn't have the power to create a pocket on his own. The one he'd used for years down near Anchor Dowt had been an old one created by some wizard traveling the void long ago, or so the story went. He remembered when Montagne was still leading a double life out of Haratus, a Fluxland near there, acting as a scenic designer for the local wizard while kidnapping a number of local women, one by one, and hauling them off to this pocket of his for who knew what purpose? Finally the bastard had picked on a woman who happened to be a drill instructor at the local military school and he'd damn near had his balls kicked off and was lucky to escape with his life.

What was he doing here?

The tiny, thin energy trail left by Cass was ragged but not hard for him to follow, since it had his personal frequency. They did not have a long ride before he suddenly raised his hand and brought the troop to a halt.

'What's the matter?' the colonel asked him, hand going to his pistol.

'See that slightly lighter area over there? That's got to be it. The trail goes right to it. I'd like to take a few troopers and scout it first. Best to know what we're getting into.'

The colonel nodded and turned. 'Fiver! Mihles! Godort! Fall in over here and dismount!'

The three soldiers, two men and a woman, looked tough and smart enough. Matson loaded his shotgun and dismounted with them. 'Stay ready,' he warned the officer. 'Montagne's range is pretty limited – he has to be looking at you to do anything – but he's too much for me to handle.' With that he and the soldiers started cautiously forward.

'Sir!' one of the troopers hissed when they were almost to the pocket's border.

'Huh? What's the matter?'

'Over there to the left. One, maybe two shapes. Guards, perhaps.'

He looked in the indicated direction and was impressed by the senses of the trooper. These were good soldiers. The figures were barely blobs at this distance, but they fanned out and moved slowly to close the net. At the point where they could finally make out the figures, though, Matson stopped, held up his hand again, and stood up, then pointed his shotgun at the pair. He knew one of them, but the other was a stranger, and he didn't know what they might have done to the one he *did* know by this time.

'All right – both of you! Stand with hands raised, facing me!' he commanded sharply.

They both jumped at the voice, then did as instructed. Cass suddenly recognized the lean figure in black. 'Matson! Thank heaven!'

'Or somebody. You understand I don't know who's been messing with your mind, so I have to be cautious. There's three more guns on you two, so come forward and don't make any sudden moves.'

They did as instructed, and soon were facing him across less than two meters. Matson reclipped his shotgun and walked up to them, staring at the larger of the two. 'I'll be damned! I thought you were a man!'

'I used to be,' Dar responded glumly.

Matson stared at him. 'Don't I know you?'

Quickly Cass stepped in, telling the story as completely as she could, while trying to spare Dar some of the most painful memories. Matson just nodded and waited for her to run out of words.

Finally he said, 'All right. So you say he's changed about twenty of the girls into his playthings, and he's got ten of the others. That's pretty fair, considering that the new ones won't know how to fight. I don't like this goat-headed fellow, though. Handling him will be rough.'

'Oh, it's been *hours*,' she assured him. 'He was going quickly, or so he said. I'm sure he's gone now.'

'We'll have to take the chance,' the stringer decided. 'All right – you two stay here for now. We're still going to keep you covered, so don't move until we tell you. Okay?'

'We won't,' Cass assured them. 'I just wish you'd brought a drink of water with you.'

'All in good time,' he assured her, and was off.

They pretty much were able to confirm the pocket's layout and general dimensions that Cass gave them from cautious observation, and a trooper was sent back to bring up the rest. Matson returned to the pair and lit a cigar. 'Okay. You sure that cave's got no outlet?'

'I'm sure,' Dar told him. 'It doesn't even go back very deep, but it's kind of squared off, arranged like a one-bedroom cubicle.'

He nodded, and the rest of the troops came up. Matson and the troopers quickly sketched in the layout and the stringer and the colonel mapped out a plan of attack. They had four submachine guns with them, and those were placed at the most likely points of breakout. Matson eyed the guns greedily, thinking of what he could have done to the cult if he'd had even one with enough ammunition. Twenty-five of the other troopers were stationed in between, so there was almost a continuous zone of fire. The others would ride right in, guns blazing, and secure positions inside as quickly as possible, with the hope of driving those inside out to the waiting firepower. If they could not within ten minutes, then the outer circle would move in with two of the machine guns taking the heights above the slabs.

Both Dar and Cass, after getting some water and a food bar each from the troopers, volunteered to go in with the party. Both Matson and the colonel were dubious. 'We can't totally trust you yet, but I *would* like somebody there who knows the layout, just in case,' the stringer said. 'How about they come in with us in the middle of the party, undressed and unarmed as they are?'

The colonel nodded. 'If they're crazy enough to do it, why not? Take the two gunners' horses there.'

Both Cass and Dar mounted expertly and brought their horses into the formation. Dar gave a dry chuckle.

'What's so funny?' Cass wanted to know.

'I just realized how much easier and more comfortable it is to ride a saddle naked if you're a girl, that's all.'

'Maybe you'll get to like it,' she returned, feeling better than she had since entering the Temple, despite the imminent battle. 'Hell, with those muscles you got bigger tits than I do by far.' And, with that, they were off.

10

Persellus

The attack was simple, direct, and quite effective because it was a total surprise. Half the riders came in from one side of the pool, the other half, almost perfectly synchronized, rode in from the other way. The inhabitants of the pocket, as hoped, were first totally frozen in confusion at the noise of the attack, then pulled in several directions, not certain what to do or who to fight first.

Several of the savages, undone by this, simply stood there uncomprehending and allowed themselves to be shot down. One, up in a tree, took the first target of opportunity and pounced down on a trooper, dismounting him. Seeing it, Dar leaped from his horse as the savage raised a bone club to deliver the fatal blow and knocked the wild animal-like woman away. Another trooper then shot her down.

It was over almost before it started, in a carefully planned hail of bullets. Part of the reason was that the newly transformed captives did nothing to fight back the attack. Some died simply because it was not immediately obvious that they were no threat, but the bulk of them simply huddled back in a large mass against the rocks and cowered in terror.

As soon as Cass hit the small grove of trees she bounded off her horse and looked for signs of Roaring Mountain and his savage creatures, but aside from the pitiful ones huddling in the rocks there were none. The riders made two passes before they seemed to realize this as well, and they met in the center of the amphitheater and stopped, several dismounting and taking up guard positions.

A rider left to gather in the encircling troops, and soon the machine gunners had set up a defensive post on the rocky flat above the slabs from which they could hit almost anything in the pocket.

Matson, still atop his horse, reclipped his shotgun and looked around. 'Where the hell is Montagne?'

The colonel frowned. 'It was too quick for him to duck out through some escape hatch. He's got to be in the cave.' The mounted troops split up into two detachments and rode to the paths on either side of the waterfall. The captain, who was the other wizard in the troop, now satisfied that his people were in control, took the right path, while the colonel, with Matson, covered the left.

'Rory Montagne!' the stringer shouted, his deep voice struggling to be heard over the waterfall. 'It's all over. Come on out now. In ten seconds we're going to start pouring lead into that cave of yours, and if a shot doesn't get you one of the ricochets will. Live or die, it makes no difference to us. Your choice.'

Suddenly great fire-breathing dragon lizards, each ten meters tall, roared out of the cave and startled the horses. As this diversion was taking place, and drawing shots, a dark figure leaped through the waterfall and into the pool and began swimming straight for the other side. The great dragons were hard for the troopers to ignore, but the colonel wheeled around on his horse and made for the far end of the pool, Matson following.

Roaring Mountain, looking quite soaked, reached the edge of the pool, pulled himself up quickly, then stopped, seeing the two figures in front of him. He shrugged and smiled at them. Wearing nothing but his medallion, he looked more foolish than dangerous. The dragons vanished.

'You didn't answer Mr Matson,' the colonel remarked calmly. 'Or were those hissing illusions your answer? Would you like to take *me* on now?'

The priest of Hell's smile faded and he studied the colonel intently. 'Answer me this first, sir, if you will,' he said smoothly. 'If I were to not take you on, what will happen to me?'

'You will be rendered unconscious, then taken to Persellus to stand trial,' the colonel told him. 'Beyond it being a fair trial by magicians of your rank I can promise nothing further.' It was clear by his tone, though, that he really hoped that the evil one would choose to fight him here and now.

The colonel's confident manner rattled Montagne. He was not, after all, a very powerful wizard, and quite limited in real, rather than illusory, magic. Nor, for all his insanity, was he stupid. One did not take on a wizard who knew your own powers and limitations while you knew none of his. 'To Persellus, you say? I understand it is a delightful place, Colonel. I shall be delighted to accompany you.'

'First things first,' Matson put in. 'Montagne, we go back a ways as you might remember, and I know you're not the big man in all this. Now who the hell is the joker hiding behind the goat's mask?'

'Jok – I don't know what you mean, dear boy. The authorities made it a bit hot, shall we say, back home when my dear little pocket was stumbled upon by a military patrol while I was away. I have scouted these obscure pockets for years, so I moved. That's all.'

Matson reached down on his saddle and unclipped his bullwhip. The dark man saw it, frowned, then looked over at the colonel. 'My dear sir, I have *surrendered* to you! I am under your protection and the merciful laws of Persellus.'

'We're not in Persellus now,' Matson said coldly. 'You killed a very good friend of mine. Worse, you stole stringer property. In the void a stringer is the law in matters concerning his train. You can answer to me, and answer straight, or take on the colonel. Your choice, I don't care which.' The bullwhip was unfurled to its full length.

'Colonel!' Montagne implored, but the colonel filled his pipe, started humming an old tune, and looked around at the scenery.

Rory Montagne sighed. 'Oh, very well. Yes, I was contacted back home one day by the one you refer to, but aside from the fact that he is one of the Seven I have no more idea than you as to who or what he is. I have seen and heard him only as you describe, in deep disguise. He made this pocket, and he sent some of his minions to bring me here with all that I had. I was to build up weapons and personnel until we were strong enough to attack and secure one of the seven gates to Hell which is not that far from here, that time to be in the rather distant future, I believe.'

Matson looked over at the colonel. 'That true? One of those things is around here?'

'So I've heard, but I've heard that since I was a kid and I never knew anybody who really knew if it was, or where it was. I been thirty years in and out of the void in these parts and I never ran into it, but I could have been right next to it a hundred times and never known it. You know how the void is.'

The stringer nodded. 'Well, it's no concern of mine if it's true or not, but I *do* want the bastard behind all this. Montagne, you seem mighty casual about going to Persellus. Any special reason?'

The madman shrugged. 'Why not? As I said, it's supposed to be a delightful place.'

'And the place where your mystery man is?'

The colonel seemed shocked by Matson's suggestion. 'In *Persellus*? One of the Nine? Without the Goddess knowing? Impossible!'

'It would be the ideal place for such a one to hide,' Matson pointed out, 'and for the very reason you just showed. All I can do is state the obvious. Whether or not you follow it up is up to you. I'm not going to be around these parts very long.'

The colonel seemed deeply disturbed by the idea, but simply said, 'It will be looked into, I promise you. At least I will bring it up in my report, and higher authority can do what it wishes.'

'Fair enough,' the stringer agreed. 'Now, then, Montagne, one more piece of unfinished business and I'll let the colonel have you. You stole a lot of merchandise from a stringer. As the recovering stringer, I am entitled to it, but I don't like damaged goods.'

Rory Montagne frowned. 'The mules are in excellent shape, and what packs we rummaged through can, I'm sure, be restored in short order.'

'Them,' Matson said, pointing to the cowering goat-women. 'Put them back the way they were.' The whip hand twitched slightly.

'Now how in hell am I supposed to remember what they looked like?' the captive retorted in a helpless tone. 'They're *women!*'

'Can you bring back their senses? Memory? Personality?'

'Oh, sure. It was a quick mass job. All I did was push them back from the control centers of the brain. What's the point unless they know exactly what's going on but are helpless to do anything about it?'

Matson and the colonel exchanged sharp glances at that. Finally the stringer said, 'Okay. It doesn't matter to me what they used to look like anyway, so long as they're people again. Just pick somebody in your head at random and make them all look like that, and bring back their minds. If they don't think and talk they're no good to me.'

Although some of the troopers were busy surveying the pocket and also repacking and readying the mules for transport, most of the others, including Cass and Dar, stood back watching the show. The latter two were enjoying every bit of it.

Montagne sighed. 'I do wish you would send someone to fetch my robe. A prisoner should be allowed some dignity.'

The colonel shrugged and gestured to a trooper, who went up, into the cave, and returned with it. It was then carefully searched but there were no pockets or concealed compartments within it and so they gave it to him and he put it on, looking quite pleased, then looked up at the colonel. 'With your permission, sir?'

They cleared a path for him and he walked towards the goat-women, who seemed to relax and greet his coming with joy.

'He won't try any tricks, will he?' Matson asked worriedly.

'It would take months to find out his particular frequencies and patterns by deduction, but once he starts I'll know if he's doing it right. You can't alter a spell, only impose a different one. If he undoes it, it has to be all the way, or the math just won't add up.'

The stringer nodded, understanding at least the basics as a false wizard.

Montagne was still a ham, and he still put on a nice show of mumbo-jumbo, chanting, and gestures, but finally he made a few basic gestures and the figures of the hapless women shimmered and changed.

'Bastard! I'll kill him!' Dar screamed, and two troopers had to restrain him.

All nineteen of the surviving members of Arden's train now looked exactly like Lani. The black magician turned, grinned, then shrugged. 'Well, after all, you *did* leave her dead in my bed. Who else did you think I'd have in mind?' He turned to the colonel. 'I'm ready to go now, sir. Take me away!'

Cass shouted at Matson, 'You *can't* make him go back with the train! You just *can't!* It'd be like you traveling with nineteen women who looked just like Arden!'

That stung the stringer, and he softened slightly. 'All right. Colonel, can we find or make some clothes for those two and let them go in with you? All in all, they've done us a pretty good service, and these will more than make up for my loss on them.'

The colonel was surprised. 'You mean you're giving them their freedom? A stringer gives something for nothing? Now I *know* the gates will be opened and the end of World is nigh!'

'Cut the sarcasm. The big one will have to face a hearing when you get home to judge his actions, both good and bad. I'll leave that judgment up to your court. Cass I'm not so sure about, but she's done me enough service to buy her way out. That's as far as I'll go.'

'Fair enough,' the colonel agreed. 'Let's see what we can do about some clothing for the two of them, then we'll commandeer two of the mules there to let them ride. You'll get them back when you reach Persellus.'

'Agreed. I need a couple of troopers to help me go back and get some packs I ditched back on the route, then we'll be headed in. I have some business in Persellus.'

'We'll see you there, then!' And, with that, the colonel went off to reorganize his troops, Montagne walking before him.

Dar was finally calm enough to be freed of restraint, but he turned his back on the now milling, chattering throng of Lanis and refused to look at them any more.

Matson came over to them, dismounted, and said, 'Well, Cass. You heard me there, although I'll never live the story down. Don't disappoint me, now.'

'I just wish I could buy my friends out,' she told him honestly. 'In a way I feel kind of guilty about this.'

'Well, you're free, but you're broke, so forget it. However, I want to warn both of you about Persellus. You've never been in a Fluxland before.'

Even Dar suddenly grew interested. 'What are they like?'

'Well, each one is so different there's no telling, but *this* one happens to be a pretty nice place filled with pretty nice folks, overall. The first thing you have to remember,' he said, his voice dropping to a whisper, 'is that every Fluxland is the creation of a very powerful wizard, one so powerful that they're like gods. Well, this one's wizard thinks she *is* a goddess. Lives up in a high tower, but really does the part. She can hear and see everything and everyone if she wants to, and she loves to. If you pray to her, your prayers might be answered if she's in the mood. If you say anything she doesn't like, or question her godhood, you'll wish you didn't. The best way to act is to steer clear of even any questions about her and for your own sakes make no even slightly nasty comments. The only way people there can get along is if they *believe* in her godhood, so they do. Even these troops and the colonel. Never mind what you know is true. Act in every way like she's a real deity, because, in real life, she is one. And do not ever accept an offer to see her, because you'll come out of it a raving religious fanatic about her. Okay?'

They both nodded, although neither was quite sure just what it all meant.

Matson left shortly afterwards to return to his train, taking a half a dozen troopers with him and his newly acquired mules, packs, and people. That last made things a little more tolerable for Dar, anyway.

The colonel proved to be a man of many abilities. When they came up with two basic trooper uniforms, one far too small for Dar and the smallest far too large for Cass, he made a small gesture and both fit as if they were tailored for the two. A second pass turned the water and the waterfall from clear water to a brown, foul-smelling substance that bubbled and hissed. Nobody was going to use *this* pocket for a refuge again, that was for sure. He did not otherwise destroy it, though, since he fully intended to send back a team of experts on void magic to study it for clues as to its origin – and originator.

Finally, they were ready. The clothes felt odd after so long without any, but they had no trouble riding as they had before. A third commandeered mule held the now comatose Rory Montagne, rendered so by a spell from the colonel that made it highly unlikely that the evil one would awaken before they were ready for him.

Finally everything was packed, inventoried, and they were off into the void once more, but with a difference. Cass was now a free woman, but in a hostile and unknown place and without resources. Dar, because of his earlier actions in the train and against Cass, was technically under arrest.

The colonel was advanced enough in the magic of Flux to find his own way in the void, although he *did* have to return via Matson's train route before he could tie in to the main trail that only a few could see or sense.

It was a slow, relaxed, deliberately paced ride, but it was still far faster than any stringer train could go, even in the speedup configuration Matson had used.

'What will you do now, Cass?' Dar wanted to know.

She shrugged. 'I'm not sure. Take each thing one at a time, I guess. Maybe I'll like this place up ahead and just settle down there. Probably not, though. If I could just find some way to earn a stake, I might like to see a little more of World now that I'm out here.'

'What we've seen so far isn't very encouraging,' Dar noted. 'It's all been pretty ugly.'

'But there *must* be nice places, maybe even wonderful places, too,' she replied. 'I mean, these wizards have the powers of gods. They can't *all* be corrupted by it, not completely. Look at the colonel and these troops here. They're pretty nice, and as human as anybody in Anchor Logh. We've seen the worst the Flux has, now it's time to see the best.'

They reached the borders of Persellus after a lengthy ride. It was not an abrupt transition, like the pocket, but a very gradual one, as the void slowly gave way to actual forms. First there was the feeling of solid ground beneath them, and the clattering of hooves on rock that seemed so odd here that it startled them. Then there were misty, indistinct shapes here and there, like landforms of one kind or another, and here and there a trace of grass or bushes. The sky lightened, until it turned increasingly transparent, although it was now an odd and unfamiliar pale blue above the fleecy white clouds, with no sign of the ever-present Mother of Universes in sight. The clear blue sky unnerved both Dar and Cass, but they soon got used to it, particularly when they didn't look up.

And, suddenly, they were completely in the land of Persellus. It was, even the gloomy Dar had to admit, a very pretty place indeed.

In effect it was a huge, wide valley with a small meandering river cutting through it. The valley itself was, perhaps, twenty or twenty-five kilometers across, and flanked by low mountains with gentle green slopes that were forested all the way to their tops.

At first there seemed little sign of people or indeed any signs of life, but after traveling a while, the road, now paved and well-maintained, took them through farms quite different from those of Anchor Logh, with broad fields of grazing cows or horses and large houses and barns of an unfamiliar design sitting back from the main road. Clearly such farms were independently managed, probably by single families. They were smaller than Anchor communes, and the buildings could not possibly handle a collective. Just the idea of independently owned and operated farms was as hard for them to grasp as was the blue sky and wizards who did magic.

'Actually,' a friendly trooper told them, 'Persellus is slightly smaller than Anchor Logh and yet it produces a good deal more. We're totally self-sufficient in food here.'

They marveled at this, but could not figure it out. It seemed so – *inefficient* somehow.

They went through one small town, strictly two streets wide and a block long, that seemed to cater to the farming community, and nowhere did they see anything or anyone who looked odd, abnormal, or out of the ordinary. About the only complaint they both had was that the light was so bright and constant here that their eyes hurt.

Still, Cass liked what she saw. 'It's peaceful and pretty here,' she remarked to Dar. 'And they're farmers, too, which is what I know best. Maybe I can get me a farm job.'

Finally they reached the outskirts of the city – the one and only city in the Fluxland. It spread out on both sides of the river valley and up onto the hillsides themselves. Here was the governmental and transportation center of the land, along with the places where light manufacturing went on, from harnesses to farm machinery to lumber and building supplies. It was far smaller than the capital of Anchor Logh, but it was the right size to serve the place. It even had its own version of the Temple, although not right in town.

Ahead, beyond the town, they could see it – a great white tower stretching up into the sky, its top hidden in clouds, its base not seeming to touch the ground. The home of the goddess of Persellus.

The houses, with their red roofs and stucco walls, seemed quite different from Anchor Logh, yet hauntingly reassuring. This place may have problems, as Matson indicated, but it was certainly no chamber of horrors.

Government House was a flat, two-story building made out of the same weathered white building material as most of the structures in the land, but it was a good block long and certainly just as deep. They said their farewells to the troopers with thanks, and followed the colonel into the building to report.

The place looked like any administrative seat, except that there seemed to be equal numbers of men and women working there and that was something of a shock as well to two coming from a culture where only men were in government and administration. The Hearing Room, however, to which they were directed, was not what they expected at all.

It was a large room, somewhat resembling a courtroom, but the entire far wall was taken up with a breathtaking and somehow three dimensional floor-to-ceiling portrait of a stunningly beautiful woman wearing white flowing robes, a small gold crown, and with an unnerving solid-looking halo over her head and an equally unnatural aura surrounding her body. Her face was looking down and smiling, her hands outstretched, and the more you looked at the thing the more you swore that the entire figure was somehow alive.

The colonel regarded it as such, entering, hat removed, then kneeling and bowing to the figure and remaining that way. Cass and Dar had already decided to follow the lead of the natives, so they did the same, wondering what happened next.

'Arise, my colonel,' said a deep, musical woman's voice that seemed somehow distant and echo-like, and which filled the chamber. 'All of you may stand.'

They did so, and faced the huge portrait. 'Holy Divine One, to whom we owe everything, this humble servant begs you to hear his report,' said the colonel reverently, all trace of the pragmatic, tough soldier-wizard gone. Clearly this man was in the presence of his god.

'Proceed, my faithful servant.' Both of the newcomers kept looking around to find the source of the voice that seemed all around them, but it was impossible to discover – if, indeed, it was there. Cass remembered Matson's description of Fluxlands. If this woman was indeed a wizard of enormous power, then she was in fact a goddess – as far as her mind could control and stabilize an area of the Flux in the image she desired. And she could make all the rules, and change or disobey them, on a mere whim.

The colonel immediately launched into his report, suddenly becoming the crisp military man once more. He obviously had enjoyed the action, and its result, and couldn't resist reliving it with relish. Cass noticed, though, that while he told about the goat-headed giant who claimed to be one of the Seven, he did not pass on Matson's suspicion that he was a resident of Persellus. Apparently the colonel had simply rejected it as too fantastic, for it was clear he would neither lie nor hold back from his goddess deliberately. The goddess let him talk, and waited until the account was complete. Then, she thanked, blessed, and dismissed the colonel, but ordered Cass and Dar to remain. The colonel kneeled again, then backed out of the room and closed the doors behind him. The two of them waited.

Finally she said, 'The evil wizard must be tried and punished according to our holy laws, and the two of you will be required as witnesses. However, in light of the colonel's account, we are inclined to dismiss the charges against you, Dar. The madness and evil you both willingly joined and aided is counterbalanced, it seems, by your later actions in unmasking and undoing that evil. However, the fact remains that you *did* take a life, and changed or jeopardized others, and that cannot be totally wiped clean. Therefore, we give you a choice, for some judgment must be rendered against you. First, are the facts that the colonel stated true and complete?'

Dar seemed nervous and a bit startled to be directly addressed by a disembodied voice and a painting, but he nodded. 'Yes, Ma'am.'

'Is there anything you wish to add to that account before our choice of judgments is offered you?'

He thought a moment. 'No, Ma'am.'

'If you please, merciful goddess,' Cass put in, trying not to stub her tongue. She was learning fast about the Flux. 'May I intercede?'

'Continue.'

'I have known him all my life. He was one of my few good friends, and I can assure you that he is a good man deep down. Any mere human could be driven mad after the sights we'd seen and the things we had done to us, and, being both fallible and human, he finally cracked under this pressure. Even then, what he did he did out of ignorance, not an intent to aid evil, and when he was given the chance to lead evil he refused and acted for the good. He will live with the terrible torture this evil priest put him through, and its consequences, all his life. Please be merciful with him.'

'We are not unmindful of this,' the goddess responded. 'Nevertheless, wrongs were done and judgment must be made. You must understand that unless these factors were present he would stand trial with the evil priest and share his fate. Still, the fact remains that *you*, for instance, and the rest of your party, did *not* fall victim to madness. A judgment must be made that will serve to remind this poor one of his own inner failings so that, if ever he reaches that point again, he will know and do the right thing.

'Dar, these are your choices. You may request a trial, which in your case would be presided over by the stringer Matson and would include random citizens, both military and civilian. We must warn you that such trials, when they occur, are held under rigid rules of law, and that the best you might expect is to be remanded to a permanent slave status with the appropriate alteration in your outlook to make you a perfect one. You *do* understand that, don't you?'

He thought a minute, and thought of the goat-women and savages of the pocket. 'Yes, Ma'am.'

'Your other choice is to throw yourself right now on my mercy, and accept as final our decision, no matter what that might be.'

He thought a moment. 'Your worship,' he said, using the form of address used for high Temple priestesses in Anchor Logh, 'I'd just like to get it over with. I feel guilty as hell – beg pardon, your worship – and I'll be mad at myself forever for being so dumb. I'll take what you dish out here and now.'

The goddess seemed pleased. 'Very well, then. What you did, you did for love of a woman. It is a very old story among humans, and the history of the human race is full of things, both wonderful and terrible, done for that reason, and for the opposite. For the love of that woman you defected to the enemy, knowing she was there. After suffering the most terrible of torments for a man, you then killed that woman, not out of anger or self-pity or revenge, but out of mercy for her own tragic state. The fact remains, though, that had you not run from the train under fire she might not have died. You will have to live with that.'

She paused for a moment, and Dar stood motionless, frozen, staring at the eerie picture. Cass felt sorry for him, but was helpless.

'It seems to us,' the goddess continued, 'that through a very strange chance, the evil one has rendered an appropriate judgment on you. We therefore, by divine spell of a sort that has never been broken by any of the gods and goddesses of World, perfect and make irrevocable your present state, as constant reminder of your own deeds and as a warning if needed to you and to others. Beyond this, no other thing will be done to you for any deeds in the past, and we declare you free and independent. We further stipulate that each of you will receive our total hospitality while you are in Persellus, for so long as you both choose to be here. Dar, you may go now and wait outside, while we talk with Cass.' It was not a request.

He bowed his head slightly. 'Ma'am, it's only justice, I guess.' He did not feel happy, but he had enough sense to remember and back out of the room. Cass was now alone with the goddess.

'You are troubled by our judgment?'

'It's pretty hard on him, I think,' she admitted. 'He's neither one thing nor the other, and he can't be happy either way.'

'That was the idea. However, we decided to explain to you our reasoning, for he will need you at least for a while. Inside him burns tremendous guilt, and with it a self-hatred. We would willingly have restored him for all the reasons you gave, but to do so without also totally remaking his mind and memories would have increased that guilt and self-hatred quickly to the point where he would kill himself. The reasons for everything he did are buried deep in his mind and his experiences, much from long before he was cast out of Anchor Logh, so to remake his mind would have been to, essentially, kill him anyway. We do not do such work for people. By making of him a hermaphrodite, oddly enough, Montagne saved his life, for then he felt punished for his own failings. He, not we, consider this appropriate punishment, and so he remains, perhaps to be useful and productive in some way. He is not without courage, only self-confidence.'

She considered it. 'I don't know much about psychology, divine one, and it seems a little mixed up to me, but I'll take your word for it. You're saying that only because he's not whole can he be sane.'

'That *is* about it,' the goddess admitted. 'Unless there is something else, you may go now.'

She thought a moment. 'Except that both of us need jobs, there's nothing, your worship.'

'You will find what you need, for you have within you a Soul Rider who guards.'

That startled her. 'A what?'

'A Soul Rider. Do not fear it, for there is precious little power it cannot command if need be, and it fights the forces of darkness on World. You must only be warned that it uses you in its fight, and so you can expect more danger and adventure. Making a living will be no problem. This is enough for now. You may go.'

She wanted to ask a lot more questions, particularly about this Soul Rider, but there was no way she was going to press somebody like this, particularly not now. She gave the bow and backed out the door, closing it behind her.

11

Haldayne

An officious-looking woman was waiting with Dar when Cass emerged from the room. Dar looked at her and said, 'Well?'

She shrugged. 'Tell you later, maybe. How are *you* doing?'

'I'm feeling a little off and my muscles ache, but I'm okay.' He turned to the woman. 'This lady says she'll see to our needs.'

'I am Gratia,' the woman introduced herself. 'Please accompany me and I will show you to your hotel and give you a brief orientation.'

They followed her out of Government House and down a central street filled with small shops and cafes, most with merchandise on racks outside or a few streetfront tables. A small hotel was two blocks down on the corner, and it was clearly a hotel and nothing else. Cass delighted at some of the displayed merchandise but couldn't help comparing what she was seeing to Anchor Logh. There was, it seemed, no equivalent of Main Street, no bars or entertainment area of any kind. The people seemed normal enough, but there was not the gaiety or spontaneity that she expected of people in a city setting. A cautious remark on the lack of some expected services brought a response from their guide.

'Our lives are lived according to the Divine Plan,' Gratia told them. 'Such things as you describe are the products of evil and are not needed nor permitted here.'

They were given vouchers of some sort, pieces of paper with numbers printed on them and another unnaturally lifelike head portrait of the goddess on them, and told that this was the money of Persellus. It was difficult to accept something as flimsy and destructible as paper as money, but this was not Anchor Logh.

They were left in a small hotel room with a map of the central city, the money stake, and recommendations for some of the better cafes and shops in the area. 'You may as well relax and enjoy your stay here,' Gratia said. 'It is unlikely that the stringer train will be able to be here in under three days, and we have scheduled the trial for four days from now. If you have any questions about anything here or have any needs in the meantime, do not hesitate to come by my office in Government House and discuss these with me.' And, with that, she left.

Dar eyed one of the two single beds in the room and shook his head. 'You know how long it's been since I've slept on a real bed? I wonder if I can do it?'

Cass laughed. 'Well, if you want to be homesick for the stringer train, then you can always strip and lie on the floor.'

A room both had originally taken for a closet turned out to be a bathroom, something both had never seen individually connected to a hotel room before. There was no power except wind, water, and muscle outside the capital of Anchor Logh, and when in that city both had stayed in communal quarters. It was some time before they even fully figured out how all the things worked, and marveled at hot water coming from taps without any pumping or pre-heating, and they spent some time flushing and re-flushing the toilet and trying to figure out just how it worked.

'As for me, that's the tiniest shower I've ever seen but I'm going to use it,' Cass decided, stripping off her makeshift uniform. 'How about you?'

Dar nodded. 'I think it's strictly one at a time in there, though. I don't think I'd fit with anybody else. I still wish it was a tub, though. My legs are killing me and I'd like to soak them.'

He undressed, and at least part of the reason for his distress was painfully evident. There was some blood on his legs, large and hairy as they were, and it disturbed him.

Cass still found it hard to get used to the sight of him like that – a true god, huge and musclebound, looking and sounding like a man who lifted weights casually and bent steel to relax, except in that one area. And that, of course, was his problem. The big, strong he-man was going to have to have periods explained to him. It was rather clear now what the goddess meant when she said she would 'perfect' what Rory Montagne had done to him.

Later, a bit cleaner, they went shopping, both picking plain, practical clothes, such as tough denim pants and simple work shirts. They also picked up toiletries and various portable packing kits for their stuff. Neither overdid it, wanting to be able to travel light if they had to. Both also picked high boots that gave good protection and support, but only Cass picked fairly high heels which gave her a little extra height. She still did not come up to his broad shoulders, but it made her feel a little more even with the world. She also selected a dark brown flat-brimmed hat with a string tie to secure it while riding, and a hand-tooled leather belt with a plain silvery oval buckle, just because she liked the look of it.

Afterward they ate at one of the recommended cafes and found the food quite good although rather plain and unvaried, except for a seeming national passion with fancy pastries. Obviously, the goddess loved fancy pastries.

After sundown, however, the whole city just plain died. There was no nightlife at all, and no real diversions. It was clear from their shopping expeditions that the people of Persellus lived for their jobs and families and did very little else recreationally. Not that they weren't an apparently happy lot, but they seemed content with everything as it was and doing what they were doing and had no real curiosity, ambition, or even much of a competitive spirit. When looking for her belt, a leather shop had directed her to another down the street, for example.

Reading matter seemed to consist mostly of book after book of the goddess's musings, aphorisms, ramblings, and the like, most of which was tough going and made very little sense. There appeared to be little education beyond basic skilled trades and reading and writing for business reasons. They didn't need doctors because when they got sick or injured they just prayed to the goddess and she healed them. They didn't need scientists or engineers, because everything worked through the goddess's magic, even the water and electricity. Smoking, drinking, dancing, gambling, even basic entertainment like plays was forbidden, and foul language was strongly discouraged, which made Dar realize what a gaffe he'd pulled in using the very mild 'hell' in the 'presence' of the goddess herself.

It was, in fact, so deadly dull a town filled with such incredibly dull people that it almost drove both of them nuts. Even the humdrum farm life of Anchor Logh was a thrill a minute compared to this place. By the end of the second day they were both so bored that they decided on the third day to rent horses and see a little of the countryside.

But the countryside, too, had the same dull sameness as the town. The only problem they had was occasional small bouts of vertigo now and then, after which something would be slightly changed. Mountains seemed a bit taller one time than another, houses seemed to grow and shrink now and then, and when they got back to town there were minor, subtle differences in the look of the buildings and even the people.

'The best guess I can make,' Cass said when they were back in their hotel room, where the furniture and fixture designs seemed very slightly different, 'is that since this land is entirely the product of the goddess's imagination, she sometimes makes little changes now and then, like redecorating a room. Or maybe it's just that, like us, she remembers things a little differently than they really were, and, unlike us, how she remembers them is how they become.'

'Still thinking of staying here and finding a job?' Dar asked her. They had not really discussed the future.

She shook her head. 'Nope. I think when Matson gets here I'll ask for some suggestions and, if I can afford it, travel along with him for a little while until I find a place I can really settle. You?'

'Oh, I'll come along, I guess. I sure can't see somebody like me fitting in around here, that's for sure. Oh, maybe if I joined the army or something like that, I might make do, but I could never call this home or fit into their family pattern. I don't think *she* had me staying around in mind.' He sighed. 'I wonder if there *is* a place where I'd fit in?'

She shrugged. 'I'm not sure. I'd like to know what a Soul Rider is, though. Nobody around here seems to know anything about it.'

'Maybe Matson will. He's been around and seen everything, and he'll be in tomorrow.'

She nodded. 'None too soon, either.' She thought a moment. 'You sure about coming with Matson, though? I mean, there'll be all those Lanis, and they sure aren't the kind of people Persellus would want.'

'I've licked that, I think. Look, I'm part Lani and part me. If I can't take people who look like her, then I may as well pack it in, right?'

She couldn't argue with it, but she hoped it was true.

They saw Matson first when they were summoned for Rory Montagne's trial. He looked clean and relaxed, although irritated that his cigars could not legally be brought into the Fluxland proper. He looked and felt naked without one stuck in his mouth.

All of them were seated in a comfortably appointed 'witness room' well stocked with cold drink and pastries while waiting to testify. They greeted Matson warmly, and he reciprocated in his usually reserved stringer fashion, but when he asked how they liked Persellus and both silently spelled out 'D-U-L-L' he had to chuckle. Finally Cass got around to business. 'How much for a ride with your train?'

Matson grinned. 'A week ago you'd have paid your arms and legs *not* to be anywhere near my train, now you're offering money to get back in?'

'As passengers, not cargo,' she was quick to point out. 'There's a big difference.'

He thought a moment. 'Well, Persellus money's not much use to me, although I could credit it to an open account here in the name of Anchor Logh and get something more transportable in return. Tell you what – if you supply your own horses and packs, and buy what supplies you'll need for at least a week's travel, I'll take you along as duggers – without pay, of course. You're both pretty good with animals and Jomo's got more than his hands full with the nearly double-sized train, even though we're going to pare it down a bit here. We'll try and give you a few shooting and close fighting lessons, too. How's that?' He paused a moment. 'But no hysterics over the human cargo, no going nuts seeing people who look like other people, things like that.'

'I'll be good,' Dar responded, knowing who that was directed towards. 'I've done some real thinking in the past few days, and I'm not the same person inside that I was.'

That settled, Cass asked, 'How come they're going through all this formal trial business for that scum? Why not just let the goddess deal with him and be done with it?'

'Well, now, that's kind of hard to explain,' Matson replied. 'First of all, he's a wizard. A real puny one, I admit, but a real one nevertheless. There's a sort of a fraternity that all real wizards belong to, mostly to protect them from each other. They've got their own rules, and their conduct has to be judged by other wizards of equal or greater rank before they can be disciplined. It sounds stupid, I know, but every one of them does things all the time that might be considered criminal to others, so they insist on being judged by their own standards. Next time one of the judges might be in the dock, so he or she wants to make sure that *they* followed the rules when *they* were judges. See?'

The door to the courtroom opened and a tall, distinguished-looking man entered. He looked to be in his late forties or early fifties but in excellent condition for that age. In fact, age had been very kind to him, and he was lean and handsome, his silvery gray hair complementing his dark complexion.

'I am First Minister Haldayne,' he told them. 'I am, in effect, the prosecutor in this case.' He picked up one of the gooier pastries and ate it. 'In a few moments we'll be calling direct witnesses. Just tell everything exactly as it happened, adding or subtracting nothing, and don't volunteer anything. Just answer what questions are asked, and let me be your guardian against defense questions. Above all, don't get emotional if you can help it, making moral judgments on the defendant or calling him names. The standards here are a bit different than in a normal court of law.' They all nodded, and he left, then returned a few moments later. 'Mr Matson, if you please.'

Matson went in and the door closed, and both Cass and Dar regretted not being able to see or hear anything. They were used to open, public courtrooms.

Matson's testimony apparently didn't last long, and Cass was called next. Haldayne offered his left hand to her to help her up from her overstuffed chair, and as she stood she noticed on his right hand a small but distinctive gold ring. Suddenly she remembered that he'd eaten the pastry with his left hand as well.

She had little time to reflect on it, though, as she was ushered into what appeared to be a traditional courtroom, although with a board of three women and two men acting as judges, and no jury. Haldayne examined her on the facts, and she told her story, almost absently, trying not to be fixated on the man himself but unable to totally betray her preoccupation. The more he talked, the more he moved, the more she was sure.

Rory Montagne looked relaxed in the dock, acting as if this somehow did not concern him at all. He had given a slight smile and wave when she'd entered, and listened to her testimony while absently gnawing on an apple. If she was right, she thought nervously, he had every reason to be unconcerned.

The defense put only a few clarifying questions to her, then she was dismissed, and Haldayne led her back to the jury room and called Dar. When the door closed again, she turned to Matson and whispered, 'That man Haldayne – he's the goat-headed boss! I'm sure of it!'

Matson frowned. 'Haldayne? But he's the bigwig around here, the most powerful wizard in the land, second only to the goddess herself.'

None the less, she outlined her reasons and her instincts, and he did not dismiss them. 'It both fits and it smells,' he told her. 'The trouble is, we'll need a lot more proof than you can give for it, and I'm not sure how to get it. Do you think he knows you suspect him?'

'He could hardly ignore it. I wasn't being very subtle, I'm afraid.'

'Hmmm … Well, even if he *is* our man, he's unassailable as he is, but if he's as good and as careful as he has to be he won't want to leave any loose ends.'

She looked at him nervously. 'You mean he might try and come after me?'

Matson nodded. 'I think you better buy what you need this afternoon and get down to my train. Just follow the road the way you came in. I'll try and clear my business this afternoon and get back there. If he's really one of the Seven in this kind of control this close to a Hell Gate somebody will have to be notified. Damn! I wasn't headed that way, but after Globbus I think we'll have to take a detour to Pericles. Well, maybe it won't be a total loss. Pericles always likes fresh young women.'

She looked up at him sharply. 'Watch it!'

He shrugged. 'No moral judgments, remember? Besides, there's a lot worse places to wind up than Pericles. But you watch it from now on. He may try anything at any time, and if he *is* our man and if he's also what he claims to be, he's one of the most powerful wizards on all World. He'd have to be just to reach First Minister in Persellus.' He thought it over. 'Still, if I were him, I *wouldn't* touch you at all. It'd give him away, where all we have now are strong and unsupported suspicions.'

She suddenly remembered the goddess's comments on her. 'Matson? What exactly is a Soul Rider?'

The question took him by surprise. 'Huh? Where'd you hear about *them?*'

'The goddess said I had one inside me.'

His mouth dropped and a light seemed to dawn in his head. 'So *that* explains it! I was wondering if I was too long in this job or what. Uh huh. A Soul Rider. Well I'll be …'

'You *do* know, then!'

He nodded. 'More or less. They are – creatures. Not much is known about them, except that they're parasites of some kind and they hate the Seven so much they get their hosts in a whole lot of trouble. One picked you, probably back in the Anchor, and most of what happened after that was at least partly its doing.'

She grew nervous. 'Parasite. Will it – hurt me?'

He chuckled. 'Well, depends on how you look at it. Supposedly they pick people, ordinary people, and get inside them, and all of a sudden those people get into a whole lot of trouble. Things happen to them that wouldn't happen to most folks in a lifetime. Now I *know* you're on to something here with this Haldayne fellow.'

She felt very uncomfortable. 'Then, it might have been this Soul Rider that caused me to find the Sister General fixing the lottery in the first place? And the reason Dar took me and only me when he ran?'

Matson nodded. 'Probably. But, remember, it's also responsible for some-how getting me to put my string on you so we could follow your trail and find the pocket. And I don't think it was coincidence that Montagne was stopped just before he changed you into one of his – creatures, or, maybe, that Dar had an attack of conscience and freed you. In fact, the odds of us finding you first were pretty slim, but we did. And now you've drawn the attention of somebody who at least thinks he's one of the Seven.'

She thought it over. 'I'm not sure I like being a puppet of a – thing.' She shivered slightly.

'Well, they're not human, whatever they are, but they're on our side. You can't expect them to act like people would, but they're not all bad. In a pinch, they're supposedly stronger than the strongest wizard, which is why, I think, the goddess won't shed any tears when you leave.'

'Still, this makes what happened to Dar even less excusable. I mean, if this *thing* caused him to do what he did …'

'Nope. You miss the point there. He did that himself. Taking you along might have been the Soul Rider's idea, but not him running out or anything else he did. In fact, he was completely on their side until it was either kill you or let you escape, in which case he had to go, too, or his neck would have been chopped. You see, it's the goddess's opinion that he only saved you because he was forced by your protector to do so.'

'Oh. I see. I'm not sure I agree with it, but I at least can understand it a little better now. I—'

She was about to continue when Dar returned, and all conversation in that direction ceased.

'Thank you for your help,' Haldayne told them, sounding sincere. 'The judg-ment will be rendered some time this afternoon or evening. I think he's far too insane for any appropriate punishment, but we'll see. You may all go now.'

They got up and left quickly, Matson following them down to the street. 'Remember – move quickly,' he cautioned Cass. 'If he's as good as I think he is, you can't even depend on the goddess for help in a pinch.'

'I'll remember,' she assured him. Dar looked bewildered, and she added, to him, 'I'll explain later. Let's get back to the hotel – we're getting out of here as quickly as possible.'

*

By the time they'd packed their meager belongings, bargained for horses, saddles, and riding gear, picked up what supplies they thought they would need, and checked out with Government House, it was close to dark. Matson had been right on one thing, though – everybody concerned seemed unnaturally glad to see both of them leave.

Although he had taken her word for the urgency and gone along, it wasn't until they were on the road out of Persellus that she felt safe enough to explain to Dar what was going on. He thought about his own brief contact with the goat-man, and admitted there were some similarities, although he was by no means as certain as she about it.

It was well into night when they passed through the small farming village, and they were grateful for the paved road as the stars gave very little light. They stopped to rest the horses, though, in a grass field near a small creek, and while just sitting there, silently, they heard sounds from the direction they'd just come, the sounds of several horses riding steadily towards them.

Cass frowned. 'This is too dead a place to have that kind of traffic.'

Dar nodded. 'Maybe it's Matson with some others.'

'I doubt it. He said he had just a little business and he said nothing about horses or passengers.' She thought a minute. 'Get the horses and let's keep very quiet and still off the road here. We can't outrun them, but they don't have to see us, either.'

He nodded and did as instructed. There was nothing particular to hide behind, but it was a very dark night and they couldn't make out the road from where they were, which was down in a slight indentation made by the creek. A small wooden bridge over the creek was not far.

The riders reached the area but did not hesitate, and they could hear the hollow sounds of hooves hitting the wood, echoing hollowly across the landscape, and then they were gone.

Dar breathed. 'Could you make out anything about them?'

'Not a thing. Just a blur. There were at least four of them, though.' She sighed. 'I wish we knew more about weapons and had some around.'

'If they reach the train and we're not there, they'll be back,' Dar pointed out.

'Maybe. But they'll have to have some excuse when they get to the train, and that should bog them down. No, I think they'll get close to the train, then lay ambush for us just up from it. It would make sense, and if any of them's a wizard they won't attract the duggers, either.'

'We could stay here until daylight. That might make it a little easier. There may be people around, and Matson'll be on his way back.'

She considered it. 'I don't think it'll work. For one thing, down this far there weren't many people. I don't remember *any*, do you? And they're not going to stay all night. When we don't show after a while they're going to come back slow and sneaky.'

'Well, what then? If we get off the road we're lost good and proper and you know it.'

'It's mostly unfenced this far along, and I guess it's not more than another seven or eight kilometers to the border and the train. The river's over there, maybe a few hundred meters. Let's follow it down. It's going pretty much the same place but it's less likely to be covered, particularly by only four people.'

Having no other suggestion, Dar agreed. They followed the creek down to the river, then nervously waded the small creek just up from its joining with the larger body of water. It was fairly deep, but not deep enough to be a problem to two riders used to horses.

The ground, however, was pretty wet, and the depth of the creek told them that the river would be an obstacle in case of any sort of attack, almost certainly too deep to cross. Fortunately, this far down there were few tributaries to worry about, and each one seemed to be shallower than the one before, telling them they were getting close to the border. They thought they were going to make it easily when the river suddenly curved away into the dark hills after making a bend bringing them close enough to actually make out the road.

They stopped to consider what to do next, and there was an ominous rumbling from off to their right. Dar looked over in that direction and saw the hills suddenly light up as clouds rolled in impossibly fast. 'Thunderstorm,' he remarked.

'Looks pretty odd for a real one,' Cass responded uneasily. 'A good wizard could whip one up, though, and light up the whole landscape and us with it. I'd say we'd better make for the road and just make a run for it as fast as we can.'

'I'm with you,' Dar told her, and they kicked their horses into action. Suddenly a great roaring wall of fire rose up in front of them, spooking the horses and causing them to stop and rear. Less experienced riders would have been thrown, but both Dar and Cass managed to stay in the saddle, if barely. The wall of fire spread, until it encircled them on three sides. With the horses already near panic, they had no choice but to take the one exit, even though they knew they were being forced into a trap.

They cleared the fire, then halted as they saw four riders on horseback ahead, spread out to receive them, guns in the hands of all four. The wall of fire vanished abruptly, and Cass cursed herself for not betting that it was an illusion and urging her horse to jump through it, but the four riders were still somehow illuminated, as were Cass and Dar.

'Just stay where you are and make no sudden moves,' one of them, a man, said. 'The fire may have been a trick but the bullets are real. You two, get down slowly and walk towards us, real slow now.'

They did as instructed, until they were right in front of the four riders, all men of middle age, all bearded and wearing farm work clothes. Cass couldn't help but remember that the goat-man, according to Montagne, had had his 'minions' move the dark priest from his old pocket to the new one. These, then, must be minions of the mad priest's boss.

'What do we do now?' Cass asked them.

The leader chuckled. 'Now, ain't that something! Look at 'em, Eck! Two pieces of ass pretending they's men. Neither of 'em look like they'd be any fun a'tall. I sure don't want 'em. Any of you?'

There were a few sniggers from the other three, but no takers.

'Then I guess the answer to your question about what to do next is to pray,' the leader said coldly, steadying his rifle.

Yeah, sure – pray, Cass thought sourly, then hope soared for a moment. Yeah! Sure! Pray! She only hoped that Dar had enough sense to roll when she did, for there was no way to tip him off. And pray she did.

'Oh, great and divine goddess, deliver us from evil!' she practically shouted, then dropped and rolled at the same time. The leader, caught off guard, fired, but neither target was there any more.

Cass had just made for the grass, but Dar had other plans. While Cass just kept praying in a low tone, he leaped up from the side and pulled one of the men off his horse. The man fell, dropping his rifle, and Dar picked it up as the others were turning to meet the threat, then dropped and rolled once more, coming up in front of them, rifle pointed at them. The fact that he had only a vague idea of how it worked or how to hit anything with it was something *he* knew, but they did not.

'Drop your weapons!' he commanded sharply.

The leader turned and grinned at him. 'Why?' Suddenly the whole area was brightly lit as if from a suspended floodlight, although no source was visible. Dar looked down and was startled to see that he was now pointing a stick at the men.

While a second helped the fallen comrade to his feet, a third dismounted and walked over to where Cass was still lying, now fully exposed, and gestured with his rifle. She got up, but did not stop praying until ordered to shut up.

'Who sent you?' she demanded to know.

'What's it to you?' the leader asked. He thought a moment. 'You know, boys, we could use a simple spell on 'em to make 'em easier to take, if you know what I mean.'

'Now you're talking, Crow,' the one called Eck responded. 'I always did hanker to screw that little milkmaid up at Gorner's. You know who I mean.'

Crow made a pass at each of them with his hand. Cass looked over and was startled to see not Dar but the vision of a very pretty and much smaller dark-haired girl. She knew it was just Dar, and that it was all illusion, but it was still startling. She wondered what she looked like to them.

'Get them clothes off now, and don't be too gentle about 'em. You won't be needing them afterwards,' Crow said ominously.

Suddenly there was a great flash of lightning, striking very near them and spooking the gunmen's horses a bit. Crow looked puzzled. 'Now what the hell is that? I didn't do nothin'!'

'Sinners! Blasphemers! Agents of Hell! You dare this in our domain!' came a familiar woman's voice, angry as they had not heard it before. 'For this you shall pay beyond your imaginings!'

'It's the goddess!' one of them cried, and Crow said, 'But Haldayne promised she wouldn't—'

'Haldayne!' thundered the goddess, and there was lightning all over the place. 'So it *is* true! Well, first we will deal with you, and then we will deal with First Minister Haldayne, formerly of Persellus, soon of Hell.' A lightning bolt came out of the sky, then split into four finger-like segments much like a ghostly hand, then struck all four riders simultaneously. All four, including the one newly remounted, toppled out of their saddles to the ground, screaming in agony as they continued to be enveloped by the electrical field. There was another flash at each of the four points, then silence.

'You were right to call upon us,' the goddess's disembodied voice told them. 'We heard you accuse Haldayne in the witness room but could not believe it. We elected to go along with you and discover the truth and now we have.'

'Those four men – what happened to them?' Dar asked her.

'Transformed. Take them along as presents for your stringer. Use them to pay for what you need. I must now attend to their master. Do not fear the four, for they are imprisoned in their own minds, unable to act or do anything at all. They are property, and they are yours, and they will now see what the other side is like.' And, with that, they sensed that the presence was gone.

Cass and Dar approached the four figures nervously, and were struck by what they found. Both she and he looked themselves again now, and there was very little light but enough to see close up.

'Well, she certainly has a single mind when it comes to punishing men,' Dar remarked.

All four men were now vacant-eyed and not very attractive but quite nude women with shaved heads and tattooed behinds. They seemed to be waiting for Cass to do something, so she finally said, 'All right, you four – mount those horses and follow us.' All four got up and obeyed their instructions exactly.

'I think we'd better get moving,' she told Dar. 'There's going to be all Hell breaking loose, literally, around this land soon and I want to be in the void when it does.'

Dar nodded, and said, bitterly, 'You know, this is the first time I really regret not being a man down below.'

'Huh? What do you mean?'

'I'd love to show *them* exactly how it feels to be on the other end of things.'

Cass had to laugh. 'Welcome to the world *I* live in all the time!' she said.

12

Maturity

Even on the periphery of Persellus they could feel the giant struggle going on inside. In one sense, Cass, Dar, and the duggers had to fight back urges to return, at least for a small distance, to the reality of the land proper to see it for themselves, but they did not. They had their responsibilities to themselves and to the train, for one thing, and, for another, they did not want to be caught up in such a fight between two supremely powerful wizards. When the land changed just because of a lapse in the goddess's memory, what might be the changes when she was directing all her energies to fighting a powerful foe with neither combatant having either much thought or much regard for the people caught in the middle?

Still, there was the sound of thunder and the ground beneath them shook like all of World had suddenly come alive and revolted. The animals grew panicky and hard to control, and Jomo and his two new assistants struggled to keep them calm.

'Maybe we'd better move completely into the void,' Cass shouted over the roar.

'Too late,' Jomo yelled back. 'We not be able to get them formed. Best just hold on!'

And hold on they did, sometimes with the help of the Anchor Logh exiles, for what seemed like an eternity. Suddenly, though, *very* suddenly, it all stopped dead, and everyting became quiet and still. After so long fighting scared animals and being in the midst of what felt like a great storm, it seemed almost unnatural to go back to the normal lifelessness they had so taken for granted.

After sorting the mess out and settling down, Dar wiped his brow, sat down on a pack, and said, 'Well, I guess somebody won. Wonder who?'

That suddenly was uppermost on all their minds. For Cass, it was particularly unnerving, since if Haldayne was the victor he would waste no time coming after her, and perhaps the whole train, to keep the news secret as long as possible, and they were up against a wall. Without Matson, none of them could navigate the void, and even Kolada, the train's 'point' or scout, could only take them back as far as the massacre or, perhaps, to Anchor Logh. That route would be pretty easy for Haldayne's people to trace.

The duggers were particularly distressed that Matson had been in the midst of all the pyrotechnics. Some doubted that he was still alive at all, but others, particularly Jomo, held that he would come. Clearly, if anyone *could* have gotten through that stuff, Matson was the one.

No matter how any of them thought, the decision to wait was easy. There simply wasn't anything else to do. Cass talked Jomo into finally reorganizing the train enough to move it completely into the void and beyond the reach of any ruler of Persellus. It was a difficult and time consuming procedure even though the total move was only a little more than a kilometer, but they agreed and, at least, it took their minds off anything else for a few hours.

It struck not only Dar but their erstwhile comrades how very easily Cass was taking over, giving more orders than suggestions now – and being obeyed by the duggers. She set up the new camp in a defensive position, then posted riflemen both front and rear. This done, she ordered a general inventory of supplies and ammunition be taken, for they didn't know how long they would be stuck there.

Jomo paid her a high compliment. 'Too bad you not know how to string. You seem sometime to be ghost of Missy Arden.'

Finally, though, all that could be done had been done. The supplies were quite promising – with the recovered material from the Arden train taken from the pocket and the subsequent recovery of the supplies dropped by Matson before coming in, they had sufficient food for people and animals for a long stay, perhaps two to three weeks if they conserved carefully. Water, however, was in shorter supply and could pose a problem. Because it was so heavy, stringers rarely took along more water than they had to, depending on their knowledge of small stringer-created water pockets to replenish their casks. There was probably one or more of these on the Anchor Logh route, but as the trip had been short enough Matson hadn't bothered to stop and so they did not know where any might be. Still, if they didn't stay too long, it was possible that they had enough water to return to the Anchor.

'What's the use, though?' Cass asked Dar and Jomo. 'We'd get back, maybe, but only as far as the clear spot – the Anchor apron. That's assuming we all didn't go nuts in the void without Matson's powers to protect us.'

Dar thought it over. 'Well, the goddess was nice enough to take our damned tattoos off, so we wouldn't be marked. The duggers would have the train to deal with in signing on with the next stringer who came along. I think you and me could talk our way back in. I don't look much like I did, and I bet they don't remember what Arden looked like all that much. You could say it was Matson who was ambushed and you, that is Arden, survived. Or you could stay with the duggers and make your own deal with another stringer.'

She looked at him quizzically. 'You want back in Anchor Logh? What on World for? What is there for you back there now?'

He grinned. 'I could always join the priesthood. *That* would drive 'em nuts, wouldn't it? At least I'd have a shot at those bastards in that bar back there, and maybe at the Sister General.'

She shook her head. 'No. As much as I'd love to see her get what's coming to her, and as much as I'd *really* love to see what they'd do if you *did* apply for the priesthood, I don't think it'll go. Somehow we've got to warn somebody of Haldayne and the threat to the gate.'

'Yeah? Who, for instance? And where? And how? And are we so sure that the bad guys won?'

'You want to go back there and find out? As to the who, well, if the gates to Hell are real, and Haldayne really is one of the Seven, then it follows that the Nine Who Watch must exist someplace, too.'

Dar chuckled dryly. 'Gates, Hell, the Seven and the Nine. Just stories. Who do we have to say they aren't? Roaring Mountain? Even his friends agree he's living in a different world. Haldayne? It's a good gag to get those that believe in the stuff but don't like it to come over to his side, but that's all. You don't need demons from Hell to be bad, but maybe the bad need the demons as much as the church does.'

That was a pretty good point, but she just wasn't ready to change her entire life view that easily, not yet. Roaring Mountain had been sought out and transported a tremendous distance to do his dirty work here. Men with power such as Haldayne's didn't grow overnight, either – clearly he had a long history and knew much of World, and such a one, whether one of the Seven or not, would have a host of enemies, probably other powerful wizards, and few friends or allies.

'Jomo?'

'Yes, Missy?'

'How long might it be before another stringer train came this way? Best case and worst case?'

Jomo was not dumb, but his mind worked in a very literal fashion. 'Best – now. Worst – never.'

She sighed. 'No, I mean, what would be your best guess?'

'Mr Matson not go back to Anchor Logh for long time. Has lot of orders for Anchor Logh. That mean train must be coming soon, yes?' He hesitated a moment. 'Unless Missy Arden plan to go back.'

And that was part of the problem. With Arden gone and her plans unknown, it might have been she who would carry the wanted materials back to the Anchor. Or it might be another stringer on his or her way here now – but how far off? Just when on his long route did Matson expect to meet this possibly imaginary train going the other way?

She sighed. 'We'll give him one day. Three meals. Then I think we have no choice but to go back to Anchor Logh and wait for another stringer, trading what we have for what we need until then. It's either that or sneak back into Persellus and get water from the river. Any volunteers?'

Jomo was unprepared to give up Matson so easily. 'I go in. Take two, maybe three slaves.'

Dar sighed and stood up. 'Oh, all right, *I'll* go. No, not you, Cass – if Haldayne's in charge you won't last ten minutes. Me he couldn't care less about. At the most it'll take a couple of hours.'

She started to protest, and realized that part of her protest was based on her still uncertain feelings about Dar deep down. He had gone over once to Haldayne's side – would he take the chance to join up again? He had quite a present to deliver Haldayne if he did – not only her, but the whole train and detailed knowledge of its defenselessness and predicament. Finally she relented, though. If he were bad, he would eventually find a way to betray them anyway. Best to find out now. 'Who will you take?'

He walked over and examined the hay wagon and its casks. 'Two should be enough, I think. It's a simple crank siphon system.' He walked back and sought out Suzl and Nadya, who had not up to this point recognized him. He brought them forward and Cass greeted them warmly. 'Look,' she told them, 'we'll try and buy your way out of this if we can, I promise. And I won't order you to do this. It might be very dangerous in there right now.'

'We'll go,' Nadya told her. 'It is far better than sitting here.' Suzl nodded agreement, and looked up at Dar. 'Might even be fun.'

They pulled out towards the edge of Persellus, Dar with the reins holding the four mules, the girls sitting on either side of him.

'It's hard to believe that you're Dar,' Suzl remarked, 'although once you told us you can see it. Wow! If you'd looked this good back in Anchor Logh you'd have had every girl begging for you, even the priestesses!'

He laughed. 'It's the magic out here. Wish I had some to use! I'd give both of you long, brown hair and get rid of those purple numbers.'

The edge region of Persellus looked the same, but as they proceeded into the land proper there was a devastating alteration. While the area nearest the border was untouched, the distant skyline showed a terrible change in the now early morning light.

Across green fields to the horizon, the land turned suddenly dark and brown, and in the distance there seemed to be dark new mountains growing up and split near their summits with cracks belching fire and smoke. Everything up ahead seemed bathed in that smoke and flame.

Dar sighed. 'Well, I guess we know who won. One thing's for sure – ain't nobody coming through *that* back this way any time soon.'

'It's pretty nice down in here, though. I guess I can sort of feel what it was like before,' Suzl commented. 'So this is a Fluxland. Even with that stuff over there, it's not as bad as I thought.'

Nadya looked up at him. 'You're the boss now. At least, some of the boss.'

They turned off the road as soon as the river was visible to them. It looked reasonably clean and unsullied at this point, since it flowed towards the capital and not away from it. They had no trouble backing the wagon down near the bank, uncoiling the sipons, and quickly filling all the casks. After, Suzl and Nadya just wanted to lie in the grass for a bit, luxuriating in the feel and smell of something real for a change. Dar came and relaxed beside them.

As he stretched out, relaxing for a moment for the first time in quite a while, the two girls snuggled up close to him. Their intent, and movements, were pretty obvious, and he felt for them. For the first time, and for this little time, they were free, unwatched, unchained or roped, in a setting that was peaceful and nearly idyllic after all that they'd experienced. He liked the situation, and he liked and sympathized with them which made it all the better. He thought briefly of Lani, and found it not painful but really more, well, nostalgic. He'd seen that group of Lani look-alikes back at the train and found that they no longer affected him much at all. That was the past, and all the terrors that had happened to him were because he had refused to let go of the past but chased it instead. No more. The future was unknown and probably bad, but living in the present was more than acceptable.

He felt himself getting turned on, and it was an odd sensation, both physically and emotionally. He very much wanted to get inside these two, but, almost at the same time, he wanted *them* in *him*. He understood what it was, and sighed. His head wanted what it always had, while his working part was sending the opposite messages. The two didn't cancel out, they coexisted, making the tension inside almost unbearable. When Suzl's hand headed for the obvious place, he suddenly forced himself. 'No!'

They both stopped. 'Why not?' Suzl asked. 'Who will ever know? Or are you still hung up with—'

'Lani? No, that's gone.'

'It's Cass, isn't it?' Nadya guessed.

He chuckled. 'No, not that, either. You remember what I said about magic? Well, I got rewarded with this body for doing the right thing, but I also got punished for doing the wrong ones. Go ahead, reach in and grab what you can find.'

Curious and a little fearful, Suzl did, and when she hit the area she felt around, disbelieving. 'Oh, by the Heavens!' she breathed, and Nadya looked puzzled. Now it was Nadya's turn. She gasped and exclaimed, 'He's a girl!'

'That part of me is, yeah. The rest is what you see.' In a way he was glad it was out in the open, particularly with them. He knew he'd faced this for a long, long time.

Suzl thought a moment and chuckled. 'Dar – were you a virgin? I mean, did you ever get the chance …?'

He grinned. 'No, I wasn't a virgin. I had a couple of times early with some older women, and Lani and me, we figured it wouldn't matter. In fact, them older women taught me a whole lot of stuff I'd never have thought of otherwise.'

'Show me,' Suzl said.

'Huh?'

'Show me.'

'But I can't—'

Both girls laughed. 'You'd be surprised. We never did it with a guy, because we just *knew* we'd wind up pregnant, but we still had the urges. So after we'd see a couple of boys we really wanted, and couldn't have, we'd sneak off and sort of, well, pretend on each other.'

And, while volcanos belched in the distance as a land was being torn asunder, they showed him, and he showed them, and what he did to them they did to him. And it felt real good and lasted quite a while.

They were still at it – it seemed impossible to stop – when, during a silent period, Dar's hearing picked up a distant sound coming closer. He froze, then rolled over and hurriedly got dressed again. 'Wagon coming!' he warned them. 'We better move it!'

'Let 'em come,' Suzl said dreamily. 'It can only get worse than this, it can't get any better.'

Dar, however, had experienced far too much to take such an attitude. In fact, his interlude with the two girls had the curious effect of energizing him, and his mind was clearer and more at peace with itself than he could ever remember. Still, Suzl was right about one thing – any wagon close enough to be heard couldn't be outrun at this stage. He went to the wagon and got the rifle, which had a clip in it. He still couldn't hit the broad side of a barn, but with its spray control, he was assured, if he just aimed in the general direction and pulled the trigger anything within range would get struck by at least one of the sixty small but powerful bullets it would spew in less than a second and a half.

The wagon approached, behind a sweaty team of horses being driven hard. It was of the canvas covered type, similar to the one they were using, and looked fairly empty from the way it rocked. The lone driver looked over, spotted them, and with some difficulty slowed his four horse team and pulled off to the side of the road, a weapon in one hand and the reins in the other.

'What the hell are *you* all doing here?' Matson wanted to know. Then he spotted the water casks and understood. 'All right – you get all my property back right now. Let's move! That mess back there is expanding and I've barely been able to keep ahead of it.'

There was a cry of joy from the duggers at Matson's arrival, and several fired shots of celebration in the air. Cass was overjoyed as well, not only by Matson's sudden arrival but also by the return of Dar and the two girls. Matson, however, was having none of it, and quickly snapped orders to get the train in line and prepare to move out. To Cass's attempt to welcome him he just snapped, 'Why are you just standing around? You're working for me, now! And where the hell are my cigars?'

It wasn't until the train was formed and well on its way, with Kolada given the string lead and dispatched ahead, that Matson relaxed at all and became approachable. Cass dropped back from her point opposite Jomo at the head of the mule train until she, on her black purchased horse, rode parallel with Matson. He acknowledged her with a nod and said, 'Jomo tells me you did the whole defensive setup and even thought about the water. That right?'

She nodded. 'I didn't know if you were coming back or not, but I had to act like you weren't.'

'It was good thinking. I got out of there barely one step ahead of the new matrix and had to outrun it for four solid hours. If I'd stayed overnight like I originally intended I wouldn't be here now. Something just told me that Haldayne couldn't resist a stab at you, and that would flush him out, force him into a revolt.'

'I hear from Dar that he won.'

'Pretty sure he did, anyway. Bubbling, boiling, smoking – that place is turning into a real old-time view of Hell. Too bad, although it's got to be livelier than it was under the old bag.'

She really couldn't argue with the sentiment, although, unlike him, she also couldn't forget the poor people whose lives, if not snuffed out, would be radically and permanently changed – and certainly not for the better.

'I brought some trade goods with me,' she told him. 'Four more girls and four good horses.' At his raised eyebrows she told him the story of the encounter the night before that had saved her but precipitated the destruction of Persellus as they had known it.

'Fair enough,' he responded. 'They'll help make up for some of the ones Arden lost in the attack.'

'Not so fast! They're not gifts, you know.'

He assumed his stoic pose, trying hard to suppress a smile and not quite succeeding. 'All right. What do you think they're worth?'

'Come on!' she chided. 'You know that I'm ignorant enough of the way the system works out here that you'll skin me in the deal no matter what. I deserve at least a little consideration.'

'Why? We're even as far as I'm concerned. More than even, in fact, considering that you've gone from slave to woman of property in record time.'

'That may be, but the fact is that we – Dar and I – aren't free just because of *your* kind generosity. Even if you hadn't freed me before, you wouldn't want anybody with a Soul Rider in your stock. I'd be a time bomb waiting to go off with any customer, and in the end you'd regret it. And, as I understand it, most of these people are not going to stay the way they are when they get delivered. They'll be subject to the magic of the land or wizard that gets them. That makes Dar a lousy property, since he's locked in that way until a stronger wizard than the goddess comes along, untangles her spells, and writes new ones. That reduces his value a lot, I'd say, so it was no big thing to free him, either, particularly since you get nineteen more than you bargained for. And, as you pointed out not long ago, we're working – for free – for our ride and using our own supplies. So what *do* we owe you?'

The smile could no longer be suppressed. 'All right. Granting that, this is still business, but don't give me any more of that poor little innocent shit. I have this feeling that even without your damned Soul Rider you'd wind up running this train anyway if I looked away for a moment or didn't read every little contract clause. Now, understanding that, you tell me what you want and I'll tell you what your four slaves and four horses will buy of it.'

She thought a moment. What *did* she want, exactly? She had the feeling she should consult with Dar, but she decided against it. Matson would just use him to rob them both blind.

'I want freedom for as many of my friends as I can buy,' she told him. 'I also want some kind of stake and passage to a place where I – we – can enjoy and earn our own livings.'

He laughed. 'You want a lot for four horses and four slaves! Now, the stake needed would depend on the place, wouldn't it? And I don't think you really *have* a particular place now, so long as you have that Soul Rider inside, anyway, and that could be for life.'

'I think I wouldn't mind being a stringer,' she told him seriously.

'I doubt it. For one thing, you're too soft-hearted. You start thinking of that cargo as *people* back there instead of just more trade goods, like horses and mules and hard goods, and you start bleeding for them. You couldn't help it, even though none of 'em can ever go back to Anchor and they'd all go nuts or die quickly in the Flux without a wizard looking over 'em. Anyway, it's a closed guild. If you aren't born a stringer, you can't be one. And if you tried to set up in competition, other stringers would get together and do you in. Part of the code, and good business. And we don't have partners, just employees. Still, I agree that you're doomed to wander. Want a job with a stringer train, then?'

She grinned. 'That might be the next best thing. But I wouldn't want a job where I had to stay out of the Fluxlands and Anchors with the mules and wagons, or where I just stayed a few hours.'

'That's not a problem,' he responded, understanding that they were in fact negotiating. 'Most duggers don't go into Fluxlands because they don't want to or they're afraid they might get kidnapped or used by the powers that be. Some of 'em are just sensitive about their looks and don't feel comfortable outside the void. As for Anchors, I've had a problem the last couple of years because I didn't have any total humans to help me with the packs going in. Had to depend on the locals, and they *charge*. The average layover is three days, and would have been back there if things didn't feel funny and if I didn't have this big human cargo to deliver down the line, eating me broke the longer I have that many on my hands.'

She nodded. 'Fine. So the Anchors allow only people they consider as human as they are inside, and you need humans. I'm human. I don't know whether Dar would pass their inspection, though.'

'Probably. They're not as fussy so long as you look normal. They have the mental image of duggers as you know them. He, or she, or whatever it is, would have to be careful that nobody found out that secret, though. Anchorfolk are so damned scared of anything different that a mob would tear him to bits and get a medal for it. You should know that.'

She nodded. 'I think he'd take that risk. I assume we work for expenses in the various places.'

'Expenses, hell! You get a salary on account. Anything you spend anyplace you get deducted. Anything left over at the end of each circuit, which is most of a year, you get credited to a stringer account. If you live long enough, don't get fired, and keep your costs down you can retire to the Fluxland of your choice someday. Or sucker some friendly wizard into making the pocket of your dreams, which is what most of 'em do.'

'So there are some friendly wizards. I'd begun to wonder. Seriously, though – how many duggers that you know of ever lived long enough to retire?'

He shrugged. 'Well, none *personally* ...'

'Uh huh. It's a deal.'

He laughed. 'Impulsive, aren't you? You decided on this first thing, didn't you?'

'Well, I admit I had it in mind. I wasn't sure whether you wanted to travel with a Soul Rider, though.'

'That's more serious than you think. But there are pluses with the minuses on that. Potentially you're stronger than any wizard, although it's useful only in defense, I hear. That's fine. What protects you protects the train. Of course, you're a magnet for trouble, but out here I'm not sure I could tell the difference anyway. At least your Rider's concern is also mine now, so maybe we'll work together to get rid of that and it'll be done with you.'

She looked at him with interest. 'Then you're going to report this?'

'Honey, I'm going to do at least that. Haldayne's bad for business right where he is, at the intersection of three good routes. He ordered an attack on, and was responsible for, a massacre of a stringer train, so nobody's safe until he's eliminated. As soon as we unload as much as we can in Globbus, not to mention alerting them there so the route from this side can be closed, we're heading for Pericles. Not the whole train – I'll just have to eat expenses on what I can't unload, although I'm going to take some merchandise with me to Pericles because I think there might be a market for it.'

'What's this Pericles?'

'The home of one of the oldest, battiest, most degenerate and powerful wizards on all of World – and, incidentally, the dean of the current Nine Who Guard.'

She gasped. 'So there *is* a Nine! But – what do you mean by "current"?'

'Nobody lives forever, even out here. I think the old boy told me once that his grandmother was one of the originals. He's barely, he says, six hundred years old.'

'Six hun – oh, my! Do you think he's really that old?'

'Could be. But he's the strongest of the Nine, and therefore the only one publicly known. If he's been around that long, and known for at least a hundred years, then he must be one hell of a wizard because that makes him automatically one hell of a target.' He sighed. 'Well, I guess that concludes our business. See if your friend wants to go along or what, but the job's open either way.'

'We haven't settled anything,' she responded. 'I just got hired, that's all. I still want some of my friends free.'

He sighed. 'You need an advance, so the four horses will take care of that for two of you. But what if I freed four of your friends in an even trade? They'd have no jobs, no defenses, no place to go, and I'm not about to hire on *six* new hands, none of whom can even shoot. All you'd do is kill 'em for sure, or give them to Globbus or someplace else for free. In the Fluxlands, everybody's either owned, if they have no Flux power, or employed if they do. If any of that lot had much power we'd have seen it by now.'

She hated to admit it to herself, but she had to agree that he was right. It was very easy to say 'You are free!' and feel good about it, but they would be free in a land where they would be at the mercy of just about everyone and powerless to prevent slavery at no gain to themselves or anyone else, and no input by anyone into how and where they would be used. If she could free them to return to Anchor that would be one thing, but even she would only be a visitor in that realm now, there at the sufferance of authorities and on a limited permit. 'Well, there are three I'd like to free, anyway.'

'Nope. Two is tops. I can't handle any more. After that the cost becomes counter-productive. The only reason I can handle four of you is that I'm sure one or two of you will screw up and never return from one place or another, at least in any usable form. And those two will work strictly for the value of the other two slaves we sell until they exhaust their accounts. Then we'll see if they are worth keeping or if they're fired. No other guarantees, no other deals than that.'

'Mister generosity.'

'I'm not generous. I'm your boss. And I'll fire your ass and that of our musclebound friend if I'm the least bit unhappy. No more lip, take it or leave it.'

'I'll talk to Dar when we stop and then let you know,' she told him. 'How far to Globbus?'

'Oh, it's about sixty kilometers from here. We average a little better than twenty kilometers a day, so that's three days. Closer than Persellus is to Anchor Logh by a fair amount. In fact, it's about the same distance to Anchor Logh from Globbus or Persellus – I had to go out of my way to do some business that, damn it, will probably never get done now.'

That 'night,' as train time was measured in the void, Cass put the proposition to Dar, who seemed interested although unhappy that they didn't get more. 'You really want to be a dugger,' he told her, 'and I can't see any other place I'd fit in. Hell, anyplace else I'm a freak, but out here I'm *normal* compared to most of 'em.'

She nodded. 'That's what I figured. Now comes the hard part, though. Which two?'

He didn't even have to think. 'Suzl and Nadya, of course.'

'Not Ivon?'

He chuckled dryly. 'That bigmouth was hiding behind a wagon while you girls were reloading rifles in the fight. He's also still scared to death of the duggers. I like him, but for all his muscles he'd never fit in around here. I think the two girls will.'

She had to agree, but found it surprising they agreed so readily on both choices. 'You three spent an awfully long time getting the water. We just about gave you up for dead. Something I should know about now?'

He sighed. 'Aw, hell. We took a three-way roll in the grass, Cass, if you must know.'

'But—'

'Hey! If the Sister General can do it, why not us? Besides, I can't help it. I still like girls. And what man is going to give *me* a tumble even if I was willing to do it? Jomo?'

She didn't argue that point, although she suspected that there were some men who'd be delighted with him the way he was. Considering the people she'd already seen in Anchor as well as Flux, that would be a minor oddity hardly worth noting. 'What I mean is, I didn't really think that those two were that way.'

He chuckled. 'They never tried the other way, but they were willing. Then they – found out.'

She was fascinated. 'What about – you? How do you feel about it?'

He grew very serious. 'It was really kind of funny. Until now I been real tight about the first time it would happen, but I knew it had to happen. Now, hell, it's like I'm free, a whole new person. I got lucky, that's all. Most folks would have turned away, or treated me like I had some deathly disease, or something, but they didn't. Funny, too – those shots must have worn off, 'cause they got real turned on, if you know what I mean.' He paused and looked suddenly concerned. 'This doesn't poison them for you, does it?'

She shook her head. 'Of course not. In fact, it says something about them that they accepted you as you were. It means they'll fit in this crazy setup. Let's call them over.'

The two girls were delighted at the news, but distressed that they were to be the only ones. 'It makes us feel so *guilty*,' Suzl told them.

'I told Cass about back at the river,' Dar told them.

Both looked slightly embarrassed. 'Is that what it is, then? Because we ...' Nadya said finally, her voice dropping off. 'But we didn't intend to. It just sort of built up in me the longer we were in that place.'

'Me, too,' Suzl agreed. 'Stronger than I ever felt before, and it didn't matter who or what. I'm just glad Dar was there. If I was alone and feeling like that I'd have screwed a horse if one came up. Nothing personal, Dar.'

He nodded. 'That's funny, though. I felt it, too. Still do. I just put it down to the shots wearing off.'

Nadya shook her head. 'Nope. None of the others have it. It was something in the air, I guess.'

Cass thought it over. 'Something in the air ... Maybe part of Haldayne's new world that was strong enough to seep through. Who knows what urges somebody like that has, or what sort of thing he likes? If the goddess could absent-mindedly rearrange a couple of mountains because it slipped her mind how they were and she liked them better that way, then his own ideas might change things as well, even without him consciously willing it. Maybe emotions run stronger than will, or at least ahead. It would make sense.'

'A whole land run like Roaring Mountain's pocket,' Dar said, and shivered a bit.

Cass got back to business. 'Don't feel that was the reason. At least, not the only one in either of our cases. I picked you two before I knew. You're both farmgirls, you know how to ride, and you're adaptable. Look at most of them

381

back there. Still mostly dead inside, just waiting for the ax to fall. That's what sets the four of us apart – we accepted what was and went from there. They are probably better off where they're going if they can't go home. We're going to beat this system, and maybe have some fun doing it.'

She went forward and told Matson of their decision and their choices. He was surprised only at one thing. 'No men, huh? Didn't pick out anyone for yourself?'

She shook her head. 'No. I gather by that comment, though, that you knew about them.'

He grinned. 'I could hardly avoid noticing. For the record, those two are the best of a mediocre lot, I think, from past judgments. They may work out, although they'll have to watch themselves in the Fluxlands – and Anchors, too, if they get into any. Attractive humans, male and female, have a habit of disappearing there. In either case I'm dealing with a wizard who has more power in his little finger than I have in my whole body or with a church with absolute control of a large population of ignorant idiots, which means it would cost me too damned much to get help and I have no real pressure. There are other stringers if I become a problem. No, I'm satisfied. Dress up the train a bit. We'll get them presentable in Globbus.' He paused. 'But what about you? If you want to blow the account, you could get some hair and maybe remake yourself if you wanted to.'

She thought about it. 'No. I've been this way and I think I'll stay this way, at least for a while.'

He stared into her eyes. 'You ever had sex? With anybody, I mean, of either sex?'

She was startled by the directness of the question, but felt comfortable enough with him to answer it. In fact, around Matson her feelings were oddly different, although she couldn't really put her finger on it. 'No,' she said softly. 'Never.'

'Never wanted to?'

'Oh, sure. I had the urges, yes. But I'm just not the sort that boys want, that's all.'

'Maybe. Maybe for *some* boys, or men, that'd be true. Most of 'em only look at the outsides in Anchor, which is why I call 'em all dumb and ignorant. If I only looked at outsides in the Flux, I'd never have the best dugger team on World and I couldn't stand ninety percent of the Fluxlands. Arden, now, wasn't pretty by some standards, although she sure knew how to make herself so when it counted. She was as bald as you, you know. Kept it that way because she said she didn't have time in the void to mess with her hair.'

The only view Cass had had of Arden was pretty ugly and not conducive to knowing anything about what she had looked like in life. 'I didn't know that,' she told him.

'You sure you're not running from sex? I've seen it before. Women who get to where they try and make themselves as unattractive as possible. Confess, now. You got rid of those shots back in Persellus.'

'Maybe you're right,' she responded, her mind a little mixed up at what he was saying, wondering if in fact it was true. 'But maybe it's just that I don't want somebody attracted to me just because I faked it all with fashions or even magic spells. This is crazy, but I really do *like* being me, and, right now, I've never been happier in my whole life. Does that sound like I've gone mad with the void or what?'

'No,' he said gently. 'No, it sounds like you did something most folks never really do, in Anchor or Flux. You grew up. Most folks never do. Most of *them* never will, never would in any case. That's the bottom line in why I took you on. Now you have to grow up one little bit more or else you're going to lose something. Either you can hide behind that boy's face and voice and keep forcing those feelings down or you can say the hell with it and let it out. If you hold it in and hide, then you'll still make a hell of a good dugger but you'll never be a complete human being.' He pointed to the regular duggers, all misshapen, most deformed inside and out. 'The Flux will just reinforce it, like it reinforces their own problems. Ever think that any of them has enough on account to get themselves done back to any human form they want?'

No, she hadn't thought of it. 'You mean they're that way because they *want* to be like that?'

He nodded. 'They're all hiding, just like you. Oh, they're not all hiding from the same things, but they're hiding all the same. We'll never know what turned them into those forms, so we'll never know what keeps them that way. But's that's *you* over there, Cass. Now.'

She didn't like that idea, but she was in a minor state of shock from his talk, and she didn't want to admit that he might be right. 'So what would you suggest? I shoot the profit making myself into a glamorous sexpot? *Who* wouldn't last long in Flux or Anchor?'

He shook his head negatively. 'No. If you like it that way, be that way. But be that way because it's practical, or comfortable, or it's just *you*, not because you're hiding behind it.'

She thought back to that time in Anchor, about all the rejection and her own attitudes and feelings. Was Matson right? Could it be true? 'So what do I do if it *is* true, which I don't think it is.'

'If it isn't, prove it. Take the plunge.'

She smiled grimly. 'Yeah, that's an easy dare. Take the plunge with who? Jomo? Nagada? One of the fake Lanis? Seems like everybody around here is either female or not exactly human.'

'There's one,' he said casually, blowing a smoke ring. 'Me.'

She stared at him as if he were suddenly some strange and terrible creature, the man she'd imagined when she first was scared stiff of the sight of him that day back in Anchor Logh. Her emotions were so jumbled up inside her she could neither understand nor sort them out. 'You?' She paused a moment. 'It's just Haldayne's influence. You got a jolt along with them, and coming on top of Arden's death ...'

'Could be,' he agreed. 'Probably at least a little. But that doesn't mean that anything I said was wrong. Look, I'm not asking you to marry me, just take a tumble up in the hay wagon. The only chance you'll have to screw your boss and get away with it. Yes, or no? It may be your only chance – I'm going to work the tail off the four of you from now on, and you've got to learn how to fight and how to shoot to be any good to me in the long run.'

'You aren't just teasing me? I mean, this is for real?' She felt oddly distant, her mind and body a confused mess and somehow out of control.

'Nope. Serious. I'll even pour us each a shot of good brandy so you won't have the cigar smoke.'

'Yes, all right,' she heard herself saying, as if in a trance.

He got up, and she followed him. They walked forward after he took a small bottle out of his own pack, and he cleared away a couple of dugger guards, repositioning them well away from the wagon. He jumped up, turned, then helped her up, and then put the tarps down front and rear, lighting a small lantern inside with a match so that there was a small amount of light.

They were in there the better part of two hours, and there was little doubt to anyone who noticed what was going on in there, but the only conversation heard was his sudden exclamation, 'I'll be damned! You really *are* a virgin!' and her soft, nearly unintelligible reply in a tone of voice she had frankly never used before and never knew was there.

'*Was*,' she responded dreamily.

13

Globbus

The next two days were extremely busy ones, offering little time for the newcomers to have their minds on anything other than business, but it was obvious to those who knew her that Cass had changed. She seemed more relaxed, more at peace with herself, and, if anything even more determined to learn what could be learned and make the most of every opportunity.

As for Cass, while she felt different she couldn't quite explain what that difference was. It was less in the experience itself than in the sense that some enormous load had been lifted from her mind. It was an odd sensation, but out here, in the void, she felt completely and totally free for the first time in her memory.

Matson had been marvelous that night, even cautioning her that the blood and mess would not happen again, but she hadn't cared about that. After, though, he hadn't really referred to it nor treated her any differently than before. He was the boss, and a pretty fair but tough one, and that was all right with her, too.

Equally gratifying to them all was the way the duggers had accepted them, although there was still some strong, underlying suspicion of Dar for his actions in the fight and they bore down on him far harder than on the others. It was clear that he would win their confidence and respect only by superior conduct in the next fight and not before.

It was also clear that the additions, two of them, anyway, made the train dugger-heavy in the sense that there really wasn't enough extra work for four of them. To everyone's surprise it was Nadya who proved the most worth, after Cass of course, helping equally with the animals, supplies and repacking, and even cooking. Although Matson had agreed that they would not have to have anything to do with their former fellow captives on this trip, since they knew them, Nadya also proved adept at the literal stringing technique and didn't mind the nasty comments and envy from the others. Suzl, on the other hand, did the minimum necessary and seemed to spend most of her time with Dar.

Still, they got some arms training, and some other fighting techniques as well, but clearly it would take far longer than the two nights and few breaks they had for the starter lessons. Although Dar proved to be the best natural shooter, it was Cass and Nadya who were presented, their last night out, with their own guns by Matson on recommendation of their dugger trainers.

The final day in would be a short one, and Cass rode up to Matson as they approached the Fluxland. 'Just wanted to know something about the place before we got there,' she told him.

'Well, it's like its name. Exactly,' the stringer replied casually.

'It's like a globbus? What's a globbus?'

'It isn't anything. It's a nonsense word. And that pretty well describes the place. It was set up by the guild the wizards have as one of three places where young wizards could study and practice and perfect what powers they have.'

'You mean it's like a school?'

He nodded. 'In a way. But no school you've ever seen before. Think of the mess a hundred or so practicing – and mostly not very good – young wizards might make, then multiply that by the number of students who went through it, and you have an idea of what real insanity is.'

'It's dangerous, then?'

He shrugged. 'If you mean in the sense of kidnap and kill, no, it's not at all dangerous. But if you think of it as a playground for a bunch of children of gods, then you get an idea of what it really is. Just remember to stay on the road, trust nobody and believe even less of it, and stick to the central district which is fairly safe and sane by comparison. Don't let one of the locals sucker or seduce you into something, no matter how innocent. They have what is known as an implied consent rule.'

'What's that mean?'

'It means that nothing you see can hurt or affect you no matter how it seems otherwise unless you give your implied consent to it. It's a game with them to get that implied consent, and you don't have to say "yes" to something to give it, which is why it's implied. Just think everything through and use all your common sense and you'll find it is something of an experience.'

She went back and briefed the others on what he'd said, but she couldn't answer their questions because Matson either couldn't or wouldn't. The only way she got the implied consent idea across to herself, as well as the other three, was to remind Dar of his experience in trust in the bar at Anchor Logh that had cost so much.

Globbus began in the manner of all Fluxlands, with things becoming a bit more solid, normal senses returning, and, finally, it opened up into a real place in every sense of the word. Or was it? It was very easy from the start to see why Globbus was nonsense.

Grass grew in multicolored striped and checked patterns. Cows and horses in the fields had any number of legs and even heads, and looked like creatures put together by a bunch of drunks and then painted in outlandish patterns. Trees in places looked like nothing they'd ever seen, and some grew upside down, roots high in the air, while others had weird looking fruit. Dogwood would occasionally bark at them, and pussywillow purred or hissed, and at one part tiny crabapples scuttled back to their branches, pincers closing. Hills and bushes were sculpted into fantastic shapes, and even the sky often changed colors and at one point was half a dull pink and half dark as night, with stars shining, some of which had the disconcerting habit of occasionally racing to new positions and patterns as you watched.

Water flowed in no particular direction, and some waterfalls flowed up. Large clouds floated by overhead and suddenly decided to make obscene gestures at the travelers below. Few people were seen, and none close up, until they approached the center of the Fluxland and its university proper.

There were buildings now, large and small, no two even remotely alike. One very normal-looking stone house was atop a high and very fragile-looking tree with no sign of a way up or down; another was a traditional cottage with peaked red slate roof, sitting upside down on its roof point. As they watched, two rather ordinary looking young men approached the house, stood there, flipped upside down in the air, then walked in the upside down door, their heads about three meters off the ground.

It was a bit much for any of them, but it was particularly stunning to the captives, for this was the first Fluxland they had ever seen. Most just gawked in disbelief or tried not to look, particularly at some of the people, who were only theoretically people. It was easy to see, looking at them, why *this* Fluxland was no inhibitor to duggers. The entire train moved into the center of what could be loosely called 'town'.

The street was not crowded, but was nonetheless a mob scene. In front of them, a small horse was riding a man, while on a porch two ugly-looking old dogs were arguing in perfect human speech about the proper solution to an abstract mathematical problem. People with two heads argued with each other, while others looked lizard-like or were part animal, part human, part something else. It was, nevertheless, less a chamber of horrors than a lunatic's view of World – no, *every* lunatic's view of World, all at once.

There was, however, an area in the center that looked normal. It was really four huge two story square buildings around a central open plaza, but that plaza had a large circular stage in the center and cordoned off areas of turf all around it. It was empty now, but it was clear that it was used often.

'That's the Market Block,' Matson told them. 'That's where we're going to unload most of our surplus merchandise in three days.'

'Three days! You mean we have to spend three days in this place?' Dar exclaimed nervously. 'I mean, two blocks over there is a square rainstorm – and it's raining *up* into the clouds!'

The stringer grinned. 'Yep. I hadn't expected to be here so early, but it's not bad so long as you can get used to the people and animals and whatever wandering about. So long as you all stay in this area, within the Market Block and the four big buildings facing it and on the streets between them, you're safe. There's shops and services available in these places that you can't get anywhere else, particularly at decent prices, because they're all practice shops for the best students with specific talents rather than the general type like the goddess or Haldayne.'

'You mean the Rory Montagne type,' Cass noted sourly.

'Yeah, like that, but service oriented rather than criminal types. It's all magic, of course, but it's all the permanent type. Just about none of this is illusion, remember. There's hotels in that building over there, as well as holding areas for the Market Block. That one next to it has a huge number of eateries of every size and type. The building across from the hotel is the services building. That's where you go if you want numbers removed or hair or a whole new you. The one across from the food pavilion is the merchandise mart. Got it?'

They nodded. 'Now, how do we draw on our accounts?' Cass wanted to know.

'First you say you're with the Matson train, then sign for it when they give you the bill. I'll let you know any time you want what your balance is, since they're all posted to the train bill at the hotel center. Most Fluxlands have their own money of some kind, just like the Anchors, but the universal unit, used here as well, is the kil. It's short for kilogram, but nobody knows now what it's a kilogram of. That's long lost in history. It's broken down into a hundred grams, of course, but don't look for it. It's all on paper, and settled on common bills paid out of established accounts.'

'Well, that's fine,' Nadya put in, 'but how do we know how much *we* have to spend of this money?'

He thought a moment. 'You don't, since I haven't sold your stakes yet. Cass, you and Dar should figure on no more than two hundred kils each, while Suzl and Nadya might have a little more – but, remember, you two girls, you have to stake yourselves out of that when we pull out, so keep it in the fifty to seventy kil range. That's for everything here except hotel, which the train picks up.'

It was clear from the central lobby of the hotel building that they were far from the only train in Globbus. In fact, there were at least four, and Matson was greeted with shouts and waves from a host of duggers, most of whom looked even worse than his, and at least one tall, dark, exotic-looking female stringer who ran up and gave him a big hug. Cass had to suppress more than a little tinge of jealousy, but she kept control of herself. It was just a reminder of the new enigma, that the unattainable, now attained, was still unattainable.

The rooms were large and comfortable; in fact, more comfortable than those Cass had stayed in in Persellus, with the floors fully carpeted and a small parlor area with two chairs and a sofa. The room had a bathroom, and Cass, who elected to stay with Nadya, had the joy of being the old sophisticate showing the rube the joys of running water and flush toilets.

They weren't needed to check in the team and cargo, so they were free as soon as they were settled in, and the foursome met again in the lobby and went first to the food pavilion to eat. The amount of choices was overwhelming, although some of the prices gave good indication of just how far a kil did, or didn't go. Although they had all dreamed of a real restaurant meal, they decided to settle, for now, on sandwiches and beer from a walk-up. They noticed, though, that the first floor only was devoted to countless eateries – upstairs were all sorts of bars, entertainment joints, and other signs of a wide-open place the likes of which even Main Street had never seen.

After eating, they decided to tend to first things first, going to the 'services' building and trying to ignore the six men and women going by who had wheels instead of legs and feet and seemed to just roll along effortlessly, as well as the woman with the body of many men's dreams and the head of some sort of short-beaked bird and other oddities. Dar did remark, though, that in *this* company he was absolutely ordinary, and there was no denying that.

The building directory listed what seemed to be hundreds of service experts, most of whom were specialists in things they couldn't make head nor tail of. What, for example, was a master of sustentation? Or a storax modifier, for that matter? And did they really want to know?

Fortunately, there was an information kiosk at which to ask for what was needed. In point of fact, the kiosk was asked directly, for it was a human-looking man down to the waist, but below it he had a huge, round mass on which he could apparently swivel. He was surrounded by a rack with all sorts of handouts, particularly accessible because in place of those legs he had four hands. He looked at them as they approached and said, 'May I serve you?'

Cass swallowed hard. 'Tattoo removal and hair growth?' she tried tentatively.

The information kiosk nodded. 'Corridor C, office 202,' he responded briskly. 'General cosmetic alterations.' One of the arms shot out. 'Right over there. Anything else?'

'How about breaking transformation curses?' Dar asked.

'General, group, specific, or personal?'

'Ah, personal.'

'Corridor F, office 509.'

They nodded and walked away. 'I'd say let's see about you two first,' Cass said to Suzl and Nadya. 'After, we'll check on Dar's situation.'

'I can meet you,' Dar suggested. 'I don't need anything where you're going.'

It was agreed, and the three young women headed for the designated corridor and office. The sign on the door said to walk in, and they did to a small waiting room. One wall was covered with pictures of all sorts of people and creatures and combinations of same involving women, the other involving all men. Obviously, this one did quite a bit more than they were after.

A small window slid back, revealing a very dark woman's face. 'Yes?'

As briefly as they could, they explained what they wanted, and Cass added, 'I guess I can stand some minor work myself.' She hadn't intended to, but there was something about seeing that lady stringer embracing Matson that just changed her mind. She knew it was silly, but it meant very little one way or the other.

The woman emerged from a rear door into the waiting room. She was stark naked, with dark brown face, hands, and feet, but her body was covered in very fine fur that was alternately black and white striped, in a spiral pattern from neck to legs. Her thick, wiry hair was snow white except for a single wide black streak running from brow all the way back, and she had long, pointed ears and a short, shaved tail with a furry white blob at the end.

When she talked, it was noted that the inside of her mouth was black with a snow white tongue.

She took note of their attention and smiled. 'Do you like it? It was one of my old teacher's last works for last year's total body collection. It didn't sell, for some reason, but I liked it so much I kept it.'

'It's – stunning,' Nadya responded truthfully, hoping not to be pressed.

The woman seemed pleased. 'Step back into here, all of you, please.'

They followed her a bit nervously through the door, Cass starting to rethink the whole proposition of any changes in this way. There were four large chairs in back lined up in front of a single long mirror. The woman indicated that they were to each pick one and sit down, and they did, growing more uncertain.

'Now, then. Most of my designers are off right now, but I think I can handle the three of you. Let's start with you,' she said, going first to Suzl. 'Nice build. A good foundation. We could do a lot with you.'

'Just some hair and get rid of the tattoos,' she told the woman.

'About twenty added centimeters and a slight body realignment will do you wonders,' the striped woman suggested. 'As it is now you'll run to fat and get chunky as you grow older.'

She actually considered it, but finally rejected it. There followed a whole series of attempts to get her to accept hair with an unusual color or pattern, but she decided on straight, shoulder-length, and black just the way it had been. The striped woman sighed and you could see she thought that Suzl had no imagination or spirit of adventure whatsoever, but she stood back, made a pass with her hands, and Suzl gasped at her reflection. It was like greeting an old friend you'd thought lost and gone forever.

The tattoo and thumb stain went with the hair. 'Now, the hair is low maintenance,' the magical cosmetologist assured her. 'It will stay at that length and style unless you change it, and if you do just wash it before changing it and it'll remain the new style. If you wish, I can have it grow normally, but right now it can be cut shorter but will always grow back to that length and set.'

'That's fine. Wonderful, in fact,' Suzl assured her. 'Now all I need are some clothes.'

'I could give you a treatment similar to mine – no design if you prefer, color of your choice – that would make clothing unnecessary up to forty degrees or down to ten below.'

Suzl passed.

Nadya got much the same spiel from the woman, who was obviously aching to be 'creative' and not finding any takers. Nadya chose a permanent dark brown pageboy and declined even the modest offer to do something about her slight overbite. By the time the striped body wizard got to Cass she was resigned. 'Just hair and tattoo, right?'

'I don't have any tattoos. They were taken care of before,' she replied. 'Actually, I'm not really sure what I want.'

The magical cosmetologist brightened. 'Tell you what. Let me try a few things out on you. No charge if you don't like them, and I'll change anything back at any time.'

It was tempting. She looked over at the other two. 'Suppose you go check with Dar? I'll meet you there or back at the hotel.'

They agreed, signed the required small papers they were handed, and were gone, although Nadya remained a moment and said, 'Don't get carried away. You may hate yourself tomorrow.'

She grinned. 'I'll remember. Nothing radical.'

But, the fact is, what was done was a lot of fun. Rejecting the exotic or freakish, the cosmetologist tried a variety of hair styles and colors, subtle facial adjustments, and body adjustments. She found out exactly what it was like to have large breasts and a sexy figure and decided that it wasn't her style. At least now she *knew*, she told herself.

But is was finally a matter of small changes that she settled on, mostly after telling Miss Rona, as the cosmetologist was known, that she was, after all, a mule whip on a stringer train who had to remain both practical for the job and human for entry to Anchor. She had an odd impulse for long hair, and finally Miss Rona suggested a reddish brown, thick and straight, coming just below the shoulders, and showed her how to tie it up or into a pony tail, the last her preferred style. Her face was softened a bit, losing a little of its boyish look while not changing all that much, and her complexion was darkened to a light olive to complement the changes. On her body, she wanted strong, hard muscles that would not have to be maintained but would not give her a mannish look, and this proved amazingly easy.

To balance, her shape was slightly recontoured, her hips slightly widened so now her work pants would hang on them at the waist, and her breasts were slightly redone so that they were still small and required no support but were clearly there and perfectly formed. In the end, most of the changes were so subtle that, except for the hair, it was difficult to really point to them, but the overall effect of the changes was to make her unmistakably female.

Miss Rona, in fact, was delighted. 'This sort of very small detail work is the most challenging,' she told her. And so was the forty kil bill, which couldn't really be disputed since the whole thing could be withdrawn with a few waves of the striped woman's hand. She sighed, decided that it was worth it but that this was *it*, no matter what, and signed the slip.

No one was at the kiosk except the kiosk, but he told her that the others had gone back to the hotel. Nadya was in the room, just relaxing, and she was enthusiastic over the change in Cass. 'Perfect! Just perfect! It's more you than you, if you know what I mean.'

She appreciated the compliment. 'For what it cost, it better be. If I have any money left, I'll buy some spare clothes. I think it's time for you to get some, though.'

She sighed. 'I suppose. It's been so long they'll feel funny just to wear.' The merchandise building, though, changed her mind, and they both spent quite a while just trying on various things. Both finally opted for practical wear, more or less stringer fashion, yet in colors other than the stringer's basic black. Although she bought a pair of boots, Nadya carried them back to the room, finding that the clothes actually made her feel human again but that her feet and lower calves revolted against footwear. For the moment, she decided to remain barefoot.

Dar and Suzl weren't back in their rooms yet, so the two women decided to eat without them.

'I forgot to ask – how did Dar's session go?' Cass wanted to know.

'Not good. They said it was powerful and complicated and would take real experts to work out. They wanted over a thousand kils up front to do it, too, with no guarantees.'

Cass whistled. 'How'd he take it?'

'Pretty well. A lot better than Suzl, I think.'

The handsome young man approached them in the bar and stood there for a second. He was young, perhaps only a couple of years older than they, and extremely human, although his hair was white save for a small reddish spot near the peak. 'Ah, you are the man with the problem?' he asked tentatively.

Dar looked up at him. 'Yeah. Are you the budding god the guy near the kiosk talked about?'

The young man chuckled and sat down. 'I suppose so, although I have no ambitions to carve out any little worldlets and preside. I am entirely interested in research, in learning everything there is to learn about these powers. Until I can get a position here, though, I have to support my researches on my own, hence my friends over at services. They get a small percentage for sniffing out people like you, pardon my language.' He looked over at Suzl. 'I can see why you are anxious to be rid of the problem, sir.' She smiled at him.

'Can you do it?' he asked.

The young wizard shrugged. 'I don't know until I take a good look. But I won't charge unless I can at least help. Is that not fair?'

Dar looked at Suzl, who nodded. 'Sounds fair to us.'

'Then come with me now, if you can.'

'We can. But how much will it cost?'

'Shall we say a hundred?'

He thought a moment. 'That's almost all I got. I have to eat for the next couple of days, you know.'

'Seventy-five, then, but no less.'

'I'll make it up,' Suzl told him. 'I'll take it back in trade.'

They left and followed the young man outside, then down a side street and out of the Market area. Dar started getting a little nervous.

'Just in here,' the young wizard told them, and they stopped by a small pyramidal building, then went inside after him. It was a small pyramid on the outside but a large rectangle on the inside, crowded with all sorts of junk as well as the remains of half-eaten meals and lots of dust. There was, how-ever, a carpeted clear area in the back near a bed that obviously had last been made when the boy arrived in Globbus. 'Now, take off your clothes.'

Dar did, and was subjected to a minute and somewhat embarrassing phys-ical examination. 'Fascinating,' the wizard muttered. 'Just fascinating.' He stepped back and looked at Dar again.

'It's superior work,' he told them. 'Among the best. I've seen many variants of this – there are lots in Globbus – but the math here is simply brilliant. Who did it, did you say?'

'The former goddess of Persellus.'

Brows went up. 'Former?'

'She was overthrown and, I assume, killed a few days ago.'

'Too bad. A great loss to the science. Still, I can follow the basic formulae.' He closed his eyes and appeared to be in deep thought. Finally he said, 'I think I have the spell's complement. If I understood what she did correctly, that is. There is, however, some risk.'

'To his life?' Suzl asked apprehensively.

'Oh, no, nothing like that. The application of the complement could, con-ceivably, go more than one way, since it's not an undoing of the spell – we don't have the weeks necessary for that and you don't have the money to shorten that period – but an effort at applying an equal and opposite spell superimposed over this one. I *think* it will work, but there is a slight percent-age that it could push him all the way to the female matrix, physically and psychologically, or it might split him – twelve hours totally and completely female, twelve hours totally and completely male. There is always a risk in this sort of thing, you must understand. That's why the specialists demand their money up front.'

Dar looked over at Suzl. 'You really want it?'

She nodded. 'I do. If you're willing.'

He shrugged. 'What have I got to lose? Go ahead.'

The young man closed his eyes once more, and his head snapped back, then forward once again. He staggered but did not fall. Suddenly he came fully erect, his eyes opening, and he seemed to struggle with his right hand. A single gesture was made with the trembling hand, and Dar felt a slight tingling. 'Now!' the young wizard shouted, and Suzl screamed.

Dar turned towards her, concerned, and the young man looked slightly upset. 'Now that's a *curse*! Damn!' Suzl fainted, and both rushed over to her, picked her up, and put her on the bed.

'What's wrong with her?' Dar demanded to know. 'She wasn't even in this, damn it.'

'I'm afraid she was, and I didn't notice it,' the wizard replied. 'That is one tricky curse you have. It took the complement and deflected it to the nearest receptor. Here – let's get these pants off her.'

They did, and Dar gasped. 'She said she wanted it, and that was all the curse needed for implied consent,' the wizard explained. 'Now she's got it, as solidly as you got yours.'

'But I still got a woman's crotch!'

'And in my judgment you always will have. And, unfortunately, she will now always have what you lost, the complement being as strong as the original.'

'But – it's so *big*! And she's so short!'

'Well, it *is* a scaled-down version of yours,' the wizard told him. 'I did what I could to keep it proportional, but it *is* the complement to your curse, and so basically your pattern. Uh – of course there will be no charge. I admit I *have* learned a great deal from this curse.'

Dar shook his head. 'And what I learn about guys in bars is of no value. Damn!'

Suzl stirred and came to, having fainted mostly from the shock. She looked puzzled, then felt gingerly in the crotch area. 'Oh, by the Heavens! It's real!' She groaned, then sat up on the side of the bed, then got to her feet. 'How do men *walk* with these things?'

'The same way women walk with breasts like yours,' Dar responded. 'You just are used to it.'

'But it's – *huge*! On you, it'd be okay. On me, it's grotesque.' She looked over at the wizard. 'Take it away! Take it back!'

The young man looked sheepish. 'I can't. It's beyond me. It may be beyond anybody but the best. That goddess wasn't only good with curses, she was devious as Hell.'

She stared at him. 'You mean I have the same curse *he* does – only backwards?'

The wizard nodded. 'That's about it. I'm afraid the curse construed you to ask for it, and since it couldn't give it to your man, here, it gave it to you. You're stuck.'

She sat down again on the side of the bed and sighed. 'And I never even found out what it was like to be a woman, damn it.' She sighed again. 'But, then, neither do men.' She looked up at the wizard. 'Will it work?'

'It's a proportional model of his. It'll work if your mind wants it to.'

She stood up and put her pants back on. 'Ugh! More shopping to do. Something to support this thing and some pants with real give in the crotch. These *hurt!*' She looked over at Dar. 'Well, it isn't exactly the way I wanted it, but I think at least in one way that you and I were made for each other.'

14

Council

'Now let me get this straight,' Nadya said, sounding confused and bewildered. She stared at the small, attractive, well-built woman and the huge muscular man in front of her. 'You, Suzl, are the man, and you, Dar, are the woman? Holy Mother protect me!'

She and Cass had now heard the complete story but still couldn't quite believe it. Even so, Cass, relaxing in a chair and chewing idly on a stick of hard candy, said, 'I have to say, Suzl, you're taking it a lot better than I would.'

She shrugged. 'I was real upset for a while there, but then the more I thought about it the more I – accepted it. You know, I think I'm the only one ever taken in the Paring Rite who wasn't really sorry to go. I used to sit there and dream of what was beyond dull, stodgy Anchor Logh. Sometimes I'd imagine myself as something different. Part horse, maybe, or cat, or something. I always knew there was something else out here, beyond the Flux wall. I imagined it as something like it is – a world full of freaks.'

They, Nadya in particular, started to protest but she silenced them, and, at the moment, she had the floor.

'Uh-huh. Freaks. You know, like in the old children's stories of fairies and trolls and all that. Well, thanks to Cass and Dar I'm out here and I'm free, and now I'm a freak. Maybe I'm Flux crazy now, but I kind of think that this was like, well, my dues. I'm one of them now, and it's not so bad. I'm still sort of getting used to it, even with the wizard's help. He said something about men and women's centers of gravity being different, whatever that means. All I know is that every time I don't think and cross my legs the old way it *hurts* like hell, and I'm always aware that it's there.'

'You'd hardly know it, what with those black denim pants hanging so low on your hips,' Nadya said.

Suzl shrugged. 'It was either that or get 'em super-baggy in the crotch. Besides, I kind of like it this way. I can still be me and still be a freak, like Dar. And you wouldn't believe how fast and how easy it turns on, with all the sensations concentrated in that one place. I think I understand men a lot better now.'

'You better,' Nadya murmured. 'Uh – have you tried it out yet?'

Suzl giggled. 'No, but I plan to. Better shape up, girls – I'm the man around here, pardon the bosoms.'

'It doesn't make any difference out here what sex you are,' Cass put in, stirring from her chair where she sat. 'There doesn't seem to be any men's or women's jobs – just jobs. That's why you two won't have problems, except maybe getting picked up by the wrong people in bars.'

'I'm swearing off bars for a while,' Dar told her. 'So far I've been in two and both haven't been exactly great experiences.'

They were about to go further when there was a sharp knocking on the hotel door. It startled them, because they weren't expecting anybody or anything as yet. Cass got up and went to the door, opened it, and found Matson standing there. He looked at her and frowned as if slightly puzzled at her new look, but he recovered quickly. 'We won't have to detour to Pericles after all,' he told them. 'The old boy I wanted to see is here in the hotel right now. He and some friends of his want to see all four of you in one hour, Room 224. Be there and we can settle this as far as we're concerned.'

'We'll be there,' Cass assured him. She hesitated a moment, then asked, 'Like the new look?'

'Hadn't noticed,' he responded curtly, turned, and walked down the hall. Crestfallen, she watched him go down the stairs.

'That rat,' Nadya commented, and she turned and shook her head.

'No, he's not a rat, just, well, unobtainable in the long term.' The ironic thing was, although they didn't seem to know it, she had obtained the unobtainable from him, knowing that he was as out of reach as ever.

'What's that all about?' Suzl asked.

'Probably another thing like the trial we told you about. Give the same information to a bunch of powerful wizards and then they'll decide something or other about Haldayne and Persellus. After today it won't concern us, though.'

Dar sighed and looked down at Suzl. 'Well,' he said hopefully, 'we still have an hour to kill.'

Room 224 turned out to be a large rectangular end room that was obviously rarely used as a place for anyone to stay but rather for small receptions and gatherings. It had been set up in this case with a head table in the front and a dozen or so folding chairs for an audience. Matson was there, as were two other stringers – the dark woman Cass had seen when they'd arrived and another, a huge, beefy man with a full beard and cold brown eyes. Also present were two duggers, obviously the chief train drivers for the other two. One was totally reptilian, down to being covered in green, scaly skin and having a snout-like face with fangs, sex indeterminable, while the other was a man whose skin was all blotched and twisted, like a long-dead corpse. The foursome sat with the duggers, nervously eyeing the reptilian one. They didn't care so much any more about the walking corpse – he looked too much like a couple of duggers in their own train.

Soon, three people entered. The first was an elderly man with long, flowing gray beard and hair that looked as if it had not only never been cut, but also never washed, combed, or otherwise cared for. He used a short cane to walk on, and seemed slow and stooped with age and infirmity. It was hard to imagine him as a wizard of power like the handsome Haldayne.

The second was a young looking woman with a rather attractive face, although she was only a meter high, had bright green skin and dark green hair, and shell-like ears, while the third was a very fat man with a nearly bald round head who looked more than slightly drunk. None were the sort of people who inspired confidence and dynamic leadership by their every look and gesture.

They took their seats up front, the old one with difficulty, and for a moment said nothing, just looked out on those whom they had summoned. Finally the fat man and the tiny green woman looked over at the old one and he nodded absently. 'The room and its contents are clean, although we have a Soul Rider present,' he croaked in a voice that was barely audible to them. Cass jumped a little at that but decided to hold her peace for now. 'That is either a very good sign or a very ominous one, depending on how you look at it.' The other two nodded slightly in agreement.

'Now, then,' the old one continued, 'I am Mervyn, the lovely one here is Tatalane, and on the other end is Krupe.' He brought up his cane like a rifle, and from it shot a tremendous spray of yellowish white energy. It struck the walls, then coated them as if a living thing, then floor and ceiling as well. When it passed under their feet it gave a very mild numbing sensation that lasted only when you were in direct contact with it. 'These proceedings are now sealed,' Mervyn told them. 'What proceeds is for our ears alone. Although only three of our fellowship of nine are present, it is sufficient for action in this matter. I am going to call upon each of you to tell me the various facts that you know directly in this matter. We will begin with the attack on the Arden train. Mr Matson first, if you please.'

Matson stood and gave a general, brief description of the discovery of the train, its grisly contents, and his conclusions from that evidence. Then Suzl and Nadya were called upon to supplement, then Cass up to the time she'd been knocked out, and, finally, Dar. He was hesitant in telling his part in the story and his feelings at the time, but this was brushed aside by Mervyn. 'Just the outline,' the old one told him, 'no moralizing or excuses. We are aware of what happened. We are reading your reactions when these things are called up in your mind.'

Eventually, in this fashion, step by step, the entire story was told to them. The three listened passively, prompting only when necessary, and made no comments or gestures at anything told them or not told them. Ultimately, with the impressions of Persellus gleaned from Dar, Suzl, Nadya, and Matson, the tale was told.

The three then lapsed into deep thought, not apparently conferring or even showing awareness of the others' presence, but finally Mervyn said, 'Stringers Hollus and Brund, what do you think of this?'

'Sounds like Haldayne, all right,' the bearded stringer commented. 'Cheeky bastard to use his own name like that, though.'

'Yes, isn't it? And you, Hollus?'

'I never had a run-in with him, but it's clear to me that he ordered the deliberate murder of a stringer and took control of a valuable crossroads. This cannot be allowed.'

The two duggers were also called on for opinions. Both, except for wishing to avenge the duggers more than Arden, echoed Hollus.

'If we were to take on Haldayne, it would require not only the three of us but an army,' Mervyn told them. 'There are enough raw souls in a land that size to make its retaking very hard. Knowing Haldayne, he would never take us on directly, but he would make his minions, his conquests, and his would-be conquerors pay dearly for each tiny bit of Fluxland. We see only two choices. Either we retake Persellus bloodily, or we act to seal it off completely and totally reconfigure the trade routes. That is, isolate it and write it off.'

There was some consternation among all three stringers at that. 'You *can't* just reconfigure those routes!' Matson protested. 'It would take *years* to reestablish new patterns and get word to everyone. Not to mention the fact that it would take one of you near there permanently just to make sure his buddies didn't break through and unseal the land.'

'And yet the object of this exercise seems to be to draw us into a direct confrontation,' Tatalane said, speaking for the first time. 'He deliberately invites attention by moving this madman and then exhorting him to attack the stringers. He could clearly see the string on Cass and could have easily eliminated it, but instead he allowed it to remain, meaning certain discovery of the pocket. He changed his shape absolutely while in the pocket, yet seemed to go out of his way to display his manner, his ring, and his left-handedness to Cass. Any one of these might be overlooked, but the combination was certain to rouse suspicion. Even so, when he could stay out of her way, he deliberately places himself in close contact with her in Persellus, then, when she could still prove nothing, sends four inept minions to subdue her, thereby proving her story. Clearly, too, Matson was allowed to see and then escape when it would have been child's play for Haldayne to have taken him, his train, and Cass.'

'Well said,' Mervyn approved. 'So he did everything but raise a flag to cover the sky of World saying, "Here I Am – Come and Get Me!" He *wants* a fight, that is certain. He knows who and what he'd be facing. That, too, leads to two different possibilities. Either he is certain he can win, or he wishes to lose. It is that simple.'

Cass frowned. Why would anyone want to lose a battle?

'Good point,' Mervyn responded, as if she'd spoken aloud. 'Why, indeed would someone want to lose a battle? Perhaps to prove to us that we saw a danger, met it, and vanquished the evil? Then we would all go our merry ways, satisfied in a job well done, and look elsewhere for the next evil. We would overlook what Haldayne really does not wish us to see.'

'But what could that be?' Hollus asked him. 'I know the crazy man said they were going to attack the gate, if there is one, but I didn't think that was possible.'

'Insofar as we know, the Guardians of the Gates of Hell have never been defeated or even tricked,' Mervyn assured her. 'Nevertheless, the conclusion is inescapable. Remember, however, that we know the location only of four of the seven gates. We do not know how many the Seven might know of – perhaps all – nor what they might have accomplished on one or more. The conclusion is inescapable. There *is* a gate lying between Persellus and Anchor Logh. We must assume that, somehow, Haldayne has access to and perhaps control of that gate no matter what logic says to the contrary. That is what he wishes to hide from us.'

'So what do you propose?' Matson asked him directly. He was growing impatient with the long-winded theorizing.

'We must recapture Persellus, if only to do what he expects,' the wizard told them. 'We must also find out what he knows that we do not.'

'But it could also just be a trap for the three of us,' Tatalane argued. 'What if it is – and he wins?'

Mervyn shrugged. 'Then we will know at least that the gate is still secure and our successors on the Nine will know and avenge us. But if he loses, then the gate is open to Hell. Haldayne has six of the seven combinations to open the gates. Hell has most certainly worked out the seventh after all this time. If he has a way in, if he can talk to the horrors of Hell, he will have all seven and need only control of the physical gates to open them. My friends, this is grave. We dare not ignore it.'

Mervyn thought a bit more. 'Hollus, have you enough duggers able to follow strings to get to Domura, Salapaca, and Modon?'

She looked back at the reptilian dugger, who nodded.

'Brund? Can you take the alarm to Zlydof, Roarkara, and Fideleer?'

The bearded man did not consult his dugger. 'No problem.'

'Are you all three willing to avenge your slain comrades?'

The three stringers huddled in whispers for a moment. Finally, Matson said, 'We are agreed that this thing can't be allowed to go on. Otherwise *everybody* will be doing it.'

Cass smiled slightly at that. That, really, was the feared stringer, the terror of Anchor and Flux – one who saw all World as a giant ledger sheet, the battling storekeeper who would leave his lady's body to rot in the void but take strong action when his trade was inconvenienced. How utterly romantic.

'Matson,' Mervyn continued, 'your train will be the point and guard along the route from here to there. We will supply equipment, explosives, and fifty good fighters to staff your outpost, all at least minor wizards.'

'Will they take orders?' he asked sourly.

'They will because we will tell them to. You three also have between you almost two hundred young people from Anchor ready for the block. We will remold them and use them.'

That got the stringers upset again. 'Who's going to pay for all this?' they all demanded to know.

'Who is going to buy them if we tell them not to?' Mervyn responded with a slight smirk. 'However, we guarantee you an equal number for the market out of conquest if we lose them. Further, we will ourselves fill any specific goods orders intended to be picked up in the old Persellus. That should restore a tidy bit.'

Mollified, the stringers sat down once more.

'Hollus, Brund, you will work with Tatalane in getting these new troops into line. Hollus knows Haldayne, which should simplify matters a good deal, while you, Brund, are particularly gifted with explosives, their transportation and use. This will have to be done in a newly created pocket between here and Persellus. There should be no traffic in either direction between Haldayne, Matson, and you, so it should be perfect – and private. We also have two Anchors to draw upon and I intend to do so. Since the four of you appear human and will pass muster at the gates, I am detaching you temporarily from Matson's service. I hate to break up a happy couple, but Dar and Nadya must accompany Krupe to Anchor Abehl, as we have no one from there here to assist. Because both Suzl and Cass have direct knowledge not only of the Anchor but the Temple of Anchor Logh, you two will come with me to Anchor Logh. There are things I must know there.'

They all four looked at each other in some distress. 'I think I know the Temple as good as Suzl,' Nadya responded. 'Why split up the teams?'

'Please do not waste time second-guessing me. We must move and move quickly. Do you not think that at this very moment Haldayne's spies aren't going mad trying to penetrate the shield on this room? However, just this once, I will explain that the rather unusual aspects of two of you are required for effect in Anchor, and both of you cannot be in the same place when the places you might be needed are three hundred kilometers apart.'

Dar looked at Suzl, who shrugged and grinned. 'Have fun. I know *I* will!'

He grinned back. 'Yeah. I always wanted to see the inner sanctums of a Temple.'

'This Council is now adjourned,' Mervyn pronounced, 'and will convene again in twenty-seven days at the proper points around Persellus. With divine help, perhaps we can convene once again in Persellus. Normal precautions have been taken so that details of this meeting cannot be picked from your minds. However, it is essential that we all get to our work and out of Globbus as soon as possible, for while compromise is inevitable we need not give the demon any advantage.'

The energy field retreated, flowing first back into the walls, then along them and back, it seemed, into Mervyn's cane. Cass and Suzl went up and approached the old wizard, as the others approached and talked to their appointed leaders and guardians. The wizard's eyes, an enigma from a distance, seemed surprisingly sharp and full of life and energy up close. 'Go, get your packs, sign out at the hotel desk, and wait for me there. We will go together. I rather imagine you are looking forward to this.'

'I'm not too thrilled with asking the Sister General for help,' Cass responded honestly, 'but at least I'll have the chance to get word to my family that I'm all right. It'll be a shock to anyone who knows us to see us again. I don't know anyone who ever met anyone who went out in the Paring Rite and returned.'

'I'm just gonna have fun,' Suzl told him. 'I can sure defile their holy Temple and surprise a whole lot of people.'

'It is true that this is an unprecedented event for Anchor Logh, but this whole business is unprecedented. Win or lose, I fear that our dear World is going to come in for some severe changes by the time this is all resolved,' the wizard said seriously.

'Damn. And before I saw most of it the way it is now,' Cass muttered.

They left him and went immediately back to their rooms. Nadya caught up with Cass as they approached their door. 'Tough luck. But we'll get together again. I sure would like to get back home and rub it in their noses, though.'

Cass nodded. 'I know – but I'd much rather be going back *with* an army than to get one. I still can't believe Anchor would ever send forces into Flux, not even on the request of the Nine Who Guard. We shall see. At least you can tell me what another Anchor is like. I've been curious to see how much they're the same and how they differ.'

'Not like Fluxlands, that's for sure. Not with the church in such control – *huh?*'

Suddenly the lights in the room went out, and both felt extreme dizziness and a sense of falling. Nadya recovered in what seemed like only a few moments, and looked around. The lights were back on, the door was closed – and Cass was nowhere to be seen.

Cass drifted in a dreamy, uncaring fog neither asleep nor awake, not dreaming, not thinking, but just so, so relaxed ...

After a while there were voices, distant and indistinct at first but growing clearer with time. She heard them, a man's and a woman's voices, but it made no impression on her.

'She is well protected,' said the woman clinically.

'She has improved her looks a good deal,' the man's voice noted. 'I guess she really is in love with that stringer. Ah! Unrequited love! Takes me back to my youth.'

'You never had a youth, love. Still, we won't get it by spell. That leaves it in my department. Good thing a drug is a drug.'

'So long as we keep it that way and there's nobody around to counteract it. It's simple and direct.'

The woman seemed to be fumbling with something, and there was a mild pricking sensation on her arm. They waited a while, just chatting pleasantly. 'Lucky for you I was here. Your crude methods would have killed her before she talked.'

'Luck had nothing to do with it. I summoned you because I needed your help. Geniuses are few and far between, my love.'

The woman snorted. 'She's under but good. Let's get that spell off her.' There was a sudden tingling, and Cass felt herself being drawn back to reality. She was aware of everything, of every noise, feeling, sensation, more aware of such things than she had ever been.

'Wake up, Cassie! It's your mom and dad here!' the man's voice called to her, and it *did* sound just like her father. She opened her eyes and saw, with some surprise, that she was under a tree in the pasture just outside her old farm, and her Mom and Dad were there, looking down at her.

'I know you're only seven years old, but you must have had a big, bad dream,' her mother told her.

'Oh, yes, Mommy! It was real *scary*, too.'

'Did you dream about the old man with the cane that shot sparks again?' her father wanted to know.

'Uh huh.'

'What happened this time after he shot sparks all over that room? You have to tell us your dream to make it go away.'

And, so, she told them, repeating the entire account verbatim, just as it happened. All about the terrible looking people and the talk of war and strategy, all the way to when she walked back to her room with her imaginary playmate and they woke her up. It was all there, better than she could have remembered it any other way.

'This is bad,' her Mommy said. 'You've been too clever for your own good, Giff. The old boy's already on to you.'

'And what'll he have?' her Daddy responded. 'Persellus and a vague suspicion and nothing else. Eventually they'll scratch their heads, maybe put extra guards around the Gate, and that will be that, for all the good it'll do them.'

Cass frowned. Her Mommy and Daddy were talking such funny stuff, the kind of stuff in her dreams, but to each other, not to her.

'What about her?' Mommy asked, pointing to Cassie. 'So long as she has a Soul Rider she's a mortal danger to us all.'

'But we can't destroy Soul Riders, whatever they are. Kill her and it just takes over somebody else whose identity we *don't* know. No, I prefer my enemy in plain sight.'

'You just can't leave her here, though. That thing could come out and attack at any time.'

He chuckled. 'Not yet. If it acts too soon it might get one of us but it'll be useless later on and it won't know the facts. No, I have a better, more effective idea. An original one.' He turned to her. 'Cass, you cannot move, but see me now as I am.' Her father dissolved into another figure, a man she also knew. Haldayne. And, beside him, the woman, too, was visible, and she knew her as well. She knew, but she couldn't believe. Sister Daji! The sexy but dumb consort to the Sister General!

Still gorgeous, still sexy, but hardly dumb. Not this one. Even the odd, ignorant tone in her voice had vanished, although she still had that very odd accent.

Haldayne grinned, and it was obvious that he liked to have his victim know who was doing it before he did whatever it was. He put out a hand on her forehead, and it was warm and wet. 'All memory flies,' he intoned, 'all that is there is null.'

Her mind literally became a complete blank. Cass no longer thought at all.

'So, genius?' Daji taunted. 'That isn't going to stop a Soul Rider when it wants to take charge.'

He grinned, and made a pass with his hands. Cass seemed to shrink down until she was very small, standing and looking up at giants.

Daji looked down, and saw a magnificent looking falcon. She nodded approvingly.

'What will you call her?' Haldayne asked.

Daji thought a moment. 'How about Demon? It seems appropriate. But what good does *this* do?'

'My dear, I said I was a genius. There is your passport back through the Guardians. They will not harm a Soul Rider and its companion. I know – I've done it once before. She is a falcon. She thinks she's a falcon, too, and will respond only to you and only to the name Demon. She is devoted to you, will obey your simple commands, and that is all. Now you just take her back to Anchor Logh, then keep her on a leg chain as a pet. Feed her mice and insects and she'll adore you forever. And, most importantly, there is no power in Anchor.'

Daji brightened. 'Oho! I see! But what if it breaks away, or betrays me at the Gate?'

'It won't. I have presented our powerful but predictable Soul Rider with a series of moral dilemmas. If it wants to learn the truth, as it must, it must accompany you all the way to Anchor. Otherwise it will never learn it, and it knows it. On the other hand, if it goes to Anchor, it is trapped, at least for the life of the bird. That should be more than enough time, I would think. Do not, however, let her off her chain. It *can* and might fly long distances, over walls and into Flux. That's what it plans on doing, you see, which is why it will cooperate with us. And, so long as you continue to perform that little chore, we are safe.'

She kissed him. 'Giff, you really *are* a genius!'

15

Hellgate

They flew from Persellus as great winged creatures of their own imaginations, out from the Fluxland now remade in his image and into the void, following first the stringer trail marks, small bands of energy seen as a criss-crossing network of lines below them, then special marks on a frequency intended for their eyes alone. Held by a small chain to the foot of one of the creatures, the falcon called Demon flew with them, having no trouble keeping up.

Finally the small lines below split and then joined again a ways off, outlining a circular pattern between them. They descended carefully, landing at the point of the first split, and their forms shimmered as they landed and became once more human figures. Now both walked forward, leaving the trail lines, to a bright point ahead that only those trained and gifted as they were could see and understand. They were almost upon it before it took true form.

The Hellgate was actually a saucer-shaped depression in the void, very regular, solid, and smooth, and immune to the void's energies and powers. A long ladder seemingly made out of the same stuff led down from the edge to the floor below, where, in the center, there was a dark circular area that was the true entrance.

Daji calmed the nervous falcon and looked down, wishing she could calm her own nerves so easily. 'You're sure this will work?'

'You got here that way, didn't you?' he soothed. 'Nothing bothered you emerging from it.'

'Yeah, but I had sent a couple of those silly novices through first to make sure. What's to prevent the Guardians from letting *her* through and killing me?'

'The Soul Rider won't allow it, because then it would never know. I do admit this is a one-time thing, my dear, but I feel much better with you not gone so long from Anchor but merely a few hours.'

Never before, since she and Haldayne had intercepted the real Daji in Persellus and substituted her as an indistinguishable carbon copy, had she met with him in the Flux. Always it was Haldayne, flying over the walls in the form of a common raven, who had sought her out. He, of course, could not change back from raven shape once in Anchor, but he could talk and discuss things with her virtually within the Temple. Now he had summoned her, through the gate, for this very purpose – to trap the Soul Rider in Anchor as he would be trapped.

'You must do it,' he told her, 'or the entire plan is lost. No one recruited you as one of the Seven – you volunteered, and you accepted my leadership freely and of your own will, without reservations. Either go back on that now, and lose it all, or trust me and go.'

She knew that what he said was true, and that if she refused it would not be merely the plan that died. Still, it was a terrifying thing to be asked to do, to enter a Hellgate from the Flux and survive. She took a deep breath. At this point she was dead either way, and only if Haldayne was correct did she have a chance. He did not risk leaving Persellus at this delicate time, even for a short while, merely to see her off. Without being able to neutralize the Soul Rider, inevitably drawn to such a scheme as this, the plan was nothing but bloody madness. She took a deep breath, let it out, then began climbing down the ladder.

The powers of Flux still operated here in this fixed bowl, but she dared not use them, for they would inevitably attract the unknown Guardians of the Gate – unknown because none had ever seen them and survived. She reached the bottom, her bare feet providing decent traction, and walked slowly and apprehensively towards that dark center spot. The falcon made a sudden fluttering motion with its wings, as if trying to fly away, startling her and almost making her fall, but her nerve held steady and she again pulled the bird back on its chain to her and then held it against her breasts, petting it and somewhat calming both of them.

Up close the dark hole showed a web-like grid of strong cables going completely around it and down into the darkness. She knew what to expect, and gingerly turned and started climbing down, the bird placed down on her shoulder and seeming a very heavy and unbalancing weight. It was not, however, far to the floor, where the webbing stopped and a tubular structure replaced it, going off horizontally in front of her. No horrible Guardians had yet appeared, and she began to relax a bit. She did not doubt, though, that those Guardians existed. Once, at another Hellgate, she watched while sacrificial slaves had been ordered in, saw the flashes of multicolored energies fly out of the dark central hole, and had heard the horrible screams of agony from the slaves as they had been destroyed.

The tunnel was long and sloped slightly downwards, but again was no problem. Although made of apparently seamless material the yellow-orange color of the void itself, it was actually sectioned, and as she reached the first section it glowed for a distance of ten meters in front of her. She walked forward, and near the end of the light, at the gaping darkness, the next section came on. When she entered it, the first section winked out. There were seven such sections, and in this direction it was a long, long walk indeed. Now, though, she reached the end, and before her was illuminated the gate itself, a great swirl that might be solid, might be energy, or might be itself alive. To her right was a large, blocky machine that did not seem to belong to this eerie place, with its hundreds of small squares and its read-out screens. This was the locking mechanism, and the ultimate trap for anyone attempting to open the gate, clearly placed here not by the builders of the gate but by someone, or something, else. To walk into that swirl, without all seven machines being fed their unique combinations within sixty seconds, would trigger instant vaporization.

But she turned away from swirl and machine, to the wall opposite the locking device. There was nothing whatsoever to mark or otherwise distinguish the wall from any other part of it, unless you knew the proper pattern. She pressed it in several spots with the flat of her hand, eventually tracing a pattern that had no meaning to her. A section of the wall glowed bright red, but she did not pay any attention to it, turning around instead to see an intricate pattern now traced on the floor of the tube, almost in front of the machine. It was a duplicate of the pattern she had just traced with her palm on the wall, enclosed in a circle of red. She walked to it, then into the center of it. There was a slight moment of dizziness, and the Hellgate vanished, replaced with the view of a dark and damp sub-basement piled high with the signs of work.

She stepped off the cleared and swept spot and into dust and debris, and as she did she felt all sense of the Flux leave her. It made her feel empty, as it always did when she entered Anchor, as if something wonderful and important had been taken away.

She had left her regular robe here when she'd left, and had reentered naked so that she would be as unencumbered as possible. She groped in the dark and found a small light switch, then pushed on it. A small, naked light bulb hanging from a wire came to life. She saw her robe on the nail, then managed to put it on, although she found she had to remove the bracelet binding the falcon's chain to her to do it properly. She had a few seconds of nervousness at that, but the falcon made no move to escape. Now she reattached it, and slid back the bar that sealed the door to outside entry. She opened it carefully, stepped out into the corridor, then reached back, shut off the light, and closed it again. She fumbled in her robe, found the key, and then locked the door again from the outside. She had spent a lot of time making the door look like nothing more than a bunch of nailed-on boards covering a crack in the foundation, and it was very convincing.

A dozen novices, working secretly at night for more than six months under her direction, had first discovered the old door, then taken up the old concrete flooring inside the room. The sub-basement was a secure area: the wardens and their monitors did not reach this far down, and, in fact, only the Sister General and the chief warden had keys to the area at all, almost never used except during the annual maintenance checks. It had been easy, though, to get the key from the Sister General's safe and give it to the raven Haldayne, who, of course, easily returned two so identical they even had the same old markings under a microscope. Things done in Flux held as they were in Anchor, within, of course, the physical laws of Anchor. No huge flying creature such as she had become from Persellus to Hellgate could fly in Anchor – it was a violation of the fixed laws of physics. But a raven was a raven, in Flux and Anchor, and so was a falcon.

She went swiftly now through back passages and service areas she knew by heart, avoiding the wardens' mechanical security sensors as only one with an intimate knowledge of the building could, then took the small back hidden stairway to the Sister General's luxurious apartment, using combinations even the Sister General had probably not bothered to learn. Explaining the falcon would not be a great problem. She had one of the very few VIP necklaces given out by the Sister General that made her immune to most of the security devices in the temple. The wardens would not necessarily see her go in or out at any time, nor would they bother to note or log it if they did.

After checking and finding, to her relief, that the Temple chief was not home, she checked the time and then the schedule on Diastephanos' desk. She had selected this time because the Sister General was supposed to be out of town visiting some of the local churches for three days, but there was no way to guarantee that the old bitch wouldn't louse her up by coming home early. Clock and calendar said that Sister Daji had cut it close, but still had a margin of several hours, perhaps a whole day, before the play began again. That would be very convenient.

She removed the falcon-restraining bracelet once more and clipped it around the brass air conditioning duct, letting Demon perch on the back of a chair. The bird still seemed very calm and somewhat confused, and that suited her fine.

She went to the intercom and buzzed the wardens' office. 'This is Daji,' she told them unnecessarily, using the vacant and ignorant intonation she always used. 'When is she coming back?' There was no need to say who 'she' was.

'We expect her any time after eight this evening,' a warden told her. Again she glanced at the clock. Barely three. 'Thanks,' she said, and switched off. Almost five hours.

She took a long, comfortable bath, then put on only the loose, open informal robe and called services. A novice was sent up immediately, who took her dirty clothes and also received a written notice signed by the Sister General for the special construction to be sent up. The novice bowed and left. Poor, brainwashed idiots, she couldn't help thinking. She recalled the ones who'd done all the work for her below. All now were Haldayne's creatures, having tested the Hellgate passage before she dared go through.

She got a bite to eat from the small kitchenette while she waited. After twenty minutes or so, the buzzer rang and two novices delivered the solid wood perch she had ordered at Haldayne's instructions days before. She thanked and dismissed them, then took it over and placed it by the Sister General's desk, then moved Demon from her odd perch and attached her to the ready-made one. She fed the bird some raw meat from the small refrigerator, then went to work on the sewing machine in her small and normally unused office area. Soon she had a scarlet hood, which fitted over the bird's head. As she'd hoped, the falcon went to sleep.

She sighed, finally relaxing, and realized that Haldayne had done his homework well. This time he'd thought of all the angles, of that she was now certain. This time, for the first time, a known and guarded gate would be totally in the hands of the Seven, making only three to go. If it worked here, it would work, with variations, elsewhere. The long centuries of frustration would be nearing an end.

Now she redid her hair, applied perfumes and make-up, then went back into her office, lifted the sewing machine off its cabinet, reached in and took out three medium-sized pill bottles. She removed one pill from each, then replaced them in their hiding place and resecured the sewing machine. She went back into the living room area, turned on the small entertainment console and took a tiny clear cube no larger than her thumb nail and put it in the device. Standing there, she dictated a long string of sentences, then programmed the device. It would play until she shut it off, but when she shut it off it would self-erase.

She poured herself a whiskey and soda, then took the three pills, then went over and turned on the recorder to playback and sat back in a large, comfortable chair, feet up.

It took several minutes for the pills to take effect, and she just lay there, relaxed, and let them do their job. The recorder kept going, and, finally, it was the only thing in her mind.

'All memory gone, floating, relaxed, so pleasant, so free of any thought, any worry, anything at all, just feeling so, so good and relaxed … You are Sister Daji, and she alone is you now. Let her come, let her become you, flow into you, so that she alone is in control …' Then came a series of instructions to Daji, an explanation of the falcon and perch, and an account of what she had been doing these past three days. She drifted into a deep, deep hypnotic trance.

Haldayne had created Daji by working in Flux with the real one, before he transformed her into another of his creatures. The Daji persona was then transferred, also in Flux, to her, where it resided, complete but separate from her. No chances could or would be taken of any compromise in her identity, which was totally submerged, inactive, until brought forth again by a special trigger command given by Haldayne or one of his agents or another of the Seven.

And so the woman who awoke with a start in the chair was *not* an agent, nor did she even know what the Seven were. She was, in fact, a carbon copy of the original Daji, a woman with the body of a goddess, the mind of a child, and an insatiable worship of and lust for older women. The agent of Hell had not minded. Otherwise, this sort of life would have been unbearable.

The woman in the chair frowned, annoyed by the prattle of the recorder. She got up, went over to it, and shut it off. The recording on it erased automatically. She popped out the small module, picked another at random and popped it in. A lively tune began playing, which she started humming along with and dancing to. Eventually she tired of the game and went into the Sister General's office and walked up to the sleeping falcon. 'Oooo, my pretty birdie! Daji's just gonna *love* you to death.'

It was well into the night, and the Sister General had long ago returned. Now both she and Daji were asleep on the bed in the next room, and the entire complex was in darkness save for a small nightlight in the commode.

Deep below the temple, below the sub-basement and foundation itself, below even the glassy-smooth rock base, something triggered on. Now there was a slight hissing noise in the sub-basement itself, and in the area marked in dull chalk in the empty and damp room a form took shape. None in Anchor could see the form, and none in Flux would want to. It was a creature of pure energy, yet so terrible was it to gaze upon that humans would go mad at the sight, could they see it at all. Slowly it looked around, not seeing as things of flesh and blood saw but sensing energy and receiving direction. Slowly, it stepped off the chalk-marked area in the floor and up to the door. Although the light was still switched off, the lone hanging bulb suddenly glowed.

It paused only a moment at the door, then seemed to flow under it and out the other side. Once in the corridor, which itself became lit as the bulbs received the energy from the creature, it moved slowly and deliberately down to the far end, where a complex of machinery whined dully. It merged carefully with the power grid, not wanting to overload it, although those still awake not only in the Temple but throughout the capital's electrically powered area frowned and noticed lights seemed to be burning brighter and electrical devices seemed to speed up slightly.

Firmly in the power grid, the creature rode it, searching the entire Temple area until it came upon the one place it was searching for. The tiny nightlight in the Sister General's bathroom glowed, then flared and burnt out, as the creature entered, but other lights came on in their ghostly fashion. In the bedroom, one of the sleeping women gave a muffled cry, turned over, and was soon fast asleep again.

The creature was not heading for the bedroom, but for the Sister General's office. The rear area was again in darkness as the lights in the office came eerily to life.

The Soul Rider inside the sleeping bird read the intense energy field and was confused. It knew the nature of the creature, but could not comprehend how it had gotten here. Still, it understood that the unknown power that directed its destiny had sent an ally, although it was unprecedented in form. The Guardians of the Gates of Hell were in fact creatures of Flux with a specific mission, and to have one detach itself from that mission was almost impossible to believe.

The Soul Rider sensed the Guardian, but had no common language to speak to it, if, indeed, such a creature had speech. Still, when the Rider understood that the Guardian was about to touch its host, it screamed out, 'No! Do not destroy the host!'

Energy touched the sleeping bird, and engulfed it, then transformed it. Matter became energy, and the stronger of the three entities now carried the other two in a manner that had no words to describe. Back again they went to the bathroom, and into the electrical system at the nightlight. Again, all electrical devices flared in the capital, and in the wardens' security office the alarm board rang. The startled warden looked up at the board, which showed every single alarm in the Temple triggered all at once, with all the tiny lights flashing on and off. 'Damn!' she swore. 'A stinking short on *my* shift!'

Below, the Guardian emerged once more from the power grid and walked to the door in the sub-basement, then flowed under it and back to the chalk-marked area. The area glowed for a moment, and then they were in the tunnel at the gate to Hell itself.

The Guardian moved swiftly up the tunnel, which blazed with light, then up through the hole and into the air above the saucer-like depression. The Soul Rider and its companion were flung high into the air and out, away from the gate and into the void.

The Soul Rider was confused and bewildered, but lost no time in acting. Having been present at the casting of the spell on its host it knew the counter, and rushed it into form, with modifications to suit the occasion. It did not understand what had just occurred, but it certainly knew why.

The energy that had been transformed from matter became matter again, reconstituted. Cass burst into sudden consciousness, remembering everything, including the details of what had happened while she was in bird form, although it all seemed distant, unreal, almost like it had happened to someone else. Her last clear personal memory had been going into the hotel room in Globbus.

Instinctively she stretched out, and was startled to find that she did indeed have wings. So she was still a bird, and it had been no dream, but she was now in Flux, thinking, remembering, and free. She wondered how she had gotten here, since the last bird memory was the Sister General and Daji playing with her, then hooding her to sleep, but here she was, suddenly whole in mind and flying through the void.

Only it wasn't a void.

Below she saw the void as wizards and stringers saw it, a criss-crossing network of complex lines of differing colors and intensities. They had an insubstantial look to them, much the same as the afterimage of a swinging light, but they were fixed in place and could be followed.

She banked and circled a moment, staring at the patterns, flying as if it was the most normal and natural thing in the world to her, but she felt some concern. She knew she had to get back, to warn Matson and the others, but which of those strings led to Globbus? Which to Persellus? Which to other places, perhaps Anchor Logh itself?

Although there were countless secondary strings, there were only three main ones, so she picked one at random and followed it, hoping it would lead eventually to someplace that would orient her. Although there were no real landmarks except the occasional patterns in some of the secondary strings, she knew that she was flying abnormally fast and realized that she was feeling neither hunger nor thirst. The Flux was supplying all the energy she required.

She was upon it almost before she realized it, breaking through into Anchor. At that moment she felt herself start to drop like a stone, and with great difficulty she turned herself back into the void, thankful that she had had enough altitude to make it in time. Strength and that curious sense of weightlessness returned. Now, at least, she knew where she was, for below her as she'd started to fall had been the apron and gate to Anchor Logh.

Now two main trails led from Anchor, and she picked the right-hand one, remembering Matson's comment that Globbus and Persellus were almost the same distance from the Anchor. She realized after a bit that she still wasn't certain if this was the route to Persellus or to Globbus, but she had no choice now but to follow it and pray that there were no other forks. Suddenly she passed over two figures, odd enough to see along any route in the void. She was going too fast to tell much about them, but banked, slowed, and approached them again, flying high enough, she hoped, to avoid their detection but just low enough that when she banked and came around again she could see more about them.

Both were mounted on horses with just saddlebags for their gear. One was a young, handsome man dressed in riding clothes who had a full, light beard. The other was a small, well-built woman, bare from the waist up but wearing a broad-brimmed hat and blue denim work pants. She recognized the figure. *Suzl!* But who was the other man? An agent of Haldayne's, or one of Mervyn's men? After all this, she decided she had to risk an appearance. At least these two, alone, would be easier to deal with if the man were an enemy than an armed and wizard-filled camp suspicious of everything and likely to shoot first and ask questions afterwards. She came around again and this time dipped low in front of them, so both could see her. She saw their faces look forward and up, and their mouths droop, but they made no hostile moves. Both riders, however, stopped, and she circled once more as they watched and landed right in front of them.

With a shock she saw that she was as large as they were, if not even larger. They stared at each other for a moment, and she wondered if she could speak. Finally she said, 'Suzl?' It sounded right.

Suzl frowned. 'Cass? Is that *really* you? Holy Mother of Universes! What in hell happened to you?'

Feeling a little relieved, she responded, 'First, who's that with you?'

The young man chuckled. 'Why, my dear, I am Mervyn.' His voice changed, taking on the old man's low, broken cackle. 'We are what we choose to be in Flux.'

She looked back at Suzl. 'Is that right?'

She nodded. 'Yeah. Second biggest shock I ever had. You're the third. What happened to you at the hotel? Who changed you into – that?'

'I'm not sure what 'that' is,' she told them honestly. 'Some sort of bird, I guess.'

'Some sort, yes,' Mervyn agreed, and made a gesture. Between them appeared a huge mirrored surface, and she could see herself.

Her body was that of a giant falcon, and her arms were wings, but her underside, raised up and facing them, was human all the way, and she had her own face, although feathers replaced hair on her head. She stared at the reflection for a moment more in wonder than in shock or horror.

'The only reason I didn't bring you down was because I sensed the Soul Rider still inside you,' the wizard told her. 'It has certainly delivered you from evil.' The mirror vanished, and both riders dismounted and sat down, relaxing. 'Now, then, tell me all that you have been through. Spare nothing.'

She went into extreme detail, although it still seemed like a dream to her. When she finished the wizard just nodded and sat thoughtfully for a moment. Finally he said, 'It is very clever. It is, in fact, diabolical. It should have worked completely, for I know that while a Soul Rider can exist in Anchor its powers there are minimal and mostly involved in influencing specific actions of others. I would love to know how you escaped, how *it* escaped.'

'I'm not sure *I* do,' Cass replied. 'I don't have any real memories between the time they stuck that hood over me until I was suddenly flying in the void, but there's a sense there of something – terrible. I really can't describe it.'

'I can read it inside you, but aside from verifying your sensations there is nothing more I can make of them. It is certainly not anything I've ever experienced from a Soul Rider before, nor are they particularly – terrible, as you call it.' He sighed. 'No matter for now. It is a question now of what to do next.'

Cass looked at them. 'If you're such a powerful wizard, how come you two are riding to Anchor Logh? Couldn't you just transform the both of you into flying things like me and make it quicker?'

'I could,' the wizard agreed, 'but, for one thing, we would arrive without bags or horses, and that would terrify the guards. There were also other factors, not the least of which was timing. I needed some time to think, and it would not do to arrive too early. If we got the aid we are seeking they would be hot to ride out immediately and on their own, and that would be disastrous. And, finally, I wanted to check this route in detail, for it forms the third arm of the triangle with Globbus, Persellus, and Anchor Logh, with the Hellgate in the center of that triangle. I wanted no surprises, and could trust none but a wizard of my rank to do the survey. I suspected that Haldayne was not acting alone. Otherwise he would not be so bold in his actions.'

'Well, you'll clearly get no help from Anchor Logh, not with dear Daji as the power behind the throne.'

'On the contrary, I think we *will* get it. This dual personality trick is a favorite of Haldayne's in Anchor, because it is impossible to detect there. By the same token, a command from a third party must be made in order to summon up the original personality.'

'But surely Haldayne and she have agents in the Temple, ones that will find out I escaped and trigger it.'

'Perhaps,' Mervyn replied, 'but perhaps not. All the Daji personality knows is that her pet escaped and is gone. This will upset her for a while, but the Sister General will console her and give her a new toy or something and she may forget all about it. The agents might never know, or never know the importance. Even if they *do* find out, they must trigger the other personality, and one or more must be taken through this intriguing gate access and then get to Haldayne, who must respond. This will take time, particularly since those agents are unlikely to be wizards of any significance. By that time we will have had our audience.'

'Maybe,' Cass said dubiously, 'but what good will that do us? I mean, if this woman is this highly placed, then she's probably got agents or corrupt innocents all over the place. That army might wind up fighting on the wrong side if at all.'

'But I don't *care* about its loyalty,' Mervyn told her. 'Don't you see? Haldayne has rigged things to lose. They will contribute and they will fight well with us because of that alone. After – well, think of this. Isn't it obvious to you by now that we must not only conquer Persellus but Anchor Logh as well?'

Both of the others looked shocked. It really hadn't occurred to either of them until now.

'And, if we do, I certainly would prefer a good share of their army out under *our* control in Flux. It'll make things a lot less bloody, I suspect.' He laughed. 'No, now that we know it all, I think we are about to give a truly bitter pill to Mister Haldayne.' He sighed and got up. 'And now we must let the others know of our plans. That will mean a slight inconvenience.'

'I could fly back with it,' Cass suggested. 'I kind of like this.'

'No, unless you were lucky enough to come across a first class wizard they would at least try to kill you, certainly not listen to what you have to say, or believe a word of it if they do. I'm afraid I must go, but this time I will take the express. You two are still half a day's ride from Anchor Logh. You go on, and I will catch up to you.'

It was Suzl who looked distressed at that. 'But how will we find our way in the void?'

Mervyn chuckled. 'That should present no problem at all. You see, as she is just discovering, Cass is a wizard herself and a fairly strong one, although limited right now to her own self.'

'What!' they both cried in unison.

He nodded. 'It took this stress and trauma to bring it out, although it has been latent all along. That is why the Soul Rider chose you. I knew it the moment I sensed the Rider, for Riders are limited to using the powers and abilities of their hosts. That is why your escape is so puzzling – Flux has no power in Anchor, as you well know. Now that you know, and now that crisis has brought it out, you can use it. You could not have found us unless you were following a main trail – correct?'

Cass nodded soberly. 'Yes, that's true. I found I could see them. But I thought it was the Soul Rider or the transformation.'

'No. It merely brought them out in you. Now, understand, you have power but no knowledge. That means that this power as regards specific things will affect only you or that which you need or which threatens you. Without much study and much mathematical training you cannot know how power-ful you really are or use it practically. But you can follow this trail, and if you need water you can find or even create it. Besides, I still want a good look at this whole route by a wizard I can trust. You fill that bill.'

'But – what about this form?' she asked lamely.

'If you concentrate hard enough, you can be anyone or anything you wish to be, with any attributes you need,' he told her. 'It will take much experimen-tation to get it right all the time, but you should at least have no problem whatsoever in becoming yourself, for you know your true form better than anyone. Try it now. Just close your eyes and concentrate on your old self. Pic-ture it, and want to be that way again. Go ahead.'

She did as instructed. She remembered herself, not as she was, but as she remembered that slightly redone Cass in the mirror at Miss Rona's. She pic-tured it, remembered it, and called up the same amazed satisfaction.

She opened her eyes. 'See? Nothing?'

'Oh no?' Suzl responded. 'Don't you feel a little – shorter? And maybe a little hairier?'

She looked down at herself, and gasped. She was, in fact, human once again. That body looked very familiar, although it was stark naked. She brought her arms up and looked at her hands. Her *hands*! She felt her head, and there was hair there, although not tied, just streaming down. 'I did it,' she said wonderingly.

'That you did. And if you need to be a bird woman again, just think of that image you saw. That's the way it works on a personal basis.'

She grinned. 'I'll be damned! Wow!' She hesitated a moment. 'But – wait a minute. I can't go into Anchor dressed like *this*.'

'Why not?' Suzl asked. 'That's the way you left it.'

The wizard shrugged. 'We'll have to teach you a few simple tricks when we can. For now –' he snapped his fingers – 'that should do it.' And, suddenly, she had on a short-sleeve red pull-over shirt, brown work pants, and boots.

'Yeah, you will ...' she breathed.

'Well, I'm off. If I'm not back before you get to Anchor, wait on the apron for me. Under no account go in there alone. Particularly not you, Cass. If word is out, Haldayne will have you marked for instant death this time, Soul Rider or not.'

16

Homecoming

They rode along for a while, just getting up to date.

'After you disappeared, and Nadya came screaming out of the room, there was holy Hell to pay all over Globbus, I'll tell you,' Suzl said. 'It was pretty clear after the initial search failed to find you, though, that you'd been snatched and carried off, and there was no problem guessing by who and where to. They met again after that and switched some things around, particularly the training and stakeout stuff, but otherwise they just accepted it. There wasn't anything they could do short of attacking Persellus then and there, and they weren't ready to do *that* yet, no matter how much we screamed at them.'

She thought for a moment. 'How did Matson take it?'

'He was pissed. Took it as a personal insult. Wanted to ride in with a rescue right away. I think he really likes you, Cass.'

She smiled. 'I wonder what he'll think when he finds out I'm a wizard? Me – that's still pretty hard to accept.'

Suzl shrugged. 'I don't know. There was always something funny about you, ever since we got caught up in that Paring Rite. Even when bad things happened to you they turned out O.K.'

'Does it change anything between us – as friends?'

'Not on my account, uh uh. Might be good to have a friend with some power around here. What about you, though? Everybody says when you get that kind of power you go nuts.'

'Maybe I always *was* nuts, so it doesn't matter. I don't know, Suzl. I guess I don't really believe it yet. Back in the gym, when we all got together and swore we were coming back and take our revenge on Anchor Logh – I didn't believe that, either. Not for a minute. And yet, here we are, heading back in, with you and me knowing that they plan to do just that. I'm really off balance, and have been all this time. I mean, just think of the others.'

'Huh?'

'The others taken in the Paring Rite, not just in Anchor Logh but all over World. Almost nobody escapes becoming somebody's slave or somebody's thing. And yet, here we are, right in the thick of great events like World's never seen before. Maybe *causing* a lot of it. I never thought of myself as any great mover and shaker. I mean, I'm still me, Cass, off the farm at Anchor Logh.'

Suzl shrugged. 'Maybe it's because we think of those big movers and shakers all wrong. Maybe we build 'em up after they're dead and gone or something into saints and angels and all that. I think maybe that all those greats really went to the bathroom same as we, and maybe got stomach aches and thought of themselves as folks just off some farm. And they probably were.'

'Yeah, but why us? Why not a couple of the others? Ivon or Kral or Jodee, for example? And why now?'

'I think it's just gotta be somebody, sometime, and we just happen to be it. I don't think it's planned. Look, the way I see it, this bastard Haldayne came up with this plot and put it into operation. This brought forth your Soul Rider or whatever it is, who picked you because you were the first one it ran into who had this power or whatever. Now, whether or not it was that thing or you that went nuts and violated the Temple we'll never know, but maybe it picked you because it knew you were the type to do just that. Who knows? This Mervyn reads minds pretty good, I think, and if *he* can, why not a creature of some kind? Once you were stuck with it, it used you and your power to unmask the plot. All because it was just floating along or something and you just happened to be the first one in the way. See?'

She sighed. 'Maybe you're right. Uh – this Mervyn and you have been riding along for some time. Did he do anything about your – problem?'

She laughed. 'I don't have a problem. Other people might, but I don't. Oh, he looked at it, decided it was too complicated, and offered to turn me one hundred percent male. *That* he could do.'

'And you refused?'

She nodded. 'I like it this way. Because you got snatched we had extra time, and I went over to one of the bars. Had a ball with it. Nope, I like it. No more periods, no more afraid of getting pregnant, none of that. But I *like* the way I look, and I *like* my tits and ass. I got the best of both worlds. There's lots of guys who only like other guys, you know. I'm the only one you know that can have it both ways and not be a pervert.' She giggled at that.

'And Dar, of course.'

'Yeah, well, maybe. But he's still pretty hung up on his maleness, and I don't think he'll ever have the kind of freedom I feel.'

'Speaking of freedom, how come the shirtless look? It's sexy with your equipment, but hardly usual.'

'Men don't have to wear shirts if they're comfortable without them. Oh, don't worry, I have a couple packed for dear old Anchor Logh. This is just kind of a turn-on. Makes me feel really free, that's all.'

They rode along, laughing and joking like two schoolgirls. When the horses seemed thirsty, Cass found it easy to identify which of the off-trail strings led to water pockets. It was all becoming very familiar very fast now. She was beginning to enjoy this newfound sense and the power it brought, and she only hoped she had enough self-control to keep from going wild with it. That, of course, was the madness of the wizard.

Mervyn still hadn't returned by the time they reached the border of

Anchor Logh. Because traffic was being stopped in Globbus and was not likely to come via Persellus, they felt reasonably safe in remaining there, just inside the Flux. Cass did not take Mervyn's warning lightly – Haldayne now would kill her on sight, since time was so crucial at this point that he would bet the Soul Rider would not find another suitable host in time to stop him.

'He seems so confident,' Cass said worriedly. 'But Haldayne's good, real good, and he knows more about his enemies than they do about him.'

'Sure, but if he's on to the fact that we know about his lady love there in the Temple, he might just give it up as not worth it,' Suzl responded hopefully. 'What's the use of fighting it out if you can't gain anything?'

Cass shrugged. 'Who knows what he thinks? I wish I knew more about what this was *really* about.'

'Huh? Sleep through your religion classes? It's all checking out in that department.'

'Well, maybe. But I've been through that gate to Hell, and I've seen the so-called sacred seal. The gate's supernatural enough, but that seal is a machine, Suzl. Real strange looking all right, but a machine all the same, a very fancy kind of machine but still a relative to the ones in the capital and the Temple. It sure wasn't put there by the ones who built that Hellgate – it just looks too different, that's all. More like something *we* would build if we knew how. Now, if the Holy Mother and Her Blessed Angels forced the demons into that hole and then sealed it with the seven seals, why did they use a machine? Why not just use the Flux power, or godly powers? And don't give me that crap about the ways of gods and demons being unknowable to humankind. *Somebody* knows. Haldayne, for example, knows, and maybe Mervyn does, too.'

'Yeah, but the old boy didn't know the gate connected to the Temple until you told him. Boy! I never saw him so shook!'

Cass nodded. 'The big thing is, if you can use this gate to get to the temple in Anchor Logh, then the odds are you can get to other Temples through other gates. That says to me that, for some reason, it's the Anchors that are important in this, not really the Flux, and I'm sure old Merv's wondering now just how many Anchors Haldayne's side already controls. He sure knows more about those gates than Mervyn and the others.'

Conversation drifted to other things as they waited. Time hung heavy in the void if only because there was no sense of it. Finally, though, a huge, dark shape came from the direction of the trail. They watched, ready to dart into Anchor if need be, but the enormous flying shape landed, shimmered, and changed into Mervyn's old man form, and they relaxed. Cass saw that there was a certain, indefinable *something* radiating from the man that marked Mervyn as Mervyn and no one else to her. Suzl, however, needed her nerves calmed, for she had none of these senses.

The wizard walked up to them carrying a small satchel. 'I've notified everyone I could find of your information – those that needed to know it, anyway,' he told them. 'We want to keep your escape secret, and I'm afraid I didn't tell them the source, so you are still officially missing, even to my fellow sorcerers. We are going to move up the attack, even though we might not have everybody, just to keep Haldayne off balance.' He put down the satchel, fumbled with the catch, then opened it and reached inside, first bringing out a cube, almost a meter square, of some undefined grayish substance. He put it in front of him, stepped back and made a gesture with his wrist. The cube shimmered, grew, and seemed to inflate as if it were some sort of balloon, until, standing there, was a full-sized living mule. 'It's so convenient when you have to to be able to compress them down to maximum survivable density,' he said, ignoring their total lack of understanding.

He reached down into the bag once more and pulled out clothing. 'We are going to have to be convincing,' he told them, 'and have easy access. Both of you get undressed here and now. We're going in undercover, you might say.'

After she undressed, the wizard handed her a robe. It was the scarlet and gray robe of a parish priestess. She put it on, and it was a bit too large for her. 'Well, grow into it. You're going to have to change your appearance totally here and now anyway. We want as many basic differences between you and your original looks as possible, and height is important because it's the first thing noticed. I want you *very* tall in bare feet – call it a hundred seventy-five, even a hundred and eighty centimeters. *Very* tall. And looking like nobody you know.'

She frowned. 'That's tough. Aside from my friends, the only women I can think of enough to concentrate on are my mother, my sisters, and those two priestesses.'

He sighed. 'Oh, very well. Stand still.' He made a flinging gesture with his hand, and suddenly the robe fit very well indeed. She towered over the very short Suzl, who stood back and nodded. 'Not bad. Maybe you ought to keep that.'

She desperately wanted a mirror – so desperately that the reflective surface Mervyn had used before materialized in front of her. She was stunning, very tall and perfectly proportioned to the height. Even her figure was absolutely perfect, and, unlike the experiments at Miss Rona's, it felt very comfortable. Her face, a near-perfect oval set off by very large, dark brown eyes and short hair of the same color, and her light brown skin made her almost the living model of religious pictures of the Holy Mother.

She wished the mirror away and was startled to see not Mervyn but another woman there, this one about halfway between Suzl's height and her own, also dark and attractive but dressed in a skin-tight outfit of what looked like red leather, with high red boots and even a cape. The strange woman was helping Suzl into a black outfit – a stringer's outfit.

'Don't be so shocked,' said the strange woman in a deep, melodious voice. 'We have to see a high priestess in a Temple. You didn't expect them to let me just walk in the way I was, did you?'

She laughed, feeling that sense of recognition she could not define. This was the third guise for Mervyn, and the most confusing of all. Since Suzl refused to permit a disguise by sorcery, she was instead going in slightly different clothing. She was soon dressed as the shortest, cutest stringer in anybody's memory. Mervyn then went over their cover names and stories and rehearsed them until they got it right. Suzl would be Sati, the name of a real female stringer that would be on the guard lists, but a stringer who had not been to Anchor Logh, being relatively new in the business. Cass would be Sister Kasdi, of Anchor Bakha, an Anchor far to the southwest of Anchor Logh but still closest in that direction, and an Anchor in many ways similar to Anchor Logh. She was given a spell-reinforced history and geography lesson that made her feel like she really had lived there. Mervyn would be Mera, a professional woman.

'Matson told me that they were anxiously looking for an electrical engineer,' he told them. 'I have some knowledge in that field and I think I can pass as a possible applicant for the job.'

Satisfied, they mounted, Cass taking the mule as was appropriate for priestesses, although she hated the side-saddle riding method that tradition dictated a priestess adopt exclusively. All set, they rode into Anchor.

Suzl had taken, apparently in Globbus, to smoking and slightly chewing on thin, crooked little cigars. While it was all part of the self-image she now had, she stuck one in the side of her mouth as they rode in and it gave a very good added effect to her stringer act. She led the mule with Cass aboard by a small rope, with Mervyn bringing up the rear. Suzl's whole expression and body took on a look of arrogant tolerance of the surroundings, like a government minister forced to tour a garbage dump, and she was obviously enjoying herself to the limit. She rode right past the shantytown of tents and dugout buildings and the small semipermanent population of duggers there and right up to the gate. A guard watched them, and when she stopped in front of the opening he called out, 'Who are you and what is your business and intent?'

'My name is Sati, stringer,' she responded boldly. 'I am still apprenticed, and was delegated to take these two from the Hollus train at Globbus, which is not heading here, up to Anchor Logh and the Temple.'

The guard vanished for a moment, then the outer gates closed with a dramatic rumbling. They waited there a couple of minutes, and then they opened again. There were now three soldiers, well armed and looking spiffy, on horseback in the gate, and they rode towards the waiting trio. Cass recognized the officer who led them as one of the men at the gate that terrible night they'd left Anchor Logh.

Suzl barely glanced at them, but reached down into her saddlebag and pulled out a small book, handing it to the officer. He looked it over, then looked at the three of them, and frowned. There was nothing unusual about such detached deliveries – they happened all the time – but his job was to ensure that these were legitimate. He rode out a bit further so he could see the guard atop the tower. 'What do you say?' he called up.

'Checks out, sir,' the guard responded. 'She's on the last list given to us by the guild, and she's apprenticed to Hollus.'

He nodded to himself and turned back to her. 'And what is your cargo?'

'Two passengers, that's all,' Suzl told him. 'Sister Kasdi was sent over here from Anchor Bakha for some specialized training in the Temple, and Miss Mera was traveling with another train when Matson came through with the word that you were looking for engineers. She decided to come on up and look your charming land over to see if she can save herself a longer trip to another job.' Cass admired how Suzl made the words 'charming land' seem like the nastiest of insults with sheer intonation.

The officer looked at the other two. Cass looked back at him, smiled sweetly, and gave him a blessing with her hand. It unnerved him for a moment. Finally he said, 'All right, will you two ladies please dismount?' They did, Cass with slight difficulty she hoped wasn't obvious. 'Stringer, you come in first and file the papers for the passes. Ladies, these two troopers will remain with you until we have passed through, then take you through with them.'

Suzl, the animals trailing, rode confidently into the gate and the officer followed. It closed, there was a pause, and then it opened once more. Suzl, at least, was back in the land of her birth.

They followed behind the troopers and into the gate, which closed behind them. One of the troopers turned and said, 'Our apologies, Sister, Lady, but we must arrange for a search. Please remain in here and do not move until someone comes for you.'

Cass looked over at Mervyn, but just got a shrug. For him it was just routine, but to her this was a new experience. She wondered, though, what all the fearful and prejudiced folk of Anchor Logh would feel if they knew how silly and useless their dreaded gate and defenses really were? It was pretty obvious that people went from Flux to Anchor and back all the time, no matter what the official line was – or even if the officials quoting that line knew it.

They waited there a few minutes, and then a priestess came into the gate. She was quite young, her robe of light yellow very plain and unadorned, saying that she was not long out of the novitiate. Clearly this was a bottom-rung job.

She approached Cass first, who outranked her by her robe's indication, then kneeled. Cass had seen this done enough to have no problems with it.

'The blessing of the Holy Mother be upon thee for eternity,' she pronounced. 'Be free and do your duty.'

The young priestess rose, bowed slightly, and responded, 'We thank thee, Sister, for thy understanding and blessing. Humble apologies to you both, but it is required that you both disrobe completely for physical examination. You have seen out there what lurks in Flux, and while we realize that it is most unnecessary on your part we can make no exceptions.'

Cass smiled, undid, and removed her robe, letting it drop to the ground. Mervyn, dressed more complexly, had more of a problem, and was assisted by Cass in reaching the same state.

For a groveling priestess not yet even allowed to have a name of her own or use the personal pronoun, she was most thorough in her inspection. Clearly she did not want to be here forever, or worse, and just one slip and worse it would be.

Finally she nodded and said, 'Please put your clothing back on, and again our humblest apologies.'

'That's all right,' Mervyn soothed. 'If you had seen what we have seen in Flux you would know just how important your job really is.'

She smiled, not realizing how totally irrelevant that job was.

The priestess in yellow led them to the other side, where Suzl waited, looking impatient and bored. Both of the newcomers were given a form to sign, and then issued passes good for one week maximum. Of course, should they be allowed by the Temple to stay, then they would be granted citizenship.

The officer and a trooper assisted Cass in remounting her mule, then they were off along the main highway to the capital. They were well along and far out of sight of the guards when Suzl finally laughed. 'So much for their security. Checked you two over with a microscope, and you both phony as can be, while they just kept shoving papers at me and never even looked me in the eye.'

'I counted on that,' Mervyn told her. 'Remember, a bureaucrat does not believe in Heaven or Hell, Church or Government. A bureaucrat only believes in paper.'

They rode on, stopping overnight in Lawder, a small town about halfway to the capital. Cass found her disguise both annoying and fun at one and the same time. Annoying, because as a priestess she had no money and had to more or less beg for food, drink, and lodging from the locals and was really prevented from going to the bar and other public rooms. It was fun, though, in that she was treated deferentially by almost everyone, and it was funny to watch them try and control their language and behavior around her. She found some diversion, though, in the fact that, as an outside priestess, everybody wanted to confess to her and this became the main agent of barter. It was obvious that many sought absolution from sin but did not relish confessing to their local priestess, who would be living in the same town with them.

Since she had been through the ritual on the supplicant end most of her life, she knew all the proper things to do and say, and it occurred to her more than once that this, more than anything else, was the most effective way in which the church had the pulse of, and control of, the entire community. They barely needed the spies and agents she had imagined when she'd seen the dossiers on that screen. All they needed was weekly updated reports from each and every parish priestess on the confessions of the faithful.

She soon had quite an earful from the locals, too. Clearly Anchor Logh was not the calm, strait-laced community she had always imagined it being. It was one thing in Flux, but here, in a place she thought she new, she began to feel a stranger.

They set out again the next morning, Suzl feeling a little grumpy because Mervyn had stopped her fun in the bar short of the payoff. She knew, of course, that this was not the time, and that there was much danger in exposure, but it still irritated her.

By early afternoon they were approaching the capital, and as they passed a large farm Suzl and Cass halted and looked suddenly serious.

'What's the problem?' the wizard asked them.

'Over there is where both of us were born and raised,' Cass told him. 'Our families are still there. I'd hoped to be able to see them, tell them I was all right.' She sighed. 'I guess I can't, looking and sounding like this.'

He thought a moment. 'If you can pull it off, not blow your cover or break down, it might be all right if you just, say, carried the news as a third party,' Mervyn said. 'Do you think you can act the part in front of people you know? They won't know you, remember, for you are someone else.'

'I'd like to try – for their sakes,' she responded honestly. 'I think, after all, this is something I *have* to do.'

'All right then,' he agreed. 'Go and do it. We will go ahead and register at the hotel. Don't take more than one hour, then follow us in. That will give us a chance to settle and get the lay of the land, as it were. Meet us there, and we'll discuss what to do next. And if anything goes wrong here, *anything*, break off and come to us immediately. I want no surprises here that we don't generate.'

She nodded. 'I will. The Holy Reverend Sister Kasdi will behave.' She turned to Suzl. 'Want me to pass on any word about you?'

She thought a moment. 'Just tell 'em I'm free and I'm happy.' She had a sudden thought. 'I hope nobody who knows me is in town now.' She alone appeared, at least, the way she had been.

'There is very little chance of that,' Mervyn told her. 'It is midweek, after all. Let's cross that bridge when we come to it.'

They left Cass there, and for a while she hesitated. Here it was – the large box she had come to check that day that now seemed so long ago, the day she had seen Matson riding in. The difference between that child and her now, although separated not really all that long in time, was an unbridgeable chasm.

She decided, though, to walk down the road, and tied up the mule at the post box. How many times had she walked down this same road to those buildings? She looked over at the pastures and could still identify and name just about every horse and cow she could see.

Finally she reached the familiar complex, and made the almost automatic turn that took her to the blacksmith's shop. The old sounds of iron being pounded and reshaped caused her heart to skip a beat, and she began perspiring despite the slight chill. Could she do it – or not? She sighed, and took several deep breaths to get hold of herself. As she had told Mervyn, she *had* to.

She walked in the barn-like open doors of the smithy and saw her father there, dunking a horseshoe in water, as two other smiths and three apprentices worked elsewhere. She approached her father, the tension rising within her. He looked up, frowned, stared a moment, then put down his work and came to her. 'Yes, Sister? What can I do for you?'

She repressed the urge to fling her arms around him and hug and kiss him as she so desperately wanted to do. Instead she said, 'You are the father of the girl called Cass who was taken in the Paring Rite?'

He suddenly went a bit tense and white. 'Yes. What's this all about?'

'I have news of her.'

He looked suddenly very concerned and she could see the emotions within him rising, despite his efforts to contain them. 'Speak,' he said hoarsely.

'I have just come through the Flux from Anchor Bakha. During that journey I met many from this Anchor. Most are suffering as expected, but your Cass is doing well.'

He looked very interested and slightly relieved, but he wanted to know more.

'I cannot tell you of the Flux, except that it is very strange,' she continued, struggling with the words. 'However, there is some opportunity there for those with special talents. Your Cass and three others from this riding have broken their bonds and now work as paid employees for a stringer, mostly tending to animals. They were healthy and seemed happy, but were anxious that I carry news back to their families.'

She could hardly believe it. Were those truly *tears* in her father's eyes? Never, ever, had she known her father to cry, not under any conditions, and she was so touched by it that she had to fight back tears herself.

'Cass also wanted me to inform others that the ones called Suzl, Dar, and Nadya are also safe, well, and have jobs and careers. Alas, for the others – there is the purging. Will you see, though, that their families also get word?'

Her father broke down at that point, dropped to his knees and took and firmly clasped her hand. It was at once both touching and embarrassing, but she knew she had done the right thing. She also knew that she'd better get out of there before she broke down completely herself.

'I must go,' she managed, voice breaking, 'but I am glad I could bring you some joy. Cass said to t-tell you s-she loved you, and missed you, but that she was probably happier now than she would have been back here.'

He didn't want to let go of her, but she managed to break free and walked out, leaving him sobbing in his shop. She walked briskly back down the road, the light wind stinging the copious tears that now flowed unchecked and unstoppable.

It was dark and she was once again in the city before she had completely cried it out.

She went immediately to the hotel, tying up her mule, and went inside. Suzl was sitting there smoking one of her little cigars and looking through the paper, while Mervyn was checking the hotel directory. They saw her, and came over to her. Suzl saw at once what sort of experience it had been for her. Her eyes were puffy and red.

'How'd it go?' she asked gently.

'It went fine. The job got done with nobody the wiser, but I'm afraid it was pretty hard on me.'

'Poor kid. It must have been tough.'

She nodded. 'Real tough, but worth it. I'll never regret it no matter what happens from here on in.'

Mervyn came up to her and whispered, 'Let's step outside for a moment, Sister.' They followed him out into the darkened street. 'All right,' he went on when he was sure they were not being overheard, 'we're in too late to do anything tonight. Sister, you will have to stay at the Temple, of course. Just relax, act the part, and get a good night's sleep. In the morning, go out and wait for us in the Temple Square.' He paused for a moment. 'I'm afraid you're going to have to go through their whole rigamarole.'

She shrugged. 'I think my lessons will hold up. Don't worry about me – I've been more places in that Temple than anybody not working there, and if your spell holds they're not going to be able to make much use of hypnotic drugs to get any information.'

'It'll hold,' he assured her. 'Go. We have a busy, and risky, day tomorrow.'

She nodded, and led her mule down streets she knew so well towards the great, lighted Temple spires.

'Any problems?' Mervyn asked her in the crisp, clean morning air when they met in Temple Square.

'None that I know of,' she told him. 'I had to do some explaining, and a lot of praying and chanting, but that's about it. It's not bad when you've got rank.

Novices to wait on you hand and foot, private rooms with all the amenities, soft feather beds. They know your covers, though – I had to tell them that.'

He nodded. 'Don't worry about it. We won't need them long. Come.'

Together all three of them went up the Temple steps to those forbidding bronze doors, opened them, and stepped inside. Cass saw that Suzl was playing the memory game from her glances. *In there is the chapel, down there is the gym where they marched us, over there are the Temple boarding rooms for young girls in town, over there is the library stairs ...* She had done much the same the night before.

Mervyn seemed to know his way around pretty well. 'They're all built pretty much the same,' he told them. Standardization. They went down the library stairway but did not make the turn to go down the next flight to the library itself. Instead they stopped, and Mervyn knocked on an unmarked door opening onto the landing. It opened to reveal a puzzled warden. 'Yes?' she asked.

'I am here to deliver a message to the Sister General. Can you take one to her from me?'

The warden looked hesitant. 'I can't just disturb her for any old thing. You can take it up with the proper channels.'

'I have no time to be put off by bureaucrats whose job it is to put me off,' he responded curtly. 'If you get this message to her, she will see me. If you do not, I will raise something of a stink that will be as unpleasant for you as for me. At the end of that time I will probably be hauled off to jail, but the Sister General will get my message in the report and then we will change places, or worse.'

The warden did not seem moved by this, and made as if to close the door. Mervyn stuck his foot in it, then pushed the warden backwards with a shove. Clearly that woman's body he'd tailor-made for himself had a lot of nasty surprises, for the larger, tougher-looking warden flew back as if struck by a sledgehammer. Aghast, Suzl and Cass followed him into the wardens' room.

Three other wardens were in there and came on the run when they saw the problem. Mervyn reached behind to his long cape and brought out an automatic rifle. They stopped, unable to believe that anyone would commit such sacrilege.

'Sati, shut that door. You on the floor – get up and get over with your sisters. *Now!* And all of you just stand there and stay away from any nice little buttons or consoles. I am a creature of Flux and I will not hesitate to shoot. If I do, the spray this thing makes in stopping one of you will kill all four of you.'

Suzl reached under her shirt in the back and pulled out a small automatic pistol, reinforcing Mervyn and freeing him to move. 'You four – come into the outer room here with us. Don't touch anything or try anything funny.'

They obeyed, hands high, but they glared at her. 'You'll fry in Hell for a thousand lives for this,' one hissed.

'I already been there, honey, and it don't scare me a bit,' she snapped back. 'Ca – Kasdi, you watch 'em and if you see one of 'em pull anything funny, you yell and they're gone.'

'You'll never get out of here alive,' one of the wardens said smugly. 'You know that, don't you?'

'If I don't, neither will you,' came the equally tough reply. Suzl, Cass noted, was loving every minute of this, and there was genuine hatred and contempt in her expression and manner. This was no act. She ached for revenge.

Mervyn studied the control panel for a moment, checked out its switches and relays, then found the master manual and thumbed quickly through it. He found what he was looking for immediately, and tapped four numbers on the intercom pad. There was a buzzing sound, then an unfamiliar voice answered. 'Sister General. What is the problem?'

'There is an urgent message here for the Sister General's ears alone,' he said into the speaker. 'It is urgent. Put her on at once.'

There was a sigh at the other end, and the connection was muted for a moment. Finally a far more familiar voice said, 'This is Sister General Diastephanos. What is the nature of this emergency?'

Mervyn looked over at Cass, who nodded. That was her, all right.

'The Seven Who Come Before have gathered at the gates of Anchor to release the spawn of Hell,' he said carefully. 'The Nine Who Guard call upon the holy church for aid.'

There was a long pause, and then the Sister General asked, 'Who is this?'

'Pericles,' he responded.

Again there was silence. Finally she asked, 'Are my wardens all right? I assume it wasn't easy to get in to use the intercom.'

'They are mad and angry and vengeful,' he told her truthfully, 'but aside from a slight bruise on one of them they are in fine shape.'

'Who's watch officer?'

He looked over at the four. One of them said, sourly, 'Daran.'

'Put her on.'

Mervyn gestured with the gun and the chief warden came over to the intercom. 'She's here,' he told her.

'Daran, this would not have been necessary if you had not refused to carry the message. These people are not criminals, nor are they committing sacrilege. How many are there?'

'Three, Your Worship,' the warden said glumly. 'Two have guns, and the third's pretending to be a priestess.'

'She may very well be one,' the Sister General snapped back. 'Now, listen carefully. You are to escort these three to my office without delay of any kind.

Understand? I want no trouble and no revenge. If there is any trouble or any action of any kind taken against them you will all be exiled to Flux immediately. I mean that.'

'But Your Worship—'

'No buts! Deliver them immediately, healthy, and with no problems and I will forgive all. Do anything else – *anything* – and you will all curse the day of your birth and the parents who bore you. That is all.'

The watch officer sighed. Mervyn smiled at her and handed her his rifle. She seemed startled, then undecided, suppressing an urge to fire anyway. Instead they walked into the other room, where Suzl handed over her pistol as well. There ensued a great debate among the four in which the watch officer had to exercise abnormal control just to keep them from tearing the three limb from limb or at least working them over with rubber hoses. Once the officer had made her decision, though, she stuck to it. When the warden who had been shoved back tried to attack Mervyn anyway, the watch officer struck her in the mouth with the rifle butt. She looked mad, but finally calmed down, as blood from a small cut trickled from the side of her mouth.

'Now, then,' sighed the watch officer, 'let's *all* go see Her Holiness, shall we?'

Leaving the guns in the security office and then locking up, they all walked back upstairs, into the chapel, then back into the sacristy. Cass had a feeling of having been here before, but now she was with someone who knew the way.

Ultimately they reached the first of three security doors. Obviously the Sister General's own area had been reinforced since Cass had blundered in. Each of the doors could be opened only from the inside, by someone who first could look at whoever was out there and take action if necessary. The wardens generally expected their way to be barred at this point, and action taken, and seemed extremely surprised when each door opened for them with no hesitation.

Finally they reached the office of the Sister General. It looked much the same as Cass remembered it, although she'd had a very different view the last time. Sister Daji was nowhere in sight, but to the left of the Sister General's huge desk the falcon perch still stood, and why not? On it was a falcon.

The Sister General looked at the mob, then said, 'That will be all, wardens. Retire to your posts and await my instructions.' They bowed, bewildered, and exited.

She looked at the three of them in turn, settling on Mervyn. 'I don't have to guess which one of you is Pericles.'

'It's been a long time, hasn't it, Des?' he responded lightly.

The tone and question startled both Cass and Suzl. It was obvious now that, somehow, these two actually *knew* each other!

She came over and hugged the wizard. 'You wore that guise just for me, didn't you?'

He laughed. 'I figured if nothing else you'd get a photo from the police with a report on my doings.'

She laughed. 'You always *were* the one for direct actions. But, enough of this for now. I'm going to have problems with my security staff for a long time over you three. What is this really all about?'

Mervyn looked around. 'Is it just us in here?'

'Yes. I cleared the rest out. Please, all of you, have a seat and we'll talk.'

'Not everybody was cleared,' Mervyn remarked casually. 'I see we have a spy over there.'

She laughed. 'Oh, Demon. Yes, my secretary went roaming in the marketplace while I was away on business and bought her as a surprise for me. Unfortunately, she seems to like the secretary far more than me. She's safe, though.'

Mervyn nodded, and Cass began to wonder if she in fact *had* dreamed the whole thing. Was it instead some odd story planted in her mind by Haldayne? Was she, in fact, loosed with false information in her mind to confuse and disrupt the Nine? She felt suddenly very confused.

'Haldayne has taken Persellus and means to move on the gate,' the wizard said simply. 'We are mounting a massive force to retake it, supported by myself and two others of the Nine.' Quickly, and in a businesslike fashion, he outlined the entire plot, leaving Cass out of it completely, though, as well as Daji and the part Anchor Logh played in it. She listened attentively, her face grim. When he had finished she asked, 'What do you want me to do?'

'How large is your troop force?'

She thought a minute. 'I don't have the exact figures, but not counting the new recruits in training after Census, about a thousand.'

'Let's count the recruits.'

'Then, perhaps a hundred more plus training instructors. But we need a minimum of three hundred to man and guard the borders.'

He nodded. 'That's fine. Give me five hundred under your best officers and noncoms. Get them in Flux and I'll see they don't crack. Once we break Haldayne's shield we'll need warm bodies to overrun and root out what's left of Persellus. He's very strong and has had time to prepare.'

'Do you think you'll catch him this time?' she asked, apparently getting caught up in the adventure of it.

'We're going to try. That's all we can do, no more. There is nothing I would like more, as you well know. Half a dozen times I've had him in my nets and he's managed to slip away. But, with your gracious help, we'll beat him this time, at least.'

'You shall have it and welcome,' she responded. 'And what will you do with it – after?'

He shrugged. 'Sister Kasdi has a great deal of talent and is now training under me. A church-controlled Fluxland in such a strategic position would consolidate quite a bit and secure the gate for some time.'

She thought about it, and liked the idea. 'A church-controlled Fluxland. It was the dream of the Founding Mothers, but somehow it's never come to pass. It would create a church-held domain over a hundred and fifty kilometers southwest.' She turned to Cass. 'You must do it! You have the best teacher in the world for it. Why, it could be the old dream – the training and university ground for the Church, as Globbus is for wizards.'

'I will consider it, Your Eminence,' Cass responded carefully, trying to make sense of all this. The idea of her becoming a Sister General wizard to a Fluxland church indoctrination center was ludicrous at best. She wondered what the Sister General would think if she knew who *really* sat before her in the guise of a tall priestess. Again she felt frustrated that she had no idea what games were being played here, only that everybody seemed to know and understand more than she did …

It was, in fact, as simple as that insofar as getting the troops was concerned. The Sister General herself would give them the commands and see them off, and they would be ready at the western gate in three days. They were ready now to leave, with a total pass from Her Eminence herself, when Mervyn asked, 'Where's that secretary of yours? I've heard some stories about her.'

She laughed. 'Daji? Around someplace, I suspect. Absolutely *gorgeous* body, but rather empty in the head, I fear. I have to keep it that way, if only for security.'

He nodded. 'I understand. But if you could spare her for these next three days she'll be most helpful, as your secretary, in clearing away bureaucratic barriers just by her presence. I can use her, so don't worry about what she doesn't know.'

The Sister General laughed. 'You're just trying to get her away from me so you can have some fun. But, all right. Take her. I'm going to be too busy for her anyway, it appears, and she only has one thing on her mind all the time, bless her.' She pressed a buzzer and there was a muffled response. 'Is Daji about?'

Again a muffled response. She nodded. 'Send her up. She's going on a little trip with some friends of mine.'

17

Sorcerers

Sister Daji had seemed quite confused when ordered by the Sister General to go with the three nice ladies and do what she was told, but after a little heart-to-heart talk in the other room she went along with it, at least grudgingly. Cass could not get over the contrast between the woman she saw now and the one she had seen with Haldayne. It seemed almost inconceivable that this bubble-brained airhead could possibly be a mistress of Hell and conniving plotter.

They went out the door and down the Temple steps, Daji clutching a small overnight bag. Some birds scattered into the air as they descended the stair, but one bird, a particularly large raven, did not. Instead, he circled and then settled atop one of the lampposts along the sides of the square itself and watched the four figures come forward. There were few people about, although there was some traffic on the streets and a couple of people were sitting on one of the benches in the square, and two yellow-robed Sisters were walking towards the Temple as the quartet walked away.

Still, Cass had an uneasy feeling she couldn't shake off. Something seemed very wrong, although things had been going well from Mervyn's point of view. It had started with the falcon still in the Sister General's office, grown worse at meeting Daji, and was now building to the breaking point. She looked around nervously, studying everyone in the square, her eyes finally reaching the two approaching Sisters. There was just something about them, something very odd …

'Everybody watch it!' she cried suddenly. '*Those Sisters are wearing boots!*'

'Caw!' screamed the raven almost immediately. 'Caw! Caw! Caw!'

The two 'Sisters' split from one another, reaching in and drawing guns at the same instant. Mervyn dropped where he was and pulled an automatic pistol, firing at the closest attacker first. The 'Sister' fell back with the force of the shots, blood soaking the front of the robe while her gun clattered as it fell. The other, however, dropped and rolled, and had time to open fire before Mervyn could bring his pistol around. Suzl had dropped at Cass's warning and now rolled towards the first assailant's fallen weapon, while Cass managed to make it behind a post that afforded some protection. Birds and people were screaming and panicking everywhere.

Daji, however, had just stopped and stood there, looking very confused. As a result, she took the full blast of the second assailant's shots and staggered back, then collapsed on the paving stones, writhing and groaning. Mervyn fired at the assassin but scored only a grazing blow. Then his gun went dead, empty. The woman in yellow, realizing this, stopped, raised her own gun, and pointed it directly at the wizard, who had nowhere to run. A volley of shots rang out, echoing across the square and against the Temple walls, and the killer spun and fell dead.

Suzl looked a little surprised that she'd shot so well from such a distance, and smugly blew the smoke away from the barrel. Mervyn, however, was in no mood for gratitude or theatrics. 'Shoot the raven!' he cried. 'The raven!' He pointed to the large bird atop the lamp, but before Suzl realized what he was saying and could make sense of it the bird launched itself into the air and was soon lost from sight to the southwest.

Cass ran over and helped Mervyn up. 'Damn!' he swore. 'It was Haldayne and we almost had him!'

Suzl walked cockily over to them. 'He almost had *you*, you mean. Where the hell did you get that pistol?'

'Trick compartment in the cape,' he told her. 'They took the rifle, left the holder, and it was still there. Damn you, though! Why didn't you shoot the raven while you had the chance? I had a spell on you that made you a great marksman. You could have had him!'

'And lost you,' she responded, getting a little irritated.

'What do I matter?' he growled. 'That raven was Haldayne. If we had gotten him we could have taken Persellus without any real losses.'

She shrugged. 'Sorry. Next time I'll let you die and shoot every damned bird in sight.' She looked around. 'Where's Cass?' They both looked, and found her kneeling beside the fallen Daji. A crowd was gathering fast, and police could be heard on their way. Mervyn elbowed his way through and knelt down beside Cass.

Daji was mortally wounded, but still alive. Gasping, blood running from her mouth, she looked for all the world a hurt and confused child. She choked once, and then something seemed to grow within her, filling her face and particularly her eyes. Her whole appearance took on a different look, and she coughed and gulped down air. 'Damn you!' she screamed, in a far different, more self-assured voice filled with hatred and fear. 'Damn that bastard Haldayne! Always the genius! Always the double-dealing genius! I should have known, you ...' She shuddered and went limp, and her eyes now held a vacancy that even Daji had never known.

Police and Temple wardens came through, pulling them away. Cass stepped back and shook her head sadly. 'It's crazy,' she said, not particularly to Suzl although that was who was there. 'I actually feel sorry for her. I don't know how I can pity her, but I do.'

Suzl shrugged. 'Well, she certainly was what you said, that's for sure. Man! That was weird, seeing her change like that.'

Cass nodded. At least she was vindicated in her own mind about it all. Daji had certainly been with Haldayne, and that meant the rest of it was almost certainly true as well. She looked up for Mervyn, and saw him with the authorities inspecting the body of the first killer. Both assassins were dead, and when the robes were opened they all saw that under those robes were two hard-looking women dressed in farm clothes.

They spent the next several hours with the police, giving statements of the events. The pass from the Sister General was absolute, and avoided many embarrassing questions about why they were there, but there were still the statements, which had to be checked, typed, and signed, and the individual interrogation of each as to the exact sequence of events. The administrative chief of the Temple showed up to clear the way for them not to have to reveal any more than they chose, and to carry back copies of everything for the Sister General, but it was still a mess. Neither killer was on the registry, nor had they any record of entering Anchor Logh. This bothered them all more than the killings themselves, as unprecedented as they were, because it meant that either there was a leak in the wall guard or else these two had come from the only place where the unregistered could possibly come from – the Temple itself.

That was not the problem of the trio from the Flux, however. 'You know this Anchor pretty well. Can we take different indirect routes back to the gate?' Mervyn asked them.

They thought about it. 'There are lots of back roads, so long as you don't mind camping out in fields,' Cass told him. 'But there's really no place to hide from somebody who knows them as well as you and also knows what you look like.'

He nodded. 'I thought as much. I'm going to pull rank with the church, then, and get us a full police guard all the way back. I want no more lopsided ambushes.'

They returned inside the police station and Mervyn composed a long note to the Sister General, sending it back with the admin chief. They waited a good hour or more, until a lower ranking priestess in admin gray returned with instructions for the police, and they had their escort and more.

There were no further attempts on them, and Mervyn wasn't surprised. 'The object of the exercise was to kill Daji first, then me if they could. You two were totally optional.'

'Thanks a lot,' Suzl grumped. 'But – why Daji? Because we had her number and maybe could have learned a lot from her?'

'That, of course,' the wizard agreed. 'I knew we were in trouble when I saw that falcon there. It was meant to confuse, but all it did was signal that they knew something was wrong.'

'It sure confused *me*,' Cass told him. 'I thought for a while that the whole thing had been a Haldayne-inspired hallucination.'

'Which was exactly the intent. But when it failed, and we arranged to have Daji come with us, they knew their subtlety had not paid off and took direct action. They could not afford one of their chiefs in my hands. She would know vital things far beyond this immediate crisis.'

'Then the plot is really foiled, huh?' Suzl put in. 'I mean, their agent's dead.'

'One agent. Someone saw us taking Daji out, and someone received orders to kill her. Haldayne might have started the killers, but he couldn't possibly have been inside the Temple. I'm afraid that all this shows is that Anchor Logh is already as conquered as Persellus, and woefully ignorant of the fact. We shall not know it all until we have dealt with all our problems, and perhaps not even then.' He turned to Cass. 'First things first. We must go into Flux and prepare you.'

'Huh? Prepare me for what?'

'Your ordination and conference, of course. It will be done by the Sister General herself in front of the troops at the west gate just before we march.'

'My *what* and my *what*? Hey! Wait a minute!'

'It is necessary for a priestess to lead the forces of Anchor into Flux. They are terrified enough now, as you would have been not so long ago. They need what is called in scripture an Adjutant to lead and protect them – a high-ranking priestess who is able to stand and use the Flux and protect herself and them. Don't worry – it's the required part of the Holy Books for all in Anchor Logh to read right now, although it's so obscure and in one of the codices that is rarely paid attention to. In short, we need a wizard-priestess. The Adjutant, when created, is second in rank only to the Sister General herself.'

'But, wait a minute! Don't *I* have any say in this? I mean, I'm not even sure I *believe* in that stuff any more, at least not the way it's taught, and I sure don't want to give up sex and the Flux power now that I've found them.'

Suzl gave a raised eyebrow at that but said nothing.

'Obviously it's too obscure for you, as well,' Mervyn responded patiently. 'The Adjutant is considered a somewhat supernatural figure. She comes from Flux and returns to it, although she is, of course, able to travel to Anchor. It exists for the very reason that a lot of the rest exists – it is convenient when the rules have to be bent. In this case, men raised to be terrified of the Flux are being asked to go into it and do battle. Think of how *you* felt when *you* first went in. It's not so bad. You'll be a High Priestess in Anchor and a wizard in Flux, and you'll need more training as a wizard than *this* job requires.'

She thought it over. 'How long has it been since the last – Adjutant – was appointed?'

He thought it over. 'Three, maybe four hundred years, I think. They all run together after a while. But now there will be two, each accompanied by a Flux warrior.'

'Huh?'

'A Flux warrior, it is said, is the reincarnation of one of the greatest warrior angels corrupted and exiled to World after the Rebellion. Because they were of the highest rank then, they are cursed to live their lives in Flux, and to be known because they differ from humans only in one specific attribute. That attribute is not defined, but that only makes it convenient for our candidates.'

Suzl grinned. 'Like me, you mean?'

He nodded. 'Like you. And like Dar.'

Cass gasped. 'So *that's* why you split them up! You had this in mind all along!'

He nodded. 'But your vanishing act nearly spoiled it. I was determined to take a dugger or whatever, but, fortunately, I didn't have to.'

Suzl giggled. 'Just think – only weeks ago we four were stripped of it all and cast out of Anchor. Now two of us are gonna be High Priestesses and the other two are angels! This is crazy but I love it!'

Cass nodded, not sharing the mirth. 'Yes, lucky – if we survive all this. Not like the rest of them marched out with us. Not like the ones in Arden's train.'

'Oh, let the dead be cremated and their ashes returned to the life of the soil,' Suzl quoted from the holy books. 'Now is now and I am me, and I'm having a ball.'

The void, which had been so terrifying before, now seemed like a welcome friend to them, offering peace and quiet and relative security. Mervyn wasted no time becoming his favorite old man's character once again, but after a short session with Suzl to brief her on just what her part in this was, he sent her back to Anchor, to the apron area, with an eye to getting as much information and rumor from the resident duggers as possible. Mervyn wanted to know how the wall leaked so easily, and it was also a way to have Cass alone for a while.

'I know you're wondering about all this,' he began, 'and that will never stop, I'm afraid, for none of us knows the answers. We, and our forebears, however, do know much more of the history and geography of World than the church permits to be taught, simply because part of our mission was to save the books and records of the past. Not all survived, alas, particularly from the earliest days, but much did.'

Humanity, he told her, had once been far greater and more numerous than now. There was once, as near as they could understand it, a great empire of humankind, which included but was not restricted to World. 'This is only one world of men, perhaps the only one left now. Once, however, there was the concept of empire.'

In this great time in the far past – fully thousands of years before – man had had a great civilization, an ideal community where all were free and had – if not directly then through machines – the powers and wonders of wizards. The forces of Hell rose up to attempt to destroy this civilization, and there was a great war, such as none today could even imagine. In the end, humans defeated the forces of Hell and pushed them back into a place outside our very universe. But the battle had not been without great cost, and the empire was shattered and destroyed and with it most of the race and most of its worlds.

'It was here on World that the final battle took place,' he said, 'and it was here, at last, that Hell was pushed out of all we know and the gates to Hell were sealed.'

'Then the machines I saw at the gate were those of that lost empire,' she responded, understanding it better. 'They were the means by which all was sealed.'

He nodded. 'However, all did not go well here, either. The church, originally set up to guard against those gates being opened or tampered with, as well as to guard all the old knowledge, became corrupted, as new generations saw it as an avenue of power. Still, the system, even with what we have lost, has held for all this time. There *were* those who disagreed with the system, however, and sought to preserve what could be preserved. Nine people, all great men and women of their time and all great wizards, copied, begged, borrowed, or stole all that they could and moved into Flux. They did not desert the church, but rather felt the church had deserted them, become too large, political, and bureaucratic. These Nine hand-picked their successors, so that when it finally came their time there was always someone ready to step in.'

'And those are the Nine Who Guard?'

He nodded. 'We guard not only against the forces of Hell but against the follies of humanity as well. None of us are saints, but we have somehow managed to do our jobs and keep the faith. Besides, it's not bad being a wizard of such tremendous power here in Flux. We also keep our hands in with the church, as it were. No one can become a Sister General or higher without spending time with us in Flux, if only to totally understand the nature and threat that Flux presents, and, of course, to read and learn the literature forbidden or destroyed in Anchor.'

'So that explains why you knew Sister General Diastephanos!'

Again he nodded. 'Yes, she trained with me long ago. Twenty years or more, I'd say.'

'She sure didn't take all the moral lessons.'

Mervyn grinned. 'Oh, it's not that terrible. The fact is, the holy books are quite a bit less strict than the rules the church now imposes. That particular section, which you'll not read in the Temple libraries, actually specifies that none will engage in sins of the flesh with any man after ordination. In the early days, for example, it was rare but not unheard of for priestesses to be widows with children, and in the early days many a "scarlet woman" or one with family problems or pregnant with a child born out of wedlock joined to

regain status and respectability. The church had such a potential to be a uni-
fying force for World. Instead, it became the dictator of it.'

This was a far different picture than the one she'd had growing up, and,
indeed, the one she'd formed since leaving Anchor. She began to realize both
the potential and the loss to World of its corruption, and it made her feel
more than slightly angry. In a sense, the church had become to Anchor what
each ruling wizard was to a Fluxland. Corrupted by power, each had inevitably exercised that power to the fullest. It was a strong vision it presented, of
a church keeping knowledge alive, and providing a moral and cultural unity
to World, while government, as a separate entity elected by Anchor, would
rule subject to the voters, not the church.

'And Haldayne, Daji, and the rest? What are they?'

'Wizards, just like the Nine and the other powers of Flux. Their organization is, in a sense, a mirror image of the Nine. In their own minds they have
a noble purpose in which the ends justify any means. They believe that
humanity can never regain its former greatness but will remain in primitive
stagnancy until, believe it or not, an accommodation with Hell is reached.'

She was shocked. 'An accommodation with *Hell*?'

'That's right. You see, even though the gates are sealed and guarded, some
slight leakage gets through. It was designed that way. It may seem strange,
but our basic power source seems to be those machines in the gates, which
generate excess energy from the seal as they maintain it and then transfer
this excess to the generators in the Temples. Without them we would have
no electricity at all, since we really don't know how to generate it on a massive scale. We keep everything working by removing parts that go bad and
giving them to wizards in Flux who are good at making exact copies of things.
Since the art of being a good wizard is mathematical, they can look at a part
that they have never seen before and have no idea what it is or how it works,
and make a copy that *does* work. They don't know how they do it, but the
only explanation is that the math is wrong on the broken one, and they can
figure out where it's wrong and make the equation balance.'

'So we depend on these Hellgates for a lot, and Anchors really depend on
Flux.'

'Interdependence. Flux is a cruel place, subject to the whims of the powerful and power-mad. It is by its very nature impossible for more than a handful
of people to be free or independent in Flux, or even remain human. It is nice
if you're a wizard, but no great discoveries arise in Flux. It simply devours a
larger number of people than it can possibly replace. Hence, the trade of
people for what Anchors need. Ideally, Anchors should be the seats of learning, where great things are produced by a free and unified people, while Flux
produces what is needed. Unfortunately, deep down, it is difficult to tell them
apart.'

'And the Seven believe that Hell is the only way out?'

'That's about it,' he agreed. 'You see, in some of the gates, because of that leakage I mentioned, it is possible for Hell to communicate with one in the tunnel. The demons of Hell are cut off from our world, but are immortal, and know how the machines work and the nature of Flux and Anchor. To early wizards frustrated by having godlike powers that were very limited over a finite piece of ground, the lure of ruling all World, as one great Fluxland under their total domination, is irresistible. And if it means selling one's soul to Hell, it seems to them a small price to pay. They are the ultimate corruption power brings, and they delude themselves that they will be partners with Hell and not make us all its last victims so that Hell will finally attain its goal to rule the universe – alone.'

They went on like this for more than two days, and in that time Cass believed she gained a true picture of what was going on. Much, as Mervyn had warned, was unknown – the nature of the Soul Riders, for example. To her, there *did* seem to be a divine plan for the rescue of humanity and its restoration to greatness, a plan subverted by the weaknesses humans had. Those who now ruled the church had all been shown this path, but all, in the end, had been corrupted by their own power or deluded themselves that they were making small changes or reforms and that any major changes would take generations. The forces of Hell were real, and on the march, but it only reinforced the church's resolve to keep things the way they were, thereby substituting the total evil of Hell with a more banal evil done by humans.

Finally, Cass was briefed and prompted on the ceremony to come, and felt she was finally ready, although it still seemed like a lot of foolishness to her. She felt a little guilty, being used as a lucky icon for a lot of scared and possibly doomed troopers.

The ceremony itself was quite impressive and flashy. A platform had been set up just inside the gate, and Cass, her horse changed to snow white for the occasion, was led in by Suzl on her black mount. Cass had made several decisions herself on this, one of which was to use her own normal form and make no more pretenses about her identity. She felt any threat to her individually was over as much as it ever would be. The reasons were no longer there.

She entered dressed only in a plain robe of white, as a novice. It was important that she be ordained in front of them, even though the Sister General already assumed it. And the troops were all lined up, as well as a great mass of common people, to see the show.

Diastephanos, who had understood Cass's role in this from the start, made it a long service, with lots of ceremony, all of the sacraments, and lots of scripture reading. It was all necessary not for its own sake, but to show the people of Anchor Logh, long taught to fear the Flux and have no truck with it, that in this case only it was the right thing to do.

Cass participated fully, finding the whole thing oddly moving to her. And, once all vows were exchanged and she was fully ordained, it was then time to accept the job, exchanging her whites for robes of lavender satin trimmed with ancient designs in gold thread, and to accept a sceptre only slightly smaller and less ornate than the Sister General's own. It was then concluded, and she turned and looked out at the crowd for the first time. All eyes were on her, and, for the first time, she realized that they had accepted all of it. In every sense of the word, even legally, she was to them and in fact a high priestess of the church.

She stepped down from the platform and went to the troops who would go with them, standing at attention next to their horses. As she passed each, she could see in their eyes the absolute confidence they placed in her. It shook her a bit, to realize the full responsibility she had been forced to take on. And when she stood before them, they all knelt and bowed their heads, and she gave them the blessing they expected, meaning it more than she intended.

'Soldiers of Anchor Logh,' she said at last, hoping her voice would carry and not tremble. 'We set out now on the most important mission in our long history. Hell is out there, almost at our gates, invading our land at will, killing our citizens and threatening us all. Do not fear the wizardry of the Flux, only respect it, for we have the strongest wizardry, the righteousness of our cause, and the support of the Nine Who Guard. The divine will is not known, except that victory is assured if we prove worthy of it. The creatures you will fight will be of flesh and blood. Some of you may die, but you will do so in a cause so noble that you will be reborn with greatness. Others will live, to enjoy the great honor that awaits. We cannot know our fate, for only Heaven knows that, but we can know and fulfill our destiny. Will you ride with us now?'

'We will!' came a chorus of responses that moved her even more.

She walked to her horse and mounted it, then held the sceptre high. 'Then mount and follow me!'

In groups, they passed through the west gate and out onto the apron. A way had been cleared from the dugger shantytown to the Flux, and they again formed up. Suzl and Mervyn, still in his old man's role, rode out of Flux to meet her, then turned to form a threesome leading the way. Suzl leaned over and whispered, 'Wow! You really look great!' Cass smiled and winked, although she was aware of the enormous weight she was now carrying, and held the sceptre up, then angled it forward. The troopers, she'd been assured, had been briefed by Suzl and Mervyn as to how to ride the void. She hoped so, for they were off.

Mervyn dropped back to the rear as the entire column entered the Flux, just to make sure there were no stragglers or unexpected surprises. Cass did not need him to lead. She felt the power of the Flux instantly, and the glowing strings of energy came crystal clear. She decided to ride as far nonstop as prudence said the horses could take, so that there could be no last-minute defections. Suzl, still dressed in stringer fashion, checked out the formation and felt every bit a stringer with a very strange train. She wished, however, she had a dozen or so duggers to help out.

They finally stopped at a water pocket, a small area undistinguished from the rest of the void except for a wizard-created pool of clear water large enough for people and horses. Mervyn, who was well practiced in elaborate magic, created the spartan food for them all. They were quite impressed, but many of them had already lost a good deal of their fear in the boredom of the void. The terrible Flux was proving only a wasteland, and the only wizardry so far was entirely on their side. By the end of the second day, Cass guessed, they would be getting both cocky and itchy from too little threat and too much boredom.

Sentries were posted and they bedded down for the night, with Mervyn agreeing to sleep first and then take over from Cass. She readily agreed, and just sat there by the pool for quite a while, looking at her reflection in the water and absorbed in thought. Suzl, acting the old hand, checked out the rest and then came over to her. 'You seem pretty quiet,' she noted. 'Problems, or does it come magically from putting on the robe?'

Cass smiled. 'Thanks. I need you, Suzl, to remind me just who I am and where I've come from. Any problems?'

'Nope. Not really. A couple of 'em made passes at me and I had a good deal of fun letting them discover why I was along and what was so different. Now they're scared silly of me. It's fun giving orders to guys the smallest of whom are a head taller than me.'

She looked at Suzl. 'You know, when that curse backfired I figured you were out of luck, but the more I look at the way this whole thing is turning out I think you got the best of the deal in many ways.'

Suzl suddenly looked at her seriously. 'What's wrong with you? Only weeks ago we were two naive farm girls scared of getting sold as slaves, who knew that if we didn't we'd be pressured into marrying some ignorant farm boy, stuck having a mess of kids and stuck in a boring job for life to boot – or joining the priesthood and having our brains mashed and everything worthwhile a no-no. You know deep down that you would never have accepted it. It would've killed you. Me, too, which is why they decided my number would come up. "Psychologically unfit for normal socialization" they once called me. I snuck in and read the teacher's report. I'm eighteen and a half and I've already lived more than I would have in ninety years of Anchor Logh.'

Cass nodded. 'What you say is true, and I don't deny it. I'm not longing for what was. I simply said that you have the best of the deal. You're free, independent, and tough. You'll roam all over World and see everything and have a ball. I envy that.'

'Well, why can't you? Hell, you're a *wizard*. You don't even need a stringer.'

'Partly because I *am* a wizard,' she replied, then added, 'and partly because I am a priestess.'

Suzl looked at her oddly. 'Now aren't you taking the show just a little bit too seriously? Me, I'm stuck as I am. Lucky for me I don't mind a bit. But you – you can be anything, do anything you want to do.'

Cass sighed, knowing that she could not explain it, particularly to one such as Suzl. Still, she said, 'No, Suzl, I'm trapped just like these poor soldiers and all the rest who got thrown out of Anchor. I'm just beginning to realize how trapped I am. You remember us talking about little people becoming important by accident? Well, I'm discovering that when you become important you get trapped as well. That's okay for now, let's drop it. I'm being forced by Mervyn and the rest to make a decision, a big one, and I'm not ready to make it. I'll have to settle it within myself.'

Suzl just shrugged and shook her head. Finally she said, 'I wonder what a battle in Flux is like?'

18

Battle

It was understood by the officers and men that the Adjutant would not lead them into battle, but would direct it instead from a command post. They didn't mind, since harm to her was the worst thing they feared. She did visit with them, though, informally. She really felt like they were her people, after getting to know some on the trail. It was now a major duty of hers to hear their confessions, because, as battle neared, they began once again thinking of this less as a new game. Unconsciously, perhaps, she wove a spell, finding that she could remember all the details of each of them.

This was far different than playing priestess back in Anchor Logh. For her, too, this was no game, and they needed her desperately. She left the strategy and tactics to others, leaving her troops only when she had to consult Mervyn on a particular spell to ease a young boy's problems. She found no trouble on an individual basis; they seemed to believe and accept everything she told them, including cautions against prejudice towards those not quite human and of Flux.

And many of them were strange indeed. The Flux wizards had strange tastes and bizarre imaginations, it appeared. And they kept coming down the road from Globbus and from the direction of Anchor Bakha, and from trails that came to the far side of Persellus as well. A mighty army had been assembled, the mightiest, perhaps, ever seen on World since Hell was sealed. A mighty army to meet an unprecedented challenge to the future of World, the one thing all of the forces, no matter how strange or inhuman, had in common.

Suzl went off for a while to see if Nadya and Dar had returned yet. Cass didn't know how long she was away, for time had lost all meaning to her in her single-minded devotion to what she saw as her duty, but one day, as Cass was walking back from another full round of counseling and confessionals, she spotted the familiar figure on the hill near the local command post.

Suzl waved and ran to her, and they hugged. 'Did you find them?' Cass asked.

'Oh, yeah. You ought to see Nadya – decked out just like you and acting just as crazy. Dar's even crazier – says he's gonna lead the attack from his side. He's going to get his fool head blown off.' She paused a moment. 'Guess who I came up with? Matson!'

Matson! The name was like a cold bucket of water in Cass's face. Suddenly that became the most important thing in the world to her. 'Where is he?'

Suzl jerked a thumb towards the tent. 'Up there. He and some of his duggers who volunteered are leading in a Fluxland crew.' She shivered slightly. 'One that's really weird. The people are the animals there, I think.'

She brushed by Suzl and walked over to the tent, then paused as she saw him, sitting on a folding chair, cigar clenched in his teeth. He was apparently waiting for someone, and glanced up at her, then away, not recognizing her at first. He looked back again, frowned, and got up. 'That you, Cass, in that church getup?'

She laughed. 'Yes, I'm afraid it is. Mervyn stuck me good.'

'We heard how you got snatched and then escaped, more or less,' he told her, not referring to Suzl's comment that he went nearly crazy at the abduction. 'I'm trying to decide whether or not to dock your pay for the period.'

'You *would*, too, wouldn't you? You stringers are a tight lot.'

He got up and walked up to her. 'Is it allowed to kiss a priestess?'

'My feet and my hand,' she responded jokingly.

'Yeah, and my ass, too,' he came back in the same vein. He grabbed her and kissed her, very long and very hard. Finally he broke away and said, 'I want you back with the company when this is through. Look, I've got to talk some things over with the old boy and the midget, but we'll meet in Persellus, you hear?'

She nodded, her head spinning. 'Yes. In Persellus.'

After she left him, she still felt in some kind of a daze. She had been, she knew, at war with herself these past few days, and she now knew which side had won. She was a wizard, and, therefore, she *could* have him, and he was everything that mattered most.

*

Before Persellus could be invaded, the three top wizards had to first break what they called Haldayne's shield. This was not a barrier in the physical sense, but more a mental zone of control. Each Fluxland was the product of the unrestrained mind of the controlling wizard, and it was as large and as stable as that wizard's will. To invade before that control was broken would only mean that the attackers would come under the will and control of the defender. There was not much profit in that.

However, breaking the shield was not the end of it. Haldayne had first broken the goddess's shield, then faced her down physically, and only then was he able to impose himself on the land. With his shield broken, the land would still remain his and in his vision. To remake the land, and make it stick, the wizards would have to progress to a point within the Fluxland where their own powers and wills could reach the farthest corners of Persellus. That ground, which might be all the way to the capital, would have to be won the hard way.

Watches had been synchronized, and the three top wizards positioned at the three decided-upon points of entry. Like most Fluxlands, Persellus was basically circular, although with jagged edges. At the appointed time, with only a small company of carefully selected junior wizards for any direct protection, all three of the chief wizards stepped into the land of Persellus, and began walking forward until they met resistance. Haldayne had to keep them out, or surrender control. Haldayne was not the type to surrender anything easily.

Behind the wizards, a good three hundred meters behind, came the leading edge of the troops. Cass had been ordered to remain behind, but as time wore on and things seemed stalled, she impatiently saddled her horse and rode toward Persellus, passing backed up troops, light artillery, and supply wagons. After all this, she decided she was not going to miss at least seeing what was going on.

What was going on was awesome and spectacular.

The countryside had changed so much she would not have recognized it as Persellus. Dark, rumbling mountains spitting smoke and fire were all around, and the countryside was covered with a fine gray ash. She finally determined where the river was, but it was mud and ash-swollen and choked with debris. Although the landscape was lit with an eerie glow that made it possible to see great distances, the sky was black as pitch, with no stars, no Heaven, nothing to break it.

Ahead, far in the distance but so enormous that it dominated all else, was a tremendous figure illuminated in lines of energy. It had the rough shape of a man, rising up from the ground, but its head was horribly demonic. It was no projection, despite the fact that it was seen only by the outline of the blazing energy, for it moved and roared a terrible, hateful sound that went

through the very ground and made it tremble. It was battling something –
three strong, solid, straight lines of force directed at it from the ground. One
struck it from behind, one from its left side, and one came from the small,
wizened figure of a man seated in a folding chair in the middle of what passed
for the road directly ahead of them.

The great energy beast was strong, and it would occasionally reach out and
grasp one of the energy beams as if it were a rope, fight with it, then force it
away, but it could not deal effectively with three such attacks from three different directions. Each time it concentrated on one, the other two took
advantage to attempt to coil themselves around its ghostly body. Still, it had
been fighting this way for hours.

Cass was enthralled with the display, and at a loss to understand why most
of the soldiers in back acted bored and uncomfortable and were not watching at all. She suddenly realized that what she was watching and hearing was
on a different frequency than normal, like the stringer's strings. The soldiers
were not interested because they could neither see nor hear it.

The great beast was clearly tiring, and the energy beams were having more
and more success. One from the side finally reached the creature's neck and
began coiling itself around that hideous face. The demon reached up to tear
the beam away, but now Mervyn shot out at the thing's legs, while the one
behind – that would be Tatalane – grasped at its arms and tried to pull them
away from the neck.

Mervyn pulled, and the beast roared and rocked, then bent over, barely
keeping on its 'feet.' A second beam now went for its neck, and then a third.
The creature screamed in agony, and there was a sudden great, blinding flare
of light in the distance and, a bit later, a tremendous thunderclap rolled down
the valley that all could hear. When Cass could see again, the far horizon was
clear.

Two junior wizards helped the old wizard to walk back to a wagon. They
lifted him in, gently, then took the reins. There was the sound of horns all
about, echoed in the distance. The shield was down. Haldayne retained his
control over what he'd had, but could no longer exercise control beyond it. If
he tried, he'd send the land back to Flux, and have nothing to defend.

The troops advanced perhaps a kilometer when they met resistance. Well
dug-in defenders of Persellus opened up on them with massive machine gun
fire, and the air all around them went chill and was filled with terrible shapes
from Hell itself.

The initial advance was cut to shreds by the fire, and frustrated by its
inability to see the enemy positions past the illusory phantoms. The defenders' task now was simple. They far outnumbered the attackers, and while they
had few decent wizards, neither did the attacking forces for a while. The
effort of breaking the shield was great, and it would be hours, perhaps more,

before any of the three chief sorcerers could be in any condition to help. Haldayne, too, was in much the same shape, but he would also regain strength the more time went on, perhaps enough to reestablish and extend his shield. Because of their inferior numbers, the attackers had to advance well into the country before this could happen, or the scenario just played out would happen again, with Haldayne able to redeploy and even by spell resupply and reform his defenders so that the next round would be just as costly. If the attackers stalled for any great length of time, each and every time, they would be wiped out.

Cass watched from her original position, well back of the fighting, but she could see everything clearly. More and more troops were filing past her and marching towards those deadly gun emplacements, then dropping and trying to dig in. Artillery was set up near her, and soon the boom of cannon fire was added to the din, as the gunners attempted to line up on the machine guns. She watched the carnage with mounting horror, saw the field littered with the dead, and was revolted as she had never been in her life. Never in her most terrible nightmares could she imagine the reality of this massacre.

She glanced over and was startled to see Matson, cigar and all, sitting high on his horse and directing some – creatures – who were hauling up some very odd-looking things. They appeared to be a large number of parallel metal pipes all lashed together. When they were in range, he gave a series of signals and smaller shapes moved up behind the tubes. In less than a minute a hundred tubes, almost at the same time, erupted with a roar and flashing smoke and fire, and ahead the gunnery positions were pounded with an entire line, perhaps three hundred meters across, of massive explosions. The roar was deafening.

The small creatures behind the tubes, whatever they were, were fast and professional and moved to Matson's barked orders. A second salvo went off, and, after the last explosion had discharged, there was a roar and cheer from troops up ahead. They moved forward. Matson's guns had pushed back or wiped out the machine gun nests, and the columns moved forward once more.

Another kilometer, and suddenly the ground opened up ahead of the advancing troops, like a giant mouth. They fell in, and it swallowed them and closed again. From behind came more withering machine gun and rifle fire, pushing the attackers back.

Less than a hundred meters from Cass's new position, Matson frowned, barked more orders to the creatures hauling the tubes forward, and rode up to the forward command group where the junior wizards were conferring with the field commanders on how to overcome this obstacle.

The stringer shouted something at them, and they nodded, and two of the junior wizards went back with him to his launchers. She waited, as they all did, to see what was up.

To her surprise, the troops were now ordered forward, and they went slowly, nervously, to the area of the trap. All defending fire stopped suddenly. When enough soldiers were on the area of the trap, it opened again, swallowing them, but at the same time Matson's tubes opened up, concentrating their rounds on the opening. This time there were no explosions, for the tubes shot not explosive rounds but huge balls of some gooey substance. The mass filled in the mouth before it could close, and as it tried it just compacted the new material, which seemed to quickly harden. Cannons opened up on the gun emplacements beyond the 'mouth' at almost the same time, and again troops moved forward. The 'mouth' shimmered and shook and tried to free itself, but it was hopeless. Matson had effectively filled it and paved it over.

It went like that for some time, although time became blurred into the sameness of death. Haldayne had a huge population to call upon, but he couldn't use them. His own volcanos had filled in enough of the valley to make any massive deployment of forces from behind very slow and difficult. The geographic strategy he had laid out to keep the attackers on a single, predictable line of march worked against him as well, and he had three sides to defend.

Mervyn, however, was still unconscious, and bird messengers brought news that Krupe, too, was still out, while tiny Tatalane was conscious but very, very weak. Still, there was no sign at all of any attempt to raise another shield, which told them that Haldayne was in at least as bad shape himself.

In what turned out to be more than nine hours of continuous fighting, Mervyn's force had gained almost fifteen kilometers, Krupe's twelve, and Tatalane's sixteen, but that last was the most important. She was coming in from the side, which had a couple of nasty volcanos in the way but was also the least defended, there being no natural road in from that point. Terrain had been her biggest enemy, but now that she had somehow cleared the mountains she was on a plain heading directly for the capital.

Cass rode back to a field kitchen and got a canteen filled not with water but with beer, then headed for Matson. He was surprised to see her, but he looked very, very tired and suddenly very old, and his shirt was soaked with perspiration. Still, he managed a smile. 'I thought you weren't supposed to be up here with the common folk,' he managed to joke.

She threw him the canteen. 'Here. Drink your damned religion.'

He caught it, opened it, and swallowed, then looked surprised and pleased. 'I'll be damned! It's *beer!*' He said that last like it was the most wonderous and beautiful word in the language.

He put it down and sighed, then looked out at the fighting not far away. They were bogged down again, this time by a very large number of well dug-in troops. 'Sure is a bitch, ain't it?' he said wearily. 'You better get back a little, though, Sister Cass. Stray bullets are carrying back farther than this.'

'I'm a whole lot more bullet proof than you,' she told him, 'and you don't look too worried.'

He turned and looked out at the battle. 'Well, I –' he began, then he was apparently hit by an invisible fist that knocked him off his horse, the canteen flying out of his hand.

'*Matson!*' she screamed, and jumped off her horse and ran to him. The entire front of his shirt had been ripped away by whatever it was that had hit him, and it seemed as if his chest were one huge bloody wound. He was still, his mouth open, blood trickling from it. She took his hand, squeezed it, and screamed at him, '*Matson! Come on, you good-for-nothing stringer! You beat the odds! You always beat the odds! You can't do this to me! Not now!*'

But there was no response. She felt a presence near her and whirled, seeing Jomo. 'Jomo!' she cried desperately. 'Get a healing wizard here! Hurry! He's been hit!'

The enormous tears in the huge blob of a man looked very strange, but the dugger shook his head, then knelt down and checked out Matson's body. 'No use, Missy Cass,' he said, voice trembling. 'He gone to see Missy Arden.'

'*No! Oh, Holy Mother above, please! Not now! Not him! Not yet!*' she sobbed. Jomo got up and tried to pry her gently away from the body. For a while he could not budge her, nor could she do anything but sob and stare at Matson's lifeless body. Suddenly she shook off the giant dugger, got up, and turned facing the battle, a strange expression on her face. She seemed to radiate power, the kind only powerful wizards do, and the dugger stepped back nervously and just watched.

She looked out at the bodies. Everywhere there were bodies, everywhere there was blood and terror and death. In that moment something snapped within her, snapped for good. Now she understood, at last, that what she had been telling Suzl was only part of the truth. She was not any victim of chance, but the one chosen. Everything that had happened said that she was the agent of divine will. She had wavered and fallen, as the church had fallen, because of human frailty and weakness, and because of this Matson had to be taken from her. She knew that now, understood that it had to be this way. Every step she had taken, every new experience, from the point at which she'd first entered the forbidden sacristy, had been directed to this one destiny.

'No more,' she muttered under her breath, looking at the fallen bodies stretched out as far as the eye could see. 'No more,' she said again, louder now, the tremendous power rising within her. It was will that brought it up, but emotion that triggered it. She stuck out her arms, palms out, as if to stop something coming down on her, but it was something different she wanted to stop. All sounds of battle, of people yelling and guns firing, vanished in a roar in her ears. There was only a single will now, and it was directed forward. She felt the power as she had never felt it.

And the Soul Rider provided the required mathematics.

Far off, in the capital, a weak Gifford Haldayne was taking a drink and waiting it out, trying to regain what strength he could. He felt it at once, and knew it for what it was, and cursed himself for it. Damn their eyes! They had a fourth World class wizard in reserve!

He frowned, then staggered, suddenly, from the force of a psychic blow. 'What the hell is *this*?' he asked aloud, amazed. Never in his entire life had he felt such power, such force, such single-minded direction of will. This was something totally new, and totally frightening. This was no doing of the Nine, or Seven, or any combination of Fluxlords. This was something new, and terrible, and beyond even his ancient comprehension. He had a sudden, queer thought. *What have I unleashed*? he wondered, but he did not dwell on it now. He knew what he had to do, and he knew he had only seconds to do it.

He released control to the new force, changed to a raven, and was out of there like a shot. He was fifty kilometers into the void before he even allowed himself enough time to realize just how close it had been.

On the battlefield, Mervyn awoke with a strange sensation inside him. He got up weakly and made it forward to the seat so that he could see out and ahead of him. The sight that he saw was as unprecedented to him as it had been to Haldayne.

Cass, in lavender robes stained with Matson's blood, walked forward towards the battle. As she did, the firing stopped on both sides, and the face of the land and sky trembled and changed. All around her the darkened and blood-stained volcanic ash changed into life itself, into fresh, green grass and flowers. It spread continuously out, touching the front lines and causing soldiers on both sides to stop, turn, and stare. The sky above lightened until it attained the dark blue of Anchor, and the landscape rippled as in Anchor as the great orb of Heaven filled the sky, sending its multicolored light down on the scene.

The wizard was awed by the power coming from her, and the total mastery of the Flux and its complex mathematics and physics despite her almost complete lack of training. He had, indeed, set the conditions up and put it all in motion, but he had never expected anything like this. In fact, he had to admit, he hadn't in the end expected anything at all.

The zone of Fluxland influence now extended from horizon to horizon, the volcanos becoming green rolling hills, the river crystal clear and running its normal course.

The soldiers of Flux and Anchor on both sides of the battle could not, in the main, sense any of the magic, yet it radiated from her frail form and touched them all. They threw down their weapons as she passed, and fell in behind her as she continued her walk.

She drew strength from the Flux, not only for herself but for them, and she walked without stop all the way to the capital, with those of both sides following silently. From the rear and from the side others streamed in from the other two attacking forces, and their enemies.

The town itself had been transformed. No longer was there a goddess's tower or Haldayne's great black castle, but in the center was a huge Temple, the largest ever seen, radiating from its perfect surface the colors of Heaven. As she entered the city limits, the townspeople lined the routes ten deep, throwing flowers at her and at all the soldiers. All fell in as the parade passed, and moved to the central Temple area, where they filed in before the great steps and back as far as the eye could see. All stopped at the base of the Temple steps, but Cass kept walking until she was at the top. Only then did she turn and face the crowd, which was suddenly silent.

'People of Flux and Anchor, hear me,' she said, and her voice somehow carried clearly throughout the boundaries of the land. 'I am the Adjutant not of Anchor but of Heaven itself. Corruption has strangled humanity long enough. There is the corruption of the church in Anchor, and the corruption of wizardry in Flux. Both have held humanity too long in their grip. You have just endured a great battle, but to what end? Hell is but the ultimate corruption of the human soul, and it flourishes and grows and feeds upon that corruption. Thousands of brave, good people have just died, mixed their blood with this land, and for what? To make things better? *No!* To keep things the same.' She paused for a moment, took a deep breath, and continued.

'To keep things the same,' she repeated, saying it bitterly. 'So what choice did we have? *We were offered only our choice of Hells!* To this I say, no more. No more. It is *evil!* I renounce such evil. I rebel at such a choice. The Holy Mother cries out to me, "No more! No more!" I reclaim this land in Her name, and with Her power, and I rename it Hope. I do not bind you to my will, for then I would be as guilty as those who now run World. Instead I offer you a partnership, and hope, and no more. It will be no easy road, to reform our ways, to rebuild our corrupted church, to make for ourselves a world of free men and women who will not fear Hell because it will have no way to gain a foothold inside us. You, all of you here, can be the vanguard that will revolutionize World. We may be weak at times, we may stumble occasionally, we might even suffer failures and disappointments, but we will *try.*'

Again she paused, allowing the message to sink in. 'Now go,' she told them. 'Go free of mind and free of entanglements so long as you are in Hope. Let all who live in this land open up their hearts and homes to those who do not. Those who wish to join in the mission, whether wizard, soldier, slave, dugger, half-human or inhuman, may meet me in this square tomorrow, either physically or in your hearts. I will know, and reach you. I was ordained by the church as Sister Kasdi, so that will be my name henceforth. Hell cannot stand against me. Only you can.' And she blessed them, turned, and walked into the Temple.

She walked straight back to the chapel and then to the altar, and knelt and prayed and performed the sacraments that only a priestess could, and reaffirmed her vows. Only then did she turn and see that there were others in the chapel. They were people that she knew. There was Mervyn, looking very spry and pleased with himself, and Suzl, and Nadya, too, in robes just like her own.

Nadya smiled and came forward, then took and kissed her hand. 'They ordained me as Sister Tamara. I, too, will keep that name and proudly.' They embraced and kissed, and there were tears in both their eyes. Finally Nadya said, 'I knew, somehow, from that very start, that we were destined for something different, something new. I would never, however, have guessed *this*.'

Cass smiled. 'I know.' She sighed. 'I guess we'll have to postpone our adventurous tour of World.'

'Only until the next life,' Nadya replied.

Cass smiled and turned to Suzl next. 'And what about you?'

'I think you're a powerful wizard and a stark raving lunatic,' she told them. 'However, this sounds interesting. As long as you can stand somebody who's psychologically unfit for society hanging around, and a cynic at that, I might just stick until I see how it all comes out. If nothing else, you're gonna need somebody around with the guts to tell you what lunatics you are, just to keep from vanishing into your own little worlds. I may not be one of the faithful, but revolution kind of appeals to my nature. Besides that, I'm unemployed. I have to sponge off *somebody* and it might as well be somebody important.'

Cass and Nadya both laughed, and Cass stepped forward and took her hands. 'All right, "psychologically unfit." As much as I think you might be dangerous to have around, considering the *real* wording of that chastity clause, I'm glad to do it.' She paused a moment. 'Have you seen Dar?'

Suzl's face grew serious. 'He's dead, Cass. He died bravely, from what I hear, saving a couple of people's lives in the process.'

She had no more tears to give to grief, but she felt it anyway. She let go of Suzl's hands and turned to Mervyn. 'Now, don't tell me you planned all this or I'll make an exception of my love rule in your case.'

'I primed the pump,' he admitted, 'but I was still surprised to find water at all, and least of all a fountain.' He sighed. 'What will you do with it all now?'

'What I said, if anybody returns, that is. Even if *nobody* returns.'

'And what of the unfinished business?'

'I haven't forgotten it, but it must wait until we're organized here. I don't think anything will be tried right away. They will be far too interested in me to think about anything else.'

'I agree,' he responded. 'I'll talk it over with Tatalane and Krupe, but I'm sure we'll all help. It *must* be done. It is long overdue. Otherwise we'll be stuck here like this forever and eventually Haldayne's bunch will win.'

She hesitated a moment. 'You know who is behind this, don't you?'

'I think I do, and my joy at this outcome cannot quite balance my grief. Still, humanity lives again. Empire is reborn as a concept, and, perhaps, as a reality. The Empire of Flux and Anchor. The concept itself is staggering.'

'Come,' said Sister Kasdi. 'We have much to plan and work out between now and tomorrow.'

19

Answers

Five hundred and fourteen border troopers had ridden out from Anchor Logh, and only two hundred and twenty-seven had returned, although, thanks to Flux magic, their wounds were healed and they felt pretty tough and proud of themselves. They were also the objects of awe among the local population and their fellow troopers, and told their battle stories time and again to enthralled audiences. Ultimately, though, even heroes have to go back to work, and they were all returned to duty.

Because they were more than a quarter of all the remaining guards, it was inevitable that, in many cases, long stretches of the border wall and the drains through it were guarded by these returning soldiers. Because of this, the invading army had little problem in breaching the wall along a more than two kilometer stretch halfway up, without, in fact, the rest of the guard force even knowing that such an invasion had taken place. They continued to guard the wall against attack from outside long after the enemy had a fully established force and was marching in strength on the capital.

There was little resistance because it was so obviously futile, and while whole families wept as the conquerors marched by they could not resist these battle-hardened veterans with anything but insults and more tears. Without guns, which were outlawed in Anchor, there was no chance of even inflicting a minor blow. Most of the population seemed dazed by it all, in fact, for this sort of thing simply did not and never had happened as far as they knew. The compact between Flux and Anchor upon which the church and its people depended was suddenly in ruins, and it was a simply inconceivable event. Anchor's own children, cast into Flux as a part of that compact, now returned to it.

The Temple was the one trouble spot, and not easy to take. It was built like a fortress of materials so hard that diamonds could not scratch it, and it was guarded from within by a force of armed wardens with electronic traps and devices. Bronze doors, however, needed far less than diamonds to blow apart; they needed only a good, solid shot from a single cannon.

Inside, confused, frightened, and dazed, the Temple staff prepared for the inevitable rapid fall. Behind still-locked doors piles of papers and other documents were burned, and the administrative section worked feverishly as the invaders conquered level after level to rid the Temple of hard evidence of its activities and files. They did as best they could, but they could not destroy it all.

One figure slipped through a little-known rear passage and went down a long series of old and dusty metal stairs and through doors that creaked and groaned from disuse to the sub-basement. For a moment it stood there, looking at the small power transformer network buzzing away, then walked over to the grid, reached down into a large bag, and picked out a small rectangular cube with two small buttons on it. The figure then pressed both buttons simultaneously and tossed the brick into the metal cage hiding the wires and transformers.

Quickly now she went up to the section of wall that seemed boarded, pressed on two spots, and the boards swung away on hinges to reveal a door. She did not wait for a key, but took a pistol and shot out the lock, then kicked the door in, then flipped on the light switch, climbed over the rubble of crumbled concrete and masonry to a spot in the rear of the room with chalk marks on the floor. She looked down at them, pistol still in hand, and mentally traced the strange and incomprehensible design. In an instant she was standing not in the room, but in front of the great machine that guarded the gate to Hell.

She paused to stare at it all for a while, now feeling no great hurry. She had never been here before, and the sight was awesome. There was something almost suicidally hypnotic about that swirling mass at the tunnel's end, giving one the same feeling as she might get standing on an incredibly tall spot. She turned, though, and walked up the tunnel, each section lighting as she passed, until she reached the wire grid to climb up and out. She realized how badly out of condition she'd become in climbing up and out, but she made it to the bottom of the saucer-shaped depression, then walked up the slope to the metal ladder there.

'There is no way out for you,' said a voice from above, at the top of the ladder, echoing across the depression and sounding ghostly and almost inhuman. She stopped, and instead of trying the ladder stepped back from it, pistol still in hand, and looked up.

'Who's there?' she called. 'Show yourself!'

A somewhat familiar figure moved to the edge of the ladder and looked down at her sadly. 'You have been in Anchor too long. That pistol cannot harm me here.'

She fired anyway, emptying the entire clip. The figure at the top of the ladder just stood there, unmarked and unmoved. In disgust, she tossed the pistol away, and it fell with a clatter and rolled back down the depression.

'I *know* you!' she shouted, frustration building within her. 'Who are you?'

'You ordained me Sister Kasdi,' came the reply.

'What do you want with me now?' called back Sister General Diastephanos.

'I want to know why. You weren't like Sister Daji, a professional undercover agent. Nobody shot you full of drugs and gave you orders to turn. You're the same woman who left Pericles full of commitment and dreams.'

The Sister General looked up at her in disgust. 'You're barely nineteen, I think. What can you possibly know? Your ordination was a political show for the benefit of the masses. You have no background in theology, let alone management. What gives you the *right* to judge *me*?'

Cass sighed. 'The same right Haldayne had to murder and rape and destroy. The same right you, in the end, used to pervert the scripture and rule Anchor Logh. *I have the power, and that gives me the right.*'

That stopped the Sister General cold for a moment. Finally she said, 'You ask me why. Why are you doing *this*? Because you see a church corrupted and a people forever stuck in one place. You can't change it. They make you so accountable, send wardens from Holy Anchor to keep tabs on you, to eliminate you if need be. You play the Queen of Heaven's game, and send her her dues, or you don't play at all. So you settle back and enjoy being dictator of your own little world, becoming fat and corrupt like the whole rotten church, or you do something. Anyone who is for the overthrow of the church is on the side of the frustrated. There is less difference between the Seven and the Nine than you realize.'

'There is less difference between the Seven and the church than *you* seem to realize,' Cass came back.

'You are so young,' the Sister General sighed. 'You may win your little revolution. It's happened before – oh, yes. But each time a better wizard comes along, or age and all those people you depend on to keep your revolution going begin to enjoy their own power, and become corrupted by it. You can't keep tabs on it all, nor can you live forever. The church, however, has had two thousand years of practice. It will entice and corrupt those it can, ultimately conquer the rest with its power to unify, and, if it cannot conquer you, it can wait you out. You can't win, but Haldayne can. When you are finally old enough and frustrated enough to realize this, you will see that the Seven is the only hope humanity has.'

'You might be right,' Cass admitted, 'but I have seen the Seven at their worst, and there is no hope at all if you are. I choose to believe that you are not right, not so much because I deny your view of human nature, which is so well proved out in both Anchor and Flux, but because the alternatives are too terrible to bear. If, in fact, we cannot win, then maybe the human race deserves what it gets, whether it's the church, or Haldayne, or Hell itself. But if we don't *try* to win, then we most certainly deserve it all.'

'You speak the beautiful dreams of youth, but, in the end, you will become me.'

'Perhaps *you* need to have some of those beautiful dreams of youth restored yourself. Come up to me, and surrender yourself to my visions. We can use your vast knowledge and experience to avoid the same mistakes.' She put out her hand over the top of the ladder.

Sister Diastephanos shook her head sadly. 'I am too old, and it is too late, for me to join a fool's parade. But, tell me, please – how did you know? Even poor Daji had no idea she was doing my work.'

'She knew, I think, as she died. She understood the depths and layers of Haldayne's tricky mind, although the full plot only came to her when he so coldly allowed her to be sacrificed on his orders. There are no windows in the Temple. The order had to be given by intercom from inside by someone who knew exactly who and what Daji really was, fast enough for a messenger to signal out the front doors before we got there. But, clearly, nothing on the scope or scale of the excavations in the basement, the vanishing of novices, the addition of new personnel smuggled in through the drainage pipes in the wall, could have remained hidden from the wardens and the Temple at large without your knowledge. Your own spies, and the spies of the Queen of Heaven, would have betrayed it.'

She sighed. 'When I saw Pericles I knew that she would eventually figure it out. That was why I gave the order to hit her first, *then* Daji. But Haldayne was outside, and he reversed the orders. I knew there would be only one chance to get Pericles, but Daji was far more of a threat to Haldayne.' She paused a moment, took a deep breath, then said, 'I believe my time is past now. I could not bear to witness your childlike innocence destroyed.' With that she turned and walked back to the black, gaping hole.

Cass gasped and cried, 'No! Come with us! We will forgive all! This need not happen!'

The Sister General paused a moment, then shook her head sadly, and descended the mesh to the floor of the tunnel. Cass scrambled down the ladder, but had barely reached the bottom when there was a sudden flare of bright energy from the hole, and a single, agonized scream, and then silence and darkness once more.

She resisted the impulse to run to the tunnel, knowing that the Guardians would not harm her, but she decided not to. There would be nothing there. Instead she turned and started back up the ladder, but as she did she began to do something that Sister General Diastephanos would never have understood.

She wept, and repeated prayers for the newly dead.

20

Questions

We are the spirits of Flux and Anchor ...

'You'll have to excuse the candlelight,' Cass apologized. 'We're trying to get a whole network of oil lamps set up so we can at least function.'

The wizard Mervyn nodded and took a chair. 'Perfectly all right. Still, it's times like these when one appreciates the ease of Flux. Just snap a finger and, *poof*, all the light you need. I often think that our ancestors must have taken electric power for granted. Otherwise, why have such a building with no windows and no manual air ducts?' It *did* smell stale and musty, but maintenance personnel assured them that enough air was moving due to pressure differentials to pose no major health hazards, although they had closed down the least ventilated parts of the Temple.

'We'll have it again some day,' she told him. 'Already we are scouring the land for experts who can rebuild the system, and there are enough Flux wizards to duplicate the damaged parts once we have them sorted out. Some of your people have already taken a look at it and told me that it is theoretically possible to have far larger storage of this energy and even transfer it by wire to smaller storage and distribution points. If possible, I would like to one day see the whole of Anchor Logh wired up.'

'I told you that energy physics was one of my hobbies. I'll take a good look at everything before I leave and then research it in Pericles. We can copy the books well enough, if only we can find a few good trained technicians to translate them into fact. In the meantime, how's it going on your front?'

'I've never seen so many people so eager to change sides. It's amazing the level of cooperation we're getting.'

'Human nature, that's all. Already the sermons are going out telling how Haldayne and the Seven had corrupted the Sister General herself, and how you are here to restore normalcy. They know you are an ordained high priestess, and things have been getting back to normal, so they'll buy it. No, I'm talking about the long run.'

'Well, Sister Tamara will be installed as the new Sister General. It will be a popular choice, since she's from the Anchor, and we can count on everyone to minimize the age factor. The first thing we'll start doing is short transfers of Temple personnel in small groups from here to the Temple in Hope, where we'll sort the bad, the good, and the reclaimable. Once we do the Temple, we'll do the parishes one by one.'

'They won't all be easy to convert. Not deep down. Not voluntarily, anyway.'

'I know that. But I and a number of others have been reading every single bit of scripture bit by bit, and there is a scholarly team compiling information. Although the whole project will take years, I've already directed them to specific areas and found some very fine and useful things. Vows, for example. In order to come back to Anchor as a priestess, all will be required to undergo the sacraments of ordination and conferrence once again in Hope, but this time with the knowledge that a binding spell will be cast at the same time. This spell will simply render them incapable of violating their vows for any reason, nor any added vow they may be required to take in the future. I don't think it will be long before we have a purified church here, no matter what their intent.'

He chuckled. 'Clever, and effective. And you?'

'I am going to be quite busy working with others on the restructuring of this society. Barbarities like the Paring Rite must be replaced by more humane practices, and we must remove this deep prejudice against Flux and its people on the part of Anchorfolk. The worst offenders we can help in Flux itself; for the rest, it will be slow, but I am leaning towards a required trip by all school-children of certain ages from here through the void to Hope. Rooting it out in the young is the best hope for a true breakdown of fear and prejudice. We're just beginning to set up our own training system in Hope, and we will need far more instructors of wizard caliber. Of course, any priestesses who show talent in that direction will be redirected there. I'm going to be very, very busy.'

'That may be true, but the Holy Anchor isn't going to be too pleased about all this. You will get inquisitors first, then demands, and finally the whole region will be excommunicated and a holy war against it declared.'

'They have to come through Flux and through areas of our control to do anything, and then they will have to break my shield. Militarily and magically I believe we are well defended. The next trick will be to spread it out, bit by bit, until we are too much of a movement to stop by any thought of direct action. It will be busy, but exciting.'

He nodded and grew very serious. 'Cass, much of this will depend on you for a long, long time. You realize that. The rest of us can help, but you will have to carry the load or it will fall apart.'

She nodded. 'I understand that.'

'What I must know is if you are really ready for this type of lifelong commitment. You're human, and you have all the weaknesses that brings with it. Heaven knows, *I* understand that. And you're a powerful wizard. Later on, when I spend much time with you in Hope, I will show you how to perfect that power, possibly the strongest on World, although that's by no means certain. It has been my experience that no matter how strong you are, eventually you find someone stronger.'

'You mean, will I turn into the goddess or worse? I'm going to try hard not to. I'm no puritan, and power for its own sake doesn't interest me. I do not want to be worshipped.'

'No, it's more than that. Look, let me hypothesize something. It's just for the sake of argument, no more, but it serves its purpose.'

'Go ahead.'

'Suppose, right now, a live and healthy Matson should walk through that door. What would you do?'

She thought of his battered and torn body there on the battlefield. 'It is a meaningless question.'

He paused a moment. 'Suppose I were to tell you that Matson was in fact still alive?'

Her heart leaped into her throat. 'Are you serious?'

He nodded. 'I'm serious.'

She seemed to shrink back into her chair and become, all at once, very small and very young once more. Her emotions grew jumbled again, and she faced the problem square for a while. Finally she remembered that Mervyn still sat there, and that he expected an answer.

'I will always love him,' she said sincerely. 'I won't disguise or mask that. But I realize that it's too late now to do anything else but what I am doing. I feel that I was *chosen* for this. I have already resolved to apply all vows, without exception, to myself. In fact, if there was a way to bind myself to my own spells I would do it. I must be an example in all things.'

The wizard nodded approvingly. 'There *is* such a spell, or at least a method. We of the Nine must use it to fully become one of the trust. But it is a terrible spell, and not one to ever take lightly, for it cannot be reversed by anyone, including yourself, under any circumstances, but it will do nothing to ease the mental pain and anguish it might cause.'

'Then you must show me how to do it. I cannot possibly ask anyone to obey what I myself am above, and it will provide the example and also prevent my abusing this power.'

He sighed. 'That is its primary purpose when we apply it to ourselves – that we may never become our enemy. But you propose a far more complex one, one that you may often regret.'

'No, you don't understand. I regret *this* situation I find myself in. I regret the responsibility. I regret the lack of freedom. I most of all regret the self-sacrifices I must make. But I understood, finally, out there on the battlefield, that I really have no choice in the matter. It was cemented by my confrontation with the late Sister General. We are losing our best to the enemy, and we are murdering our future and our hopes. What I said to her I was really saying to myself. Only once in many generations, I think, does somebody come along with the right combination of luck and will to get into a spot where they can revolutionize things, change things for the better. When it does come about, you can turn your back on it, in which case you are guilty of the most terrible of sins, putting yourself before the future not of others but of the race. Or, you can try without total commitment, without any willingness to sacrifice yourself and what you love, and wind up like Diastephanos or Haldayne. Or you can accept it and devote your all to it. Those were my choices, and I know which one I now have to make.'

She paused a moment, and then added, 'You know, the more I have thought about this, the more I'm convinced that I'm not unique. In fact, I suspect that somebody has this sort of opportunity fall into their hands in some way quite often. Maybe it's just somebody on a local level who says, "this is stupid, or cruel – let's find another way" or something like that. They just don't have the nerve to make a total commitment, and so evil prevails as usual.'

'You're probably right,' he agreed, 'but you *are* unusual, you know. Very few make such a total commitment.' He sighed. 'Would it help if I told you that I have no idea if Matson is dead or alive?'

She gasped. 'But you said—'

'I said, "Suppose I were to tell you".'

'That's – cruel.'

'I had to know. And, I think, you did, too.'

She sighed. 'You're right, of course.'

'The stringers attempted to recover all of their own. Matson's body was not among those logged with us. It's barely possible, but not likely, that he lives. I just thought you should face that fact, not only for the obvious reason but for the other.'

'I know, and I thank you for it. Uh – what other reason?'

'Cass – you're pregnant.'

That hit her with more of a shock than the idea that Matson somehow survived. 'That's impossible!'

'You're still a virgin?'

She coughed. 'Uh, no, but it was only once, with Matson, out on the trail. My first and only time. I thought the odds were against you getting pregnant anyway, and certainly not on the first try!'

He shrugged. 'That's a young girl's self-delusion, common as long as there has been a first time. Yes, the odds are way against it, but so long as there *are* odds they hit somebody. I suspect that your own power, which has a mind of its own, might have been operating there as well. Subconsciously, at least, you wanted his baby, and in Flux, for a few of us, wishes can come true.'

'But – after all this? The transformations, everything … It isn't possible!'

'It is and you are and that's that. There's nothing improper about it. It was before any vows were taken.'

She nodded. 'But – it's impossible! How can I manage it? And how do I explain it? The new Sister General of the Reformed Church has a child.'

'You should learn by now that heads of churches can sell any rationalization they want to the devout, particularly when it doesn't violate true scripture. It *would* be a tough thing to explain to the old church, whose general practices forbade any but virgins becoming priestesses, but we are returning to basics here.'

She sank back in the chair once again. 'Damn!'

'High priestesses don't curse in front of others,' he cracked. 'But, seriously, you will be in Flux most of the time. It is not necessary to have it.'

'But it *is*! Don't you see – it's the only thing left of him. He wanted one, and it was supposed to be Arden's, but she was killed. No, somehow I will manage.' She sighed. 'I need to be alone for a little while with this. Then I have to start getting things ready for Sister Tamara's installation.'

'I understand,' he told her. 'Don't worry. I'll be around if you need me.'

The candles blew out when he closed the door on his way out, but she did not get up and relight them. For quite a while she just sat there, being, for a moment, little Cassie, alone in the peace of the darkness.

We are the spirits of Flux and Anchor, and some call us demons …

She had the spell memorized. It was incredibly complex, and she did not understand it, but she understood its meaning. Now she knelt at the altar in the Temple at Hope, completely alone, and performed the full sacramental service. In the midst of it, she paused, and without hesitation executed the spell.

'I am a priestess of the Holy Mother of Universes and an instrument of Her Holy Church and will,' she said softly. 'I vow that I shall always be a priestess in all things and in all ways, and that I shall never violate my sacred trust nor deviate from my cause.

'I vow that I shall devote my life and my power to the uplifting of humanity and the reformation of the Holy Church. I vow that I will never use that great power for selfish gain, but only to further the sacred causes and the divine will.

'I reaffirm my vows before thee, that I shall in all things obey scripture as regards myself and others; that I shall live as the humblest of my priestesses, owning nothing; that I shall keep and never violate the sacraments; that I shall go beyond thy vows and be in all ways forever after chaste.

'I further vow that I shall never ask of another anything which I myself am not willing to do, nor be false to myself, my flock, or my faith in any way. To these things I bind myself, willingly, now and forever.'

She continued with the service, but there was a new, strange light in her eyes, for she could see the future in her mind's eye.

We are the spirits of Flux and Anchor and some call us demons. It is possible that we are such, for certainly we know not our nature or our origins …

In the great golden palace at Holy Anchor, Her Perfect Highness, The Queen of Heaven, was looking over the account books and scowling. There was a sudden fluttering in the window nearby, and she looked up, irritated, to see a large, fat raven perched there. She stared at it and frowned. 'Be off, bird!' she snapped. 'Shoo! I have too many headaches right now to fool with the likes of you!'

'You haven't begun to know what a headache really is,' the raven squawked back. 'We, my dear sister, are in deep, deep shit …'

Slowly, sparing no details, he explained the new situation. She listened attentively, nodding now and then and asking an occasional question, but otherwise letting him tell it. Finally, he was finished, and she sighed wearily.

'I suppose you have a grand new design for dealing with this?'

'Of course. But I'm willing to hear alternatives.'

She thought a moment, then said, 'With much patience, and a great deal of pressure, this might be yet turned to our advantage. An uprising will panic the Fluxwizards and Anchorfolk alike all over World. A holy crusade could cement our control.'

'You mean to contain it, then? I thought of turning it instead.'

'We will try containment first. If that doesn't work, then we will try your more devious ways. Do not worry, my brother. I know exactly what to do …'

THE IDENTITY MATRIX

*This one's for my
technical advisors,
Bill Hixon, Dave Weems,
Ben Yalow, Ron Bounds,
and Mike Lalor, to whom
all nasty cards and
letters should be sent.*

This time the horror was an old woman.

She ambled down the little street that was like all slum back alleys in every city in the world: garbage-littered, closed-in, filled with the cries of babies, the yells of aimless adults, and smelling like too many people were cramped into too little space, a fact further attested to by the long lines of frayed washing hung from fire escape to fire escape.

She toddled along, dressed in a faded green and very baggy print dress decorated with faded orange flowers, garb that seemed to accent rather than hide, the effects of age and improper diet. The dress itself was rumpled, as if she slept in it and removed it only for an occasional super-bleached washing.

She halted in the middle of the street as some wisps of wind broke the heat of the day and rolled discarded trash from one side to the other and looked cautiously around.

A lone young black male, barely fifteen, dressed in old, faded shorts that had been cut off from a well-worn pair of blue jeans, and little else, was idly humming an incomprehensible tune as he tossed a little red rubber ball against the wall and caught it.

She stopped to watch him for a moment, her kindly face breaking into a satisfied smile as it squinted to observe the young man.

She liked them young, and he looked in excellent health.

The solitary ball player hadn't even noticed her; he didn't notice as she positioned herself carefully behind him and took one last glance around.

After a few more seconds the kid threw the ball against the cracking brick facade a little too hard and ran into her as he chased the flying red missile that sailed overhead. She fell, then muttered something he couldn't hear under her breath and started to pick herself up.

The kid was extremely apologetic, and she smiled a toothless smile at him.

'That's all right, boy,' she told him kindly, 'jest hep me back up to my old feet.'

She held out her hand, and he took it, pulling her up.

Suddenly, so quickly that he didn't even have time to think, he stiffened, then shook himself and looked down at the old woman again.

She appeared to have fainted and lay collapsed in a heap in the middle of the street. Carefully, he knelt down beside her and groped for something strapped to her leg, a small case, held in place by an elastic band.

Carefully removing the case, he opened it and removed a hypodermic needle. Taking her limp arm, he found a vein, then stuck the needle into it and pushed the plunger slowly, injecting air.

Satisfied, he walked down the street to where it came to another, larger and busier one, and dropped the syringe down the sewer so casually without stopping that no one would have noticed that anything had been discarded.

A little farther down the street a young white woman waited tensely at the wheel of a yellow Volkswagen, motor running.

Without a word, the young black man opened the passenger door, got in, and settled down. Without even a glance, the woman started the car forward, and, within a minute, was out of sight, lost in a sea of thousands of little cars heading into and out of the inner city.

He walked into the old morgue with an air of confident authority. A police sergeant greeted him just inside, and after exchanging a few words they made their way down a long, echoey hall lined with ancient marble, their footsteps ghostly intrusions on the quiet.

They entered the main room and both shivered slightly, for it was a good deal colder here than in the rest of the building and in extreme contrast to the heat of the muggy August night.

One wall was filled with what looked like huge airport lockers of a dull gray. The sergeant checked the names and numbers, then nodded and turned the shiny aluminum handle on the third from the bottom.

The compartment slid out on well-greased rollers revealing a body wrapped in a clinical white sheet with the city's seal on it. Methodically, the sergeant pulled back the cover to reveal the body of an elderly woman, Jane Doe #8, wearing a faded green flowered dress.

The man nodded gravely then removed a small fingerprint kit from his suit pocket and took her index finger's indentations carefully.

The sergeant recovered the body and slid it back into the refrigerated compartment, while the man reached into his inside jacket pocket and took a small card from a worn leather billfold.

He put the card next to the one on which the old woman's prints stood out clearly, nodded to himself, and grunted, a sour expression on his face.

'It's her, all right,' he said disappointedly. 'That old bitch beat me again.'

CHAPTER ONE

I should have known better than to go to a bar on a Friday night, even in Whitehorse, Yukon territory.

Whitehorse has that aura of backwoods pioneer behind it, but about the only evidence of roughing it left in the now modern, metropolitan city are a few multistory apartments made of logs and the prices you have to pay for everything. Long ago the old frontier gave way not just to traffic lights but traffic jams, parking meters, and modern, plush motels and restaurants. The motel I was in might as well have been in New York, or maybe Cedar Rapids, with its neon, its prefabricated twin double beds and little bands reading 'sanitized for your protection' and several channels of cable television – in color, of course.

The bar, too, wasn't much different than anywhere else in North America these days – dark, with a small band (one would think that any act reduced to playing Whitehorse would find a better way to earn a living, but, what the hell, they'd never dream of leaving show business) playing all the latest pop-rock dance tunes pretty badly while lots of the young men and women dressed in suits and designer jeans mingled, talked, and occasionally danced in the small wooden area in front of the stage and barmaids continually looked for potentially thirsty patrons at the tables. About the only rustic touches were the stuffed and mounted moose, elk, and bear trophies over the bar (probably made in Hong Kong) and a few plastic pictures of the Trail of '98 on the walls, all impossible to see clearly in the deliberately dim light.

I sat there, alone, looking over the scene when the barmaid came over and asked if I wanted another drink. I remember looking up at her and wondering what factory made motel barmaids for the world. The same one that made state troopers and cab drivers, probably.

I *did* need a drink and ordered a bourbon and seven, which arrived promptly. I sighed, sipped at it, and nibbled a couple of pretzels, surveying the people in the bar.

There *were* a few differences, of course. Some old people – I mean *really* old people – were incongruously about, looking like retired salesmen from Des Moines and haggard, elderly grandmothers of forty-four kids, which is probably what they were. What they most certainly were were tourists, part of a group that was one of thousands of geriatric groups that came to Alaska and the Yukon every year on the big cruise liners and by fast jet and motor coach combinations. Most of their party would be at one of the 'authentic' old frontier bars down the street, of course, all about as authentic as Disney-land; but these were the leftovers, the ones whose arthritis was kicking up or who'd been on one too many tours today and just didn't have any juice left. I reflected that it was a shame that most of those romantic-sounding cruises to exotic Alaska always looked like floating nursing homes, but, I suppose, that age was the only one where you had both the time and the money to do it right. Somebody once said that youth was wasted on the young, who had neither the time nor resources to properly enjoy life, and nowhere was that more graphically illustrated than here. Still, these people had worked hard and lived full, if extremely dull, lives and shouldn't be begrudged for this last fling. They were lucky in a number of ways, at that.

Most people never get the chance to go coast to coast, let alone to some-place far away like Whitehorse, and, of course, their lives had been satisfying to them, anyway.

Lucky ...

I knew I shouldn't have gone to a bar on a Friday night, not even in White-horse. You sat there, drinking a little, watching the beautiful people – and the not-so-beautiful people pretending they were – drift in and out, mix it up, watch couples pair up and others mix and match. You sat there and you watched it and you drank a little more, and the more you watched and the longer you sat the more you drank.

It'd be easier, I often thought, if I were physically scarred or deformed or something like that. At least you could understand it then, maybe come to grips with it then, maybe even find somebody who took pity or had sympathy for you so you'd meet and talk and maybe make a new friend. Harder, far harder on a man's psyche to have the scars, the deformities within, hidden, out of sight but no less crippling or painful.

I finished the bourbon, and, leaving a couple of dollars for the barmaid, left the place. Nobody noticed, not even the barmaids.

It was a little after midnight, yet the July sun shone brightly outside, sort of like six or seven anywhere else. It was hard to get used to that most of all, because your eyes told you it was day while your body said it was really late and you were very tired. One of the tour groups was struggling into the lobby looking haggard, turning the place briefly into a mob scene. I just stood and watched as they bid their goodnights, some laughing or joking, and made their way to the elevators to turn in. None noticed me, or gave me the slight-est glance, and I waited there until they'd cleared out before going up myself. No use in fighting that mob, not with only two elevators.

I got a newspaper and glanced idly through it while waiting for the eleva-tors to return. Nothing much, really. Internationally, the Russians were yelling about something the CIA supposedly did in some African country I barely knew, the Americans were yelling about a new Russian airbase in the Middle East, there was some sort of local rebellion in Indonesia, and the Common Market was debating the duties on Albanian tomatoes. An earthquake here, a murder there, the U.S. President was pushing for some new missile system, and the Canadian Prime Minister was in the Maritimes trying to keep Newfoundland from seceding. Big deal. I suspected that this same newspaper could be used, with perhaps a few names and locales changed, for roughly every third day of the past two decades.

The elevator came and I got in, riding it swiftly up to my room, still glancing through the wire-service laden local paper. NORAD scrambled in Alaska when a UFO was sighted south of Fairbanks, but it was gone when they'd gotten there, as usual. Ho hum. UFO stories seemed to run in ten-year cycles, with a particular rash of them right now. I remembered meeting the ambassador to Uranus once in San Francisco, really a balding, gray-haired little man with thick glasses who might never really have been anywhere near Uranus, or even Pittsburgh, but got a lot of attention by saying he had so often he almost certainly believed his fantasy himself by now.

I unlocked the door to my room, went in, and flopped on the bed. All the lonely people … That was a line from a song once, when I was growing up, and it was certainly true. The world was full of such people – not the nonentities downstairs, both old and young, who live but might as well not have lived, but the lonely ones, the ones who fly to Uranus in their minds or maybe become flashers in Times Square or take a crack at killing a politician. There were degrees and degrees of it, from the horrible to the hilarious, but those nuts had found a release, a way out. For a few there was no release, no way out, except, perhaps, the ultimate way.

Some just got naked in cold, plastic motel rooms and jerked off to some private fantasy they might not ever want to actually experience.

I got up after a while and walked into the bathroom. It was one of those kind with a full-length mirror – you couldn't even shit without watching yourself doing it – and I stopped and stared at myself as I had so many times before.

Behold Victor Gonser, I thought. Age – thirty-five. Height – five eight and a half, something like that. Average. Overall – average. Caucasian male who'd always been almost scarecrow-thin and still looked that way, only now there was an incongruous double bulge at the tummy that looked totally ridiculous. Most people gained all over, or at least had heavy asses, but, no, mine ballooned around the navel like some hydrogen gas bag.

There wasn't much hair left, and the thin moustache, all I could ever really manage, gave me one of those mild-mannered accountant looks. Truth was, I looked weak in all areas, the face a patsy's face, the kind of face that told you you could walk all over this guy. And even this Caspar Milquetoast was something of a fraud. The uppers were kept in a jar overnight, and I peered at myself from a distance of six inches through glasses that looked like the bottoms of Coke bottles.

There'd be no release tonight, I knew. I was too down, too depressed, too sober despite the double bourbon. It was, I thought, a ridiculous situation for somebody like me, but, damn it, there it was.

Somebody once said that a few of my colleagues envied me, and that had shaken me up for quite a while. The people in question were better looking, more outgoing, seemed to enjoy their lives. Envy? Me? But, of course, there were the things they saw that I'd attained that I'd once also seen as wonderful, only to find they were meaningless once you had them.

Money, for example, was always envied, and I'd had nothing to do with that department. Dad had been a corporate lawyer with a really big-shot firm and he'd made a bundle in his time. Home to me would be a mansion to most people, sitting in the very wealthy Virginia suburbs of Washington, D.C. In a place where a two-bedroom shack was a quarter of a million; we had twenty-two rooms on fourteen wooded acres, complete with pool, riding stable, tennis courts, you name it. It was a lot – particularly when you consider that Mom had to have a hysterectomy for a cancerous condition only a year or so after I was born and that left just the three of us on the place. Two, really, since I guess we saw Dad for about an hour a night and maybe every sixth weekend. That was another of life's little jokes on people, I always thought. Self-made men who worked damned hard and made a couple of million dollars were always so busy they never were home enough, never had time enough, to enjoy any of that money. And, when they started realizing this, as Dad finally did, they'd wind up dropping dead of a heart attack just when they've decided to take it easy and enjoy life.

As Dad did. Dead at forty-six. No geriatric cruises, no graduations, weddings, sailing, none of that for him. That was left to the nonentities, the retired feed grain salesmen from Des Moines with the IRA account.

Life was always full of cruel jokes like that, I thought glumly. And, when I'd stood there, watching him being lowered into the ground surrounded by enough big shots to buy California, I'd felt no loss, no pain, no sense of grief, and I'd felt guilty for that, but damn it all, it's hard to grieve for a man you barely knew.

Mom, now, she was a different case. I had to hand it to my father that he'd remained married to her all that time, although he was no TV sex symbol star himself. She was plain, beyond the best beauty and fashion consultants money could buy, and she'd been poor. They both had been when they'd married just out of college, and she'd gone to work and supported him through law school. There was a bond there, between these two seemingly plain, ordinary people from Moscow, Idaho, one that didn't fall apart as his spectacular law school grades had attracted a large firm well connected to Senator Carlovich and which he'd ridden to Washington and the seats of power. I don't know if it was love – I was never sure of that – but it was more than a strict Catholic upbringing that kept them together. I think, perhaps, that they each had what they wanted out of life, or thought they did. Money, power, prestige.

But Mom wanted more than Washington social life, more than the routine of being married to the powerful and well-connected, more than her polit-ical activities and championing of liberal causes. I was the only child she had, and, by damn, I was going to be somebody, too!

A private all-male military style prep school, one of the best, shielded from the world, from the ordinary folk and the roots both she and Dad had risen from, only the best training and prepping for Victor Leigh Gonser, yes, ma'am! Hell, I was eighteen before I even *met* a girl in other than the most rigidly controlled social situations, and by that time it was getting too late. I discovered that I simply didn't know what to do. I hadn't had a childhood, I'd had a mini-business adulthood, so protected from my peers that I could hardly identify with them. It's in the teen years, particularly, that you learn the rules society has set down – how to meet and mix with other people, all the social and sexual signals, the anthropology of your culture. Without them, and out in the world, you find you're as well prepared for socializing as you would be if you were living amongst a New Guinea tribe. You're not a part of it, you don't fit.

And, of course, when you fail out of ignorance to respond to the rituals of society you get pigeonholed and stereotyped and promptly ignored. In my case the men, and women, at college at first thought I was gay, then decided, finally, that I was sexless, a neuter without the needs they all had. God! How I envied them.

So I threw myself into my studies, for that was all I had, and ignored the social life and activities that the rest of the world enjoyed around me. The work was absurdly easy, even at Harvard – money-hungry universities had gone for the least common denominator in a generation where such basics as reading and math were largely irrelevant, and it had reached even here. Not that there wasn't some intellectual stimulation, but it was the rare professor and the rare course that offered it, and you could tell *those* men and women were not long for the academic life. They did the inexcusable at a modern university – they thought, and, worse, promoted thinking among those with whom they came in contact.

I excelled at university studies, not merely for this reason but because it was the only thing I had to do that I could take some pride in accomplish-ment. I took massive loads, partly because I was interested in practically everything but also because I had nothing outside the academic life to occupy my time or mind, and the heavier the workload the less time I had to dwell on my lack of humanity. Oddly, the social sciences held the greatest attraction for me, as if, somehow, I could find what was lacking in my own being by studying others in a clinical, professional pattern. I studied human behavior the way the biologist studies the workings of a cell or the life of a paramecium. I wound up graduating *summa cum laude* with double majors in psychology and sociology and a strong minor in political science. For graduate studies I concentrated on psychology simply because I felt that I understood the interaction of human beings in groups as much as anyone did up to then. It was the individual mind, the human psyche, that somehow eluded me. Yet it was political science that I finally got my doctorate in. The truth was, everybody I met in the psychology department was definitely nuts, and a good deal of modern psychology exposed too much of the human being studying it to others – the essence of psychology, of course.

This is not to say that I didn't try analysis. On a one-to-one basis I could be frank, open, and free, but the problem was that I generally seemed to know as much as the psychiatrist and more than many. The foundation of clinical psychology is to get you to admit and recognize the causes of your problems so that you can work them out. My trouble was that I *knew* the causes of my problems, understood myself quite well, but that I could articulate what I needed to join human society only to another similarly afflicted. The rest just couldn't really understand.

Just after my twenty-fifth birthday something truly disenheartening happened. I had graduated, received my Ph.D., and I was ready to make my own way in the world from an academic standpoint, but not at all prepared to do so on an emotional level. I was a twenty-five-year-old sexually repressed virgin. There seemed only one thing to do, and I did it, back home in Washington, when outside a restaurant on Connecticut Avenue I was approached by an attractive black woman, nicely dressed and finely featured. I actually approached the proposition clinically, as I did everything, reflecting that I had little to lose with almost no money on me if it were a set-up for a rob-and-roll, and, what the hell …

It was legit, and it was fascinating, and it was as coldly businesslike as any academic lab exercise on both sides. It broke my cherry, but it was neither satisfying nor particularly pleasurable in the end. All it showed me was that I was a normal male with the ability to perform; it did nothing to integrate me into the lives of real people.

I was offered an instructor's position in political science from a number of places, but selected Johns Hopkins in Baltimore partly because it was close to home and familiar surroundings and partly because it was the most prestigious institution offering me anything. I did a couple of books that sold moderately well, mostly examinations of political attitudes, and while I found the faculty politics and undergraduate standards at Hopkins to be a mini-Harvard, I managed to find myself a niche. Although my political writings weren't really popular with my colleagues, I was non-threatening, never rocked the boat, and found it easy to say the right thing at the right time to the right person to keep it that way. Not only the psychology, but all those years growing up around Washington hadn't been totally wasted. Still, I tended to associate more with faculty in other, unrelated disciplines than with my own immediate colleagues. It made it easier to keep out of arguments and office politics, and, of course, it helped satiate my never-ending curiosity about practically everything.

And so, I guess, those who could not know what was going on in my head (and no one else could) could envy me – rich, with a solid position at a top school, and with a modest amount of national fame through my books and occasional TV talk show stints. They especially loved me for voter analysis around election time.

Mom died when I was thirty-three. Funny – she'd always been paranoid about cancer since that operation so long ago and it had become a passion with her. So she died of a heart attack on the tennis court at age sixty-one.

I felt real grief for her, even though she was at the heart of most of my problems. She had meant well, and she'd been proud, and, I guess, she'd been the only real human being I could relax with. I considered an offer from American University so I could live in the house, but one look at the place with just me and no social life made that idea ridiculous. I just rented it for a fantastic sum to the Majority Whip of the Senate, who needed it, and took a large old brownstone near Hopkins.

Mom's passing, though, had a serious effect on me. For the first time in my life I was totally, utterly, truly alone. There was no one else now (I suppose Mom went to her grave bewildered that her frenzied matchmaking did no good at all) and every time I looked in a mirror I saw myself growing older, falling apart a little more, losing my last chance at ever joining humanity. I was becoming, had become, not human at all, but a sort of friendly alien, a creature that was nonhuman in all respects and, like Marley's ghost, could only wander the world watching happiness it could not share, existing but somehow apart. I moved through crowds, the only one of my kind.

I often envied women, and even occasionally fantasized myself as one. Not that I was gay, as I said – this was different. It seemed to me that women had an innate social advantage in a society that was male created and, despite years of liberation, still predominantly male dominated. Women, even the most sheltered, were raised to know the rules of the game. Oh, it might be as a warning – if this guy does this, watch out! – but they all knew. They had more options than men, too, in a curious way. I suppose that was why many men feared the women's rights movement. Society – not codified laws, cultural laws – now gave them all the options. Marriage was an option. Children, in or out of marriage, was an option. They could work, with the full backing of the law and the courts, in any field they wanted competing directly with men, or they could opt to be supported by men. Men, on the other hand, had none of these options. The courts still put the burden of divorce and child support on the man while granting custody to the woman, no matter what the relative age or income. Men couldn't have children. Men could not opt to be supported by women if they so chose.

And, in any case, no woman seemed to be in my position in a crowd. Women could walk into a motel bar and be the center of attention, no matter what they looked like, of lonely men on the make. A female colleague of mine once confessed that she'd dropped a bundle in Reno and was left with nothing but a bus ticket home – yet men bought her breakfast, lunch, and dinner with only a little prodding, and she'd made out quite well, thank you. And she was as ugly an old bag as you could imagine.

It wasn't the sexual part of a woman's life I craved, it was the social interaction that was seemingly almost automatic. Academically I knew that there had to be some women, somewhere, who were in my kind of fix, but I couldn't conceive of them in real-life terms.

I wanted a wife, children, parties, dancing, mixing, socializing, feeling, love, tenderness, togetherness with another human being.

And there I stood, looking at reality, in a motel john in Whitehorse and knowing it just wasn't going to happen.

Since Mom died I'd gone away for the whole summer, conscious of the fact that neither of my parents had lived to a very old age and that I could go any time. If I couldn't participate, at least I could visit.

My first year I'd gone on the Grand Tour in Europe. I'd been there before, of course, but this time I poked into everything and anything. I spoke passable German and my French was very good indeed and it helped a lot.

And this time I'd decided on Alaska and the Yukon, mostly because it was already dramatically changed from when I was a boy and I had this strong feeling that, if I didn't see it soon, I'd come back to find it domed over and paved, a chilly California. I'd salmon-fished at Katmai, took a trip into Gates of the Arctic National Park, walked the garbage-strewn streets of Barrow, taken a boat down the Yukon, and now, after a flight from Fairbanks, it had been more than worth it – the place, spoiled or not, still was absolutely the most scenic area in the whole world.

And huge, and wide, and lonely.

I loved the place, but knew that July was not January, and I wasn't so sure I'd like it in the opposite season.

From Whitehorse I intended to take the once-a-day tourist train of the White Pass and Yukon Railway to the trail head at Yukon National Park on the Canadian side, then make my way down the Chillicoot Pass, a reverse Trail of '98, way down to Sitka at the bottom, where I could catch the ferry south. The trail was excellent, thanks to the National Park Service, and while I couldn't have hiked a hundred feet up it the way the pioneers did in the gold strike days, I was wonderful at walking *down* trails. It was a natural capstone to my Alaskan Grand Tour, as it were, and one that I'd have hated myself for passing up. I looked forward to the walk, but not to its ending, for that boat would take me to Seattle and a plane home. I didn't want to go home, really. That bar had brought it all back to me, and, in a sense, represented what home and 'real life' was.

I didn't really want real life any more, not that kind, and lying in bed, in the stillness of the early morning, I wondered if I really wanted life at all.

The White Pass and Yukon Railroad owes its existence and continued huge fortune to the gold rush. One look at the Chillicoot Pass showed that only the hardiest could climb it under the best of conditions – yet tens of thousands did, carrying all that they owned on their backs. The lucky ones made it to the top without collapsing or being robbed by Soapy Smith and other professional crooks, but, as with all gold rushes, even the lucky ones who made it to the headwaters of the Yukon River and the boats that men like Jack London piloted downriver to Dawson and the gold fields, rarely struck it rich. Those who did, though, were faced with problems as well, for never had gold been so remotely located and so hard to get not merely out of the ground but out of the area once you did. As the boomtowns grew, their new, swelling populations also needed almost all manufactured goods – and it was due to this that enterprising business pioneers, in a stunning feat of engineering, built the narrow gauge railroad all the way from the port at Skagway up, over the mountains, to Whitehorse and the river and road connections. Although the gold fever was now long gone the railroad prospered, supplying the growing population of the Yukon and dealing now in new, less glamorous but no less needed resources of the burgeoning north country. So big was the business that they'd been trying for years to get rid of the one tourist train a day, as there was still only a single track and it was needed for more profitable goods, but, while service was not really what it once was, that train still ran.

At the beautiful headwaters of the Yukon River, in a bed of glistening lakes at the river's source, the train stopped at the old station where once the gold-seekers had transferred to glittering stern-wheelers, only now it was to feed the captive tourists a captive lunch and allow northbound freights to pass. It was here, though, that I got off with a pack and little else, since, just around the lake over there, was the top of the Chillicoot. It was a warm day, around 60 degrees, which meant almost hot down in Skagway, only a few miles for the eagle to fly but a long, long way down. The air was crisp and cleaner than most people have ever known, and, near the trail head, you could look down through scattered clouds and see the Pacific far beyond gleaming in the sun.

Although it was a long walk, with all its switchbacks, it was an easy day trip from this direction – three or four for the one in great condition coming up the way the pioneers did – but I had been trapped by the tourist train's schedule and it was past midday. My ferry wasn't due in down there until after 7 P.M. the next day, so I was in no hurry and planned to stop at one of the convenient Park Service campgrounds about halfway and say goodbye to the wilderness experience in some grand style.

I met a few people as I descended, mostly young couples or two or three young men, but it was not a busy day for the trail. More would start two days hence, when the ferry came in and disgorged its load, but, for the most part, I had the trail, the views, the clean air and whistling, soft wind to myself the way I wanted it. Finally, leisurely, I reached the camp I'd selected before starting out and was delighted to find no one else using it. It was one of the best according to the parks guide, with a stunning view of Skagway, tiny and glistening below, its harbor, and out past the last point of land, past Haines Junction, to the Pacific and the Inside Passage.

I'd packed light; all cold stuff, prepacks, the sort of thing; for minimum gear and minimum weight, with a small, light folding pup tent I'd already used often on this trip. Still, I had a tiny little gas jet and pot for boiling water, since I couldn't conceive of a day without coffee to get me going, and it not only worked nicely but also provided the added joy of being able to make a cup of bullion.

I sat there for a long time in the late-evening daylight enjoying the view, the solitude, watching a couple of brown eagles circling lazily in the sky, and I thought of what a contrast it was between here and that bar back in Whitehorse. Here, perhaps only here, I was at least partly human, as close to nature and the world as I could get. Here there were no pressures, no social rules, no sign of beautiful people and the kind of normalcy I had never known.

I did very little thinking, really. I just lay there, at peace for the first time in a long, long time, looking out and around and becoming one with nature, riding with the whispering winds, soaring like those eagles, at rest, and free.

I didn't want to go back. I knew that for a certainty. This sort of peace and freedom was beyond me in any crowded, social setting. Soon it would be back to the cities and the bustling humanity and a world that was very much like that bar, a world in which I was not equipped to live and join and mingle, but only to sit silently at endless dark tables sipping, sipping my drink that might bring forgetfulness while observing the rest of the world in a manner oh, so very clincal and so damnably detached from myself.

I thought again about women, oddly. I'd more than once taken a woman to dinner and had pleasant conversation, or to a show, but after they'd eaten and watched, they'd walk off with somebody they met in the waiting room or at intermission. Oddly, I had no trouble going places with women – they considered me safe, nonthreatening, nonsexist and nonsexual, which, in a way, I was. I didn't even want to go to bed with those women particularly, but it hurt me terribly to watch them going to bed with everybody else in the world except me. More than one grad assistant had put the bite on me for a loan, or propped up my ego so I'd buy them dinner, only to use the money to treat somebody else to a date. I was a soft touch and often used, and I knew I was a sucker, but, damn it, if all hope vanishes what's left?

But I realized, late that night, in the deepening gloom over the mountains above Skagway, that I *had* lost hope. My scars were too deep, too painful, and would never heal, and they had me in agony. I was a human being! Why, then, did everyone around me insist on being treated as a human being but never even think to treat me like one? Hurry! Hurry! See the robotic man! He walks! He talks! He thinks! But he never feels …

But I felt, all right. Every single time was another scar on my soul – no, not a scar, a festering, rotting, infected wound that would never heal, never subside, could only be compounded more and more until the pain grew unbearable. I could feel them now, those wounds, growing worse and worse as I approached a return to civilization and society, already near the threshold of pain. Weeping slightly in my lonely tent, uncaring as to what would happen, I finally, mercifully drifted into sleep.

The sound of horses woke me, and I groaned, turned over, grabbed for my glasses, and glanced at my watch. A bit after seven in the morning, I noted, and rolled over, squinting to see what the noises might be. It was unusual to find horses on a trail like this – it'd take an expert to navigate them on the winding, rough terrain and I didn't even realize that the Park Service allowed them. Still, there they were, coming slowly down, two men and a child, it looked like, on three brownish-red horses breathing hard in the morning chill, nostrils flaring.

I crawled out of the tent and went over to my small pack, where I'd left a pot of water the night before fetched from a small waterfall nearby. I lit the little gas jet, then went over and scooped up some icy cold water from a rivulet on the rocks and splashed my face, trying to wake up and look at least moderately presentable. Only then did I turn to the approaching trio and give them a good looking-at.

Both men looked like hell and neither looked like they should be on a trail in the Alaska panhandle. Both wore suits, although the clothes looked like they'd been slept in for days, and both looked dead tired and somewhat harried. The child, I saw, was an Indian girl, perhaps twelve or thirteen, with long, black hair almost to her waist, but still pre-pubescent, although she was certainly on the verge of turning into a woman. She looked a bit more normal, in a ski jacket, T-shirt and faded, well-worn jeans, with extremely worn cowboy boots that might have been tan at some point in their past.

The lead man had only now spied me, looking somewhat wary and suspiciously in my direction, eyes darting to and fro as if he expected others about. Both men looked to be in their forties, with graying hair and lined faces; the kind of men you'd expect to see in business offices in Juneau or Anchorage but not out here and not looking like that.

'Good morning!' I called out in my friendliest tone. 'You look a little tired.'

The lead man nodded glumly and stopped near me. The other seemed mostly interested in surveying the terrain not only around the camp but also back along the trail. For a fleeting moment I thought they might be escaping bank robbers with their hostage, and their manner did nothing to reassure me. The Indian girl looked impassive, as if either resigned to her fate or uncaring of it.

'Mornin',' the lead man responded to me. 'Yeah, you're right about being tired, I'll tell you.'

'Want some coffee?' I offered, trying to stay as friendly as I could. No matter who these people were my best chance was to keep innocently on their good side and let them go.

'Coffee …' the lead man repeated, almost dreamily. 'God! Could I use some coffee …'

'You sure you wan'ta stop, Dan?' the other man put in, speaking for the first time. 'I mean, we don't know …'

The man called Dan sighed wearily. 'Charlie, after you been here a while you'll see things differently. I'm so damned tired and sore that if I don't get something in me I'm going to fall down to Skagway.'

The other shrugged. 'O.K. Suit yourself.' He sounded nervous and not at all convinced. Both men got off their horses, though, and stretched. I couldn't help but notice as Dan, the nearest to me, got down there was more than a hint of a shoulder holster. I think he realized what I'd seen as well, and I could see him weighing in his mind what to say to me.

'Don't be alarmed,' he said at last. 'We're not criminals. Not really, anyway. The truth is, we're federal officers.'

That stopped me. 'Huh?'

He nodded. 'What you see here is the culmination of a lot of skullduggery in what might be the most minor diplomatic incident in recent memory.' He looked over at the boiling pot. 'Coffee ready?'

I nodded idly and went over to the pot. I had only two telescoping plastic cups, so I fixed two cups of instant and decided I'd wait until they were through before having my own. I felt bad about the Indian girl, though, still sitting there atop her horse.

Dan went over to her, sipping hot coffee with a look of extreme ecstasy on his face. She looked down at him quizzically and asked, well, something like, '*U chua krm sbi?*' It was a guttural language pronounced in a manner that would give me a sore throat. In fact, Dan's response would, I'm sure, be beyond me.

'*Gblt zflctri gaggrb,*' it sounded like. '*Srble.*'

Whatever it was, she nodded and dismounted, approaching the pot. Using a little ingenuity, I'd managed to refill it about halfway from the rivulet in which I'd washed my face.

'You know about the Tlingit Indians?' Dan began at last.

I nodded. 'A little. The local tribe, I think, along the panhandle.'

'That's putting it mildly,' he responded. 'Fact is, they aren't like any Indians you ever heard about in your history books. They're nuts. More like the Mafia than the Sioux. In the early days they sold protection to the Hudson's Bay Company. The Company'd pay 'em or their trappers just would go into the wild and never come out. Then the Russians moved in, and they decided the Russians were competition for the protection racket, so they went to war and massacred 'em – the Indians massacring the Russians, that is. Real sneaky, real clever. Used the money to buy all sorts of manufactured goods and to throw huge parties. They even started the gold strikes up here just to bring in people so they coule extort more money.'

I just nodded, letting him tell his curious story. I couldn't imagine where he was going with it, though.

'Anyway,' Dan continued, 'today they ride around in huge fishing trawlers. Rich, well-educated, and still as clannish and as trustworthy as the Mafia. The girl, there, is the son of a big shot – chief you might call him. He and his wife had a big falling out and she took a hike with the kid up the Pass to relatives in Whitehorse. The old man threw a fit. Declared war, more or less. Started trying to ram Canadian boats, caused all sorts of trouble, which brought us in. The family's so strong, rich, and powerful we couldn't settle them down without the U.S. Marines and you know what *that* would look like in the papers.'

I nodded again, seeing his point exactly. Wouldn't the Russians, for example, have a field day with Marines shooting it out with Indians in this day and time?

'Well, the old lady was stubborn, and the Canadian government wanted no part of it, so we did the only thing our bosses decided we could do. Like common criminals, we snatched the kid and are taking her home to Daddy.'

'I gather this wasn't supposed to be your way out,' I noted.

'You said a mouthful,' he came back. 'Hell, all of Momma's relatives are on our trail, not to mention the Mounties, and if we don't beat 'em down to Skagway there's gonna be a *hell* of a stink.'

I sighed and shook my head. Your U.S. government tax dollars at work, I thought glumly.

'Dan!' the other man hissed, and got up quickly. 'I think I heard horses!'

The other man got up and looked around, also concerned. I strained my ears and, after a moment, thought I *could* hear sounds back up the trail.

'Damn!' the leader swore. 'I guess we better get moving.'

'Hey, Dan – wait a minute,' Charlie said thoughtfully. 'You know, they're looking for the girl most of all. I know there's only one, but we might meet more. It'll mix 'em up, anyway.'

The leader paused and considered it. I wasn't following their conversation, but I *did* want them to move. The last thing I wanted was to be in the middle of what might well be a shooting match.

Don turned quickly to the girl, who by this time had also gotten up. '*Grtusi shm du krttha nsi,*' he said to her. Her eyes widened a bit, then she nodded, turned, and looked at me with the oddest expression on her cute little face.

Finally she said, '*Grtusi, mckryss, ka,*' nodded, then walked up to me. I couldn't imagine what was going on and just stood there like an idiot, wondering.

A tiny brown hand reached out, took mine …

My entire body seemed to explode and crackle electrically. There was a searing, all-encompassing pain as if every nerve in my body suddenly cried out, then one massive blow that seemed to explode inside my head. It was as if the entire fibre of my being were being somehow drawn, or sucked from my body, leaving, in an instant, only oblivion.

CHAPTER TWO

I awoke feeling groggy and totally numb, except that my head pounded with a thousand off-key variations of the anvil chorus. I groaned slightly, but couldn't move for a moment.

I opened my eyes and saw only a terrible blur, but, after a moment, my vision seemed to clear and I could see off in the distance. Off – and up. Clearly I had been hit over the head or, perhaps, shot, and my body had been thrown off the side of the cliff. Luckily, I'd landed on a flat patch wedged between rock outcrops, probably the only thing that had saved my life.

Still, I wasn't sure if I were really awake or still dreaming. For one thing, I was *seeing*, and it was perfectly obvious that I was wearing no glasses. The colors, too, seemed slightly wrong, a little darker and different in texture than they should have. Still, my vision was crisp and clear, and, after a moment, I was convinced that in fact I *was* seeing through my eyes. Could the blow and the fall somehow have restored my eyesight? It didn't seem possible, yet there seemed no other explanation.

Still, I was too numb, too stunned to move, and I was aware that I was in shock.

Voices came to me – men's voices from above, where the camp was. Then, suddenly, I heard the sound of rifle shots, their crisp crackle echoing and re-echoing from the rocks around, and there were men yelling. One of the men in the camp came to the edge of the cliff and I tried to call out to him, to tell him I was here, but all I could manage was a weak gurgling sound. I prayed that he would look down, see me lying here, but he wasn't looking at me. He had a very nasty-looking semiautomatic rifle and he was looking out and down, away from my position.

There was something oddly incongruous about his appearance that made me think it might have been a dream after all. He looked like neither Indian nor Mountie, nor anybody else. He seemed to be dressed in a black suit more out of the 1890s than today, wearing a derby and sporting an outrageously large handlebar moustache. In my shock and delirium I thought perhaps I was seeing the ghost of Soapy Smith – but the rifle he held was very modern indeed.

He didn't look down but turned back to unseen others and yelled something. There was a scramble and a rush, and I heard horses moving out, down, and away from me. Far off in the distance I thought I could hear the sound of a helicopter, and that, at least, gave me some hope. Tlingit kidnapping, indeed. Federal officers indeed. They were what I first suspected, I knew. Fugitives from some crime above, probably in the Yukon. Well, they wouldn't get far, I reassured myself – they were descending into the most totally escape-proof box canyon ever devised by nature, and Skagway had barely 1500 people. Still, if they had copters looking, it meant that I might be able to attract their attention – if I could move, and if I hadn't broken every bone in my body.

A sense of cold came over me, and numbness gradually subsided, to be replaced by aches over much of my body. Still, it was encouraging, and, after a while, I tried once again to move and managed to get somewhat to a sitting position. Almost immediately I felt a sense of wrongness, of something unthinkably different about myself. For a moment I put it down to the after-effects of the blow and fall, but now, as shock wore off and I became more fully aware of myself, I realized at once that several things were terribly wrong.

I had no glasses, yet I saw, sharply, everywhere. I had teeth in the top of my head – not the omnipresent upper plate, but real teeth. And, as I moved my head, I felt weight and something of a drag and I reached up and took hold of a large mass of glossy, coal-black hair.

My reaction to all this was curiously schizophrenic. At once I knew for a certainty that I, now, somehow, was that little Indian girl I'd seen ride in with the two strange men – yet, of course, I knew too that such a thing was unthinkable, impossible. The human mind was an incredibly complex organism – how could you possibly change it for another? I sat there, awe-struck and trembling slightly with the certainty that, were I not mad, such an exchange was not only possible but had happened to me. Happened because that girl had wished it to happen – no, had been *ordered* to make it happen.

What kind of a monster was she? What sort of thing, creature, whatever, had the power to trade bodies as casually as it changed a suit of clothes? This went beyond any ESP or similar powers, real or imagined in parapsychology. It smacked, almost, of demonic power, of the supernatural in which I had never really believed. I went back to my memory of her sitting there atop that horse, oblivious to me and to the others.

Relax, keep calm, think it out, I told myself. Consider only the facts first.

Fact: that girl could and did trade bodies with me. My memory and all that I thought of as me seemed unimpaired in even the slightest detail. If any-thing, my mind seemed clearer, able to recall more detail about more things than I could ever remember.

Fact: at least one person could trade minds. Maybe more, but at least one.

Fact: somebody else knew it. Those men with her – bodyguards? Allies? Or could they, too, be possessed of that power? But her protectors weren't the only ones who knew. Others knew, and were pursuing them even now, if they hadn't caught them already. So they could be killed – perhaps even cap-tured, although that seemed hard to imagine. Physical touch had been required, that's for sure. The girl had reached out and taken my hand – my *hand!* – and that had done it. That meant no disembodied spirits in the dark. They could swap bodies, but they needed bodies in which to live. They were as mortal as we, and that alone gave me some comfort.

Was she, then, some sort of mutation, some freak of nature or the result of some unknown experiment? She – not the girl, surely. What did the creature look like at birth? Who or what was it? Certainly that was many bodies ago. But such a one would be enormously powerful, almost godlike, I told myself.

And the girl, clearly, hadn't been in charge. Hadn't even spoken any lan-guage resembling any one I'd ever heard. The lead man, Dan, *he'd* been the boss. Charlie was the new man. Dan had remarked to him, 'When you've been at this as long as I have' or words to that effect. This hadn't been the first time, then.

The UFO report in the paper came back to me – although even if that were related it was hard to see how something that far away could have wound up here. Unless … Unless NORAD hadn't lost the object, but almost captured the occupant that it dropped. Come close enough, in fact, to force a wild chase through the bush. If those men's job was to get that alien passenger down to civilization, and if their covers were blown, they might just criss-cross enough, trying to shake pursuit, and so wind up almost anywhere. For the same reason that Skagway was a trap it'd also be the last place most government agents would look for fleeing fugitives.

I considered that angle. Whatever they'd tried hadn't worked. The government – probably both governments, U.S. and Canadian – were on to them, chasing them, closing in. Ordinarily they'd just change bodies and identities and slip into the crowd, but they hadn't – until now. Why? Because too many leftover innocents in wrong bodies would be a trail in itself? Because it would blow their existence wide open, causing panic, suspicion, paranoia. They swapped when they had to, not otherwise. They'd swapped with me because the girl had been a dead giveaway. Now they might split up, two men going one way and one the other, probably losing the horses, playing cat and mouse in the rocks, trying to surprise their pursuers, get one or two off by themselves and swap.

And that left me. First of all, I was no longer who I used to be, possibly forever. My past was gone, everything was gone. Oddly, I felt pangs of regret about that, despite my depression and loneliness, for now, it came home to me, I had lost the one thing I had always had – security. Of course, I could hail the pursuers, those who might understand what had happened to me – but would they? Did they really know or understand the power they were facing? Were they, in fact, a killing party? If so, they'd be looking for an Indian girl and they might shoot first and ask questions later. I couldn't take a chance on it.

Still, what were the alternatives? I stood up, somewhat unsteadily at first, and felt the sore points on my new body. Miraculously, nothing appeared broken, although I knew I was going to feel the bruises even worse as time went on. I checked the pockets of the jacket and jeans but they were empty, except for one stick of chewing gum. Curious, I thought. Or was it just there from the body's original owner?

The fact was that I was now, and possibly forever, suddenly female. That seemed at least interesting. It certainly couldn't be worse than I'd been. I loosened the jeans and felt the area around my crotch. How strange, how different it was. I refastened the pants and felt my chest, where, it seemed, two incipient breasts were just beginning to push out slightly.

I looked at my reddish-brown hand and arm. I was also an Indian, a pureblooded Indian. That didn't really bother me so much, but it *did* mark me socially. In my old circles it would have been a real plus, but up here – the government controlled a lot of Indian life, and there were certainly people who didn't like Indians.

Finally I was twelve, perhaps, certainly no more than thirteen. Just edging into the teen years – but there were drawbacks, too. Mentally and culturally I was a thirty-five-year-old associate professor at Hopkins and graduate Ph.D. from Harvard. Goodbye degrees, unless I somehow got the chance and was willing to do all that work again. If I were picked up, I'd look like an Indian escapee from seventh grade. Going through *that*, at my age, in some Indian orphan asylum – or, worse, being returned to the parents of the original girl – was not something I wanted at all.

I started looking around to see what else they might have tossed down here. I spotted the tent forty or fifty feet below me, which gave me some hope that they'd just tossed everything over in the hopes of disguising the fact that there had been a switch at all. I spotted my pack on another ledge, a little down from me, and, after a pretty precarious climb I managed to reach it. I generally stuck my wallet and other personal things in the pack when sleeping outdoors, both as theft protection and because they were uncomfortable to sleep on. I rummaged around and came up with several things – my spare pair of glasses, for example, which I took out and looked through. My whole head almost was able to fit between the frames, and the world was a horribly blurred, indistinct mess with them. I tossed them away.

Finally I found it – both my wallet and my checkbook! The wallet contained a little over three hundred dollars in U.S. and Canadian cash, and *that* was a godsend. The traveler's checks I regretfully had to conclude were worthless. Even though I could sign them – who'd believe that a little Indian girl was Victor Gonser? Still, it was hard to abandon over five hundred more dollars, and I decided to keep them for a little while. You never knew – one time I might find somebody willing to take them.

The credit cards, too, seemed interesting, but I finally decided against them. They'd just think I stole them. I didn't want to wind up in the clink, an Indian juvenile delinquent, for stealing my own stuff. The checkbook, though, was another matter. If I could make it somehow back to the lower forty-eight I might be able to manage, through my bank in Maryland, a by-mail transaction.

So, keeping only the money, travelers checks, and checkbook, I started to make my way back up to the campground. It was not easy. I hadn't really realized the weight of so much hair, the drag on the neck muscles, and I didn't have the reflexes to automatically compensate that someone born to the body would have had. Too, my arms never *were* very strong, but I found myself positively feeble now. It took me better than an hour and a half to make it back to the top.

Aside from some droppings from several horses there was no sign that anybody had been there, as I expected, and the ground was, overall, too rocky to see much in the way of footprints. Here a crushed cigar, there a couple of cigarette stubs, and that was about all.

I listened for the sounds of people, of gunfire, of, perhaps, the helicopter, and heard nothing. In all the time it'd taken me to get to the pack, then back here, the chase was far beyond now, if not over. I went over and drank some water from the rivulet still flowing nearby as if nothing momentous had happened, then turned and walked back to the ledge up which I'd just climbed. It was a terrible drop down there, with precarious and tiny holds. I realized for the first time what luck I'd had in surviving at all, and noted that what had supported my sixty- or seventy-pound frame on the way up might not have supported my old body. My survival, though, had been a real freak of luck, and I shivered at the thought. No wonder the pursuers hadn't bothered to look down!

I turned away and walked around a little, trying to get used to the balance of my new body, gain some sort of mastery over it. Even the boots had higher heels than I'd ever worn and took some getting used to. Finally, though, I knew I was as ready as I could ever be and started cautiously down the trail. I was determined to hide if at all possible, keep out of sight of any possible pursuers. But, on the long trip down, I met only one person, a park ranger, who simply nodded and continued on up, giving me not a second glance. My biggest problem was a few gusts of wind that occasionally threatened to blow my slight body over, and my constant struggle to keep from falling off my own boots.

The trail became wider now, the slope still sharp but broad, with no sheer cliffs to contend with. You could see almost clear down to Skagway now, and, while anyone else could also see me, there seemed no real way around it. Besides, I had the best vision I could ever remember, and I felt confident that, at least, nobody was going to sneak up on me or lie in hiding.

Approaching Skagway, but still a ways up, you suddenly hit trees and I was thankful for them. Although the chances of ambush were greater, I felt confident in moving off the trail and paralleling it in the brush. Still there seemed no one around, either pursuer or pursued, to threaten. Wherever the battle had gone, it was still ahead of me.

But, then, where would my danger lie? They couldn't put an army in here without alarming the population and making headlines. No, if they were looking for the three fugitives they'd do the obvious things. They'd stake out the train station and probably the rail yards as well to avoid a double-back. They'd stake out the tiny airport, the only place you could fly out of in this small valley surrounded by sheer mountain cliffs two miles high. They'd stake out the ferry terminal, of course, to make sure you didn't get out that way, and the little marina. And they'd start a new team down both the White and Chillicoot Passes from the top just to make sure.

But – would their trap work on such beings as these? Assuming the insane for the moment that these were, indeed, alien beings from some other world, they'd be perfect actors. I saw no signs of a device in the transfer – it was something absolutely natural with them, something they did because they were born with the power to do it. Perhaps they were creatures of pure energy, parasites who invaded bodies – but, no, then why would the process be two-way? Obviously, then, such creatures had to have evolved this power as some sort of natural protection. I wondered, idly, what sort of world it would take for such an ability to evolve? A terribly harsh and competitive one, almost certainly. One with so many enemies that, to survive, it had to learn how to become its enemies.

That was a sobering thought. These would be no pushovers, these alien body-swappers. They'd be tough, accomplished, perfect mimics. About the only problem they had as far as I could see was, in this instance, the new-comer, the one dropped by spaceship, was totally unfamiliar with Earth and its people and customs and hadn't even yet learned the language. The other two, though – they were something else. If 'Dan' and 'Charlie' were actually creatures like the girl had been and not merely hirelings or agents, they'd become your best friend and you'd spill all your secrets to them.

And they'd kill you without batting an eyelash.

I felt certain that if they'd gotten this far the government or whoever those pursuers were would fail to bottle them in.

But they certainly could bottle *me in*, I realized suddenly, feeling a touch of panic once more. They *knew* what I looked like, certainly – and they'd be watching for me.

I stopped dead and sat down wearily on the grass, cursing softly. Skagway was a trap, all right, but it was a trap for *me*. How the hell was I going to get by them?

I wondered what seventh grade in an Indian school would be like – if they let me live that long.

The sheer impossibility of my situation was sinking in on me, and I felt despair rising within. Damn it, I was tired and cold and achy and hungry, and I'd had a lot of water and one stick of gum all day, and I didn't even know how the hell to pee without a toilet without it running all down my legs …

CHAPTER THREE

It occurred to me that, had I been in a large city, not merely a New York or San Francisco but even Anchorage, I'd have had little trouble. I had money, although it wouldn't last long, and I could mix with a crowd, even perhaps enter a shop and buy less conspicuous clothing. Even putting my hair up would be a big help, but I simply didn't know how to do it. The conclusion was obvious and inescapable: to survive to find my own new path in this world, I'd have to get out of the trap that was Skagway.

Air was out, of course. I briefly considered the train – it would be possible to hitch a ride in a boxcar, say, jumping on at one of the slow turns as it went into White Pass – but that would only take me back to Whitehorse, a town as isolated and as staked out as Skagway – and one in which the real little girl's parents and friends might reside. There were no roads out of Skagway. The highway through the pass, long a joke in the region, had been killed forever when most of the area had been made a national park.

Skagway itself was a living museum with its 1898 buildings and boardwalk main street. It might have been possible to do something had there been a horde of tourists, but it was a slow day. I briefly toyed with the idea of waiting for the ferry's crowds to come in, using them as at least a mild shield behind which I could get some sort of disguise, but this was quickly dismissed. They would remain with the area staked out until they accounted for all those they were searching for. The danger was acute here, less the further away I got. That meant that, somehow, I had to go along with my original plan to take the ferry southward in the evening, and that posed its own problems.

Skagway ended a good quarter to half a mile from the water's edge. The area from the end of Main Street, except for some boxcars, was clear and open and absolutely flat. There would be no way to even get close to the boat short of swimming for it – and the water temperature was 50 degrees at best and probably far less than that. Still, I made my way down towards the harbor keeping close to the main line railroad tracks which offered some concealment, trying to see if anything was even remotely possible.

It was late; my stomach fairly growled and writhed in hungry pain and I was somewhat dizzy and exhausted, yet the ferry was now due in only a couple of hours and something had to be done fast. Most of the ferries stopped at the highway connection at Haines Junction; it might be two or three days before the next one put in here.

The railroad yard personnel were busy, it seemed, but it took a moment before I realized what they were doing. A large crane-like device hovered overhead, and, occasionally, it would lower slowly its grasping apparatus over a boxcar. There would be a series of loud metallic *chunks* and then the boxcar was lifted into the air – no! Not the boxcar! Just the top of it …

Containerized cargo. Load the box in a yard, lift it onto a truck flatbed, take it to the Whitehorse rail yard, lift it off the truck and sit it down, securely clamped, on a railroad car frame and wheels, pull it to Skagway, then take it off that rail frame and …

And put it back on a truck frame. There was only one truck cab, though, being used to pull the trailer frames away and back new ones into position, and I counted. Six – no, seven large trailers were lined up in a row there, yet there was no freighter in the railroad docks. I felt hope rise within me once again. Why all this work now when there was no freighter in? Why load them onto trailer chassis at all? The only answer had to be that these were being readied to be placed on the ferry. If I could slip into, or somehow get on, one of those trailers, I might be pulled right into the belly of the ship beneath the noses of my watchers!

Slowly and carefully using as much of the railroad's equipment as I could for a shield, I made my way towards those waiting trailers, fearful that at any moment watchers in the yards, or trainmen, would spot me – or that they would begin taking the trailers over to the ferry dock itself. There was a small stretch of open space I had to get to, but it was extremely cloudy and there was a light mist falling by this time, and it seemed worth the risk. Judging my time as best I could, I sprinted for the trailers, adrenaline pumping, and made them, stopping in their shelter to suddenly gasp for breath and get hold of myself.

After a few moments, I looked them over, finding that being four feet tall placed the heavy truck latches out of reach. I might get to one by standing on the ledge and stretching, but it might take more effort than I could muster to move them – if they weren't locked.

My very tininess, though, might serve to some advantage if I could ride in on the undercarriage. I ducked under and checked that possibility out. There were spaces and grooves in the solid steel frame where I might fit, but the handholds would be precarious at best and I would have a long, bumpy pull under the least comfortable of circumstances. I knew, though, that I'd have to chance it. I had no real idea where I was going or what I was going to do once I got there, but I knew for damned sure that any alternative was worse. The only people who would believe my story and accept body-switching were the aliens, who'd tried to kill me, and their hunters, who'd think me one of their enemy and would take no chances, of that I was certain.

Choosing the 'shoe' area which helped support the rear axle, I picked one of the lead trailers and wedged myself in as best I could and I tried to relax, waiting for the inevitable.

How long I waited there, so precariously perched, I don't really know – but several times I heard men's voices and heard and saw legs and feet walking between the trailers. Once or twice I heard latches thrown, and loading doors on the trailers thrown back, including the one I was under, but they didn't see or suspect me hiding beneath. Some of the trousers looked too fancy and new to be trainmen, and I was suddenly glad, despite the pain and discomfort, that I hadn't tried to sneak inside one.

I heard the ship come in, a mighty, echoing blast from its air horn signalling arrival at its furthest outpost, but I dared not peek at it. I knew what it looked like, anyway – a great blue ship, more like an ocean liner than a ferry, a representative of the most luxurious, yet necessary, working boats in the world. I waited stuffed inside my precarious perch, hunger and fatigue temporarily recessed as the tension built within and around me. It seemed like hours there, although it must have been far less than that, and I heard the roar of vehicles getting off, the bumps against the concrete and metal ramp, and the myriad voices and shouting that accompanied loading and unloading. Then it was still, for a while, as the ship made ready to load and begin the long journey south once again. At least I knew this one's itinerary – there would be an empty stateroom aboard this time, the one I would have occupied.

Finally, after an eternity, I heard the start-up of engines on the dock and heard the loading begin. There would not be many from Skagway – you couldn't drive anywhere from here – but they would have to be carefully arranged, as Alaska's ferries stopped at all the cities and towns of the panhandle and arranging cars and trucks so they would be able to get off at their proper destinations was a skill in itself.

Finally there was quiet once more, and I became afraid that I had misjudged the situation, that these trailers, after all, were not due to get on. With the fear came a new awareness of the pain in my position was causing, and I shifted slightly.

Suddenly I heard the roar of a diesel cab and was aware that it was backing up to the trailer under which I hid. The rear of the cab slid under as I watched, then stopped with a bump that almost spilled me. A man got quickly out of the cab and walked back, operating the hydraulic couplers, linking the trailer to the cab, then plugging in the air brakes. He looked under to check his work, and I feared he would spot me there, but his mind was on business, and I got lucky. He walked back and got into the cab, then slammed his door and put the truck in gear. The shock of sudden movement spilled me and I grabbed frantically at the metal, trying to pull myself back up before I fell to the ground and was left. I know I cried out in pain and anguish as I did so, but the noise was more than masked by the roar of the diesel. Scraped, with part of my jeans torn, I managed to get back up into the ridiculously small perch and hang on for dear life. Had the truck been in any but the lower gears I know I couldn't have stayed there no matter what I would have tried.

Still, now we roared onto the dock, turned, and moved slowly towards, then into the great ship. Once inside its massive car deck, the truck went through a series of slow maneuvers, backing up and then going forward, then repeating, again and again, until it was in its proper position and lane. Quickly and professionally the driver jumped out, disconnected the air brakes and lowered the hydraulic coupler, then sped out to pick up the next.

There were people all about in the deck area, both passengers and crew, but I wasn't about to wait to be discovered. I got cautiously down, wincing slightly as I discovered that my knee had been badly skinned, then using the trailer as a shield, looked cautiously around. It was obvious that I would have to cross some open deck to get to the stairway up, but I really wasn't concerned. The purser would still be out on the dock – and only he would know or be likely to remember who came aboard. I decided that the best defense was simply to walk over as if I belonged there legally and naturally and hope I made it. After some hesitancy, I took a deep breath and went for the hatch marked 'To Passenger Decks' trying to look as if I belonged.

Whether or not I seemed out of the ordinary, nobody gave me a second glance, and the hardest thing I had to do was bear the burning pain as I walked up those interminable stairs, then pushed back the sliding doors at the top, and walked onto the deck of the ferry. The door hadn't been easy – the latch was very high and I'd had to stand on tip-toe to get at it, then push the door back with all my might. I was reminded once again of my new physical situation.

I walked down the corridor, past closed stateroom doors, heading towards the rear of the ship where I could figure out where everything was. I reached the end of the corridor and found a diagram of the ship, a sort of 'you are here' thing, and again had to strain, as it was fully eighteen inches higher on the wall than the top of my head.

Nerves suddenly started to get the better of me, and I realized now that this was going to be something new, something I hadn't given any thought to until now. I'd made it – but that fact gave me little comfort. Everything I had done up to this point was borne of necessity and desperation, but now I was reentering society as someone totally different, someone I didn't even know. I was a small, prepubescent Indian girl now to everyone else, and I knew that I would have to *be* that person, act like her, react like her, to be both accepted and inconspicuous.

I'd ridden the ferry on the way up from Seattle to Juneau, but somehow the ship seemed to have doubled in both size and scale, even though this was a smaller ship. Everything, I was discovering, looked larger than life. Nowhere was this brought home more forcefully to me than when I met my first human beings close up. How much we forget of what it's like to be a child in an adult's world! How gigantic the ordinary-sized adults look from four feet or less and perhaps sixty plus pounds.

Aft a bit I saw two illuminated plastic signs that said MEN and MEN'S SHOWERS, and I almost went in until I realized that those signs, which I'd been so conditioned to look for, were now the wrong ones for me. I walked back up, crossed through an intersecting corridor to the other side of the ship, and went into the women's john.

Although hardly a baby, I was so tiny and thin that I almost slipped into the toilet, and my legs barely touched the floor. Still, the relief was the same – or more so, since there seemed even more pressure now.

I had some problem with the latch to the shower – too high again – but managed to get in and close the door. A dressing room and two stalls. I looked around and found a tiny bit of somebody's leftover soap. Not much, but it would have to do. I undressed and, using the dressing room mirror, looked at my new self for the first time. How thin, frail, almost fragile I looked, with ribs you could count and a waist almost impossibly small. My reddish-brown complexion did a lot to hide the many bruises I had, but the aid was only cosmetic – they told me now constantly that they were there. The scrape from falling from the truck looked and felt nasty, but I'd had worse and it'd stopped bleeding.

It took several tries before I got a good hold on the water handles, but the shower felt good and the soap helped loosen the grime, wilderness pee, blood and whatever else had accumulated, and I felt my new body tingle with the warmth and the spray. I had no shampoo, but my long hair was already wet because I couldn't reach up far enough to adjust the shower nozzle and I rinsed it as best I could.

It wasn't until I was reluctantly through that I realized I had no towel, so I had to stand there in the dressing room letting myself drip-dry as good as possible, while wringing my hair out again and again. I hadn't had much hair for a number of years, and never as much as this, and I hadn't really realized just how saturated it could get. As I was doing all this I heard the distant sound of the ship's air horn, felt the slight engine tremble accelerate, and realized that we were under way.

I got back into my clothes, still slightly wet. They clung, but it wasn't so bad, and all but my hair was dry in minutes. The hair would be a major problem, I realized now. Before, I hadn't given much thought to women's long hair, but now I saw that its care and management was a major skill needing tools.

I remained there a moment, thinking of what I should do next. Get something to eat, certainly, and, if the ship's store was open, maybe pick up a couple of things I'd need. Then head for the lounge and try and get some sleep. I'd need all I could get for the days ahead.

The diagram said there was a cafeteria in the rear upper deck, so that was the first place to go. I went out on deck hoping that the wind would help blow-dry my hair, which currently seemed to resemble a tangled and sticky wet black mop.

It was raw-cold, suddenly, and extremely windy. The wetness of the marine climate was all over and went right through you. Away from the shelter of the mountains, the weather was rough even for July. Still, while I was aware that it was cold, made particularly so by the wind, it didn't really affect me as much, while before I'd had to have a sheepskin-lined parka if it dropped to fifty degrees. I recalled seeing pictures once of Eskimos running around in the snow barely clothed, and I recalled that some Oriental skin was colored such because it contained thin layers of insulating fat between the layers of skin. Either my greater tolerance was due to that, or my youth, or a combination of same.

My hair was damp – it would be for hours – but manageable, and I knew that a high priority would be a comb. Despite my near starvation level, I headed amidship for the ship's store, which wasn't going to be open very much longer. Once we stopped and loaded at Haines, it'd pack up for the night.

Amidst the piles of souvenirs were several things I needed, although I had some problems with the large number of people crowding into the very small space and the fact that I was so small myself. Still, a cheap shoulder purse with a ferryboat on it, a comb, box of tissues, toothbrush and toothpaste, and some spray-on salve for the skinned area were easy. They also had some kid's sized T-shirts, a head band that might keep my hair manageable and looked very Indian despite the fact that it was stamped 'Singapore' on the back, and I looked at jackets, too. Most were adult sizes at highly adult prices, but there were some kid's thin windbreakers – again with Alaska tourist symbols – and a blue one that fit. I also picked up a small sewing kit, although I hadn't much idea how to use it, in the hopes of patching the tear in my jeans. The place, after all, was a tourist trap, not a clothing store.

I approached the cash register shyly, because I *was* feeling very small and very nervous and insecure, but the gray-haired lady just smiled and took all the stuff and totalled it up.

Fifty-seven fifty. Gad. And the three hundred bucks or so had looked like a lot of money …

Still, I had to pay it, and, without saying a word, I gulped and frankly surprised the woman by peeling out the crumpled bills, which she took, handing me the change. I walked out, away from the people, and, heading again for the trusty john, I sorted out what I had, put the money and other stuff in the purse, then reluctantly removed my original warm, thick ski jacket and left it on a hook, putting on the thinner, cheaper windbreaker. Finally, I laboriously combed my hair, finding it a real and sometimes painful struggle.

While in the john others would enter, and several times I had an involuntary shock at seeing women enter. It would take some getting used to, both their presence and their casualness once inside. I felt like a peeping tom, but forced myself to ignore it as much as possible. I would have to get used to it – I was one of them, now.

Finally I completed what I could and headed back aft to where I longed to go from the start, the cafeteria. My head was barely level with the lowest shelf, but the sight and smell of food almost overwhelmed me. I felt my stomach almost tie itself in knots. What I wound up with was a cheeseburger – at almost three bucks! – and cocoa (mercifully sixty cents) and I found I couldn't really finish the burger. It wasn't my size; my stomach had gone without food for so long it could only barely recognize it any more. The cocoa, however, went down well and tasted fantastic. Now, relaxed for the first time, I felt totally exhausted and slightly dizzy. The clock, which my tired eyes could barely read, said it was almost midnight, which meant that I'd been without sleep, really, for almost forty-eight hours – and who knew how long before that? Still, I couldn't sleep quite yet. I walked forward on this deck, looking over the general passenger lounges, finding hordes of people sprawled out asleep on the floor, on the couches and in the chairs, some just sprawled, others with air mattresses and, in some cases, sleeping bags. There was an area, too, with a lot of gigantic lounge chairs, reclining types like on first-class long distance airlines, and a few were empty. I hadn't seen anyone who looked even vaguely familiar, and no one who looked in the least interested in me except for a few smiles and patronizing glances, and I decided that I was reasonably safe. It was warm here, and quiet. I climbed into one of the lounge chairs, so large it almost engulfed me, and curled up, intending just to rest for a couple of minutes.

The next thing I knew, the sun was shining brightly through the side windows and it was early afternoon of the next day.

I creaked a little from sleeping curled up in a tight little ball in the big chair, and my head was filled with cobwebs. I had the experience of waking out of the deepest sleep humanly possible and, for a while, it felt as if I hadn't slept at all. Some of the bruises were still very much there, but the skinned knee, at least, seemed to have scabbed. I made my way back to the cafeteria once more and found, again, that I felt only slightly hungry. How small *was* my stomach now, I wondered? I got a horribly overpriced bun and some coffee, despite the protestations of a busybody in line with me that I was too young for the stuff, and went over to a table. The sun had already vanished once again, hidden by clouds and monstrous mountain walls that gave the huge ship very little clearance on either side. The Inside Passage was extremely deep, but very narrow in many parts, and I was startled to see trees on the left side actually tremble as branches brushed against the deck railings.

The bun and coffee positively bloated me, and I discovered that my taste had certainly changed. Sweet stuff seemed to taste much sweeter, and satisfied tremendously, while the coffee, although waking me up, tasted terribly bitter and more acidic than I'd ever remembered. I thought of complaining, then realized that the coffee was probably perfectly all right – it was just that *I* had changed.

And not just taste, either. I'd noticed from the start that color perception was quite different. Oh, red was still red, green was green, and so forth, but they were *different* reds and greens. My big brown eyes definitely saw things a bit differently than my old, weak bluish-gray ones had. Smells, too, seemed sharper, richer, more distinct and in some cases overpowering, yet different, each and every one. A fact that only someone who'd lived in a different body could learn – people's senses were quite different from body to body.

After, I played with my hair, using a couple of purchased rubber bands to make a sort of pony tail and fitting the headband. I was determined to change my appearance as much as I could. It had occurred to me from the start that not only the government agents, or whoever they were, might be aboard but the aliens as well. The only people I feared meeting more than the government men were Dan or Charlie – or, perhaps, myself.

That idea unnerved me a bit. I had hardly been happy with that body, but it *was* me, had been me my whole life. To run into it with somebody else inside, somebody not quite human, would be more than I could have stood, I felt sure.

Still, here I was, heading south, out on my own, with a couple hundred bucks and not much else. Where was I going? What was I going to do?

The coffee was acting like a pep pill on me, the caffeine making me hyperactive, hypersensitive, and a little jittery. I decided to walk the length and breadth of the ship, to see if I could spot any potential threats, and perhaps, work off this nervous energy. I resolved to stick to cocoa after this, anyway.

The ship was crowded now from many stops, crowded not only by the tourist crowd but also by family groups and lots of young people in rugged clothes who'd been on Alaskan vacations or trips. I stopped by the store again and, despite the prices, blew five bucks on a small red cowgirl's hat with a tie string to keep it on in the wind. It made me look kind of cute, I decided, and it also further changed passing perceptions of me. It was the most I could do to change my looks without help and more resources, and I hoped it would be enough.

I ran into a bunch of kids my physical age and younger playing in the lounge – tag or hide-and-seek or something like that – and while I declined to play several crowded around, asking me if I were a *real* Indian and ooing and ahing when I told them I sure was. I got away from them fairly quickly, but I felt reasonably satisfied. I'd run into a group of my apparent peers and they hadn't noticed anything more unusual about me than my fine, dark Indian features.

Still, it brought me back to the question that lurked about me now, one that I couldn't avoid for very long. What was I going to do now? This ship, in three more days, would put me into Seattle, but then I'd be on my own. Being Indian I could accept. If I made my way back East it'd be an asset instead of the handicap it was west of the Mississippi. Being female, too, I could accept, although it would take a lot more adjusting to. But there was no way around the one central thing that I was that stood in the way of any job, any way to a new life at all. I was at most thirteen years old, for God's sake! Too young for a social security card, driver's license, *any* of the things needed to turn labor into money. Child labor laws stood in the way of any gainful employment, and I wasn't even legally responsible for anything. The world was quite certainly effectively organized to deny any of the basics of life to a thirty-five-year-old pre-teenager.

An hour or so wandering with such gloomy thoughts brought me to an outside stairway on the upper stern deck that I hadn't noticed before. I climbed it, curious, and reached the top deck of the ship, an area which looked flat and barren for a moment, dominated as it was by the giant dark blue smokestacks and mast. But – no, not empty of interest after all, I saw. There *was* an area behind the stacks with people, open on this side but closed on the other three sides and with a roof. The sign said it was the Solarium – which I discovered, was filled with plastic-slatted chaise lounges and camping gear and was heated, sort of, by strong, bare coils attached to its roof.

I ran to it and into it, perhaps a bit too exuberantly, and immediately tripped over somebody's backpack, which in turn sent me sprawling right into someone.

'I – I'm sorry,' I mumbled, then looked up.

It was a young woman's face, perhaps eighteen or so, that I saw smiling sweetly at me. She was dressed in a heavy red flannel shirt with red stocking cap, tough-looking jeans and hiking boots, yet she was without a doubt the most beautiful woman I had ever seen in my entire life. Her reddish-blond hair hadn't a hint of dye, her bright, deep blue eyes sparkled with life and inner beauty, and her face, bereft of makeup, was both tremendously sexy and yet somehow angelic. *Angelic.* The word might have been created for her.

'Well, young lady, you were really in a hurry to go nowhere, weren't you?' she said laughingly, her voice soft and musical. 'You're not hurt, are you?'

I picked myself up and sat on the cold deck, arms around my knees. 'It's kinda wet,' was all I could manage, unable to take my eyes off her.

She picked one of the chaises and sat down, looking at me. 'You're an Indian, aren't you? What tribe?' She was being friendly with just a hint of patronizing that was inevitable when talking to someone of my age.

I nodded. 'I'm a Tlingit,' I told her, echoing Dan's lie. For all I knew it could be the truth.

'A Tlingit! Then you come from around here.'

I nodded, drawing a little more on Dan's story. 'Admiralty Island,' I told her.

'Then you'll be getting off soon,' she responded, gesturing slightly to her right. 'There's Admiralty over there.'

'No,' I told her. 'I'm going all the way to Seattle.'

'Seattle!' Her patronizing tone was growing and getting a little hard to take, but I had to grin and bear it. Like it or not, I'd better get used to this sort of thing. 'What takes you there?'

I considered my answer carefully. Until this moment I hadn't really considered a cover story, and my creativity was being sorely tested. Still, I had to gamble sometime on somebody else – and she seemed as good as any and less threatening than most.

'They were gonna put me in an orphanage,' I told her as sincerely as I could. 'Daddy was killed in a boat accident and Mommy's been – gone – for some time. Do you know what kinda orphanages they got for Indians? Horrible, drafty places out in the middle of nowhere run by a bunch of white bureaucrats – no offense – who are just there for the fat paychecks. A *prison's* better than those places.'

She looked suitably concerned. Blonde and blue-eyed young women generally felt a lot of social concern at this stage in their lives. I'd taught enough of them to know that it wasn't much of a gamble to play on her inevitable social conscience.

'Oh, come on. I've been to a few orphanages in my time and they aren't that dreadful at all.' She pronounced 'been' as 'bean' and I marked her as a Canadian.

Looking as sadly indignant as I could, I responded, '*White* orphanages. Whites are people. Indians are wards of the state. I'm thirteen now, but as far as the government's concerned all Indians are thirteen forever.' Now the *coup de grace*. 'Aw, what's the use? You couldn't understand anyway.'

It hit home, I could see that. Thanking my entire social science and teaching background fervently, I waited for her move.

Her face was serious now, and she looked at me thoughtfully. 'So you're running away,' she almost whispered. 'How'd you get this far?'

I told her some of the story, altered to make it believable. I said I'd stowed away on a fishing boat north and gotten stuck in Skagway. Realizing I was in a deadend trap, I'd then used the truck trailer gambit to stow away again coming south, this time as far as possible. I told her, too, that the Bureau of Indian Affairs men were looking for me, which is why I had to be careful. I even showed her my torn jeans and skinned knee. The hardest part wasn't the lie, which was less a lie than the truth would have seemed, but keeping to contractions and a slightly more childish vocabulary. I still came out sounding awfully bright for my age, but that was O.K.

The truth was, I really didn't know why I was telling her all this in the first place, nor had I any clear idea of what I could gain by all this. Mostly it was the insecurity, the terrible loneliness of my condition, and my sense of helplessness about it that craved some company, some companionship, some concern. I needed somebody now, even for a little while, more than I had ever needed anybody in my whole life.

'You aren't gonna turn me in, are you?' I asked warily.

She was genuinely touched and concerned, and it showed. 'Come,' she said. 'Sit by me,' and I did. She lifted me into her lap and put her arms around me. It felt warm and secure and good. I was so overcome I felt myself starting to cry, and, try though I might, I couldn't really stop it. No gold, no wondrous prize of any kind, could replace that hug. It was a need beyond price.

After a few moments just lying there, weeping slightly, cradled in her arms, I looked up at her, bleary-eyed, and saw that she had tears in her own blue eyes.

'No,' she whispered kindly, hugging me tighter, 'I won't give you away. But – where will you go? What will you do?'

'I'll go somewhere where they won't send me back,' I told her. 'Get in a city, maybe do a little begging. I'll get by.'

She sighed. 'Well, I'll do what I can as far as I can,' she told me. She let go and reached down into her bag, coming up with some tissues and a hair-brush. 'Let's start by untangling your pretty hair.'

She brushed and combed and took out the tangles, and did the sort of things I wanted to do but hadn't known how.

'I'm Dorian Tomlinson,' she told me as she brushed and combed. 'My friends call me Dory. What's *your* name?'

I hadn't thought of a name yet, but one seemed obvious. Fortunately my male name had a feminine equivalent, as most did. 'I'm Vicki,' I replied. 'Just Vicki – not Victoria or anything like that.'

'Vicki what?'

I could hardly use Gonser, and it seemed better for the moment to just cop out. 'You'd never pronounce it,' I told her. 'Let's just keep it on a first-name basis like real friends, O.K.?'

She laughed softly, 'O.K., friend.' She turned me around, straightening my crumpled clothes. 'Well, you don't look so bad now you've been groomed. Now let's go downstairs to the ladies' room and I'll see what I can do about patching your pants.'

My little sewing kit in expert hands made short work of the rip, and we adjourned to the cafeteria. She'd spotted the money when I'd reached in for the kit and I'd had to think fast and tell her it was my father's secret savings jar money. As I sipped cocoa and she tea I managed to turn the conversation away from me and towards her.

She was a college student, had just turned twenty, and she'd accepted an invitation by a classmate – a boyfriend – to go hiking and camping up in Glacier Park. She wasn't too clear on why they had a big fight, but I guessed it was more than just sex since she had to know he'd have some of that on his mind all out there in the wild, but, anyway, they'd fought and she'd stalked out and caught the next plane back to Juneau and caught the first ferry through. As a walk-on she had no chance at a stateroom and the solarium seemed to be the most private place other than a stateroom on the ship. She wanted to be alone, to think things out, she said.

For some reason I felt a consuming jealousy for that nameless young man. I couldn't really explain my emotional reaction, but the longer I was with Dory the more she seemed to loom ever larger before me, like some sort of goddess I was joyful in worshipping. It was much later before I realized that I was develping a mad, passionate crush on her, one caused by her beauty and compassion, my need for a friend, my frustrated (male) previous life, and, probably, the glands of the near-woman I now was.

And I'd eaten a whole hamburger just because she'd asked me to.

As we walked around the ship afterwards, poking into things and looking through the little shop, this feeling grew ever stronger within me. Her merest gesture, word, glance, was heaven to me.

I was totally, madly, completely in love with Dorian Tomlinson.

We walked and talked for most of the afternoon, and generally enjoyed each other's company. I was too busy acting like a lovesick schoolgirl to have to pretend to anything, and later on, when the fatigue wouldn't go away, I went sound asleep in her arms, cradled against her warm, soft breasts.

'We'll be in to Prince Rupert before noon,' Dory told me gravely. The comment sobered me, bringing me down from my secure high of the past day and a half. Dory was going home to Calgary, a long train trip from Prince Rupert but definitely out of my way.

'What happens then?' I asked apprehensively.

She sighed. 'Well, I can't very well desert you here, and yet I have a train to catch.'

'Let me come with you, then,' I pleaded. 'I don't eat much, and I could probably smuggle myself aboard any old train or something.'

She laughed. 'I don't think we're that hard up. But, yes, you're right. The only thing I can do now is take you. I have a small efficiency apartment just off campus you could stay at, at least for a while. Think you can talk your way past customs?'

'Sure,' I told her. 'Nothing to it. An Indian kid in Prince Rupert?' I was anxious, even eager for this. It seemed the way out of all my problems, even if it did shift the burden onto someone else. In my situation, I *had* to be dependent on someone, anyway, at least until I grew 'old' enough to make my own way. And I certainly didn't want to leave Dory – anyplace she was was where I wanted to be. It looked like things were really working themselves out, and I wandered forward in the lounge, feeling content, wondering idly what the small crowd in front was watching. Curious, both Dory and I approached, and I suddenly froze solid, gripping Dory's hand as tightly as I could.

The crowd was watching a man do card tricks. He was quite good at it, and seemed to be having a good time. He was a medium-sized, ordinary-built man, but he'd stand out in any crowd. He was dressed in an old-fashioned black suit and string tie, wore a bowler hat, and had a huge, black handlebar moustache.

Although I'd only seen him briefly and at some distance, he was impossible to forget – although the last time he'd been gripping a semiautomatic rifle and peering off a cliff on a trail above Skagway.

Dory caught my fright and looked down. 'What's the matter?'

'That magician,' I whispered nervously. 'I don't know what's with the funny get-up but he was with the men looking for me.'

She frowned and looked at me like I was crazy, but shrugged and turned. 'Let's just go back to the lounge and sit for a while, then, O.K.?'

She had no argument from me. We started to walk casually back, away from the strange man's performance. I was beginning to wonder about my original assessment of the pursuers as FBI or somesuch, though. Not only did the man dress outlandishly, but the patter I heard with his card tricks was in an unmistakable Irish accent.

What the hell *was* going on here, anyway?

I wondered when he'd gotten on. I'd pretty well cruised the ship since Skagway time and time again and I'd watched the passengers very carefully. Nobody looking like that had been anywhere around, I was sure of it. If he'd been on from the start, he'd kept himself locked in a stateroom – but, if so, why come out so publicly now? The only possible answers weren't pleasant. I *knew* that he was a pursuer – and that implied that, if he were aboard, so were those he was chasing. He and his people had probably spent some time surveying the passengers even more closely than I had, but hadn't had any luck so far. Although their quarry could be literally anybody, they seemed at least reasonably satisfied that the aliens or whatever they were were still aboard, and they hadn't been able to smoke them out. Moustache, then, would have kept out of sight up to now because he was easy to spot – but now we were only hours from Prince Rupert and through road, rail, and bus connections. Now Moustache would have to make his move, publicly reveal himself, try and get his quarry to panic, make a mistake.

I looked around at all the big people standing around the lounge area with renewed suspicion. Two men in particular caught my attention, one lounging on each side of the doorways going aft, looking relaxed but eyeing everybody who passed with more than idle curiosity. Moustache's pals, I knew instinctively. The ones who wanted to see who turned and ran when they spotted their easily recognizable boss.

There seemed little choice but to try and ignore them and walk right by. After all, they'd probably been on since the start and hadn't picked me up yet. I just held onto Dory's hand and kept going. They'd never catch these aliens like that – but I was damned resolved that they wouldn't catch me, not now, not when I was so close.

Now we were past them and walking down the corridor, and I turned my head slightly and glanced back. One of the men was slowly and casually walking behind us, then stopped, took out a cigarette, and lit it as we continued walking.

There was a stairway ahead, just before the lounge chair section. 'Let's go down a deck,' I suggested nervously, 'and use the ladies' room.'

Dory sighed, not having seen what I'd seen and having a sense only that I was paranoid. Oh, Dory, if you only knew the truth!

There were footsteps on the stairs behind us and I turned again, seeing with some relief a middle-aged couple, obviously tourists, instead of Moustache and his boys. We reached the bottom of the stairs and continued on when suddenly I heard a shout and we both turned.

How he'd gotten ahead of us I don't know, but it was Moustache, who'd been flattened against the wall near the stairs. Now he whirled and grabbed at the middle-aged man, who snarled, then yelled, *'Gfrhjty tig smurf!'*

Dory said, 'What?' but I dragged her forward. 'Come on!' I implored. 'For God's sake get into the john!'

I opened the door and practically dragged her in, closing it behind us. The six-stall john was apparently unoccupied.

'Wha – what's going on?' Dory gasped, but before I could answer the door opened again and the middle-aged woman burst in, slamming it behind her. She had a wild look in her eyes and we both just stared at her in mixed apprehension and fear.

The woman reached into her purse and pulled out a shiny-looking .38 pistol. 'Just relax,' she snapped, gasping for breath. 'Oh, that bastard, that devil!' she added, talking now to herself rather than us.

I let go of Dory, who was standing there petrified and speechless. 'You may as well just give yourself up,' I told the woman with the gun. 'Moustache's men will be here any second and you're trapped in here.'

The woman grinned evilly. 'Not necessarily,' she responded, and I knew exactly where her thinking lay.

'We won't do you any good,' I pointed out. 'They saw us come in here.'

It was too much for Dory. 'Vicki – who *are* these people?' she asked, amazed and frightened.

The 'woman' considered what I said. I could almost see the wheels turning in her stolen brain. Idly I wondered if this were Charlie's or Dan's. She looked at me with a nasty expression on her face. 'We should have finished you back there on the trail. Why the hell did you have to follow us?'

'You stole what was rightfully mine,' I came back. 'What the hell did you expect me to do?'

Dory was confused but she'd overcome her initial fright. She knew that, somehow, Moustache and his men were some sort of cops and that this woman was a fugitive, and that we were now hostages. Initial fear was replaced in her by a sense of indignation, even anger.

'Put that gun away!' she told the woman. 'You're not going to shoot us in here. It'd bring everybody running.'

'Dory! No!' I almost shouted. 'That's just what she wants! Believe me!'

The woman with the pistol grinned, knowing the truth of what I said. Still, she relaxed rather than tensed and I knew that she was quickly writing the script. 'It's the only chance I got,' she said, almost apologetically. The pistol came back up, trained on me.

'*No!*' Dory screamed, and launched herself at the woman, hitting her and knocking her back against the door. I rushed forward, grabbing at Dory to pull her away.

Again there was that terrible explosion in my head and the total numbness of body, the feeling of electrocution, almost combined with something pulling, on me ...

And I lapsed into shock and unconsciousness.

CHAPTER FOUR

I awoke, this time, in a bed. The terrible headache and numbness was there as before, but it seemed less severe this time. Maybe I was just getting used to it, but maybe, too, it became easier the more times you did it. The aliens or whatever they were seemed to have no blackout at all.

I just relaxed, groaned slightly, and let it pass. A soft bed, at least, was a lot easier to take than hard rocks and bruises. Still, my first thought was, *it's happened again. God in Heaven, they got me again!* But who was I? Three of us were involved this time. I could easily have stirred, tried to see, but I found myself unable to do it. It wasn't the shock, I just couldn't make myself do it. It wouldn't matter to the alien, of course. She was counting on the rescuers coming in, finding three unconscious bodies, and making the switch in the confusion. I wondered if the creature had.

It struck me that, for such super-powerful beings, they were awfully ordinary crooks. They got neatly cornered – part of their ego, I suppose, catching up to them – but when they pulled guns they were no Buck Rogers ray guns, just standard old .38s.

The door opened and Moustache looked in. I grew apprehensive suddenly, not knowing where I stood with him – or who or what he was. Even if he were a government man, he'd touched that other alien on the stairs. Who was he now, I wondered, and in whose hands had I fallen? We. Poor Dory, I thought. What a monster I was to get her involved in all this.

Moustache smiled and fully entered the cabin. 'Ah, I see that you're awake once more,' he said in a friendly tone that retained the Irish accent if not quite so pronounced. He *sounded* like the same man I'd seen doing card tricks in the lounge.

He sat on the edge of the nightstand and looked down at me. 'First,' he continued, 'let me introduce myself. I'm Harold G. Parch, I'm a federal officer, and I know for a fact that you're in the wrong body. That make things easier?'

I nodded hesitantly but said nothing. I'd met 'federal officers' before.

'First of all,' he went on, 'let me assure you that we have all three of them. Two, unfortunately, are quite dead, but we have a third in better condition, strictly controlled and out of this world on some drugs we have found effective with them. What I need to know from you first is who exactly *you* are.'

I sighed. There was no use in concealing anything no matter who he really was. 'Victor Gonser,' I responded, my voice sounding odd to my ears, lower in pitch than I'd gotten used to. I started to have a real bad feeling about all this.

He nodded. 'They got you somewhere on the trail, then. Swapped you with the Indian girl. That figures, although we weren't really sure. We found several bodies along the way and, while we knew that one of you had to be the Indian we really didn't know which.'

'Bodies?' I managed weakly.

He nodded. 'I'm afraid so. They rarely slip up, you know.' He took a small spiral notebook from his back pocket and flipped through it. 'Yes, I'm afraid so. They usually like to make it look like a heart attack – hypodermic full of air into the bloodstream – but they were harried and rushed. They blew your brains out with the pistol, I regret to say.'

I seemed to sink deeper into the bed. Somehow, somewhere in the back of my mind, I harbored the idea that, sometime, I might get back. Now that door was forever closed. Victor Gonser was dead, murdered on the trail in the wilds of Alaska. The final door was shut – there was no going back, ever.

'I'm afraid we played a bit unfairly with you,' Parch continued. 'We missed you on the trail, but spotted you a couple of times as you came down. At first we thought you were one of them, but you just didn't act like it, and so we simply kept an eye on you. When you passed that park ranger and didn't body-swap we knew we were dealing with a human being, and we got curious. If you could get on the ferry, which we were prepared to let you do, we hoped that you would spook the dybbuks – what we call them – who thought they'd finished you off. And we were right, although it was a close call. I finally had to make an appearance in full regalia to unnerve them a bit.'

'You unnerved me, too,' I noted.

He nodded. 'I had no idea if you knew what I looked like, but it worked out well. You stopped and turned, and they must have felt surrounded. They followed you with the intention of either killing you as they thought they had done or finding out if you were a part of some trap they should know about. We spotted them easy then, since the one was still too new to speak anything except that impossible jabber of theirs.'

'I – I saw you leap out and grab the man,' I said. 'How did you get ahead of us? And why couldn't he change with you?'

Parch smiled. 'As to the first, why, 'twas a simple matter. I simply watched you all go, then ran forward, down one flight, with the idea of approaching from the other side. My boys had everybody "made" by then. As for the second, well, that's why they are so damned scared of me that they have little shit fits at the sight of me. You see, I'm immune. Scares the hell out of 'em – somebody they can't switch with. I suppose I'm the boogeyman in spades to them, the one who hunts them yet can't be disembodied, as it were.'

I envied him that distinction, and that immunity. 'But why didn't you tell me?' I asked. 'At least I wouldn't have gotten Dory sucked in.'

He didn't reply immediately, and exhaled audibly. Finally he said, 'We would have interceded if you attempted to leave the ship. But you must understand the situation. First, we didn't know who you were – only that you were not one of them. We didn't know who *she* was, either. Remember, these people can be anybody. Whatever, it's twenty-twenty hindsight right now.'

I had gotten the courage, finally. I sat up and turned, sitting on the side of the bed. The mirror was directly across from me and it told the story.

'Oh, my god. Does Dory know?'

He shook his head negatively. 'She hadn't awakened as yet when I last checked. One of my people is looking in on her and they'll call when she comes around.'

I just stared blankly into that mirror for a few moments, and watched Dorian Tomlinson stare back at me. I felt unclean, somehow, and a little sick. Finally I asked, 'Who – which is Dory now?'

'The Indian girl,' he responded. That made me feel a little better – the thought of Dory trapped in the body of that old lady was more than I could have borne. My conscience was killing me as it was.

'Apparently what the dybbuk did was swap with Dory, then you, then back to the old woman again. They don't go into shock or anything when they switch – it's easier than changing hats to 'em. We were lined up outside and burst in the moment we heard the commotion, only to find all three of you apparently out on the floor. Fortunately I was the one closest to the old lady, and she suddenly got very awake and tried the swap with me. We plugged her on the spot. Messy.'

There was a light tap on the door. Parch opened it and I heard a man's voice say, 'She's coming around.' The agent just nodded and turned back to me.

'I think I'm going to have a very difficult job right now,' he told me. 'I don't want it, but it has to be done and I'm the boss. I'd like you to come along if you feel up to it.'

'Of course,' I responded, and followed him. I felt a little dizzy and unbalanced, but that was to be expected.

Of course, Dory would be a much tougher job than me. I, after all, had been there before and knew what was going on. And, I thought glumly, my old body hadn't been a lot to lose when you came down to it. Dory had lost far, far more.

We approached the next cabin door and Parch turned to me and whispered, 'I think it'd be best if you stayed just outside here until I prepare the way. Listen in if you want.'

I nodded understandingly. She was going to have enough shocks without staring herself in the face the moment she woke up. A man stationed at the door opened it for him and closed it behind, leaving it slightly ajar. I moved nervously to it, slightly irritated at the guard's leering glance in my direction.

Parch greeted her in the same soft, friendly fashion he had me, and introduced himself. I heard a thin, weak voice ask what had happened to her, what all this was about.

Parch cleared his throat. 'Something impossible is what happened and what all this is about,' he began a little nervously. I didn't envy him this job. 'Ms. Tomlinson, we are at war, in a way. A funny war, although not comical. Our enemies are from a place we don't know and their weapon is a terrible and formidable, if impossible one. But it is not, alas, impossible. This – enemy – has the power to change minds with you. Yes, now I know what you're thinking, and that's what our own reaction was the first time. We don't know how long it's been going on, either, since they normally kill those with whom they swap. A few times they slipped up, and that's what finally made us aware of their presence. We still don't know how many people just plain killed themselves or are locked up in crazy wards who may also be their victims. Your friend was such a victim – and now, so are you.'

I heard her gasp.

'That's right – sit up,' he invited soothingly. 'Face the mirror and the truth and the worst will be over.'

I heard movement and a sharp little cry, then silence. Finally I heard her say, in hushed and unbelieving tones, 'It – it's not possible. I'm mad. This can't have happened, can't be happening!'

And then she broke into tears and it was a long time before they subsided. I heard Parch pulling tissues and a nose blow, then silence for a moment. She was a brave woman, I told myself. She'd launched herself at that – thing – to save me. She would accept it.

Finally I heard her ask, 'My own – body. What's become of it?'

Parch explained the three-way switch and the outcome, ending with, 'So, Vic – Vicki has your body now, and you have hers.'

'Where is she?' Dory pressed. 'Can I – see her?'

I sighed, swallowed hard, and stepped slowly into the room.

'Oh, Dory – I – I'm so *sorry*,' I sobbed, fighting back tears. She just stared at me with those huge brown Indian eyes for a while, then sighed and shook her head unbelievingly. Finally she took a couple of deep breaths, swallowed hard, and said, firmly, 'Well, it's done. I can't believe it but I've got to accept it.'

'You can see why I couldn't tell you,' I tried lamely. 'You would have said I was crazy.'

Suddenly she got up and ran to me, put her arms around me, and held on tight, sobbing again. I pulled her gently into me and started crying, too. Finally she was all cried out, although I wasn't, and let go, stepping back and grabbing a tissue, wiping her eyes and blowing her nose. 'You – you weren't originally that Indian girl, were you?' She said more than asked it.

I shook my head. 'No. But I'd accepted having to live my life in that body,' I imagined, trying to get hold of myself. 'I'm sorry, Dory. I had no idea they were still around. Damn! It was all going to work out, too!'

She tried a wan smile. 'Who were you – originally? I think I have the right to know that.'

'You have the right to know anything,' I told her sincerely. 'I was Victor Leigh Gonser, Ph.D., Associate Professor of Political Science at Johns Hopkins University.'

I saw Parch chuckle at that last. Dory gasped slightly. 'You – were a *man?*'

I nodded. 'More or less. A bald and ugly little nebbish, really.' This started her laughing hysterically, and we let it run its course.

Finally she calmed down and managed, 'I don't believe this. It can't be real.' She turned back to me. 'I used one of your books – last semester.' She sat back down on the bed, still shaking her head. Finally she turned to Parch. 'What happens – now? To us, I mean?'

Parch shrugged. 'Not my department. I have to get our live friend and his two dead companions out of here, of course. That's pretty tricky because we're in Canadian waters, but we'll manage. You have the run of the ship – enjoy. But don't get off at Prince Rupert. In a couple of hours I'll have my instructions.' He softened a bit, realizing how harsh he was sounding. 'Look, it'll be all right. We won't abandon you or lock you away or anything. It's just that – well, there are things I can't discuss right now until I get word from my own people. As soon as I know, I'll tell you – O.K.?'

Dory frowned. 'I'm not sure I like being the property of the U.S. government,' she said with a trace of annoyance. 'I'm not even a citizen.'

'Right now you are both non-persons,' he pointed out. 'You, Ms Tomlinson, can hardly go home and pick up where you left off. You're a thirteen-year-old Indian. And you, Gonser – what'll you do? You can *be* her, body or not, but you can't just go off and be somebody else, either, because the person you appear to be legally exists. Please – just trust me for a few hours. I'm not the enemy.'

I looked at Dory and she at me and we gave almost simultaneous sighs and shrugs. Parch was right – we were stuck, at least temporarily.

'All right – we'll play it your way for now,' Dory said. 'I assume, though, that your government is now picking up the tab?'

He grinned. 'Expense account. You're welcome to these two cabins, of course, and if you need any money just ask one of the boys.'

There was a knock at the door. He opened it, said a few words, then turned back to us. 'We're coming in to Prince Rupert,' he told us. 'I'm going to be busy for a while. Stay here or walk around all you want. We'll talk when I'm through.' And, with that, he was gone. For the first time since the switch we were alone.

Dory got off the bed and stood facing me. She turned up her nose a little and looked around. 'Everything's so much higher all of a sudden.'

I nodded. 'I know what you mean. Oh, hell, Dory, I feel so guilty about all this. I've mucked up your life like they mucked up mine.'

She smiled up at me. 'Look, that's going to get us nowhere. We're stuck and that's that. I thought about it just now in the way Parch said – it's a war. That old woman was going to shoot you, maybe both of us. In a way we were lucky, I guess. Maybe one day they can put things back again – at least for me. Until then let's accept the fact that we're innocent victims and go on from there.' She paused a moment, looking at me with a somewhat critical eye. 'In the meantime, maybe I can make a real woman out of you.'

I laughed in spite of myself. 'What on earth do you mean?'

'The way you're standing. The way you walk. I put a lot of work into building that body and I'm going to see that it's taken care of and treated right while I'm not in it. In the meantime, let's go get something to eat.'

I just stared at her, open-mouthed. She was some kind of woman, I decided anew. I envied her confidence and resilience. She opened the door and saw the guard standing there. 'Hey! We're going to eat,' she told him. 'Parch said to tap you for the money.'

The man stared a little, a bit put off by this tiny girl giving him orders, but he took out his wallet and gave her a bill. She looked at it, then said, 'Uh uh. More. None of that cafeteria crap. We're going to the main dining room.'

We talked mostly about inconsequential things through the meal, a very good one in the big, fancy dining room with the very artsy glass seal sculpture in the middle. I was impressed by the quality of the food, compared to the cafeteria, and the fact that prices were actually lower. I was also interested in the fact that I was hungrier than I'd been in some time and ate far more than I had as the little girl. Dory showed that the birdlike appetite I'd experienced was all that that body required.

She was fascinated with the things I had been – the differences in color perception, all the senses, really. As for me, I found Dory's eyes a bit closer to my original ones in color perception – we both had blue eyes, not brown – but I found she was slightly nearsighted, and my sense of smell was a degree different from either my former male self or the Indian girl's. The world was a subtly different place depending on the body you wore, that was for sure.

Dory was making a try on some chocolate ice cream – for some reason, whether weight or complexion or something else, she hadn't had any for a very long time – and I was lingering over a coffee that no longer tasted foul and bitter when Parch joined us. We were already out of Prince Rupert and still headed south. The ship had to get in and out fast, it seemed, because Prince Rupert's single ferry dock was needed for the CN overnighter to Vancouver Island. We sat on the dining room side facing the dock, and had noticed a couple of ambulances pull up and some stretchers being wheeled off, and knew that Parch had done his job efficiently.

He nodded and sat down with us, looking far more relaxed. I took a moment to study his face and decided that there was something very slightly wrong about it, although I couldn't put my finger on it.

'I radioed my field office in Seattle,' he began, ordering just coffee. 'The IMC wants you, it seems, as I figured. There are very few survivors and we'd like to examine and interrogate you as to the – ah – experience.'

'IMC?' I prompted.

He nodded. 'You'll find out. We have a pretty big operation going, you must realize. We've been at this over six years and it's not an easy job.'

'Six years,' Dory put in. 'That's a long time to hide something like this.'

Parch chuckled. 'You have a childish faith in democratic institutions.'

'I'll concede that,' I agreed, 'but it still seems hard to conceal. There's the press, political leaks, you name it.'

'I'd have expected more cynicism from a political scientist,' the government agent laughed. 'Yes, you're right – covering up is a lot of the work. But, you see, this is one area where everybody in the know is in agreement. If this came out, and was believed, the panic and paranoia would be beyond belief. Be frank – knowing what you know, could you ever trust a crowd of strangers again? When your best friend might not be? See what I mean? It can give you nightmares – and on a national, even global scale ... Well, you see how it is.'

'You're pretty free talking about it in a public dining room in normal tones,' Dory pointed out.

He shrugged. 'Who would believe it in this context? Right now the ship's abuzz with the three kidnappers federal agents nabbed and that's excitement enough for them.'

'But who – or what – are they?' I asked him. 'And what's their game? They seem awfully lame to be such a huge menace, what with little old ladies and 38s.'

'They're a bundle of contradictions, all right,' Parch agreed. 'And there's no easy answer to any of the questions. We've captured a very few, mostly by sheer luck, over the years, and while they haven't been very helpful we know that one group calls itself the Urulu. We don't know where they're from or what they're like naturally, but they definitely aren't from anyplace any of us have ever visited.'

'One group?' I put in, getting a sinking feeling.

He nodded. 'There's more than one, that's for sure, and they don't like each other much. Or so the Urulu maintain, but who knows what we can trust? We can knock 'em out, but they don't respond to much of anything in the way of truth serums or any other stock information techniques. Their story is that they're the good guys and they're here to root out the bad guys. You will understand why we take this with a grain of salt.'

We both nodded and Dory articulated the thought. 'The good guys indiscriminately kill us and pull guns on us. All things considered, how bad can the bad guys be?'

'That's about it,' Parch agreed. 'And, of course, we have nothing but their word that there's another group. We've certainly not seen any. Either they're more efficient than the Urulu or, more likely, they're part of a convenient cover story and don't really exist.'

There seemed little to add to that, so I changed the subject. 'You're not an American,' I noted. 'Not originally.'

'Not native born, no,' he replied. 'Originally I was from Belfast. When I was a wee lad the IRA blew up my parents for the crime of being Presbyterian and leading a peace march. To save me from the orphanage some relatives in Philadelphia offered to take me in and I finished growing up there. But – enough of me. My sort of job may seem very glamorous and dangerous, but it's rather boring, really. A year of plodding routine for one brief moment of action.'

'What of us, then?' Dory asked. 'I mean – after this exam. What kind of lives can we expect from now on?'

He sighed. 'Look, I won't kid you. After the examination, though, which won't last all that long, you can remain and work with us on this problem or we'll set you up somewhere. New identities, complete bios and backgrounds. You can walk out and start new lives on your own that way, or keep within the security of IMC and find a place with us. The choice *will* be yours.'

I considered what he said. My thoughts were emotional and confused, but I knew what my decision should be. I had fulfilled a fantasy of sorts, even though it wasn't quite the one I'd imagined. I was young, attractive, definitely the socially accepted type. I'd been oblivious to things when Dory was Dory, but I was already aware of being constantly eyed by men of all ages. I had a free, new start, and it had to be better than my miserable loneliness of so many years. Hell, I'd have been satisfied as the little Indian, really, as long as I didn't have to worry where I was sleeping. So what if I were female? Being male hadn't brought me much; this just *had* to be better. But there was one real hitch in this bright new future.

It was *Dory's* body I wore, and she definitely wanted it back – and I would have to give it back if it were possible. Hell, I was responsible for involving her in this. I couldn't just walk out now, particularly since Dory was such a fantastic person. I still loved her, perhaps more now than before, because of the respect she'd earned by her reaction to all this. The plain truth was that I was less in control of my destiny than I had ever been. The decisions were hers to make, not mine. I was an interloper, a usurper, however involuntary, and my life and future were in her hands.

'Actually,' Parch went on, 'I hope you'll join us. Both of you have very sharp, open minds; that's rare in this day and time. We need people like you.'

We spent the rest of the day just relaxing, doing very little and talking less. We were in a waiting phase, really, a holding pattern. Neither of us were yet really free.

We got Dory's things from the solarium and she went through them, taking what was worth saving. Parch had promised us some time in Seattle to shop for what we'd need, so it wasn't much. There were cosmetics, though, and I got something of a short course on their uses and application, and also some criticism on general mannerisms. 'No, don't walk like that – more like *this*.' Dory had begun her lessons in 'making a woman' out of me and I was an eager student. No matter what, I expected to be one for the rest of my life.

A car met us at the dock after we got into Seattle and Parch took us to a a fancy downtown hotel and checked us in. He also gave us, to our surprise, a thousand dollars in blank travelers' checks.

'Go out on the town,' he told us. 'Buy yourselves new wardrobes, all the essentials.'

Dory looked at him playfully. 'Aren't you afraid we'll just up and leave?'

He didn't seem disturbed by the idea. 'You could, of course. But that money wouldn't last long, and what would it get you? Just take care and be here in the morning – I'll have a wake-up call put in.'

He left us then, but both of us knew that he would take no such chances. We might never see them, but we'd never be out of sight of one or more of his operatives.

Dory looked around the luxurious room. 'Wow! They sure do it up right when it's the taxpayer's money.' She jumped on one of the twin queen-sized beds and seemed almost lost in it. She bounced up and down a few times on it, looking and sounding exactly like a thirteen-year-old kid. She seemed to realize this, and rolled over on her stomach, propping her head on her hands and looking very, very cute.

'Look, if I gotta be thirteen again I may as well enjoy it,' she said lightly. 'There's some advantages to it. You can act like a kid with nobody looking twice because you *are* a kid.'

I chuckled at this and sat down, signing the top line on the travelers' checks. There were a *lot* to sign, and Parch had told me to go ahead and sign them 'Dorian Tomlinson,' using Dory's driver's license as back-up. I felt a little odd about it, but it was the best way to handle it, I knew.

Finally I was finished, and turned to Dory, who was fooling with the television. 'Enough of that,' I told her. 'Let's go spend this money.'

She giggled, turned off the set, and bounded up, ready to go.

Dory was relatively easy to do, since a kid looks like a kid in practically everything that fits, and she opted for the continued informal look of jeans and T-shirts, buying several pairs in different colors, plus some sandals and tennis shoes. She also made one change in her looks, getting her hair cut to a shorter Indian-style with bangs. Having had to manage that ton of black hair I could hardly blame her, although if anything she looked more Indian than ever now.

She spent a lot of time on me, though. I'd never had to shop for women's clothing, let alone wear any, and bowed completely to her advice. It was clear that she still considered this body of mine her own, and she was redesigning it from an unusual vantage point.

By the time I was through I looked like a fashion model. Dorian was, as I'd mentioned, a beautiful woman, and Dory bought, fitted, and matched clothing, cosmetics (about which I had a lot to learn), and the like until I hardly recognized myself. Every time I looked at myself in the mirror it was like looking at somebody else, gorgeous, desirable, stunning. The figure in the glass was everything I'd ever dreamed about in a woman, not only my but many men's fantasy woman come to life. The only trouble was, it wasn't my fantasy I was seeing, it was *me*. *I* was the girl of my dreams, not her lover.

Years ago I'd discovered that people judged you by how you looked, dressed, acted, with no regard for the person inside, the important part of a human being. Women, even beautiful, desirable women, would find the inner me, would come to me with their problems and confidences, make friends with me. But they'd always go to bed with Handsome Harry down the hall, even though his insides were hollow. Everybody does it, even when they condemn it. The cover is everything – what's inside rarely matters at all, and never matters until later.

We wound up still with a couple hundred dollars, and blew that easily on some jewelry for me and a petite watch. Dory insisted on, and got, a Mickey Mouse electric.

We went back, got a meal, then watched a little TV and went to bed. After a short time, Dory said she felt a little lonely in that bed and asked to shift to mine. I agreed readily, and we talked for a little bit, hugged, kissed, and finally drifted off to sleep.

We were up before the wake-up call, and Dory picked out my wardrobe. Now I looked at myself once again in a mirror and marvelled anew at what I was seeing. My blondish auburn hair had been restyled into a sexy set of curls and bangs, and small crystalline earrings set off my almost perfect Madonna-like face to which cosmetics had been expertly but discreetly applied, and Dory applied a little perfume in the right places.

The clothes were tight-fitting, a black satin pants-suit set off by a gold-colored belt with sunburst pattern, going into long leather boots.

'You're crazy, Dory,' I told her. 'You've made me into a hell of a sex symbol. I'll have to fight everybody off. Christ! I think I'm madly in love with myself. Is all this really necessary?'

'I told you I was going to make a real woman out of you, Vic Gonser,' she responded somewhat playfully. 'For as long as it takes you're going to be *me*, the me I never was but always wanted to be. You might as well learn to play the part. And, when I get it back, I'll know what I'm like and you'll know everything about being a woman.'

I couldn't really find a response to that. She was obviously neurotic about me, although I couldn't blame her for being a bit odd after what she'd gone through – and what she'd lost, which was what I was seeing in the mirror. I kept wondering why *I* wasn't off myself – or, perhaps I was and just didn't know it. But, damn it, I *owed* her, and she was the boss. I wanted it that way. If she wanted me to be her surrogate self, living her life for her, then I'd do it.

I almost understood it.

Just joining Parch for breakfast gave me a real taste of what being this surrogate was like. Heads turned in my direction when I entered the coffee shop; men cast rather obvious covetous glances at me, women a different sort of look. People scrambled to open the glass doors to the restaurant for me despite the fact that I was not only capable of it myself but had to step carefully to keep from tripping over them, and waiters seemed to vie with one another to offer me a chair in their territory. I was the center of attention, no doubt about it. And, I found, I kind of liked it, too.

Everything I'd done in my whole life was an attempt to escape the psychological barriers to humanity that my sequestered youth had built up. I had never broken free on my own, not with my learning, my books, my position of respect. Suddenly it had been done to me, and for me, without me having to even lift a finger. It was, in a way, the confirmation of my whole dismal view of human behavior. Not one of those people scrambling for the door or chairs or eyeing me either lustfully or enviously knew who I was, what I did or didn't do for a living, whether I was rotten or nice, brutal or gentle, any of these things. It was irrelevant what I was; only what I looked like really counted.

Parch had been surprised and a little taken aback at my appearance. Still, he remained rock-solid, as distant as always, barriers up. I wondered about him – his strange background, his odd vocation, his outlandish moustache and manner of dress. Somewhere in that head was a very strange mind, I knew, and a tremendously private one hidden behind granite layers as mine had been. I couldn't help wondering if it was as fragile as mine, or, perhaps, hid something far darker. No matter what, all we could see of him was a carefully crafted and totally masked *persona*.

'Where to from here?' I asked him over eggs and coffee.

He put down his knife and took a long drink of brewed tea. 'South, eventually to IMC, if only for your own protection. No telling if there might be more around, tracking us, trying to find out where their comrade has been taken. I can tell you no more now – you will be thoroughly briefed after you arrive and settle in.'

'What's this IMC you keep mentioning?' Dory wanted to know.

Parch just smiled. 'You'll find out soon enough.' He glanced at his watch. 'After ten. We'd best be going, I think. I'll ring for a car to pick us up and we'll be off.'

This was quickly done, and a nondescript blue Ford soon pulled up and two serious-looking men got out and helped us load our new baggage and Parch's one small case into the car. Dory insisted on sitting up front and I found myself in the middle of the back seat sort of squashed between Parch and one of the security men. The stranger bothered me a bit, mostly because he kept making subtle moves directed at me. His arm somehow kept finding its way around me, and he seemed to press in on me a bit more than was necessary. I found it more than irritating but couldn't think of anything to do; Parch seemed oblivious and gazed idly out the window. I could only pretend I didn't notice, try to squirm out when possible, and make the best of it. Dory, I noticed, looked back at me from time to time, saw the problem, and seemed somewhat amused by it.

It wasn't a long ride. As we neared the Seattle-Tacoma Airport we turned off on a side road, then went up through the freight terminals and over to a small building that bore the insignia of an Air National Guard unit. I sighed in relief as we got out, then noticed Parch take out a small walkie-talkie and speak into it. He looked up, and we followed his gaze, seeing a small helicopter in that direction now turn and go swiftly away from us.

Parch turned back to us and put the walkie-talkie away. 'No obvious tails,' he told us with a little bit of disappointment in his tone. 'I think we're safe.'

We walked through the small building with all of us getting curious looks from the uniformed servicemen there and me getting some different kinds of looks, then quickly out onto the tarmac. Waiting for us was not the military plane I'd envisioned but a sleek Lear Jet.

The interior was wonderfully appointed; it looked like it had been decorated by Gucci for a millionaire. Parch told us it was a VIP plane used for ferrying congressmen, senators, Pentagon bigwigs and the like. It had a bar, music system, and wide and comfortable seats, which, fortunately, were individual and of the swivel-type, so I didn't have to put up with any amorous security men there.

Once airborne, Parch served some coffee and cookies and seemed to relax quite a bit. 'No more problems for now,' he almost sighed, and for the first time I got an idea of the tension he'd been under.

'All right, then – what is the IMC and where is it?' I wanted to know.

'Nevada,' he responded unhesitatingly, telling me that we were heading now straight for the place. 'It's near where they used to test atom bombs years ago. We still have what is referred to as a 'Nuclear Research Facility' there – that's IMC as it appears in the federal budget, Pentagon budget, official ledgers and such. Initial funding was a bloody bitch – we took a little from just about every DoD program – but, since then, our maintenance budget hasn't really been out of line with what we're supposed to be. That's one way we get away with it. Most senators and congressmen are simply too busy and too rushed to check out every single project, particularly established routine expenditures, and we can get pretty convincing should one ever decide to inspect the place.'

'I still can't believe you can keep such a thing secret,' I told him. 'You said DoD – that's defense. *Somebody* has to know.'

He chuckled. 'You'll see that we can be most effective there. But, you see, it has to be that way. There's perhaps half a dozen senators and two dozen congressmen who can keep a secret. The rest would cause more stupid, ignorant panic than anything else. Our work depends on secrecy, not really from our own people although that is necessary, but from the aliens. We can, after all, be penetrated. We don't know who's who – let's face it. That's why it's essentially a sealed facility, like a good top secret research project working on anything dangerous. Once in. you're in until we feel we can let you out.'

I wasn't sure I liked the implications of that. I wondered just how free our choice was going to be, but I said nothing.

'IMC,' he continued, 'stands for Identity Matrix Center. When we dis-covered that we had been penetrated, invaded, whatever you like, by aliens who could body-switch it was the logical choice. Heretofore body-switching had been considered a total impossibility, a fantasy thing and nothing more. The very concept was unthinkable, for it meant that no one anywhere could be trusted and literally nothing could be safe for long. We were then forced, by a couple of blunders like the one that left you alive, to confront the reality of the thing – and there seemed only one logical response. In the for-ties this country decided upon an atom bomb, found the money, got the best experts on atomic physics together with as unlimited a budget as was pos-sible, and told them to design and build one. They did. In the sixties, we decided to put a man on the moon and created NASA. It was more public, of course, but the approach was the same – get the money you need and the top experts in the field together in the best research facilities you have and tell 'em to do it. They did and there's American flags all over the moon now. The same approach was tried with the Alternate Energies Task Force, although that's been underfunded. The same thing is applied to IMC. Body-switching exists. It's possible. Therefore, we need a defense against it as priority number one. A secondary priority is to learn how to do it ourselves if we can – for obvious reasons.'

I nodded, only beginning to see the scope of this thing. 'And have you made any progress?'

He shrugged. 'We know *what* happens when they do it, but not *how* they can do it. I am living proof that they have made a lot of progress – I was not *born* immune to the aliens. The trouble is that it still requires enormous tech-nological backup to do even that to one person. Mass protection is still practically impossible although theoretically we could do it. What we lack the most is concrete information on our enemy – how many they are, where they come from, just what they're doing here. Without those we're still some-what defenseless, since we assume their technology to be far in advance of ours. Were we to just go to a big program, let the cat out of the bag as it were, they might well easily invent a counter and then we're worse off than we were. See what I mean?'

'You're military, then?'

He chuckled. 'Oh, no. Most of the boys you've met are FBI, of course, and the Defense Intelligence Agency actually manages the security of IMC, but I'm the top watchdog. I'm the Chief Security Officer of the General Services Administration.'

CHAPTER FIVE

IMC didn't look like much from the air – miles and miles of miles and miles, composed of yellow, red, and orange sand, mostly flat, with a few high sharp mountains far in the distance. We passed Yucca Flat, where long ago the first atomic weapons were tested – you could still see the ghostly remains of old mock villages and protective concrete bunkers as we circled for a landing.

Twenty or thirty miles from all this an airstrip loomed ahead on the barren desert. There was no question it was in use – a squadron of sleek fighter-bombers was berthed in two concrete parking areas and a couple of huge transports were parked near the tiny terminal, nearly dwarfing it. The base itself was small – a few dozen squads at best of what looked to be regulation Air Force barracks, all looking like long veterans of continuous occupation. All badly needed paint at the very least. I felt something of a letdown and said so.

'That's only the top of it,' Parch laughed. 'The main base is underground, going down more than half a mile. They built them deep for the atomic stuff, and we made it even deeper. Our computer banks alone run for miles under the desert, a couple thousand feet down and very isolated from any outside influences.'

I frowned. 'A computer that large? I thought that went out with the integrated circuit.'

'Ordinarily that'd be true,' he admitted, 'but even when you consider that a hand-held computer with a phone plug can do almost anything, it's limited by the amount of information that can be stored in it. Consider the human brain, then, with every single thing in it reduced to computer bytes. That's what that computer – computers, really – down there is for. We need mechanical equivalents of human brains plus. There's never been a computer complex like IMC.'

We rolled up to the little terminal building, almost under the wing of one of the giant transports. Again a car, this time from the government interagency motor pool, picked us up and drove us from the plane to one of the barrack-like buildings. Entering, we discovered it was a complex of small offices. Nasty-looking Air Force guards with menacing automatic rifles, checked us out and quizzed us every fifteen or twenty feet. I had the distinct feeling that, if Parch didn't give the correct response each time – and each was different – we would all have been shot down where we stood.

A huge and incongruous freight elevator was in the middle of the first floor, with two more Air Force guards on either side of the door. Again the routine, then both guards plugged in keys on opposite sides – too far, I noted, for any one person to do it – and turned together, opening the elevator door. We stepped aboard and the door rumbled closed once more. Parch then punched a numerical combination in the elevator wall, there was a click, and he extracted from a small compartment yet another key and placed it in a slot, turning it not like a key but more like a combination lock. I began to feel very, very trapped.

We descended, and, passing the next floor, then the next, and still another, I knew we were sinking into the Nevada desert. Level five was ours, but I had the impression that the shaft continued on a lot further, and walked out into a long, lighted tiled corridor with an antiseptic smell. The ceiling was lit with indirect fluorescent lighting, and except for the lack of windows it looked like any modern office building. Uniformed Marine guards seemed to be everywhere.

Parch led us down a side corridor, then through a series of double doors. I saw that we were in some kind of dispensary, although that wasn't quite right.

Men and women in medical whites looked up at us and one woman walked over and had a conversation with Parch. Finally he came back to us.

'Processing first,' he told us. 'Just believe it's all necessary. It won't take long, anyway.'

He waited while the efficient team photographed us, took our fingerprints, retinal patterns, EKG and EEG, blood sample – the whole thing. The end result was going over to a small window and receiving two small cards, one for each of us, that looked like credit cards. On the front was our photographs, fingerprints, and a lot of zebra-stripe coding, the back was entirely coated with a magnetic surface.

'Guard those cards,' Parch told us. 'To get into and out of your room, or anywhere here, you'll need them. They contain everything about you that we know now, all linked to a cross-checking computer. You'll need them even to eat. There's some paperwork to fill out, which I have here, but I'll take you to your quarters and get you settled in first. You can fill it out there and give it to me later.'

We followed him down another corridor and the decor changed a bit. The floor was even carpeted and the doors were evenly spaced. 'I feel like I'm in a motel,' I noted.

'You are,' he replied. 'The IMC Hilton, we call it.' He went up to a door about halfway down with the number 574 on it. 'No keys, though. Go ahead, Gonser – try your card in the little slot there.'

I hesitated, then put the little plastic card in the small, narrow slit next to the door. The card went in about halfway, then something seemed to grab it, pull it all the way in, and there was a click. I didn't immediately try the door, expecting the card to come back.

Parch realized the problem. 'Just go on in. It keeps the card until you leave the room and close the door. When the computer control senses the room's empty it'll offer the card back to you in the slot. Take it and it automatically locks. Neat, huh?'

I shrugged, turned the knob, and opened the door.

The quarters were quite nice, like a luxury hotel suite. There was a single queen-sized bed, dresser with mirror, nightstands, a table and couch, a couple of comfortable-looking chairs, lots of lights and lots more closet space, and, in the other room, a large bath with shower. The main room even had a color TV and there were remote controls for it and all lights beside the bed. Parch showed us everything like an experienced bellman, even trying the TV to make sure it worked.

In back of the parlor area was a small portabar which was mildly stocked and a miniature refrigerator for ice, also containing some fresh fruit, milk and juice, and the like. A cabinet held glasses.

I was impressed. It was far more than I'd expected from the U.S. government. Parch just shrugged it off. 'Look, we have some of the top brains in biophysics, biochemistry, computer sciences, you name it – and, in some cases, their families as well. We can hardly take such people and lock them away in some fallen-down barracks, can we? All your things have been brought here and unpacked, by the way, along with a number of extras in your size; lab whites, that sort of thing. You'll notice the phone has no dial – it's not a line to the outside. But there's a directory there, so you can call anybody in IMC, even arrange wake-up calls. There's daily maid service and the bar and fridge are kept stocked. If you need more, or pharmacy items, anything like that, the numbers to call are there.'

Dory looked around the room with a mild look of disapproval. 'The bed's for both of us? Don't you have a king size?'

'This is Ms Gonser's room, not yours. You have an almost identical one next door in 576.'

'Why can't we stay together?' we both asked, almost together.

'Rules,' Parch told us. 'Get used to them – there are a lot of them, I'm afraid.' He hesitated a moment, looking a little apologetic. 'Look, you'll be next door and can visit all you want. The only thing is, well, you're still on probation, so to speak. Please go along with us for now and trust me that there are good reasons born of past experiences behind those rules. O.K.?'

There seemed little choice but to accept it – for now.

'Come, Ms Tomlinson, I'll show you your room,' he said, turning to Dory. 'And I'll leave the papers here. Take a little time, stretch out, relax, fill the things out, and after I check in and tend to my own business we'll get together again. Take advantage of this time – you're going to be very busy soon.'

They went out and the door closed behind them. I went over to it and saw that there was one difference between it and a motel that made me vaguely uncomfortable – no inside lock. I finally just sighed, turned, and went over to the bed. Hell, if you can't trust a setup as guarded as this a puny little lock wasn't going to help, I told myself.

Finally I explored the room. In addition to the other features I found a clock, a radio, some recent magazines, and the day's Las Vegas newspaper.

I checked the clothes, all neatly unpacked and put where they should be. I got undressed, then stood there, looking at my nude body in the dresser mirror.

Damn it all, I told myself, I still turn myself on.

Suddenly, on impulse, I got up, lugged one of the chairs over to the door and propped it against the knob. It made me feel better, even if it made no sense. I wanted no sudden surprises, and the guards in the local area I'd seen were all male.

I took a brief shower, which felt good, then just plopped on the bed, looking at that supine reflection in the mirror.

It was no good, I thought moodily. I've joined the human race, all right, but I've joined the wrong half. Oh, it might be fun to act like a woman – all the way, with my choice of men, just to see what it was like, but, somehow, I didn't think so. It wasn't my body – it was *hers.*

As much as I enjoyed the attention now being paid to me, the courtesies, the fact that I was the automatic center of attention, the ogled rather than the withdrawn and hopeless ogler, I couldn't pretend that my inner self had really changed. Mentally, I was still male. All those handsome young men I'd met that morning hadn't done anything for or to me. I still looked sideways at some of the cute and attractive women we'd passed in Seattle, and the only time I'd felt any sort of sexual stirring was in the women's room of the coffee shop back at the hotel. I still was attracted to women. I would rather be in bed *with* this reflection than *be* this reflection.

I reached over and flipped on the TV. It was the news, something I usually immersed myself in. The usual was going on. Two dead in hotel fire … Secretary of State hopes for new arms treaty with the Russians … President of the Central African Republic shot in coup attempt … And so it went. Somehow, it just didn't seem important anymore.

I flipped off the TV and lay back face up on the bed, closing my eyes for a moment. What the hell kind of future did I have? I was a gorgeous sex symbol who was the opposite of what I appeared to be. In a sense, nothing had really changed. I was still the alien, the outsider, the non-participator in society because my inner and outer selves were so damnably different.

Idly, I became aware that parts of my body were reacting to my inner thoughts, a pleasurable tension building, and I was only half aware that my hands were touching, stroking those parts. My nipples felt like tiny, miniature erections, and responded to rubbing with a tremendous feeling of eroticism. I kept rubbing one, almost unable to stop, and reached down between my legs, doing to myself what I *wanted* to do to myself. I could imagine me – the old me – here, in bed, next to this beautiful sex goddess, doing this to bring her to a fever pitch, then penetrating, thrusting ... I grew tremendously wet, my finger feeling so good, my thumb massaging the clitoris, until, finally, I experienced an orgasmic explosion that shook my entire body. It felt so good I kept at it, accomplishing it several more times. It felt *so* good and I think I just about screamed with ecstasy at the repeated orgasms. Finally I stopped, a sudden fear that my outcry had been overheard bringing me down a bit, and I just went limp, breathing hard on the bed, savoring the afterglow. Male and female orgasms were certainly related experiences, but very different in the way the sexual sensation was transmitted. It was a wonderful feeling, but it did little to snap my depression.

For it was still me inside this sensuous body, me, Victor Gonser, male, all by myself, alone in the quiet of the room.

After a while I managed to get up and went over to the desk to look at the forms to be filled out. There were a *lot* of them, and they were very detailed about my past life, work, interests. I filled them out almost haphazardly, not really caring very much.

The phone rang and I picked it up. It was Parch, asking me to come down to his office. 'The guard will show you the way,' he told me. 'We'll have a light dinner, then I want to go and wake up our prisoner.'

'He's *here*?'

'Oh, yes – and still sleeping like a baby. We've prepared a special room for him and it's about time we tried to find out what we can.'

'Is Dory coming?'

'No, just me and you, then a couple of specialists. Don't worry – she's fine. You can visit her later on tonight if you like.'

I hung up, got up, and looked through the clothing. I had never appreciated before how much trouble women go through to look the way they do. It all felt funny, cumbersome, and slightly uncomfortable. The bra was the most uncomfortable of the lot, but with my ample chest I thought I needed it.

I went through the clothing Dory had bought for me and cursed her for it. All the stuff was clingy and sexy and that was not what I wanted, definitely. I looked over at the added stuff and decided on it for the moment, choosing a pair of white pants, a plain white T-shirt, and sandals. It looked just as sexy as all the elaborate stuff, but, what the hell, it was comfortable and practical. With my shape I hardly needed a belt, didn't see one that worked, and decided against one. Finally I brushed my hair, which I hadn't washed, nodded to myself in the mirror, then walked over and pulled the chair from the door. I opened it and spotted the Marine guard at the end of the corridor. I stepped out, letting the door shut behind me. There was a click and a whirring sound and my card reappeared in the little slot. I'd almost forgotten it, but I removed it now and stuck it in my hip pocket.

The guard gave me the kind of look that betrayed every thought in his licentious mind, but he was *very* disciplined and directed me down the corridor to another, small elevator. The guard on that one had been expecting me and inserted and turned his single key. I stepped in, was told to punch the next level up – four – and the door closed. It was more like a normal elevator than the other, but, I noted, the buttons went only from levels three to sixteen. No way out on this one.

I punched four, noted the implications of level sixteen, and was quickly taken up. The guard on four directed me to Parch's office, which proved to be a large affair, with two secretaries in the outer office, teletypewriters chattering away, computer terminals like mad, and lots of different colored telephones. It looked more like the city desk on a newspaper than the office of a man like Harry Parch.

He was carefully putting his costume back on as I entered. I noticed more comfortable military khakis draped over a chair, and a makeup and dressing table resembling an actor's off to one side.

When he turned around he was the Parch we'd seen from the start – but now knew. I wouldn't recognize the real Parch from Adam in any group of men. No wonder I hadn't seen him on the ferry earlier than that showdown day – he probably was all over the place, but as someone entirely different. The blue eyes were special contact lenses; I saw a pair of glasses on the table. The moustache was one of several different types he kept in a small case, and there were more wigs and a wardrobe of differently styled clothing in a rear closet.

Everything, I realized, about Harry Parch was phoney.

He brightened and smiled. 'Well! You certainly have adjusted well. Most folks in your – er – situation go a bit off the deep end, you know. Some worse than others.'

I nodded. 'I think Dory's a bit off. Nothing serious – but she's not quite herself, I'd say.'

He shrugged. 'Could be worse. We have an entire psychiatric unit here just to treat problems like that. They're good, but nobody can work miracles. I suspect we'll let them take a good long look at your friend when you take the routine tests tomorrow. Maybe they can help her adjust. She's going to be no good to anyone, even herself, unless she does.'

It was clear as we walked down the hall who was the boss here. Sentries snapped to when he approached, nobody once questioned him about anything at all, and he walked to a small executive dining room like he owned the place. In a sense, he did. The dining room with its own chef and fancy meals, was obviously for the select few at the top.

'Why the costume?' I couldn't help asking him as the salad came.

He smiled softly. 'Symbols are important to anyone. I head the people who track the dybbuks down, and I'm immune to their biggest trick. I'm not Superman, though – a bullet does the same thing to me that it does to you. They both hate and fear me – and so I let them hate and fear *this*. It affords a physical magnet for them that also serves as a terror symbol – the man with the stake out after the vampire, so to speak. And it protects me as well, of course. If they knew my real identity and appearance I could never venture anywhere without an armed guard.'

'The accent – is that phoney, too?'

'Oh, my, yes, ducks!' he came back in thick Cockney. 'Any bluddy toime y'want, luv.' He chuckled, then switched to Brooklynese. 'Dem bums ain't gonna know wud I'm like.' He switched back to the familiar soft Irish he normally used. 'You see? I've studied accents for years. Makeup, too. In my younger days I was going to be a great actor. Maybe I am. I like to think so.'

'That Belfast story – it was a phoney, then?'

He thought for a moment, and I wondered if he were deciding whether to elaborate a lie, invent another, or tell me the truth. Would I ever know? This strange man exuded something vaguely sinister, something I couldn't really pin down intellectually but felt, deep down. Perhaps it was his total lack of anything real – or was that cold and analytical tone the real man coming out? In his own way, Harry Parch was as chameleon-like as the alien dybbuks he chased.

'Yes, I'm a naturalized citizen,' he said hesitantly. 'The early part is genuine. I'll be quite frank, Ms Gonser – that experience shaped my entire life. You have no idea what it's like to grow up with the army on every street corner, neighbor against neighbor depending on what church your folks went to, not knowing whether the next parked car contained a bomb or the next ordinary man or woman you passed wasn't going to turn and blow your kneecaps off.' His tone grew very serious. 'You have no idea what it is like to see your parents blown to bits before your twelve-year-old eyes.'

There was nothing I could say to that, but I couldn't help thinking that he was either being honest or was one hell of an actor.

'Those early nerves – Belfast reflexes, I call 'em – stand me in good stead now. Coming down that trail up north, not knowing who was who ... And

I'm well-suited for this battle, I think. I *always* doubt strangers, but only a Belfast boy doubts his old friends.'

I more or less believed him, but it didn't make me feel any better about him. I had the strong feeling that Harry Parch loved no one, trusted no one, lived in a violent world where all could be enemies. If his story were true he was undoubtedly so paranoid as to be in many ways insane; if it were not true, then he was even worse – a man who loved the game, to whom patriotism, ideology, and human beings were all just words to him, labels on chess pieces to be moved and sacrificed at will. I wondered which he was. A little of both, probably. Pragmatically, governments need people like Harry Parch, I reflected, but always as agents of someone else, never as the boss.

We continued talking as dessert came, but it was all small talk. That was all I was going to get from Harry Parch, on himself or on anything else. I was just another pawn to him in his grand game and I would get only what he decided I should get.

We left the dining room and he led me back to the elevator which we took three more levels down. The new area looked like a clinic – which, in a sense, it was. Three people met us – two women and a man – all dressed in sharp medical whites. He talked with them for a minute, then introduced me to them, and finally said, 'Well, I have to go in there with him. I'm supposedly immune but you never know – so what about a password?'

I thought a minute. 'How about – Machiavelli?'

He laughed sharply, although I could see he was somewhat nervous. 'Machiavelli it is, then. You all hear that?' The others nodded and I was a little surprised to see that it was the two women who drew nasty-looking pistols from their pockets. One I recognized as a vet's dart pistol, the kind used for putting zoo animals to sleep, but the other was a vicious-looking magnum.

We walked down another corridor and entered what looked like a recording studio. No, I thought again, maybe like the place where police hold line-ups of suspects for witnesses. There were several comfortable seats in front of a thick pane of safety glass, with microphones in front of each chair. The two women took positions on either side of me, putting their weapons in swivel vises, then opening small doors in the glass window through which the pistols could protrude. I saw that there was a wire mesh on the other side of those tiny openings, preventing anyone from touching the weapons. For a moment I was uneasy about this, since I wondered if these aliens might not be some sophisticated collection of microbes, an alien symbiote or parasite – but I quickly dismissed the idea. Not only would they have known that, at least, by now but the odds of any alien organism being able to affect humans was slight to none.

Behind the glass lay the man, on a hospital bed, a bottle of some clear fluid hanging on the side, dripping a little bit of itself into the unconscious figure through a small needle inserted in a vein in his wrist. The body was strapped securely to the table.

Parch and the male technician in white slid a number of bolts and locks from the door to one side of the glass – I could hear each lock give – and Parch stepped inside. The door closed behind him and I could hear every lock going back into place. Only when that was done did the inner door open electrically, allowing Parch to step into the chamber.

'Now, everyone, I'm going to slowly bring him around,' Parch's voice came from the speakers, sounding oddly distant. 'I'm simply going to prompt him with some elementary stuff, perhaps sprinkled with some little white lies, so we can get the measure of him a little better.' He took a deep breath. 'Let's do it.'

I had to admire Parch's coolness, even though he was clearly a little nervous. Carefully he removed the needle from the dybbuk's wrist and hung it to one side, then quickly left. I noticed that the medical technician who remained outside gazed anxiously at an electronic console. Obviously the alien's body was monitored – and perhaps Parch as well.

'Now, no shooting unless my life is in danger,' Parch ordered, and I realized that it was his fellow humans, not aliens, that worried him. 'Also, please no one say anything until and unless I ask you to. He can not see you; the glass is one-way.'

We sat there, waiting expectantly, intently watching the figure on the hospital bed. It took about five tense minutes before the man seemed to stir, groan, then, finally, groggily open his eyes.

Abruptly, his eyes focused, found Parch, and widened in what I could only think was fear. He struggled to get out of his bonds but got nowhere.

'You'll not break those shackles very easily,' Parch warned him. 'You should have chosen a weightlifter or someone else more muscular. However, that still would do you little good. You're covered by both a sleep gun and a magnum, and both would be used as unhesitatingly on me or on you.'

The man – a rather good-looking man of thirty or so, with sandy hair and a ruddy, outdoorsy complexion – looked around the chamber and stopped struggling. 'Where am I?' he asked in clear and accentless American English.

'You're at IMC, and at IMC you'll stay,' Parch told him. 'It's where your folks have been trying to get to all this time anyway. Well, you made it. Now, let's be civil about this – introductions?' He looked around with annoyance. 'I should remember to bring a chair in here.' He sighed. 'Well, I'm Harry Parch, Security Officer for IMC – but I expect you know that.'

The man just stared at him.

'What do we call you?' Parch asked, shuffling a bit from foot to foot.

'My name would mean nothing to you – literally,' the man on the table responded. 'For general purposes, I use the name Dan Pauley.'

I started slightly. So this was Dan, the leader on the trail.

Parch nodded to him. 'All right, then, Mr Dan Pauley it is. You know, this is the first time I've ever had the chance to talk civilly to one of your kind. This *is* quite an occasion. Sorry I forgot the champagne.'

'You've killed a lot of us, though,' Pauley almost spat.

Parch assumed a mock-hurt look. 'Oh, come now! *I'm* not the one who picks innocent people and shoots air bubbles into their veins after stealing the bodies they were born in.'

'I never liked the killing,' Pauley responded in a sincere tone. 'At first, I admit, none of us gave it a second thought – to them you seemed barely higher than the apes, if you'll pardon the expression. But I've lived here a long time, got to know this place, and it became more and more unpleasant. We simply had no choice if we were to stay undetected.'

'Oh, my! Pardon me!' Parch responded, his tone if anything more cynical than before. 'Isn't it fortunate that the first of you that we capture in one piece is a moralist, an idealist, and even has a guilty conscience! My, my!' His tone suddenly changed to chilling hatred. 'And I'm so glad that all your murders were necessary! How much comfort that is to your victims, their spouses, children, friends. How *very* comforting.'

Pauley sighed. 'All right, all right. But don't make such a moral crusade out of it yourself. The human race hasn't been very kind to any of its own who happened to be in the way if they were more primitive than the civilization moving in on them. To a race that practices genocide on parts of itself that differ only in color, or religion, or some other trivial thing I think we're pretty civilized about it. We killed only when necessary, and we killed only to safe-guard our own mission.'

Parch had started pacing a bit, but suddenly he stopped, turned, and looked directly at the man strapped on the table. 'Ah, the mission. If the kill-ing and body-stealing is an abhorrent necessity, then you must have quite a good reason for doing so, at least in your own mind. What? Anthropology? Conquest? What?'

The man thought for a while, obviously wrestling with his inner self. If he told too much he'd betray his people to his worst enemy. If he told nothing he would be unable to escape the moral corner into which he'd painted himself. I felt a little sorry for him. He couldn't know that he was not the first Harry Parch had caught nor, I suspected would he.

'Look,' he said at last, 'my people – we call ourselves Urulu, which just means people, really – are in trouble. In many ways we're quite different from you, maybe more so than you can imagine, but in some ways we're the same. We evolved on a life-sustaining world, became dominant, and built a civiliza-tion. Finally, we reached the stars, as you may someday do, and began looking for other civilizations. We found a lot, but none capable of interstellar flight, and things went along pretty well for a while. Like most expanding cultures, we stole from the civilizations we discovered, but not anything you might guess. We stole ideas – art, new ways of looking at things, scientific break-throughs in areas we never considered, things like that. They're the true treasures of a civilization, and we could steal them to our profit without injuring any other cultures. They never really guessed we were there.'

'Like Earth.'

'Well, not really. Frankly, Earth is just a bit too primitive and too alien to have much to offer us. But, finally, we bumped into another civilization, a far different one, also spreading out to the stars. We frankly don't know much about them, although they're technologically our equals. In many ways they seemed like us, even to the body-switching capabilities, but when they'd reached our level they had made different choices about how to use their powers. They weren't a civilization you could even talk to, identify with, or really understand. They were – well, missionaries, I guess, interested only in converts. When we met they tried it on us, we resisted, and war resulted. A gigantic war, really, on a no-win scale. They won't surrender – they *can't* sur-render, it wouldn't be something they'd comprehend – but we're so strong militarily that they can't win, either. This state of perpetual stalemate has existed now for thousands of years. And we can't win, either – they're too many and we too few.'

Parch's expression was both grim and thoughtful and I saw him nod once or twice to himself. I had the feeling that Pauley was confirming what Parch had been told by others, and I thought I could see how his mind was going. Either the Urulu had one hell of a convincing and consistent cover story or they were telling the truth – and they seemed too egocentric to bother con-cocting anything this elaborate. It would be hard for them to imagine being caught like this. And if this war were true – where was the other side?

'How does all this involve the Earth?' Parch wanted to know. 'Are we now the front? Or might we be?'

'I – I really don't know. There's no front in the normal sense. We have a mili-tary stalemate, remember – and destroying a planet doesn't get you anything but one more dead planet. The war now is a battle for the minds, the souls, if you will, of various planets. There's some evidence that they are active on Earth, but it wouldn't be a high priority item for them. You're very rare in the galaxy, you know. Most – maybe 95 percent – aren't like you at all. Most races couldn't exist here in their natural forms, we included. But there are enough planets with what you might call humanoid life to make it worth their while – and ours. We have few allies, and those we have are much closer to our form of life than yours, and we occasionally need, well, warm bodies to work those planets. You're out here on a spiral arm, pretty far away from the action, but you're the closest, most convenient source of warm-blooded mammalian oxy-gen-breathers we have.'

I was appalled, and even Parch looked disturbed, at all this.

'We're your spare parts depot, then, for humanoid worlds,' Parch said more than asked.

Pauley nodded slowly, a sheepish look on his face. 'Look, this world's massively overpopulated anyway, and I think you'd admit that most of those people are vegetative – subsistence farmers, primitives of all kinds. They die young, of curable diseases and terrible customs, sometimes of starvation, and it makes absolutely no difference whatsoever to your race, your history, if such people live or die. We try to concentrate on people like that – we really do. Most of the bodies we take are from people who matter not a bit to Earth but they matter a great deal to us. In a sense, we give them purpose.'

'At the cost of their lives,' Parch responded darkly.

'This is a war! You'd react the same way and do the same things if you were in our shoes! You *know* it!'

Parch didn't reply to that because he knew as well as I did that the whole of human history supported the alien's point of view. We really weren't that different after all.

'So those people on the trail and in Skagway and on that ship – they were all expendable?'

Pauley sighed. 'Look, I was a – station chief, I guess you'd call it. I've been here a very long time, and I was due to go home as soon as I could break in my relief. That's who I picked up in Alaska – but something went wrong. You know more about that than I do. We got chased halfway across Alaska and the Yukon by you, no matter what tricks we tried. I wish I knew how you did it, I really do. All those we left – well, it was them or us. You'll understand that a body-switching race doesn't face death easily because there's a good chance it won't happen.'

Parch nodded at that, and I considered it. A race of body switchers *would* be potentially immortal, subject only to accidents and acts of violence. Particularly a spacefaring race with access to all the bodies of many worlds. It was a staggering concept.

'Now what happens?' Pauley asked. 'You can kill me, of course – and I admit the thought terrifies me. But I'm a soldier and a volunteer – I'll die if I have to. You can keep me prisoner, but that won't gain you much, either. I don't mind telling you the general things but there's much, the important parts, no amount of coercion can get from me. You can try torture, but I can shut down the pain centers – I have far more control over this body than you have of yours. You can't use drugs – although I'm sure you'll try. All you'll get is a Urulu mind and unless you know Urulu, a language with few common references to yours, it'll get you nothing but a lot of bad sounds.'

'Or I could let you go,' Parch said softly.

To my surprise that caused the alien to laugh. 'Come on, Parch! You and I both know I couldn't do anything now if I wanted to. You have me in your sights. You have some way of tracking me – how I can't imagine. I'm not about to betray my people.'

'We have your matrix, you know,' Parch said in that same soft tone.

The man stiffened. 'My ma –' He seemed to collapse, to deflate as if a balloon newly pricked by a needle. 'So you've come that far,' he managed weakly.

'You started it, you know,' the IMC agent pointed out. I wished I knew what they were talking about.

Pauley seemed to regain a little of his composure. 'I suppose we did, although it's hard to believe you're advanced enough to manage it. I wish my people knew. It might change everything. Make us allies instead of adversaries.' He hesitated a moment, thinking. 'Maybe that's what *they* are doing here. We thought it was just to try and cut off our body bank, but if *they* even guessed …' Again a pause, then, 'You may be in far more danger than you realize.'

'If they know – and we have only your word that they even exist – we're already doomed,' Parch noted. 'I rather suspect they do not know, Mr Pauley, if you didn't.'

'Which brings us back to question one,' the Urulu said. 'What do we do for now?'

'Well, I can't trust you, of course, for I have only your word on these matters, and you can't trust me, since you can hardly place your faith in my hands childishly. What I think we shall do for the moment is leave things as they are while we get to know each other better. For now, I'm going to release you from this bed, and we have rigged up a small apartment in back, through that door there. It is, of course, totally bugged and monitored and is not the world's most comfortable accommodations, but it should do. Food will be passed in to you. Automatic and human-controlled weapons will be trained upon you at all times, of course, so please keep that in mind. Just consider yourself, well, a prisoner of war.'

The man nodded. 'I understand.' Parch undid the straps holding the alien down and Pauley got up unsteadily, rubbing the places where the tight restraints had cut into him. Finally he got unsteadily to his feet and went over to Parch. 'Truce?' he asked, and put out his hand.

We all tensed, knowing what Pauley was trying to pull. Parch did not hesitate, taking Pauley's hand and shaking it vigorously, a wide smile on his face.

'Now that we have that established, yes, a truce,' Parch told him.

Pauley looked more than a little astonished and somewhat worried. 'The only people I ever knew that were immune are other Urulu, who can consent or not, and our enemy,' he said suspiciously. 'Which are you, Parch?'

For the first time I understood just why Harry Parch was such a terror figure to them. They knew all their own people on our little world, so Parch, who had the power to block a switch, had to be their enemy in human guise. It seemed to me that Parch, too, must have thought of that, perhaps long ago. For a second I wondered if it might not just be true, but I quickly dismissed the idea. That way lay madness, and you could be paranoid enough just knowing what I knew.

'I'm no alien,' Parch assured him. 'I was born in this body on this planet, I promise you. I am – a prototype, you might say. A few of us have been rendered immune to you, although at great cost.'

Pauley just stared at him and I did likewise. 'Cost?' The alien repeated.

He nodded. 'I am totally immune. I am myself – forever. Forever, Pauley. You yourself mentioned the promise of immortality from the process. You can see, then, why so few working on this project have been willing to take the cure.'

Pauley's mouth dropped slightly, and, for the first time, I understood IMC's problem, why the defense wasn't 'perfected' as Parch had said. If we really *could* learn how to switch bodies then immortality, at least for some, would be attainable. Attainable, yes, like the Urulu – but not for Parch. Never for Harry Parch ...

'I must leave you now,' the agent told the alien. 'However, I'm assigning someone directly to you, to talk to you, discuss ways out of this mess, give us some common ground. I think you two will get along famously – considering you are responsible for her being in the body she's in. Your partner, anyway. Does the prospect interest you, Ms Gonser?'

I almost jumped at the sound of my name. Finally I leaned over and keyed the microphone. 'There's nothing I'd like better,' I told them both.

CHAPTER SIX

I was escorted by Marine guard back to my room, and I decided to drop in on Dory and fill her in. I went to her door and knocked, finally hearing a muffled question. I called out who I was and heard the sound of something being pulled back from the door. The motion made me chuckle a bit, and feel a little better, too. I wasn't alone in my privacy demands, it seemed.

Finally the door opened a crack and Dory said, 'Come on in. I'm not really fit for those gorillas at either ends of the hall.'

I pushed the door open and walked through, shutting it behind me. She was nude and had a towel wrapped around her hair. The TV was on, and I saw a mirror, scissors, and make-up kit on the bed.

It was already getting hard to remember myself in that slight, dark body, and I reflected how odd it was that I'd adjusted so easily to all this. Humans were adaptable animals, all right.

She was extremely thin and quite cute in an exotic sort of way. Although not quite there as yet, you could tell she was going to be an attractive, if small, young woman.

'What've you been doing?' I asked her.

She went over and snapped off the television. 'Sitting around, mostly. Watching T V. They got a couple of movie channels here I never saw before – one's all porn. Interesting. I've been sitting here doing my hair and taking notes for when I can use it properly.'

I smiled and took a seat on the couch. 'Did you get anything to eat?'

'Oh, yeah, hours ago. One of the Marines came by and we went up to the dining hall. The food's not bad, although I have a thing against cafeterias. They got some setup here, though. Bar with dance floor, movie theater with first-run stuff, game rooms – you name it. Like a luxury hotel. Swimming pool, jaccuzi, saunas, you name it. Even tennis courts. They live pretty good here, I'd say.'

'I'll have to see it,' I told her, then proceeded to fill her in on my evening. She followed my story with rapt attention, occasionally breaking in with questions. When I was through she considered it all for a while.

'You know, you sound like you really *liked* that alien thing,' she noted.

I shrugged. 'I don't know what I think. I *can* say that I found him reasonable, at least. I don't like the idea of my planet being a body bank for some alien species, but I can understand his point of view without approving. I think, inside, we're more alike – his people and us – than either of our groups wants to admit.'

'Or he just understands humans better than we understand his kind,' she responded a bit cynically, then changed the subject. 'Any idea what happens next to us?'

I shook my head. 'Parch said we'd spend most of the day tomorrow taking a battery of tests.'

'Tests?'

'Psychological tests, mostly, I think. They want to find out if there's anything wrong with our minds after the switching, how we look at ourselves, the world, that kind of thing.'

She nodded. 'I guess I understand. The truth is, I've been looking a little at myself lately. I'm not really sure I know myself anymore, if I ever did. I mean, it's kind of funny, but the more I think about all this the less I *mind* it. Isn't that weird?'

I frowned. 'I don't understand what you're saying, frankly.'

'It's – well, it's hard to explain. I think maybe you'll find out for yourself.

But, well, things weren't going right for me. I was pretty screwed up inside, and I didn't really know where I was going, only that I couldn't really go back to my old life, my old friends, be the kind of girl they wanted. It's – well, hard to explain. But life was getting to be such a pisser this wasn't so bad – once you get over the shock. For a day or two I really went off the deep end, particularly with my old self standing there in front of me. It's passed, though. I keep thinking that this was the best thing that could have happened to me – becoming somebody else, that is.' She hesitated, realizing she wasn't getting through. I had the impression that there was more to this than she was telling me, some missing piece of the complex puzzle that was Dorian Tomlinson. For my part, I couldn't imagine a nineteen-year-old stunner of a woman with money, brains, and looks having any problems I could recognize as problems.

'What about you, Vicki? How are you holding up? I mean, you had a lot more of a change than *I* did. All I did was lose some height, about six years, and gain reddish-brown skin.'

My own sense of loneliness and isolation, of being out of place, returned to me with a vengeance. The interlude with Parch and the alien had allowed me to temporarily push it to the back of my mind, but it never really left, and now here it was back full once again. In a way, I thought, I was worse off than I was before, for the only way I got any release was by pretending I was doing it to somebody else. I felt a need, almost a hunger, to share this feeling with somebody and Dory was, now, closer to me than anyone else in the world. I began cautiously, but eventually it just poured out, my whole life story, my frustrations, the whole thing. 'I feel as alien as that Urulu or whatever it is in that cage,' I told her. 'Just like I always have. God, Dory! I have such a need to *belong*, somewhere, just once.'

She came over to me and kissed me softly on the forehead. 'Poor Vicki,' she sympathized, 'you really have the worst of it, I think.' She curled up into a cute little ball on the couch opposite me, looking at me thoughtfully.

'You know,' she said, 'it's really crazy. I never knew you as a man and I have a tough time thinking of you in those terms. You're *mannish*, yes, in your movements and gestures, but not *male*, if that makes any sense. Part of that's my own conditioning, I guess. I knew a lot of women who dreamed of being men, but you're the first man I know who admitted fantasizing being a woman. It's the old image thing, I guess. Women say they want men to be more emotional, tender, all that – but you got me to thinking that maybe that's all wrong. Maybe men *are* all those things women are, but it's all locked inside somehow. Maybe we contribute to it – I know many of my friends say they want a warm, tender man but they only go to bed with macho types.'

I nodded. 'That's my bitter experience. Men who really *are* what our liberated women say they want are often friends, confidants, of those women – but never sexual partners. That was my experience. I always wondered if the male stereotypes everybody decries – the macho types, that sort of thing – aren't reinforced by women's behavior towards them. A man with normal sexual drives who tries to be a warm, friendly human being to women only to see them march off with what they say they abhor might *become* more of that macho type himself. In the process he loses his humanity, and maybe his pride, which makes him inwardly bitter, but he does it because he's forced to. And then there were those like me who *couldn't* lower themselves that way, and so became the permanent outsiders. You have no idea the hurt it causes – and the cynicism it breeds against women in general, fair or not.'

She considered that. 'So you envied women. The pretty ones got all the attention, while the more open economy gave them all equal competition with men in the marketplace and other options. You know, I wonder if we haven't hit on one of the basics of human behavior. Still, you know, it's a man's world in most respects. Men still run the country, most of the businesses, make most of the decisions, make more money and seem generally freer to us women. Male culture dominates so much that the successful business-women really get there and stay there by imitating the men, being as aggressive, as macho, maybe, as they are.'

'We begin as little babies, but there it departs. Everything in a boy's life is competition – winning. Sports. Fighting to establish pecking orders in gangs. Showing off. But, you see, the necessary basic training is there because men can't do anything else. Women now have the same career choices as men, but they can opt not to work, to have and raise babies, their choices clear early in life. Men have only that sense of purpose in the job. Even if they marry, the law gives the man the obligation to support the wife and kids, and in a divorce gives the kids almost invariably to the mother while making Dad pay for it, even if Mom's a cultist murderer with a fifty-thousand-dollar-a-year job while Dad's a kind, devoted, loving ten-thousand-dollar-a-year janitor. He has no rights, only responsibilities, and no real options. No wonder men die so much earlier than women.'

'It's no picnic as a woman, either,' Dory responded. 'We get the dolls, the toy stoves, the frilly little dresses. We rarely get the attention our brothers do, the preparation for something big. Then along comes puberty and you get periods that make you feel yucky, and suddenly you can't go to the store alone. If your parents aren't scared for you then you soon get scared yourself. Rape becomes a threat you live with. You envy your brother going downtown alone to pick up something at the store or take in a movie. The boys see you as a thing, not a person, and usually have only one thing in mind. I was seventeen before my parents would trust me out on a date after dark! And most girls have to decide in the college years – career or family. The pressure's big, you get hurt fast and often, and if, like me, you're good looking you're even more limited. It's understood you'll work for a while until you get married and settle down, but aside from modeling or show business or something like that you can *get* any job – if you want to pay the price for keeping it, and if you don't expect to go anywhere.

'Pretty women aren't supposed to be smart, and they don't have to be. You quickly learn what you're expected to do to get what you want – and you either do it, or don't and go nowhere, or get married and settle down. You get a dozen passes just going to lunch. You wind up a prisoner in your own skin without options at all. You know, I really envied men. I had two older brothers and I really wanted to be one of them. Come and go when you please, free to pick and choose careers, free to be left alone in a crowded party if you wanted to be or go on the make if you felt like it. No period, no danger of getting pregnant, none of that.'

I shook my head sadly from side to side. 'The grass is always greener. You wonder how anybody winds up happy in this life, or satisfied, or content.'

'Luck, mostly,' Dory decided. 'Enough people, enough combinations. But not either of us, it seems.' She chuckled dryly. 'How did two such miserable outsiders wind up together in this fix?'

I looked at her without comprehending. 'Surely you were better off comparatively than me. You had a lot more of your life ahead of you, were still far along from making those choices. You had the *potential* to find happiness, a potential I really ended.'

'No, Vicki,' she responded gently. 'It wasn't that way at all.' She sighed and was silent for a moment, as if making a decision. Finally she shook her head slightly and mumbled to herself, 'O.K. True confessions time, I guess.' She looked back up at me. 'What I'm going to tell you I've never told a living soul. I just really got to telling myself a few days ago, for real.'

'You don't have to tell me anything you don't want to.'

She shook her head. 'No, I *want* to tell you. Particularly now.' She sighed once more and looked a little thoughtful. 'Look, I knew what growing up was supposed to mean, supposed to feel like. I had a lot of girl friends in the neighborhood, and they all had crushes on big pop stars or TV actors, things like that. Even on some local boys. I never did, but I figured I was just more picky, smarter, or something. I just stuck mostly with my girl friends, never really feeling too comfortable around boys. I was a virgin until I was seventeen – that's weird in this day and time, but I never really thought it was until I hit college. I was sure horny all the time – the tension inside me was unbelievable. I tried a couple of boys in college – after all, I had my pick – but it just didn't do much for me. I never got off and hardly even got wet. I got to wondering if maybe most of this stuff I'd heard was bullshit, that women just faked it but didn't really get out of sex what men seemed to. But I could get *myself* off, and it felt great – but I felt like a freak.'

She paused here but I said nothing, having a feeling as to the direction she was going. It was most difficult to remember that she'd been in college only a year – and so all this was only fourteen or fifteen months at most, still very fresh to her. Despite the tiny thirteen-year-old body and childish voice she seemed so very much older than nineteen.

'After school ended last May, we had a big party off-campus to celebrate,' she continued. 'Lots of stuff around. Booze, pot, pills, coke, even opium, would you believe? I never really was much into that whole thing, but it was that kind of party, you know, and I drank a hell of a lot more than I should and did a little hash with the group and the next thing you know I'm rolling around on the floor making out passionately ...' She sighed. '... With Mary Forester.'

I nodded, although it felt very strange to hear it. She looked up at me and there was genuine anguish in her face.

'You see? Well, when I woke up on the floor much later there, I got out fast and went back to my little off-campus apartment. I was sick at myself as well as being hung over. I kept telling myself that it was the booze and drugs, and I had myself halfway believing it, but I didn't want to see any of those people again. I was embarrassed, afraid, I guess. I just wanted to run, get away – not home, either, although that's where I went. My folks were glad to see me, of course, and Mom was trying to fix me up with dates while Dad was talking about my future and all that and all I wanted to do was crawl into a hole and die.'

'And after a month of hiding out, with your family pressing you to get out, you decided to pack off to Alaska.'

She nodded. 'Tommy Coyne wasn't at the party – he'd already gone home to Vancouver. I decided to call him, he invited me along on his trip to Glacier, and we managed to con my parents – not hard to do – into believing it was a summer trip for college credit. There really *was* a course like that so I had all the brochures. Tommy was a nice guy who had the hots for me but we'd never made it. I figured this trip would not only let me sort myself out but maybe reassure me.'

'It didn't, though,' I guessed.

She nodded grimly. 'It was worse. Even worse because he *is* such a nice guy. I knew it even before. That roll with Mary Forester had unlocked something in me and I found myself looking at women in a whole new way every time I passed them, talked to them, whatever. Look, I didn't *want* it. God! Here I was a sexy young woman in college with a bright future someplace and then *this* Of course, once I came face to face with it I could see that it'd been that way all along. I just hadn't considered it, hadn't wanted to think about it. And now my whole world was crumbling around me. Choices closed, options closed. I walked out on Tommy without explaining – I just couldn't think of what to say, how to tell him – and caught the next boat through. I could've flown, but I wanted the trip, the time to think things through and sort things out. All I could think of was that I couldn't tell my parents – they wouldn't understand, couldn't understand. They're conservative, solid, all that. The scandal alone would have killed Mom, at least. But I couldn't just turn my back on it, either. I wasn't cut out to be celibate. I was still trying to make my decisions, find a way out for myself short of suicide, when you showed up and gave me somebody else to think about. You know the rest.'

I nodded. 'And what about now? Has anything changed for the better?'

She smiled thoughtfully. 'At first, as I said, I was real upset. I wasn't *me* any more. I wasn't really free. But where had I been going, anyway? The more I've thought about this, the better it seems, the more like a godsend. I'm somebody else and somewhere else. Cut off from the past completely. No matter what I do now, it's not my old problems. In a way this has solved my problems. I don't know if I'm going to still feel the same sexually or not – I rather think so – but I don't care any more. I can live that life if it's divorced, now and forever, from my family, friends, classmates.' She sounded genuinely relieved, sincerely satisfied, although it was as if she herself were seeing all this for the first time. 'Dorian Tomlinson is dead,' she breathed. 'I'm free.'

I looked at her and tried to smile a little. Dorian Tomlinson was dead and she was free, yes, perhaps. But Dorian Tomlinson was also looking at her and sitting very near her this very moment, imprisoning a very different sort of person with a different problem not at all resolved.

CHAPTER SEVEN

Most of the next day was taken with the testing we'd been told to expect. It was quite involved and elaborate, with all sorts of written exams – some forcing pretty bizarre choices – plus interviews, extensive questions on personal background and attitudes, everything. There were even a couple of very involved I.Q. tests, and those results they were willing to tell us. Mine was 162, down a couple of points from my old tests but well within the margin of error. Dory's was 144, lower than mine but still well above any norms, confirming my opinion of her. She was a little disappointed. 'Not quite a genius,' she grumped. 'The story of my life.'

We hadn't had much time to talk to each other, but after it was all over, a little after 5 in the afternoon, and we were in the cafeteria getting a bite to eat, she brought it up briefly.

'You know our talk last night?'

'Uh huh.'

'I was pretty free with the same information today. I tell you, Vicki, it's like a gigantic weight has been lifted from my shoulders. I didn't even flinch at the word. I really do think, maybe for the first time in my life, that I like myself, that I'm at peace with myself.'

I squeezed her hand. 'I'm glad for you,' I told her, and I really was.

She smiled back. 'I know. The funny thing was, they didn't seem at all bothered by it. Lesbian. Such a weird word. They even told me there might be nothing really wrong at all. One of 'em said it was partly physiological – a function of brain development. I want to find out more about that angle. If I could know that for a fact it would kind of, well, knock out the last guilty stab wound.'

I admitted I didn't know much about it, but I pointed out that IMC was probably the greatest assemblage of experts on the brain and human behavior ever assembled in one place – certainly assembled with such facilities and such a budget. She'd get her answers here.

We had the evening free, and Dory delighted in showing me around the luxurious facilities. She was almost a different person, half girl-child, half wise adult, but I knew that she'd probably slept solidly and without real worries or guilt for the first time in a couple of months the past night.

I found, too, that she was right about this body I wore. I don't know how many passes men made – I'm sure I missed some of them – but it was not only annoying, I really did begin to feel like some kind of object, a pretty piece of art or sculpture. A part of me wanted to take one of them up on it, to really *be* a woman, but I wasn't one, not really.

We'd gotten up early and were, therefore, tired early. I had a message from Parch that we were cleared now and that we had tomorrow for the grand tour and then to work. Dory would be placed in a training program for technicians – she'd have her choice of several types – while I'd begin the process of making friends with, and trying to draw out, the mysterious Dan Pauley. I was looking forward to that.

In one way, at least, Dory's own revelations, her own emotional outpouring and honesty about herself to others, had done me some good. She no longer dreamed of getting this body back, and I was no longer a caretaker. That made things a little easier on me – I could begin to think of this as a permanent condition and make my plans accordingly. Still, I didn't want to think much beyond IMC, at least not right now. In a sense, I was where I would have wanted to be had I known of the place in my old existence. An encounter with aliens from another world was the most momentous act in the history of modern man, one that would forever change the way human beings saw themselves and their place in the universe. I was *still* a social scientist, and still wanted to be one, and, for that field as well as the others here, this was the place to be.

Parch met us after breakfast and took us down to Level 10, lower than we'd ever been allowed before. We were ushered into a large, spacious office even grander than Parch's, and the sign on the glass door read, 'S. Eisenstadt, Ph.D. – IMC Project Director.' I was a little shocked at that name – hell, I *knew* Stu Eisenstadt! He'd been on the faculty at Hopkins until mysteriously leaving for 'government work' four years ago. Now I knew what that work was and where he'd gone.

He came out to meet us and I couldn't help thinking how little he'd changed. He always reminded me of a fat Albert Einstein, even to a thin, reedy, and slightly accented voice. He'd been in the United States most of his life but he still couldn't tell the difference between a V and a W.

He stopped when he saw us, gave a look of slight distaste, I thought, to Parch, then eyed us, eyes lighting up and a large smile growing under his bushy white moustache. 'Vell, vell, vell! You bring me two beautiful ladies!'

He was the kind of person who was charismatic in an odd way, exuding a grandfatherly warmth you could feel. He had always been among the most highly regarded men I could remember by those who knew him, always doing favors, always willing to listen, sympathize, give advice. His father, a Lutheran minister, had died in a concentration camp during World War II and he remained a deeply, if inwardly, religious man, seeing no conflict between his science and his faith. He never pushed it on you; he just lived it and that was far more impressive.

I went up to him and offered my hand. To my surprise he didn't shake it but took it gently and kissed it. 'Dear lady,' he said softly, and suddenly I was yanked back to the present and my own new form. This wasn't Hopkins, and he was seeing a far different person he'd never known.

'Stuart, it may be hard to believe, but inside this body is Vic Gonser, an old colleague of yours.'

He grinned broadly, and there was added twinkle in his eyes. 'My! *Victor!* How you have *changed!*' He turned to Dory. 'And you must be Miss Dorian Tomlinson.' He bent down slightly and repeated the hand-kissing routine.

I cursed myself for underestimating the wily old bastard and not remembering that 'Project Director' title on his door. His often comic personality masked a brilliant mind fully as devious as anyone's. Of *course*, he'd known all about us, who we were, how and why we were here, all the facts well ahead of time.

He gestured to chairs and we all took seats except Parch, who excused himself and left with a few whispered words to the professor we couldn't hear. I couldn't help noticing that the others in and around the office kept glancing nervously at Parch, while the security chief was anything but deferential to Stuart. When Harry Parch left, he seemed to take a black cloud with him.

Eisenstadt sighed. 'Vell, Victor! So – it is a great improvement, this change in you. I find you positively radiant to look at.' He turned to Dory and said with mock seriousness, 'He was a bald little schmoo of a man ven he vas a he.' She giggled, and I could see she was falling under his spell.

'Stuart, I may look different and you the same, but I have to say I'm surprised to see you here – surprised and pleased,' I told him. 'Project Director, huh?'

He nodded. 'This is vere it's all done. Parch, he chases the aliens and keeps us a secret, but *here* ve find out how they do it, what they do, and open up the frontiers of knowledge. I tell you, Vict – Vicki – that here ve have already taken quantum leaps – quantum leaps! – in man's knowledge of himself, the most important frontier you can imagine.'

I was interested. 'You've made real progress, then?'

'Wery much so. I'll be glad to explain it to you, but first ve begin at the beginning, yes? Some old college biology. Ve have not vun brain in our head, you know, but three. Vun, the medulla oblongata, is the first, the basic, the *primal* brain from our reptilian ancestors. It controls much of our automatic functions. Then there's the cerebellum, our mammalian brain. Body temperature, blood pressure, voluntary muscles, that sort of thing. If you have both these you are perfectly equipped to be an ape, yes? A primitive ape, anyway. Memory data, too, is mostly stored here. But to use it for anything but the most basic stuff you need the cerebrum, yes? In computer terms, the cerebrum is the programmer, the cerebellum is data storage, and the medulla is the electric company, you see?'

I had to laugh at the analogy, which was simple but apt. I would like to admit that such basic stuff was unnecessary, and it was to me, but I could see that Dory was getting her memory jogged.

'Now, that's a simplified model – extremely so.' Stuart continued, 'but it's vat ve need for our purposes. Ve will keep to the computer analogy for all this, but it is important you not think of the brain as an integrated whole but a series of assembled components. All right?'

We both nodded.

'All right, then. Ve have known for a long time that the memory process is basically holographic – you see complete, integrated ideas or images in your cerebrum, not individual data bits. Ve had some success back at Johns Hopkins vith feeding additional information into the brain in such a manner, but it vas child's stuff. But this holographic idea vas a wrong direction, even though it was right. No, don't look at me like that. I mean it. It meant ve didn't ask the right question next.'

'And that was?' I prompted.

'How that information is *stored* rather than how it is *processed*', he replied. 'Look, basically we vould have claimed that what we can now do vas, if not totally impossible, then unlikely in our lifetime. What shocked us all was the self-evident fact that complete memory and personalities could be changed with no apparent physical harm. Incredible! Impossible! But a fact. The process itself is so complex that it defies rational explanation among my colleagues. The fact is, like gravity and magnetism, ve're not quite sure *how* it works but ve know it does.'

'You *can* do it, then?'

He shrugged. 'Not vat these aliens do, no. They do in moments vat it takes this entire complex of the most sophisticated computers to do. No machines, no vorry, just touch and *pfft!* It is something inside them, something to do with the nature of what they really are. I think they are some sort of energy creatures, bound together in a complex pattern, that needs a body to vork. They are born in bodies, yes, same as ve, but they are not that body. They are symbiotic organisms inside animal bodies, although they can not exist outside bodies at all. So, vat they do naturally ve are not physically equipped to do. But if they can do it to us, there is a vay, vith technology, for *us* to do it to *us.*'

'I'm sitting here listening to all this,' I said, 'in a body so different from my own it's incredible, yet it's still hard to believe.'

He nodded. 'I know, I know. I don't believe it myself sometime. But, let's make a try at it, yes? Let's start by saying that the brain is everything. The most incredible, complex, and vonderful computer ever designed. It is made up of cells called neurons that are so densely packed that there are one hundred thousand of them in a square inch! And interconnected by ten thousand miles or more of nerves. The whole brain contains over ten trillion neurons – a staggering number, bigger than ve can really conceive. So much ve don't live long enough to fill it all up.

'But the brain is a prisoner, you see, an isolated thing with no sensations, not even pain. It is totally input-dependent for its information, and this input comes from everyvere else in our bodies – eyes, ears, nose, throat, and the nerve cells that cover our bodies inside and out. It can be fooled – that is the basis of hypnosis. If it can be convinced by its receptors, its input, that something false is true, it accepts it. It has no independent vay of checking out that information.'

I glanced over at Dory and saw her rapt attention. Stuart was a good teacher, and he was obviously relishing the role once more.

'Now, input – sensory data, whether it be light, shape, color, anything – is sent to the brain and routed to the proper place for it,' he continued. 'It indexes by area. There's really no difference in the neurons, but our genes set up a pattern, a matrix if you will, that the brain follows as its own unique coding and indexing system. Evolution, in other vords, produced an incredibly efficient indexing system. Each individual matrix is unique, like fingerprints, and so our first problem is how to discover how the brain indexes for each personality – their identity matrix, you might call it. Ve do this by a sophisticated probe – actually millions of tiny energy probes – that finally find the right place and are able to plug in, as it were, to the individual's brain. The process is new – invented here – and quite complex.'

'You don't have to shave the head and drill, then?' Dory put in.

He chuckled. 'Oh, no. At the start, yes, but no more. It is necessary only to establish a direct, electrical connection to the brain. The Urulu, they do it at almost any set of nerve ends in the body, but ve believe there is actual entry by the Urulu organism along the nervous system and into the brain. Ve based our own work on that hypothesis and it vorked. Our computer system and probes is the mechanical replacement for the organic, as it were, Urulu.'

'But you said each matrix was unique,' I pointed out. 'So how can you replace one pattern for another?'

'Vell, ve start by shooting tremendous amounts of stimuli into the cerebrum directly. You say "name" and your name is brought forth into the cerebrum. The computer seizes on that and follows it back, and so on. But after a vile it can ask questions far faster than ve, and it asks millions of them per second. Ultimately it learns the code, the matrix, for the information center and can track down miscellaneous material until it has complete access to memory storage. It generally needs an external stimuli – like us asking questions – to start, then it takes over, and, at computer speed, it still takes twenty or more minutes, sometimes longer, to completely map a matrix. At the end it is just recognizing the existence of data, of course, not caring vat that data is.'

I was starting to feel a little uneasy about what he was saying. The idea of mapping the memory, the very core of being, of an individual like Rand McNally did roads was unsettling.

'Now, let's go back to the brain itself,' Eisenstadt went on. 'Although retrieval is holographic, storage is not really so. The hologram is constructed in the cerebrum from retrieved data. How is that data stored? Vell, all the input, all the information from your senses, goes to the cerebrum – but not as you perceive them. All external stimuli are instantly converted into brain language – and that brain language is chemical in nature. But there are two languages. One, the holographic one, is transmitted to the brain. There it is broken down into bytes of information and recoded. Each byte becomes a synapse, a chemical messenger that is hustled along and routed by a tiny electrical impulse. Each little messenger gets to the brain where neurons route it, according to the matrix, to its proper place. When it gets to that proper place the individual neuron in charge, as it vere, makes a tiny copy in its *own* individual language. All this at incredible speed, you understand. Like trillions of tiny chemical tape recorders, infinitely specialized, who record the message ven the chemical messenger runs past its little recording head.

'Ven you remember something, or use something, or need to retrieve something, then the command is sent out from the real "you" – your cerebral cortex, or command center – and, instantly, the little bits of information that apply rush back with copies of the information needed – copies, note, the original stays there – where the cerebrum reintegrates this information into a holographic picture. An idea. A memory. You name it. Naturally, the information that is most frequently used is easiest to get at. The less it is used the more difficult it is to get at that information – you "try to remember" but can't, quite, because you have had no need for it for so long the track is overgrown with veeds. It has to be this way. Most information you get from cradle to grave simply isn't needed or relevant, no matter how big it vas at the time, and it is stored avay in the cranial closet, so to speak, to make room in the more efficient areas for more pressing stuff. Once out of the main matrix and off in that closet, it becomes hard to find, like any attic overfilled with unused and unvanted stuff, becoming even harder as you grow older as those closets fill with all the junk. That's why much of the brain appears to be doing nothing and ve don't even miss some of that stuff if it has to be removed, say, in an operation.'

'Does the brain ever – erase?' Dory asked hesitantly. I got the impression she was a bit unsettled by all this, too.

'Oh, yes,' he replied. 'Sometimes it's accidental. Sometimes it's the result of an injury – repairs inside the brain may require it. Self-repairs, I mean. In fact, some of it is automatically erased very qvickly. Vy should it bother to keep instructions it gave to the gastrointestinal tract for digesting a specific meal when you vere three? So, after a decent interval, it erases and generally keeps this sort of expendable information in one area for constant re-use. So, to sum, the neurons store the information, the synapses feed the input to the brain, copy and transmit stored input, and erase. They also do much more, of course – they create enzymes that do different things in and to the brain and the like in response to stimuli.'

'That explains the brain in layman's terms,' I agreed, 'but not how the Urulu swap minds.'

'Ah, the Urulu. Vell, vat they do seems to go something like this. By simple touch they are able to plug into anyone's nervous system the same as our computer. Automatically, in no more than a few seconds, they are able to do vat ve vith our huge computer take half an hour or so to do – get a complete picture of your matrix, and, as such, know exactly vere and how your information is stored and processed. And they know instinctively what to ignore – the automatic functions, for example. Then they are able to order the neurons to disgorge this information and it flows in an electrochemical rush to the point of contact and from there to the Urulu brain. The same thing happens to the other matrix, which flows, simultaneously, in the opposite direction. The amazing thing is not only is the exchange complete in both directions, without disrupting the body functions, but it is accompanied by a 'carrier' signal, as it were, which is the exact opposite of the information being extracted. In other words, the neurons receive a signal that is absolutely complementary to the chemical code they already are storing – in effect canceling it out. The effect is that each brain rearranges itself into an exact chemical copy of the other. *Not* a hundred percent, mind you – memories, personality, yes, but not vat is necessary to keep the body going, to manage the unique physical body into which it is now placed. Vether this is an actual transfer of information or vether this is simply a rearrangement is something ve don't really understand yet, although ve tend to think it is a rearrangement rather than an actual exchange considering the speed at vich it is done. If memory, personality, whatever is chemically stored, then prior information is duplicated by the other brain and then totally erased in the original by giving such commands to the cerebral cortexes of each brain and a channel through which the information needed may be exchanged.'

'Then – I'm not really Victor Gonser at all,' I said, feeling a little hollow and distant. 'Dory's mind just thinks it's me. And that Indian girl, whoever she was, just thinks she's Dory.'

Stuart shrugged. 'If all that vas you, your id, ego, super-ego, all the memories and bits of information that went into forming them, your identity matrix, in other words, is duplicated exactly – vat is the difference? I think of it as an exchange of souls in a marvellously mathematical way.'

'These chemical messages – you already said false ones could be sent and that total erasure was possible,' Dory put in, thankfully changing the subject. 'You also said that the computer can figure out our entire filing system. Does that mean what I think it means?'

'If you are thinking vat I think you're thinking, then, yes. An unforeseen side product, but a revolutionary discovery. In its own vay the equivalent of atomic energy – with the same potential both vays.'

I suddenly felt very stupid. 'What are you two talking about?'

'Selective memory,' Dory responded. 'If that computer tells you you're Joan of Arc you'll set the fire yourself.'

'It is a fact,' Stuart admitted. 'Ve can read out the mind and record it, even store it like Beethoven symphonies are recorded. Feed it into any mind. It's still very primitive right now, and there are too many risks to try it on humans, but it is coming, it is coming!'

I felt sick. 'And anything that can be digitally recorded can be selectively doctored.'

Stuart nodded, apparently not bothered by that. 'Oh, yes. Ve have high hopes that ve can bypass brain disorders, cure cerebral palsy, for example, epilepsy, and other such things. Do away vith dyslexia. Perhaps, eventually, be able to order cancer cells to self-destruct. The potential for ending much human misery and suffering is unlimited!'

I grew increasingly uneasy, and I could see Dory was the same way. 'You could also turn an entire population into loyal, loving, obedient slaves.'

The scientist shrugged. 'Like all discoveries, the potential for abuse is awesome. It is our responsibility, our trust, to see that it does not happen. Fortunately, ve have much time – the technology involved in such a thing is not yet here, and, for now, ve alone have it. But ve cannot unlearn vat ve have learned, cannot undo vat ve have done any more than the atomic genie could be pushed back into the bottle once released. It is a grave responsibility, but it is no more grave than other great discoveries of mankind. Ve have the responsibility vether ve vant it or not, and, as always, ve puny little fallible humans have to deal with it. Considering how far ve have come to now, I think ve vill.'

An assistant brought Stuart and Dory tea and me coffee. I couldn't help thinking about the potential, and wondering about the possibilities of abuse. I looked around at the people at IMC and thought about the others I'd met. Except for Parch they seemed very ordinary people, middle-level bureaucrats in administration, technicians and scientists and their families as well. Not evil threatening people. Not headed by Stuart, particularly, one of the finest men I'd ever known. Still, they would worry me, particularly Parch. In the hands of such a man as he, the pontential was horrible.

It was Dory who shifted subject again, possibly partly in self-defense against thinking too hard on what was bothering me.

'What about genetics?' she asked Stuart. 'I mean, you can't change the genetic code when you change this information in the brain.'

'I'll admit that is a puzzle,' Eisenstadt admitted. 'There are so many things about a person that are determined by his physiology and science is no closer to solving the heredity-versus-environment debate now than twenty years ago. Perhaps people like *you* vill eventually solve the puzzle, although there is debate even on that. After all, your personalities were shaped by your original genetic and other makeup and might by this time be too fixed to be measurably changed. Maybe not. If you find out vill you tell us?'

We both laughed, and Dory kept to this point for a reason I slowly started understanding.

'What sort of things are you certain are genetically caused?' she asked him.

He shrugged. 'Studies vith tvins have shown a little but it is more puzzling than before. They make a great thing about identical twins separated at birth using the same shaving lotion – but might that not be because their taste and smell are the same so the same stuff vould be pleasurable? Ve don't know.'

'What about – sex?' she pressed, becoming obvious.

'Sex is obviously genetic in the most basic sense,' Stuart replied, at first missing the real question. 'The degree of sex and of sexual response is partly a matter of enzyme and hormone production, stuff like that. You *can* be over-sexed or undersexed, for example, even in the drive, as determined by your genetic make-up. Beyond that, though, so many cultural factors go into it that it is hard to say. Victor, here, vas Victor for thirty-five years and is now Vicki, but not in the usual sex-change vay. Fully functioning, with all the body's genetic drives, hormones, that sort of thing. I vould suspect the head to respond to vomen and the body to men, vich vill give you the life of a real svinger for a vile – but you vill settle down into vichever pattern body and mind compromise on, feel best vith, over the long run.'

'That was *my* body,' Dory pointed out.

'I'm avare of that.'

'Doc – I was a lesbian.'

That stopped him, but only for a moment. He thought over the possibli-ties, then said, 'Vell, that puts a little more of a strain on Vicki, here. There is a tiny area in the cerebellum discovered in 1980, a small group of neurons that is normally sexually consistent – it looks vun vay in men, the other in vomen. It came out of studies to see if the male and female brain differed in any significant vay. Now, this is not the cause of all homosexual tendencies – much of it is psychological and environmental. But it has been found that some vomen have the male configuration – not many, but some – and some men have the female. Who knows vy? A mistake in genetic coding? A muta-tion? Something the mama drank? Extreme sexual mirror-imaging vas found in hermaphrodites, but a small but important percentage have the thing tilted a bit towards the wrong sex, if you'll pardon me. It might cause extra – complications – for Victor if that body's sexual identity center is more male than female. Only time vill tell – or, of course, ve could do a computer scan and find out.'

'You mean hook me up to your computer? Uh uh, Stuart. Not now, any-way. I've had enough fooling around with my mind for the time being.'

He chuckled softly. 'Come. I vill show you the heart of IMC and maybe you vill not feel so bad.'

We got up and left the office, going down a hall to a set of large double doors with all sorts of security warnings on them. He ignored them and held the doors for us to pass inside.

The room was huge, looking more like the control center for some space system than anything related to biology. An orange wall-to-wall carpet went around the floor in a semi-circle, but it was almost obscured by the computer terminals, control centers and chairs, that made it seem like Mission Control. They all faced a raised semicircular platform carpeted in light green, on which sat two large chairs looking like nothing so much as dental chairs with large beauty-parlor hair dryers attached. Enormous masses of cable ran from the chair assemblies into the floor.

'The soul of IMC,' Stuart told us with obvious pride.

We walked onto the orange-carpeted area and Stuart went over to a large and forbidding looking console. He opened the top and reached down, removing from it a ruby-colored translucent cube perhaps a foot square. He handed it to me and I looked at it curiously. It weighed no more than two or three pounds at best. I handed it back and asked, 'What is it?'

'A digital recording module,' he replied. 'Inside it can be stored over ten trillion bytes of information. In a sense, a couple of these can hold the sum total of a human brain's knowledge and experience. It is a revolutionary vay of storing information and the key to our progress here. The equivalent of tventy thousand kilometers of magnetic tape fifty centimeters wide. Two or three of these, in the computer system, and ve can record and play back a human mind.'

I shivered. 'Then you can actually remove information from the brain, like they can?'

He nodded. 'Yes, yes, ve can do that. It is simply a matter of applying the correct electrical signal at the correct point in the cerebral cortex. Ve can now get a readout.'

I looked down at Dory and thought that her expression must be matched by my own face. 'So can you – switch minds?'

'Ve are not *that* far along yet, although ve are very close. So far ve have managed first to copy someone's identity matrix and store it on the cubes. Then it was but a short step to learning how to erase as ve recorded. Ve can take it out and erase now, and put it back in the same head from which it vas took, vith no apparent loss. In fact, ven ve do that the person always remembers much more of their life, seems to think a bit more clearly. Remember – ve are cleaning out not only the active memory and personality but also that attic full of forgotten junk, opening new pathways to it and for it. It becomes accessible again. But only for a vile. Since it vas stored there in the first place because it vas no longer needed, it fades with disuse, in a veek or two at the most.'

I nodded to myself. 'Yes, I remember the first time I got switched. I seemed to remember things back to babyhood and everything seemed so crisp and clear, like my I.Q. had been doubled. But it faded.'

'Can you – put people back into other bodies?' Dory asked hesitantly.

He saw her concern and smiled reassuringly. 'No. Not yet. Not really, anyvay. Tolerances are too critical. Ve just don't know enough. There is anyvere from a ten to fifty percent insertion loss, or the information is there but can't be gotten at. The roadblock seems to be the brain vaves, the woltage inside the head. It, too, is different for different people and the old values won't do since that would interfere with the autonomic functions of the body ve don't touch. The values of the new body aren't matched to vat the old matrix system is used to. It appears there is an almost no-tolerance compromise between vat the input needs and the new body requires that is unique with each individual. But the Urulu find it – find it and automatically match it in moments. Vun day, perhaps soon, ve vill find it, too.'

And, somehow, I knew he would. I shuddered at the idea of an 'insertion loss' of ten to fifty percent. An I.Q. 150 might become a below-normal I.Q. 75.

Stuart had to go about his business after that, and we left him in the command center of IMC. We headed for the cafeteria, although neither of us felt like eating. I, for one, felt the need to sit down and get control of myself for a few moments.

'It scares the hell out of me,' I told Dory. 'Right now he can read us out and store us in little cubes. You know it won't be long before they'll know how to switch. Considering how far they've come in such a short time now, it could be today, or tomorrow. Certainly it's a matter of months, not years. And all that will be put in the hands of men like Harry Parch. Worse. Can you imagine them with a bunch of bodies, clearing them out, then feeding Parch's recording into all of them? An army of Harry Parches. He wouldn't need his makeup kit any more.'

'It's worse than that, if you remember our earlier conversation with Eisenstadt,' Dory replied. 'Look, I own – used to own – a good digital tape recorder. Puts the signal on tape as a binary code, millions of tiny dots, each representing a single element of the music. Mine won't edit much – it's a cheap model – but at the store where I got it they had this real fancy kind, the kind professional recording companies and TV companies use. They had a string quartet – four instruments playing together – on tape. They used to show what you could do with an editor by removing one instrument – the violin, say – and replacing it with a piccolo playing the same part. Sounded stupid and weird, but that computer tape recorder-editor of theirs could figure out which little dots applied *only* to violins – even reverb, echo, you name it – then separate it from all the other sounds and replace it.'

For a moment I didn't see it, but suddenly it hit me. Holographic memory ... That meant that the brain didn't store your name, for example, in a billion places. Inefficient. It stored that in one place and went to it when forming its thoughts. If they learned which little digital dots, which bytes of information, were which, and could locate your name as easily as the musical engineer located Dory's violin, they could replace that information when reading it back into you. Edit your memories.

'You see what I mean,' she said gravely. 'They could redo everybody. We'd be happy little robots. And Dr Eisenstadt seemed so *nice*.'

'He is,' I assured her. 'I'm sure he and his colleagues are thinking along the lines he said. Curing disease, treating hopeless mental illness, that sort of thing.'

'These people – the ones we've met – they seem like decent sorts, I guess. They have husbands and wives and kids and many live on the surface, in normal homes, having normal family lives. They join the PTA, play tennis, laugh at comedies, bowl. Am I wrong to be so afraid?'

I reached over and squeezed her hand. 'No, you're not. History is on the side of your nightmares, I'm afraid. Oh, I doubt if anybody here, even Parch, is acting from selfish, power-seeking motives. Whatever they do with this power they will do for the best of reasons, from the purest of motives. Their psychiatric screening is damned good, as good as for the guys who fire the nuclear missiles in case of atomic war – and we've never had one fired incorrectly yet. But good motives don't make actions good. These people aren't monsters or crazy dictator types, they're worse – middle-level government bureaucrats and naive scientists. But consider – I'll just bet there is, or soon will be, a Genetic Research Center that's the equivalent of IMC somewhere. So that IMC and GRC combined can produce the sanest, healthiest, most perfect human specimens government bureaucrats can devise. Perfect people made to order – a glorious ideal. Without hatred, without prejudice, all equal. And all somebody else's idea – and ideal – of perfection.'

She shivered. 'What a horrible idea. Surely there must be *something* we can do about it.'

I shook my head slowly from side to side. 'There isn't much. The only thing that might undo it would be the full glare of publicity. And, no matter what Parch said, we're prisoners here, really, Dory. They aren't going to let us out of here until they can be assured of our silence. And as long as they are in a wartime type situation, with everybody concerned with meeting an alien menace from the stars, they'll have a Harry Parch around to make sure nothing gets out.' I sighed. 'We're in the position of knowing the danger, but we have to sit back and hope somebody else blows the whistle. It's out of our hands, damn it.'

'At least they aren't there yet,' she said, trying to convince herself that there was some light at the end of the tunnel.

That very afternoon they put me to work. By this time Dan Pauley had been transferred to a more automated and more secure glass cage, and I was able to work without a lot of gunslingers around. Remote monitoring would stop Pauley before he could do just about anything; a rat caught in a very frustrating trap.

This left me with Jeff Overmeyer as the one man always there for my sessions with the alien. Overmeyer was a nice young technician who oversaw the technical aspects of my talks, made certain the recordings were clear and that all systems in the alien's security were working properly. Although officially Parch's man, a security man, he was neither as sinister nor as secretive as his boss and generally tended to be a really nice guy. It wasn't an act, either, and more than once I suspected that the usual government games were being played and that he might be Eisenstadt's man in Parch's organization the same as Parch undoubtedly had people with Eisenstadt's technician crew. Both men were coequals who often got in each other's way, and both would be always trying to circumvent the other.

As for Pauley, he seemed to enjoy talking, particularly with me, although never about things he didn't want to discuss. Overmeyer assured me that they had already tried the drugs and other tricks short of physical torture on Pauley and found him not only impervious, as he'd said, but infuriatingly amused by their attempts. It was up to me.

Some things I learned explained a little. The Urulu didn't like airplanes, for example. I found it amusing that a race that flew across countless light-years of space was terrified of airplanes, so much so that they'd gone from car to train to horseback to ferry in Alaska rather than easily circumvent Parch by switching bodies secretly and taking a plane south. It was an odd bit of alien psychology that helped remind me that this normal, pleasant young man was neither normal nor a man. The best explanation I got was that the normal Urulu form was so different from ours that their normal environment posed its greatest threat in changes in pressure. Although unaffected physically by small changes while in human form, their inborn alien fear of such a thing was so great they couldn't bring themselves to do it. It was a handy fact, anyway, as Overmeyer pointed out. It meant they didn't have to check airplanes and airports as much, and that a really good test of whether a body was taken over or not might be to take them for a plane ride.

They'd played pressurization games on Pauley here, but it hadn't worked. The terror was so complete that the knee-jerk reaction he had was to pass out cold. Nobody won again.

As to how the Urulu switched bodies, he was no help at all. Not that he withheld much information – he just didn't know. It was like raising your right arm, or blinking, or anything else normal – you just *did* it, that's all.

About the Urulu he was no other real help, although he was willing to discuss his enemies, a group that translated out as The Association. The master races of that alliance had apparently developed the technique mechanically, much as IMC was trying to do, and had hit upon our wildest nightmares.

It was odd, in fact, how much Dan's description of the Association matched Dory's and my own fears about IMC. Theirs was a race – the original one – that had used the process to create 'perfect' people according to an idealized standard. It was a dull, soulless, mechanical society but everybody was happy because they couldn't be anything else, and nobody had any doubts, fears, jealousies, nor love, hate, or any of the emotions we would recognize. Their sole drive, their sole aim, was to bring that driving 'perfection' to all sentient races in the universe. They would find a race on a world, study it in cool, computer-like terms, analyze the 'imperfections' of the society and the race – and the world – and then slowly, surreptitiously, they would worm their way in, gain converts, create a force of native devotees, and eventually they would gain the seat of power in each and every nation, tribe, you name it. The world, then, could be easily remade.

'That's why the very existence of IMC worries us,' Pauley told me. 'We don't think they've found it yet, or infiltrated it yet, but it's tailor-made for them to take over. If, of course, it doesn't become a homemade and home-grown version of The Association without their help.'

That last, I think, disturbed me more than any external threat. I asked him what his people would do if they discovered IMC.

'Destroy it, certainly,' he responded instantly. 'But not the minds who created it. Just the physical plant. With that done, they would then try to enlist the Earth as an ally against The Association. Space and potential immortality in exchange for fighting a war Earth had a stake in winning.'

'That didn't seem your direction as of Alaska,' I pointed out coolly.

He shrugged. 'Alaska was another era. If my people now knew just of IMC and how much progress it had made they might well destroy the entire planet, writing it off as lost to The Association.'

That was a chilling thought. 'So we have the cooperation of the dead? Some alliance!'

'No, no! You must understand Earth, as I said, is very peculiar. Evolution went a wildly different way here. That's why we needed the bodies and had to come all this way to get them. Maybe ten, fifteen planets out of tens of thousands, went your way. There is some, well, prejudice there, of course. The belief that such a world and such a race can't develop the kind of human qualities we see as valuable. You see, the mother race of The Association was more like yours than ours. My people would have to be convinced that Earth wouldn't inevitably take The Association's path. Soulless, we call such races. But I've been here. I know you're capable of the kind of qualities we value so highly – individuality, love, warmth, feeling, caring for one another. They looked and saw only the bad points – the terrible hatred and prejudices on such petty grounds, the dehumanizing philosophies, the cruelty and hatred and suspicion. If my people could be convinced that you are not on one side of the ledger but poised on the line, able to go both ways, they'd fall over backwards to make sure this planet developed its true potential for greatness.'

'And who will convince them?' I asked skeptically. 'You? If we let you go will you usher in this great new era? Even if you could, why should we believe you? Why trust you to do that?'

He just shook his head sadly. 'No, I *don't* know if I could convince them. I'm not sure how to do it in the limited amount of time we'd have to make a decision. Even if I'd get listened to by somebody who could make such a decision.' He hesitated, then concluded, his tone one of total defeat, 'And I have no way at all to show that I'm not a dirty villain lying through my teeth. That's what's so frustrating, Vicki – knowing what has to be done, and knowing that you can't do a damned thing about it, not even knowing if you could if you had the chance.'

I nodded sadly. I knew exactly what he was feeling. It was close enough to home I felt more comfortable changing the subject.

'Dan – why do your people need live bodies at all? Why wouldn't cloning do as well?'

'It won't work,' he told me. 'Don't ask me why but it won't. An experienced, complex mind just doesn't mesh right with a cloned body that has no history of its own. If you raise the clone as a total individual, yes it'll work – but not an unused mind grown for that purpose.' He looked apologetic. 'When you think of Earth people the way most Urulu do, as little more than complex animals, it's easier just to nab bodies as you need them.'

Every day I was continually fighting off men's advances. I began to realize what Dory meant by beauty being a curse. All men seemed to think they were God's gift to women, none seemed to think I could do anything for myself, and, since very few knew that I was not born in this body, all assumed I was 'making it' regularly with somebody or other. Trouble was, this damned body looked good in a potato sack.

I found what relief I could in masturbation but couldn't bring myself to anything more overt, although I hardly lacked for opportunity even with a few of the women around, lesbians themselves. They were more tolerant of such things at IMC, where the brain was the object and the subject. Ultimately, though, I knew I would have to face up to the problem, since my body was more and more insistent and had far greater needs than my old one had, and, of course, I badly needed some sort of companionship in this cold, underground city. Dory was around, of course, but not much after a while, as her training program took her to far distant levels and required a lot of practice and studying. Besides, I told myself, she'd *found* her new life, her new start. I still felt that I owed her, but she didn't necessarily feel the same towards me, and I couldn't blame her.

I was also, now, experiencing menstruation, and it still shocked me every time my 'period' came. It was messy, smelly, uncomfortable, you name it, and every month on the first day of it I got the most horrible, debilitating cramps I'd ever experienced. The IMC medical staff prescribed some stuff which helped enormously, but I was still experiencing the underside of what it was like to be a woman, and the physical discomfort and mental shifts were far greater than I'd ever realized from the viewpoint of being a man.

I was pretty well reconciled to being in this body the rest of my life, though. That, at least, grew easier every day. I no longer awoke with a feeling of surprise at who and what I was, and I'd long ago gotten used to the bras, the odd feeling of women's undergarments, not to mention all the cosmetic stuff, hair care, and the rest. Real high heels were still a bit beyond me, but I was practicing, in the private places, and I was also consciously studying and imitating women's mannerisms, ways of walking, that sort of thing. I was a long way from being completely natural, but it was coming. I wanted to fit.

And that, finally, brought me to the decision point. I *had* to know about myself, and that meant taking the plunge.

There was no question as to who would be the first experiment. Jeff Overmeyer had been the closest thing I had to a confidant and friend since Dory'd gotten so busy, and he was young, experienced with women, knew my background but didn't mind, and had never once pushed himself on me or treated me as other than an equal. I liked him a lot, even if I didn't fully trust him, and although I hesitated for weeks I was the one who finally made the first move.

After, coming back to my quarters, I saw that Dory was still up and went in to tell her.

'Well, you don't look any worse for wear,' she noted. 'What did you think?'

'I don't know what I think,' I told her honestly. 'It was – well, strange. On the one hand, I'm now convinced that women get a little more out of it than men. A man's only got one place to feel it, while we've got four.'

'We,' she noted. 'You *are* adjusting.'

I shrugged. 'On the one hand, it felt really good. On the other, well, it felt *wrong*. I kept wanting to be the aggressor, for one thing. And while the preliminaries were fine, during intercourse I kept wanting to stick it in, to feel that total sensation, and instead I had a whole different set of feelings. Not unpleasant, in any way, but not what I knew *he* was feeling. Put it down to mixed reviews, I guess I haven't gone sour on the deal, although the idea of a blow job is pretty repulsive.'

'Did he come?'

'Yes.'

'Did you get off?'

I hesitated, then replied, 'No.'

She just nodded for a moment, then asked, 'Did he use a condom? Or have you started on the pill?'

I felt a slight shock go through me. 'No on all counts,' I said uneasily.

'Jesus! How far along are you? How long since your last period?'

I thought a moment. 'Two weeks. I'm about mid-way.'

'Holy shit! You took a chance there! Or do you plan to have his baby?'

I just sat there, stunned, for a bit. It simply hadn't occurred to me.

Dory whistled. 'You're really in the club now. You got two weeks or more of heavy sweating to do. As much as you hate your period, you're gonna be praying for it to come. And if it doesn't, and the feds don't do abortions here, you're gonna go through more than I ever did. *Now* you're *really* gonna find out what it's like to be a woman.'

CHAPTER EIGHT

The next three weeks were among the most miserable of my life. I grew increasingly nervous and irritable, and even throwing myself into the reports and mounds of paperwork on Pauley and the Urulu didn't help. I screwed up form after form, couldn't type worth a damn, and every little thing made me furious where in other circumstances I'd have laughed them off. I was a holy terror to be around and I knew it, but I just couldn't help it.

I certainly didn't blame Jeff Overmeyer. In fact, I didn't even tell him, although he didn't quite escape blame in my mind. I was irritated with myself, of course, for not thinking things through, and the primary blame was mine, but there seemed something unfair about the fact that he had assumed that I had taken precautions rather than think along those lines himself. Score another one culturally for men, I thought sourly, realizing that, as a man myself, in my very infrequent sexual acts not once had I considered any kind of male birth control.

Dory tried to cheer me up by noting how much against the odds any inter-course leading to pregnancy was, but I was sure that the venerated Murphy's basic law would apply. When I was a week late, I got one of those home pregnancy test kits from the pharmacy and tried it, only to get some chemical confirmation of my worst fears.

I was pregnant.

The very news, knowing for sure that the worst had happened, calmed me a bit, since, at least, it outlined a series of actions. I knew from the start that I wasn't ready for this sort of thing, not yet, anyway, and that left abortion as the only option. The trouble was, the medical facilities at IMC were entirely governed by government regulations, and while they see-sawed on the abortion question and had for many years they currently didn't allow it in government facilities except to save the life of the mother. I was furious at this – *they* didn't have to carry the kid, let alone bear it under these circumstances – but they wouldn't let me take the only obvious way out. There seemed a particular irony to my problem, since we were of undetermined status (although officially on the government payroll) at IMC and it had been many months since either Dory or I had seen the sun. I wasn't about to take this, though, and finally confessed the problem to Jeff.

He arranged an appointment with Harry Parch.

I'd seen almost nothing of the man since the first few days at IMC, and I'd had the impression that he'd been away more than here which suited everybody just fine, but walking into his office once again I found him the same cool fish, only more cruel and infuriating than ever.

'So you got knocked up and you're stuck,' he said with a trace of amusement. I grew furious at his tone and felt myself becoming flush with anger, yet I held it in. No matter what kind of slimy eel the man was, he was the only one who could help.

So instead of yelling at him, I just replied, 'I'm in trouble, I have a problem, and my status here keeps me from resolving it. I'm asking – pleading – for your help. It's only a problem because of your goddamned government restrictions.'

He nodded. 'I'll agree that the situation is complicated beyond normal bounds. Just what do you want me to do about it? I can't order the clinic to ignore those policies – the folks that slap them on pay our bills and our salaries. Frankly, my influence just doesn't extend into the medical field.'

'I know that. They already explained that to me. But we're in Nevada, a state with liberal laws on almost everything. I've talked to several women here, and they tell me there are abortion clinics in Las Vegas.'

'I thought it was something like that.' He sighed. 'I don't mind telling you that you present me with a real problem, since you certainly know too much at this point for true security's sake.' He paused, hands together, thinking it over. Finally he said, 'However, I can sympathize with your situation. If it were strictly up to me, there'd be no problem. I doubt if you could do much harm anyway, unless you ran into some Urulu. You're too trusting, too much of an idealist. Tell you what, though – I'll pass this on to the full Directorate of IMC, which includes myself and Dr Eisenstadt, and recommend we allow it. It could be a little while, though, so you'll have to just grin and bear it until then. Everyone's not here right now and I have to leave again shortly for Washington.'

I had a sinking feeling. 'How long?'

He shrugged. 'As soon as possible. That's all I can promise.'

'It'll have to do,' I agreed, resignedly.

I had, naturally, talked all this over with Dory, and she seemed interested in the idea of me getting out, however briefly.

'Look, I've been in lots of places you haven't,' she told me. 'I told you about some of the things I've seen.'

She had been giving me regular reports, since my own areas of IMC were now routinely familiar but off the beaten track. It was clear that IMC was experimenting on human beings, starting with some terminally ill volunteers from various government hospitals. Close to death and without hope, these people had allowed themselves to be placed in the two sinister chairs downstairs. Early results, rumor said, had been very encouraging. Finally some volunteers who were themselves on the project had been tested – with horribly mixed results. Bright young men and women who now had pieces of themselves missing, muddled, or scrambled, now kept around in whatever menial tasks they could do until the bugs were worked out. Eisenstadt, it had been said, opposed the experiments at this point but was overruled by the Pentagon bosses in Washington who were desperate for results. Now he was working eighteen-hour days and seven-day weeks to break the puzzle, because, of course, those damaged people had had their 'identity matrices' recorded prior to the experiment. He was determined to restore them.

It rang true to me, first because it sounded like Stuart, and also because the pressures *would* be mounting. From my security contacts, mostly through Jeff, I had learned of some independent confirmation that a second alien group might well be operating and that the Urulu story might not be just a common bluff. If the Urulu scared them, The Association practically terrified them, not just because of its philosophy (since we had no real way of knowing if the Urulu were any better) but because it represented Earth as a potential battleground between two superior alien forces and technologies, helpless to do anything about it. The pressure to crack the last bits of the identity matrix puzzle would be enormous.

That they would do it neither Dory nor I doubted. But when they did – what would they do with it, these faceless, nameless Pentagon bosses? It made some sort of public disclosure even more imperative.

Time passed, though, with my own problems taking on more urgency than the larger, global picture. If they went too long without a decision, I might have to have a far more dangerous and drastic type of abortion and that scared me most of all. I began to think that, in spite of everything, I might have to bear the child.

Six weeks after that fateful intercourse I finally got a summons to Parch's office once again. He looked tired and haggard and not at all in the mood for trivialities like me. Still, he said, 'All right. They approved it. We've made an appointment for you at one of these places for one tomorrow afternoon, and will, of course, deduct the considerable cost from your account here.

Overmeyer will drive you there and stick with you. It's almost a three-hour drive, and who knows how long there, so we've approved your staying at a motel in town for the night, then driving back in the morning. I picked Overmeyer because he's at least partially responsible for this, but it'll be his head if anything, and I mean *anything*, goes wrong. His and yours, too. Understand?'

'I understand,' I nodded glumly.

'Oh – the motel's on you, too. We'll pay for the gas.'

'Thanks a lot,' I muttered sourly, and left him.

I met Dory for lunch – she was now working in one of the computer centers as an operator, seemingly enjoying it, although she had some problems with everyone taking a thirteen-year-old kid seriously as a co-worker – and told her the news.

She brightened at the news I was getting out. 'Look,' she whispered, her tone becoming somewhat conspiratorial, 'while you're there you can get word out.'

I was startled. 'To who? And how? I'm not going to be alone – except for, well, you know …'

'You've gotta know somebody's home phone number. Send a telegram by phone and charge it to that number.'

I considered it. It actually sounded plausible. My own old number would, of course, have been long disconnected, but there *were* a number of people whose numbers I knew and who wouldn't even notice such a charge on their bill. 'But who?'

She thought a moment. 'How about Harl Calvert?'

I thought about it and the more I thought the more sense it made. Calvert was the biggest syndicated muckraking columnist in Washington. He'd sell his soul for a story like this if he hadn't already sold it long ago – but once he had it he wouldn't let go. And he was listed, so they could phone in the telegram without my having to give specific addresses.

Still, I was extremely nervous about the abortion and this only doubled my anxiety. Yet, the abortion might disguise my actions, and it was worth a try. That was all I could promise. I'd try.

I won't dwell on the ride into Vegas in the scorching sun, nor the abortion experience, except to say that Jeff seemed as worried and depressed as I was, so there was little conversation, and the clinic was the most dehumanizing cattle barn I'd ever been in, with loads of miserable looking women, mostly teens it seemed, sitting around waiting to be called. The experience itself was administered by doctors who had the same regard for you as they did for a piece of meat and it was painful and horrible to undergo, and more of a shock to my nervous system than I'd expected.

It was also, in a more personal way, very depressing. No matter what my liberal feelings on abortion, they'd sprung from the viewpoint of being a man, one who would never have even the threat of undergoing one himself and not the slightest idea of what it was like. And, somewhere deep inside me, I realized I'd always bear the cross of the action, always feel like I'd killed, if not someone else, then at least a little part of me.

Jeff was solicitous and left me alone when I wanted to be. We were registered in as 'Mr and Mrs Jeffrey Overmeyer' which, I supposed, was only fitting. It was odd, somehow, that the most abnormal combination of circumstances imaginable gave such an air of total social normalcy.

Still, he left me alone in the room to sleep a little – I was pretty slicky still and hadn't slept at all the night before – and, were I was, alone in the motel room with a motel phone.

I admit I lay there on that bed staring at that phone, knowing what I had to do but also knowing that if I waited much longer, Jeff would return and my chance would be gone.

Finally I got up the nerve to do it.

I charged the telegram to my father's law firm. Although he was long dead the firm continued and even prospered and it'd never much changed its number. I took a chance in identifying myself as George Lloyd's secretary, since it'd been long enough she might not still work there, but they took the message and didn't seem to have any problems.

I sent, 'Top secret government mind control project well underway in Nevada desert near Yucca Flat. People held virtual prisoners to security there.' I didn't sign it, of course.

But it was done – and now it was up to Harl Calvert.

I had barely finished when the key rattled in the door and I almost jumped back into bed as Jeff opened it. The initial scare was followed by some relief – if he were this close he couldn't have been overhearing me at the switchboard, and if he were lurking just outside he would have come in earlier.

He brought the local papers and seemed totally free of suspicion. 'How are you feeling?'

'Much better,' I told him, and I was, although a bit weak. 'I feel starved, though. What time is it?'

He looked at his watch. 'About seven thirty.'

I got up, and found myself slightly dizzy. 'Umph. Still a little weak. They said it was all in the mind, though, so I guess my mind decides what's important. What's for dinner?'

He laughed, looking relieved. 'Glad to see you more like yourself again. Look, there's no room service in this dump, and none of my instructions covered barring the doors. Parch is pretty convinced you could shout to the rooftops "the aliens are coming!" and only get thrown in the asylum anyway.

What say we make the most of tonight? Go down to a good restaurant, hit a casino, then get a good night's sleep.'

I smiled. 'That's the first bright spot I've had in weeks,' I told him with total sincerity. 'Just let me get dressed.'

I dressed quickly, not only because I genuinely *was* anxious to get out but also because I feared that something would go wrong, that they'd call back and inquire about a telegram or something.

And it *was* a good night, although I was still feeling slightly weak and it didn't last very late. It was the first time since Seattle, so very long ago, that I'd been out in public, and I was a different person now even if in the same body. It was fun to be out *with* someone, to walk arm-in-arm down a casino-lit strip, to let go a little and hug him when he hit on the crap table. Being with him I felt very normal and very secure. I was still aware of the heads turning, the admiring glances, but it didn't bother me that night.

And, later, in the motel room, he held me when I wanted to be held and we kissed goodnight and I thought that he was probably the only man who had any understanding of me.

I wasn't falling in love with Jeff, and still felt no real sexual passion for him, but I liked him a lot, not just for being a nice person but for understanding. I didn't really know myself yet, or what I wanted or even could be, but I *did* know that Jeff had brought me, in the worst of circumstances, the closest I'd ever felt to belonging, to fitting in, to being a part of the human race, and I owed him for that.

It almost made me feel guilty that I had betrayed his kindness and trust in me with the telegram. Almost, but not quite. For looming behind Jeff was IMC, and Harry Parch, and I certainly felt the same about them.

I had taken the risk and done what I could, and I could do no more. It was out of my hands now. But I had some satisfaction in the wording of the message. Parch had been right – had I even mentioned 'alien invaders' or 'body switching' in my telegram it would have been tossed right in the circular file with the other nut cases. But I hadn't. I had lived in and around Washington too long to make that kind of mistake. I had offered instead the irresistible.

We had been taken to IMC in July; it was now February of the next year and things were still running according to routine. I'd long since finished with Dan Pauley; I had no idea where he was or even if he still was anyplace. I was now working with the computer techs on assembling a basic history and psychological profile of the Urulu and it was proving fascinating to me, although it would probably have driven most people nuts to go through all that minutiae for some little scrap here and there. Much of what I found confirmed the essentials of Pauley's own statements, although, I had to note, they had all been the most casual, friendly talkers any interrogator would want and yet they'd told precious little anybody wanted to know.

I also turned twenty in February, according to Dory – February 16. Dory remained in the technicians' ranks, mostly by choice. She had never had much interest in some grandiose career or the joys of college learning; she was far more practical-minded than I was and found a hands-on job far more satisfying. She'd grown a little, and near the end of the year had begun the final stages of passage into puberty, the change into womanhood bringing out an innate beauty in her.

My telegram had been sent in late October, apparently to no avail. I'd lived in some fear of discovery for weeks after, but now my greater fear was that it had either not reached its intended party or had been disregarded by Calvert's column. All I could tell Dory and myself was that I had tried, done what I could, and it just hadn't been enough.

It was, therefore, a major surprise late in February when the whole of IMC was abuzz with the news: a big-shot congressman, Chairman of the House Intelligence Committee, Phillip Kelleam, was paying us a visit – and, word was, there would be at least one reporter with him.

The rumors were soon confirmed as we were commanded to attend little after-hours seminars by Parch's people on what to say and what not to say, who we could talk to and who we couldn't.

I had continued to see Jeff Overmeyer, although not romantically, on a social basis and got more details.

'Somehow, Calvert – that Washington columnist with spies in every department – got wind of IMC,' he told me. 'We don't know how, but, then again, it's a miracle something this big has managed to escape the public this long. He dug up enough supporting stuff to make a real stink and threatened to go public with it unless he got the whole story and could be convinced not to run it. That got Kelleam involved, since it's his ass as much as anybody's, and so they're orchestrating this little tour. All Parch wants is for nobody except hand-picked people to say more than polite nothings to them and leave them to him.'

'He'll get that much,' I noted. 'After all, who wants to be the one that broke the rules who's still here with Parch after they leave? But I think you're blown now, Jeff. Even if Kelleam's in on this Calvert won't sit still no matter what bullshit he's fed. If he finds out the truth he'll splash it over the whole world; if he doesn't, he'll mount a massive attack on us as a wasteful extravagance.'

Overmeyer just sighed. 'No, I don't think so. You just don't *know*, Vicki, what we can now do.'

He wouldn't go any further, but it worried me.

Kelleam turned out to look like everybody's favorite uncle; he was a twenty-four-year veteran of the House and one of its masters, in line, some said, for the Speaker's chair. I stared at him, going around, shaking hands like anybody here could vote for him, and being so much the saccharine politician that I knew he was anything but what he appeared. He was a damned smart and shrewd political manipulator, a power-lover with guts, and one of the few men who'd know all about IMC. As different as the two men appeared on the surface, if Harry Parch had a friend and soul-mate in this world it was almost certainly Phil Kelleam.

He brought an entourage, of course, mostly bright-looking young men and women, his aides and yes-men whose very souls he owned but who had dreams one day of being at the center of power themselves. How much *they* knew of IMC's true job was unknown, but, courts or no courts, I bet myself that every one of their phones were tapped, their every waking moment spied upon or monitored by somebody.

Calvert was by himself, nobody else allowed from his side. He looked much older than the little picture they always put with his column and not at all well, but his brown eyes darted everywhere and his expession showed that he was not here for any pleasure trip.

When Parch, Eisenstadt, and another man in a business suit whom I'd not come across before but who was, obviously, IMC's own chief of administration, Joe Parks, shook hands around with the party, it was Calvert who spoke up.

'I want to know the truth about this place,' he snapped to Parch in a somewhat threatening tone. 'You have a lot to account for, you know. The budget for a whole nonexistent nuclear aircraft carrier is here and the public has a right to know how you can float a ship in Nevada.'

Parch didn't seem at all disturbed. 'We'll show you everything,' he assured the columnist. 'Answer any questions, anything you want. Even give you demonstrations. At the end, if you still think this place should see print at this time, we'll do nothing to stop you.'

Calvert just nodded dubiously and walked to catch up with the Congressman. From my office I just watched the group fade down the long hall until they were gone.

Something definitely stunk to high heaven, though. The level of cover-up necessary to fool somebody like Calvert just hadn't been done at IMC, and Harry Parch had sounded a little *too* confident of himself. I began to worry a bit. Would they dare kill Calvert? I hoped not, not only because I'd feel like a murderer but also because it would mean a sense of power here beyond any in the country. But, no, I told myself, they wouldn't do it anyway. All you'd need to blow this place irrevocably would be to have Calvert die in the course of its investigation, even by the most accidental of causes.

I didn't see them again, but Dory did, twice, and what she saw made us both even more nervous.

'I saw Calvert twice,' she told me. 'Once on the same day you did, then again two days later when they were leaving. It was incredible, the change in him, Vicki. I swear to you that I heard him talking to Kelleam and Parch like old buddies and assuring him that he'd do everything in his power to keep the lid on! Calvert!'

I felt defeated. 'You think this is all an act of his, then? That he's really with them.'

'He wasn't with them, wasn't acting, when he came here,' she responded ominously. 'Oh, Vicki, I'm *really* scared now. I think they've done it – broken the roadblock wide open! I think they did what they told him they'd do – show him around, answer every question, and give him a demonstration. I think they demonstrated all right – on him!'

I was wrapping up my work in early March. They seemed quite pleased with it, despite my own estimation that it was full of holes in all the important places. We were winding down now, though, and I expected to find out in another few days what my next assignment would be.

I, therefore, wasn't all that surprised late one afternoon to get a summons to Parch's office. Technically I worked in his area, although far removed from his nastier jobs, and it would be from him or one of his administrative assistants that I would get my new assignment.

I was, however, surprised to find Dory there, and I got a very uneasy feeling. As I walked into that familiar office I noticed an immediate change. The secretaries and technicians were nowhere about, but present were several well-dressed men who could only be some of Parch's agents.

Parch himself looked grimly at us and gestured for me to take a seat. Still, his opening remark was very routine. 'You've finished the master report?'

I nodded nervously. 'It just needs to be correlated and printed out.'

'That's good, that's fine,' he responded. I glanced anxiously at Dory but she had the same nervous look I was feeling and her eyes and expression told me that she had no idea what this was about.

Parch leaned back in his office chair and sighed. 'Ms Gonser, Ms Tomlinson. The time has come to discuss both your futures, I'm afraid. You've been most helpful to us in a number of ways, and I'd like to just pay you off, give you new identities, and be rid of you. Unfortunately, I cannot. You have also been a wee bit harmful, I'm afraid, and even if we could overlook or fix that part, neither of you are very trustworthy when it comes to making my job easier. I am charged with keeping this installation secure. I do not believe that this is possible were I to let you go, even if we could, somehow, erase the location of it from your minds.'

'I don't know what you're talking about, Parch,' I managed, my mouth feeling suddenly very dry.

He shook his head sadly. 'Look, I'll not play games with you, nor can I spare the time in needless cat-and-mouse talks. We know you sent the telegram to Calvert. It was quite a good try, really. We had no idea at the time, but once his people got to poking and probing we managed to get into his files and discover the text of it, then compare it with Western Union. Although it was charged to a Washington law firm – your father's old one, I believe – the official file copy contained the number from which it was placed. That proved to be where, from its date, we already suspected – the Mirage Motel in Las Vegas, Nevada. It was not nice, Ms Gonser, to abuse our hospitality like that.'

He had me cold. There was really nothing to say. He turned to Dory. 'As for you,' he continued, 'while we have few places totally monitored on a routine basis, since this place is so large, we did, because of your psychological profile, take extra precautions with you. During your initial medical exam here we placed a tiny micro-miniature transmitter under your skin. It ran down a week or so ago, finally, but we have a nice tape recording of your conversations with Ms Gonser, particularly one just before she went for her abortion.'

'You bastard,' she muttered.

He shrugged off the insult. 'Now, even with all that, I wouldn't normally be worried. But, as I said, we can't really remove IMC from your minds, not all the people, physical layout, you name it, unless we induced amnesia from the point of the final switch on the ferry. That I could do, but it wouldn't mean much to your futures and your life. It simply wouldn't be fair.'

'Since when has something like fair play ever been a part of your behavior?' Dory snapped, and a little part of me cheered.

He sighed. 'Look, I'm not the evil mastermind you think me, I assure you – for all the good it does. I do not make the final decisions, although discretion is left to me on how those decisions will be carried out. If it were strictly up to me, I would just let you continue until the time, here, when we know enough to go public and face down our threats. But it's come down to a matter of security. The Urulu were telling the truth, in one regard, at least. They are at war with another alien power and that war is reaching us more and more. Because we lack the defenses we cannot yet meet the threat. The security of IMC is important now first and foremost because either of those alien sides would destroy it in an instant and the warfare would become open and blatant. Millions of lives are at stake, I firmly believe – and in that condition, what can a few individuals count for? Not only the two of you, but me, anyone here, no matter how high and mighty.'

'The land of the free and the home of the brave,' Dory sneered.

Again he was surprisingly defensive. 'Yes, it *is* ironic that we claim to be defending freedom and yet must resort to unfree methods. Still, free has a whole new meaning now. We're talking about the potential for the most absolute form of slavery – tyranny of the mind of every human being on earth by an alien power.' He grew quite intense, and I began to think that, perhaps, he really *didn't* like all this. 'I believe that what we are doing here will determine forever whether or not the human race can be free. I cannot, will not, allow personal feelings or considerations to jeopardize that sacred trust.'

There was silence for a moment. Finally, feeling wooden and empty, I said, 'So you're going to kill us, then.'

'No, I'm not,' he replied, sounding a little hurt. 'First of all, both of you are already dead. The Indian girl is forever just plain missing, of course, but any records traceable to her original identity were removed totally. Fingerprints, footprints, you name it. They appear on no official record anywhere. You, Gonser, are dead and buried as you know. And as for the Tomlinsons, a bit of scouring morgues throughout the northwest turned up a decent candidate. You, Ms Tomlinson, missed your train at Prince Rupert, decided to hitch-hike, were in an accident and burned almost beyond recognition. You were identified by your personal effects, and are buried in Parklawn Cemetery, Winnipeg.'

Dory started, and I was almost as surprised.

'Again, records were gotten to, but, this time, other data was substituted. Ours is a society of records, of bureaucracy. Both of you, as you currently are, are anomalies in the world today – people on whom not a single solitary record exists.'

I felt sick, like I was going to throw up.

'However, this is the United States of America, not Soviet Russia or China or some two-bit dictatorship. We simply don't shoot and dump people, at least anywhere I'm in charge.'

'Then you're going to imprison us here? Maybe for years?' Dory gasped, and, odd as it sounds, there was a note of hope within her. If we remained alive, there was always a future.

'We have no budget for such a thing, and no authority,' Parch told us. 'Besides, it would be controversial here and it would be such a waste. No, there is another way, a way that will make things as right as they can be, allowing you to live normal lives while keeping us secure and you removed as any possible threat. We have come a long way technically here, as you certainly have guessed by now. It was the only reason we could deal with your Mr Calvert. Unfortunately, the remedy for him, as I said, is not possible with you. You're still not at peace with yourself anyway, Gonser, and you, Ms Tomlinson, shouldn't be cooped up here, perhaps for years, unable to live any sort of life.'

'You're going to make us into robots, slaves,' Dory gasped, horrified.

'No, nothing like that. Consider it from my viewpoint. We can not continue as before. It's bad for you, and it presents a continual risk to us. We can't morally justify killing you. It would be almost as criminal to have you both wake up strangers with a nine-month gap in your memories, not to mention embarrassing things that are possible if you *did* decide to return home and convince people you're who you really are. To imprison you would be illegal and unconscionable. To process you like we did Mr Calvert and a couple of Kelleam's aides would be impossible if we were to release you because we can't be that selective, and anything like that would open up one of the possible cans of worms I already mentioned. We can't simply turn you around to our point of view, either, since you have been here nine months, gotten to know a very large number of people, and such a personality change would be noticed, they'd put two and two together, and we'd get a holy stink from Eisenstadt's crowd.'

'What, then?' I wanted to know, just wishing it was all over with.

'Dr Eisenstadt and his top people are all in Washington for a conference,' Parch replied. 'We arranged it that way. The rest of his people who are not also *my* people are, interestingly, not working this evening. In the course of research, our people took the matrices of a huge number of people. Thousands, I'd say. They didn't know what was being done, of course, and the process isn't important. We were looking to see the differences, of course. To compare them. When it became clear that we would reach this point, my people started working on looking at those matrices, taking parts from various ones, literally creating *new* identity matrices, complete people who never lived.'

'Violins,' Dory mumbled.

Parch ignored her. 'Each of you received quite detailed individual attention. We needed real people – that is, ones that *might* be – and we needed ways of life for each of you that would allow you to live normal, if obscure, lives, out of the mainstream as it were, where you wouldn't be likely to even be discovered by accident.'

'A retired salesman from Akron and his homemaking wife,' I sighed, resigned to almost anything now.

'Huh?'

'Like the people in bars and dance saloons, on vacation. The kind that go to Vegas on a four-day, three-night package holiday. The normal folks who live and die and nobody cares.'

He looked at me a bit puzzled. Finally he said, 'This is the best way, believe me. Best for you, too. No more sexual or identity hangups. No more learning how to walk in high heels. No more lusting after other women, either. I'm aware of its partial physiological basis, but it can be overridden. The brain can be fooled into almost anything.'

'I'll bet,' I said sourly. I was shaking slightly and I couldn't stop.

'You'll be real people,' he went on. 'You'll remember your pasts, you'll fit in where you're put comfortably, and you'll live your lives with not even a thought of us, a hint, a lingering memory.'

'When are you going to do this to us?' I asked him.

The men in the back of the office stepped forward. 'In a few minutes,' he said. I felt a prick on my arm and turned with a jerk to see a man already holding a spent syringe. Dory had received the same treatment.

'Wha –' I managed.

'You'll be fully conscious,' Parch assured us. 'We need that. But we find this drug will make you much less inclined to argue and much more eager to cooperate. Just relax and let it take hold.'

Already I could feel it working. A strange numbness came over me, as if my whole body were going to sleep. My eyelids grew heavy and finally closed, my mouth became dry, my tongue felt thick and limp, and I struggled unsuccessfully as my thoughts seemed, also, to go to sleep. And yet, as Parch said, I was somehow fully conscious, a lump of clay.

'Open your eyes,' Parch said gently, and I stirred slightly and did so. 'I'm your friend,' he told me. 'I'm the only really good friend you have.'

Yes, I knew him now. He was my friend. My very *best* friend.

'You trust me,' he continued in that same soothing tone. 'You know I won't do anything to hurt you. I want to help you. I want only good things for you. You'd trust me with your life, wouldn't you?'

I nodded, both awake and not awake. He was my very best friend and I trusted him with my life.

'You'll do anything I tell you to do, won't you?' he prodded. 'Just *anything*.'

I nodded eagerly. I'd sure do anything at all he asked me to do. He was my very best friend and I trusted him.

'Now, get up from the chair and go with these nice men. They are your friends, too, and mine. Go with them to where they take you and do what they ask. You *want* to go, don't you?'

I smiled, nodded, and got up. Such nice men. Friends of my very best friend. I trusted him so I trusted them, too. I'd go with them anyplace they wanted and do just what they said.

One of them took my hand. 'Let's go,' he said, and we walked out of the office. Behind me I could hear Harry Parch speaking to Dory, but it just didn't concern me and registered not a bit.

They seated us in the large chairs on the raised, green-carpeted area of the lab center. A tiny part of me seemed to know what was going on and tried to fight against the drug, but it was hopeless.

Seated where I was, I could see part of the lower level. The consoles were all on, with thousands of multicolored switches thrown, some blinking, some changing colors, while CRT screens showed everything from odd patterns to rows upon rows of print. Technicians sat at the different consoles, many with headsets, fiddling with dials, controls, and keyboards.

A white-clad technician came up to me, fixing straps around my arms, legs, and below my breasts, securing me in one position in the chair. Then she reached behind me, there was a clicking sound, and the large helmet-like device came down over my head. The technician guided it with one hand while fixing my hair in a certain way for ease of the probes, I suppose.

Parch came into the room and looked around, then nodded. He went over to one of the technicians.

'Gonser first,' he told the man at the screen. 'You set up?'

'All systems normal,' the man responded, then, into his headset, 'Loud cubes. Memory insertion modules six through eight. On my mark. Now.'

The screen flickered. Idly I thought, *he isn't even looking at me. He has his back to me.* It was an independent thought and I tried to grab onto it, cling to it, but I failed. I steeled myself for what might come next, marshalling as much will as I could. It wasn't going to work. Somehow, they were going to blow it. Somehow, I was still going to be me, that little part of myself not drugged cried out.

'Initial I.M. sequence, probes out, Chair One,' the chief technician said, and suddenly I was aware of a tremendous vibration from the middle of my forehead up and all around me. The humming sound was quite uncomfortable.

'Matrix probes go, report on probe lock.'

My whole head started to feel funny, like millions of tiny needles were being stuck in it. Actually there was nothing physical at all; there would not be until one of the little light probes found what it was looking for.

The humming subsided, to my relief, and so did the odd, ticklish sensation of the probes.

'Probe lock on,' a voice from one of the other consoles said crisply.

'Probe lock, aye,' the chief responded. 'Prepare primary sequencing.'

'Prepared. Locked on.'

'Stage one. Begin manual stimulus.'

The woman who had strapped me in and lowered and adjusted the helmet now spoke to me.

'What is your name?' she asked. 'You needn't respond to these. Just relax. Do not answer the questions.'

I struggled against the drug, against everything, but it was no use. Every time she asked a question the answer would always come to mind, the same way it was impossible not to think of the word 'hippopotamus' once you'd been told not to think of it.

'Where were you born? Sex? Mother and father?'

The questions went on and on, like a job questionnaire you didn't have to fill out, only read. The questions, however, covered a wide range of my personal life and experiences, my attitudes, quite a bit more than the basics with which they'd started. It was frustrating to realize what they were doing – locating holographic keys, master bits of cross-referenced material which the computer itself could trace from there. There was no sensation.

'We've got sequencing!' Somebody shouted, and the woman stopped asking me questions and stepped back. I recalled Stuart's explanation and knew what they were doing now. The computer had located enough key pieces of information that it was now asking the questions itself, asking them directly of my brain at a speed so fast my consciousness wasn't even aware of it. I have no idea how it works, but I have no doubts about it.

It seemed to go on forever. Finally a buzzer sounded somewhere and the chief technician, still huddled over his console, nodded.

'Initial sequencing completed. Begin recording on one, two, and three,' he ordered. 'Read out on my mark … now!'

Again there was no sensation, but there wouldn't be. The brain had no senses of its own, and this was a read-out, a copy of what was there, not anything actually being done to it.

For the slowness of the first stage, this one seemed to be over before I knew it. Again the buzzer sounded.

'Recording complete. Analysis. Run two-six-five.'

'Running.'

'Analysis completed.'

'Run comparator with new I.M. on 4-5-6.'

'Running … Completed. Comparator confirmed. Some slight adjustment in levels required. Got it. Matched. Go.'

'Very good,' the chief technician said. 'Prepare for manual check.'

'Manual check ready, aye. All systems stable and normal.'

'Begin manual check.'

Again the woman technician next to me spoke. 'What is your name?' she asked.

'Victor Leigh Gonser,' I responded aloud, and with it I felt some triumph. The drug was wearing off! I felt sure of it! If I could just hold on I could break this control!

'What is your name?' she asked again.

'Misty Ann Carpenter,' I replied, feeling more confident now. It wasn't working!

'How old are you?'

'Thirty-six,' I responded.

'How old again?'

'Twenty – just.'

'What sex were you born, Misty?'

'Male.'

'What sex?'

'Female.' Dumb questions. I was beginning to relax. They couldn't do anything to me! Maybe it was the double switch, but I was sure now I was immune.

'And where were you born?'

'Alexandria, Virginia.'

'Where?'

'Cedar Point, Oregon.' I was feeling relaxed now, the tension easing out of me. It wasn't going to work. Sooner or later they'd realize that. I didn't know what Parch would do then but at least I would still be me.

'We've got it,' a technician called. 'No problem. Run program.'

'Running.'

Yes, I was still me. I was still Misty Ann Carpenter, twenty, female, from Cedar Point, Oregon, and I damned well was gonna stay that way.

CHAPTER NINE

I woke up slowly, as if from a very deep sleep. For a minute I didn't know who or where I was, but it all came back to me as I opened my eyes and looked out the large window of the Greyhound bus.

Ain't it funny how things go, I thought, and, for a moment, I just lay there, leaned back in the seat, and remembered.

Cedar Point was a small logging town. Just that. Daddy was a logger, and his Daddy'd been one, too. There weren't nothin' else to do. Mama was right pretty, but she didn't have much schoolin' and they got hitched when she was just sixteen. Three of us kids, me the only girl, later they closed the logging. Made a park outta it. Daddy, he didn't have nothin' and no place to go, so he started drinkin' hard. When he was drunk he was mean, and when he was mean he beat us, Momma hardest of all, and he was drunk more and more of the time. I remember him, all big and fierce and mean, with the blaze of drink in his eyes.

Mama, she was so pretty even after that, but she cried a lot and tried to bring us up proper, sendin' us t'church Sundays and doin' what she could on the welfare and the food stamps. 'Cept Daddy kept gettin' 'em and tradin' for booze. One day he didn't come home at all, and they come and tole us he was in jail for killin' a man in a drunk fight. Things was better after that, but Mama she just couldn't get ahold of us.

Me 'specially. I kinda felt bad about it now, but what's done is done, as Mama us'ta say. In my teens I skipped school mor'n I was in it. It was dull and I never was too good at that readin' and writin' stuff, anyway. The boys, now, that's what I was good at. I finally just quit school, said the hell with it. Why go? I was just gonna finally find the right boy, get married, and have my own mess of babies. Didn't need school for that.

That's how I'd finally got in with Jeremy Stukes. He was a big hunk of muscle, real strong, and the biggest prick I ever did see. I fell for him like a ton of bricks, and, afore I knew it, I was listenin' to his big dreams about goin' to the big city and makin' a pile. I was seventeen then and the most I'd been from Cedar Point was Klamath Falls, once, with Mama when she had trouble with the food stamps.

Jeremy, he and me made plans, and one night we got the big escape. I snuck out with a bag, and he picked me up in this real big, fancy car. I was so took I never even asked whose it was. Turned out it was stole, damn him. A cop picked us up goin' south and we beat him out, all right, but by then I was both scared and mad as hell at him. I started tellin' him what I thought of him and, 'fore I knowed it, he'd throwed me outta that car and drove off, leavin' me there in the middle of nowhere with a bag and a couple of bucks.

Well, I was plenty scared, sure, but I wasn't gonna go home, either. For all I knew they might 'a thought I stole the car, and, besides, wasn't anything to go back to anyways. So I just started hitchin' – found it was real easy. Hell, I always knew I was pretty and stuck out in all the right places, so I didn't have much problem.

One ride was this nice salesman, and I needed a shower and he was *real* friendly, so we stayed overnight in a motel together. I knew what he had in mind, but I kinda needed it myself, and the only real surprise was that he give me twenty dollars when he let me off. I hadn't really thought of it before, but suddenly I saw there was lots of lonely men out there and somebody like me, well, she could maybe help 'em out and make some bucks at the same time.

I finally made Sacramento, but I got busted kinda quick there and it scared me. They couldn't tell how old I was, though, and they weren't real tough, just told me I hadta get outa town right fast. This one vice cop was real friendly, and him and me made it together, and he told me I should go to Nevada, where what I was best at wasn't a crime.

So I worked the roads up to Reno, only to find that it was legal everyplace *but* Reno and Vegas. Still, I had no place to go and nothin' else to do, and the money was good enough that I managed to pay the fines. Got to be a regular down at vice. Funny, though, cops in vice ain't like real cops. I kinda think they don't like some of the laws they carry out. Anyways, this one cop introduces me to this other guy he knows and, last week, I get an offer from this place called Cougar Lodge. This guy tells me I can get four hundred a week free and clear plus room, board, clothes, you name it, by turnin' one trick a day, minimum, more if I wanted. All nice an' legal.

After almost two years on the streets, makin' it for peanuts as a free-lance, I knew I'd either hav'ta hook up with one of the pimps in town or I'd finally get tossed in the joint for real, not just do a few thirty-day stretches in County Jail like usual. My cop friend told me this Cougar Lodge was a high-class house, run right and with state exams and stuff like that. I'd already had to use the free clinic a few times, for one abortion and lots of times for VD checks, and while I was clean still I knew it wouldn't last. Not with the kinda Johns I was gettin'. So I tole the guy O.K., I'd try it, and he took me to his own Doc – a fancy one – and I came out clean. And then I got this bus ticket, and here I was, goin' south to who knew what? Who cared, either?

'Stateline, Nevada casinos,' the driver called out, and pulled in. I looked around. So this was Tahoe, I thought. Looked like the Reno Strip in the Oregon mountains.

I got off and found it was real cold. I didn't expect that, although I had my heavy jacket on. Reno was cold, but we'd been goin' *south*, for Christ's sake!

The same guy I'd met in Reno was there to meet me, all bundled up, and he got my bag, real gentleman-like, and we walked to his car. It was somethin' else, I'll say. A big, fancy Mercedes all shiny and new. Maybe, Misty old girl, you got hooked up right. Maybe you finally got the breaks.

His name was Al Jordan, a little, fat guy about fifty or so puffin' a big fat cigar. He was the manager, he told me, and went over the terms once more. I reminded myself that I was twenty-one, at least to him, since at twenty I was still too young for the legal stuff, but I'd been lyin' about my age for a while now.

The place was real beautiful, up in the mountains and all. Kind of a winter resort, with snow and everything. I didn't mind, since Cedar Point was sure colder'n this sometimes and Reno wasn't exactly Miami Beach in February.

The place looked like a big old hotel, which I guess it was once. It was real pretty inside, too, with a big hall, blazin' fireplace, bear rug, all that. But I really knew I was in the big time when I saw that they took all the big credit cards. That was a giggle. Wonder what they put on the little slips?

I got introduced to the staff by Al, then we went into his big, fancy office and he gave me a bunch of forms. I looked at 'em but had a little trouble readin' 'em, and he helped me. They was the damndest things. Tax withholding forms, social security, shit like that. I really started feelin' like I'd found a home.

'You'll work a six day week, with Mondays off,' Al told me. 'But you'll get six days around your period off, and you can go anywhere you want, stay here, go into Tahoe, whatever. You're paid once a month, at the beginning of your break, into a bank account in your name – that's one of the forms there, the yellow one. You can take as much out as you want any time at the desk, or let it stay. It'll be in the bank, making money for you, until you want to use it.'

That sounded fine to me.

I had my own big room, with bathroom, and big, round bed. Al let me decorate it the way I wanted, on the Lodge, and I had a lot of fun doin' that. We also went on a shoppin' trip to Tahoe, with me pickin' up a buncha really sexy clothes and all.

The other girls were real pretty, too. Some were real smart, some came from the streets like me, but all looked *gorgeous*. I never got along much with other girls – men was my style – but they was nice enough as a bunch and we each had our own room and place.

Al brought this one guy to me who was a beauty expert, they said, and I really got the works. After he was through I almost didn't know myself, and when I got into my workin' outfit I decided I was at least as sexy as the other girls.

The workin' outfit was real high heels, panty hose with black mesh, and a kinda bikini, plus nice, long earrings, a sexy hairdo done for us by a guy who came through a lot, cosmetics, and the like. We was told to let our hair grow long, keep our fingernails long and them and toenails painted, and all that.

When a customer – we was told never to say trick or John – came in, we kinda paraded in the lobby struttin' our stuff and he picked whichever of us he wanted. There was some bad feelin' among some of the other girls against the ones that got picked most often, but as I got picked a lot I didn't mind. Let 'em eat their hearts out.

The guys weren't real kinky types, either. Oh, a couple, but mostly those types were weeded out. We serviced the best in the West, Al always said – salesmen, big shots, show-biz people (sometimes even makin' house calls down to town for them types). Some were into bondage and S&M, which was cool, as long as they didn't hurt *me*. Al knew which way we all bent and he tried to steer the customers to the right girls when he thought he should. He seldom made mistakes.

I never liked the S&M types, and so I never got 'em. Oh, once, a goof, but I put that straight. Bondage, though, I didn't mind, and all the other kinky stuff, the role-playing and other games, that sort of thing. Some of the guys got off just from the mirrors I had all around, includin' on the ceiling.

I told myself every day when I woke up, around two or so, that I had found paradise, maybe for a lot of years. Carole, for example, was thirty-seven, looked younger, and still goin' strong. I could do it forever. I made a lot of lonely guys happy, gave high-class sex to guys who hardly knew how to fuck, and I couldn't get enough. I really liked the ones on power-trips, though. I was so submissive bondage was just an extra turn-on, and I loved it. I couldn't get enough.

The rest of the time I just stayed home, mostly, watchin' TV and shit like that, including the porn movie channel to get ideas. Every once in a while I'd go down to Tahoe, 'specially after the weather got warm and the ski bums cleared out, to swim a little in the pools of the big hotels, gamble some, and, once in a while, get picked up and treated for a night, sometimes for a freebie but mostly not. I spent some dough, though, not so much on that – I found I never really had to buy a meal – but on pretty clothes, jewelry, that sort of thing.

Hell, I had nothin' else to spend it on, and I could die young or somethin' and what good would it do me? At the end of a year I got a big raise, too, so it kept buildin' up. I bought mink and jewels and fancy, sexy clothes and still had money in the bank, even after the government took out its cut.

Over that first year, though, a real funny thing happened. It was so grad-ual-like I didn't even think about it 'cept when buyin' clothes, but here I was, a growed woman, and I outgrew my bra!! Got thinner at the waist, too. Changed a bit. My 35-24-35, which wasn't bad, became a 42-23-36, which was real weird at my age. I was always sexy, but I started bein' almost always horny, even always dreamin' of sex. I thought maybe Al was puttin' somethin' in the the food, but even he and the other girls noticed it and said somethin' after a while. I never really tried to figure it out, but while it was better than ever for business the big boobs sometimes made my back hurt and I started findin' myself rubbing my workin' parts just sittin' around. It was like I was becomin' an *animal* or somethin', and it worried me a little. I told Al, but he just said this life was what God had made me for and now that I'd found it I'd just turned completely on. 'All your juices are flowing full-tilt,' he said.

But it *was* a change. My voice was a little lower and all-the-time super-sexy without me even havin' to shift gears, and I knew my moves were all super-sexy, animal-like. But as time went on I worried less and less about it. I got lots of customers every day, and a lot of repeat business, and a couple of the big show-biz stars started wantin' me only. Pretty soon I stopped worryin' about things, or even thinkin' much about anything except fucking and pleasing men and getting as many as I could.

Finally, after I'd been at the Lodge a long while, one of Al's friends, Joe Samuels, who ran a fancy strip club in town, asked me if I'd ever thought about doin' that. I told him I had – I'd watched them fancy strippers and really liked the idea of takin' it all off while all them men watched.

It turned out that Al owned part of the Copa Club and didn't mind. He was such a sweet guy. I got up a little early and went to school again, but this was a different kind of school. A stripper's school – only they said 'exotic dancer' or some such shit. There was a lot more to learn than I figured. Not just the dances, the moves, but the timing. When to turn, when to drop this or that, all that.

So I started stripping for the Copa Club part of the time and as I got to be more of a draw I got less and less of the walk-ins at the Cougar, stayin' only with my old regulars and the really big shots.

I loved stripping almost as much as fucking, and there was no reason not to do both. I was goin' up in the world I loved, and I was havin' a ball at it.

I got recognized on the street, not just for bein' sexy but for bein' a big shot, a *celebrity*. I got a rush just lookin' at the Copa Club's big sign now, with a picture of me on it and just one word, 'MISTY.' All capitals like that. I didn't like to read and never read much of anything but that one sign I read over and over.

I got a driver's license – I don't think the testing guy was payin' any mind at all to how I was doin' – and credit cards and a little sports car in a fancy pink shade.

Pretty soon Joe was gonna open a new, bigger Copa Club in Vegas, and he and Al wanted me to go down there. I liked it in Tahoe, but Vegas was big time, and I couldn't say no. Besides, it was warm, even in the winter.

I didn't want to leave Al, and it was kinda a tearful goodbye, but I knew I hadta go. I went down a couple weeks early to get settled in and look around my new home town.

It was Reno and Tahoe all rolled into one. I had no troubles there, even if I wasn't really known yet – I knew I'd own this town, at least the part of it I wanted, real quick. I stayed at the Sahara while lookin' for my own place and I had a lot of fun cruisin' the strip, tryin' to have a good time each night without liftin' a finger or payin' a dime.

My third night in town, I met this nice-looking young guy, said his name was Jeff something-or-other, and we went out on the town and had a real good time, even if we did lose at the tables. After, we went up to my room at the Sahara and, well, one thing led to another, and I was gettin' all set, when I turned my back on him for something or other and felt a sharp sting right in my ass. I let out a sharp 'Ow!' and started to turn around, but the whole world just blacked out.

CHAPTER TEN

'Run program!'

Again there was no sensation, no idea that anything was going on, but funny things, lots of big words and memories and all sorts of stuff, rushed back into my head.

An elderly man who looked like Einstein, only fatter and older, stepped up to me. 'How do you feel?' he asked gently in a soft accent that was central European, I guessed. I seemed to know him from somewhere, and I struggled to recall.

'Stuart,' I managed.

He smiled. 'Excellent! You know me. Now – who are you?'

I tried to think. Who? It was all so mixed up. 'Mis-ty Vic-tor Gon-ser Carpenter,' I managed.

'Which is it?' he prodded. 'Which one are you?'

I tried to think for a minute, sort things out in my head, and they wouldn't quite come together. It upset me, not knowing, not being able to put it all together.

I tried to think. I remembered Misty Ann Carpenter and her life perfectly. I *was* Misty Carpenter and it *was* my life. On the other hand, I was also Victor Leigh Gonser, male, mid-thirties, somehow in the body of Dory Tomlinson. I tried to look at my body, feel my body. It was Dory's body, yes, but it was also *my* body. Misty's body, Vicki's body. It felt both natural and odd.

'I – I'm both,' I said in wonder.

Eisenstadt nodded again. 'Good. Very good to come so far so fast. I think that as you go on the two parts of you vill more and more come together. You vill be a new person, not Victor, not Vicki, not Misty, but a blend of all three. I think that is all ve can hope for, and I think it might just be for the best.'

He signalled and the apparatus was lifted from me. He offered his arm and I got up from that chair, that damnable chair, and unsteadily followed him back into his office. He gestured for me to sit down, then poured a little brandy for me which I gulped greedily.

'Do you know how long it's been?' he asked gently.

I shook my head, still trying to get a grip on myself. 'Long, I think. The only attention I've paid to time recently was when to take the yellow pills and when to take the green ones.'

He chuckled, then grew suddenly serious. 'It's been more than three years.'

That stunned me. Three *years!* I was twenty-three now, then, and Dory would be almost seventeen ... That brought up a thought. 'Dory?'

He turned and gestured behind me, and I recognized an older Jeff Overmeyer enter with a strange, dark young woman. She was a tiny woman, not just in height but she seemed so small and fragile, with dark reddish-brown skin, wide, flashing eyes that looked almost coal black, and long, almost blue-black hair. But she was extremely attractive, narrow-waisted, small-boned yet somehow with the toughness of leather about her. Her face was a classical Amerind beauty's, with high cheekbones and the look of the exotic, almost mystical, about her. She wore tight, faded jeans and an old T-shirt with some Indian design, showing small but firm breasts beneath. A faded pair of cowboy boots seemed perfectly in place on her.

'Dory?' I gasped.

She just stood there a moment, staring at me, wide-eyed. 'Vicki?' she responded, unbelievingly. 'Is that *really* you?'

I got up, she ran to me, and we hugged and held each other close. I found that I was crying, and, looking at her, I saw that she was, too.

I was conscious of how different I now appeared to her, and felt a little odd about it. We finally let go, and Eisenstadt offered her another chair. She just sat there for a moment, staring at me.

The scientist looked past us. 'Jeff! You might as well come on in, too.' The agent came over and took another seat, facing us. He looked older, I thought, but still the same. Only Stuart never changes, it seemed.

'I can't believe it!' Dory said in an amazed tone. 'What did they *do* to you? You shouldn't look all that different after three years.'

'I can explain that,' Overmeyer said. 'Parch arranged with a man named Al Jordan, who runs a high-class sex palace up in Tahoe, to take on a new recruit. Jordan has some ties to organized crime, and was nailed a number of years back, but never spent any time in jail. Instead, he does favors for the U.S. on occasion, from sexual blackmail to taking on people like Vicki here – or should I still call you Vicki? It doesn't seem the same any more.'

My mind was reeling from all this. Al a Parch man? It didn't seem possible! I felt somehow betrayed and used. Still, Jeff's question deserved an answer. Which one was I?

'Make it Misty,' I told him. 'I've been her for a long time now, and it's the only real identity I have. It seems – *right*. I dunno.'

'O.K., Misty. Anyway, knowing where you were going, they fiddled with some areas of your brain. Doc? You know more than me about that.'

He nodded. 'Yes, they changed the orders to parts of your body. Increased hormone production, that sort of thing. It's wery complicated to explain, but easy to do. Basically, they adapted your physical body perfectly to your, er, occupation, in the same way they might increase steroid production in a bricklayer to develop bigger muscles. They overrode the genetic instructions – but while it is permanent it is not inheritable.'

I was shocked, but also oddly relieved to find the changes in me explained. Still, I said, 'A tailor-made *nymphomaniac?*'

He shrugged apologetically. 'That is the potential of this process, I fear. Tailor-made anything. That is vy ve had to find you both and get you back now. They are to the point vere they are starting to process the staff here, actually *inwiting* big shot politicians to come in, that sort of thing. They are out of control. Acting now vas a big risk, but acting later may have been impossible.'

Overmeyer nodded. 'I'm due next week. Oh, not for processing, not officially. Just having my matrix taken, they say. But I know better. I've seen the people they've been processing lately and it's scary.'

'Wait a minute! Let me get my breath and bearings!' I protested. 'We – we *do* have some time, don't we?'

'A little,' Stuart replied. 'I took a leaf from Herr Parch's own book. Only their routine duty staff is on right now – and I have some of my people at key stations. Ve are not being monitored here, and the big vuns in Security, like Parch, are all back East until tomorrow.'

I relaxed a little. I had to trust these two men, since I knew so little myself about this labyrinthine place.

Labyrinthine, I thought idly. Misty wouldn't even be able to *think* of the word, let alone pronounce it.

I looked at Dory. 'What – where did they send you?' I wanted to know. 'Speaking of changes – you're some little sexy bomb yourself. If I'd known I was gonna grow up to be that I wouldn't have changed bodies.'

She laughed a little. 'It is hard on me, too,' she replied. 'But, for the last few years, I've been growing up on an Indian reservation in northeast Arizona. A school for Indian orphans. Oh, they knew I wasn't Navaho, but they finally sort of accepted me. While you were having all that fun, I was going through high school again – or a poor excuse for one. It's terrible what's been done to the Indian, and they're such good people. I wasn't much of a student anyway. All I knew was I'd finally get married to some buck and we'd live in some hovel out in the wilds and have babies and try and manage.'

I nodded, seeing the pattern of Parch's 'placement' concept. 'You sound different, you know,' I told her. 'Sort of an accent there.'

She nodded. 'They programmed me with Navaho – a real bitch of a language, by the way – and Corho, which is a northwest language so it'd seem right, but not much English. I was supposed to be a half-breed by their standards – half Navaho, half Corho. A good part of me, maybe proportionately more of me than you considering our ages, is Delores Eagle Feather, and everything I say is sort of filtered through Navaho. I find I think in Navaho, mostly, where there are word equivalents, but my whole English and French vocabulary is there for the asking.'

'So are you Dory – or Delores?' I asked.

She screwed up her face a little. 'I never liked Delores much, although, like you, it's the only legal identity I've got. I'm going to go back to Dory, I think. It's gonna be harder getting used to you as the old Vicki, though. You sure don't look like I remember.'

'I'm not the old Vicki,' I told her. 'But I don't know who I am yet, either.'

'Both of you have some adjusting to do,' Stuart said, 'and it vill take some time. It vill come gradual, not in one *woosh*. I had the option of restoring you vere you left off or just feeding your old matrix back in on top the new, and I decided it vas best to do the latter. You should know your whole life, and, particularly in your case, Vic – Misty, the new parts of you are better equipped to handle that body of yours. I could erase the new encoding for the genetic instruction override, but it vouldn't be a service. Your body vould be out of balance. It vould cause fat, and your enlarged boobs they vouldn't shrink, just kind of deflate and sag. Better ve keep both of you in at this stage.'

Dory nodded. 'I prefer it that way anyway. I'm not the same person I was when I left here, but I think I'm the better for it in some ways. I feel more Indian now, and that's good, not only because of what I now am but also because, for all the terrible life most Indians have, they still are a great people. I learned a lot from them, and I'll always be a part of them.'

I looked at Stuart. 'You must have had more of a reason than this to bring us back now. Where do we go from here?'

He looked at us seriously. 'Listen, the both of you. A lot has happened in the past three years. For vun thing, obviously, ve can do anything they can do and at least as vell. Parch, and the people over Parch, are mad vith power. If they aren't stopped, I don't know vere it vill lead. I fear that I, too, might be put under my little babies out there after a vile. Eventually – vell, the whole country? The vorld?'

'But there's an equal threat,' Overmeyer put in. 'This Association, or what-ever, is on the march. It's winning. You can't really see 'em, just smell 'em, in a nasty way. Last month the four largest religious cult organizations, different as night and day, all merged into one huge body. Their followers can't be deprogrammed by anybody short of IMC. Their combined assets are in the *billions*, their followers fanatical and growing, and they're everywhere, not just the U.S.'

I frowned. 'But most of the world is communist. That wouldn't work there – unless you're suggesting a war.'

He shook his head. 'Not a war between us and the communists, no. But they're working there, too. A whole new Chinese philosophical group has arisen, cultlike, and has gathered powerful friends in Peking. It appeals to the ideals of communism and argues their present attainability. The Soviets will probably be the hardest nut to crack, but even there we see similar forces at work. They're patient, this Association. I think they'd be willing to simply grow up into powerful positions in the party until they *were* the leadership. Once in charge of even a single Soviet Republic, their work efficiency, dedi-cation, and production would propel their leaders to the top in Moscow – and in that kind of society people can be ordered to be processed.'

I shook my head, a feeling of hopelessness coming into me. How much nicer, more comfortable, to be Misty Carpenter, to not worry about things like this or even be able to conceive of them in her little world.

'What can we do?' I asked.

'Ve can do the only thing possible,' Stuart responded. 'Ve can take the biggest gamble in all of human history. Listen, you remember long, long ago, interviewing the alien Pauley?'

I nodded.

'Vell, remember vat he said? That the Urulu vould save us if they could be convinced ve vere vorth saving?'

I strained to remember. It seemed a long time and another life ago. Still, I nodded. 'Go on.'

'Vic – Misty, look, ve have talked about it and ve think now that it may be our only hope. Ve must contact the Urulu, somehow conwince them that ve are vorth redemption, and get them to come in. To destroy IMC and face down this Association before it is too late.'

My old conversation came back to me now, and I was dubious. 'But he said there was a chance they'd just decide we were infested and destroy the entire planet.'

'Misty, the planet's already *being* destroyed,' Overmeyer put in. 'Weren't you listening? Ten years, twenty, and you might neither recognize nor want to *be* human on this planet, if that word has any long-term meaning. IMC is making the enemy's task easier here, although you can't convince them of it. The world isn't going to collapse tonight, or tomorrow, or next year, but it's rapidly reaching the point of no return, when they'll be in such control that this sort of plan will be impossible. The Urulu have to see us humans the way we are, not the way we'll be remade. Dr Eisenstadt and the rest of us who are sick at the way things are going are convinced that we must make our move now.'

'Which brings us back to what we have to do with this,' Dory responded. 'Why us?'

'I vould like to say it's because I love the both of you, vich I do, but it goes deeper than that. This fellow Pauley, he was the most reasonable of the vuns they caught. The most *human*, you might say. He'd lived vith us a long time and understood us a bit better. Also, according to your own reports, he seemed to feel some sort of guilty conscience, particularly around you. Ve think he is our only hope. Ve intend to free him – and, vunce ve do, you may be the only hold on him ve have.'

Dory looked dubious. 'I don't like it. I can still remember the absolute *contempt* that woman, that alien, on the ferryboat had for us. I can't imagine that they'd be any better than the enemy.'

Overmeyer looked at her. 'They are because they *have* to be – don't you see that, Dory? If they're no better, then we're already lost. It's a gamble, sure. Lots of things could go wrong. They might be as bad as the others – they can't be any worse. They might not listen. Pauley might just say to hell with us and leave. They might blow us all up. But *what is the alternative?*'

She didn't like the idea despite the arguments, that was clear, but she could only shrug. 'I'm just along for the ride.'

'Not qvite,' Stuart told her. 'There vere several reasons for taking the added risk of bringing you back, all carefully vorked out and thought out. For vun thing, if Pauley *does* feel real guilt about – Misty – then you are a double dose, and a reminder to him. She will also need somevun to help and support her. It is a big burden to carry alone. And, of course, you are more practical than she – sorry, my lady, but it's true. *You* came up vit the plan for the newspaper-man, yes? *You* had better sources of information within IMC than did Vicki, who vas in a much higher place. You complement each other. You are a better team than either alone. You see?'

I was a little put out by Stuart's assessment of me, but the more I thought of it the more I had to agree, particularly now. I was being raised from the dead, as it were, and entrusted with the fate of the whole human race, the heroine of a bad thriller that just happened to be so damnably *true*, and I needed somebody badly.

'How do we begin?' I asked them.

'First we talk with Pauley,' Overmeyer said.

'He's *here?*'

He nodded. 'Always has been, on a special security level with the few others we have. It's computer-monitored and watched, but we have the computer here, and if we can feed false data into brains it's no trick at all to feed false data into security pictures, sound monitors, and the like. Once we spring him, we arrange the computer so you walk right out of here. It's the wonderful thing about relying on computerized security systems – they only work if the programmer's honest. We've had time to prepare this, Misty.' He reached in his pocket, pulled out several cards and handed them to us. I recognized them at once – the same credit card-like security keys as before. 'Your voice codes we'll give you in a few minutes, and we'll arrange for instructions to reach the elevator guards ahead of time. Isn't bureau cracy wonderful? As much as it obscures and slows, it also makes things painfully simple – if you understand it, and if you get the paperwork right. You will be able to leave – but once you're in that parking lot upstairs you're on your own.'

'You're not gonna be able to keep this from Parch for long,' Dory pointed out. 'Even if we get out, he'll know when he gets back.'

Stuart nodded. 'Yes, but ve vill give him a little something to puzzle over first. It is time ve vill buy, no matter how little. An hour, a day, can make the difference.'

I looked down at myself. 'Some getaway,' I commented. 'Super low-cut slit, sparkling green evening dress, high heels ... I'm really going to be inconspicuous.'

'You couldn't be inconspicuous anywhere,' Jeff noted. I smiled sweetly at him. How different it would be for the two of us now, I thought wistfully.

I looked over at Dory. 'Well? What do you think now?'

She smiled and shook her head in wonder. 'God! You're so *sexy!* I can't believe it!' Then she turned back to the two men.

'Let's do it,' she said.

CHAPTER ELEVEN

Stuart and Jeff left us to prepare our going away party. I felt uneasy about it all, but, as Jeff had said, there really wasn't any choice in the matter. The alternative was that Parch or this Association or both would take over, remaking us into happy little robots. I only hoped that the two of them were up to matching Parch trick for trick; otherwise, I'd still open Joe's new joint in Vegas and Dory would be opening a beads and trinkets stand on U.S. 89.

The trouble was, a part of me wanted nothing to do with it all. I had what I really wanted now, popularity, adulation, fun ... It didn't seem fair, somehow, to wrench me back and load the world on my shoulders.

'Three years,' I said to Dory. 'It doesn't seem possible. All that time, such a different life.'

She nodded. 'Out of curiosity, why the long peroxide curls? I always thought my fluffy auburn hair was real pretty.'

'It was and is,' I told her. 'But it's – professional. The big body, big boob look seems to require a blond. Look at all your past sex symbols.'

She sighed. 'I suppose so. I'll tell you, though, that I would not have recognized you. I still can't really believe it. You've changed so much ... Inside as well as out. That sultry voice, those moves. I can hardly wait to see you eat a banana. They said you were a high class prostitute. Was that true?'

I nodded. 'It's not nearly as bad as it sounds. Lately I'd moved up into stripping. I was going to headline a new club in Vegas. Dory, this may sound funny, but I *like* my new self. If – *when* we get out of this, I'll go back to it. Still, speaking of changes – you're a small package of dynamite yourself. You really grew up with the right stuff – again. But you seem a little more thoughtful, more reflective, more comfortable with yourself.'

'Maybe some of this did us a favor. The blend of new and old made us new people, but whole ones.'

Whole people. I liked that idea. Victor Gonser had never been a whole person; he was all act, introspection, aloof from the humanity he craved to join, but could not. Vicki Gonser, too, had been trapped in a nasty transsexual web, out of place and time. Misty Carpenter, the original, had been shallow, dumb, totally self-centered and egotistical, a hollow person, somehow. Parch's idea of what women should be – beautiful, sexy, seductive, submissive, and without a brain in their heads.

Dory, too, had been trapped in her old body, cut off from the society she wanted to be a part of even more cruelly than Victor had been; sexy, attractive, bright, and lesbian, not confident of herself, her future, her place in society, facing a new kind of life she didn't really want but couldn't avoid. I looked at her now with a great deal of affection, and felt a few unbidden tears rise inside me. Whole people.

I suddenly reached out, grabbed her, hugged and kissed her once more, and cried softly.

Victor wouldn't have done that, and the old Misty wouldn't have understood why.

'I'm so very glad to see you,' I whispered softly.

She hugged me and kissed me again, and I could see that there were tears in her eyes, too. 'Me, too, Vicki Misty Gonser Carpenter.'

I laughed and we hugged and kissed and touched and, in that moment, I think, we both did become truly whole.

The battle was for the minds, Pauley had once told me, not the shells.

Stuart came back in. 'Ve have located him and talked to him,' he told us, and I had no doubt who 'him' was. 'Ve brought him up to date. He seems quite agreeable, and particularly anxious to see the two of you. Ve told him vat happened to you both.'

Jeff Overmeyer stepped into the room and I looked at him. 'How will you get him out?' I asked.

'He already *is* out,' Jeff replied, and I froze. There was something terribly wrong about him, something I couldn't quite put my finger on.

'Oh, *no!*' I almost sobbed.

'Yes, it's true,' he sighed. 'I'm not Jeff. We switched. But it was voluntary, I promise. He knew what he was doing.'

Both Dory and I were on our feet now, staring at him. 'But – why?' I looked at Stuart.

'Ve discussed it early on. Somebody had to do it. Jeff has been on the outs vith Parch for some time. He couldn't get avay and he knew it, but if he stayed he vould go under the computer. This way his mind, at least, is safe – for a vile – and no Urulu are missing. That extra time is bought a bit more, but it is bought dear, yes?'

I nodded glumly. 'Dear indeed.'

'Oh, come on,' Pauley said, sounding relaxed and sure of himself. 'My old body wasn't much older than Jeff's and is in good shape.' His tone grew grimmer. 'He was a dead duck and he knew it. Better this way than no way at all.' He walked over to us and looked us over. 'Let me take a look at you.'

Involuntarily, we both stepped back, away from his grasp. 'Don't you touch me!' Dory snapped.

'Wait a minute! I'm not going to switch with you – I promise.' He saw we were still hesitant. 'Look, if we're going to do anything at all together we have to trust each other. If you don't trust me now then we're lost before we start.'

I shivered slightly, but stood still. 'All right,' I said nervously.

He took my hand, then placed his other hand, fingers spread, on my forehead. I could feel nothing. Finally he nodded to himself and let go, turning to Eisenstadt. 'Interesting. You have it all now, although some of the approaches are unique. Dory? May I?'

She took another step back nervously, but steeled herself finally and let him repeat the process. Finally he said, 'All right. I sense the conflict within each of you, the problem of integrating two lives. Being holographic, your brain still has trouble handling both and is frantically re-sorting, re-filing, and trying new and different pathways. But it'll work itself out. You may find your mind playing little tricks on you but it won't matter in the long run. I think they're capable, Doctor. Shall we get out of here?'

'Wait a minute!' Dory exclaimed. 'If Jeff's so hot how do you expect to get out of here as him? And if you switch, it'll leave a real loose end.'

'That is true,' Stuart admitted, 'but, you understand, if it vas only Jeff and myself this would never have been possible even to now. Misty, Dory, these are *good* people on the whole. Normal, decent people. Even Parch, in his own odd way, is no monster. But there *are* monsters in the chain of command – ordinary, normal fellows vith vives and kids who vorship power. It is, in some vays, like Hitler vithout Hitler – the monster cannot be pinned down, but he is there. Now ve, of IMC, have vun chance to show that ve are not just good Germans, following orders no matter vere they go. Every vun looks for the Hitler, but it is the banality of evil that makes it so insidious.' He stepped to his door and gestured. Two technicians came on the run.

Stuart nodded to them. 'These brave fellows are John Castellano and Villy Stroyer. Johnny, here, is my chief administrative aide. Both are too young to know the horrors of vich I speak first hand, yet they are vith us. They know the horror that is *here*.'

Castellano, a small, dark, hawk-nosed man with long black hair, spoke. 'We're volunteers, Miss. And we have clearance to leave if we want.' He turned to Pauley. 'Which do you want?'

Pauley looked both surprised and impressed, both by their commitment and their casual acceptance of him. 'Either of you married?' he asked.

'No sir,' the other man, a bit older but still a decent-looking man with a fine-lined Nordic face and a slight paunch. 'I was – once.'

Pauley considered it, then turned to Eisenstadt. 'Why not you, too, Doctor? John – you've worked with him. Think you could *be* him? Until we come back, anyway, and can get you into a younger body?'

Castellano looked nervous – they both did – but he sighed and said, 'I think ve can pull it off, yes.'

The voice was all wrong, but he had the tone, accent, and inflection down pat.

Eisenstadt stared at them and I thought I saw the tiniest glimmer of a tear in his eye. 'You vould do this?'

Castellano nodded. 'Doctor, I don't want to see you under that thing with Parch at the controls. I was ready to do it as Jeff Overmeyer, I'm willing to do it now.'

Pauley became all business. 'Lie down on the floor, then – all three of you. Good. Now, grip each other's hands tight. Just relax – it won't hurt.'

We watched, fascinated. For the first time I was going to see the Urulu exchange bodies without being a party to it.

It was very odd to watch. Pauley alone was not knocked out by the process, but Pauley kept changing from body to body, so three would be out cold and the fourth would move, then drop and another would move, and so forth. I realized he was trying to put the right people in the correct, although wrong, bodies. Suddenly it was over, and Stroyer got up fairly confidently. 'We'll have to wait for them to come around,' said Dan Pauley. 'Partly to see if I got it right, and partly so we can see how convincing it all is.'

It took seven or eight minutes for the first to come around, the Jeff Overmeyer body which was now occupied by the original Stroyer. He rubbed himself, groaned, sat up, shook his head, and tried to get a grip on his new self. I could sympathize.

Castellano's body was next, with the same trouble, but with a slight difference in manner and tone.

'Whew!' gasped Stuart Eisenstadt. 'Ven ve do it it's slower but not such a jolt to the central nerwous system!'

His own body was last to revive and had the most trouble adjusting. 'The biggest problem, though, will be remembering that accent,' Pauley warned him. He looked pleased.

'Well, now we have left them a Dan Pauley, a Jeff Overmeyer, and a Stuart Eisenstadt, all of whom would be missed. And two technicians will leave at the end of their shift as normal, not to be missed at least until they fail to show up tomorrow morning.'

Stuart nodded. 'Yes. I have the codes in my head, so ve are safe there. But – see, you vomen – give me your cards.'

We were a bit puzzled, but handed over the little plastic keys he'd given us not long before.

'Let us make it look *very* right,' he said conspiratorially, and went to his inner office where there was a computer terminal. He switched it on, began typing, then stopped and inserted one of the cards in the slot on the side. There was a rat-tat-tat noise, and the card popped out again. Now he inserted the other card and repeated the process.

Finally he handed the cards back to us, took his own – that is, Castellano's – card and punched in, then Stroyer/Pauley's. I looked at mine but could see no differences.

'Ve are now married,' he said with some amusement. 'Me to you, Misty, and Dory to, ah, Stroyer. Isn't bureaucracy amazing? There is now even a statement on file in the computer files of Las Vegas County to that effect.'

I shook my head. 'But – why?'

He grinned. 'It vill register now on the computer record that ve vere met by our vives, who vere cleared to this point, and left with them a couple of hours later. When they do a cross-check by computer, they vill find ve *are* married and things vill look normal. Every little step ve cover is important.' Besides, he added, giving a mock leer, 'I feel so much younger and better and now the feeling it is legal.'

For such an absolute security prison it was remarkably easy to just walk out as we'd walked in so long ago. The right words were spoken, the right combinations turned in the elevators, and all went smoothly. Stuart was right, I realized. The most burglar-proof safe in the world is no better than paper if someone wanting to break into it knows the combination.

'Ve'll take Castellano's car,' Stuart suggested. 'It is the largest.' He stopped a moment. '*If* you have the keys, Pauley, in his pocket.'

Pauley looked surprised, fumbled, came up with a small key ring, and we all sighed.

Although large by today's standards it was still a small car, and while Pauley took the driver's seat and Dory the front bucket Stuart and I squeezed in the back. There was little room.

'Where to?' the Urulu asked.

'Avay. Out of here,' Stuart replied. 'Vunce on the vay ve vill make better plans.'

He started the car, backed out, and switched on the air conditioner. I was already starting to bake, and the hatchback in the rear gave the little compressor a real workout. We drove out of the parking lot and down the base road.

'Gate coming up,' Dory warned.

The sentry came out as we stopped at the gate, gave us an odd look as he saw the assemblage in the car, but after looking at all four of our cards he waved us on. In twenty more minutes we were on U.S. Route 95, headed south.

We'd done it!

Take that, Harry Parch! I thought smugly.

'Where are we headed for?' I asked.

'Sign back there said Las Vegas 250, which I assume means kilometers,' Pauley replied. 'Not much in between, either. We could use a road map.'

Stuart was a little worried. 'I don't like the idea of going to Las Vegas,' he told us. 'Too much Harry Parch there.'

'Well, I could turn around and head north,' Pauley suggested, 'but I remember there's even less there. We're on the wrong side of the mountains and they could cut us off fast on any of those roads. I'd say Las Vegas is our best bet – we have lots of options from there.'

'Most of my stuff's in storage there,' I noted, 'but I've got a room at the Sahara with a change of clothes. I'm not gonna get anywhere dressed like this.'

Stuart frowned. 'I don't like it. If anything goes wrong it'll be the first place they look.'

'That's true,' I agreed, 'but, remember, I'm *supposed* to be there. Poor Joe – how will he take his opening big act skipping out on him?'

Stuart thought about it. 'Yes, there is something in that. Tell you vat, Dan. Let's go into Vegas, then try to change cars if at all possible vile Misty tends to her affairs. I think you could cover her from the street and help in case things go wrong. Misty – how much money do you have?'

I laughed. 'I don't have much need for it,' I told him. 'But I've got a bunch of credit cards.'

He shook his head vigorously. 'No. No credit cards except maybe to check out. They can trace you easy from those cards. I mean *cash*.'

I thought a minute. 'Misty – the old Misty – never paid much attention,' I told him. 'Most of it's in savings, just a little in checking.'

'Hmmm … The banks vill be closed by the time ve get there. But ve need money. *Any* idea how much you got?'

I shook my head. 'Only roughly. Ten or fifteen thousand at least.'

Everybody seemed to react in shock at once. Dory whirled and said, '*That* much? In three years? You *must* be something!'

I shrugged. 'I started at four hundred a week, but top-draw strippers make a lot more.'

Stuart sighed. 'Veil, I don't like it, but it looks like ve have to stay in or near Las Vegas until the banks open tomorrow morning. Ve need that money. Dan?'

'I have to agree,' he told us. 'We'll need travel money at least. And if I can't contact a station tonight, which is unlikely – we used to change 'em every month or two anyway – it might be a long trip finding which is active.'

I looked at Stuart. 'You didn't say I had to finance this whole thing. Couldn't you at least have thought of the cash angle?'

He looked defensive. 'I said the plan was *good*, not that ve had thought of everything.'

We drove along, and I had to look at my companions and marvel a bit. What an unlikely team out to save the world, I thought: A well-meaning, idealistic scientist who could change the world from a computer terminal but forgot things like money, an alien cut off from his species and an unknown quantity beneath his slick veneer, a Navaho girl of uncertain personality and little background for any such intrigue, and a former male political science professor now happy as a voluptuous blond bombshell of a stripper. What an insane team.

And me – just who was I, anyway? I knew the answer almost instinctively, from every cell and nerve in my body. I was Misty Ann Carpenter, queen of the strippers and sometimes lady of the evening, that's who. And I felt comfortable and right that way.

What had happened to Victor Gonser, I mused, as the miles of desert and mountain roared past. Where had he gone? I was Misty Carpenter – but she didn't exist. She'd been created in that same computer by Harry Parch and his technical crew. Was I real – or some embodiment of a male sexual fantasy? Certainly I wasn't what the average woman wanted to be or admired. I was a toy, a pampered pet, a plaything for other people, a mistress, a lover, too good to be true for the common male libido. And I *liked* it. If anything I alone was setting women's liberation back twenty years or more. And I didn't *care*.

So, in a sense, Parch had won a victory over me even with my old memories restored. And because it worked, it didn't really matter.

But where was the old Victor Gonser? I looked for him, but found only traces here and there. Oh, I remembered my past all right, but it seemed distant, remote, as if it'd happened to somebody else, like in a very long, boring movie or something.

Data. Computers again. I had the data of Victor's life. The data but not the – matrix? Soul? I couldn't be sure. I tried to think back to when I was he – how long? Four years? I was that person for thirty-five years, my present self for four, so why was he so less real to me than Misty Carpenter?

I thought back, tried to get inside him, and found I could not. Even the little things – being much taller, stronger. It just didn't relate. All the episodes of his life were there, but I could only see myself behind those eyes that witnessed it. I tried to remember the sex and even there I couldn't get it right. I'd remember the woman, remember the room, everything, but when it came to doing it I was always being penetrated, not the other way around. I couldn't even remember what it had been like to even *have* a penis. Why couldn't I?

Memory is holographic. The phrase echoed in my mind, but now I began to understand what Stuart and Dan had been talking about. Your data wasn't stored redundantly, over and over. The brain would quickly fill despite its huge capacity. But if reference A were stored only once, and all the bits and pieces were stored only once, the cerebrum would simply pull from those spots to create a picture, a complete thought, in the mind.

Or a self-image.

And that was what was happening to me. The Gonser data bits were there, of course, complete and ready for use, but the core of me, my self-image, could either fragment into two totally split personalities, in which case I would be schizoid, or one would attain dominance, would establish itself in the primacy seat of the identity matrix.

Did anything of Victor Gonser remain? Well, Misty Carpenter was a stripper and prostitute who could discuss Von Clausewitz, A.J.P. Taylor, and the fine points of Jungian psychology before going to bed with you.

'We're coming into Vegas,' Dory announced, bringing me out of my thoughts. I opened my eyes and looked out, seeing the bright lights in the distance although it was still twilight. Vegas was beautiful by night, I thought, but ugly as hell in the daytime.

'Two motels, fairly near but outside the Strip,' Stuart suggested.

'Why two?' I asked.

'If they are avare of us they vill be looking for four,' he explained. 'And off the beaten track the rates are cheaper and the traffic thinner. Better ve stay extra cautious and get avay.'

There was no argument for that, although I, at least, felt a little more secure. I had walked the Strip for almost a week and checked it out, and I was a legitimate visitor.

We dropped Dory and Dan off at one little motel, a nothing sort of place, really, a few blocks off Las Vegas Boulevard, and they registered without problems. I was glad to see Dory accepting it so well considering her ill-concealed distrust of Pauley. She had guts, I had to admit that.

Stuart and I took a room in another place just down the street. It looked O.K., and after we were all settled in we met again at a Sambo's for a bite to eat and some discussion.

'I think I should go directly to the Sahara and get my things,' I told them. 'The longer we wait the more the risk.'

'Agreed,' Pauley replied. 'Look – no use in all of us going. Doctor, you and Dory stay here – I'll drive Misty down close to the Strip and let her off. She can walk down to the Sahara and get what she has to.' He paused, looking at me seriously. 'This and the bank tomorrow will be the riskiest part of this stage of the trip. Be extra careful.'

'I will,' I assured them all.

Dan let me off quickly and sped away, but I knew he was just going to stash the car in the Sahara's back lot. I walked slowly but confidently towards the hotel-casino, acting like I had every right to be there – which I did. I took it slow and easy, though, to allow Dan enough time to park and make his way around to the lobby area.

Walking into the casino was like coming home, the sights and sounds and bright lights, the clunk of slots turning and stopping and the bells going off signalling jackpots, seemed like lost friends welcoming me back. Three guys tried to pick me up on the way to the elevators, a little above average, but nobody looked particularly suspicious. That didn't mean much, of course, since Parch's agents were visible only when they wanted to be. It would be up to Pauley to protect my rear.

There *did* seem an abnormal number of people just lounging about, though, and it gave me pause. For the first time since hitting Vegas I started getting nervous, looking sideways at people. Was that clerk the same one as yesterday? Was that guy with the racing form lounging against that post over there ogling me surreptitiously for the right reasons? I suddenly didn't feel so sure.

I reached the elevators and punched the button, conscious of eyes on me that, perhaps, weren't friendly or lustful eyes. It seemed to take forever for the damned car to come, but finally it did. I stepped in, and as the door started to close two men ran for it. I stepped back involuntarily, fear shooting through me as the lead man caught the door, hit the rubber safety stop, and, as the doors went back, got on with me. The other man followed.

I had already pressed 6, my floor, and now I cursed myself for it. Who were these men, these strangers so insistent on riding With me?

One man pushed 8, the other 11. Higher floors than mine. Could they be planning to walk back down from 8 and surprise me at my door?

The elevator stopped at 6 and I got off, not very relieved that the two men stayed on. I fumbled for my key in my small purse and almost ran to my room. I put the key to the lock, then hesitated once more. Were they waiting for me inside? Would Harry Parch's chilling voice greet me when I opened it?

I had no choice, but still I hesitated. I wished Dory were here, or Dan, or somebody. I was suddenly feeling very alone and frightened. Finally I took a deep breath, put the key in the lock, turned it, and pushed the door in.

It was dark in the room, and I quickly and apprehensively turned on the lights. Nobody there. It didn't reassure me. Closets, bathroom, they could be anywhere.

Scared to death now and cursing myself for insisting on this little side trip, I cautiously explored the entire room. Nothing. I sighed, knowing it might only be a brief reprieve. Quickly I hauled out my smaller suitcase and looked at my wardrobe. Finally I hauled out the big one, too, and started sorting. Undergarments, panty hose, toiletries, cosmetics, all went in the small one, along with some different shoes and some miscellaneous outfits. For now I decided that the simple, casual look was appropriate. Some blue jeans, sandals, and a thin sweater over just a bra.

The rest of the stuff I threw into the large suitcase. I hesitated on the short mink jacket. It was too warm and I wasn't dressed for wearing it, but it seemed like it might come in handy when we left the desert. Somehow I managed to cram it into the small suitcase and get it shut.

I tried picking them up but while the small one was barely manageable with two hands, the big one was impossible. I would need help.

Feeling that the world was closing in on me, I thought frantically for a moment, then realized that I would have to have a bellman. I sighed, picked up the phone, and called the bell captain.

A young man was up very quickly with a small cart – too quickly, I thought with suspicion. He quickly loaded the bags and took them down to the lobby. I began to think the worst, that, perhaps, they *were* on to me, all around me, but wouldn't pounce. They were waiting for me to lead them back to the others.

I checked out, and at least the cashier was a familiar face and a woman. I found that I could leave the large case in hotel storage, at a few bucks a day, until I sent word of where to send it, and that relieved my mind a bit. I had them put two weeks worth on the credit card and signed it, hoping I'd remember to keep up payments. I really didn't want to lose all that good stuff.

I looked for Dan in the lobby and finally spotted him, but tried not to look directly at him. He was down a bit towards the casino, playing the slot machine nearest the lobby.

I managed the small suitcase as best I could, and it was only a moment before a middle-aged man came over and offered to help. In any other circumstances I would have been delighted, but I found myself wondering if this was legit or not. But I couldn't move that thing very far – my back was killing me anyway – and I accepted his help to move the bag to the main entrance, where cabs normally lined up.

I thanked the man and he responded, 'Any time at all, Babe,' which sounded sincere and natural enough and then he went back into the casino.

Cabs weren't prevalent, but one pulled up in five minutes or so which I told to take me to the bus station. At the station, I walked in, waited until that cab had picked up another fare, then came back out again, thanking God that it wasn't too far to lug the case. I got in another cab and took *it* to the Sambo's where we'd eaten. He thought it was an odd destination, but didn't argue. I waited there a long twenty minutes or so, and finally a small car, a red one, pulled up and Pauley stuck his head out. 'Misty! Get in!'

I frowned at this car change, but lugged the case to the curb and managed to lift it in to Dan. I got in and he took off.

'What happened? Where'd you get this car?'

'It's not good,' he told me. 'I think we got away with this but by a whisker. I was just heading back to the car when several cop and plainclothes cars pulled up front and back of the Sahara. One local boy, probably proud of himself, was already standing at the car and some of them ran to him. I checked the front and saw others rushing inside. I knew you were away, so I just walked away, slowly and naturally. Finally I found this one, parked and unlocked on a side street, and I stole it. Somebody'd gone into a laundromat and left the keys in. So it's hot, and I'll have to ditch it. Look, I'm taking you back to the room. Brief Stuart, then have him get Dory and come to your room, or you do it. I want to find out what's what in this city, and I have to dump this far away. O.K.?'

'All right,' I replied, sounding worried. 'Look – take care of yourself. Without you this is all for nothing.'

He pulled up in front of the motel room and surprised me by leaning over and kissing me. I was startled. Then he winked, took my suitcase out with one hand, and said, 'You just sit tight. Nobody catches me twice. Just get Dory with you and don't move from that room until I get back no matter what – hear?'

I nodded, and he roared off. Off in the distance I could hear the wail of sirens, off in the direction of The Strip.

I knocked on the door and Stuart opened it cautiously, saw me, then came out and helped both me and my suitcase inside. I quickly filled him in on the developments.

'Probably poor Castellano,' he sighed. 'He probably forgot the accent and let New Jersey come through.'

'We have to get Dory,' I told him, but he held up his hand. 'No, let's do it the smart vay.' He pointed to the telephone. 'No sense in all of us getting exposed.'

I was so rattled I could hardly think straight, not to mention dead tired and achy. I was damned glad to have Stuart around to do the thinking for me.

I called Dory. She answered almost immediately and took the news pretty well, but she said, 'Look, I'm just about to get in the shower. Give me twenty minutes or so. I'll be over then. I'll knock twice. O.K.?'

'O.K.,' I responded, hung up, and told Stuart the news. Then I sat down on the bed and found myself suddenly trembling, unable to stop.

Stuart came and sat beside me and put his arm around me. 'Poor Misty,' he said as gently as possible, 'you are not equivipped for this sort of thing. Vell, neither am I. But ve do vat ve must, yes?'

I nodded and squeezed his hand very hard. He held me tightly, and I needed to be held, and made me feel at least a tiny bit secure.

Dory was almost on schedule, still dressed as before but with a large motel towel wrapped turban-like around her hair. 'They didn't have much time to grab anything of mine when they snatched me,' she explained. 'No loss, though.'

Something in my manner seemed to betray my recent attack of nerves, and she came over and squeezed my hand, then looked at me face to face. 'Huh. I'm almost as tall as you when you're in sandals.' She grinned. 'I don't think I'm ever gonna make five feet, though, so you got me by three inches.'

It broke the tension a bit and I relaxed a little more, laughing at her. I began to have even more respect for her now, knowing she realized how tightly wound I was and diverting me with trivialities.

Finally she sighed and looked at the two of us. 'Look, I don't know about you but I'm really dead tired. I haven't been to sleep in almost two days and that shower was the last straw. Would you mind?'

'Of course not,' I said. 'Pick a bed.'

She stripped without hesitancy, noting that her clothes had to last her a while yet, and climbed into bed. Stuart idly started looking through the Las Vegas promotional literature, and I finally relaxed enough to get undressed myself. I flexed my back muscles, which were really starting to ache, and Stuart, seeing this, came over and started giving me what felt like the most orgasmic backrub I could imagine.

'It is the breasts,' he explained, although I'd already figured that out. 'A lot of veight pulling you forward, a bit more than your genes designed your back muscles for. Unless you get reduction surgery it's something you'll have to live vith.'

I nodded. 'I know. Maybe someday I'll be settled down, not need 'em so much any more, or the back will finally get to me and I'll do something.' I lifted them up with my hands and looked down at them. 'Good Lord, Stuart – was there ever a woman born naturally who grew a pair like these? Sometimes I feel like a cow.'

He chuckled. 'Thousands, probably. But few in such delightful combination.' He sighed. 'Ah, if I were only thirty years younger!'

I looked over at Dory in the other bed. She was out like a light, mouth open slightly, totally oblivious to the world.

'But, Stuart,' I whispered, 'you *are* thirty years younger.'

He started a moment, then looked thoughtful. 'So I am,' he said, wondering, then undressed himself.

God! I needed him!

I was tired, and he was tired, but we lay there in the darkness after, neither of us really able to sleep, thinking about things that the past few minutes, at least, had helped us forget.

I stirred a bit. 'Why do I always get the wet spot on my side?' I whispered.

'It's a male plot. Ve're trained to work it out that vay,' he responded lightly, and we both chuckled softly and were silent for a moment.

'Still vorried?' he asked.

'A little,' I admitted. 'About a lot of things. Not just tonight, although that's bad enough, Lord knows.'

'Vant to tell your doctor about it?'

I smiled in the darkness. 'It's me, Stuart. Since I – came back – today, I've been struggling with myself, with who I am.'

'Ve've varned you about that.'

'No, no, it's more than that. In the car this afternoon – I *knew* that I had undergone a profound change. Victor Gonser is dead. Gone. And not just physically. There is only me, and I'm Misty Carpenter.'

He thought for a moment. 'No, I think you have the right solution but the problem it is backvards.'

'Huh? What do you mean?'

'The solution, the *only* solution for you, is to be Misty Carpenter, now and forever. It is not only a person you like but one you *must* be, for you will be Misty Carpenter to the vorld no matter vat. The problem you have is that this Victor fellow, he is not as dead as he should be. You are looking at yourself through his mind, his morality, and you think, vell, it is wrong that I like being a voman, like being Misty Carpenter, like the heads turning, doors opening, the sex, the exhibitionism. Because he is not dead, this Victor, he makes you feel guilty, doubt yourself. Look – this Victor fellow ve both knew. Did you like him?'

I considered the question. 'No. Well, not exactly. I didn't mind *him* so much as the way he was forced to live.'

'He vas an egomaniac and an insufferable bore,' Stuart responded. 'A man who lived in his own private little hell, vich he built himself, and preferred self-pity, vallowed in it, even kind of enjoyed it. So – you start! Vy should you care? You are not he, you are Misty Carpenter!'

I tried to respond to that, but I was all confused inside now. It had seemed so *simple.*

'You see? Now *vy* vas he such a bore, a stick-in-the-mud? He never could join. He was dark, not very good-looking, bald, and had a pot belly. No girls paid him any mind. He had built such a mountain of defenses against a lonely childhood and a possessive Mama that he could not break them.'

Tears came unbidden into my eyes as his comments brought back a lifetime of anguish and bitter loneliness.

'So now he is gone, *pfft!* And in his place is Misty Carpenter. She, too, has her problems, but they are not Victor's problems. Heads turn ven she valks into the room. Men fall over themselves to gain her favor. Misty can never be lonely. A dancer? Look at those big, beautiful eyes! Everyvun vants her. Everyvun loves her. Money? Vatever she vants she gets. Inhibitions? No. She loves the crowd and they love her – she valks naked in their midst if she vants. Is she used? Exploited? No, not really, for she loves vat she does and does it by choice, yes?'

'You make it sound so trite,' I said bitterly.

He hugged me. 'And so it is! But that is *all* it is. You have a golden opportunity here. Vat have you done so far? You have taught. You have done brilliant research, written many books that have caused young people to think – a very rare thing these days. That alone is more than most human beings *ever* accomplish. Far more. Now, you are born again, yes? You experience anew, are able to give anew, learn and grow in new and impossible vays, vithout losing any that you have already accomplished. This is not bad – it is vunderful. The only hard part to understand is vy you feel guilty about it. You should be *proud*, not ashamed! Trite? Perhaps, perhaps not. But if they are trite they are the trivial things as vell, yes? They are not the main things in life. But joy is important, *love* is important, *caring* is important. Yes – become Misty Carpenter, body and soul. You must. For only then can you live and love and give and get.'

I sat there quietly for a while, digesting what he said, and he left me alone to do it. He was right, of course. I was Misty Carpenter because I wanted desperately to be Misty, who was always adored and never alone.

Stuart was right, though. Victor was not dead. Victor was transformed, raised up. A part of me would always be Victor and should always remember him, understand him in order to know and help all the Victors of this world. But I was not Victor. I was *me*.

I kissed him with feeling, then turned and my hand touched the little plastic alarm clock on the nightstand. I took it, suddenly, and looked at it. 'Stuart – it's almost one-thirty.'

'So?'

'Dan's not back yet.'

'That has been on my mind, but I haven't let it get to me. He vas tough enough to trap on your boat, yes? He vould be almost impregnable in a big city. I think he is spying for us.'

'But – suppose he doesn't come back? Suppose he just takes off?'

'If he'd vanted to he could have done it any time, yes? If he has, then ve have lost, of course. But I think not. He vill come back.'

'I almost hope he doesn't,' I said. 'Then we would be out of this.'

'For a vile, yes; for a very short vile. But then the campaign begins. And ve – you, me, Dory, all of us – vill be its wictims. No – he *must* return. He *vill*! And you must hope so, too, deep down. No matter who or vat you are you have a responsibility.'

'I didn't ask for it.'

'No, but few of us *do* ask such things. Fools, perhaps. You studied history. It is not extraordinary men doing great things. It is, mostly, ordinary men propelled by events, by circumstance, into extraordinary positions.'

I could almost hate Stuart then. He was too insufferably *right* all the time.

Finally I said, 'Stuart – when he does come back, what then? If the alarm's out and they know I've been to the Sahara, have the car, then the bank is out. I have less than twenty dollars left in cash. Dory has almost nothing. And you've got – what?'

'Tvelve dollars and sixteen cents,' he admitted.

I nodded. 'And we have no car now. They'll be looking for us anyway. We need money and a way out. I don't know about the way out, but I *can* get us some money. More than we got, anyway.'

He knew what I meant. It didn't really bother me, of course, but I couldn't help thinking of Dory.

Stuart understood. 'Look, you forget – you who should of all people not forget – that she is a twenty-three-year-old voman, yes? A modern voman. You are not – you are vat you vant to be, a concept of a voman, but not of her background. She is not naive, nor stupid. She was raised on the tradition that vomen can do anything, be anything. You are in some vays the old model, she the new. You have decided vat is the right sort of vomen you vant to be – you can not change that, nor can you act on vat is right for her. That is her choice.'

'But – I – we – damn! It's kind of weird, but, Stuart, I'm in love with her! I have been in love with her ever since I first met her. I don't want to hurt her!'

'So? Vat is so veird? She loves you, you love her. You two of all people are the best sort of lovers. You know it's vat's *inside* that counts, not the body you vear.'

'But I like – men.'

'So again? Sex is love, maybe? Since ven? Sex can be vith love or vithout it. You should know. But vun is not necessarily the other.' He sighed. 'Still, if you must do it for us, you must, even if she vould have some hurt – vich I'm not too sure about. Our responsibility is to those people who can not know vat is going on. They have no choice, and so neither do ve, if they are not to become wictims, yes? First ve do vat ve must. Then ve decide our own lives. So vat is the alternative? Ve all shack up vile you get a dance job and the rest of us sveep floors, yes? Or?'

'What would I have done without you, Stuart?'

'The same thing – only more slowly, and vith more pain.'

I hoped that he was right, not so much for his sake but for mine.

The night wore on towards morning, and, in spite of ourselves, we finally fell asleep.

A gentle knock on the door awakened me. I glanced at the clock – a little after five. Not even light yet. I began to think I'd dreamed it when the knock came again, a little more insistently. I got up as quietly as I could and went to the door, checking to see that the chain was on.

I opened it a crack and whispered, 'Who is it?'

'Dan,' came a hissed reply. 'Let me in – quick.'

I undid the chain and he slipped in, then I closed it and chained it again. I stared at the shape in the dark, which looked smaller, different, somehow. 'Dan – is that really you?'

'Yes,' he responded. 'I – had to switch, Misty. It was a close call. Turn on the light and get ready for a shock. We better wake the others, too.'

I reached over and flipped the lights on and gasped. The figure in the room was a tiny one, wearing a brown monklike robe with hood and sandals.

Dory and Stuart stirred with the light, woke up, and looked blearily in our direction. Both saw the new Pauley and gasped.

'Relax – it's Dan,' I told them, and I really hoped it was.

He reached up and pulled back his hood. The head was totally shaved, even the eyebrows, and the face, which once might have held some human attraction, looked bony and emaciated.

'Are you – male or female?' Dory asked, staring in wonder.

'Female,' he responded, 'although sexless is more naturally true.' Speaking aloud his voice did have a feminine tone to it, but the inflection, the manner, was all Pauley's.

'Who or what was *that?*' I wanted to know.

Pauley sighed and collapsed tiredly into a chair. 'Look, I'll tell you the whole thing from the beginning. I ditched the car on the north side, in a motel parking lot, then started walking back towards downtown. Thank God they have buses all night here, and one came along and I grabbed it, heading back for the Sahara area. I *had* to know what they were doing. I tried to be as inconspicuous as possible, but I no sooner entered the casino when I spotted a very familiar figure across the way talking to a couple of security men. It was Harry Parch.'

'Parch!' Dory gasped, then turned to Stuart. 'I thought you said he wouldn't be back until late today.'

'Something must have tipped earlier than planned,' the scientist responded. 'They got him back here on the next plane.'

'Well, anyway, there I was in a known body, target number one, fifty feet from my worst enemy. I turned to walk out the door and as soon as I hit the street this girl in this long robe, here, comes up to me and starts a pitch to sell me flowers. I tried to put her off, but a glance back showed Parch and the security men heading my way, so I eased her down towards the parking lot. I couldn't help noticing how nice, how *trusting* she was, smile always on her face. Well, there was this dark area, and I got ready, figuring at least I wouldn't have to kill anybody. No use hiding with Parch around. So, I reach out to her, and, by God, she reached out and grabbed me first! Not just her hand – I mean with her mind!'

'She was Urulu?' I gasped.

That strange face was grim. 'No, not Urulu. But *I felt the push* – it's hard to describe. Let's just say she let her mind flow out, flooding mine. I had an instant reaction, first an instinctive block, then I rushed in and made the switch on my terms. Her ego – her matrix – was so simple, so uncomplicated, that I damned near crushed it, and I left my old body sitting in the phone booth with a stupid smile on his face.'

'But she could make the svitch, like you, yes?' Stuart prodded. 'But this ve have not yet developed. I vould know it if ve had.'

Pauley shook his head. 'It wasn't IMC, either. It's a new wrinkle, but an old pattern. I wouldn't have guessed it, not yet – but it is The Association.'

I thought back to the tapes, and the conversations we'd had, and shivered.

'So ve *are* under attack after all!' Stuart murmured.

Pauley nodded slowly. 'The war is here. How long it's been here I can't tell – we've all been out of circulation for three years. That's why I can't just contact Urulu here. I tried a couple of the numbers but they were disconnected.' He turned to Stuart. 'Tell me about the Redeemers.'

The scientist shrugged. 'Ve have had such cults around this country for years. They are mostly young, mostly made up from runaways, former addicts, teens vith unhappy homes.'

'I remember the Children of God, the Moonies, lots of others, from when I was growing up,' I added. 'I suppose Hari Khrishna is still around.'

'Most have merged,' Stuart told us. 'This new church svept them up, a big movement. You cannot escape them, and, thanks to the courts and the First Amendment, you can't interfere with them. Many of the older ones have come together vith them. They own huge tracts of land, are rich and pervasive.'

'I know how rich they must be,' Pauley responded. 'I left the mongol sitting there and went over to this cart that read "Flower Power for Love and Godhead." I saw two others similar to myself working further down the airport, and I checked in my pocket. There was almost $230 there.

'That much was good. You ought to have seen those APs when I tried to sell them flowers! I even pressed Harry Parch himself!'

'You didn't!' Dory gasped. 'And did he buy one?'

'He looked at me kind of funny for a minute, and I thought I'd gone too far, that he knew who I was despite all. But, I'll be damned if he didn't gentle up and buy a nice carnation! I even chivvied him out of his change for a "contribution."'

'Dan!' I scolded. 'You shouldn't have! How did you ever –?'

That strange, shaven head came up, and I'd swear there was a definite change in the form. It seemed to be eerily transformed, to shrink, change, become someone else.

It rose, an incredibly sincere pleading in its eyes.

'Buy some flowers?' this plaintive voice asked, so genuine and convincing that we all seemed to pull back a little. 'Would you convert some money to beauty?' it pleaded, so genuinely that it scared the hell out of me.

Suddenly the effect was gone, replaced by Pauley's confident manner and smile that shone through that odd body. He chuckled.

'My God! That's *incredible!*' I managed.

His face turned serious. 'You see,' he said, 'my people developed the IM transfer without mechanical aid, as an evolutionary device. We were weak, our brains our only defense in a world unremittingly hostile. Our brains gave us IM if we needed it, and gave us a certain illusory power as well. There would be this terrible creature, ready to eat us, and we'd activate this protective circuit. Suddenly we weren't Urulu food any more, we were a plant, another carnivore, something like that. We can still do it – the power of the Urulu is all in the mind. We've been fighting all our existence, and we still have it.'

It was unsettling to all of us. Frankly, Dan Pauley had been a real person, even in different forms. He was not a friend on the trail or on the ferry, but he'd become a nice sort of guy in imprisonment and escape.

But he wasn't a nice sort of guy at all, I thought.

He was an alien creature whose very thought patterns were different from us. He was simply imitating us, giving us what we wanted him to be. That's why everybody liked Pauley, everybody felt comfortable with him.

Stuart, ever practical, broke the mood. 'Did you keep the money?' he asked.

Pauley smiled. 'Sure. Two hundred and thirty flower power bucks plus five from Mr Harry Parch.'

'But what good does it do us?' I protested. 'We're still known, and now Parch knows we're in town. He can smoke us out – it isn't that big a place. And now The Association will know that a Urulu is here, too.'

Pauley shook his head. 'No, not much threat from The Association at this stage. These are drones. Their minds have been drained, the useful information, if any, filed, and they have been given identical, empty *personas*. They're robots, that's all. That's why the girl's mind cracked when I resisted. It simply wasn't equipped for it. The other two won't even recognize that one of their own is missing. They'll go on until relieved, then go back to their living quarters. Nobody will notice or care. The biggies will only show up to make sure everything's going right and collect the money. They won't even count. Individuals don't exist in The Association.'

I started to press for more information on the enemy but Stuart was ever practical. 'The fact remains that Harry Parch is here and he knows *ve* are here. He can lock up this town tighter than a drum but very qvietly, vith full government authority. Ve have to get out of here. As the crow flies, ve are less than eighty miles from IMC.'

'Well, we've gotten this far – we can't give up now,' Dory put in. 'I won't give that son of a bitch another crack at me!' She started thinking. Finally she said, 'Look, I'm the least known and most unobtrusive person here. Parch hasn't seen me since I was a kid and my odds of meeting him head on are pretty slim anyway.'

There was no arguing with that.

'O.K., then,' she went on, fire in her tone, 'so we've got $235, plus whatever we have left over. That's a lot. Now, when the stores open, I'm gonna take that money and buy us a way outta here.'

Check-out was noon, but, despite some nervousness, we needed a little more time and I managed to sweet-talk the manager, a kindly old guy. I was a little apprehensive about letting Dory out alone, but Dan and I were both conspicuous, for different reasons, and even if Stuart's current face wasn't familiar to them, which it was, he would have been lost on such a shopping expedition.

She came back in a taxi with a pile of stuff we had to help unload. I looked over it, somewhat approvingly, the only one who, at least, didn't need a wardrobe.

'I kept it simple,' she told us. 'Things we needed, things for a good disguise, all from the discount stores except the wigs, which I had to pick up at Sears.'

We sorted the stuff out and I was amazed at the variety. She handed me a package. 'Mix it,' she told me. 'It's hair dye. Sensual Auburn, it says. Seems stupid to dye it its natural color, but I couldn't stand black on you, red always looks phoney, and it looked the best.'

I took her advice, although with a bit of regret, and filled the sink.

A bit later she took over the bathtub and started pouring in small packets that turned the water into what looked like really thin mud. 'What,' I asked her, 'is *that?*'

'Skin tint,' she replied. 'You mean you never saw it? It was just getting to be the in thing a few years ago. It's out now, I guess, but it's still around. It's a dye, it won't wash off, and this particular batch is called "Bronze Goddess." You can get 'em in any color – even blues and pinks and stuff like that.'

I looked at it dubiously. 'How *do* you get it off, then?'

'You can use an alcohol sponge, but most folks just let it wear off. It fades out in a couple of days. Now, strip and get in – we got to cover every part of your nice, white skin with it.'

The stuff actually didn't look bad *on* the skin, or in it, or whatever it was. Like a really deep suntan, a real golden bronze. She spent a lot of time making sure I had a complete coat, using a sponge applicator. When she was finished my skin and hair just about matched, although my blue eyes were a little incongruous. Dory was even prepared for that. 'I knew you might have sunglasses,' she said, 'but not with a light frame.' She handed me a pair and they looked pretty good. A golden nail polish and light lipstick completed the job, and I had to admit, looking at myself in the mirror, I looked like an entirely different person. With my hair now up and back, my ears showing, I looked exotic, all right, but not like Misty Carpenter. I decided to stick to the jeans, sweater, and sandals. It was simple, and comfortable.

She had gotten Pauley a short brown wig that looked pretty good, some false eyebrows that gave the Urulu a more human look, and a simple jeans and T-shirt outfit. 'You'll have to wear the cult sandals, though,' she apologized. 'I couldn't guess your shoe size.'

For herself she put her hair up and fitted a black Afro wig over it, applied some judicious cosmetics, and got some new jeans and a souvenir T-shirt but she added a matching denim vest. 'Had to go to the children's department,' she grumped. She stuck to her boots, on the theory that she still was the least recognizable, and pulled out a denim cowgirl-type hat with fancy stitching.

Stuart was the hardest, since we couldn't change him much. A complete change of clothes made him look touristy, a light jacket, more sunglasses and a brown cowboy hat completed the picture. He had a two-day growth of stubble, and we suggested he not shave for a while. We did, however, give him a dye job, changing his black hair to a browner shade, with just a touch of gray on the sides. It made him look different enough that he seemed satisfied.

Pauley was amazed. 'How did you even know the sizes?'

She grinned. 'When you've been a woman all your life you get to guessing other women's sizes pretty well.'

We stood back and looked critically at one another. 'What do you think?' Pauley asked.

'They'll do,' Dory replied. 'Look, it was the best I could do for a hundred and fifteen dollars. You never had problems, I am least likely to be known, Stuart – well, if he came face to face with somebody who'd known the original owner he'd be in trouble, but not casually, or from an I.D. photo. No, Misty's the only one with problems.'

'What do you mean? I think I look terrific!'

'Yeah, you do – as usual, which is the problem. Honey, you have a forty-two-inch bust on a twenty-four-inch waist. There's no disguising that. Your every move is an advertisement. One sex goddess attracts as much attention as another – and attention is what we don't want to attract.'

'What can I do?' I wailed. 'This is *me*.' I felt that it was a ridiculous position. Who'd ever thought that not being noticed, being nondescript, fading into the background, being very common and ordinary, would be such an asset?

Where are you, Victor Gonser, when I really need you?

'Let's get something to eat,' Pauley suggested. 'The usual place, I think. It's a good test, since our old selves have been in there before – *your* old selves, anyway.'

I nodded, then had a sudden thought. 'What about my suitcase? It's got all my stuff in it!'

He sighed and looked at it. 'You can't even lift it,' he pointed out. 'I'd say take what little you can in your purse and forget it.'

'Forget it hell! That's my *life* in there!'

'Or it might be your life if you keep it,' he shot back.

I sighed and almost cried when I thought of the stuff I would be losing. But one thing I wouldn't abandon. I opened the thing and took out the mink jacket. It was a nice brown and would go with my dyed self.

'Wow!' Dory whistled. 'Is that *real?*'

I nodded. I also took the jewelry case, opened it, and dumped it into my shoulder bag, along with the contents of the smaller purse I'd been going to use. The rest was really nice, and had some fond memories attached, but it could be more easily replaced. I looked at it sadly and shook my head, then sighed. 'O.K. Let's go before I start bawling my head off.'

Stuart and I went first, dropping the key off and then going off arm-in-arm. It served to draw some attention away from me to him for having me on his arm, which was good psychology.

Dory and Dan followed a few minutes behind, and we met in a corner booth at the restaurant. At the end, after figuring the bill, we figured we still had about $120 and some change. That was only $30 apiece. Not very much at all. Not even enough for bus tickets.

'We'll have to split up and get out of town,' Pauley told us. 'I don't like it, but they'll be looking for groups. Ordinarily, I'd say Misty and Stuart were the ideal couple, but not here. Putting our most recognizable people together would be a mistake. Better he and I – much less visibility that way, since they won't know me at all – and you and Dory.'

I nodded. 'Sounds O.K. to me.'

'I'd still not travel around too close together while in Vegas,' Pauley went on. 'You've got to face it, Misty – even in a city full of beautiful showgirls you get noticed, and that could cause them to put you and a smaller Indian woman together.'

'We'll take it easy,' I promised him. 'Look – you two take care of yourselves and don't worry about us. I think we can handle ourselves in the city.'

'O.K., then. I'll leave it to you how to get out. Train, plane, and bus stations are bound to be watched closely, as will all rental car agencies.'

'They can plug right into the computers,' Stuart put in. 'Get a readout – and you'd have to use your right name and driver's license and credit cards.'

'I didn't say it would be easy – for any of us. I'd say bus is the best bet – it's the one thing we can probably get for the money we've got, although maybe not all the way. Take separate busses. Let's see ... This is a Thursday. We'll meet in Los Angeles, at the Farmer's Market, at noon.'

'Tomorrow?' I asked.

'Every day until we all link up,' he replied. 'But don't give it too long. Anybody not there by, say, Monday, you have to write off. If I can get out of here and get a little money I'll check a safe house we have between here and there. Maybe I can make contact.'

'And if not?' Dory asked him.

He sighed. 'Then we've got real big problems. Not insurmountable ones, but a lot harder. Look, I'd rather not go into that now. Better you don't know until you have to.'

I saw what he meant.

The hot, bright, cheery look of Las Vegas was, somehow, suddenly more sinister. I began to feel the fear again, gnawing inside me. *They're out there*, I thought. *Out there looking for me.*

Suddenly it wasn't quite so much fun being Misty Carpenter.

CHAPTER TWELVE

Dory and I paid our bills and left them there, then walked out onto the street. We didn't even look back to see where they went. It was better that way.

And lonelier.

I took Dory's hand and squeezed it tight. She looked up at me and gave a confident smile, and I felt better.

I wasn't alone. It was the two of us against the world, at least, and while that wasn't much it was far better than just one.

She looked down the bleak highway. 'It's a ways down to the Strip and the bus station,' she noted. 'May as well start walking.'

Nobody walked in Las Vegas, not from this far away from the casinos. There wasn't even much provision for sidewalks, and the gleaming towers of the Strip looked ugly in the distance, set against the bright sun and dirty sand and hills. It should never be day here, I thought.

'We can't do it this way,' I told her. The Strip was there, but it was a good mile away. A couple of hotels and casinos were closer, but they weren't where we had to be.

'Yeah,' Dory agreed sourly. 'My feet won't take this, and I'm sweating like a stuck pig.'

'C'mon!' I urged. 'I've got an idea!'

We ran across the street when traffic allowed, and stood there.

'If I'm going to be a sex goddess,' I told her, 'I should be able to get us a ride.'

And I did. As a matter of fact, the guy almost lost control of the car. I had a hot thumb.

He leaned over and opened the front door, and we both squeezed in. It wasn't a big car, but it was air conditioned and felt good. I was in the middle, so I put my arms behind the two.

'Where you girls heading?' the guy asked pleasantly. He didn't look like a gambler or tourist. More like a salesman, I thought.

It took no effort at all to turn on Misty Carpenter's full charms.

'Down to the Strip,' I said in my best voice. 'Going to look around for a while.'

'I have to go over to the residential section,' he replied, regret evident in his voice. 'I'll run you down to the Frontier, though. That ought to put you in the center of things.'

The trip by car was too short for many questions, and I made sure he didn't think of any. It was so *easy*, I thought. It amazed me, this power I had. Not just that it worked, but that it didn't have to be worked. It was there when needed.

We got out, and I made his day by kissing him.

Las Vegas at 2 P.M. isn't the world's most thrilling town. This place ran by night, came alive by night, although it was always open.

I shifted my shoulder-purse, which seemed to weigh a ton – and no wonder. Even after giving a little of my best jewels to Dan to pawn when he cleared town, I had a lot in it. Mink was also warm at eighty-one degrees.

'Well, we can't stand out and fry,' I said with a lightness I didn't feel. 'Let's go in where it's cool.'

Once inside, with the clank of slot machines and the ringing bells and flashing lights, I felt nervous again. Everybody seemed to be looking at me, but instead of the admiring glances they probably were I saw each as a Harry Parch spy.

I noticed Dory was staring at me. 'What's the matter?' I said, suddenly concerned.

'I'm trying to figure out just what you do, how you do it,' she replied.

'Do what?' I asked.

'That's what I mean,' she said sulkily. 'The moves, the stance, the walk, everything.'

'Oh,' was all I could manage at first, relief sweeping over me. Then I added, 'Besides, you're too young for that.'

'Like hell,' she retorted.

I remembered Stuart's words and frowned. We needed more money, certainly, and I could get it. It was here, available. Vicki Lee shouldn't need money at all.

I looked at Dory, and she read my thoughts.

'If you do it, I will, too,' she said, teeth clenched.

And that upset me for some reason I couldn't understand. 'No,' I said in the same tone.

'You go ahead,' she urged. 'I'll watch. Then – well, I'll meet you in the L.A. bus depot, that's all. Don't worry. Remember, I'm twenty-five and this body's *ready.*' She paused. 'I go *both* ways now, you know.'

I started to protest, to argue, then turned and walked away from her, towards the bar.

She was small, but she was a well-developed seventeen-year-old. They wouldn't have any problems believing her old enough, particularly with that manner and speech, and an experienced woman.

Which, of course, she was.

Even this early in the afternoon, I didn't even have to sit down before I had to choose which John looked most promising.

His name was John K. Jessup, he was about forty-five, paunchy and slightly gray, dressed in a brown tweed suit and matching tie. He was there for a convention, he was lonely, and he had the bread.

He reminded me a lot of Victor Gonser. I wondered if the old Misty would have targeted him, or whether this was *because* of the resemblance.

It was right out of the books and old movies. He was a machine tool salesman, of all things, from Iowa City, of all places, and he bought me some drinks until we both felt good, and he talked of his business and his life while I just gushed all over him.

It was simple. I just stopped thinking and it worked on impulse.

Then we gambled a little, caught a nice little lounge act, danced a bit after – he really wasn't a bad dancer – and he had the time of his life. Everyone was looking at him, envious of him, wondering why they couldn't have such luck.

For that was my protection – in context, I was a cypher, a symbol, a thing, a precious object that was coveted.

But not a wanted human being, sought by certain people.

Then a nice dinner, a few more drinks, and up to John K. Jessup's room, where he fulfilled his fantasies.

It was a life I liked, would have gladly stuck with.

But I was wanted in this town, I had a responsibility, and I had an appointment in L.A.

He didn't want me to go, begged me to stay at least to breakfast, but I couldn't.

I never once asked for money, I never once asked for anything.

He slipped me some money; insisted I take it, and seemed slightly embarrassed by the action.

I was in the elevator before I looked.

It was two hundred bucks.

That easy.

For having fun.

For giving somebody else a good time, too.

I walked to the bus station, the hot night air feeling just great, me feeling just great.

There was a cop car parked around the corner from the bus station, and a suspicious-looking guy in sports shirt and slacks leaning on the wall near the door.

Suddenly I didn't feel so good anymore.

I was alone, all alone.

And Misty Carpenter feared that most of all.

I backed away from the streetlights, back into the shadows and waited, barely daring to breathe. I was trembling slightly, and I turned and walked back down the street, back into the Strip, which somehow seemed now to be threatening; the garish lights and weird sounds loomed and swooped and pressed in at me.

I realized suddenly that I'd started to run, and slowed to a nervous pace.

People passed me on the street, the heads turning as always to look at me, only this time I didn't want them to look, didn't want them to notice. I felt like I was lit up, an advertising billboard, which, in a way, I was.

I needed a drink and a place to sit down for a few minutes, and I turned into a small bar and slot machine parlor on the fringe of the Strip. It was crowded, and heads turned when I entered, men staring, gesturing.

'Hey Babe! Lonely?' somebody yelled out, and I turned, pushing back out onto the street, that suddenly cold, lonely street.

Misty was, in herself, a trap.

I reached an intersection turning off to a small, dark street. As I turned the corner, not thinking of where I could go, not thinking of anything but getting away from the lights, a figure suddenly loomed before me, strange and horrible.

'A pretty flower for a pretty flower, both to glorify God?' piped a voice. It was one of the Redeemed, and I almost screamed, and pushed the poor creature out of the way.

There are no really bad sections of Las Vegas, but there are some not so well lit, not so garish, not so public, and I was in one of these now.

I was cloaked in the darkness, and for a moment, it felt good.

Suddenly a man came out of the shadows, a bottle in his hand.

'Hey! Honey! Wanna drink?' he called out in a filthy, ugly voice as he reached for me. I almost screamed, but evaded him. He followed me, and I started running again.

Finally I came to a corner and rounded it. There was a house and some small trees watered by a sprinkler, and I quickly crouched down in their protective, dark shelter, and held my breath.

He came around the corner seconds later, and stood there for what seemed like forever, breathing hard and looking around.

So this is what it's like, I thought. Is this what every woman feels and fears if she ventures out alone? Is every walk in a strange place a potential threat, a promise that, perhaps, horror is lurking there?

Victor Gonser wouldn't have hesitated in walking into that bar, down this street. Victor wouldn't be crouching, trembling in fear as some bastard stalked him. Men couldn't comprehend this terror, as I waited breathless, certain I would cough, or fall and give myself away to this man of the dark.

He drained the bottle, and threw it into the yard. It hit the tree, and landed just a few inches from me.

I heard him mumbling something to himself, then he turned and walked slowly down the street toward the Strip.

I remained there for some time, shaking terribly, realizing that while Victor Gonser hated being alone, I, Misty, could not *survive* alone.

I heard a clock somewhere strike three. Three in the morning, and I was crouching in the darkness of somebody's front yard.

Just as I could not turn Misty off physically, I could not shed her mentally, either. She was not cut out for this and she was terrified, out of her element completely, overcome with that emotionalism that now worked against me.

I shuddered, and forced myself to stop crying, to calm down. I took deep breaths, and tried to regain control.

Think, dammit, think! I told myself over and over.

Cautiously, I made my way back to the walk, and could see nothing, nobody but a few cars going to and fro.

Now the Strip was closed to me as well. *He* had gone that way, and I must go the other.

I walked, forcing myself to be slow and deliberate, afraid as I walked under every streetlight, more afraid of the darkness between.

I was suddenly out of sidewalk and streetlights again, and walking on the sandy shoulder of what the sign said was State Route 6. How long or how fast I'd walked I didn't know. Over to the right of me I saw the start of an Interstate highway, and beyond it a cluster of lights in the darkness.

Route 6 and the Interstate seemed to get further apart, so I cut overland, crossing the dark gulf between; desert grass and brush stung my feet, and I felt in total despair.

Then, suddenly, I was at the big highway, which was carrying a moderate amount of traffic. I looked over and saw that the lights I'd seen were not merely lights but a truck stop of some sort.

It was difficult crossing the highway, and there was a slope down the other side which caused me to fall more than once, but I was over, and walking toward the bright lights.

Frankly, I was in a state of shock yet, had been since the man had almost caught up to me. I could just think of the lights, of people, lots of people, with no dark places.

The place smelled of diesel fuel and a young attendant rushed around checking green pumps, using extenders to wash the windshields of the big rigs.

Even so, it was fairly new, and one of those complete types – a restaurant, complete with slot machine banks, and a trucker's store of sorts. I walked in and headed first for the women's bathroom, which was fairly difficult to find. This was still mostly a man's world.

Once inside, the shock seemed to wear off a bit, and I almost collapsed, bracing myself against a sink. Slowly my head came up and I looked at myself in the mirror.

My God! I thought. I looked like hell, and even looking like hell I looked sexy.

I straightened myself up and went into a stall. I sat there for several minutes on the toilet, trying to get ahold of myself.

Now what? I asked myself, fearing that the answer was that I was doomed to wander forever like this, cut off and alone.

Something within me seemed to snap. *No!* I told myself suddenly, and dried my flowing tears of hopelessness.

I was back in control, tired but thinking once more. The terror wasn't gone, but it had been superseded by desperation. If the terror came, then it would come. I had to accept that. But, if that was all I could look forward to, I might as well slit my throat right here, now.

That's where Victor Gonser had been, back up on the trail, I realized. Thinking about jumping off a cliff, wasn't he?

I fumbled in the big, cheap purse. Some makeup there, yes, a small towel, and about $230.00. All my worldly goods.

I straightened myself up and went out over to the trucker's store. It was mostly men's stuff, but I found a cute straw cowboy hat that looked really nice, some hankies, deodorant, and other toiletries. Even a spare couple of shirts. They stuffed the bag to bulging, but it was much better.

I went back into the john and used what I'd bought, carefully brushed my hair, cleaned up, got looking and smelling nice.

Terror there might be, but I had a mind inside this body, and I had this body, too.

I walked into the restaurant. It was mostly empty except for a few truckers talking in a special area reserved for them, sipping coffee or eating hamburgers.

The waitress came over, and I asked for coffee and some eggs, all I thought I could manage.

But I radiated, and I knew it. Nature abhors a vacuum, and I had a vacuum on both sides of me, while nature was staring from the trucker's lounge.

One of them, a tired-looking man in his mid-forties dressed somewhat cowboy-style, a day or so's growth of beard giving him something of the rugged look, called over.

'Hay!' he said loudly, in an accent that was strictly hillbilly. 'Hay Sweet Thang! You lonesome? C'mon' over!'

I drank my coffee and pretended to ignore him. Finally he got up, mostly, I think, at the whispered taunting of two other drivers, and came over.

'What's the matter, gal? Troubles?' he asked pleasantly. 'You look too sad sittin' here like that with that expression on yore face.'

I turned to him. 'I'm stuck, if you want to know the truth. I used to dance at the Mauritania Lounge here, but the boss decided he wanted to use me in another end of his business, and I quit. I've just been drifting around all night, trying to think about what to do next.'

He seemed genuinely sympathetic. 'I know what you mean, I think. Where y'all headin' now?'

I sighed. 'I was thinking of getting a waitress's job or something,' I told him. I had seen a sign near the front door. 'Now, I don't know. I have a lot of friends, but they're all back in L.A., and I have no way to get there.'

He rubbed his chin, and looked about as sincere as I was.

'Well, now,' he thought. 'No money?'

'Some,' I replied, then told him about the encounter with the would-be rapist. I told it straight, sparing nothing except the fact that I was not about to go back into town for entirely different reasons than the fear of meeting him again.

He nodded sympathetically, and there seemed real concern in his voice.

'Look,' he suggested, 'I've just dropped a load at the air base here, and I'm deadheadin' back to Barstow. You're welcome as far as there. After that, well, I don't think we got a problem gettin' no ride into L.A. for a beaver pretty as you, ma'am.'

And it was as simple as that.

He was a perfect gentleman all the way, and I slept the not so long ride to Barstow.

Once he got in C.B. range of the 1-15,1-40 junction, he got on the radio and described me in incredible, somewhat colorful language, and explained my need.

The others didn't believe him, and so I got on myself and asked for help.

I hope I didn't cause a smash-up somewhere, but finally the man with the strongest radio got through the jam and we linked up. I kissed my savior good-bye, and changed trucks.

The new man was not as nice or as gentlemanly, but he seemed satisfied to pet and snuggle as best he could with fourteen gears to control, and damned if he didn't wind up driving miles out of his way to drop me at the Farmer's Market!

I had made it with two hours to spare, not costing me a thing, and I was dead tired but little else.

Meeting in the Farmer's Market, I found, was more difficult than anyone would think. It's a huge place, full of stalls selling just about everything, and crowds of people all about. I finally decided that I was too tired to hunt; if I was going to be a magnet, I might as well be one and let them find me.

I got a small bun from a Greek-style bakery stall, and some strong coffee and sat down at one of the picnic tables that were spread all over the inside of the place.

People were all around, and I got the usual looks, but nobody bothered me. *This* kind of crowd, the tourists and the locals, was the kind I liked best right now.

About 11:15, wandering around just looking at things, I heard a familiar voice shout 'Misty!' and before I could move Dory was all over me, kissing and hugging. I finally calmed her down and we found a place that, while not exactly quiet, was at least out of the mainstream, and sat down.

'Well,' I said to her. 'You don't look exactly worn down and away. Tell me what happened after we split up.'

'Well,' she echoed me, 'after you went off with Mr Middle America I stood around for a while, then walked into the bar – and immediately got challenged for my I.D.! I didn't believe it, but I had to leave, and they escorted me completely out of the casino.

'So, there I was, out on the streets with no place to go. I saw some of the Redeemed selling their flowers, and I wanted to get away from there.'

'I know,' I responded with a slight shudder. 'I saw some on the way here. It's a wonder they aren't all over here.'

'They wouldn't allow it,' Dory said flatly. 'They're selling, so they'd have to have a stall.' She twisted in her seat a bit, getting more comfortable. 'So, anyway, I didn't want to be around those creeps, and so I headed for the bus station. I saw all the stakeouts, but I figured that if this getup wouldn't get me past them then I was gone anyway, and they gave me barely a glance!'

I took a deep breath, thinking of my own fears and what that had led to, and said nothing.

'Well, there I was, so I bought the ticket and started to come here. They were pretty thorough – had somebody at the ticket counter and bus gate, too. Well, anyway, I passed, and got a seat, and a few minutes later this young black guy, a real cool sort, took the seat next to me. He tried to look disinterested, but I've been around. We got to talking, and he was very nice.

'So we got in about a little after one in the morning, and we took a cab to his apartment—'

'Dory! You didn't!' I exclaimed.

She smiled. 'C'mon, I *said* he was a nice guy. I spent the night there, he had a real nice place. A computer programmer, I think he said. He played some records – Man! Are they ever weird now! – and blew some smoke and had a real great night. He was gone to work when I got up, so I fixed myself some breakfast and came on over. You know, I heard they didn't have any buses in L.A., but they do – occasionally. I got here, and that's all there is to it. What about you?'

I hesitated, feeling a little funny. I didn't know exactly what I felt, or why I felt it, but it was a crazy sort of combination. Joy that she was here, and safe, and without any problems, some resentment that she'd done it all so easily after what I'd gone through, and, for some reason, a touch of possessive jealousy, strange from someone like me.

I tried to push it back and considered how much to tell her. In the end, I felt a little mad at myself and thought, hell, this is *Dory*, dammit. I told her everything, sparing nothing, and she listened in quiet concentration. When I was through, she sighed.

'You've had it rough, even though most of it was of your own making. After all, you had over two hundred bucks. Hell, you coulda taken a *cab* to L.A., at least to Barstow, anyway.'

I was thunderstruck. It simply hadn't occurred to me. Now that she'd said it, I saw a dozen easy ways that a girl with money could have gone.

Blind, dumb fear had done it to me.

I started to cry, and this upset her. 'Now, don't do that, or I'll feel bad and we'll both be bawling,' she said sharply. 'Look, you just went through something that every woman grows up with, has to face. It's the real world. Men can sympathize, but they can never *feel* it, so they can't ever understand how limiting it is to be a woman.'

There was nothing I could say. Once I'd written of my hatred and contempt for all restraints, for anything that limited choices.

But there were some decisions you couldn't escape from.

Unless you went Harry Parch's route, or The Association's, and gave up *all* choices.

I glanced over at a clock nearby, and gasped. 'It's after twelve,' I said suddenly.

We moved out into the mainstream again, got some drinks, and started staring at the increasing crowds of people milling about, eating, and going back and forth.

Over two hours later we were still waiting.

I couldn't conceal my mounting agitation, and neither could Dory. Neither of us, though, would say it for some time more.

When it got to be three o'clock, she finally uttered the unspeakable.

'I don't think they're coming,' she said softly.

I sighed. 'So what do we do now?'

'I think we take a bus and go shopping for some clothes with that money of yours, then find a place for the night,' she responded.

I nodded glumly. 'Then?'

She shrugged. 'We come back here tomorrow, same time. And the next day, and the next. If they don't show by then, I think we both go out and get jobs.'

CHAPTER THIRTEEN

A hundred bucks doesn't go far these days when you're shopping for clothes, but Dory was ever the practical one and it's surprising what you can get at big discount and drug stores.

For another forty we found a room at a cheap hotel, not the kind of place I really liked but the most we could afford in these days of $150 rooms. That left about $70 for food, transportation, and emergencies. It wouldn't last long, but it only had to last until Monday, when, I hoped, I could find a pawn shop.

By early evening I was dead on my feet and just about passed out. I think I slept ten or eleven solid hours, but, despite a headache, I felt better than I had since I'd last been in Stuart's little chair at IMC.

It was a little after ten on Saturday. Dory came into the room from the outside, newspapers in hand. 'Well! Sleeping Beauty awaketh!'

I managed a smile, and shook the sleep from me. I took a cool shower to get fully awake, then got dressed, sticking to the casual outfit. It was warmer in L.A. than I'd expected.

Trying to manage with the city's less-than-great mass transit system was a pain, but we couldn't afford cabs at today's prices, not now. We got to Farmer's Market just before noon, and I managed to get coffee, a danish, and some aspirin. We idly read the papers, thin for a Saturday, which contained little of interest to us, and waited.

Suddenly, thumbing through the inside back section, Dory let out a little gasp.

'What is it?'

'Listen. "Man, Woman Die in Flaming Crash. Victorville, October 2. An unidentified man and woman were killed tonight when their car swerved to avoid a pedestrian and rolled over, bursting into flame. The car had been reported stolen in Las Vegas hours earlier. Highway Patrol officers are investigating." ' She looked up at me, a pained expression on her face.

'You don't suppose ...' I managed, supposing exactly that.

She nodded slowly. 'Sure. It fits. Although it's almost certainly not the way it really happened.'

I thought sadly of poor, gentle Stuart, and of the strange alien who called himself Dan Pauley. I couldn't bring myself to believe it, although, deep down, I knew it was true. Stuart, in particular ... The thought of a world without him was almost unbearable.

They were gone.

I fought back tears, not very successfully. 'So it's over. The great expedition to save the world is over. Well, if anybody saves it, it won't be us, now.'

Dory nodded glumly. 'No use hanging around here any more.'

'What do you want to do?'

'Get drunk, or stoned, or both. Then wait for the Sunday papers and see what's available.'

'Like hell I will,' I snapped, getting mad now. 'Damn it, I'm through running. Where's a phone booth?'

She looked at me strangely. 'What ...?'

I stalked over to the booth, picked the receiver up, fed it a quarter, dialed

0 and got the quarter back. 'Operator? Give me Al Jordan, Stateline, Nevada. I don't know the area code but I know the number.' I gave it to her. 'Collect,' I told her. 'Tell him it's Misty Carpenter.'

I listened for all the relays and operator-connected conversations. I was using Al's private number, though. If he were there – and he almost certainly was about this time, I'd get him.

'Hello! Misty! Good to hear from ya,' he enthused.

'Listen, Al, don't give me that bullshit,' I shot him. 'You're a no-good son of a bitch in the pocket of Harry Parch and I know it.'

'Hey! Wait a *minute*, Baby!'

'Just shut up and listen, Al. I know you can call Parch. He's in Vegas, most likely. You call him and tell him to call off his dogs. We surrender. We want to have normal lives. I want to open that club, Al! I want to pick up where I left off! And I don't want any Harry Parch or his type whiskin' me off anywhere in the dead of night. You tell him Dory and me'll keep quiet, we'll be good girls and he can check on us all he wants, but we've had it, we're through, all we want is to be left alone, as we are – *as we are*, Al – to live normal, decent lives. Y'hear me?'

He was silent for a moment. Finally he said, 'Jesus, you can get mad! O.K., O.K., I won't bullshit you. I can get ahold of Parch. But I dunno if he'll buy it – or if you can trust him if he says he'll buy it, Babe.'

'He's a skunk and a rat but I think he *will* buy it, Al. How long do you figure it'll take to get hold of him?'

He thought a moment. 'Give me 'til eight tonight, at least. Call me back then or give me a number.'

'Uh uh. I'll call. Talk to you later, then. And, Al ...'

'Yeah, Babe?'

'I can't do anything about Harry Parch or to him. But I wrote down a whole list of names and dates of some pretty big customers at Cougar over the years and I got it so it'll hit the papers if I disappear. You got that?'

'Take it easy, Babe. I'll do what I can!'

I hung up on him, feeling a lot better.

Dory, I found, was standing next to me, and she was staring at me, open-mouthed. 'Wow. I didn't think you had it in you.'

'Neither did I but, damn it, I'm tired of being pushed, shoved, brain processed, chased, and all. We done what we could and that's that.'

'Your grammar slipped, you know,' she noted. 'You sounded like a whole different person, accent and all.'

I nodded. 'Meet the real Misty Carpenter.'

'Think Parch'll buy it?'

'I think so,' I told her honestly. 'If we're in Vegas we're under his thumb, so to speak, and he has nothing to gain now. In his own way he's a reasonable man. We just don't matter any more, Dory.'

'I hope you're right,' she said sincerely.

I wasn't about to call Al from the hotel, but we went back there to settle down and wait for the magic hour.

We didn't say much about the future, or the risks involved, nor did I, at least, dwell on them. I think I'd just been tensioned and pressured out. I was just too sick and tired of this to be scared any more. I'd had plenty of sleep, yet I felt completely worn out, inside and out.

There wasn't much on TV and we finally went through the papers, and, for a while, we just sat around listlessly, letting it all wear off. Finally I said, 'I think I'm going to take a shower and just wind down.'

Dory looked over and smiled. 'Want company? We can save water and do each other's backs.'

I laughed and said 'sure' and we did. In the process, the tension seemed to lift, and we got to playing around with each other, scrubbing the sensitive spots, and when we got out and dried off we both flopped nude on the bed.

'Misty?'

'Yes?'

'What happens if Parch buys the deal? What happens then?'

'I use the credit cards for a plane to Vegas, we rent a car – mine's still up in Tahoe – and pick up all the left luggage. Then we check into the best hotel suite we can find and get the best dinner in Vegas.'

'No, not immediately. After. In the long term.'

'I make a pretty good living, and I have a lot of contacts from my old clientele,' I told her. 'I got a solid four-week contract with the Imperial Lounge, which is Joe's place, which I can parlay into a lot more, either with Joe or some of the others there, if I'm a hit.'

'You'll be a hit. With those moves you're the best in the business, I bet.'

I smiled. 'And, if I get long-term work, we find a condo or something there and settle in. Buy furniture, clothes, you name it.'

'And where do I come in? I mean – what's *my* future? Yours is pretty secure.'

'As long as the looks last,' I admitted, turning on my side to look at her. 'But I don't see what you're concerned about. You can do anything you want to do.'

'I'm not sure just what I *do* want to do. Since – coming back – I really haven't allowed myself to think about the next day. Now I have to – and I have no place to go, no money, no job, not even a real cover identity so I can get a driver's license or social security card or anything like that. No high school diploma, nothing – and I at least deserve that, having gone through it twice.'

I looked at her strangely. 'Dory, you have a place. Wherever I am you have a place, money, whatever you need. I can't hack this world alone, not any more. Maybe the original Misty could, but I can't. I need you very badly.'

'Sure, for now. But when you get the big time and all those big-shots are around with their flashy everything, it might be different.'

I sat up, turned, and stared at her. 'Dory, you little idiot! I'm in *love* with you! Don't you understand that? I've been in love with you since the first day we met on the boat. I need you terribly, with me, always. Without you, all the rest doesn't mean a thing.'

Her face broke into a broad smile and she got up and hugged me. 'Oh, Misty! That's all I wanted to hear!'

And we made love there, for the first time, an act stronger than sex but which made sex all the better. It was as Stuart said. It wasn't who you were on the outside but who you really were, on the inside, that mattered most, that was the only thing that was really important.

And the lovemaking lasted and lasted and lasted ...

I would not give up men – and possibly she wouldn't, either. A part of me, at least, required the physical act. But I knew then that I could love only this one, and make love only to this one person, this individual, this wonderful human being.

And after we just lay there, caressing each other tenderly, saying very little for a while. Finally Dory sighed and said, 'Misty? You know, after all this, I *finally* found it.'

'Found what, honey?'

'My place. Normalcy. A real life. For the first time I *like* myself, see a real future. I'm whole, Misty! I'm not a freak any more! I'm a real person and I'm very, very happy.'

I smiled, recalling my own conflicts. Whole people. Neither of us would ever have been whole or happy as our former selves, doomed to go through life slightly askew. The Urulu, although it wasn't their motive, had accomplished a lot, and, oddly, so had IMC, even Harry Parch. Not deliberately, of course, but it was there all the same. I didn't know, had never known, two people as much in love and so filled with caring for each other as Dory and I were now, yet, even there, those external forces had twisted and turned us for the better. I rid myself of my male-ness, so to speak, and became a real woman, while Dory faced down and made peace with her inner demon. And, knowing that body-switching was not only possible but was practiced by all sorts of creatures, including the U.S. Government, removed any last stigma that might linger in the mind about love between two women. When men could be women, or women, men, at the flick of a switch or the touch of an alien hand, what difference did your body really make? Tall, short, fat, thin, old, young, male, female, black, white, red, yellow ... all irrelevant.

Was this, perhaps, the Urulu promise? A civilization that never looked to the outside, only *inside?* Who saw and reacted only to the real person within, regardless of physical form? It was an exciting possibility, one made all the more likely by the Urulu's own nature. Would *any* race that evolved with this ability pay any attention to looks or superficialities at all? Not among their own people, certainly.

I wondered again what they were really like. Not at all like us, certainly. And not totally free themselves of prejudices and hang-ups, since they had so little regard for us warm-blooded mammals.

And there was the rub. The authoritarian empire they had encountered had been led by a race like ours, a race that had itself discovered, rather than evolved, the mystery of the identity matrix. Had evolved with our concept of physical, superficial differences being important. Their prejudices, like those of Harry Parch and those who pulled his strings, shaped their use of the identity matrix, and had distorted and perverted its potential. No wonder the Urulu couldn't grasp us as a race worth saving! They couldn't see how we could evolve except into a new mini-Association.

And they might well be right, I told myself. Certainly we had failed, but, damn it, we had done our best. Done everything that was asked of us, to the best of our ability. We could only hope now that there were others to take up the fight and that one of them would succeed. A pity, though, I thought. We – Dory and I – were, I felt, closer to the Urulu, or at least its ideal, than any other human beings on Earth. Stuart, though, poor Stuart, had at least seen this potential.

Suddenly I had a thought and sat up, grabbing for the clock.

'What's the matter?'

'It's after nine! I didn't call Al back!'

Dory got up and shook her head. 'We were at it for *hours*. Wow.'

I kissed her and jumped out of bed. 'And it was wonderful, too. But I have to make that call.'

I was still only half-dressed when the telephone rang in the hotel room. I jumped at the sound, then turned and stared at it for a moment. It was one of those internal things, without even a dial. Who would be calling *this* room?

Hesitantly, I picked up the receiver. 'Yes?'

'Miss, ah, Carpenter, when you failed to call at eight I decided to wait a bit, but finally decided to call you, instead,' said Harry Parch.

I almost dropped the phone. Dory saw my horrified expression and I mouthed Parch to her. That made her sit up fast.

'Go on,' I told him, trying to sound brave.

'I took this step as a demonstration of good faith,' he continued. 'As you can see, we know where you are, and could have picked you up at any time if we'd wanted. Actually, I must congratulate you. We did not pick *you* up at all, and I have no idea how you got where you are. However, we had excellent photos of your friend from the Indian school, and we spotted her when she boarded the bus. From that point we just followed her directly to you.'

I nodded glumly to myself. It *had* seemed all too easy. 'So why didn't you pick us up yesterday?' I asked him.

'Basically, we wanted to see what you'd do. We have not been kind to the two of you, who are the most innocent people in this mess, and we would prefer not to do any more. You *didn't* go to the papers, you *didn't* run around hysterically, you just accepted things, and that is what we wanted to know. Miss Carpenter, when I received your message today I can not tell you how happy it made us. You have chosen the best course for you, for us, for every-one. I believe we can finally end all this, or, at least, your part in it, and you and your friend can go about the rest of your lives.'

I felt excitement and relief rising in me. I covered the mouthpiece and whispered to Dory, 'He's going to buy it!'

'Then we're free to leave? To go back and pick up our lives?'

'Yes, indeed. You understand, of course, that we will keep a watch on both of you, and that if you cause trouble in the future this arrangement may have to be modified. But, as long as you don't rock the boat, neither will we.'

'That sounds fair enough,' I told him. 'But there's one minor point you could help with.'

'Oh?'

'Legal identities. I'm sort of real, but Dory's got real problems. She needs proof of citizenship.'

He sounded surprised. 'Why, she's got it – and so have you. We don't do things halfway. There really *was* a Misty Ann Carpenter, but she died at the age of three months and is buried in Cedar Point Cemetery in a pauper's gravesite. Delores Eagle Feather had a similar fate in Yakima, Washington, but her birth certificate's on file there. Use those. No one will ask or question you about them. It's done all the time.'

I nodded to myself. Finally, I said, 'Parch – one more last thing on this matter.'

'Yes?'

'Pauley. He said the Redeemed were the enemy and that they could switch.'

He sighed. 'I know. They use the First Amendment as a weapon. But we're working on it, that's all I can say. It's not your battle now. Go find a home. There are others more qualified to carry the burden. Goodbye, Miss Carpenter.'

'Goodbye, Mr Parch.'

And that was that.

It was, in fact, as easy as Parch claimed. We blew the last of the cash on a quick flight back, called the Sands for a minibus, and were settled in in less than four hours. I was relieved to find that not only was my big wardrobe still in storage, but the nice old geezer at the motel still had the bag I'd left.

The city lost its ugliness and was alit with neon splendor at two in the morning, open and doing business all around. There are no clocks in casinos, and they work on a timeless schedule which many of the restaurants and other places also follow.

On Monday we went to the bank and then on something of a shopping spree. It was far different than before. Las Vegas was its former glamorous, unthreatening self once again, and we had each other and were no longer alone.

A black, heavy weight had been lifted from both of us and we were like kids. Both of us had ourselves practically done over, the only complaint from Dory that I needed my hair blond and curly again, and Dory seemed almost born anew. She had her hair styled into a pageboy, bought some really nice clinging fashions, and, in a slinky, satiny silk dress, heels, and some jewelry transformed herself into a stunningly beautiful woman.

We wrote for our birth certificates and got them, applying for passports, the ultimate stamp of legitimacy although we didn't feel like going anywhere, got her a driver's license, and had her name added to my charge accounts and bank accounts, and found a small but comfortable apartment away from the Strip in a nice, safe neighborhood.

Joe was delighted to see me and launched the club with a big publicity blitz. It was a real class show in a real class setting, and a damned good location – no gambling, of course, but sandwiched between two busy casinos. We did really great business, and Joe was so happy he offered me thirty weeks for thirty thousand. I took it, of course, but not before Dory looked over all the contracts, deals, and exclusions. It was clear I was the star and centerpiece of the show, she said, and if I could establish my dominance during that run the place would be so identified with me that they'd wind up eventually giving me a piece of the club.

She got around the high school problem by taking the G.E.D., a real snap according to her, then enrolled in night courses in business administration. She became my manager, more or less, making most of the decisions, controlling the money and spending, even getting me on some local TV and, through that, an agent with powerful connections.

Nobody raised an eyelash at our obvious intimate relationship, not in Vegas, although some of the guys I knew couldn't figure out how I could go to bed with an attractive guy and obviously enjoy it and then go home to my 'wife.' Dory seemed to understand and not to mind my promiscuity as long as I always came home to her. For her own part, she didn't seem interested in anybody but me – although I hardly could have stood in her way – and she seemed happy and content. I might have been the star, but she was the boss in the household, no question about it, and I liked it that way.

If anything, our relationship deepened even beyond what I would have thought possible. At times we almost seemed two different sides of the same person, knowing what each other was thinking and feeling, understanding each other and trusting each other totally.

On her official eighteenth birthday she came of legal age for most things and applied for a legal change of name, from Delores Eagle Feather to just Dory Carpenter. I was flattered, but she did it because she wanted to and I didn't object. She had a lot of fun changing names on accounts and her driver's license and even passport when it came through. She had taken the last step, that of becoming her own person and not somebody else, and she was radiant.

The publicity campaign paid off. I got written up by one columnist as 'The Queen of Las Vegas' and I loved it. I did talk shows and supermarket openings and loved to shock the hell out of people by proving myself an intellectual, conversant with a lot of topics, although never in the act. That wasn't the image the public was buying.

Again the old hang-up, of course. What I was outside was what was important to the masses.

Dory had been right, too, about the club's dependence on me. When I made a move to leave, they jumped, had long discussions with my agent, and, since they really couldn't offer me more money – without a casino, which a strip club couldn't have under the weird laws there, their top gross was limited – but they did wind up offering me a slightly lower salary and a profit percentage, which we took, along with the biggest piece of ego I could imagine – a name change to 'Misty's Harbor,' complete with large, sexy portrait of me framed in Vegas neon.

The only dark spot was the numbers of the Redeemed that seemed to be growing everywhere. You couldn't go anywhere without running into them with their flowers, candy, shaved bodies and raped and gutted minds. They had bought large buildings, huge tracts of land, and were gaining political influence, the kind that comes with massive amounts of tax-free money and power. They swelled in membership and never seemed to lose converts, a fact that actually attracted more young people and lost souls to the movement. As usual, the press was mixed, the conservatives upset at losing their kids, the liberals shocked at the gutting of a generation's spirit, but with Constitutional guarantees there was nothing, it seemed, that could be done to slow them.

They were spreading worldwide, in the Latin countries, in Africa, in Europe and parts of Asia, tailoring their public beliefs to fit local concerns. It was hard to tell what they were doing in the Iron Curtain countries, but I had no doubt they were there and working successfully.

The cult alone soon had a worldwide following estimated at more than twenty *million*. Dory and I watched the TV and headlines and understood anew what Dan Pauley had meant. The Association planted, and grew, and moved out to conquer all.

I couldn't believe that Parch and IMC would take this lying down, and I wondered if, somehow, they'd just discovered an enemy they could not fight without making themselves into the enemy. It must be frustrating, I thought more than once, to *know* and have the power and be so impotent.

We'd been living our own life of peaceful glamour for more than two years now, and it showed no signs of slacking off. Some tentative investments Dory had made in local real estate had already paid off, and we were very comfortable and secure. To celebrate our second 'anniversary' I'd taken some time off and we'd gone to Hawaii and Tahiti, a sort of belated honeymoon, just the two of us doing what all lovers do – or would like to do, if they had the time and money.

Coming home from the club late one night, about four or so, I was feeling a little off and just wanted to get in, eat, and relax. On such days Dory would have a light supper waiting, and I could just relax and unwind.

I walked in and saw nothing cooking and Dory in the living room avidly watching TV. For a moment I just thought she'd got engrossed in a movie or something, but then I realized it was a newscast and that she was very intent on it. I frowned. A newscast? At this hour?

She looked up as I entered, looking worried and haggard, and I grew concerned. 'What's up?' I asked. 'What's happening?'

She got up and came over, giving me a hug and a kiss. 'You haven't *heard?* You don't *know?*'

I shook my head. News didn't travel much in my circles, at least not while it was happening.

'They shot the President!'

'*What?*'

She nodded. 'He was comin' out of a hotel in Chicago where he was campaigning and they zapped him!'

'What? *Who?*'

'The Redeemed! About an hour ago. Opened up on all sides with automatic weapons! Mowed down a *huge* crowd.'

My God! I thought, and sank back into the sofa. What insulated lives we've led. I wasn't a fan of the President's, but I still felt a deep sense of outrage at the deed.

'Why would they do it?' I asked aloud. 'It doesn't make sense for The Association to do something like this.'

We both went over and turned back to the TV. They were showing an instant replay of the thing – it seemed to have been in front of the network cameras. It was a stunning, horrible, grotesque sight. 'They're all *smiling*,' I breathed, unable to tear myself away from it. 'Oh, my *God!*'

They switched back to the studio, where a tired-looking anchorman, not one of the regulars, continued the story.

'Vice President Arnold was awakened and told the news at 3:45 Pacific Time. Arnold immediately cut short his campaign swing through California and is expected to fly to Washington later on this evening. His motorcade is already getting ready to go to the airport and he is expected to leave for there as soon as possible.

'Repeating our earlier story. President Long is dead, shot to death by gunmen waiting for him with submachine guns outside the Trevor House Hotel in Chicago where he had been in an early morning political strategy session with Illinois Republican bigwigs. He emerged from the hotel at about six fifteen Chicago time and was immediately cut down, along with at least twenty-six others, by a squad of at least six gunmen with automatic weapons who were allegedly members of the Church of the Redeemed. All six were killed. A complete list of the dead will follow shortly.

'President Long had to fit the session into a crowded schedule, and scheduled it only as a last-minute bid to end party bickering in the crucial midwestern state. The unusually early time was caused by his schedule. He was due to fly to Kansas City at eight Central Time.'

I did a mental calculation. If he was shot at 6:15 Central, it was 4:15 here – only twenty minutes or so before I got home.

The announcer was going on and on about the whole thing. The list of dead included the Secret Service agents, some well-known press people, his top campaign aide and two Congressmen from Illinois.

'FBI and Secret Service agents immediately went to the local and national headquarters of the International Brotherhood Church of the Redeemed, but spokespersons for that organization deny any responsibility for the slaying and state categorically that they are as shocked as the rest of us.'

'I'll bet,' Dory grumbled.

I thought a moment. 'No. Wait a minute. Maybe they are.'

'Huh? You know those idiots don't do anything without orders!'

I sat back, feeling stunned. 'Dory – suppose it *isn't* The Association. Suppose it *isn't* the Redeemed.'

She looked at me quizzically. 'What do you mean? You saw 'em. You remember how Dan looked: Who else could it be?'

I thought furiously. 'Dory – who's the Speaker of the House?'

'Huh? I dunno. Why? I guess I can look it up in the almanac.' She got up, rooted around, found it, struggled with the contents, then found the right page. 'Well I'll be damned,' she said. 'Phillip J. Kelleam.'

'Arnold's a dead man,' I told her. 'If not today, then as soon as possible.'

'I don't get you.'

'Dory – if the President *and* Vice-President are killed before a successor be named, the Speaker of the House becomes President.'

'Oh, Jesus!' she breathed. 'It's Harry Parch!'

I nodded.

'We gotta do something. Warn the Secret Service or something!'

I shook my head sadly. 'We can't. He's probably got our phone tapped and us monitored very closely right now. Besides – who'd believe us? And why would they?' I got up, went over to the small bar, and poured myself a stiff one.

Dory came over and looked at it. 'Pour me one, too. A good stiff one. I think we both need it.'

In the background, a remote announcer was saying, 'The Vice-President is emerging now, absolutely covered by Secret Service agents. He's in the car – they're roaring off. They want to take no chances tonight.'

But, as night passed and the dawn rose over the desert, my prediction was already true. More of the so-called 'Redeemed' had planted a huge series of bombs on a key overpass any limo would have to take to get to the airport. It exploded as Arnold's limo went over it, then dozens of the Redeemed, all smiling, closed in and machine-gunned everything that moved. Some of the cops who survived finally got them – it was a suicidal attack with none of them even trying to find cover – but they had done their job.

And so had Harry Parch.

In a way, it was a master stroke. Kill the two top men. Put your own man in power, probably backed up by a huge contingent of people either on the inside at IMC or those who had been invited out to scenic Nevada for a demonstration ... Kidnap some of the Redeemed and reprogram them. Make sure it was on national television, the nightmare of young, hollow faces in robes and hoods smiling as they shot those people down in cold blood. Knocking off both the top spots absolutely demonstrates the conspiracy in the public mind, allowing Kelleam to take control and move decisively, as a result of massive public outrage and pressure, to close down the Redeemed. Was it any coincidence that the bomb-planters had waited to be cut down at that bridge when they could have easily slipped away?

So all we could do was sit there and get very drunk so we wouldn't have to decide whether or not Phil Kelleam and Harry Parch were really any improvement over The Association.

We awoke hung over when the phone rang the next afternoon. I reached blearily over Dory and answered it. It was Joe, of course, telling me that the club would be closed for a few days, through the funerals, anyway. I just told him I expected it, hung up, and rolled back on the bed again.

I felt really lousy, but Dory was even worse, so I struggled up, finally, sticking some coffee on, then flipped on the TV. The usual stuff, mostly, what you would expect under these conditions.

Kelleam had wasted no time while we slept, declaring four days of public mourning, scheduling the unprecedented double funerals, and, almost before he was sworn in, authorizing the FBI and Secret Service to move in on the Redeemed all over the country with National Guard and regular military supporting them. He had almost unlimited power for the moment to deal with the obvious menace, and he was making good use of it – to the applause of Congress and the people. He moved so efficiently that you'd almost swear he'd been expecting something like this and had the plans already drawn up.

Most everything was closed, even in Vegas, except the casinos, of course.

Dory struggled into the kitchen, groaning, and looked like I felt. She reached into a drawer, took out a plastic bag, and rolled a joint. It didn't make the hangovers go away, but we didn't care so much about them anymore.

The TV showed the military moving on Association buildings, temples, and holdings with exceptional speed and thoroughness. Tens of thousands were being rounded up, and large camps were being established in different parts of the country to hold them all. A quick session of Congress had authorized exceptional emergency measures, thereby reinforcing what Kelleam was already doing by executive order. Many other countries were moving, too, either frightened by the Redeemed or using the events in the U.S. as an excuse to move. All over the world the cult, which had enjoyed such fantastic success, was being rapidly and systematically crushed. Rumors were already circulating that really strange things were being discovered in examinations of church papers and property; implications were being made that this was far more than the simple religion it appeared.

About five that afternoon we'd both come down sufficiently to eat something and function in a more or less normal manner, but we both felt down, depressed, and helpless. It seemed obvious to us that the country was being softened up in order to be faced with the threat of alien invasion, an invasion by mind control which needed defense.

It would take a while, of course, to build the pressure up and do it right, but it wouldn't be a very long time. They would want to capitalize on the emotional shocks and the resultant national mood. They would introduce the devices all over the country, the processors that would make you safe from the aliens. They were probably quite rapid and efficient now, and maybe even portable. People would beat down the doors of government demanding protection, and they would get it. Yes, they'd get it – and what else? A few ideas, a few attitudes, perhaps, that they didn't have before? Neither of us could fully shake the feeling that it wasn't the beginning of the end.

'Don't worry,' Dory said, trying to put as cheery a front on things as she could, 'you're proof positive they'll have exotic dancing and sexy women in their brave new world.'

But I still wasn't sure if I wanted to live in a world run by men who would cruelly cut down their own leaders and program the rest. Still, *our* life would continue, somehow, and there was nothing we could do about it, anyway.

'Let's take a little trip,' I suggested. 'Just the two of us.'

'Where?'

'Away. Someplace without a lot of people and newscasts. It's the middle of the summer.' I glanced at the calendar. 'In two days it'll be six years since we first met on the ferry.'

'Think you can get away?'

'Sure,' I told her. 'I don't have anything big scheduled, nothing I can't cancel. And it's a hundred and eight out there, for Christ's sake! Things aren't going to be normal for some time.'

'Where are you thinkin' of?'

I went over some possibilities in my head. 'Why don't we just get in the car and drive? I'd like to go to the ocean, I think. Maybe the Sonoma Coast of California. Nice and deserted, and I haven't been there in a long, long time.'

'Well, it beats sitting around here gettin' stoned,' she agreed, and it was settled.

I had some trouble getting hold of Joe, but no real trouble in getting three weeks. With the club closed for the next four days, he had plenty of time to line up some good alternates and put in a little last-minute plugging.

I still had my little Fiat sports car in shocking metallic pink, a car I'd been attracted to in the first place because it was one of only two or three convertibles you could still buy. We packed and got a road atlas and got started the next day.

It felt funny driving north, since we drove along the boundaries of Nellis Air Force Base and Test Range, beyond which, buried under thousands of feet, was IMC. When we passed the small, nondescript road leading off into the dry hills to the east leading to it I felt a slight shudder, but nothing more.

We stopped for the night in Stateline, mostly for old time's sake, although I didn't go up to the lodge. I was afraid that if I ran into Al up there I'd ring his pudgy neck.

The next day we hit San Francisco, officially in mourning but still functioning, and I showed Dory some of the sights. We had a good seafood dinner near Fisherman's Wharf and rode a cable car hanging to the outside like only tourists do, but it was still too filled with people and news and reminders of the world situation, not the least of which was a San Francisco in which not a single member of a cult was on the street corner trying to peddle you something. In *that* town their *absence* was bizarre.

The next day we took California 1 up the coast. It's never been a good road, being two-lane, winding and twisty, but it is, I'm convinced, the most scenic road in America, perhaps anywhere. Built originally by the Spanish starting back in the 1600s, it follows the winding coastline at the edge of the Pacific providing unlimited scenery as well as a real test of driving skills. It had changed since my youth, becoming more developed with fancy houses on many of the scenic bluffs, but it was still really pretty most of the way.

It was warm but not hot, a really refreshing change from what we'd been used to, and the salt-smell, sea birds, and sound of crashing breakers on the cliff walls far below the road acted as something of a tonic.

Out here, it seemed, bad things couldn't happen. Out here was only the sun and sea and the creatures of nature, true peace and quiet. Traffic, too, was abnormally low because of the mourning period, and the only reminder of the larger world were the flags we occasionally passed, all at half-staff.

We stopped often at the frequent turnouts – it's a little better driving south than north, as you're on the ocean side of the road – and once we climbed down to the rocky beach below, played a little, and played tag with the waves at the water's edge. For a moment, at least, it was good to be alive.

Finally, late in the day, we reached the coastal town of Fort Bragg, a resort and logging town despite its military name dating from Civil War days, and took a motel room for the night, agreeing that we would neither buy a newspaper or watch TV, and we didn't. We had ourselves, and we occupied ourselves with each other, and we had a good time. Finally, we fell to sleep.

The ringing phone awakened me, and, for a moment, I thought I was back home and started to reach over Dory for it, only to suddenly realize where I was, groan, get up and walk over to the phone on the dresser. I didn't know what time it was, but it was still dark.

Cursing whoever it was for getting a wrong number, I picked it up, ready to give the caller a piece of my mind. 'Yeah?' I snapped.

'Misty?' responded a low, pleasant man's voice. 'This is Dan Pauley.'

I dropped the phone.

CHAPTER FOURTEEN

'What is it?' Dory called sleepily.

'There's a man on the other end who says he's Dan Pauley!' I told her, picking up the phone and getting a little mad. 'Listen, you,' I told him, 'I don't know what the game is but we quit, remember? Harry Parch said to leave us alone!'

'I'm not from Parch,' the voice replied. 'I really *am* Dan, Misty. I'm not dead – and neither is Stuart Eisenstadt. Look, I'll explain everything but not on the phone. You're still being shadowed, particularly now, and I don't know how much I can do like this. Look, the Surf Motel, about a half-mile up the road from you, has an all-night pancake house. Meet me there in half an hour and I'll explain everything.'

I started to say something, but the line was dead. He'd hung up on me.

I detailed the conversation to Dory, and she was even more dubious about this mystery man than I was. 'You have to learn not to answer phones in hotel rooms where nobody's supposed to know you,' she grumped. 'Still, I guess we better get dressed.'

I picked up my watch. 'It's four in the morning!'

'Yeah,' she responded sourly, 'but we gotta go anyway. If it's some kind of Parch trick we're better off in a place like that than here. And if it's not, well, we'll always wonder.'

I nodded, knowing she was right. 'You're the boss,' I told her, then turned on the lights, pulled on some jeans, a sweater, and sandals, gave my hair a quick brush, and was ready.

Dory looked at me critically. 'You let it all hang out like that and you'll drive the truck drivers wild.'

'I don't plan to be too long,' I shot back.

'Yeah, well, just don't jog anyplace, huh?'

We left, got in the car, and drove up Route 1. It was dark and deserted, with almost nobody on the road. It was fairly easy to spot the place, though, on the right hand side, and we pulled into the parking lot and looked around. After a minute or so, I turned to Dory and said, 'Well, we haven't been arrested or anything yet. Might as well go in and get some coffee.'

She nodded, and we walked nervously into the place, picking a booth and looking around. It was nearly deserted, only a few people sitting at various tables.

A young man entered looking like something out of a bad old movie. Long, black hair, frizzy beard, leather jacket, motorcycle helmet under one arm, studded black boots and even, so help me, a tattoo on the back of his right hand. A cigarette dangled from his lips, and he looked around the place, his eyes finally settling on me.

'Oh, boy,' Dory breathed disgustedly. 'For this we get up in the middle of the night, right?'

He finally sauntered on over to us, as I knew he would, and looked down, almost dripping invisible slime. 'Hi, mind if I join you ladies?'

Frost was too mild for my tone. 'Buzz off, buddy. We're waiting for somebody.'

'You're waiting for me,' he mumbled, then straightened a little, his tone becoming clearer, more normal. 'I'm Dan Pauley.'

'*That'll* take some doing,' Dory snapped nastily.

'Yeah, I know what you must be thinking, but it's not. Look – mind if I sit down? There's a cop coming in and he may give me a pain.'

Seeing that Dory wasn't going to give ground, I shifted over a bit and he sat. 'It's good to see you both again. I – owe you a lot of explanation.'

'Yeah, at least,' Dory responded. 'How do we know you're who you say you are, anyway? Or, if you *are* Dan, if you haven't been turned around by Parch and his buddies?'

He sighed. 'You can't. You'll have to trust me. What motive could I have, anyway? You got off pretty free by facing up to them and adjusting. You've done pretty well, I know, both of you. You've got no real kick coming.' He turned to me. 'Look at you. The Queen of Las Vegas.' He turned back to Dory. 'And you, the Indian paramour and real estate genius. But, you're right. I *do* owe you an explanation.'

'At least,' I agreed, adjusting to the fact that his tone and manner did sort of remind me of Pauley, what I'd seen of him, anyway.

'Why weren't you at the Farmer's Market?' Dory asked.

He nodded. 'O.K. From the top. After you left the restaurant, the Doctor and I wandered down to the Strip. I decided he should go to the bus station first, while I could cover – they didn't know me at all, remember, in that body and that disguise. He bought his ticket O.K., but in the line to get on the bus two of Parch's men just slid up on either side of him and walked him off. I couldn't do a damned thing without jeopardizing myself, and maybe you. I made a good fifteen agents in that station, including some working the counter. All I'd get would be another dart or maybe a shot in the head. It was damned frustrating, but there wasn't anything I could do. The only thing I could think of was to wait for you and see what happened then. About half an hour later Dory came in, bought her ticket, and made it onto the bus. I was pretty sure they'd made you, but they let you go. I had to ask myself why.'

She nodded grimly. 'They made me, all right. All the way.'

'Well, I waited as long as I could for Misty, but you never showed, and I couldn't live in that station without somebody getting suspicious, so I got my ticket and rode out. Nobody made me, since they weren't sure who they were looking for. I had to figure Misty'd been picked up, too, and that Dory and I were going to be on our own. I headed straight for the Farmer's Market when I got in, then staked out the area. Imagine my surprise when Misty walked up to a counter in the inner courtyard.'

I nodded. 'I remember.'

'Well, I waited, and finally Dory came, too, but I spotted her tails. I suddenly realized why they'd let you slip through, Dory. You were bait. Bait for me. You were the only way they could get to me, since I could be anybody, even if Stuart blabbed. Of course they couldn't afford to let *him* run loose, but you, well, you weren't really important to them. I tailed you all day, kept watch on Parch's tails, and when I saw just how well covered you were I knew that I would have no chance if I contacted you. He even had somebody on the hotel switchboard ten minutes after you checked in.'

I nodded, and even Dory seemed to be warming a bit to him. The waitress brought our coffee and we sipped at it while Dan continued his story.

'Well, I'm sorry for how it sounds, but I was just forced to write off getting to you. I hocked those diamonds you gave me, Misty, and that gave me a little money to work with. I was still in trouble – I had no idea how to contact my people and almost no money, so I did what I had to do. I cased a small sub-urban bank, picked a victim, studied her for a couple of days, then intercepted her on her way to work, switched with her, tied her up, and, using her master keys, managed to steal several thousand dollars. I left, switched her back, and left her there. Poor woman. Either she's in a mental ward, or maybe in jail, but it was the only way.'

'You could've gotten a *job*,' Dory snapped.

He sighed. 'Look, we've been down that moral road before. Maybe Parch got wind of it and cleared her. I hope so. Anyway, I knew about the planted news item where we were apparently killed, and I figured you'd take it at face value. Parch obviously wanted to see if you had a contingency place to run to that would lead him to me or other Urulu, and he got fooled. I think at least half the reason he let you go back to your life was that he still hoped that, sometime, I'd contact you. It cost him very little.'

I was starting to get paranoid again. 'Are we still being tailed?'

He nodded. 'Oh, I don't think he's paid much attention to you for the last year or so, but when you took off on a trip at this critical time he had a man on you. *A man.*' He grinned. 'I'm him.'

I gasped. 'And what is he – now?'

He smiled. 'A member of the Redeemed. I got the drop on him, switched, tied him up, then called the cops. He's been hauled to the local slammer by now.'

'Where'd you find one of the Redeemed?' I asked. 'I thought they were *all* locked up by now.'

'Mostly,' he admtted. 'But I never changed bodies. There wasn't any need to, so I didn't. It was the same one I'd nabbed back in Vegas. You know, the eyebrows grew in but the hair never did. They must have used a chemical or something. That's gonna make it even easier for Parch to round 'em up.' He paused a moment. 'You know, they didn't come up with a bad plan. This'll set The Association back years here. They'll have to devise a whole new strategy, start over – unless they take the military option. IMC's gambling they won't, and I kind of agree. A major force moving this way would alert the Urulu, and it really isn't worth that kind of a fight. It can be won other ways.

If it weren't for the fact that the same scheme to discredit the Church also was cleverly disguised to put their people totally in power and soften up the population for IMC's debut in their hands, I wouldn't even be here now.'

We let that go for a moment. 'Where did you go after you robbed the bank?' I asked.

'Well, we had a safe house and station in the desert near Death Valley. An old abandoned government installation. Missiles or something, but over-grown with weeds and overrun with sidewinders after the years. I figured that was my best bet, so I took the tourist bus out to Furnace Creek, then hitched down to where I had to be. I walked over that hot desert for several hours and finally reached the place. It was gone. Destroyed totally.'

'Parch?' I asked.

He shook his head no. 'Not self-destruct, either. The place was melted, fused together. A high energy weapon from the air beyond what you have and very different from what we would use. The Association had hit it quick and hard.'

'So you were still stuck,' Dory noted.

He nodded. 'Stuck was right. I almost died in that damned desert just get-ting back to the road. I thought a car would *never* come along. I was sick for two days. But I recovered, and eventually worked my way around to two other isolated safe houses, one in Utah and one in northeastern California. Fused too, into nothing. Oh, I could have gone on around the continent and maybe overseas, but I got the message. They'd made us, somehow, and attacked all locations simultaneously and so thoroughly that there was little use. That left me only one way out, and I didn't want to take it.'

'Which was?' I prompted.

'There's an emergency ship out there, in orbit,' he told us. 'It's pretty well disguised and its screens would keep anybody from The Association to NORAD from getting curious. The type of attack they launched, the signs that it'd been at least a year earlier, maybe more, and the fact that there had been no Urulu reprisals told me that nobody, probably, got away. Maybe there's a few loose like me, but, if so, they're laying so low they wouldn't make a move. Besides, even if they took the emergency craft they'd arrange for another. No use stranding some of your own people for nothing.'

'Won't your own people start wondering and check up on you?' I asked him.

He shook his head. 'Not unless they get a real distress signal. This is off the beaten path, considered not worth bothering about. The only way they'll come is if somebody gave them a call and asked them in, like from the emer-gency ship.'

'Dan – why haven't you just gone to that ship?' Dory wanted to know. 'Why wait so long? And why come back and see us – now?'

He sighed. 'Look, if I'd taken that ship out and filed my report on what I knew, they might just write Earth off, or, instead, they might come over and wipe out every man, woman, and child on the planet in the same way as a doctor would kill disease germs. I've been here too long. I like the people, and I see the potential here for it to go either way. Look – long ago, I was in a similar situation far away from here. Different world, different kinds of people, night and day, but it was still comparable. I took the easy way then, and that world got destroyed. I simply can not bear the responsibility of that twice, at least not without trying to do something about it. But once I report, I have about as much influence in the final decision as an army sergeant in the field has with his commanding general. You see my problem?'

We nodded, and, still, Dory pressed the questions that were on both our minds. 'So why now? And why *us?*'

He hesitated a moment, then replied, 'O.K., I'll put it right on the line. IMC's moves have pitted them directly against The Association. They've written us off and joined battle directly. I think the nationalism, petty jealousies, prejudices, and rivalries of this world favor The Association hands down, but, in the long run, it makes little difference to humans who might win. It forces my hand. I know neither of you liked being in the position of having to decide the fate of the planet – the responsibility is too terrible. But *I've* had that choice dumped on me, and I can't avoid it any more. I think Dr Eisenstadt was right in the beginning, but we were a lot more naive then and the timing was wrong. It may still be, but I think we've reached the deadline, and I feel I've got to call that ship and report. I want you two to come with me. I want them to see you, talk to you, examine you. I think you two are the only hope left for saving this planet.'

I shook my head unbelievingly. *'Us?'*

He nodded. 'You know the process. Neither of you are what we call "body-native" so you'll be more acceptable. And, frankly, I think, as Dr Eisenstadt did, that you two, particularly now, have grown so much inside that you best represent the qualities my people will be looking for.'

'I find that hard to believe,' I told him sincerely. 'We're not in the least representative of humanity.'

'Exactly,' he agreed. 'That's why. With so much at stake we have to rig the game a bit, but you'll admit I know my people better than you. I know what I'm asking. Risk again. Putting yourself on the line, maybe your lives. At the mercy of an alien race so different from you that they aren't superficially human, like me. I can't force you. You have to make your own decision.'

I didn't know what to think or how I felt, and I could only look over at Dory. Her face was inscrutable, but her big brown eyes met my gaze for a moment, and I knew, then, what we would do.

'You're going anyway, aren't you?' she asked me. He nodded.

She sighed. 'Then I guess we really have no choice.'

And she was right, of course, although it seemed like nothing had really been our choice for the past six years. It just didn't seem *fair*, somehow, to risk all that we now had, to ask us to do it, because of some duty, some responsibility, to the future of the human race. The human race had never felt much duty or responsibility for us. They had felt no responsibility for poor Victor's plight, certainly, when and if they recognized it at all – it just wasn't any of their business. They were forcing Dorian Tomlinson into extreme personal agony, to live a life in some sort of gray ghetto cut off from family and friends or, perhaps, commit suicide somewhere in what would have been a terrible waste of a wonderful individual. Even Misty Carpenter was really a cypher, a cartoon in the public's mind, an object of lust because of what was really a physical deformity of the sexual parts of her body. Would those lusting people still be around when I grew old and saggy? Did one of them even think of the physical pain, the back strain and other side effects, I lived with because of that?

Stuart's old, original face seemed to come to my mind. *He* cared. And Pauley, too, telling Harry Parch that most people's lives were so empty, so devoid of meaning, that they might as well have never lived at all. Make your life matter, Stuart had said. I thought of history, of the faces and personalities that marched forever in our minds for good or ill. History was the account of people who *mattered*.

Dory was right. We *had* to go.

'What next?' I asked him. 'I mean, that agent will be missed no matter what.'

He nodded. 'But we have a long journey to complete. There's only one place for me to call the ship. We have to return to Alaska.'

Full circle, I thought. *For better or worse, it will end where it began.*

CHAPTER FIFTEEN

There seemed to be very little point in subterfuge. If Parch really wanted us, he could have us, although it seemed we'd have to either keep some distance from Pauley as long as possible while headed in the same direction. We agreed that the best way to handle it was to go back and go to bed – as if I were capable of anything else at that point – and proceed normally up the coast. Since we weren't supposed to know about our tail, we just had to act as if we didn't have one. Had the tail vanished and we with him there might be a big outcry – but if we continued openly and normally up the coast and made no effort to hide, they could never be sure that their man's disappearance was directly connected to us or not.

Pauley checked our car, found a small electronic tracer, and decided to leave it there. The more open we were, the better. We agreed on an itinerary for each night up the coast, and Pauley warned us that he would certainly have to switch bodies again but would pace us all the way.

Dory was a bit upset at this. 'You're gonna do to somebody else what you did to *us*,' she protested.

He nodded. 'Or worse. But it *has* to be done, Dory.'

'You mean – *kill?*'

'If I have to,' he replied. 'I want no trails. There's too much at stake. Dory, all I can promise is that I'll try my best to cause as little harm and pain as I can.'

She was irreconcilable, but he left us shortly after that and there was nothing either of us could do or say.

The next day we continued on up the coast, not going too far because of our lack of sleep, then continued on U.S. 101 now, still along the coast for a while. We continued to hit the sights although our mood was far different from the previous few days at the start. Finally, though, we relaxed and had a really good time, perhaps being even more carefree and uninhibited than normal as it went on. Deep down, neither of us knew if we'd ever be able to do this again.

We finally cut over in Washington State and reached Seattle, a pretty city that had changed little in six years. We were back in civilization again, for a little bit, anyway, but things were already starting to return to normal with the funerals now over. Only the still half-staffed flags reminded us of the momentous change that had taken place.

A ferry was due to leave for Alaska in two days, but, in July, a stateroom was just out of the question and taking the car even less possible. The fact was, the tourists and their agents had the best all sewn up every year, and, unless you were very lucky the only thing you could get was a general ticket, which entitled you to go on board but little else. Although we were told that a cabin could be squeezed in between Ketchikan and Juneau we decided, what the hell, we'd rough it. I arranged with a long-term parking agency to keep the car and we went on a shopping spree far different than the one we'd gone on in Seattle so very long ago, haunting the best camping supply dealers for sleeping bags, air mattresses, and a small portapump of light plastic. We were delighted to find one that slept two, and took it. With Dory's slight build and my disproportionate one we decided against backpacking, but the whole thing was put in a large, thin casing with handles that, although it weighed a ton, was manageable. We also bought some heavier-duty clothing for the trip and seemed set, finally heading down to the huge blue ship at the dock in the late afternoon.

Because we were getting on in Seattle we had among the first choices of location, and chose an inside place in the forward lounge, just putting our suitcases and bedroll there so that others wouldn't usurp it. Flying was never considered as an option in our talks with Dan; he still wouldn't fly unless his life depended on it, and maybe not even then, and that gave us the excuse to be nostalgic.

We'd been bothered with men most of the trip, and I was used to cooling them down anyway, but I think we were so openly and blatantly affectionate on shipboard that it scared a lot of them off. Oh, the occasional 'You never had a *real* man' slob, sure, but nothing we couldn't handle. Still, it always irritated me that men had more relative freedom than women. I doubt if either Dory or I had gone anywhere without a little can of mace and a portable scream alarm in our purses, and you were never sure whether the next guy you met was a nice fellow, a jerk, or a would-be rapist. It was infuriating to be walking to my car back at the club and then have to drive home even if it was a nice night, but I always was conscious of how damned lucky I'd been, and I'd known a few women who hadn't.

That, I guess, was why it was nice to be alone with Dory on a trip like this. The undercurrent of fear was still there, but it didn't seem intrusive when you were with someone.

There had been no sign of Dan Pauley during the whole trip, but we suspected he was never far away. We also suspected that Parch's men – two, probably now, at least – were also somewhere about. We didn't let it worry us.

The ferry was a different one than the one on which we'd met, larger, fancier, but it was similar enough in design to make us a little nostalgic and bring back the old memories. The topside solarium, the gift shop, cafeteria, you name it – and the young campers, backpackers, and hordes of tourists.

It took three and a half days to reach Haines Junction, end of the line in this case, and I couldn't suppress a look to the east, where, out of sight beyond high mountains, Skagway and the Chillicoot Pass lay.

It was another day's bumpy bus ride from Haines to Fairbanks, but it was new territory now for the both of us and we enjoyed it while we could. Still, there was tension underlying the journey now, building with each passing kilometer marker on the highway, as we knew that we were approaching the moment of truth.

It occurred to me that Parch might well know, or at least suspect, where we were heading, and that worried me. He could be there, waiting, as he had been when the shuttle had landed six years before to disgorge another occupant for an Indian girl's body.

We stayed the night in Fairbanks, still very much on schedule, and in the morning rented a car and drove south along Route 3 past Mt. McKinley National Park – the mountain was socked in and we could see nothing – to Cantwell, then turned east on Route 8, a good dirt road with occasional paved spots, for several miles.

Traffic had been heavy on 3 but aside from an occasional pickup truck we neither passed nor were passed by much on the dirt road.

We proceeded until we hit Milepost 12, then stopped, turned around, and proceeded back a mile. If all was well, Pauley should be waiting with a signal by the side of the road, a sign reading, 'Need a lift to McKinley,' which would be fairly natural except that this wasn't exactly the world's best-travelled road, and a code-phrase to double-check.

At almost the 11 Milepost we saw somebody. He was a tall, thin, black man in his forties dressed casually, and he was holding a sign.

'Need a lift to McKinley.'

'I'll be damned,' I muttered, and came to a stop. He ran up to the car, looked in at us, nodded, and said, 'Screw Harry Parch.'

'Get in,' I told him, and Dory popped up the back door lock for him. He got in and said, 'Just go a few hundred yards further up – there's a tree with a white mark on it. Stop there.'

I saw it as he said it and pulled over once more. He got out, removed some very substantial-looking brush, revealing a rough and overgrown dirt track. I drove up it, and he quickly replaced the brush, which seemed wired together, and rejoined us. 'Just follow the track to the end and park under some trees,' he ordered.

I did as instructed. The road curved and twisted and hadn't been used in what looked like years, and it took all my reflexes to keep us on track. Finally, though, it ended at a small stream under a clump of small trees. This was not really tree country, but it offered some concealment.

He got out again and beckoned for us to follow, which we did. There was a small trail, hardly noticeable now, once you crossed the stream, leading a half a mile or so farther along to an open meadow strewn with large and small rocks. He studied the area for a moment, then went over to a particularly large rock and strained to lift it.

'He'll never lift *that* boulder,' I said, and, as I said it, the whole thing seemed to flip up. We went over to it curiously and saw that the rock was something artificial. Revealed now was a faceplate with several sets of ringlike markings on it. His fingers tapped on the rings in what looked like random order but had to be some prearranged code, and suddenly one of the rings glowed a dull red. He nodded again to himself, looked satisfied, and closed the 'rock,' then exhaled deeply.

'Well, that's that. You don't know how I had nightmares that I'd find this place booby-trapped or melted or the power gone.'

I looked up at the sky. 'How long before it gets here?'

He thought a moment. 'An hour, maybe more. It'll have to sneak itself out of wherever it's hiding and figure the best emergency approach in and out. We don't want to attract missiles or any other attention until it's too late.'

'You don't *know* where it is?' Dory asked.

He shook his head. 'Nope. It's a pretty smart little mechanical bugger. It thinks for itself pretty much. I just hope it comes before we have company.'

I looked around nervously. 'You think we will?'

'Oh, sure – sooner or later. Later, I hope. The only tail you had as far as I could see was the one pickup truck and you passed it. I expect they're discovering you're gone right about now, but until our baby lands they won't find us unless they spot the car from a helicopter. It's a risk we had to take.'

I shivered. This was going to be a *nervous* hour.

'Who did you kill for that hunk?' Dory wanted to know.

He shrugged. 'No appeasing you, is there? If you *must* know he was a pimp and a drug pusher in Eureka I happened on. Believe me – he's no loss to this world. I picked him for that, and also because he was a black male, which gives us physically three major races and both sexes.'

'Is that important?' I asked him.

He nodded. 'Trust me. I'm trying to load the dice as much as possible, like I told you.'

We sat and waited because there was nothing else to do. The temperature was comfortably in the seventies, and the only sound and annoyance around seemed to be the buzzing of some particularly large mosquitoes. Swatting at one brought another thought to mind.

'Dan – your people. The Urulu. What are they like? Physically, I mean.'

He thought a moment. Finally he said, 'Do you have any prejudices against jellyfish?'

I shivered slightly. The fact was, I *did* have a little against them. Every summer in Chesapeake Bay the stinging sea nettles would make water fun impossible without a protective net. 'You're a jellyfish?'

He chuckled. 'No, not really. Nothing like one, actually. But the Urulu might remind you, superficially, of jellyfish.'

'Whew! That's a relief,' Dory responded sincerely. 'I had visions of scaly horrors with big eyes and nasty teeth.'

We both just looked at her strangely.

'I always liked monster movies,' she said defensively.

'Dan – shouldn't you brief us?' I asked him. 'I mean, we're going into this pretty cold turkey.'

'It's got to be that way, Misty. If you're coached they'll know it and we'll blow it. Don't worry – I'll be there to lend support. Just be yourselves. I don't think either of you really realizes what really superior human beings you are.'

There was no reply to that. Neither of us believed it for a minute but it was pure balm for the ego.

The time did not pass quickly, partly because we expected to hear a helicopter screaming overhead or the bark of guns from the brush at any moment. It was incredible we'd gotten this far.

Finally, however, the thing came. It came in a crazy, impossible fashion, coming in incredibly fast just above ground, keeping distance from whatever terrain, and then stopping on a dime as if for all the world the laws of inertia had been repealed. There was a *crack* sound, once.

It wasn't large – in fact, it wasn't much bigger than a small truck – and it wasn't saucer-shaped. It looked, rather, like a stylized, very thick pair of wings, or perhaps a boomerang, with rounded corners. It hovered there, a couple of inches above the ground making no sound at all. Pauley approached it, and although that computer or whatever had never seen him before in that body it seemed to recognize something. One of the 'wings' rotated with a slight humming sound, revealing an opening about four feet square.

'Let's go,' he shouted. 'In the hatch as quickly as possible and move down!'

I hesitated a moment, but then heard the sound of helicopter blades not too far off and the sound of engines in back of us. Both Dory and I ran for the opening which Dan had already entered. He reached down, pulled her in, then strained to help me. There was a strong vibration all around us, and I lost my balance as the hatch rotated closed, falling on the smooth, seamless floor.

And then, quite suddenly, Dory gave a yelp and fell, too, and before I could do or say anything a giant fist seemed to slam us back down hard. I could already feel the bruises.

We seemed held there, unable to move, breathing with difficulty, for a fairly long time, and then, just as suddenly as it appeared, the pressure lifted. I picked myself up, groaning a little, and rubbed my rear end. 'Ow! I wonder if I'll be able to sit down tomorrow,' I said.

'Don't expect any sympathy from me,' Dory responded weakly. 'You got a *lot* more padding than I do, and you were already down!'

I got to my feet and helped her up as well. The whole ship vibrated slightly, but otherwise there was no noise, no sensation of anything at all. We seemed solidly anchored to the deck, too.

'Damn! At least I thought we'd get to find out what it's like to do it in no gravity!' I pouted.

The ceiling was just a couple of inches above my head – my hair rubbed against it when I stood up, and the chamber we were in was quite small, no larger than, say, the back of a pickup truck. There seemed no doors or windows, and I looked around. 'Now what? Where's Dan?'

She shook her head. 'He headed forward as soon as he dragged you in.' She looked at the solid wall. 'How, though, I don't know.'

The wall shimmered, and Pauley stepped through, having to crouch down to get in. 'Sorry for the fast lift,' he told us, 'but I had to give the go-sign. They were already shooting at us. Come on forward and we'll relax a little.' He turned and more or less duck-walked through the wall.

I shrugged. 'If he can do it I guess *we* can, too.' I went up to the wall, hesitantly, and pushed against it. I felt a tingling, and the place I touched seemed to shimmer and become intangible. I stepped through, getting the overall sensation of walking through a vibrating shower. It felt pretty good, really.

The other side was not much larger than the entry chamber, but had a soft, furlike padding all over it that you kind of sunk into a little. It was all over, a nice baby blue, on the walls, floor, ceiling. All over. There was nothing else in the room. Pauley was sitting against the wall, watching me with faint amusement.

Dory entered and looked around the chamber with the same surprise I did. 'I expected a big, fancy control room or cockpit,' she noted. 'But, then, I guess a padded cell *does* fit better.'

Pauley laughed. 'Take a seat. Anywhere you're comfortable. This thing wasn't built for anything except fast landings and fast getaways, I'm afraid. We're in the half set up for humans – the other side is for Urulu.'

'Where do you pilot the ship from?' I wanted to know.

'We don't. It does it itself. I just tell it what I want and it does the rest.'

'Where are we?'

He shrugged. 'I have no idea. It took the fast way out – sorry for bumping you around, but I didn't know if that helicopter had some nasty weapons, or if they were training missiles on us at that very moment.'

I shivered. 'You're forgiven. But – you mean this is it? No great pictures of Earth from space? No fancy stuff? We just sit here for who knows how long in this blue room?' I seemed to remember it'd taken three days just to get to the moon.

'I'm afraid this *is* it,' he answered. 'I mean, we have ships with those kind of things but this isn't designed for it. Sorry – not very exotic, I know. But we've already left the Earth's magnetic field, and, in a few minutes, the ship'll have all the data it needs for a jump – allowance for gravitational forces, solar wind, stuff like that.'

'Jump?' Dory said uneasily.

He nodded. 'Don't worry. It's a little too complicated to explain, and since I don't understand it myself there's no use in me explaining it. When the ship's ready, it'll give us a warning, then you just lie down flat on the rug, here, and relax.'

'Faster than light drive,' I noted. 'So Einstein was wrong.'

'As far as I know nothing can exceed the speed of light except for some little subatomic particles that do nobody any good,' he replied. 'No, the way it was explained to me once was that the ship kind of punches a hole in space/ time, goes through it, closes the hole behind it, travels along until it gets to where it wants to go, punches another hole, re-emerges, and that's it.'

I frowned, 'Dan – where does it punch a hole *to?*'

He shrugged. 'Damned if I know. All I know is that it isn't in *our* universe, that's for sure. I'm not even sure anybody knows – it just *is*, that's all, and you can use it. The ship flies at about two-thirds of light speed there, then emerges.'

'Two-thirds of light speed,' I echoed. 'That's damned fast – but unless we're staying in the solar system we're going to be *years* getting to where we're going!'

He nodded. 'Probably fifty or sixty at least. But, don't worry, you won't feel a thing. We'll be in a nice, safe, state of suspension. Physically we won't age a bit.'

'But we'll get back a hundred years too late to help Earth!' Dory protested.

'Nope. That's the crazy thing about this no-space business. We'll re-enter this universe about two or three minutes after we left it. I admit it wouldn't have been practical without the state of suspension, but it's convenient, and seemingly fast. Just wait and relax. You'll see. The effect is almost as if it's instantaneous.'

Dory shook her head and looked at me for help but I couldn't say a thing. It made no more sense to me than to her.

There was a sharp, irritating buzzing sound. Dan looked up, although there was nothing to look at. 'O.K. – here we go. Just lie down flat, face up and comfortable, on the floor here, and relax.' He did it himself, and we did like-wise. I didn't know how Dory felt, but I felt queasy as all hell, and I found her hand, took it, and squeezed it. She squeezed back.

There were two short buzzes, a slight pause, and then the world went green. No, I don't mean the rug changed color – everything was a sparkling, translucent green, including the air inside, and it all seemed to shimmer slightly. A tingling went through every part of my body much like the feeling I'd had passing through the wall or whatever it was – very pleasurable, like an all-over vibrator.

And then, suddenly, the green clicked off, and all returned to normal again. There was a long buzzing sound.

Pauley stirred, sighed, and got up to a sitting position, stretching. 'Well,' he said, sounding a little hoarse, 'that's it. We're here.'

I turned slightly. My mouth felt really dry and my eyes hurt a little like they had mild eyestrain, but otherwise I felt just fine.

'That *it?*' I managed, sounding a little hoarse myself. 'That was barely a couple of minutes – not fifty years.'

He smiled. 'It was really a long, long time. It just doesn't seem that way. We need some fluids, though, and fast. The process is very dehydrating to human type bodies.' He reached over against the wall and a small hinged panel revealed itself. Reaching down, he brought up a large cube with a strap attached to the top, put it in front of him, and touched a small area on the side. The top slid back, and he took out three tall canisters, about a liter each, and three small wrapped blocks. Dory and I each took a canister and followed Dan's example, turning the top until a slot appeared.

'Go ahead – drink it,' he urged, and took a swig of his.

I put it hesitantly to my lips, then drank, overcome with sudden thirst. I drank quite a bit, then put it down for a moment. 'It tastes like orange juice!'

He nodded. 'That's because it's basically orange juice, with additives that'll help get your body quickly back in balance. The stuff's matched for each race likely to use this thing. The cakes look and taste like gingerbread, by the way, but will give you a lot more than plain old gingerbread ever did. My predecessor, who set up this ship for Earth, liked the tastes.'

I tried the cake, and it *was* good. My stomach felt as if it had a lump in it, but the juice and cake seemed to go down quickly and dissolve the lump in a matter of minutes. The thought of fifty-year-old, half-digested food had a sort of repulsion about it, but I'm not quite sure I bought Pauley's explanations and time-frame anyway. I wondered if they would give anything real that might clue in some future Earth scientist in the way IMC had been born.

The buzzer gave several short bursts. Pauley nodded to himself, then said, 'We're within range of a perimeter ship now,' he told us, 'and the ship's made contact.'

I was disappointed. 'I was hoping we'd see a Urulu world,' I told him.

He chuckled. 'You couldn't go there anyway. The closest to it would be something like Jupiter in your own solar system. A big gas giant with beautiful multicolored bands of gases and a lot of heat from the pressure caused by the weight of the incredibly dense atmosphere.'

'Your people could live on *Jupiter?*' Dory gasped.

He shook his head. 'Probably not. It's not the right mixture. But most of our worlds are similar *looking*, anyway. My own home has a beautiful multiple ring system, like Saturn.'

'And you live on a dark ball underneath all those gases?' I pressed, trying to understand.

'No, no. There *is* a planetary solid there, very dense, but we don't live *on* it. We live in the middle of the atmosphere itself, kind of like fish in water. It's quite hard to describe, but on many gas giants the protein molecules that form life are found in wide bands of gases heated by radiation from the pressure below and maintained there. We don't ever touch the solid below – the pressure alone, not to mention the heat, would kill us.'

'And yet you somehow found the means to get there, even mine there, or you'd never have ships like this, space travel, or any mechanical things,' I pointed out.

'That's true,' he agreed, 'but it's a long, complex story. Maybe, one day, when your people and mine can sit down as friends, we will be able to study the history and development of your people while you study ours. But now is not the time.'

We both nodded, understanding what he meant. The sense of high adventure, of new worlds and new experiences, faded swiftly as the reason why we were here really came back to us hard.

When your people and mine can sit down as friends ...

That might well depend on what we said and did in the next few hours or days.

There was a thump, and a shudder went through the ship. *'Jgur abrix!'* an eerie, nonhuman voice that I can not describe came to us.

Pauley sighed. 'O.K. We've docked. This ship is giving the physical requirements for us. When the mother ship has a chamber prepared for us that won't kill us, we'll go through. It's pretty fast – we have to be set up to handle a variety of races and requirements, obviously.'

Obviously, I realized. Body switchers who sped between the stars at near-instant speeds would need a lot of technical knowledge and skill about an incredibly varied number of lifeforms.

A clanging sound came from the wall behind us through which we'd entered. Pauley sucked in his breath for a moment, showing his own nervousness, then stood up as well as he could and headed for the wall. 'Stay here,' he told us, 'until I see what's what.' The wall shimmered obligingly and he vanished behind it. I turned to Dory. 'Scared?'

'A little,' she responded nervously. 'You?'

'Frightened to death,' I said honestly. 'But what's done is done. Here we are – wherever it is.'

She squeezed my hand tightly and kissed me lightly.

Pauley was gone for some time, but, finally, he returned and sat down on the blue carpeting, looking a little grim. 'Look,' he began hesitantly, 'I warned you that humans weren't exactly common and that we were very different.'

We nodded.

'Well, they've got a chamber for us, but it's little more than a big bubble inside Urulu atmosphere. I got them to darken the floor so we have some solid grounding, but it's going to be like being in a giant fishbowl. Just take it easy and remember that you're perfectly safe there, and there's a good deal of machinery maintaining proper air, gravity, and pressure, and a damned thick wall between you and the rest of what you see.'

My nerves were getting the better of me. I wanted this over with, and got up.

'I want you both to take your clothes off,' Pauley said, starting to undress himself. 'I'm afraid you're going to have to play by the rules, and that means you bring nothing in you weren't born with.'

'Well, you said it would be a fishbowl,' I sighed, and complied.

'In more ways than one,' Pauley responded. 'You will literally be the object of a lot of curiosity, both professional and just plain gawking.'

We were totally stripped now and I looked at him. 'Hmm ... Well hung, Dan.'

He grinned, turned, then looked back at us. 'You're going to feel a real tingly sensation as you pass out of the hatch,' he warned. 'Decontamination. A dry shower, sort of. Don't worry – it won't hurt you or your unborn children.' With that he stepped through.

I looked at Dory. 'Ready?'

She nodded. 'Let's get this *over* with!'

I stepped through first, then she. I reached the open hatch and paused, bending down and looking out. I let out a gasp and felt Dory just behind me, also peering out.

Pauley's description of his home as something like Jupiter was fairly close. The world swirled around us, a sea of thick gases that were mostly yellows, reds, oranges, and purples. It was as if somebody had put a stick in Jupiter and stirred it up.

I stepped out and helped Dory down. Immediately we felt the 'shower' and it was no different or worse than the other odd feelings we had had. Turning, looking forward, though, we walked out onto what appeared to be a long, flat piece of dull aluminum, circular and about ninety feet across. The air smelled fresh and sweet, the temperature was warm and comfortable, but there was no visible boundary between the 'bubble' and the atmosphere of the rest of the ship.

The floor did not feel cold and metallic to my bare feet, but like soft rubber, with some give to it, and it was at air temperature.

The only features of the bubble were a shiny round protrusion in the center and four seatlike pads around it. Pauley was already at the center and gestured for us to come to him.

The eeriest thing was the silence. It was so quiet we could hear ourselves breathing and the sounds of our bare feet against the odd flooring material. I was glad that Dan had gotten them to color the floor – I felt exposed and off-balance as it was, with nothing save the floor and the protrusion in the middle to get bearings from.

Suddenly there was a loud sound behind us. We stopped and turned as one, watching as the whole rear wall shimmered and a blackish shape receded and disappeared.

'Hey!' Dory called out.

I looked at her. 'The ship's gone. We're trapped in here!'

We held hands and approached Pauley. 'Don't worry,' he said reassuringly. 'You're safe.'

'I'm beginning to wonder how I got talked into this,' I told him with more seriousness than he took it. I looked at the big center protrusion. 'What's that?'

'We'll get food and water from the middle – the hub flips back. The water will be distilled and the food won't be very appetizing, but it'll do.'

'I don't exactly feel very hungry,' I mumbled, looking around. I felt adrift on a platform, lost in some nightmarish sea of colorful clouds. I had the sensation of moving because of that swirl, and it made me slightly dizzy.

'Dan – I hate to say this,' I said hesitantly, 'but I have to pee.'

He laughed and pointed to one of the pads. 'Just reach down and flip it up.' He saw my hesitancy, and reached down and pushed against the top. It swung back noiselessly and revealed a rubbery-looking tube. 'Just sit on it – it'll support you,' he told me. 'Then go.'

Dory looked upset, but I was in no position to argue. It worked fine. Dory, though, seemed irritated.

'Damn it,' she grumbled, 'I think this is a little *too* public! I'm not sure I *like* shitting in a fishbowl!'

'Well, you're going to have to,' Pauley replied. 'At least until this is over.'

'Dan? Where's the toilet paper?' I asked.

'There is none,' he told me. 'See that little indentation there by your right elbow? Just keep seated and push it.'

I did as instructed, and got the damndest erotic sensation I'd *ever* had – but whatever it did, it worked. I was dry and sanitized.

I got up and lowered the lid. 'Now what?' I asked him.

'We wait. I – whoops! Company!'

We turned to see what he was looking at, and got our first view of what I guess was an Urulu.

In some ways it *did* remind you of a jellyfish – a large umbra, but multicolored, below which was suspended a huge brain case of some transparent material, then a chamber I guessed had something to do with digestion, and, oddly, an iris-like opening that changed. From the region where the umbra met the brain-case dangled hundreds of incredibly thin tentacles that seemed to be composed of countless tiny translucent blue beads. The whole creature swam effortlessly in the sea of gases, and was partially obscured by them, but it was *big* – perhaps ten feet across at the umbra, with the brain-case and other organs beneath three or four feet long, and the tentacles reaching down at least fifteen, maybe twenty feet. The umbra undulated constantly and the creature looked incredibly graceful, almost beautiful.

'Here comes the messenger-boy,' Pauley said. 'I'll be talking to him for some time, so excuse me. Just amuse yourselves.'

'Never have I felt less like amusing myself,' I grumbled.

Pauley went over to the edge of the bubble. The Urulu approached the same spot, and suddenly a tentacle shot out and touched the side of our shield against its world. A small, brownish disk shape appeared where it touched, and Pauley reached out and put his hand on the disk. Almost at once he stiffened and seemed to go into a trance. I realized that the two were talking in some way, perhaps related to the identity matrix transfer itself using that area as a conductor to replace physical contact.

Dan said he might be a long time, and his conversation or whatever it was dragged on and on. We sat on the spongy floor and waited, having nothing else to do and no place else to go.

As it went on, we began to see other shapes, other Urulu floating by, a few at a time. Although no eyes were evident – the iris beneath was almost certainly a mouth – there seemed no doubt after a while that we were the object of curious attention.

'You know,' Dory remarked, 'they really have a kind of graceful beauty about them, don't they? I wonder what it's like to float in all directions and glide through that? Kinda like a bird.'

I nodded, not mentioning that I was beginning to feel like a zoo animal. Still, there was a great fascination in the huge creatures, and I began trying to deduce things from them.

It seemed impossible that such creatures could have built great machines that would fly to the stars. How would they even *see* stars in this kind of atmosphere? I thought they were probably much older than mankind, even on a relative scale. Progress, which for humans had come in comparative quick jumps, had to have come very, very slowly to such people. But – how could such as they have even developed the means to get to, let alone mine, a hot planetary center under huge pressure? Was it possible that Pauley had been giving us another untruth, or at least half-truth, about their history when he said that they had developed the body-switching technique as a defense against predators? In their element, they looked more than capable.

But what if life had developed in a layered system within a gas giant? Or what if they bred forms of life, weaved them from the floating nucleotides of their gaseous environment, that could take those pressures? Took what might have been a sophisticated communications process and discovered from it the secret of the identity matrix?

I would imagine them moving, then, from layer to layer, their minds travelling through those new creatures they made at each step tailored for that particular environment, until, in one direction, they reached the planet and in the other saw the stars. Could their sophisticated powers, then, have developed not as a result of predators but rather as the result of a frontier psychology? Would we ever really know these strange people?

They, then, would see bodies mostly as tools, form following function, a concept that would eliminate a lot of the root causes of hatred, prejudice, divisions which marked our own terrestrial people. In our society form followed function only in our tools; in a sociological sense, function followed form, as was so graphically illustrated by my own self. The fact that Victor looked like a wimp made him something of a wimp, but also produced, through social pain and introversion, a social scientist, author, teacher, whose work had to be everything in his life because his form, socially, turned him inward. I, on the other hand, was a buxom beauty who turned people on when I walked into a room. And what did *I* do for a living?

If I were at all right in my theories of the Urulu, it explained why our form of life and theirs had taken such different paths, and why the Urulu themselves might hardly believe we could have a meeting of the minds.

I shared these ideas with Dory, but she just shrugged and shook her head. Life, I knew, was simpler for Dory than for me. Things were practical – what was, *was* – or they were beautiful, ugly, that sort of thing. She was the hardhead and I was the dreamer, which is why, I think, we complemented each other so well. Without her practicality, her good common sense, her ability to face life on its own terms as a series of practical problems to be solved, I'd not be able to survive. But without people like me to wonder and speculate on the unknowable, there would be not only no science, but no poetry, either.

'I wonder how they fuck?' she mused, showing the difference between us.

I managed a chuckle. 'They probably lay eggs. Or they might not even have sex as we know it.' I put my arm around her. 'We just have to hope that they have love.'

Pauley finally disengaged and seemed none the worst for wear. He came back over to us and sank down wearily. His Urulu contact floated off and was soon lost in the billowing gases.

'Well?' I asked him.

He shrugged. 'All I did was report. Gave a readout, as it were, of all my experiences, feelings, and conclusions. Now it'll be taken higher up, then again higher, and so forth, until it finally reaches the people who make the decisions.'

'There seems to be one universal law,' I noted, 'if even the Urulu have a complicated bureaucracy.'

We rested and we waited for quite some time. Food came, and it was as tasteless and as filling as Dan had warned, and more time passed, and hordes of Urulu kept swimming by, giving us the once-over. Except for feeling like a specimen, I didn't really care about that, but I was a little worried about Dory. She seemed to shrug it off, though, after a while, perhaps concluding that these weren't really people – not her kind, anyway. And we could do little about it, anyway. Still, we felt very exposed, and I wished for some privacy.

We finally slept, and food came again, and I began to worry about things. Why was it taking so long?

'You have to remember they have to digest an enormous amount of data, sort it, analyze it, you name it,' Dan consoled. 'It all takes time. It's possible they might pass the buck to higher-ups, which means physically leaving and going, since radio waves would take forever. We just have to be patient.'

Of his people and my speculations Dan would neither confirm nor deny anything. I understood. Deep down he was still the military man in a war, and this was a military ship.

Finally a Urulu did approach the communications point again; maybe the same one, maybe not. Dan went over and went through the touching ritual again, but did not stiffen. They were talking, somehow, not anything more.

He let go after a moment, turned, and walked back to us. 'Misty, Dory – they want confirmation of my feelings, which is a really good sign. They want to examine the both of you.'

Dory frowned. 'Examine us how?'

He smiled reassuringly. 'Look, it's nothing, really. Wait until the Grandfather gets here, then just do what I've been doing.'

'Grandfather?' we both echoed.

He nodded. 'That's the closest I can come in English. Call him, well, a venerated old man, a commanding general, a political leader – a lot of things – and you get some idea.'

'What, exactly, is this examination like? Will we be asked questions?' I wanted to know.

He shook his head negatively. 'Nothing like that. What he's going to do is read out your matrices. He'll know the both of you better than you know yourselves.'

'I don't want anybody messing with my head again!' Dory exclaimed.

'No, no. It's like taking the recording. There's no sensation, particularly, and he's not going to do anything *to* your matrix, just copy it.' He paused a moment. 'It's the only way.'

I sighed. 'All right. When?'

He looked up at the swirling gases all around us. 'I'd say almost any moment. See?'

We looked, and for a moment I didn't realize what he meant. Then it registered – the hordes of curious Urulus, the gawkers, had gone. There was nothing at all to be seen except the swirling colors. The boss was coming – they were scurrying back to look like they were busy.

And then the boss came, majestically through the mist. He looked like all the others, but seemed much, much larger; so huge he almost dwarfed our little bubble. All of us could have stood in his brain-case with room left over.

I realized that Urulu just kept growing as they got older. I suppose gas giants give you a lot more room.

A huge, cablelike tentacle snaked out and touched the communications plate. Pauley went over and touched it, again casually, talking rather than anything else. Finally he let go and turned back to us. 'O.K. – who first? Don't worry – he doesn't bite.'

Actually, it wasn't the huge creature or the idea of having my mind read out that bothered me the most. It was the knowledge that what this being learned, or thought he learned, from the likes of Dory and me might well determine the future of Earth – *would* determine it, for better or worse.

For, in the end, these were not godlike beings, but *people* – a far different sort, but people all the same.

I stepped up to the plate. 'Here goes,' I muttered, took a couple of deep breaths, and put my right palm flat on the plate.

Considering my IMC experience I had expected no real sensation whatsoever, but there *was* this time.

Half of me stood there, but the other half seemed floating free in space, hovering in air of spectacular beauty and fluidity. My vision was fully 360 degrees and, even as I was aware of myself, standing there in the bubble, I also saw myself, and Dan and Dory, as if from a different place. I felt reassured, warm, comfortable, yet I could sense in the great being a tremendous feeling of concern, of responsibility, which was there, tangible to me, yet just out of reach, a frame in which I was the picture.

Oddly, this feeling, this confidence, reminded me somehow of Stuart, and I felt more comfortable, more at ease.

And then, suddenly, it was over, and I was just touching plastic. I let go with some regret, and Dory hesitantly approached.

'It's all right,' I told her. 'It's – a real experience.'

She touched the plate and stiffened, and I knew the process had, once again, begun. It seemed to take a terribly long time, but Dan assured me that, no matter how short it had seemed to me, it was no longer than mine.

'How was it?' Dan asked me.

'It was – interesting,' I replied. 'It seemed like I got a little into his head, too. Dan – do you miss it? Floating free like a bird or a fish, seeing a wider and different spectrum, communing with the others of your kind?'

He nodded seriously. 'Sometimes I do, very much – like now. Remember, I was supposed to come back years ago.'

'Will you stay, then?'

He shook his head sadly from side to side. 'No, I doubt it. Not if it goes the way we hope. They'll need somebody who understands humankind, at least as well as anybody can, and I'm the only likely candidate left alive and free. I'll have to train others and ease them in. Still, I like the idea a lot better than before. It's a nicer, cleaner kind of job – to build bridges, rather than blow them up. Harder, though. *Much* harder'

Finally Dory, too, was let go, and returned to us with a dazed expression in her eyes. 'Wow!' she breathed. 'That's really *something!*'

Dan went over and 'talked' to the Grandfather again. Then he let go and the huge creature rose majestically and vanished in the billowing clouds, causing a riot of colorful patterns as he went.

'What now?' I asked Dan.

'Now we wait some more,' he sighed. 'While the Grandfather and *his* bosses and the computers analyze the data.' He crossed his fingers. 'And then they'll tell us if I played it right.'

I realized then what tension he, too, was under, and I recalled his tale of being responsible for another world, far away, being destroyed. He had told that one with too much sincerity and anguish for me not to believe him. I felt a little sorry for him, really, since I knew that this meant almost as much to him as it did to us.

And so we waited, and waited, and waited …

A convulsive shudder went through the ship, starting the interior gases swirling even more and knocking us to the floor of our bubble. I was afraid for a moment it would crack, or, at least, break free and go hurling off into the void, but it soon settled down to a steady vibration.

Dan looked apprehensive but hopeful. 'We're moving,' he told us.

How long had we been there, I wondered. A day? A week? It was hard to tell from the food cycles and the sleep cycle had changed for us anyway, in response to boredom and the almost hypnotic effect of those clouds.

A Urulu approached the plate, and Dan went to it. He returned in a few moments, looking cheerful. 'We've done it! Misty! Dory! They bought it!'

He talked feverishly, excitedly. A small task force was being assembled, he told us, to proceed to Earth directly. The first priority, he told us, would be to hit IMC, to wipe it off the face of the Earth.

'It won't mean that they'll be destroyed,' he cautioned. 'It'll just set them back a few years until they can build a better computer. But it'll be a demonstration of power. Then we're going to contact those leaders of yours, not just in the U.S. but key leaders worldwide. They're going to get an ultimatum of sorts.'

I was nervous. Invasion from outer space might guarantee cooperation but hardly a friendly attitude, and I pointed this out.

'No, it won't be that kind of grandstanding,' he assured us. 'We are going to demonstrate our power for them, once in each key country. Then, *quietly*, we will contact them. The message will be simple, yet startlingly complex. We're going to leave them alone, but we will offer complete protection against The

Association – for a period. The key to the identity matrix is known now to your people – at least some. When the facts are clear, the others will start to work on it, or steal its secrets – whatever. Then we're going to sit back and watch what you do with it.'

I was aghast. 'But – Dan! They'll misuse it!'

'That's the one thing we plan to point out to them. If they misuse it, if they go the way of The Association, we will abandon them to the enemy, for there won't be a dime's worth of difference between them anyway. But as they learned to fear the atomic bomb so much they have never used it against one another after the first time, so they might do the same here with the identity matrix. If they use it to learn, to grow, to change their society and their attitudes, then they make history. They become the first race of their type to transcend their physical limits, their petty hatred and prejudices. If that happens, humanity will gain not only a host of friends, but the stars – and inner rewards you can't even dream of right now.'

I shook my head. 'It's no good. We'll blow it. We always blow it. Besides, totalitarianism seems to be the natural trend of mankind.'

He smiled humorlessly. '*They* think so, too. But they're willing to give you the chance.'

I looked at him. 'What about you, Dan? What will you do, now?'

'I'll be there, with you,' he told us. 'Like I said, training others, putting evaluators in place, so we'll *know*. God bless Stuart Eisenstadt! How I'd love to find him and give him the news.'

That brought me up short. 'You might kill him. He's probably in IMC.'

He nodded. 'I thought of that. But so are some of our people, remember. Don't worry – the odds are we won't kill anybody. It's the *computer* we're after.'

'And we're heading home *now?*' Dory asked, sounding anxious.

'Soon, anyway. They'll warn us when they make the jump. Then be prepared – the three of us have some work to do.'

'Huh?'

'Well, *my* people can't go into IMC. They can't even breathe there.'

CHAPTER SIXTEEN

When we arrived off Earth they brought a small ship for our use. The interior smelled like it had been put together expressly for us, which it might have been. If Pauley was really serious about the amount of physical time needed to traverse space, they'd have loads of time to refit whatever was necessary if they just didn't go into suspension in one part of the ship until they finished what they were doing.

It was larger than the one that had brought us – Dan could stand in it – and had one of those combination food and water dispensers and johns as well, not to mention three very comfortable form-fitting chairs. It also had a small screen that showed us where we were heading, but little else. The carpeting was yellow instead of blue.

Dan was getting information from a small hand plate near his chair. I tried it once, but the images and language were far too confusing and just made me dizzy.

'They found The Association's base,' he told us. 'It was pretty far out on a chunk of rock that's one of Neptune's moons. No ships got off successfully, so they think they cleaned out the nest. It wasn't a big operation, anyway. They didn't need much.'

'They sure did a lot of harm for a little bunch,' Dory commented, and I nodded.

'It's not numbers but technique and knowledge, experience, that counts,' he noted. 'The cleanup below will be a lot tougher. Thanks to Parch the leaders have already gone underground down there and will take a lot of digging out. I'm not worried, though – they have no place to go now.'

We looked at the screen, filled now with the great blue-white ball of our beautiful world. It looked just like the pictures from the orbital stations.

'Dan – how are we going to work this?' Dory asked. 'What's the procedure?'

'O.K. First the big ship will move into position in orbit and assume a stationary orbit over IMC. They will train a beam on an area of about twenty square miles around IMC, essentially putting every living thing in the area into a suspension similar to the one we use for space travel. It might cause some deaths or injuries – people driving, like that – but it's far less damaging than any other thing we could come up with and its very ease should scare the hell out of the government. In the "showers" we've been getting we've been coated with a compound that permeates the skin and will render us impervious to this kind of suspension field. The task force will cover us and the big ship, vaporizing any missiles, planes, or other nasties that might be thrown at us.'

'All right,' I said, 'but what do *we* do?'

'See those plates next to your chairs there? Put your hands on them when I tell you.'

I looked nervously at mine. It'd given me only gibberish and headaches when I'd tried it.

'They have your matrices, remember. They're going to link up through you, attuned to you. It won't last more than a few hours at best, but we shouldn't need very long.'

'But the electronic security – we don't know the *codes!*' Dory protested.

'You won't feel it, but you're going to be linked to the most powerful portable computer I know of,' he replied. 'Just let *it* do the thinking. Once inside, I want you, Dory, to head for the programming department. You worked there and know it best.'

She nodded.

'You, Misty, get down to that chamber with the chairs. Think you can find it?'

I nodded. 'If the elevators work and the doors will open.'

'Good. I'll free the Urulu, and we'll all meet out in front of the access building.'

I frowned. 'But – Dan. What do we do when we get to these places?'

'You'll know what to do when you get there. Just let us guide you. Clear out as soon as you're finished, get upstairs and outside.'

'Seems like a lot of extra-elaborate trouble to go through,' I noted, 'when you could just short out the computer from the air.'

He nodded. 'But that's not the point of the exercise. There are loads of easy and quick ways to blow IMC, but *this* involves technology and demonstrations totally beyond the powers of your people. It's designed for maximum effect, to illustrate their impotence. It'll scare the hell out of 'em so badly they'll have to listen to us.'

'All right,' I sighed. 'When do we get it over with?'

'We're approaching the terminator now,' he responded. 'It'll be late night at IMC, which is best for us.'

Dory looked around. 'Uh – Dan? Where's our clothes?'

He looked sheepish. 'Damn. My people don't use 'em, and I guess they were tossed out when the emergency vehicle was cleaned. I just plain forgot.'

'You mean we have to do all this in the *buff?*'

'They'll all be frozen anyway,' he replied. 'You'll be safer than anywhere else on the planet including your own bathroom.'

'But our *keys*, driver's license, credit cards …?'

He shrugged. 'They can be replaced. Ready? Here we go! Put your hands on the plates *now!*'

We landed and went to the rear where the hatch opened, letting in a sudden mass of dry, incredibly hot air. We were in the middle of the parking lot and had to run barefoot across still really hot asphalt to the main building.

Everything was lit with an eery, purplish glow, which seemed to sparkle a bit with some sort of pent-up energy.

Everybody inside was frozen stiff, it looked like, suspended like still pictures in most cases, although some people had fallen over if not balanced. Even a police dog was frozen, caught in the act of a big yawn.

We walked down the hallway in eerie silence, although the lights remained on and we could hear the occasional clatter of automatic teletypes and the like still functioning even with their operators stiff.

We reached the freight elevator, with two burly Marine guards standing there, and Dan removed one key and I the other from the two men, then put them in the slot and turned. The elevator door slid open. Inside, he reached into the little compartment for the interior key, put it in, and started very slowly twisting and turning it, almost like a safecracker. Suddenly, the elevator started to move.

'It was an easy set of circuits to analyze,' Dan commented, and I suddenly realized that it wasn't *he* who analyzed it, but the computer we were all theoretically connected to. I felt nothing except a slight, odd feeling of buoyancy, of unreality about it all. There had been no sensation when we'd touched the plates.

Our destinations were on different levels. Dory got off on 4, I on 12, and Dan continued down to the IMC dungeons. I was alone, heading towards Stuart's old office and that terrible theater of the mind.

Passing people frozen there, and occasionally stepping over them, was something of a novelty and a turn-on. I had a great urge to do something to them, maybe undress them or put them in obscene poses, but I barely repressed it. This was business.

I looked in at Stuart's office – it still had his name on the door, which made me feel a little better – and saw a number of technicians around, but not Stuart. I headed for the control room.

It was an odd feeling, walking into that place once again. Here Misty Carpenter had been born, Victor Gonser killed, sort of, in a cold, mechanical and technical process. It still gave me the creeps, even though I liked myself and who I was these days.

There were only a few people around, looking in the process of straightening up the place, and I sat down at the master control console, my back to the chairs. It was in this seat that a dispassionate engineer had called the shots for my, and who knows how many others', reprogramming. It felt cold on my naked skin, but, then, the whole air-conditioned place did. I had goose bumps.

Now, though, I wasn't sure what I was supposed to do. I looked at the massive screen and all the controls and keyboards but didn't know what to do next. I just put my hands out, typewriter style, and much to my surprise they started working. I had no knowledge or control of what I was doing; I was just a passenger, now, watching my hands control, adjust, throw switches, type in messages, read out outputs, and punch more messages. Academically, I *did* realize what was going on – the bosses up in orbit and their master computers were learning about this one, probing and testing and analyzing, comparing the information with what they already knew and were learning from Dory's end – and, perhaps, from Dory's matrix. She'd worked these things and had a lot of training on them.

Suddenly I stopped, but the CRT screen didn't. It filled with line after line of numbers, symbols, and the like, faster now than my eyes could follow, but it would pause occasionally and a single phrase would appear, but for a moment.

'Garbage dumped.'

Then it would resume, again and again.

I felt now that I could leave it to its own devices, and got up without any hint of resistance from above. I was finished.

I headed back down the hall, stopping in on Stuart's inner office and seeing his nameplate, pipe, and even a spare lab smock. I didn't know whether, or if, Parch had done anything to his mind, but I felt certain Stuart was all right.

I headed back to the elevator, which now opened for me as I approached it. The Urulu, then, were now in complete control of the computer.

'Hey! Wait!' I called out, although I didn't really know to who. 'If there's time – stop at Level 4.'

The elevator seemed to jerk slightly, then continued, and opened at Level 4. I looked around. 'Thanks.'

I walked down the still halls, heading for one particular place. I found it easily – I knew the way well enough. Harry Parch's office. How *very* much I hoped to find him in.

But he wasn't. The office hadn't changed much, but there were only a couple of secretaries there, frozen in the act of typing. In the inner office I looked around for any sign of who or what he really was, but there was only the make-up table, the wigs, false moustaches, and wardrobe closet.

I was tremendously disappointed, but, I told myself, it didn't really matter. Parch, Kelleam, and the others involved in all this – it was more than personal. It was worse, in a way. If they hadn't found Harry Parch to do their dirty work, they'd have found somebody else. The country, the world, had no shortage of them, and the Phil Kelleams and the rest, the bureaucrats and technicians who followed the system blindly, each a small part of the whole they never really allowed themselves to think about. It was the Eisenstadts and Jeff Overmeyers and those assistants of Stuart's who were the rare ones, I knew. The horribly outmatched people of vision and all that seemed good in the world on whom the only hope of Earth's future rested.

I turned and walked back to the elevator, meeting Dory there. She turned and smiled. 'All done. I figured you couldn't resist comin' up to *his* office.'

I shrugged and smiled sheepishly. The elevator door opened, and then closed and took us back to the surface.

Pauley waited for us just inside the door, between the desk staff, security men, and the still yawning police dog. He had seven other people with him, four women and three men, all of whom looked pale and drawn but happy.

'We did it!' he called out happily.

I looked around at the strange faces, suddenly conscious of my exposure. They all wore loose-fitting clothes. 'Now what happens, Dan?' I asked, not waiting for unnecessary introductions.

He looked at the others. 'I've told them what's going on,' he said, 'and they have all pretty well agreed to stay on and help. We're going to send them up for debriefing and a little reorientation, then they're all coming back to work for us.'

Dory nodded. 'What about *us*, though?'

He leaned over the counter and pulled up some car keys. 'Why don't we all go home to your place? The three of us, that is.' He looked at the big clock. It said 23:40.

'You mean – drive into Vegas? Like *this?*'

He shrugged. 'We'll get in about 3:30 in the morning, hunker down and take some back streets. Maybe we'll shock a few neighbors of yours but I think you can stand that.'

'What about Parch?' I asked, suddenly worried. 'He's sure to come after us.'

'If he does he's in trouble,' Dan replied. 'Parch's bosses are at this moment getting the word from on high. They'll leave you alone, Misty. They're going to be scared stiff of you. You have powerful friends.'

I nodded, hoping he was right. 'I *still* would like some clothes,' I grumbled.

'Don't get modest now,' he laughed and pointed. Dory and I both looked around and gasped. Until this moment I hadn't realized, hadn't remembered, the security cameras, which were automated and, therefore, still running.

'You mean – we've been *televised* the whole time? Like *this?*' Dory blurted out.

He laughed. 'Just think of yourself as an honorary Urulu,' he replied, and the others laughed, too.

Dan looked at the others a moment, particularly at one young woman who was particularly well-built and attractive. 'You know, I've been getting an idea about the domestic angle of my evaluations,' he said.

Driving home was a little nerve wracking, but we made it, in a nice Air Force station wagon. I kept worrying that we were going to be hauled over by a cop or something, but the only problem we had was at one traffic light in Vegas, when a couple in the car next to ours got more than their money's worth.

Dan picked the lock on our door with the government credit card in the glove compartment used by the normal driver for fuel purchases, and we entered, both of us making mental notes to install dead-bolt locks from now on.

Things looked pretty well undisturbed, although Dan assured us that there were signs of a thorough search. My little electric calendar said it was July 20, so we'd been gone less than three weeks. I chuckled. If Dan were right, I was due back at work the day after tomorrow.

I felt tired, but very good inside, and Dory seemed the same. 'You know,' she told me, 'I've been thinking. This may yet be the kind of world I'd want my kids to grow up in. Maybe it's worth bein' an optimist, just this once.'

I stared at her. 'You do what you want to do, honey.'

Five years. Five years ago and a world away, it seems. Mankind still hasn't changed much, but it hasn't changed much for the worse, either. Things go on almost as if nothing has happened, and I wonder, after that massive cover-up the government pulled, whether we'll ever know what effect our actions had on them, on Parch, on the scientific community that creates our wonders and the political community that directs and controls them.

Parch, if he's still around, has not bothered us one bit. I hope he got some jollies out of seeing Dory and I jiggling around IMC on those tapes! We haven't heard from anybody connected with IMC, in fact, although Kelleam just won his second term last year and Stuart is in the papers, I think. At least, I suspected when I saw the trim, youngish, somewhat sexy new National Science Advisor to the President on a talk show that he was all right. The fellow, who was Dr Blumberg, we were told, had a most interesting set of mannerisms and a crazy accent that was mostly Americanized but had real problems with 'w's and occasionally 'v's.

When nothing happened to us, Dory relaxed quite a bit and really started talking seriously about children, a family. Of course we couldn't have each other's children, but that was easily remedied. She's had two beautiful, dark Indian babies now, with different fathers but they both look very much like her, and she's settled into what appears to be very happy domesticity. I love them so much I kept dreaming of having my own, but pregnant strippers don't make it and we were not yet secure. We are, now – Joe's little club has turned into something of a colossus, with heavy interest in casinos here and in Reno, Tahoe, and Elko, and a mini-chain of high-class strip joints now in twenty cities. My Dory-negotiated five percent interest in the original company is now worth a couple million, making us more than comfortable.

We have a pretty home now, in the mountains outside of Vegas, with a pool and other comforts and enough privacy that we could walk nude without being observed by anything but jackrabbits, yet only forty minutes from the Strip.

As for me, I'm heading towards thirty and finally decided it was now or never. I'm in my ninth month and feel like a bloated cow with a giant watermelon stuck in her stomach, and my tits have started swelling with my tummy to incredible proportions, but I can hardly wait. I could know the sex and all that, but I want it to be a surprise, like Christmas. The way it feels it *must* be a boy, and if so, I'll name him Victor Stuart Daniel Carpenter, I think. Or, maybe, I'll just have three boys … I don't know. The world is fantastic right now, and I don't want anything to spoil it.

The pregnancy gave me the time, finally, to write this book. I wanted to write it, although I have no idea if it'll ever see print, at least in my lifetime. I'm forty-six, you know, going on twenty-nine …

I'd like it to get published somewhere, although they'll probably just label it science fiction or something. Who would believe? Only the people who know, and Kelleam's still damned popular.

As for Dan and the Earth-based Urulu, we see them often, not only as guests at the ranch but in other capacities as well. He seems to have worked out an interesting idea for getting his people around the western world, anyway, meeting the common people in city after city, noting news reports, gossip, you name it for their reports. I wonder what people would say if they knew? The government knows, of course, but they can't do much about it. At least they can't say that the Urulu aren't earning their keep.

Tonight, in fact, I'm going down to Misty's Place if I can lug this *really* out-of-balance body there and take a night out without getting *too* tired, and watch the Las Vegas debut of Danielle Dynamite, the Red-headed Rocket from Rhode Island, finally here after her first big national tour.

I wonder if Harry Parch will also be in the audience?

CODED – TOP SECRET – PRIORITY A
DISPOSITION – MASTER PENTAGON FILE HYDRA ONLY
FROM – DIRECTOR, HYDRA
SUBJECT – OPERATION 'TRIPLE PLAY'
COVERAGE – GENERAL SUMMARY AND EVALUATION
    OF OPERATION

It should be clear from the attached memoir that, despite impossible odds and tremendous risks, 'Triple Play' succeeded beyond our wildest dreams. A combination of brains, luck, and tremendous dedication and sacrifice were necessary for it to succeed, and for those of some future time who might wonder at why such incredible risks were taken, let me assure you that the finest minds of this country supported by the most sophisticated computer analysis found that, while the operation had, frankly, less than a fifteen percent chance of being totally successful, there was simply no other alternative. The fact that it worked is certainly the ultimate justification, but those who might question what we did and how we did it should also consider the fact that no suggested alternative gave odds which could even be recognized as such.

Consider: quite by accident, or, if you will, sloppiness, this government was faced with two incontrovertible facts. First, that we had, in fact, been penetrated by alien beings from off this planet whose abilities and technology were far in advance of our own and whose behavior indicated that they were hostile to humankind. Second, that these beings could trade minds with us or with each other as they chose. Further, they knew enough about us to easily pass our most stringent muster, yet we knew nothing about them.

Naturally, this information was not given to the public, as the panic and paranoia it would cause would only aid the enemy. In fact, only a special team composed of the heads of the CIA, FBI, DIA and other security organizations and the Joint Chiefs were ever informed, and were directed by the President to create a crisis management team, code-named Hydra, to combat the menace. It is almost certain that, at no time, did the number of unsecured top personnel – that is, those with liberty and not living in a secured environment – exceed a dozen.

The first task, of course, was to create a security force capable of at least recognizing the enemy and perhaps placing a bit of pressure on them. This was organized under Chief Inspector Harold G. Parch, who had supervised the original team that had exposed the first aliens. Parch is a strange man, as accurately pictured in the Gonser narrative, but he is both fiercely loyal and intensely patriotic. He is also, quite certainly, dangerously psychopathic, but in a manner useful to us. I would in no case wish Parch to date my daughter, but he is the first one I would trust with the family jewels, and he was perfect for his overall security role. We owe Parch not merely for the success of Triple Play, but also for our own necks, since, in the course of the operation, all of us violated our most sacred oaths and principles in what we believed and believe to be a desperate cause.

In addition to security – which included not only tracking the enemy but also securing their existence from the outside world – there had to be a concurrent operation to find a defense against this body-switching ability. As a result, IMC was formed, with the finest minds and finest machines available at all times. As the Gonser manuscript makes clear, while we never did find out how they so easily did it, we did find a way to do it mechanically. Show the finest minds in a field that someone else can do something they can't and give them almost unlimited funds and resources and they will almost certainly do it.

Of course, just when we found a proper defense we discovered that we had not one, but two hostile alien powers, both with this switching ability, on our hands. We were, then, on the horns of a dilemma, since we found ourselves the innocent civilians in the midst of a war between superpowers we could barely understand. Obviously the only thing we could do was pick a side and try and arrange it so that it would take us under its protection. A very subtle task, not only because we had to at all costs prevent a military confrontation with either side that we would inevitably lose while, at the same time, we had to evaluate and choose the lesser of two evils among the alien powers. Since we had a number of captured Urulus but none of the opposition, we had to start with the Urulu side. Gonser/Carpenter's early work with 'Dan Pauley' and her complete evaluation of them helped enormously, and the relationship developed between the two formed the cornerstone, as it were, of Triple Play.

Our problem, of course, was that time was against us, and there was strong evidence that the Association, at least, was actively engaged in influencing our affairs while the Urulu were not. It became fairly easy to tell them apart, since the Urulu switched minds totally without fail, while the Association seemed more concerned with the by-product of the process, the selective editing of the memory and personality. Faced with clear evidence of active opposition by one side, we felt we had no choice but to opt for the Urulu as our 'friends.'

The trouble, of course, was that the Urulu were, at best, indifferent to us and had no desire to be our friends, nor did they consider our planet and race worthy of concern no matter what was happening. In the meantime, intelligence clearly showed the Association patterns in the cult's growth and, almost by accident, stumbled on the evidence that the Association had actually penetrated the White House.

At that point Hydra's hand was forced, since the President knew of IMC and Hydra and, therefore, our liquidation or takeover despite our best efforts was only a matter of time, perhaps very little time. To buy that time, it was necessary to take drastic measures.

Triple Play, of course, was already in motion at that point. Having decided that Gonser/Carpenter and Tomlinson were the best lead to the Urulu leadership, an intensive study of what the very alien Urulu valued in other people and other civilizations based on our prior work was condensed to specific personality points, and from those we created the human personality with values and outlooks we believed would hit the Urulu where it counted. The original personality recordings of Gonser and Tomlinson, then, were edited, altered, and rewritten so that, when added once again to their created new personalities they would become the kind of people the Urulu, it was hoped, would identify with and want to help. And since they would be, hopefully, the samples, the Urulu might well take them as representative of the human race itself.

We then 'discovered' them in their new security-created lives, added our modified recordings of their past selves, and arranged to have this 'Pauley' broken out of IMC.

And it was here that the ultimate gamble had to be taken. We could not afford to have 'Pauley' immediately spirit the women to his superiors for evaluation, since to a race that swapped minds as easily as we snap fingers the psychosurgery we had so recently performed would have been painfully obvious. Therefore, the women had to be allowed to live as their new selves for a while, to settle in and *become* those newly designed psyches we counted so much on. This, however, meant potentially losing 'Pauley,' and we thought we had completely blown it when so much time elapsed. Fortunately, the Association ships and those of the Urulu are quite different, and we detected no Urulu ships arriving after the escape period, nor any departing. We knew, also, that the Association had hit the isolated Urulu bases hard, thanks in part to the fact that we leaked what we knew of those bases via the President to help them out. This served several purposes. For one, it kept Pauley a fugitive and made his escape from Earth extremely difficult. Second, it convinced him of the scope of the Association's subtle attack. Third, it confirmed once and for all that the President – and, alas, as we discovered in the same way, the Vice President – were already controlled by the Association. And, finally, by leaking that information we gave the Association a reason for letting Hydra and IMC continue, at least for a while. We represented no direct threat and were a source of information on their enemy.

Finally, however, we simply were forced to act. Evidence showed that the Association was poised for a much deeper penetration of government and that Hydra and IMC were in imminent danger not of being dismantled but of being taken over by the enemy. Since Speaker Kelleam, thanks to his visit and 'demonstration' of IMC, was very much *our* man, our survival became obvious. The assassinations we arranged and the terrorist attacks we perpetrated caught the Association off guard. It was pretty easy not only to break the news to the public but also smash their political apparatus. Of course, we knew this would be a temporary solution, but we were banking on them not having a significant military force deployed for us. This was one time when it really paid to be a primitive jerkwater island off in the fringes of a war.

The actions had the effect of reviving Triple Play, on which we had almost given up. Seeing what was happening, Pauley took our bait and contacted the two women. We had, thank God, judged him correctly. Knowing that, eventually, the Association would return in force, and having lived with and made friends with some of our people, he opted, as our profile predicted, to try and convince the Urulu to intervene on our side.

The foregoing manuscript shows that he, and therefore we, were successful. The personalities we created went unsuspected and contained the elements necessary for a command decision in our favor to be made.

You can certainly argue that the personality and lifestyle of 'Misty Carpenter' is not one one would like or accept. *I* certainly am not comfortable with such a casual and, well, immoral lifestyle, but I'm old and very old-fashioned.

But we have a younger, more pliant, more tolerant generation, and as one of those who created Misty Carpenter as she is today I can hardly kick. Thank God we always have that younger, adaptable generation! And, of course, she would be terribly shocked at my own actions in this matter if she knew them. If this is the newer generation, I might not accept – but I will not resist. Social evolution, no matter what the cause, has generated more suffering from the resistance to change than to the acceptance of it.

But it's still not *our* world, it's ours only by sufferance of the Urulu who are, I might point out, alien, not friendly on the whole, and not really any more our friends than the Association, for as long as we primitives remain at their mercy and sufferance we control not our own destiny.

It used to be simple in the old days. Two armies would march out, fight it out, and the best force would win. Or we'd plant our spies, they'd plant their spies, and we'd battle for advantage in the shadows. But a war where one superior adversary has to be tricked into taking out another superior adversary – well, nobody in history ever had to fight this sort of war before, and I think we can be damned proud of ourselves despite the ugliness we had to perpetrate. History, we all feel, will be kind to us – if, as Carpenter darkly suggests, we do not 'blow it.' Like her, I suspect we will – the Russians and Chinese in particular are climbing the paranoid walls even now. But we have the only defense. The rest of the world can either take the cure from us or go nuts. And, when they *do* take the cure, and get not only protection but also a little change in attitude as a bonus, then, maybe, we can allow the Carpenter book to be published. Probably not, though. We don't want anyone planting the idea of judicious editing of the mind right about now.

But we've come this far, and the great enemies in the totalitarian societies are, of course, the most fearful and paranoid of all. They've all got their own IMCs now, of course, but they're ten years or more behind in the hardware necessary to do it right and many years also behind in experimentation we've already done. When the rulers even now are afraid to shake hands with their closest aids or go to bed with their wives or mistresses, they will eventually *have* to come to us. And when *they* do, we'll have little trouble with their general populations.

What we need, and have hopefully bought, is time. Time to bring the rest of the world around. Time to educate the population. There's talk of introducing the IM process into medicine next year, for treatment of brain disorders, and after that it'll be mated with teaching machines, then ... In our time, we hope, people will take the IM treatment so much for granted, like they now accept plastic surgery and home computers, that they'll be ready to accept the idea of routine body-switching. That, of course, will transform society beyond our imagination. And, by that point, our Urulu watchdogs will themselves consider the process so normal and so positively used that there will be no further trouble with them. At the very least the IM will double our IQs, a tremendous leap – children might learn to read again and like it, and without the severe international tension and nihilism rampant through our century they might get the chance to use it.

The hardest part, of course, is that we remain, of necessity, behind the scenes, unknown and unrecognized. I doubt if the Hydra report can ever be known until that social revolution takes place – if it does. Still, it *will* all come out one day. Hydra and IMC are generally safe, though. We can be just about anybody – and sometimes are. Fewer still know the real identity of Harry Parch, and what he really looks like. Still, I doubt if any of us can ever pass a burlesque house or strip joint again and feel totally secure.

As for me, I am prominent now, but with a little IM work perhaps my telltale speech patterns will vanish into, say, Brooklynese, and I hope soon to abandon the public life and restart my research work at the new IMC in Colorado, already hard at work – as it has been since before the Urulu kindly saved us the trouble of demolishing the old Nevada IMC, obsolete as it was.

But when the Urulu find out one day at last that a couple of very primitive old apes made suckers out of their godlike selves, I will be very, very hard to find. But that will be a while. Perhaps, by then I'll know how *they* switch and we can leave our dependence on machines forever behind.

Respectfully submitted,
Stuart J. Eisenstadt

Dear Dr 'Blumberg':

Caught you on TV the other night. A nice performance, but you still can't tell a 'v' from a 'w.' Still, with you up there with the high and mighty ones, I feel like the human race is really going to become something great. My best to you,

Dan Pauley

Dear Dan:
War is hell, son.

Eisenstadt

If you've enjoyed these books and would
like to read more, you'll find literally thousands
of classic Science Fiction & Fantasy titles
through the **SF Gateway**

✱

For the new home of
Science Fiction & Fantasy . . .

✱

For the most comprehensive collection
of classic SF on the internet . . .

✱

Visit the SF Gateway

www.sfgateway.com

Jack L. Chalker (1944–2005)

Jack Laurence Chalker was born in Baltimore, in 1944. He received an MLA from Johns Hopkins University and taught history and geography for over a decade before becoming a professional writer in 1978. He was active in the fan community from his teens and though he published work as an editor and critic, it is for his fiction that he is best known. He was a prolific author, writing across genres successfully, and was nominated for the Hugo and John W. Campbell New Writer awards, among others. His major work is The Well of Souls sequence, comprising ten books across two series, and featuring the 'godgame' narrative device that was his signature. He died in February, 2005.